MILLER'S
INTERNATIONAL
ANTIQUES
PRICE GUIDE

1987 AMERICAN EDITION

MILLER'S
INTERNATIONAL
ANTIQUES
PRICE GUIDE
1987 AMERICAN EDITION

COMPILED AND EDITED BY
JUDITH AND MARTIN MILLER

VIKING

HOW TO USE THE BOOK

Miller's uniquely practical *International Antiques Price Guide* has been compiled to make detailed information immediately available to the consumer.

The book is organized by category of antique: eg Pottery, Porcelain, Furniture, etc. (see Contents List on page 8); within each major category there are sub-categories of items in alphabetical order: eg basket, bowl, candlestick etc., and these in turn are ordered by date. There are around 10,000 photographs of antiques and collectibles, each with a detailed description and price range. There is also a fully cross-referenced index at the back of the book.

In addition to individual entries there are special features throughout the book, giving pointers for the collector – likely condition, definitions of specialist terms, history etc – together with general articles, chapter introductions, glossaries, bibliographies where further reading is important, tables of marks etc. As all the information – text and pictures alike – is new every year the selection of items included quickly builds into an enormously impressive and uniquely useful reference set.

PRICES

All the price ranges are based on actual prices of items bought and sold during the year prior to going to press. Thus the guide is fully up-to-date.

Prices are *not* estimates: because the value of an antique is what a willing buyer will pay to a willing seller, we have given not just one price per item but a range of prices to take into account regional differences and freak results.

This is the best way to give an idea of what an antique will *cost*, but should you wish to *sell* remember that the price you receive could be 25-30% less – antique dealers have to live too!!

Conditions
All items were in good merchantable condition when last sold unless damage is noted.

ACKNOWLEDGEMENTS

Judith and Martin Miller wish to thank a large number of International auctioneers, dealers and museums who have helped in the production of this edition. The auctioneers can be found in our specialist directory towards the back of this edition.

Copyright © M.J.M. Publications Ltd. 1986
**Viking Penguin Inc.,
40 West 23rd Street, New York,
New York 10010, U.S.A.
Penguin Books Canada Ltd.,
2801 John Street, Markham,
Ontario, Canada L3R 1B4**
Designed and created by
M.J.M. Publications Limited
Sissinghurst Court
Sissinghurst
Cranbrook
Kent, England
in association with
A.G.W. International Ltd.,
Chicago, Illinois.

All rights reserved
First published in 1987 by Viking Penguin Inc.

Published simultaneously in Canada
Library of Congress Catalog
Card Number: 86-40373 (CIP Data Available)
ISBN: 0-670-81606-X

Typeset in England by The Final Word Limited,
Tonbridge, Kent
Printed in Spain by by Graficas Estella, S.A.,
Navarra, D.L.N.A. 282/1986

Editors' Introduction

by

Martin and Judith Miller

We started *Miller's Antiques Price Guide* in 1979 as a small cottage industry. We believed that there was a great need for a guide that illustrated photographically a very large number of antiques and collectibles that had recently actually been on the market, and that gave good precise descriptions and realistic prices. We wanted to produce the book, because it was the book we wanted to buy and could not find. Obviously we were not alone, because the 1986 Edition of the guide, which we produced – as we did the previous six mainly for the British market, sold well over 100,000 copies and is now used daily not only by huge numbers of consumers but by major antique dealers and auction houses around the world as a standard reference work.

Two years ago we decided to produce a new edition especially for the US market. We have both travelled extensively and have always been convinced that, although there are obviously regional differences in the world of antiques, it is very much an *international* world and an *international* market – a fact borne out by the fact that the major auction houses in New York and London are the same companies. Dealers and collectors buy from all over the world directly or indirectly, and this makes a real impact upon the choice available everywhere. It really is a world without national barriers.

The first US edition followed the tradition of the original book. What we have produced was, we believe, by far the most comprehensive and practical book on the subject. Good, clear photographs of over 10,000 antiques and collectibles accompanied by detailed descriptions, masses of background detail, and researched price ranges made the book a standard reference for collector and professional alike.

The first two US editions of Miller's proved so successful in meeting the growing needs of the collector, dealer and enthusiast alike, that we have continued with this 1987 edition. The 1987 Guide has the added advantage of 96 pages of colour photographs.

We constantly stress that *Miller's International Antiques Price Guide* is a GUIDE and not a LIST. There is no set price for an antique but *Miller's* will give you the best pictorial and descriptive guide there is, and a realist price *range*. (See *How To Use the Book*, opposite).

We believe in a visual approach to the subject – how can you possibly judge the likely value of the item you wish to assess on the basis of comparative descriptions alone, except in the case of a few numbered collectibles? – so we change every photograph every year. This means that if you buy *Miller's* for a few years you will build up a fully comprehensive visual encyclopedia of every major category of antique and collectible with no repetitions from edition to edition.

We never use the standard photographs of museum pieces you will see in some guides. In any case these pieces are well covered in standard thematic reference books. All the items in *Miller's* are 'available' – they have actually been bought and sold during the past year. So we really do give a guide to the market, not just a theoretical survey.

Many people have helped us to compile the guide. However we could not possibly list everyone who has helped to make this book what it is, but their help has been invaluable. Because it is impossible for two people to have all the expertise to compile a general international price guide, we are in constant touch with salesrooms and dealers all over the world to check and recheck our facts. Catalogues from all over the world pour into our headquarters here in Kent, England, for assessment and sorting. Trends are predicted, anomalies resolved, final selections made. *Miller's* is a never ending task – but one which we find fascinating and personally rewarding.

We hope to show you something of the inside world of antiques and that you enjoy the book and find it a profitable companion throughout 1987 and beyond.

CONTENTS

Pottery	9
Porcelain	91
Lowestoft	153
Goss & Crested Ware	156
Oriental Pottery & Porcelain	157
Glass	179
Oak & Country Furniture	189
Furniture	244
Clocks	352
Barometers	376
Scientific Instruments	377
Cameras	384
Art Nouveau	387
Doulton	411
Royal Doulton	412
Lalique Glass	416
Art Deco	420
Silver	435
Wine Antiques	471
Silver Plate	480
Tortoiseshell	508
Metalware	508
Ivory/Shell	527
Marble	528
Terracotta/Stone	530
Wood Carvings	531
Antiquities	532
Rugs & Carpets	539
Textiles	544
Dolls	556
Automata	561
Dolls' Houses	562
Toys	564
Models	577
Games	580
Musical Instruments	581
Musical Boxes	583
Phonographs	584
Gramophones	585
Boxes	586
Enamels	591
Electrical	591
Transport	593
Sport	596
Crafts	599
Tribal Art	601
Ephemera	604
Scripophily	607
Oriental	608
Russian Works of Art	638
Wine	641
Lighting	642
Papier Mâché	643
Sewing	646
Miniatures	647
Coins	648
Pine	650
Kitchenalia	661
Arms & Armour	667
Jewellery	676
Directory of Auctioneers	683
Index	687

A green-glazed model of a tower in three detachable sections, the top section with a ridged and tiled roof, triangular windows and square doors above a larger section fitted with a door moulded with a taotie mask and fixed-ring handle above a pierced galleried stand, supported on a square base with four arched feet (restored), Han Dynasty, 38in (97cm). This piece realised $11,000 at Christie's, London on 21st April 1986.

A pair of English delft blue and white bowls, painted in the Oriental style with flowering chrysanthemum and bamboo, within a band of trellis pattern and stylised foliage, the crenellated rims enriched in blue, one with hairline crack, c1750, 9in (23cm) diam. **$1,400-2,600**

A Liverpool delft bowl, decorated in blue and manganese, the interior reserved a Chinese figure, with prunus blossom border, the exterior decorated 2 Chinese ladies in gardens, 18thC, 10½ in (26 cm) diam. **$800-1,500**

A Liverpool creamware bowl, printed and painted with a ship in full sail and inscribed 'Success to the Valentine 1783', and the exterior printed in black with the Sailors Farewell, The Soldiers Farewell and the Triumph of Neptune and Venus, c1783, 11in (27cm) diam. **$600-1,200**

Liverpool 'Ship' bowls were produced in delft, pearlware and porcelain as well as creamware. All types are keenly collected.

A Liverpool creamware bowl, the interior painted in black with a sailing ship, 9in (22cm) diam. **$300-600**

Less valuable than a bowl which includes the name of the ship.

An early Staffordshire blue and white transfer ware fruit bowl, with Buffalo pattern, with scalloped edges, c1790, 9in (22cm). **$80-180**

A Prattware fish bowl, c1800, 10 in (25 cm) diam. **$1,300-2,400**

A pearlware blue and white bowl, printed with American Indian figures, a stag and martial trophies and the interior rim with Prince of Wales feathers, c1820, 7 in (17.5 cm) diam. **$200-450**

Pearlware was introduced c1780 as a cheap alternative to porcelain. Painted or printed chinoiseries are common. The glaze is often quite blue due to the addition of cobalt. Wares are purchased for their decorative quality rather than their collectability unless bearing unusual decoration including a name, date or political slogan.

A blue and white Delft bowl, decorated with European figures in landscapes, 18thC, 12½ in (31 cm). **$2,000-4,500**

A rare bowl in good condition made especially collectable by the European landscape decoration.

◁

A George Jones majolica punch bowl, with Mr Punch lying on his back supporting the holly-decorated bowl in his arms, cobalt blue with pale blue interior and naturalistic colouring, impressed with 'G Jones' cypher and monogram, very small chip to one foot, c1875, 14½ in (36 cm) diam. **$5,000-9,000**

A rare and highly collectable piece in spite of the slight damage.

A majolica oval pedestal bowl, with putto handles and suspending floral swags, 21in (52.5cm) wide. **$400-900**

A Wedgwood Fairyland Lustre bowl, the interior decorated with mihrab columns, elves, fairies, sailing ships and castles, the exterior decorated with woodland elves at play, painted number Z5340, 8in (20cm) diam. **$1,000-2,000**

Fairy lustre wares remain a popular collecting field.

Busts

A Nevers 'bleu' shallow bowl, painted in white, ochre and yellow with birds and flower-sprays on the blue ground, rim chips, late 17thC, 9½in (23.5cm) diam. **$800-1,500**

Cf W B Honey: European Ceramic Art, *pl 79a, for a similar bowl in the Victoria and Albert Museum.*

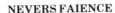

> ### NEVERS FAIENCE
>
> ★ the term Nevers faience refers to a region rather than a single factory
> ★ Italian potters came to the region after 1565 and by 1600 a flourishing potting industry had developed
> ★ early products were in the style of Italian faience
> ★ Nevers bleu grounds became popular after c1625 and were produced in large quantities throughout the 17thC
> ★ most common form of decoration on Nevers bleu ground is of birds and flower-sprays
> ★ such wares are sometimes, incorrectly, termed 'Persian' but they have no connection with Persian decoration

A good quality Staffordshire library bust of Shakespeare, by Enoch Wood, late 18thC, 17 in (42.5 cm). **$1,300-2,400**

A Yorkshire pearlware portrait bust of an officer, in bright blue jacket with yellow collar and frogging, chip to side whiskers and epaulette, c1800, 12 in (30 cm). **$1,800-3,800**

An unusual and collectable figure. Both English and French soldier busts were produced during the period when the two countries were engaged in hostilities.

A Prattware bust of a French ▷ officer, early 19thC, 11½ in (28 cm). **$1,300-2,400**

A Staffordshire figure of Handel, by Ralph Wood, c1800, 9½ in (23.5 cm). **$600-1,100**

A very rare Staffordshire named figure of the Duke of York, c1800, 6 in (15 cm). **$400-750**

A Yorkshire pearlware portrait bust of an unnamed actor, in blue jacket and ochre, green and blue spotted waistcoat, c1810, 8in (20cm). **$1,000-2,000**

Cf John and Griselda Lewis, Pratt Ware, *p.138, where a possible solution to the identity of the sitter is discussed.*

A Staffordshire bust of Rousseau, in coloured enamel finish, mostly blue, green and brown, c1810, 9 in (22.5 cm). **$600-1,200**

A Staffordshire pearlware portrait bust of the Duke of York, named on the reverse, in iron-red jacket with yellow frogging, the socle with lion supporters and the initials GR, enriched in colours, socle restored, c1810, 6 in (15 cm). **$400-900**

A bust of Admiral Duncan, decorated in underglaze blue, black and yellow, possibly Yorkshire, c1810, 9 in (22.5 cm). **$600-1,200**

A Staffordshire bust of an unknown person, c1815, 8½in (21cm). **$500-900**

A good English pottery bust of Sir Francis Burdett, 16in (40cm). **$1,800-3,800**

A rare pottery bust depicting Rev William Clowes, Methodist, in enamel colours of black, grey and flesh tones, manufactured by Barker, Sutton & Till, c1835, 11 in (27.5 cm). **$1,300-2,400**

A Robinson and Leadbeater parian bust of Lord Kitchener, on square base, impressed marks, 8½ in (21 cm). **$100-250**

A Staffordshire pottery bust, probably by Wood & Caldwell, depicting Tzar Alexander, with iron-red tunic and white sash, on a marbled socle base, 10½ in (26 cm). **$200-450**

A Wedgwood terracotta bust of ▷ Locke, some restoration, impressed mark and inscribed on the reverse, c1785, 8½ in (21.5 cm). **$400-900**

This model is taken from the bronze by Michael Rijsbrack.

A rare Wedgwood black basaltes library bust of Lord Byron, 19thC, 14 in (35 cm). **$400-900**

Commemorative

A creamware teapot and cover, probably Wedgwood, printed in black, on one side with John Manners, Marquis of Granby and on the other with a battle scene, surrounded with trophies of war, slight damage, late 18thC, 4½ in (11.5 cm). **$600-1,200**

A commemorative Nelson jug, in mint condition, c1790-1800, 5 in (12.5 cm). **$400-750**

A brown and cream glazed stoneware jug, moulded in relief with scene from Battle of Acre depicting Capt Sir Sydney Smith, 7 in (17 cm). **$80-180**

11

A Liverpool creamware inscribed and dated armorial jug, transfer printed and enamelled in colours with 'Colonel Tarleton' named below, standing before a cannon, the reverse printed in black with 'The Watchtool Makers Arms' and the motto 'By Hammer and Hand All Arts Do Stand' and with the initials EMH and date 1792 beneath the spout, with green line rim, minor cracks to rim, 1792, 5½ in (14.5 cm). **$1,200-2,100**

Colonel Tarleton was a native of Liverpool and a distinguished cavalry officer during the American War of Independence in the 1780s. He was later returned as MP for Liverpool on various occasions from 1790-1807. The print is taken from his portrait by Sir Joshua Reynolds.

CREAMWARE

★ a low fired earthenware first produced c1740
★ Josiah Wedgwood perfected the body in the mid-1760's. This perfected body he named Queen's Ware in honour of Queen Charlotte
★ Wedgwood sold Queen's Ware in the white and with overglaze enamel decoration
★ the body was well suited to overglaze transfer printing
★ other potteries also produced creamware in large quantities, notably Leeds, Melbourne, Cockpit Hill (Derby) and Liverpool

---

A creamware jug, printed on one side with an interior scene of named people and groups, entitled 'Separation of Louis XVI from his family', on the other an execution scene, inscribed 'Massacre of the French King' and 'La Guillotine or the Modern Beheading Machine at Paris, by which the unfortunate Louis XVI (late King of France) suffered on a Scaffold, Jan 21. 1793', 7½ in (18.5 cm). **$600-1,100**

A pottery jug printed in blue with the ghost of Napoleon before tomb upon St. Helena, 8½ in (21cm). **$80-180**

A pottery jug printed in blue with portrait of Wellington and battle trophies, slight chip, 8½ in (21 cm). **$180-300**

A pearlware blue and white dish, the centre printed with the busts of George III and Queen Caroline, inscribed 'A King Rever'd A Queen Beloved', 'Long May They Live', 7½ in (18.5 cm). **$600-1,200**

A creamware Queen Caroline commemorative jug, printed in black, the reverse side with a political parody based on a popular nursery rhyme, some chips, c1821, 5 in (12 cm). **$400-750**

The verse on this jug refers to supposedly spurious evidence brought against Caroline to support a bill brought forward in 1820 aiming to dissolve her marriage to the Prince Regent on the grounds of adultery. In 1821 she was prevented from attending the coronation and she died later that year. The verse indicates how far public sympathy was on the side of the Queen.

A blue and white transfer printed and band moulded harvest jug, decorated with opposing panels of a View of Shipping in the Avon Gorge, possible Pountneys of Bristol or South Wales Pottery, early 19thC, 11in (27.5cm). **$500-900**

A rare portrait jug of Napoleon Bonaparte by Stephen Green of Lambeth, marked to underside 'Stephen Green Lambeth' in an elaborate cartouche, c1830, 7½ in (18.5 cm). **$300-600**

A Swansea Irish commemorative jug of 'Dan O'Connell Esq', and 'The Very Reverend Father Matthew', commemorating the two great regenerators of Ireland, unmarked, c1829, 5in (12.5cm). **$300-600**

A Staffordshire copper lustre and yellow-ground jug, transfer printed in black on both sides with a portrait of General Jackson, 'The Hero of New Orleans', named above and below, the yellow-ground enriched with foliage, c1830, 8in (21 cm). **$600-1,100**

A Royal Doulton pottery jug, printed in colours with portrait of George Kinloch Esq, MP and 'Reform' and inscription, 8 in (20 cm). **$80-180**

A Staffordshire mug printed in puce with a crown above flowering vines, flanked with half-length portraits of William IV and Queen Adelaide, commemorating their Coronation in 1831, 4in (10cm). **$400-750**

A pottery mask jug printed in black with 'The Deliverer', and 'Gratitude' between moulded scrolls and decorated in blue, for the 1851 Exhibition, 8 in (20 cm). **$80-180**

A Sunderland lustre frog mug, with a Crimean War illustration, c1860, 5 in (12.5 cm). **$300-600**

An Alcock & Co jug with black transfer decoration depicting scenes from the Crimean War, gilt decoration with inscription 'Sam Joinson – Nantwich'. **$200-450**

A Scottish pottery Crimea Peace jug, printed in black with allied servicemen, and a home-coming scene depicting kilted serviceman and inscription, 8½in (21cm). **$100-250**

A Staffordshire pottery Crimean War bowl with heavy foot, printed in blue with a young portrait, naval scenes and inscribed 'Mess No. 56', 6½ in (16 cm) diam. **$200-450**

A pottery jug, moulded in relief and decorated in colours and lustre with portraits of Sir C Campbell and Sir H Havelock, 8½in (21cm). **$80-180**

l to r

1 An Alliance pottery jug, printed in black with a military scene entitled 'Light Cavalry Charge at Balaclava', and also 'May England Forever such unity boast', decorated in gilt, 8in (20cm). **$200-450**

2 A pottery jug, printed with a military scene entitled 'Charge of the Chasseurs D'Afrique, at Balaclava', decorated in gilt, 8 in (20 cm). **$200-450**

3 A white saltglazed pottery water jug, moulded in relief with a scene depicting Florence Nightingale (?) attending the wounded Turk, 11½ in (29 cm). **$200-450**

4 A Staffordshire pottery saltglazed jug moulded in relief with 2 sentimental/military scenes entitled 'Home and Abroad', 7 in (17 cm). **$150-250**

5 A Sunderland lustre pottery jug, printed in black with a naval scene entitled 'Jack's safe return to his True Love' and inscription, chipped, 5 in (12 cm). **$150-250**

6 A brown glazed stoneware jug, in the Gothic style moulded in relief with 4 sentimental 'Home-coming' scenes, 7½ in (19 cm). **$300-600**

An unglazed parian jug with extensively moulded decoration, including portrait of Prince Consort and Royal Arms on blue grounds, wreaths, orders and inscription, 9½ in (23 cm). **$300-600**

A pottery jug, moulded in relief with equestrian portraits of Garibaldi, decorated in blue and cobalt blue, hairline crack to handle, 1864, 8½in (21cm). **$80-180**

A Disraeli Memorium pottery jug, printed in black and decorated in colours with portrait, inscription and book titles, hairline cracks to base, 1881, 6 in (15 cm). **$200-450**

An 1887 Jubilee pottery plate, the centre printed in brown with portrait arms and inscription, 10 in (25 cm). **$80-180**

STAFFORDSHIRE MOULDED STONEWARE JUGS

★ manufacture commenced c1825
★ increasingly popular with collectors
★ generally made in 3 sizes
★ body can be buff, pale blue, grey, pale green or white
★ manufactured by many Staffordshire potteries
★ marked examples particularly popular
★ value significantly affected by damage and quality of moulding

A pair of Robinson and Leadbetter white parian illumieré busts of Edward VII and Alexandra after W C Lawton, 1902, 16 in (40 cm) high overall. **$400-750**

An 1897 Jubilee pottery plate, printed in brown with young and old portraits, Royal Arms and national flora, 9½in (24cm). **$80-180**

A 12-sided 1902 Coronation porcelain plate, printed in blue with an all-over design including portrait, trophies and details of Empire, and decorated in gilt, the reverse with inscription, 10½ in (26 cm). **$200-450**

A Paragon porcelain 1935 Jubilee plate, the centre printed in brown and decorated in colours with portraits, arms and inscription, 10½ in (26 cm). **$100-250**

A Minton's 1937 Coronation porcelain plate, the centre printed in brown and gilt, and decorated in enamels with profile portraits and inscription, limited edition no. 101/1000, 11 in (28 cm). **$100-250**

A Dudson blue ground stoneware vase, decorated in white with applied moulded portraits of Col Baden Powell and Sir Redvers Buller, between crossed rifles, 7 in (18 cm). **$200-450**

A Ringtons Tea octagonal blue and white pottery biscuit jar and cover, produced for the 1929 North-East Coast Industries Exhibition, Newcastle-on-Tyne, 5½ in (14 cm). **$80-150**

A Gray's pottery plate, printed in brown and decorated in colours with Royal Arms, national crests and inscription, 1939, 11in (27cm). **$60-120**

A rare Staffordshire pottery castle spill vase, c1825, 5½ in (13.5 cm). **$900-1,700**

Cottages

A flower-encrusted pastille burner, in the form of an octagonal house, c1835, 5½in (13.5cm). **$600-1,200**

A lilac pastille burner of octagonal form, enriched with gilding, c1835, 7 in (17.5 cm). **$800-1,500**

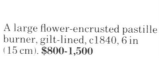

A large flower-encrusted pastille burner, gilt-lined, c1840, 6 in (15 cm). **$800-1,500**

A very unusual Staffordshire blue pottery cottage pastille burner, c1840, 6½ in (16 cm). **$900-1,700**

A rare pastille burner modelled as a church, with pierced windows and 3 iron-red doorways, the detachable base modelled with flowerheads and outlined in gilt, 6in (15cm). **$1,000-2,000**

An octagonal cottage, with central orange chimney and detachable roof, the gilt-lined base modelled with flowerheads, 4½ in (11 cm). **$600-1,100**

An octagonal cottage, with 4 brown doorways below a pierced roof, on separate circular gilt-lined base, 5½ in (13.5 cm). **$600-1,100**

A Staffordshire cottage, c1850, 7½ in (18.5 cm). **$300-600**

A pastille burner, with 2-tiered roof, above 5 pierced windows and an iron-red doorway, 5½ in (13.5 cm). **$400-750**

A rare pastille burner, the roof supported by trees, the pierced windows outlined in blue, on circular green and gilt base modelled with flower-sprays, the roof detachable, possibly Spode, 5 in (12.5 cm). **$1,000-2,000**

A Staffordshire purple lustre castle, c1860, 7 in (17.5 cm). **$300-600**

Cow Creamers

A Staffordshire cow creamer, some restoration, 18thC, 6 in (15 cm). **$1,200-2,100**

A Whieldon type creamware cow creamer, 18thC, 5in (12.5cm). **$1,300-2,400**

A Staffordshire cow creamer, 18thC, 5½ in (13.5 cm). **$1,400-2,600**

For a well modelled and brightly decorated example in perfect condition.

A Pratt type cow creamer, modelled as a cow with ochre and brown markings, standing before a tree, a calf at its feet, 7in (18cm). **$3,200-6,000**

This unusually fine example, in good condition, brightly coloured and with unusual bocage, fetched $5,500 at auction due to fierce competition between two would-be purchasers. An example of how auction rivalry can stimulate price levels particularly in the case of rarities.

A Prattware cow creamer, with hobbled back legs and milkmaid, decorated in yellow, grey and green glazes, lacking cover, c1785, 5½ in (13.5 cm). **$1,400-2,600**

A fine Staffordshire cow creamer and cover, with sponged decoration in yellow and grey-brown, green washed slab base, c1785, 5 in (12.5 cm). **$1,200-2,100**

A pair of early Staffordshire cow creamers, c1790, 6 in (15 cm). **$2,600-5,300**

A Staffordshire cow creamer, with sponged decoration in yellow and black with green washed base, c1790, 5 in (12.5 cm). **$1,000-2,000**

A Pratt cow creamer, decorated in underglaze ochre and black sponging on a green glazed base, replacement cover, c1790, 5 in (12.5 cm). **$1,200-2,100**

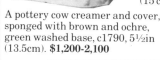

A cow creamer and cover, modelled as a standing cow with pink lustre and brown markings, on shaped rectangular green mound base, 6 in (15 cm). **$400-750**

A pottery cow creamer and cover, sponged with brown and ochre, green washed base, c1790, 5½in (13.5cm). **$1,200-2,100**

A fine Prattware cow creamer, sponged and patterned in ochre and grey, with milkmaid in blue and yellow, on a green washed base, c1790, 5 in (12.5 cm). **$1,400-2,600**

A pair of Staffordshire cow creamers, with ochre and brown sponged decoration and milkmaids with green dresses, damage to horns and milkmaid on one creamer, late 18thC, 6in (15cm) long. **$2,600-5,300**

It is unusual to find a matching pair of creamers.

A pair of early Staffordshire cow creamers, c1790, 6 in (15 cm). **$3,200-6,000**

A cow creamer and cover, modelled as a standing cow with copper lustre and pink lustre markings, 5½ in (13.5 cm). **$400-750**

A Staffordshire cow creamer of scarce type, painted with alternate red and black motifs on a green washed base, restored, c1810, 5 in (12.5 cm). **$900-1,700**

A large Staffordshire cow creamer, decorated in brown and blue, on shaped base with green lining, c1830-40, 6in (15cm). **$800-1,500**

A pair of early Staffordshire cow creamers, c1810, 5in (12.5cm). **$2,600-5,300**

A cow creamer in brown glazed pottery, cover missing, c1840, 4½ in (11 cm). **$800-1,500**

Cups

A very rare pottery coloured saltglaze tea bowl and saucer, c1755. **$900-1,700**

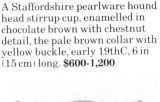

A Staffordshire pearlware hound head stirrup cup, enamelled in chocolate brown with chestnut detail, the pale brown collar with yellow buckle, early 19thC, 6 in (15 cm) long. **$600-1,200**

A Staffordshire slipware inscribed and dated loving cup, the dark brown body overlaid in cream slip and incised with the initials IBE, the reverse with the date 1763, rim repaired, c1763, 7 in (17.5 cm). **$4,000-6,800**

A Staffordshire dog's head stirrup cup, with black markings and pink muzzle and the rim decorated in solid pink lustre, c1825, 4½ in (11 cm) wide. **$1,400-2,600**

A Staffordshire pug's head stirrup cup, painted in pale brown and the lip decorated in solid pink lustre, c1825, 3½in (8.5cm). **$1,600-2,800**

A pair of Staffordshire pottery fox mask stirrup cups, inscribed inside 'C.P.1858', 19thC, 5 in (12.5 cm). **$800-1,500**

A Staffordshire stirrup cup, c1825, 4 in (10 cm) long. **$500-900**

Did you know
MILLER'S Antiques Price Guide builds up year by year to form the most comprehensive photo-reference system available.

Figures – Animals

A Staffordshire pottery cricket mug, 19thC, 5in (12.5cm).
$400-750

A Castleford-type mug, c1810.
$300-600

A pottery bull baiting group, by Ralph Wood Jr, the base decorated in overglaze enamels and applied with shredded clay foliage, the beast coloured with large splashes of iron-red, ears and left horn damaged, 5½in (14cm).
$1,200-2,100

An Obadiah Sherratt bull baiting group, with male figure and 2 dogs, 13in (32cm) long.
$4,500-9,000

An Obadiah Sherratt bull baiting group titled 'Bull Beating', 'Now Captin Lad', much restored, 13½ in (33 cm). **$1,800-3,800**

A rare animal figure which would have been given a much higher price if in better condition.

An early Staffordshire bull baiting group, c1790, 7½in (18.5cm).
$1,800-3,800

A Staffordshire pottery cow and calf bocage group, early 19thC, 5½ in (13.5 cm).
$600-1,100

A Staffordshire cow group, marked Walton, c1820, 5 in (12.5 cm).
$600-1,200

A Ralph Wood model of a doe, the coat enriched in brown and white, extensively restored, c1770, 6 in (15.5 cm). **$1,000-2,000**

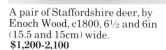

A pair of Staffordshire deer, by Enoch Wood, c1800, 6½ and 6in (15.5 and 15cm) wide.
$1,200-2,100

A pair of Staffordshire pottery greyhounds, the bases coloured in turquoise enamel, their coats vibrantly splashed in black enamel, enamel flaking, mid-19thC, 10½ and 11½in (26 and 28cm).
$1,800-3,800

A pair of standing greyhounds and hares, one restored, c1860, 10 in (25 cm). **$600-1,200**

A pair of Staffordshire dogs, with free standing front legs, c1850, 9 in (22.5 cm). **$300-600**

A greyhound on blue base, c1850, 5½ in (13 cm). **$200-450**

A Staffordshire figure of a greyhound, c1840. **$200-450**

A Staffordshire dog, by Ralph Wood, c1800, 7 in (17.5 cm). **$1,400-2,600**

An early Staffordshire dog, c1800, 6½ in (16 cm) long. **$600-1,100**

A pair of rare, well-modelled spaniels with brown markings, wearing gilt collars, on unusual shaped rectangular pink-ground bases, modelled with leaves, 10in (25cm). **$2,200-4,200**

C F Anthony Oliver – The Tribal Art of England, *pl 102.*

A rare majolica pug, some restoration, c1880, 17 in (42.5 cm). **$1,000-2,000**

A pair of spaniels with brown markings, wearing gilt collars and chains, 10½in (26cm). **$400-750**

A pair of groups of poodles wearing gilt collars, with puppies, on blue and gilt bases, 8in (20cm). **$600-1,200**

A pair of early Staffordshire dogs, in orange and white, c1840-50. **$300-600**

A Prattware model of a ram, thinly potted and decorated in semi-translucent glazes, mainly green, orange and black, c1785, 5 in (12.5 cm). **$1,200-2,100**

A Ralph Wood model of a ram, on a high mottled yellow base, his body and horns enriched in mottled tones of grey, small chip to base, c1770, 6½ in (16.5 cm). **$1,700-3,000**

An early Staffordshire group, in mint condition, c1790, 4½ in (11 cm). **$1,800-3,800**

A Staffordshire pair of Enoch Wood sheep, copied from Derby examples, 5½ in (13.5 cm). **$1,600-2,800**

A pair of early Staffordshire Walton sheep, with bocage, c1830. **$800-1,500**

An Enoch Wood model of a lion, his left paw resting on a yellow ball, his coat and mane enriched in yellow and light brown, the base moulded with stylised foliage and painted in imitation of marble, base cracked, chips to teeth and base, c1790, 11½ in (29 cm) wide. **$1,800-3,800**

A Yorkshire Prattware figure of a sheep, shepherdess and lambs, 6 in (15 cm). **$1,800-3,800**

A rare model of a lion standing, its left forepaw resting on a yellow ball, on rectangular marbled base, 10 in (25 cm) high. **$1,400-2,600**

A Staffordshire pair of figures, a ewe and a ram, marked Walton, bocage in mint condition, c1820, 6½ in (16 cm). **$1,600-2,800**

ENOCH WOOD OF BURSLEM

* one of the most productive potteries of the late 18th early 19thC
* Enoch Wood started work as an apprentice in the pottery trade in the early 1770's
* in 1784 commenced a pottery with his cousin Ralph Wood
* in 1790 established a new firm, Wood and Caldwell
* in 1818 the firm became Enoch Wood and Sons
* produced good figure models generally using overglaze colours (earlier Ralph Wood and Whieldon figures used muted in-glaze colours)
* overglaze colours sometimes produce a matt surface
* also produced blue-printed wares and exported large quantities to the USA

A rare and unusual pottery figure of a recumbent leopard, its front paw resting on a piece of knarled flesh, decorated in overglaze brightly coloured enamels, damaged, early 19thC, 8½in (21cm) long.
$2,000-4,500

A rare pair of lion and tiger figural groups by Obadiah Sherratt, c1820. **$22,000-40,000**

Obadiah Sherratt of Burslem produced some of the most collectable types of Prattware animals and figure groups. His models are often larger than those of contemporary factories. This unusual pair of a lion and tiger attacking a missionary and a native may have been intended to have a satirical content.

A Wood and Caldwell figure of a lion, on a black enamelled rectangular base, wearing a gentle expression and with its tail curled around its body, its coat enamelled in two shades of brown and with brush-stroked mane, some restoration, 5 in (12.5 cm) wide.
$600-1,200

An early English slip decorated pottery cat, covered in a honey coloured glaze with brown spots, on oval base, one ear repaired, other chipped, c1680, 6in (15cm).
$800-1,500

A Whieldon type tortoiseshell glazed figure of a seated cat, covered in a manganese tortoiseshell glaze, c1760, 3½in (9.5cm).
$1,300-2,400

An Obadiah Sherratt group of a lion attacking a child, the lion with grey mane and yellow coat, on oval marblised base enriched in green, repair to its tail and one leg of child, c1820, 8in (20cm) long.
$3,200-6,000

A pair of spill vases modelled as horses, with foals recumbent at their feet on oval coloured gilt-lined bases, 12½in (31cm).
$600-1,100

A pair of horse spills, c1880, 13 in (32.5 cm). **$500-900**

A pottery figure of a cat, its coat sponged in black and yellow enamel, 3½in (9cm) wide.
$200-450

A Staffordshire pottery horse, finished in chestnut and brown with green shaded base, restored, c1840, 5in (12.5cm). **$400-750**

A Staffordshire game bird, 18thC, 10½ in (26 cm). **$200-450**

An early Staffordshire pottery bird, c1790, 3 in (7.5 cm). **$500-900**

An early Staffordshire pottery bird whistle, c1790, 3in (7.5cm). **$900-1,700**

A Ralph Wood model of a polar bear, standing on an oval high green rockwork base, his coat enriched in grey, 2 minute chips to rim, c1770, 3½ in (9.5 cm) wide. **$1,800-3,800**

A good Ralph Wood model using muted in-glaze colours as opposed to overglaze enamels.

A Staffordshire pottery elephant, c1850, 9½in (23.5cm). **$1,700-3,000**

A pair of rare figures of goats with brown markings, standing on oval coloured gilt-lined bases, 5 in (12.5 cm). **$600-1,100**

A pottery figure of a giraffe, on a grassy base delineated in gilt, before a palm tree, damage to ears and tree, 4½in (11.5cm). **$300-600**

A pair of zebras on oval coloured gilt-lined bases, 8½ in (21 cm). **$400-750**

A pair of squirrels, 1890-1910, 6 in (15 cm). **$300-600**

A pair of rare figures of rabbits with black markings, recumbent facing right and left, eating lettuce leaves, 5 in (12.5 cm). **$4,000-7,500**

Figures – People

An early Staffordshire group of George and the Dragon, by Ralph Wood, some restoration, c1780, 11 in (27.5 cm). **$1,800-3,800**

A group depicting St. George and Dragon, some repair, impressed mark Wood & Caldwell, Burslem on rear of base, well coloured in enamels, 1790-1800, 8in (20cm). **$1,300-2,400** (Depending on condition)

23

A rare English grey stoneware spice dish, 2 figures with repairs to waist, minor chips, 17thC, 9 in (22 cm). **$1,800-3,800**

A Staffordshire white saltglaze figure of Eve, her eyes enriched in brown and her hair and body lightly enriched in blue, c1750, 4½ in (11 cm). **$1,000-2,000**

Cf Bernard Rackham: Catalogue of the Glaisher Collection of Pottery & Porcelain, pl 55D.

A Yorkshire figure of the Madonna and Child, she in brown dress and with a blue-edged ochre shawl, the Child in a blue robe, c1790, 9½ in (23.5 cm). **$400-750**

◁ A Yorkshire figure of a man, in brown hat and striped trousers holding a bag and a cudgel, standing before an ochre tree stump, c1790, 5in (12.5cm). **$500-900**

▷ A Yorkshire Prattware figure of a woman with a child, 18thC, 9½ in (23.5 cm). **$900-1,700**

◁ A Yorkshire group of George and the Dragon, c1790, 11 in (27.5 cm). **$1,800-3,800**

An early Staffordshire Leeds-type pair of gardeners with urn, 6½ in (16 cm). **$1,000-2,000**

A Ralph Wood Jr, Staffordshire figure group of Vicar & Moses, blue and manganese, cream and green glazes, 1770-95, 9½ in (23 cm). **$1,600-2,800**

An early Staffordshire figure, sometimes known as The Orator, c1795, 10 in (25 cm). **$1,000-2,000**

A Ralph Wood group, Vicar & Moses, the translucent decoration in mainly brown and grey, base unglazed, untitled, c1785, 9½ in (23 cm). **$1,400-2,600**

An early Staffordshire figure group, possibly by Neale & Co, in good condition, c1800, 8½ in (21 cm). **$1,400-2,600**

An important Lakin & Poole group depicting Cephalus & Procris, with fine detail enamelling to figures and base, c1790, 10½in (26cm). **$1,800-3,800**

A Staffordshire figure of Simon, impressed Wedgwood, c1800, 9½ in (23.5 cm). **$800-1,500**

A pair of Staffordshire pottery figures of classically draped maidens, on leaf moulded bases, late 18thC, 7in (17.5cm). **$600-1,200**

An early Staffordshire group entitled Vicar & Moses, probably by Enoch Wood, c1800, 12 in (30 cm). **$1,000-2,000**

A Staffordshire figure in a chair, c1800, 4 in (9.5 cm). **$600-1,100**

A Staffordshire double Rural Pastimes group, c1810, 11½ in (28.5 cm). **$2,200-4,200**

A pair of early Staffordshire Leeds-type figures, c1800. **$600-1,200**

A Staffordshire figure, Hurdy Gurdy, impressed mark Enoch Wood, c1800, 8in (20cm). **$300-600**

An early Staffordshire group of musicians, c1800, 7½ in (18.5 cm). **$1,000-2,000**

A Staffordshire classical figure of a lady holding a baby and attendant child, c1800, 9in (22cm). **$100-250**

Two Yorkshire figures of ladies, one dressed in a riding habit, the other in décolleté dress enriched in blue and yellow, standing on high green mound and octagonal bases, both plumes, one hand and one base restored, c1800, 11 and 11½ in (27.5 and 28.5 cm). **$1,800-3,800**

An early Walton type Staffordshire group depicting Abraham sacrificing Isaac, well decorated in many enamel colours, c1815, 10½in (26cm). **$1,000-2,000**

An early Staffordshire group, entitled 'Friendship', in mint condition, 8in (20cm). **$1,600-2,800**

A marked Walton group of
'Songsters' with large bocage
support, 1815-25, 9 in (22.5 cm).
$1,400-2,600

One of this maker's rarer pieces.

A pair of Staffordshire groups
depicting Sailors Farewell &
Return, c1815, 9½in (24cm).
$1,000-2,000

*Note that the sailor's dress is
different in each group which is
quite normal on a pair.*

A Staffordshire group of musicians,
c1815, 9 in (22.5 cm). **$900-1,700**

A Staffordshire spill holder, 'Return
from Egypt', impressed mark
Walton, c1820, 8in (20cm).
$1,400-2,600

A pair of early Staffordshire figures,
'Widow' and 'Elijah', marked
Walton, in excellent condition,
c1820, 12 in (30 cm). **$1,600-2,800**

A Staffordshire Gretna Green
group, on a rectangular base, with
the inscription 'John Macdonald
Aged 79 A Scotch esquire run of
with a English girl aged 17 to
Gratnal Green the old blacksmith
to be married' (sic.), restoration to
lovers' arms, tree and blacksmith's
hammer, c1820, 8in (20cm).
$1,000-2,000

A Walton group of a Sultan and a
Sultana, on a grassy mound with 12
resting sheep, marbled serpentine
stand with floral border and bracket
feet, 8 in (20 cm). **$3,200-6,000**

A rare set of Sunderland lustre
figures of the Seasons, marked
Dixon, Austin, c1820, 9-9½in (22.5-
23.5cm). **$3,200-6,000**

A pair of Walton-style pottery
figures depicting 'Flight' and
'Return', coloured overall in
overglaze enamels, damage to limbs
of Joseph and donkey, boy's head
missing, Joseph's head and the base
restuck on 'Return', 10in (25cm).
$800-1,500

Two Staffordshire pottery figures of small girls, on low rectangular bases delineated in red enamel, both damaged, early 19thC, 3 in (7.5 cm) wide. **$150-300**

A Staffordshire pottery figure entitled 'Fruitboys', standing on a blue green mound base, the boy flanked by flowering bocage and wearing blue tunic and wide yellow trousers, base chipped, early 19thC, 5½ in (14 cm). **$500-900**

A Staffordshire group of dandies, Walton, enriched in colours, standing on square base, some repairs, c1810, 8½in (21cm). **$800-1,500**

A Walton group of 'Friendship', impressed Walton to reverse, c1820, 7 in (18 cm). **$1,000-2,000**

A Walton pottery figure of a putto, reverse impressed Walton on a scroll, restored, 6in (15cm). **$200-450**

An early Walton-type group of gardeners with implements, decorated in green, red-brown, purple and blue enamels, 1815-20, 7 in (17.5 cm). **$900-1,700**

A Staffordshire new Marriage Act group, c1820, 7in (17.5cm). **$1,600-2,800**

A Staffordshire Walton-type figure of the Shepherd, c1820, 4½ in (11 cm). **$500-900**

A Walton-type figure of 'St. Peter', backed by large bocage with double flowers, mainly coloured orange and yellow, with green base, c1820, 10 in (25 cm). **$900-1,700**

A Staffordshire group of Dandies, wearing brightly coloured costumes, c1820, 7½ in (18.5 cm). **$800-1,500**

A very rare Staffordshire group, The Lovers, of Walton-type, c1820, 5 in (12.5 cm). **$600-1,200**

An Obadiah Sherratt figure of 'Venus', naked except for a yellow and puce drape, slightly damaged, 10 in (25 cm). **$1,000-2,000**

Obadiah Sherratt of Burslem was one amongst a number of makers of colourful figure groups decorated overglaze in bright orange, blue, green and brown. These figures are sometimes called Prattware figures after Pratt of Lane Delph who was a leading manufacturer of such pieces. Other leading makers were Ralph Salt of Hanley and John Walton of Burslem.

An Obadiah Sherratt group of the Gretna Green marriage, decorated in multi-coloured enamels, the lady figure a replacement, c1825, 7½ in (18.5 cm). **$1,200-2,100**

In perfect condition $2,200-4,200

A rare Obadiah Sherratt figure of Summer, with typical flower decoration to dress, c1825, 7 in (17.5 cm). **$400-750**

An Obadiah Sherratt 'Grecian and Daughter' group, showing the chained and manacled Cimon being offered sustenance by his daughter, c1830, 10in (25cm). **$4,500-9,000**

It is interesting to note that the actual auction prices of two almost identical figure groups were $4,000 and $1,300 . This difference cannot readily be explained by condition, though the higher priced group was in slightly better condition and more pleasingly painted. The more expensive group was sold in London some few months before the second group.

An Obadiah Sherratt group of The Courtship, she wearing wide brimmed bonnet and iron-red flowered dress, he in green jacket and puce patterned trousers, the base enriched in green, iron-red and grey, the base applied with a jardinière, minor repair to the rim of her hat and branches of tree, c1810, 8in (20cm). **$3,200-6,000**

Cf the example in The Earle Collection of Early Staffordshire Pottery, no. 650.

An Obadiah Sherratt figure entitled 'The Reading Maid', c1825, 11½ in (28.5 cm). **$1,000-2,000**

A naive Staffordshire group of musicians with numerous animals, topped by crude bocage, c1825, 7½ in (18.5 cm). **$800-1,500**

This is a charming attempt to copy Walton.

A Staffordshire group entitled 'Rural' by Enoch Wood, with enamel decoration, 8in (20cm). **$600-1,200**

This is derived from earlier examples by Ralph Wood Jr.

A Staffordshire group of The Sacrifice of Isaac, Abraham standing about to sacrifice his son seated on an altar applied with an inscription, enriched in bright enamels, minor restoration to dagger, c1830, 10½ in (26.5 cm). **$600-1,200**

Cf Reginald G Haggar, Staffordshire Chimney Ornaments, pl 79.

A Staffordshire Obadiah Sherratt Bull Baiting group, c1825, 9½ in (23.5 cm). **$4,000-7,500**

See other examples in pottery animals section.

A Staffordshire Tithe Pig group showing the farmer's wife offering one of her offspring in lieu of a pig, decorated in underglaze colours, c1830, 6 in (15 cm). **$900-1,700**

This has an unusual base.

A pair of Staffordshire figures of a shepherd and shepherdess, modelled by Lloyd Sheldon, c1840, 5½ in (14 cm). **$600-1,100**

A well modelled figure of a man standing wearing a blue neckerchief beside a donkey laden with sticks, the base entitled 'Beesums' in gilt-moulded capitals, 10½ in (26 cm). **$400-750**

A Staffordshire pottery figure of a man seated on a tree trunk playing the bagpipes, early 19thC, 6 in (15 cm). **$200-450**

A Staffordshire pottery group, The Sacrifice of Isaac, with trunk vase at the rear, on oval base, 12 in (30 cm). **$150-250**

A large Staffordshire pottery figure of Little Red Riding Hood by Thomas Parr, c1860's, 15 in (37 cm). **$600-1,200**

Modelled after the painting by James Sant.

A Staffordshire pottery figure of a child with a cradle, c1860, 6½ in (16 cm). **$200-450**

A Victorian Staffordshire figure of a kilted Scots hunter with stag and hound, raised on an oval plinth base, 13½in (33.5cm). **$80-180**

A later Victorian edition of an Enoch Wood group known as The Drunk Parson and Town Clerk, c1860. **$400-750**

A later Victorian edition of a Ralph Wood group known as Vicar & Moses, c1860. **$400-750**

A Staffordshire figure 'Gipsy Boy' on a dun horse, 19thC, 9 in (23 cm).
$80-180

STAFFORDSHIRE FIGURES

★ period of production c1835 to 1895
★ figures made with 'flat backs' or 'in the round'
★ material used varies from pottery to porcelain type body
★ many figures do not appear in the standard reference book 'Staffordshire Portrait Figures' by P D Gordon Pugh. However, some collectors only buy figures which appear in Pugh
★ many fakes and restored pieces appear on the market
★ value is affected by damage, poorly defined features, flaked overglaze enamel or rubbed gilding
★ unusual animals and theatrical figures particularly collectable

Victorian Staffordshire

A. British & Foreign Royalty

A Staffordshire group of the Prince of Wales and Princess Royal, repair to waist of princess and wheel of carriage, c1845, 7in (17cm) long.
$400-900

Cf Gordon Pugh, Staffordshire Portrait Figures, *pl 47 fig 143*.

A Victorian Staffordshire group of Royal children with bird, c1850, 8in (20cm).
$180-300

A rare well modelled group of Albert and the Princess Royal, the former standing to the left wearing blue jacket and full length iron red ermine edged cloak, on oval gilt lined base, 9in (22.5cm). (A56/172).
$400-750

A rare figure of Victoria and the Princess Royal, the former standing to the right wearing a blue bodice and tartan skirt, 10in (25cm). (A57/179).
$300-600

A Staffordshire pottery figure of the Princess Royal, Empress of Prussia, holding a dog and a bird, on circular base, 17½in (43cm).
$400-750

A pair of figures of the Prince and Princess of Wales, 10in (25cm). (A76/225,226).
$200-450

A Staffordshire pottery portrait figure of the Prince of Wales, decorated in colours, on oval base, 18in (45cm).
$180-300

A Staffordshire pottery figure of the Prince of Wales, 8in (20cm).
$200-450

A figure of Britannia seated, flanked by a shield and the British Lion, 6in (15cm).
$400-750

A pair of Staffordshire figures of Queen Victoria and Prince Albert, c1848, 8½in (21cm).
$600-1,200

A Staffordshire flat back figure, gilt name to the base 'Empress of France', in underglazed blue and enamel colours, late 19thC, 10in (25cm).
$200-450

A Staffordshire figure of the Prince of Wales with bird, c1848, 5in (12.5cm).
$200-450

A Staffordshire figure of the Princess of Wales with cradle, c1848, 5in (12.5cm).
$200-450

B. Statesmen & Politicians

A well modelled figure of Wellington, on raised pink lustre marbled base, 13in (32.5cm). (similar to B2/19).
$400-900

A rare figure of Theobald Wolfe Tone, beside a pedestal entitled 'Who Fears to Speak of 98', the oval base named in gilt script, 13½in (33cm). (B16/51).
$600-1,200

A well modelled coloured figure of Wellington, wearing a blue jacket and holding a scroll in his right hand, 12in (30cm). (similar to B4/25).
$800-1,500

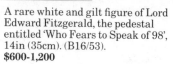

A rare white and gilt figure of Lord Edward Fitzgerald, the pedestal entitled 'Who Fears to Speak of 98', 14in (35cm). (B16/53).
$600-1,200

A rare white and gilt figure of Henry Joy McCracken, the pedestal entitled 'Who Fears to Speak of 98', 13in (32.5cm). (B16/52).
$400-900

A Staffordshire portrait figure, named 'Washington', c1850, 15½in (38.5cm).
$1,000-2,000

A Staffordshire group of 'Uncle Tom and Eva', Eva's right foot missing, c1852, 8in (20cm).
$600-1,200

Cf Gordon Pugh, Staffordshire Portrait Figures, *pls 28, 29 figs 87-90.*

A large white and gilt figure of Benjamin Franklin standing before rockwork, the oval base entitled 'General Washington' in gilt script, 16in (40cm). (B23A/70A).
$1,000-2,000

A high price because of the American association.

A rare figure of 'Aunt Chloe' standing, holding a basket in her left hand, the circular base named in gilt script, 8in (20cm). (B26/82).
$200-450

A rare equestrian figure of Gholab Singh, wearing an iron red jacket and yellow waist sash, holding a scimitar in his left hand, on shaped gilt lined base, 8½in (21cm). (C27/68).
$400-900

A Staffordshire group from Uncle Tom's Cabin, showing Eva and Uncle Tom, 7in (17.5cm).
$200-450

C. Naval Military & Exploration

A rare group of Topsy and Eva seated, arm in arm on oval scroll moulded base, entitled 'Topsy and Eva', 8in (20cm). (B26/84).
$300-600

A figure of Captain Cook, wearing captain's full dress uniform, holding a manuscript, resting on a tripod table at his side, on shaped gilt lined base, 7½in (18cm). (C5/4).
$2,200-4,200

A rare well modelled figure of Campbell, standing in full military uniform, 10½in (26cm). (C56/144).
$600-1,200

A rare equestrian figure of General Simpson, wearing full military uniform, 13in (32.5cm). (C56/150).
$800-1,500

A Staffordshire pottery fortress, named Sebastopol, Crimean War, c1860, 10in (25cm).
$500-900

A Staffordshire figure group of a soldier from the 21st Lancers and a sailor, c1898, 12in (30cm). (C340).
$300-600

A Staffordshire figure group of 'Eugenie and Napoleon', c1854, 12½in (31cm). (C80).
$300-600

D. Religious

A Staffordshire figure of Moody, the American evangelist, c1873. (D9a).
$200-450

This figure is one of a pair.

A Staffordshire flat back figure of John Wesley, in enamel colours and gilt, clock face on oval base, c1875, 12in (30cm).
$200-450

Religious figures are amongst the least popular figures in the Staffordshire group. However a rare example will still command a good price.

E. Theatre, Opera, Ballet & Circus

A rare figure of King Henry V, wearing a long tunic, blue ermine-edged jacket and yellow gauntlets, beside a pedestal surmounted by a sceptre, the rectangular base entitled 'Henry V Trying On the Crown', 13½in (33cm). (E12/29).
$5,500-9,000

Cf John Hall, Staffordshire Portrait Figures, *pl 27.*

A Staffordshire flat back figure of 'C H Spurgeon', enamel colours, raised name on base, late 19thC, 11½in (28cm).
$200-450

A well coloured group of 'Othello and Iago', 11½in (28cm). (E13/31).
$800-1,500

A figure of John Philip Kemble as Hamlet, standing holding a skull in his left hand, the circular coloured base entitled 'Alas, Poor Yorick', 11in (27.5cm). (E13a/32a).
$400-750

A figure of Madame Alboni as Cinderella, wearing a plumed hat, blue cloak and green skirt in an elaborate pumpkin carriage behind a horse, 8½in (21cm). (E20/43).
$600-1,200

Cf Antony Oliver, The Victorian Staffordshire Figure, *colour pl 7.*

An unusual hollow Staffordshire figure of Falstaff, c1845, 6in (15cm). (Similar to E25).
$180-300

◁ A rare group of trick riders, probably portraying Andrew Ducrow and his wife, Louisa Woolford, 11in (27.5cm). (E68/131).
$400-900

A rare group of Masaniello and ▷ Fenella, 11in (27.5cm). (E111/221).
$300-600

A rare group of Mr Barton and Miss Rosa Henry as Giaffier and Zuleika, on oval gilt lined base, 12in (30cm). (E28/60).
$900-1,700

Cf Antony Oliver, The Victorian Staffordshire Figure, *pl 145.*

A rare figure of Mr Pickwick, standing wearing a dark blue tailcoat on shaped gilt scroll moulded base, 7½in (18cm).
$300-600

A figure of a gentleman wearing striped trousers, yellow jacket and turban, seated, a tiger dead at his side, on an elephant before a stream, on oval coloured base, 8in (20cm).
$1,000-2,000

A figure of Jenny Lind as Marie, her right hand holding a green hat, wearing a blue bodice and striped skirt, the shaped base entitled 'M. Lind', 7½in (18cm). (E83/164).
$800-1,500

A rare figure of Sarah Eggerton as Helen MacGregor, holding an axe in her right hand, a shield in her left, on oval gilt lined base, 9in (22.5cm). (E74/146).
$400-750

A rare Staffordshire portrait figure of the lion tamer Van Amburgh, titled, the subject standing surrounded by a pride of lions, a leopard on his back, c1840, 6in (15cm).
$6,000-12,000

A Staffordshire group of the Elephant of Siam, enriched in green, iron red, blue and grey, c1840, 6in (15cm) wide. (E156). **$600-1,100**

A Victorian Staffordshire theatrical figure group, c1845, 9in (22.5cm). **$200-450**

A Victorian Staffordshire girl mandolin player, c1845, 10in (25cm). **$180-300**

F. Sport

An early Staffordshire figure of Tom Cribb, c1830. **$1,800-3,800**

A pair of Staffordshire figures of the boxers 'Heenan' and 'Sayers', in mint condition, c1850, 9½in (23.5cm). **$800-1,500**

A pair of Staffordshire pugilist figures, modelled as the boxers Mollineux and Cribb, both wearing ochre breeches, Cribb's left arm and base restored, c1810, 8in (22cm). **$4,500-9,000**

A Staffordshire sporting group, of two pugilists 'Heenan and Sayers', as raised names on base, enamel colours, 10in (25cm). **$400-750**

A figure of George Parr, standing wearing an iron red and blue peaked cap, a cricket ball held in his right hand, flanked by a jacket, stumps and cricket bat, on oval gilt lined base, 13in (32.5cm). (F7/13). **$800-1,500**

Figures depicting cricketers are particularly collectable.

G. Crime

A Victorian Staffordshire pair of figures of Dick Turpin and Tom King, 9½in (23.5cm). **$400-900**

A Lambeth delft blue-dash Royalist portrait charger, the centre painted predominantly in blue with a portrait of Queen Anne, her dress, orb and sceptre enriched in yellow, standing in a green field flanked by sponged trees, within a blue and yellow line cartouche and blue-dash rim, restored, c1705, 14in (35cm).
$6,000-12,000

Cf Frank Britton, English Delftware in the Bristol Collection, *pl 3.53.*

A London delft plate, with a Chinaman kneeling with yellow bushes and manganese circle, with floral border, c1740, 9in (22.5cm).
$400-750

A London delft Royalist blue and white plate, painted with the rose and thistle tied with ribbon beneath a crown and the initials 'GR', within concentric blue lines, crack and chips to rim, c1715, 9in (22.5cm).
$1,800-3,800

CF F H Garner and Michael Archer. English Delftware, *pl 66A.*

A Lambeth delft ballooning plate painted in blue, green, yellow and manganese, within a blue 'feuille-de-choux' rim, minor glaze flaking to rim, c1785, 12in (30cm).
$3,200-6,000

See F H Garner and Michael Archer, English Delftware, *pl 119A.*

A Liverpool delft blue and white commemorative dish, the centre painted with The Taking of Portobello beneath a wide border, within an ochre rim, the reverse with blue pennants, slight cracks to well at 1 o'clock, minor chips and glaze flaking to rim, c1741, 12in (30cm).
$2,600-5,300

Cf Anthony Ray, op cit pl 10, no 28, also Frank Britton op cit pl 10.48 and Bernard Rackham, Catalogue of the Glaisher Collection of Pottery and Porcelain, *pl 118E.*

A Liverpool delft Fazackerley palette plate, with Flowers and Fence pattern, 9in (22.5cm).
$500-900

Two Liverpool delft plates painted in Fazackerley colours with central flower sprays, c1760, 9in (22.5cm).
$400-750

A London delft blue-dash tulip charger, painted in ochre, yellow and blue within a yellow line and blue-dash rim, the reverse with a pale green glaze, some glaze flaking, c1700, 14in (35cm).
$3,200-6,000

A delft dish, painted in green and yellow outlined in manganese, London or Bristol, c1760, 11½in (28.5cm).
$300-600

A Staffordshire saltglaze tartan-ground Royalist teapot and cover, with loop handle and faceted spout, painted in sepia with a bust length portrait of Prince Charles Edward Stuart, restored, spout chipped, c1750, 5½in (14cm).
$20,000-30,000

Above A lead glazed pottery stove tile, moulded in relief with the Royal Coat-of-Arms, mid-16thC, 13½ by 10in (34 by 25cm).
$3,200-6,000

Below A Staffordshire two-handled slipware posset pot, late 17thC, 4in (11cm) high.
$8,000-15,000

A Southwark delft armorial salt, painted in blue, the ends moulded with the arms of the City of London, one foot repaired, chips to rim, second quarter 17thC, 5½in (13cm) wide.
$10,000-18,000

Very few salts such as this would appear to be recorded.

Right A saltglazed punch bowl, decorated in scratch blue with sprays of flowers, inscribed E. Saddler and dated 1759, 11in (28cm).
$10,000-18,000

Below l. A Yorkshire pearlware oviform jug, with portrait of Lord Nelson, c1800, 5½in (13cm) high. **$800-1,500**
c. A Yorkshire pearlware oval portrait plaque of Admiral Earl Howe, c1795, 7½in (19cm).
$1,400-2,600
r. A Yorkshire pearlware oviform jug, c1795, 5½in (13cm). **$1,000-2,000**

A Staffordshire pottery garniture of 3 figural spill vase groups, in the manner of Ralph Wood, the younger, c1790, 10½ by 9½in (26.5 and 23cm).
$2,600-5,300

Left A rare Yorkshire money box in the form of a ram, attendant and dog, c1800-20, 6in (15cm).
$2,600-5,300

Very few pottery money boxes in this form appear to exist.

A Ralph Wood Toby jug, representing Lord Howe, mould mark '63' impressed under base, c1770, 9½in (24cm).
$4,000-6,800

A Yorkshire cow group with girl attendant, 6in (15cm). **$1,800-3,800**
Below A pair of Liverpool delftware candlesticks, c1760, 9½in (44cm).
$20,000-30,000

An Obadiah Sherratt model of Politos Menagerie, impressed 'Menagerie of The Wonderfull Burds and Beasts From Most Parts of the World', c1830, 13in (32.5cm). **$14,000-24,000**

Below An Obadiah Sherratt group of Politos Menagerie modelled as a stage, inscribed, restored, one parrot and monkey missing, chips, c1830, 12in (30cm).
$34,000-54,000

Above, far left & left Two rare Staffordshire pottery groups of musicians, seated on high graduated grassy bases before flowering bocage, one showing a piper and lute player both wearing feathered bonnets, the other modelled as a flautist and lute player, a stream and swan at their feet, 8¾in (22cm), early 19thC.
$4,500-9,000

Above A Staffordshire pottery figure of Charity in a floral robe and yellow sash on a shaped grassy base before a stump support, with two children at her feet, some paint flaking on base and tree, 7½in (19cm).
$600-1,100

One of the rarest forms of cow creamer, having a large impractical bocage support, unusual acorn-bedecked leaves and large calf, probably from Yorkshire c1780-90, 9in (22.5cm).
$3,200-6,000

Above A fine Prattware figure of a cavalry officer, mounted on a prancing horse, wearing a deep blue jacket with yellow sash, yellow breeches and brown boots, his helmet embossed with the cypher GR, on a textured green mound base edged in ochre, 8¾in (22cm).
$4,500-9,000

Left A rare Staffordshire (Lloyd) group of Isaac Van Amburgh, wearing Roman gladiator dress, with a leopard, a lion, a lioness and a cub, c1830, 5¾in (14cm). (E100/200).
$6,000-12,000

'The new Marriage Act' by Obadiah Sherratt, decorated in typical Sherratt enamel colours, made at the time of the Act, 1822, 6½in (17cm).
$2,000-4,500

A Bristol delft blue and white documentary bowl with encircling inscription 'Joseph Springall: whole:sale: potter; in; mattshall: in: the: county: of: Norfolk:' minor chips and restorations, c1735, 14in (35cm).
$18,000-26,000

A pottery plaque decorated in underglaze colours with unglazed buff earthenware back, Whieldon School, Staffordshire, c1755, 7 by 8½in (17.5 by 21.5cm).
$6,000-12,000

A pair of pottery birds sitting on tree stumps with flowers in relief, decorated in underglaze colours, Whieldon type, Staffordshire, c1755, 7in (18cm).
$26,000-45,000

A delftware bottle with finely painted European landscape scenes, Liverpool, c1760, 10in (25cm).
$3,200-6,000

A Wedgwood 3-colour jasper figure of a reclining child modelled by William Hackwood after Della Robbia original, damage, c1785, 5½in (14cm) long.
$20,000-30,000

A Minton garden fountain, 'Amorini Fountain', modelled as a pair of cherubs sitting on a rock, impressed 'Minton 911' and date code for 1868, 26in (65cm) high.
$9,000-15,000

Right A Minton urn, with moulded decoration in high relief, impressed Minton 980, date code for 1864, 38½in (96.5cm) high.
$40,000-66,000

A Minton jardinière and stand, designed by Albert Carrier de Belleuse, naturalistic polychrome colouring on a cobalt blue ground, jardinière impressed 'Minton 990' and date code for 1882, 68in (168cm) high.
$50,000-90,000

Above right A pair of large Minton two-handled urns, with 2 relief panels below the rim with Bacchanalian scenes, impressed 1359 and date codes for 1872 and 1876, 23½in (59cm) high.
$10,000-18,000

A large Minton two-handled vase, minor chips, impressed IA, date code for 1859, 28in.
$18,000-26,000

41

Above An Hispano Moresque blue and copper lustre deep dish, with central IHS monogram in lustre, Valencia, mid-15thC, 19½in (48cm) diam.
$90,000-150,000

A Deruta blue and gold lustre a candelieri dish, some glaze repair to centre, rim chips, c1520, 16½in (42cm).
$10,000-18,000

Below right A Böttger polished brown stoneware baluster coffee pot and domed cover, with scroll handle, minute chip to spout, c1715, 7in (17.5cm).
$20,000-30,000

Below A Brussels faience boar's head tureen, cover and stand, minor rim chips, traces of S.L.M. mark to base of tureen, mid-18thC, stand 16in (40cm) long.
$11,000-18,000

The mark of this piece refers presumably to a member of the Mombaers family who were active in Brussels from 1705 until well after 1750.

A Safavid tile panel, with a black field and figure of Sagittarius surrounded by palmettes and flowering vine, some repair, framed, 49 by 34in.
$20,000-30,000

A pair of Luneville lions, in a rich blue glaze, enriched in white, minor repairs, some chips, c1750, 17½in (42cm) long. **$9,000-15,000**

A Bow blue and white ink pot, the top pierced with 4 holes, slight staining, indecipherable mark in blue, perhaps a circle, 1750, 3½in (9cm) diam.
$20,000-30,000

A Bow circular tureen and cover, the loop handles with incised frowning mask terminals, the cover with twig finial, chips to rim, finial repaired, unglazed base with incised R mark, c1750, 26in (66cm) wide.
$13,000-22,000

A pair of Bow figures of a cock and hen, the cock with minute chip to tail feathers, the hen with restoration to neck and chips to tail feathers, c1758, 4in (10cm) high.
$8,000-13,500

A Chelsea 'Hans Sloane' botanical plate painted with hibiscus, with a shaped chocolate line rim, some minute rubbing, red anchor and 43 mark, c1755, 9½in (23.5cm).
$10,000-18,000

A pair of Bow cherubs amidst bocage, c1765.
$1,200-2,100

A Chelsea oval sauceboat with scroll handle, painted in the manner of O'Neale with fable subjects, the interior with a bouquet and scattered flower sprays, red anchor mark, c1753, 9in (22cm) wide.
$28,000-48,000

l. A Chelsea lobed beaker, c1750, 3in (7cm).
$14,000-24,000

Only one other example would appear to be recorded

c. A Chelsea octagonal bowl after a Kakiemon original, c1752, 4in (10.5cm) wide.
$6,000-12,000

r. A Chelsea fluted beaker painted in the Kakiemon palette, rim minutely chipped, c1750, 3in (7.5cm).
$5,000-9,000

A Chelsea lobed teaplant beaker, minute rim chips, c1745-49, 3in (7.5cm).
$10,000-18,000

A rare Chaffers Liverpool phosphate mug, decorated in enamels, c1760, 5in (12.5cm) high.
$1,700-3,000

A Derby part dessert service painted with foxhunting scenes, comprising: a two-handled oblong compote, sugar bowl, cover and stand, 4 shell dishes, 12 plates, some minor rubbing to gilt, iron red crown, crossed batons and D marks, c1790.
$24,000-45,000

A rare Chelsea set of 4 cattle, 2 bearing red anchor marks, c1755, 1½ to 3in (3.5 to 7.5cm).
$6,000-12,000

A Longton Hall grape box and cover, c1755, 5in (12cm) wide.
$18,000-26,000

A Minton part dessert service, c1878. **$4,000-7,500**

A Worcester quatrefoil baluster vase, c1758, 6½in (16cm) high. **$18,000-26,000**

A garniture of 3 Minton vases, painted with flowers and with fine gilding by Thos. Steele, c1820. **$5,000-9,000**

A Worcester flared wine funnel, painted in a 'famile verte' palette with an Oriental holding a fan, the interior with a green diaper and flower-head pattern border, minute rim chip and fritting to inside rim, c1755, 5½in (13.5cm) high. **$24,000-45,000**

Above A Derby yellow ground tête-à-tête, each piece painted by John Brewer with animals and butterflies, blue crown, crossed baton and D marks, c1800. **$14,000-24,000**

Right A Pinxton yellow ground trio, in the manner of William Billingsley in puce with 'In the County of Wicklow, Ireland, Pinxton Church, Derbyshire and Beauchiff Abbey, Derbyshire', minute chip restored to foot rim of teacup, red mark P113, c1800. **$2,000-4,500**

A Worcester yellow-scale saucer-dish, painted with exotic birds and insects within gilt vase- and mirror-shaped cartouches, within gilt line rim, c1765, 7¼in (18.5cm) diam.
$8,000-13,500

Two Worcester blue-scale cabbage-leaf moulded mask jugs: One painted with bouquets and flower-sprays within gilt vase and mirror shaped cartouches, on a well-defined blue-scale ground, the handle with pink flowers and 'feuille-de-choux', slight chip to spout and foot rim, c1765, 8in (20cm).
$1,800-3,800

The other similarly decorated with garlands and flower sprays, slight chip to spout, c1768, 8in (20cm).
$2,000-4,500

Left: A pair of Worcester blue-scale oviform vases and covers, 2-handled, painted with phoenix and dragons among flowering plants in Oriental style, in rococo panels within richly gilt scroll borders, the necks with narrow bands of formal flowers in underglaze blue and gilt, floral knops and scroll handles, square seal marks in underglaze blue, c1765, 6½in (16cm).
$4,000-7,500

Below: A rare set of 12 Rockingham dessert plates, made to royal order, the centres painted in colours and gilt with the arms of King William IV suspending the Order of St George, puce printed 'Griffin Rockingham Works, Brameld, manufacturers to the King, Queen and Royal family,' within an elaborate cartouche and the date 1832 in gilt, one with repair to rim, 2 with hairline cracks, 9¼in (23.5cm) diam.
$40,000-75,000

A pair of Worcester circular butter tubs, covers and stands, painted with festoons and sprays of flowers in mirror and vase shaped panels outlined with gilt rococo scrolls on a blue-scale ground, the tubs with scroll handles and the covers with floral knops, square seal marks in underglaze blue, c1765.
$4,000-6,800

Left A Worcester quatrefoil two-handled chestnut basket, pierced cover and stand, painted in the atelier of James Giles, the base with blue '8', the cover with blue 'q' mark, some minor repairs to flowers, c1770, the stand 10½in (25.5cm) wide.
$9,000-15,000

Right An extensive Worcester, Flight, Barr & Barr, dinner service, the borders painted with meandering flowers in underglaze blue, overglaze iron red and pink enriched in gilding, within shaped gilt gadrooned rims, some damage, impressed and printed marks, c1820.
$74,000-120,000

Left A Worcester yellow-ground honeycomb moulded oval dish, with vinestock and leaf handles, the centre with scattered flower sprays, the border with reeded arcading painted with flowers, c1765, 12½in (30.5cm) wide.
$11,000-18,000

A Royal Doulton bone china plate, for the Coronation of Edward VII in 1902, with coloured portraits and unusual fluted edge, 8in (20cm).
$150-250

Right A Chamberlain's Worcester porcelain jug, the tapering body with gadroon moulded flutes, painted in sepia with a view of 'Worcester 1798', as seen from the river, the flutes of alternating white and cobalt heightened with gilt leaves, the neck with gilt oval monogram reserves against a ground of cobalt heightened with gilt fleur-de-lys, gilt Chamberlain's Worcester mark on base, body crack, 7in (17.5cm) high.
$300-600

A Fulda figure of a lime seller and a grape seller, standing holding baskets, minor chips to basket of lady, blue cross mark, c1770, 5½in (14.5cm) high.
$18,000-26,000

A pair of Frankenthal figures of Scaramouche and Columbine, modelled by J. W. Lanz, on shaped rococo scroll bases edged in pink and gilt, minute chips to bases, blue rampant lion mark and impressed PH monogram of Paul Hannong and N and 3, 1756-1759, 5½in (14.5cm) high.
$12,000-21,000

A Meissen sugar box and cover, painted in the Höroldt workshop, blue KPM and crossed swords mark and gilder's No.38 to each piece, 1723-25, 4in (10.5cm) long.
$18,000-26,000

An early Meissen chinoiserie coffee pot and cover, painted by J. G. Höroldt, the cover with flowers issuing from rockwork, slight losses to glaze, c1723, 6½in (16.5cm) high.
$18,000-26,000

A Meissen teapot and cover, painted with landscapes and river scenes, with horsemen fording a stream, and figures outside a house, in shaped panels outlined with scrolls in lustre and gold, the ground with indianische Blumen in colours, the spout issuing from a mask and the handle with foliage terminals, the cover painted with a coastal scene with shipping, KPM mark and crossed swords in under-glaze blue, both teapot and cover with gilder's numeral 11 in gold, 1725, 4½in (11cm).
$40,000-75,000

A Meissen bowl, the inside with solid gilding, the outside with 3 groups of chinoiserie figures, in ciselé gold, resting on scrolls and strapwork, with gold borders edged with scrolls, 1725, 7in (17.5cm).
$8,000-13,500

A Meissen gold-mounted
circular bombe snuff box and
cover, with gilt base, gold
mounts, with the Master's
mark of Louis Métayer,
c1730–40, 6cm diam.
$40,000-75,000

l. A Meissen apple green ground cup and saucer with white
and gold shell and scroll handle, blue crossed swords mark,
c1740.   **$7,000-12,000**

c. A Meissen lime green ground coffee cup and saucer, blue
crossed swords and gilt 20, c1740.   **$10,000-18,000**

r. A Meissen turquoise ground coffee cup and saucer, blue
crossed swords, c1742.   **$4,000-7,500**

Above left A pair of Louis XVI ormolu mounted Meissen figures of a cockerel and hen, naturalistically
modelled by J. J. Kändler and coloured on tree stump mound bases applied with coloured flowers, the shaped
oval ormolu bases with flutes and acanthus, repair to the cockerel's tail feathers and beak, minor chips, blue
crossed swords marks, c1745, the cockerel 12in (30cm) high overall. **$18,000-26,000**

First modelled in 1741.

A Meissen plate from the Christie-Miller Service,
with 4 oval quatrefoil panels en camaïeu rose,
with scrolls and shells in gold and chocolate, with
gilt rim, blue crossed swords mark, Pressnummer
22, c1742, 9in (23cm).
$24,000-45,000

Above right A Meissen chinoiserie powder box, with 3
vignettes of Chinese figures on 'Laub-und-Bandelwerk'
supports in Böttger-lustre, iron-red, puce and gold, with
blue crossed swords mark, c1735, 4½in (11.5cm) diam.
$5,000-9,000

A Meissen teapot and cover, the mask spout enriched
with gilding, the sides painted by P. E. Schindler, blue
K.P.M. and crossed swords mark, base and cover with
gilder's mark 36, c1723–25, 7in (17cm) wide.
$24,000-45,000

A Meissen group of Chinese lovers, modelled by J. J. Kändler and P. Reinicke, some restorations, c1745, 5in (13cm) wide.
$8,000-15,000

Right A Meissen figure of a jay by J. J. Kändler, some damage, blue crossed swords mark, c1745, 15in (39cm).
$22,000-40,000

A Meissen group of lovers with a snuff-box, by J. J. Kändler, minor chips to leaves, blue crossed swords mark under base, c1745, 7in (17cm) high.
$10,000-18,000

Two Meissen snuff boxes with gilt metal mounts:

l. Blue crossed swords mark to interior, c1745, 3in (7cm).
$14,000-24,000

r. c1750, 3in (7cm).
$6,000-12,000

A Meissen group of Tyrolean or Dutch dancers, modelled by J. J. Kändler, with Louis XV ormolu mounts, his right shoulder repaired, chip to underside of base, blue crossed swords mark, c1745, 8in (19cm).
$18,000-26,000

A Nymphenburg Crucifixion group modelled by Franz Anton Bustelli, Christ-figure with repairs to both legs and left arm, impressed Bavarian shield mark to Mater Dolorosa, c1756, 8in (21cm) long, on ebonised wooden base.
$22,000-40,000

A Meissen Papal tea caddy and cover
from the Benedict XIV service, bearing
the Royal Arms of Saxony, the arms of
Lambertini and the Papal tiara and
crossed keys of St Peter, Pressnummer
49, c1748, 5in (12cm).
$50,000-90,000

l. A Meissen coffee cup and saucer painted after G. P.
Rugendas, blue crossed swords mark, c1740. **$8,000-15,000**
c. A Meissen teabowl and saucer, blue crossed swords, gilt 50
mark, c1740.   **$8,000-15,000**
r. A pair of Meissen coffee cups and saucers, blue crossed
swords, c1740.   **$18,000-26,000**

A Paris, Nast, part tea and coffee service, finely painted with
birds, with iron red and gold marks, c1810.
$14,000-24,000

l. A Vincennes milk jug and cover, marked
with blue interlaced Ls enclosing date
letter C for 1755, 5in (13cm).
$10,000-18,000

c. A Sèvres cup and saucer, blue
interlaced Ls, painter's mark of Evans
and date letter M for 1765.
$2,000-4,500

r. A Vincennes sugar bowl and cover, blue
Ls, date mark for 1753, 3in (8cm) diam.
$6,000-12,000

A Sèvres-pattern garniture with gilt metal
mounts, imitation interlaced L marks to
covers, c1890, the vases 29in (73cm) high.
$18,000-26,000

A green-glazed pottery model of a farmhouse tower in three sections, various restorations, Han Dynasty, 23in (59cm).
$40,000-66,000

A green-glazed red pottery model of a house, one door hinged, interior shelves, some restoration, Han Dynasty, 16in (41cm) wide.
$8,000-15,000

A large Yüeh ware olive-glazed oviform jar, chips restored, 6thC, 10in (26cm).
$14,000-24,000

A painted red pottery figure of a court lady, minor restorations to extremities, Tang Dynasty, 17in (44cm).
$100,000-240,000

Dating of this piece confirmed by thermoluminescence test.

A Sancai pottery horse, restorations, Tang Dynasty, 30in (77cm) high.
$460,000+

A Northern celadon bowl, borders cracked, Song Dynasty, 8½in (21cm), fitted box.
$8,000-15,000

A Sancai glazed ambrosia bottle, chips to lip, base and foot, Tang Dynasty, 9in (22cm).
$24,000-45,000

An early Sancai glazed pottery warrior figure, with old damage and breaks, Tang Dynasty, 29in (74cm) high.
$14,000-24,000

A Sancai figure of a court attendant, with restorations to his hat and base, Tang Dynasty, 40in (101cm).
$50,000-90,000

An early Ming dish, Yongle, 18in (45cm).
$200,000+

Right An early Ming vase, meiping, extensively repaired, Yongle, 11in (28cm).
$30,000-54,000

A Jun Yao Bubble Cup, Southern Song Dynasty,
4in (10cm) diam.
$34,000-54,000

A late Ming blue and white figure of
Budai, the God of Happiness, original
firing cracks across the waist, Wanli,
9in (23cm).
$6,000-12,000

A Guan Yao foliate wine cup, Song Dynasty, 3in (8cm) wide,
with box.
$14,000-24,000

A Ming green and black enamelled
brush rest, fritted, chips to
extremities, late 16thC, 8in (20cm).
$2,600-5.300

A pair of large 'famille verte' rouleau
vases, minor chips, one with areas over-
fired, Kangxi, 29in (73cm), wood stands.
$20,000-30,000

A Transitional blue and white
sleeve vase, the shoulder and foot
incised with narrow bands of foliage
and chevrons, mid-17thC, 19in
(46cm).
$8,000-15,000

A massive blue and white fish-bowl, painted in the manner of the Master of the Rocks, rim fritted, star-shaped body crack, early Kangxi, 24in (60cm) diam.
$11,000-20,000

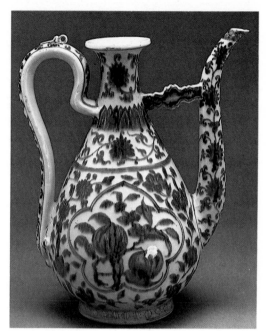

An early Ming ewer, some fritting, first half 15thC, 11in (28cm) high.
$50,000-90,000

A pair of 'famille verte' hexagonal puzzle jugs and covers, one finial and spout restored, Kangxi, 9in (22cm).
$4,500-9,000

A very rare 'famille rose' plate for the Dutch East India Company, some rim chips and a hair crack, fitted box, Yongzheng, 9in (23cm).
$20,000-30,000

Three large baluster vases and domed covers, fritted, one vase and cover damaged, another cover with damage to the unglazed inner rim, Kangxi, 22in (57cm) high.
$8,000-15,000

A 'European Procession' punchbowl painted with mounted figures in late 17thC dress, the interior painted with flowers and central bouquet, Qianlong, 16in (40cm).
$40,000-84,000

A cylindrical vase, painted in underglaze blue and copper red with spotted deer in a landscape, minor damage, large Qianlong six-character seal mark and of the period, 19in (48cm).
$20,000-30,000

A pair of Chinese Imari fish bowls, the sides set with biscuit lion-mask handles, one restored, c1750, 24in (60cm).
$40,000-90,000

A pair of export models of crouching hounds, crisply modelled, ears restored, Qianlong 6in (15cm).
$8,000-15,000

A pair of green dragon jars and covers, Qianlong six-character marks of the period, 8in (20cm).
$18,000-26,000

A Kakiemon oviform vase, cracked and riveted, a small hole filled and 2 distinct firing blemishes, c1665, 10in (26cm).
$10,000-18,000

l. A Kyoto oviform vase, signed Kinkozan zo, late 19thC, 8in (20cm). **$5,000-9,000**
c. A Kyoto dish, signed, late 19thC, 13in (32cm). **$5,000-9,000**
r. A Kyoto-Satsuma koro and cover, signed, c1900, 6in (16cm). **$5,000-9,000**

A pair of garden seats, body cracks, late 18th or early 19thC, 18in (47cm).
$4,000-7,500

A model of a roistering Dutchman, originating from a Dutch Delft design for Bacchus, base of goblet chipped, 18thC, 14in (36cm).
$24,000-45,000

An Imari ship's plate and cover, Genroku period, 10in (25cm) diam.
$2,000-4,500

Left A Chinese export punchbowl probably for the American market, the interior painted in sepia and gilt, c1790, 14in (36cm).
$4,500-9,000

A set of 3 green spirit decanters in papier mâché stand, each bottle with gilt simulated wine label, c1790, stand 9in (23cm) high.
$1,700-3,000

A blue sucrier and cover, with gilt label and decoration, c1790, 6½in (17cm).
$800-1,500

A set of 3 spirit bottles with silver mounts and stoppers, hallmarked Birmingham 1845, in a silver plated stand, with 3 silver wine labels for port, claret and madeira, hallmarked London 1822, stand 17in (44cm).
$1,000-2,000

Right A cream jug and sugar basin, the bowl with gilt inscription 'I Wish you Well', rubbed inscription on jug, c1820, jug 5in (13cm) high.
$600-1,100

A roemer-style wine glass on folded conical foot, c1780, 4½in (11cm).
$300-600

Right A flute-cut decanter with star-cut base, cut mushroom stopper, c1840, 10in (25cm).
$400-750

A flute-cut claret jug, with strap handle, c1840, 12in (30cm).
$500-900

A 'Nailsea' carafe, with crown glass body, c1860, 11½in (29cm).
$400-900

Three 'Nailsea' bells, c1860:
l. 12in (30cm).
$300-600

c. 13in (32cm).
$300-600

r. 12in (30cm).
$300-600

l. A gilt-decorated wine glass on double series opaque twist stem, c1760, 6in (15cm).
$400-900

r. An ogee-bowl wine glass on lace spiral twist stem, c1770, 6in (15cm).
$2,000-4,500

A Nailsea mug in bottle glass, with applied handle, c1780, 4in (10cm).
$150-300

A Wrockwardine bonnet glass and hat of bottle glass, the glass with red and white inclusions, the hat with blue inclusions, c1810, 2½in (6cm).
$400-750

A set of oval blue glass salts, with star-cut bases, c1780, 4in (10cm) diam.
$400-900

A satin glass scent bottle with raised gold floral decorations, silver mount marked Sampson Mordan London, 1885, 4in (10cm).
$600-1,100

Two St Louis weights, **$4,500-9,000** Three Clichy weights, centre, c1850, **$8,000-15,000**   **$4,000-15,000**

Above A Bristol or South Staffordshire scent phial, c1770, 3in (7cm).
$500-900

Right A set of 6 wine glasses, marked 'Richardsons Stourbridge' under feet, c1880, 5in (12cm).
$1,000-2,000

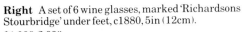

Two unusual potichamanie rolling pins:

l. With amethyst background, c1870, 13in (33cm) long.
$200-450

r. With orange background, c1870, 11in (28cm) long.
$180-300

A small Venetian enamelled flask from the atelier of Osvaldo Brussa, mid-18thC, 3½in (9cm) high.
$6,000-12,000

A pair of Liverpool delft plates, the centres decorated in blue with Chinese peony and rock groups, one hair crack, c1760-75, 13in (33cm).
$500-900

A blue and white transfer pottery platter, Chinoiserie Ruins, impressed Stephenson, c1805, 19in (47.5cm) wide.
$500-900

A pottery plate in dark blue and white transfer ware, entitled 'Sheltered Peasants', by R Hall, the title on a branch, 8in (20cm).
$60-120

An English pink lustre plate, c1850.
$30-60

An English delft charger, painted in blue, green and ochre, the border with blue lines and the reverse with an ochre glaze, probably Southwark, a plaster reconstruction riveted to the rim at 10 o'clock, crack, chip and glaze flaking to the rim, mid-17thC, 15in (37cm).
$1,400-2,600

Cf Michael Archer and Brian Morgan, Fair as China Dishes, *pl 8, and Michael Archer,* English Delftware, *pl 17.*

A British Marine pottery soup plate, in blue and white transfer ware, c1830, 10in (25cm).
$60-120

A blue and white pottery plate, transfer printed with the Shipping series, 10in (25cm).
$100-250

Cf Coysh and R K Henry Wood, p 335.

Make the most of Miller's

Miller's is completely different each year. Each edition contains completely NEW photographs. This is not an updated publication. We never repeat the same photograph.

A rare Staffordshire blue and white meat dish, printed with bathing carriages at Monks Rock, Tenby, 18½in (46cm) wide.
$400-900

A rare Staffordshire blue and white meat dish, printed with the Durham Ox pattern, 22in (55cm) wide.
$1,000-2,000

A Wedgwood plate, with moulded decoration of 4 standing angels, naturalistic colouring and variegated mottling, chip to one wing, impressed Wedgwood and registration mark for 1861, 12in (30cm).
$1,000-2,000

A Wedgwood charger, the cobalt blue ground with raised polychrome decoration, impressed Wedgwood, 15½in (38.5cm).
$1,700-3,000

A Wedgwood fish platter, with
moulded decoration in imitation of
wickerwork with seaweed and sea
shells, polychrome on a white
ground, impressed Wedgwood mark,
26in (65cm) long.
$1,200-2,100

A Wedgwood pearlware dish,
painted by George Eyre with The
Quarrel between Sancho Panza and
Don Quixote's Niece and
Housekeeper, after Doré, impressed
mark, signed in monogram, c1870,
9in (22.5cm).
$400-750

Eleven Wedgwood creamware
shaped plates, painted in colours by
William Wagstaff with scenes after
John Leech's sketches for Punch,
impressed marks and date codes,
c1868, 9½in (24cm).
$2,200-4,200

Cf Maureen Batkin, op cit pl 105.

A rare Dutch majolica pale blue
ground dish, painted in colours with
a parrot perched on a branch, the
border with manganese and ochre
dots, Rotterdam or Amsterdam,
minor rim chips, early 17thC,
13½in (33.5cm).
$10,000-18,000

A Dutch Delft polychrome plate,
restored rim chip, and minor chips,
c1700, 7½in (18.5cm).
$600-1,100

A Dutch Delft polychrome dish,
painted with a bird perched on
flowers in a yellow vase on
rockwork in a landscape, rim chips
and repair, early 18thC, 13in
(32cm).
$200-450

*Dutch Delft tends to make a higher
price when sold in Holland.*

A Dutch Delft blue and white
strawberry dish and stand, the
pierced dish on 3 feet, minor rim
chips, blue mark of the Porseleyne
Klaeuw and 70 mark, early 18thC,
9½in (23.5cm).
$800-1,500

A Dutch Delft polychrome dish,
painted with pagodas and sailing
vessels in a river landscape, rim
chips, early 18thC, 14in (34.5cm).
$300-600

A Dutch Delft polychrome Royal
portrait dish, painted with the head
and shoulders of Prince William V,
rim chips and repairs, 18thC, 14in
(34cm).
$800-1,500

A Dutch Delft polychrome dish,
with yellow and iron red rim, rim
chips and repairs, early 18thC,
14½in (36cm).
$300-600

A Dutch Delft polychrome plate,
painted with a deer in blue, in a
double circle with coloured flowers
and insects, rim chips, first half
18thC, 9in (22.5cm).
$300-600

A Dutch Delft polychrome plate, in the Kakiemon manner with prunus issuing from hay bales, minor rim chips, blue P mark of perhaps Johannis Pennis of De Porceleyne Schotel, 18thC, 9in (22cm).
$1,200-2,100

A rare example of Dutch Delft in the Japanese style.

A Dutch Delft blue and white plate, painted with a deer amongst plants surrounded by foliate and dot-and-dash border at the rim, De Grieksche A factory, rim restored, slight chips, mark of WVDB3, mid-18thC, 10in (24.5cm).
$200-450

A Dutch Delft blue and white dish, painted with a vase of flowers on a border of Oriental figures and flowers, 14in (35cm).
$300-600

A pair of Dutch Delft blue and white dishes, painted with vases of flowers within borders of flowerheads and leaves, 13in (32.5cm).
$400-750

A Dutch Delft hunting dish, painted in blue with a huntsman, hound and quarry among sponged foliage, 18thC, 14in (35cm).
$800-1,500

A Delft blue and white shaped oval dish, painted with flowering shrubs, 15½in (38.5cm) wide.
$300-600

An Hispano Moresque dish, with raised central boss, painted in copper lustre with a bird with outstretched wings, 14in (35cm).
$800-1,500

A Bayreuth blue and white armorial plate, blue B.K.C. minor glaze chips to rim, c1735, 9in (22.5cm).
$4,000-7,500

A Rouen bleu Persian shaped dish, decorated in the Gillibaud style in white relief with flowers and insects within borders of scrolls, minute rim glaze chips, c1700, 14½in (36cm).
$800-1,500

An Hispano Moresque dish, with raised central boss and leaf moulded border painted in copper lustre and blue with stylised flowers.
$400-750

A Rouen large dish, painted in blue and enriched in manganese, the rim with stylised lappets, small rim chip, 18th C, 16in (40cm).
$1,000-2,000

A pair of Castelli dishes painted with the Prodigal at Prayer, the other with Neptune, within borders of putti and scrolling leaves, 9in (23cm).
$3,200-6,000

Make the most of Miller's

For a larger section on Italian maiolica see previous editions of Miller's Guides

A South German blue and white dish, painted with a bird on a flowering branch, the border with symmetrical scrolling flowering foliage, hair crack, minor rim chips, blue S. mark, c1760, 18½in (46cm) long.
$1,000-2,000

An Urbino Istoriato alzata, painted with the Dream of King Astiages, the reverse inscribed in blue 'Dil Vechio Astiage Re L'alta visione 1551', damages to rim, repaired, 9½in (23.5cm).
$10,000-18,000

The composition on the present dish is very close to the Pesaro dish by Sforza, lost during the Second World War from the Herzog Anton Ulrich Museum but described by Lessmann in her appendix I, pl XXXIV and dated 1576.

An Urbino Istoriato dish, painted with the Rape of Proserpine, the nymph in yellow and ochre dress carried off by Pluto naked and bearded, the reverse inscribed in blue 'Diplutto et Proserpina', in half and repaired, c1555, 10in (25cm).
$6,000-12,000

Derived from Ludovico Dolce's woodcut in Le trasformazioni di Ovidio *published in Venice in 1553.*

Two Turin (Rossetti) plates, painted with chinoiserie figures in landscapes, rim chips, c1760, 10in (24.5cm).
$3,200-6,000

Jars

A Turin (Rossetti) saucer dish, painted with a horsedrawn carriage approaching a palazzo, minor rim chips, c1760, 8½in (21.5cm).
$1,200-2,100

A Lambeth delft blue and white drug jar, for 'U: SAMBUC', c1740, 7in (17.5cm).
$500-900

A London delft dated blue and white wet drug jar, for 'S. CICHOREI. SYMPI', with fluttering pennants below enclosing the date 1659, with scroll handle, spout lacking, rim chips, 8in (20cm).
$2,000-4,500

This would appear to be the earliest example recorded of a dated wet drug jar with this angel's head cartouche.

Cf Agnes Lothian, 'Vessels For Apothecaries', Connoisseur Year Book, 1953, where the dating is discussed and also Louis L Lipski and Michael Archer, Dated English Delftware, pl 1600 for the first recorded example of this type dated 1660.

A Bristol delft jar of acorn shape, the sides painted in blue, green and iron red, glaze flaking to handles and rim, c1710, 5½in (14cm).
$1,600-2,800

Cf Antony Ray, English Delftware Pottery, pl 66, no 130, for a jar of similar shape.

A Lambeth delft blue and white wet drug jar with scrolling strap handle, for 'S:E: CORALLIIS', chips to foot and some glaze flaking, c1680, 7½in (18cm).
$1,300-2,400

A Staffordshire jar and cover, painted in apple green with the word 'Honey' in gilt, 12in (30cm).
$400-750

A London delftware wet drug jar, with a cherub and shell label, 7½in (18.5cm).
$500-900

A London delft blue and white drug jar, named for 'CONF. DE. OVO', rim flaking, c1680, 7½in (19cm).
$1,000-2,000

A London delftware dry drug jar, with a cherub and shell label, early 18thC, 8in (20cm).
$500-900

A Dutch Delft blue and white tobacco jar for 'SPAANSE', metal cover, rim chips, blue V mark, first half of 18thC, 9½in (23.5cm).
$600-1,200

A Staffordshire jar with blue and gilt scoll handles, painted in blue and gilt with stylised vines, entitled 'Leeches' in gilt, 7in (17.5cm).
$400-750

A Dutch Delft blue and white oviform drug jar, entitled 'SPAANSE', and another similar entitled 'RAPPE', 9in (23cm).
$1,300-2,400

A Venice waisted albarello, painted with a saint seated in a C-scroll and foliage cartouche, reserved on a blue ground with sgraffito scrolls and yellow and blue painted mask and trophies, restoration to neck and foot, c1550, 11in (27cm).
$1,000-2,000

An Italian pottery jar and cover, with gold cartouches on a speckled blue ground, the pedestal foot and cover with matching decoration, foot repaired, 39in (97.5cm).
$1,600-2,800

A Dutch Delft blue and white large tobacco jar and brass cover, named in blue 'VARINAS', the brass domed cover with ball finial, mark of the claw in blue, 21in (54cm).
$3,200-6,000

A French faience cylindrical tobacco jar, with pewter screw cover, named in manganese 'Tabac' and painted in green, yellow and manganese with tobacco leaves, the screw cover with carrying handle, c1740, 17½in (43.5cm) high overall.
$3,200-6,000

A salt-glazed stoneware three-gallon jug, by Edmands & Company, Charlestown, Massachusetts, c1850-1865, with impressed mark and '3', 16in (40cm) high.
$1,500-1,800

A salt-glazed stoneware five-gallon butter churn, by Thomas P. Chollar, Cortland, New York, c1844-1849, with impressed mark, with wooden cover and dasher, 18in (45cm) high.
$350-550

A salt-glazed stoneware four-gallon jug, by D.P. Shenfelder, Pennsylvania, mid-late 19thC, painted with cobalt stylized floral spray, with impressed mark and '4', 14½in (36cm).
$350-400

A salt-glazed stoneware five-gallon jug, by John Stewart, Great-Falls, New Hampshire, second half 19thC, with impressed mark and '5', 18in (45cm) high.
$350-400

A salt-glazed stoneware two-gallon jug, by O.L. and A.K. Ballard, Burlington, Vermont, 1856-1872, with impressed mark and '2', 14in (35cm) high.
$250-300

A salt-glazed stoneware jug, probably New York State, first half 19thC, unmarked, 15in (38cm) high.
$250-300

Miller's is a price Guide not a price List

The price ranges given reflect the average price a purchaser should pay for similar items. Condition, rarity of design or pattern, size, colour, provenance, restoration and many other factors must be taken into account when assessing values. When buying or selling, it must always be remembered that prices can be greatly affected by the condition of any piece. Unless otherwise stated, all goods shown in Miller's are of good merchantable quality, and the valuations given reflect this fact. Pieces offered for sale in exceptionally fine condition or in poor condition may reasonably be expected to be priced considerably higher or lower respectively than the estimates given herein.

A salt-glazed stoneware jug, probably by Jonathon Fenton, late 18th/early 19thC, impressed with a cobalt-enriched fish, unmarked, 15in (38cm) high.
$800-1,000

Jugs

A Staffordshire saltglaze bear jug and cover, modelled as a crouching bear, covered in frit and with brown trailed slip collar, his eyes and paws enriched with brown slip, crack to cover, muzzle repaired, both front paws restuck, repair to back right paw, c1740, 10in (25cm).
$4,000-6,800

These brown bear jugs were traditionally thought to represent performing bears. See A Catalogue of English Brown Stoneware from the 17th and 18th Centuries compiled by Jonathan Horne.

A Staffordshire saltglaze bear jug and cover, covered in frit and enriched with dots of brown slip to its neck, muzzle and cub, cover repaired and with piece lacking, one leg lacking to cub, head and arm of bear repaired, pieces lacking to foot and ear, c1740, 10in (24cm).
$3,200-6,000

A Nottingham brown stoneware bear jug, with detachable head, holding a dog in his arms, reputedly representing bear baiting, repaired, c1740, 9in (22.5cm).
$1,700-3,000

An English mediaeval globular jug, covered in a greenish ochre iridescent glaze, chips to handle and rim, some glaze degraded, 14thC, 11½in (28.5cm).
$800-1,500

A solid agate baluster jug, the body formed of marbled white and red clays and covered with a rich glaze, the body with incised line decoration, perhaps Newcastle-under-Lyme, handle, spout and chip to rim restored, c1745, 7in (17cm).
$600-1,200

A Wedgwood creamware pear shaped milk jug, painted in colours by James Bakewell with sprays of tulips in puce, yellow and green, with beak spout and entwined strap handle with foliage terminals, impressed mark and potter's marks, painter's mark in puce NB, c1770, 7in (18cm).
$2,000-4,500

James Bakewell, enameller at Wedgwood from 1769 to 1773 is best known for his freely painted flowers in puce monochrome.

A Jackfield black glazed large jug, painted in gilt with a horse and hounds in a landscape, the body with the initials 'I+A' and inscribed 'True Blue', 11in (28cm).
$1,200-2,100

A Wedgwood Whieldon cream jug, cauliflower moulded, naturalistically coloured, c1765-70, 3½in (8.5cm).
$1,300-2,400

A Staffordshire slip decorated jug, c1765, 6in (15cm).
$1,200-2,100

A coloured saltglaze cream jug,
c1755, 3in (7.5cm).
$600-1,100

An early Staffordshire Whieldon
cream jug, c1770, 5in (12.5cm).
$800-1,500

A fine Prattware jug, depicting
Grooms Carousing, the reverse An
Offering to Peace, c1790, 6in (15cm).
$500-900

A Pratt jug, decorated in the usual
underglaze blue, ochre and green,
depicting Sailors Farewell and
Return, c1790, 6in (15cm).
$400-750

A Ralph Wood Bacchus mask jug,
cracks to rim and chips to rim and
base, c1775, 9½in (23.5cm).
$800-1,500

A Pratt jug, depicting field sports,
possibly not of Staffordshire make,
decorated in brown, green and
yellow, c1795, 6in (15cm).
$500-900

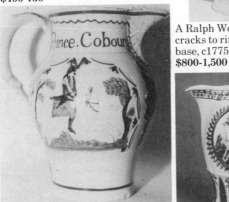

A Pratt jug, depicting 'Prince
Cobourg', the reverse the Duke of
York, with coloured underglaze
decoration in ochre, yellow, blue
and green, c1793, 6in (15cm).
$400-750

A Prattware jug, with peacocks in
landscapes enriched in blue, brown,
green and ochre, the lower part with
a band of stiff leaves and bell
flowers, the rim with a band of
foliage, c1790, 8in (20cm).
$600-1,200

A pearlware jug, illustrating The
Dandies, c1810, 5in (12.5cm).
$500-900

A Portobello Napoleon and bear jug
(Napoleon and the Russian Bear),
early 19thC.
$1,000-2,000

A Liverpool Herculaneum
creamware large jug, transfer
printed in black with the farmer's
arms and inscribed below 'In God
our Trust', small chip and star crack
to one side, c1800, 13in (33.5cm).
$4,000-7,500

Two Staffordshire blue and silver resist jugs, one transfer printed in blue with a hunting subject after Morland, the other with 'Women grinding Corn' named below, reserved on the silver resist ground, c1810, the larger 5½in (14cm) high.
$1,000-2,000

A Staffordshire yellow ground jug and 2 waste bowls, the jug transfer printed in iron red, small hairline crack, 5in (13cm) high, the bowls painted in iron red and green on the yellow ground, the lobed rims in iron red, both with repairs, c1820, 6in (15cm) diam.
$400-750

A rare silver lustre blue and green grape decorated jug, early 19thC.
$500-900

An English earthenware sporting jug, the cream body coloured in copper lustre, pink and turquoise enamel and moulded in relief with 2 sportsmen seated with hounds during a pause in shooting, reversed with sportsmen holding a rabbit surrounded by hounds beneath a band of moulded grapevine, c1810, 6½in (16cm).
$200-450

Two Staffordshire lustre jugs, one enriched in colours and pink lustre with a sporting subject between yellow line borders, the neck with a band of copper lustre, small rim chip to spout, the other boldly painted in pink lustre with flower sprays, small rim chip, repair on spout, c1820, the larger 4½in (11cm).
$150-250

A Sunderland lustre cherubs and goat jug, c1835, 6in (15cm).
$180-300

A Staffordshire pink lustre sporting jug, enriched in green, iron red, brown and black, the neck with a band of foliage reserved on the pink lustre ground, c1810, 6in (15cm).
$400-900

Two Staffordshire pink lustre jugs, one transfer printed in puce with English country houses in landscapes reserved on the pink lustre ground, enriched with foliage, c1820, 5in (13cm).
$400-750

A rare Leeds silver lustre Robin jug, c1815, 5½in (13.5cm).
$1,200-2,100

A set of 4 Staffordshire copper lustre jugs, illustrated with Royal coat of arms and animals, c1840, from 4-7in (10-17.5cm).
$1,200-2,100

A large copper lustre jug, with coloured print, c1840, 11in (27.5cm).
$900-1,700

A Sunderland pink lustre jug, with a Sailor's Farewell scene with inscription and verse, c1840, 7in (17.5cm).
$400-900

A blue and white pottery transfer jug, c1830, 4½in (11cm).
$60-120

A Swansea pottery jug, with lilac transfer design, with mark, c1835, 5in (12.5cm).
$100-250

A Mason's Ironstone jug, with dolphin handles, restoration to handle, c1825, 12in (30cm).
$1,000-2,000

Two identical transfer printed earthenware jugs, in perfect condition, probably made at Ashby-de-le-Zouche, c1850, 6in (15cm).
Large $80-150, Small $60-120

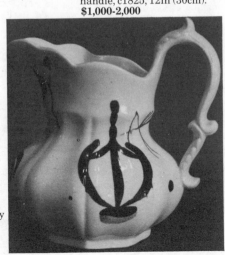

A Swansea jug, possibly incompletely painted, c1840.
$80-180

A Hanau blue and white pewter mounted enghalskrüg, the strap handle enriched in blue, the hinged pewter cover with ball thumbpiece, hairline crack to handle, c1750, 13in (33cm).
$1,800-3,800

A Brownfield jug modelled as a goose, the handle modelled as a standing monkey pushing open its beak, with naturalistic polychrome colouring, impressed Brownfield, c1860, 14in (35.5cm).
$600-1,200

A Wedgwood black basalt jug, the body with a band of cherubs watering within borders of engine turned bands and with silver rim, impressed lower case mark, 8in (20cm).
$800-1,500

A Brownfield jug modelled as a cockatoo, with white plumage, yellow crest and naturalistic colouring, impressed Brownfield, small chip to crest, 9½in (24cm).
$800-1,500

A Westerwald blue and grey stoneware jug, with contemporary hinged pewter cover and foot rim, moulded with a mask spout and circular flowerheads on a blue ground, hair crack to neck, 17thC, 9in (22.5cm).
$600-1,100

A dated Rhenish stoneware armorial bartmannkrug, moulded with a bearded mask and 3 oval armorial medallions, each dated 1599, and covered in a mottled brown glaze, crack through base restored, rim chips, 9in (22.5cm).
$600-1,100

Toby Jugs

A good Ralph Wood Toby Jug, with flaked translucent glaze decoration, 10in (25cm).
$1,200-2,100

An Ewenny pottery jug, inscribed mark, incised Jones Bridgend, c1900, 10in (25cm).
$80-180

'Na werth Nef er benthyg byd' (Don't sell Heaven for things on earth).

A Whieldon Toby Jug, in predominantly brown and green glazes, holding a pear shaped jug, typical of this type of jug, c1770, 9in (22.5cm).
$1,000-2,000

The shallow base has a 'step' underneath.

A rare Thin Man Toby Jug, possibly made at Leeds, decorated in semi-translucent glazes of green and grey, holding a brown jug, c1765, 9in (22.5cm).
$3,200-6,000

Plaques

A Staffordshire saltglazed stoneware mug, with applied profile medallion of George II with letters 'GR', scratch blue foliate decorations and banding, hairline crack, c1750, 6in (15cm).
$300-600

A Dutch Delft mug, painted in blue with a stag hunting scene, early 18thC, 3½in (8.5cm).
$1,300-2,400

A Ralph Wood portrait of The Duke of Cumberland, with yellow edged shirt and green drapery, the border moulded with a band of foliage enriched in green, pierced for hanging, cracked, c1770, 6½in (15.5cm).
$1,000-2,000

A Ralph Wood pearlware plaque, of a Greek philosopher, on a brightly coloured green background, c1780, 12 by 9½in (30 by 23.5cm).
$1,800-3,800

A Wedgwood & Bentley blue and white portrait medallion of George III, the dipped pale blue ground moulded in white relief, chip to underside, impressed lower case mark, c1775, 2½in (5.5cm).
$400-750

A Wedgwood & Bentley polished blue jasper oval plaque of Benjamin Franklin, attributed to William Hackwood, impressed Franklin, reverse impressed Wedgwood & Bentley, c1775, 3½in (9.5cm).
$3,200-6,000

A pair of Wedgwood & Bentley black basalt oval portrait plaques of Vespasian and Nero, named 'T. Vespas. Avg' and 'Nero Avg' within self moulded gadrooned and reeded borders, Vespasian with minute rim chip, c1777, 8in (20cm).
$4,000-7,500

First listed in Wedgwood & Bentley's fourth catalogue in 1777, Class VI, Nos 6 and 10.

A mantel ornament in the form of an architectural clockface plaque by Obadiah Sherratt, base and putto surmount damaged, 2 angels' wings chipped, c1830, 11½in (29.5cm).
$1,800-3,800

A Spode pottery panel, reverse side impressed with manufacturers mark, indistinctly signed, all mounted in gilt frame, 20 by 13in (50 by 32.5cm).
$900-1,700

A Wedgwood lilac jasper rectangular plaque, after Flaxman, impressed Wedgwood, 2½ by 7½in (5.5 by 19.5cm).
$400-750

A Castelli plaque, painted in colours in the Grue workshop, minute rim chips, c1720, 10 by 8in (25 by 20cm).
$1,000-2,000

A Wedgwood blue and white jasper portrait medallion of William Pitt The Younger, impressed mark, glazed wood frame, c1790, 3½in (9.5cm).
$1,000-2,000

Cf Robin Reilly and George Savage, op. cit., p.276.
This model has been variously attibuted to Flaxman, Lochée and Tassie, the original dating to circa 1785, on the evidence of style the Lochée attribution is considered the most likely.

A portrait medallion in blue jasper of Sir Eyre Coote, modelled by Mountstephen from a bust by Nollekeus in 1779, 4 by 3in (10 by 7cm).
$1,800-3,800

See Dictionary of Wedgwood by Reilly and Savage, p 246; also see illustration.

Pots

A Bristol delft blue and white 2-handled posset pot and cover, the handles enriched with blue lines and the spout with whorl pattern, spout, cover and part of rim restored, minor glaze chips, c1730, 9½in (23cm) wide.
$2,600-5,300

Provenance: S M Taylor.

A pearlware bough pot and pierced cover.
$1,300-2,400

A Bristol delftware polychrome posset pot, restored, c1730.
$1,000-2,000

A yellow lustre chamber pot, made by Deptford or Balls Bros., c1860, 8½in (21cm) diam.
$300-600

A rare Wedgwood moonlight lustre pot pourri vase and cover, pierced lid missing, c1815, 12in (30cm).
$800-1,500

A Dutch Delft polychrome shaped oval plaque, painted with Chinese figures standing on a terrace before a fence and a screen, restoration to finial and base, early 18thC, 9½in (23.5cm) wide.
$3,200-6,000

A Staffordshire pottery child's tea service, comprising 6 cups and saucers, 1 sugar bowl and 2 plates.
$300-600

An Ashworth's ironstone part dessert service, with dark green ground, comprising: 5 comports and 2 plates, impressed and transfer marks to base, one comport damaged.
$500-900

A Victorian ironstone dinner service decorated in Imari style, comprising: 4 tureens and covers, 1 stand, 8 meat plates/stands, low comport, 12 soup plates, 12 dinner plates, some chips and cracks. Impressed marks BB new stone and pattern No. 6028 in red.
$1,300-2,400

A Doulton Lambeth faience coffee service, comprising: coffee pot and cover, sugar bowl and cover and a milk jug, printed Doulton and P.O.D.R. mark for 29th May, 1879, painted 'HH' and 'WJ' monograms, 10½in (26cm) coffee pot.
$600-1,100

A black basalt part tea service, comprising: a teapot and cover, spout with minute chips, a milk jug and cover, minute chip to spout, a sugar bowl and cover and a slop basin, c1800.
$600-1,100

A Victorian ironstone china part dinner service decorated in iron red, blue, green and gilt, comprising: 12 dinner plates, 12 side plates, 6 soup plates, 3 graduated meat dishes and a similar vegetable tureen and cover.
$1,800-3,800

A miniature Wedgwood blue and white printed Willow Pattern dinner service, comprising: 6 dinner and 6 soup plates, tureens and covers, 2 serving plates and a sauceboat and stand, impressed mark, one cover finial damaged, second quarter 19thC.
$500-900

A Staffordshire part dinner service printed and painted with iron red foliage on a blue cell pattern ground, comprising: 4 meat dishes, a square shaped bowl, a sauce tureen, 10 soup plates, 15 dinner plates and 11 dessert plates.
$2,000-4,500

At present there is a strong market for extensive and reasonably complete services if they are early and decorative. The illustrated service was estimated at only $300-600 but due to fierce competition in the saleroom fetched $4,500.

A George Jones tea set, comprising: a teapot, coffee pot, milk jug, sugar basin with lid and a tray, the pale blue ground decorated in relief with naturalistic colouring, marked with monogram 'GJ' and registration lozenge for 1873, damage to teapot lid, tray 22in (55cm) long.
$2,200-4,200

WEDGWOOD BLUE PRINTED POTTERY

★ rapid growth in production by other factories commenced c1780
★ at first Wedgwood bought in printed wares from other factories, e.g. Minton
★ Wedgwood first produced blue and white printed pottery in 1805
★ first pattern was Blue Bamboo
★ series of floral patterns introduced from 1805-11
★ from 1811-21 Chinese landscapes produced
★ products given impressed marks, normally Wedgwood plus numbers, letters or symbols

Tankards

A South German small cylindrical tankard, with contemporary hinged pewter cover with ball thumb piece and with pewter foot rim, painted in blue and manganese, hair cracks, minor glaze chips, first half of the 18thC, 6½in (16cm).
$1,200-2,100

A German faience blue and white tankard, with contemporary hinged pewter cover and foot rim, probably Bayreuth, glaze chips and repair, mid-18thC, 6½in (18.5cm).
$400-750

A German polychrome faience tankard, the white glazed body decorated with simple green swags, orange and brown lines, pewter mounts and domed cover with knop finial, the cover inscribed 'M.D.4' and with a small medallion, 18thC, 9in (22.5cm).
$400-900

A Hannoversch-Münden faience tankard, with contemporary hinged pewter cover with ball thumb piece, the tankard inscribed 'Es liebe mein Mädchen', hair crack, minor rim chips, mid-18thC, 8½in (21.5cm).
$600-1,100

A German polychrome faience cylindrical tankard, the white glazed body painted with a man smoking a pipe in a garden with flowering plants, pewter mounts and domed cover with acorn finial, inscribed on lid 'M.G.L.1770', marked on base VX, cover slightly faulty, 18thC, 9½in (23cm).
$1,300-2,400

Tea Caddies

A Staffordshire square saltglaze tea caddy, minor repair to rim of neck, c1755, 6in (16cm).
$1,200-2,100

A Pratt tea caddy, decorated with Macaroni figures, late 18thC, 6in (15cm).
$600-1,200

Good to find one with its original top.

A Whieldon pottery tea caddy in green and brown glazes, 18thC, 5in (12.5cm).
$800-1,500

A rare dated and inscribed blue and white Leeds creamware tea caddy and cover, one side inscribed 'Ann Colridge', the reverse with the date '1797', cover and one of the cherub busts to the corners with repair, dated 1797, 6in (16cm).
$1,800-3,800

A Dutch Delft blue and white tea caddy, minor chips, blue MS marks on base for perhaps Joris Mes, pewter cover, c1680, 7½in (18cm).
$1,800-3,800

A Leeds creamware square tea canister, the corners enriched in blue with flower sprays, one side inscribed 'Elizh, Hal(istay)', small chip, dated 1798(?), 7½in (19cm).
$1,300-2,400

Tea and Coffee Pots

An Astbury redwear coffee pot and domed cover, minute chip to spout, c1750, 9½in (24cm).
$600-1,200

A saltglaze coloured teapot, c1755, 5in (12.5cm).
$1,300-2,400

An Astbury armorial cream jug and cover, the rich brown body applied with the Royal coat of arms in white relief, the cover with 3 crowns, cover restored, c1750, 5½in (13cm).
$1,400-2,600

A Whieldon teapot, c1775, 5in (12.5cm).
$1,000-2,000

An early Staffordshire saltglaze teapot, with bird decoration, c1755, 4in (10cm).
$1,300-2,400

A Leeds creamware teapot and cover, enriched in blue, green and yellow, the scroll spout moulded with formal foliage, minor chip repair to rim of cover, and tip of spout, c1770, 8in (20cm).
$1,000-2,000

Probably decorated at the Rhodes Enamelling Studio.

A Whieldon type tortoiseshell glazed miniature teapot and cover, splashed in manganese, green and grey blue, minor chip to tip of spout, c1760, 5½in (14cm) wide.
$1,200-2,100

A Whieldon type tortoiseshell glazed teapot and cover, covered in a brown and greyish blue tortoiseshell glaze, minute chip to interior of rim, c1760, 7in (18cm) wide.
$2,600-5,300

A Whieldon type teapot, shaped like a cauliflower, c1760.
$800-1,500

A Whieldon type tortoiseshell glazed teapot and a cover, small chip to tip of spout, finial repaired, c1755, 7in (17cm) wide.
$1,200-2,100

A Staffordshire yellow ground ▷ teapot and cover, transfer printed in black, c1810, 8in (20cm) wide.
$400-900

A Rothwell Yorkshire creamware teapot, decorated with mottled translucent glazes, c1700, 6in (15cm).
$1,000-2,000

An early Wood creamware teapot, c1800, 6in (15cm).
$800-1,500

A Leeds creamware teapot, c1800, 5½in (13.5cm).
$800-1,500

A Leeds creamware teapot and cover, painted in colours and gilt with Aurora and her chariot, enriched in iron red, puce, green and yellow with flowering foliage in landscape vignettes, minor repair to tip of spout, c1780, 8in (21cm) wide.
$1,300-2,400

A miniature pearlware teapot, c1800, 4½in (11cm).
$300-600

A black basalt tea kettle and cover, spout and cover chipped, c1800, 10in (25cm).
$600-1,200

A barge teapot, c1888.
$600-1,200

An English majolica teapot, c1875.
$800-1,500

Tiles

Four medieval lead glazed floor tiles, 13th/14thC, 4½in (11cm).
$600-1,100

A pair of Bristol delft blue and white stove tiles, painted in blue with a statesman in Roman dress, some repairs, c1700, 10in (25cm).
$1,800-3,800

Possibly intended as candle niches.

A Bristol delft tile, painted in blue, mid-18thC, 5in (12.5cm).
$40-90

A Bristol delft tile, painted by John Bowen, c1750.
$80-150

A Liverpool delft tile, painted in black by Sadler, c1760, 5in (12.5cm).
$100-250

A Liverpool delftware tile, 'pencilled' and painted in manganese and purple, c1765, 5½in (13.5cm).
$200-450

Polychrome, chinoiserie and animal subjects are scarce and consequently of greater value than more common biblical or pastoral tiles.

A Liverpool delft tile, painted in a 'Fazackerley' polychrome palette, c1765, 5in (12.5cm).
$200-450

A Liverpool delftware polychrome tile, c1765, 5in (12.5cm).
$300-600

A Liverpool delftware tile, painted in blue, mid-18thC, 5in (12.5cm).
$30-60

78

A set of 25 English tinglaze tiles, decorated urns on pedestal feet joined by husk swags, late 18thC.
$800-1,500

A European brown glazed stove tile, covered in a honey brown glaze, chips to rim and glaze, 16th/17thC, 9in (22.5cm).
$800-1,500

A pair of Rotterdam manganese tile pictures, painted with Abraham dismissing Hagar and Jephta's Return, Aelmis workshop in De Bloempot, damages, c1770, 31 by 26in (78 by 65cm).
$2,600-5,300

Tureens

A tureen with ladle, bat printed in black with rural scenes, factory unknown, early 19thC, 6in (15cm).
$300-600

A pair of Staffordshire bird tureens, naturalistically modelled with incised feather markings enriched in yellow, turquoise, iron red, brown and blue tones, one cover repaired, c1800, 7in (17.5cm) long.
$2,600-5,300

A Rogers pottery tureen and dish, with Zebra pattern, c1820.
$180-300

A Staffordshire dove tureen, the bird with raspberry pink plumage, early 19thC, 4in (10cm).
$800-1,500

A Staffordshire pigeon tureen, c1840, 6in (15cm).
$600-1,100

A creamware soup tureen, c1780.
$900-1,700

A John Meir & Son soup tureen and stand, the Italian scenery pale blue with floral borders, mid-19thC, 23in (57.5cm) diam.
$80-180

With lid **$200-450**

A Spode ironstone soup tureen and cover with acorn finial, printed and painted with coloured flower sprays, 13in (32.5cm) wide.
$400-750

An unusual Staffordshire elephant tureen and cover, with restored base, c1860, 8½in (21cm).
$1,000-2,000

An English Brownfield pottery butter tub, 1868, 4½in (11cm).
$500-900

A George Jones majolica game dish and cover, the brown ground moulded with dead birds and trophies, the cover with a fox crouching before a swan on bracken, raised cartouche mark, 11½in (27.5cm) wide.
$1,400-2,600

There has been a great increase in interest in 19thC majolica over the last year.

An Ewenny pottery casserole pot and cover, in brown with cream slipware decoration, some damage, inscribed, dated 1910, 9½in (23.5cm).
$80-180

A French faience cauliflower tureen, cover and stand, enriched in tones of green, blue and pale yellow, some repairs, firing crack, c1770, the stand 12in (30cm) wide.
$4,500-9,000

Cf Hans Haug, Les Faiences et Porcelaines de Strasburg, *Strasburg 1922, pl xxib.*

A German faience asparagus tureen and cover, naturally modelled and coloured and tied with a manganese string, minor chips, mid-18thC, 7in (17cm) long.
$2,000-4,500

An Erfurt faience cow tureen and cover, naturally modelled as a recumbent cow, with blue markings, blue 3 mark to each piece, repairs to horns and ears, minor chips, mid-18thC, 8in (20.5cm) long.
$1,700-3,000

Vases

A Dutch Delft polychrome butter tub and cover, with bud finial painted with fruit and flowers in panels and garlands within black and yellow lined borders, cover and handles repaired, 18thC, 5in (12.5cm) long.
$200-450

A Ralph Wood dolphin flower-holder, decorated in translucent glazes, c1770, 7½in (18.5cm).
$1,000-2,000

A pair of sponge-ware vases in blue and ochre, early 19thC, 5in (12.5cm).
$600-1,100

A Dublin delft blue and white baluster vase, delicately painted with a fountain in a continuous rocky river landscape with trees and trailing shrubs, beneath 2 swags of flowers and foliage suspended from the rim, c1750, 13in (32cm).
$2,000-4,500

Cf Castletown Exhibition Catalogue (1971), pl 11 for a wall-cistern with a similar style of painting.

A purple lustre spill vase, impressed mark Sewell & Co, c1815, 8in (20cm).
$600-1,100

A Wedgwood dark blue jasper vase, with pierced domed cover, the side with a band of white reliefs of allegorical figure and shrubs, the everted rim and socle base edged with bands of acanthus leaves, impressed Wedgwood, 13½in (33.5cm).
$900-1,700

A pair of Wedgwood 3-colour jasper vases and covers, the dipped sage green grounds moulded in white relief, the bodies with dice pattern with yellow flowerheads divided by bands of berried foliage, impressed marks, one rim repaired, one cover cracked, the other with finial restuck, c1860, 13in (33cm).
$4,000-6,800

A Wedgwood pot pourri vase and cover, the black jasper-dip sides sprigged with a procession of 8 classical dancing women, impressed mark, late 18thC, 10in (25cm).
$400-900

A pair of Wedgwood creamware baluster vases painted by Emile Lessore, the necks, rims and bases with ochre and iron red bands, signed, impressed marks, one with rim chip restored, indistinct date code probably for 1865, 5in (15cm).
$1,400-2,600

A pair of Wedgwood Fairyland Lustre-type vases, painted with river landscapes and trees, printed marks, Z5464, 9in (22.5cm).
$1,600-2,800

A Wedgwood & Bentley black basaltes vase, the body moulded in relief with Venus in her Car drawn by mythical birds through clouds, impressed Wedgwood & Bentley, slight damage to left handle, 17in (42cm).
$4,500-9,000

Make the most of Miller's

Unless otherwise stated, any description which refers to 'a set' or 'a pair' includes a valuation for the entire set or the pair, even though the illustration may show only a single item.

A pair of Hicks and Meigh ironstone vases, transfer printed in underglaze brown with a continuous Japonaiserie water garden scene, all painted in underglaze blue, iron red, gilt, green and brown, transfer mark in underglaze brown, Real Stone China, a ribbon below a crown, 20in (50cm).
$4,000-7,500

A pair of large English pottery vases and domed covers, painted on each side with a rustic landscape incorporating buildings and figures within a scroll-moulded panel, upon an overall deep cobalt ground heightened with elaborate gilt scroll, and feathered leaf motifs, 35in (88cm).
$3,200-6,000

These vases appear to be of previously unrecorded form.

A pair of Mason's Patent ironstone china vases, potted in the Chinese style and decorated in gold with insects on a deep blue ground, 14½in (36.5cm).
$1,000-2,000

Wemyss

A large white Scottish Wemyss ware pig, 19thC, 11in (27.5cm).
$800-1,500

A Plichta middle sized pig, painted with roses by Joseph Nekola, 20thC, 8in (20cm).
$600-1,100

A Wemyss ware small black and white pig, impressed 'Wemyss' and printed mark of 'T. Goode & Co.', 7in (17.5cm).
$400-900

A Wemyss mug, painted with sweet peas, impressed Thomas Goode, 19thC, 5½in (13.5cm).
$400-750

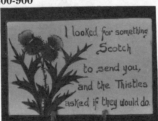

A small plaque, painted with thistles, 20thC, 7 by 4in (17 by 10cm).
$100-250

A Wemyss impressed pin tray, c1920, 5in (13cm) long.
$80-150

A Wemyss heart-shaped tray, impressed, c1930, 12in (30cm).
$150-300

WEMYSS WARE
c1883-1930

★ Robert Methven Heron introduced a group of continental artists into his Fife pottery in the 1880's. The very characteristic nature of Wemyss derives from their influence although roses, apples and cherries had been stiffly painted before

★ most of the artists returned home but Karel Nekola remained. Wemyss was always wanted by the rich and the ware was well supported by Scottish Lairds

★ Wemyss was fired at low temperatures to produce a biscuit body which would absorb the delicate brush strokes. Then it was dipped in a soft lead glaze and fired again at a low temperature. This accounts for the fragility of Wemyss and the relative rarity of exceptional quality pieces

★ Nekola trained James Sharp, David Grinton, John Brown, Hugh and Christina McKinnon and they were later joined by Nekola's sons Carl and Joseph

★ Karel Nekola tended to paint the large important pieces and also the commemorative pieces from Queen Victoria's Jubilee in 1897 until the Coronation of George V in 1911. He died in 1915

★ Edwin Sandiland became chief decorator in 1916. The change in public taste after the First World War, with the introduction of the Art Deco movement, saw a move away from the traditional Wemyss designs. Various new designs were tried but by the time Edwin Sandiland died in 1928, the end was in sight. The Fife Pottery closed in 1930

★ the Bovey Tracy pottery in Devon bought the rights and moulds of the Fife pottery and gave employment to Joseph Nekola, who continued the familiar decorations to a high standard until his death in 1952. Royal Doulton subsequently acquired the rights

A Wemyss bucket with lid, from a washstand set, painted with roses, impressed, 19thC, 11in (27.5cm).
$400-750

A Scottish Wemyss basket, painted with cherries, 19thC, 12½in (31cm) long.
$600-1,100

A large Wemyss bulb bowl, painted with sweet peas, 19thC, 14in (35cm) diam.
$800-1,500

A Wemyss matchbox holder, painted with roses, impressed, 19thC, 3in (8cm) long.
◁ **$200-450**

A pair of Wemyss brush vases, painted with roses, impressed, 19thC, 6in (15cm).
$300-600

A Wemyss preserve pot, painted with strawberries, impressed, 19thC, 6½in (16cm).
$150-300

A large Wemyss brush vase, ▷ painted with thistles, impressed, 19thC, 11½in (28.5cm).
$400-900

A small Wemyss brush vase, painted with a pastoral scene with a cow, 19thC, 4in (10cm).
$150-300

A Wemyss hat pin holder, painted with carnations, 19thC, 6in (15cm).
$150-300

Carnation paintings are rare.

A Wemyss skep (beehive), painted with bees, Scottish, 19thC, 7½in (18.5cm).
$800-1,500

Miscellaneous

A Liverpool delft blue and white cornucopia wall pocket, lightly moulded with a bird on a flowering branch, c1760, 8in (20cm).
$800-1,500

A Bristol delft bulb pot, with chinoiserie scenes, 5in (12.5cm) square.
$1,200-2,100

A Staffordshire pearlware box and cover, modelled as a dog wearing a yellow collar inscribed 'Venture', the cushion lustred in pink with green, yellow and iron red band, the screw cover with the initials 'ET' in black, minor chips, c1815, 2in (5cm).
$2,200-4,200

Cf W D John and Warren Baker, Old English Lustre Pottery, *pl 34B.*

A Staffordshire yellow ground oval tobacco box, cover and inner lid, moulded with the Kill and applied with fox head handles, the inner cover with recumbent lamb finial, impressed 2, repair to both finials, chip to foot rim, c1800, 4in (11cm) wide.
$1,300-2,400

A Bristol delft flower brick, with blue chinoiserie scenes, c1760, 3in (7.5cm).
$500-900

A rare Bristol delft blue and white brick of unusually small size with ogee feet, c1730, 5in (12.5cm) wide.
$900-1,700

A Staffordshire cradle, 3½in (8.5cm) wide.
$200-450

A Pratt grandfather clock, late 18thC, 6in (15cm).
$900-1,700

A Yorkshire clock group as a money box, on oval grass mound base enriched in ochre, manganese and blue, repair to figure of girl, c1800, 8½in (22cm).
$1,800-3,800

An unusual pearlware bough pot and pierced cover, in the form of a mausoleum, the body painted in pink lustre with three landscape views, cover cracked, early 19thC, 10in (25cm).
$1,300-2,400

A Rockingham or Brameld group of bird whistles, c1835, 9in (22.5cm).
$1,200-2,100

A purple lustre watch holder, with lion at the top, c1815, 8in (20cm).
$1,200-2,100

An Ewenny money box, with sgrafitto decoration, with cockerel and other birds applied to body, no mark, some damage, c1830, 8in (20cm).
$300-600

An unusual English pottery item, part of a supper set, with high glaze blue and white chrysanthemum transfer, 4in (10cm) wide.
$60-120

This could be Swansea.

An early Staffordshire Prattware watch holder, c1790, 9½in (23.5cm).
$1,400-2,600

A Staffordshire watch holder box, with slip mouldings, 9½in (23.5cm).
$500-900

A Walton castle spill, depicting bridge and river below, in coloured enamels, Walton mark on back, c1820, 6in (15cm).
$600-1,100

A rare money box, modelled as a chapel with blue roof and 2 chimneys above 6 windows and 2 doorways outlined in yellow, the rectangular base supported on 4 ball feet, 7in (17.5cm).
$900-1,700

Cf Anthony Oliver, The Tribal Art of England, *pl 183.*

A number of modern fakes have appeared on the market in recent years.

A Staffordshire model of a coiled snake, with a brown and yellow splash glaze covering the green scales, c1800, 2in (5cm) wide.
$300-600

A Staffordshire puce-printed money box.
$600-1,200

An English pottery pocket flask, with classical scenes, 18thC, 6in (15cm).
$600-1,200

A Staffordshire blue and white pottery dog's dish, in the Florentine pattern, 19thC, 10in (25cm).
$400-750

A Wedgwood comport, in browns, yellows and greens, impressed Wedgwood and date code for 1884, damage to spout of one dolphin, 17in (42.5cm).
$1,700-3,000

An unusual pottery spirit flask, decorated in dark red, blue and green, with transfers of Dr Franklin on either side, possibly of North-country origin, c1840, 8in (20cm).
$400-750

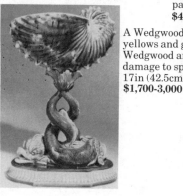

A Wedgwood & Bentley white stoneware pestle and mortar, impressed lower case marks, minute chip to rim, c1780, the pestle 5½in (14.5cm) long, the mortar 3½in (9cm) wide.
$1,400-2,600

A Wedgwood black basalt Egyptian inkstand, the exterior moulded with wings and scale pattern, impressed mark, c1810, 12in (30cm) wide.
$5,000-9,000

A Victorian cheese dish and cover, naturistically modelled and coloured in the form of a straw bee skep, on square rustic pattern stand, unmarked except for Patent Registration Mark, stand chipped on one corner, 13in (32.5cm).
$1,200-2,100

A pair of Wedgwood majolica wall brackets, modelled as putti supporting drapes on turquoise grounds, 10½in (26cm).
$1,000-2,000

A black Jasperware half stilton dish and cover, second quarter 19thC, 10½in (26.5cm).
$300-600

MINTON MAJOLICA

★ Joseph-Léon-François Arnoux appointed art director of Minton c1848
★ before 1850 Arnoux introduced a ware imitating 16thC Italian maiolica
★ opaque white glaze over pottery body as surface for polychrome painting in opaque colours
★ in 1851 Mintons displayed wine coolers, flower pots and stands 'coloured in the majolica style'
★ transparent coloured glazes of green, yellow, brown and blue often used over patterns moulded in low relief. These are in imitation of wares produced by Bernard Palissy in the mid-16thC but are sometimes mis-named majolica
★ rival firms copied majolica wares but Minton examples usually bear the name Minton impressed
★ game dishes especially popular with collectors
★ other collectable factories include Wedgwood and George Jones

---

A George Jones sardine dish and cover, with moulded decoration of a sardine on each side, seaweed and coral reef on the corners, impressed monogram GJ and registration lozenge for 1862, 4½in (10.5cm).
$1,200-2,100

A George Jones jardinière, cobalt blue with turquoise interior and naturalistic colouring, impressed G. Jones within crescent shape, hair line crack, 13½in (33cm) high.
$1,300-2,400

A George Jones ashtray, modelled as a finch on bulrushes, the green ground with naturalistic polychrome colouring, impressed GJ and with registration mark for 1871, beak restored, 7in (17.5cm) long.
$500-900

A Clews pottery bed pan, transfer-printed in blue with Fonthill Abbey, Wiltshire, impressed Clews, printed title mark, 16in (40cm) long.
$400-750

A Minton pottery salmon dish, with majolica type glaze, the handle in the form of a lemon, coloured predominantly in pale green with salmon coloured highlights, impressed Mintons and numerals, c1860s, 23in (56.5cm) wide.
$1,800-3,800

A Minton butterdish and stand, in green, brown, blue and white. Dish and stand with impressed marks Minton 485 and date ciphers for '1867', 7½in (18.5cm).
$6,000-12,000

A Minton majolica game dish and cover, of tapering oval form, the sides brown glazed and moulded to simulate basket weave, interlaced with green oak leaves, the interior turquoise glazed, impressed Minton, date code for '1867', 12½in (32cm).
$1,200-2,100

A majolica jardinière in Mintons style, with rams head and cupid mounts on oval base, date code for June 1856 (?), 36in (90cm).
$2,600-5,300

A Mintons jardinière, with moulded relief decoration of stylised flower heads on a turquoise ground surrounding 4 cream panels painted with multi coloured flowers, transfer and impressed factory marks to base, late 19thC, 15in (37.5cm) diam.
$400-900

A large Minton jardinière in the oriental style, with stylised owl masks, pale blue with dark blue bands, yellow and mottled brown, pink interior, impressed Minton 1620 and date code for 1872, 20½in (51cm).
$1,300-2,400

A Minton jardinière on 6 lion feet, with pale blue body, maroon rim, pink interior, and naturalistic colouring, impressed Minton 1023 and date code for '1865', some restoration, 18in (45cm).
$1,800-3,800

Cf Victoria Cecil, Minton Majolica, 1982, No. 118, illustrated.

A Minton footed jardinière, cobalt blue and naturalistic colouring, pale blue interior, impressed Minton 1429 and with date code for 1884, 14½in (36cm).
$4,000-6,800

A Minton jardinière, the handles modelled as intertwined snakes, pale blue with pink, yellow, green and white, the snakes naturalistically coloured, impressed Minton 532 and date code for 1876, 18in (45cm) diam.
$3,200-6,000

Cf Victoria Cecil, Minton Majolica, 1982, No. 50.

A large Minton jardinière, modelled as a giant pale blue nautilus shell with pink interior, the base aubergine with 2 colours of green, impressed Minton 437 and date code for 1867, 18½in (46cm).
$1,800-3,800

Cf Victoria Cecil, Minton Majolica, 1982, No. 101, illustrated.

A Minton jardinière and underdish, cobalt blue with polychrome naturalistic colouring and pink interior, impressed Minton 1685 and date code for 1874, 16½in (41cm) diam.
$1,400-2,600

A Minton jardinière and underdish, in pink with pale blue interior and yellow rim, the bulrushes naturalistically coloured, square underdish en suite, impressed Minton 1096 and date code for 1865, 9½in (23cm).
$1,400-2,600

A Minton pedestal, with 6 vertical panels and pierced Chinese style decoration, polychrome colouring on a pale blue ground, impressed Minton 451 and date code for 1865, 32½in (80.5cm).
$1,300-2,400

◁ A pair of Minton pedestals, decorated in relief with ribboned swags festooned with fruit and flowers on the upper half and a bank of acanthus leaves below, naturalistic polychrome colouring on a pale blue ground, impressed Minton 891 and with date code for 1872, 37½in (93.5cm).
$5,000-9,000

▷ A Minton pedestal in the Japanese manner, with pierced decoration of flowers, fish, fans, and tied scrolls, green, mustard colour, pink and white on a cobalt blue ground, impressed Mintons 2081 and with date cipher for 1883, 29½in (74cm).
$2,600-5,300

A Minton jardinière, with oak and acorn border under the rim, pink with turquoise interior and naturalistic colouring, impressed Minton and with date code for 1867, 11in (27cm).
$1,600-2,800

A Minton majolica stand, painted in bright enamel colours on a dark blue ground between narrow bands of leaves, the top with matching decoration, impressed marks with the date code for 1867, slight damage, 19in (47cm).
$1,700-3,000

A Minton majolica jardinière upon stand, in green and white, with red, blue and white background, stamped Minton A1007, 19thC, 32 by 43in (80 by 107.5cm).
$5,000-9,000

A Minton Secessionist majolica stick stand (Robert Pugh), c1902, 16in (40cm).
$200-450

A Minton Secessionist majolica jardinière, c1902-14, 10½in (26cm).
$400-750

A pair of Minton majolica tazzas modelled and painted with flowerheads on yellow, brown and blue grounds, impressed marks, date cipher c1867, 11in (27.5cm).
$2,600-5,300

A Minton bowl, in naturalistic polychrome colours, impressed Minton 874 and with date code for 1863, 13in (32.5cm) diam.
$4,000-7,500

A Minton honeycomb dish, modelled as a beehive with bees crawling on it, naturalistic polychrome colouring, impressed Minton 1499 and date code for 1877, 7½in (18cm).
$4,000-7,500

Cf Victoria Cecil, Minton Majolica, 1982, No. 119, pattern illustrated.

A pair of Minton full figure Toby Jugs, in naturalistic polychrome colouring, on circular mottled green and brown bases, impressed Minton 1104 and 1140 and with date stamps for 1867, restored, 10½in (28cm) and 11in (28.5cm).
$1,400-2,600

A Minton majolica oval dish and cover, the cover modelled as a crab between seaweed, the dish painted with alternating panels of blue and brown, 15½in (38cm).
$4,000-7,500

A pair of Minton majolica oyster dishes, modelled with turquoise coloured shells, impressed mark, 10in (25cm) diam.
$200-450

A miniature Minton majolica amphora, impressed marks, with date code for 1859, 7in (17cm).
$800-1,500

A Minton majolica ewer, with mask head handle, modelled with drinking figures in white relief on a blue and brown ground, impressed mark date cipher 1874, 14in (35cm).
$1,200-2,100

A Minton wall plate, the central boss decorated in relief with a rose and mistletoe, the border with holly leaves separated by 4 panels with cherubs engaged in Christmas pursuits, in naturalistic polychrome colouring, impressed Minton date code for 1859, 16in (40cm) diam.
$2,200-4,200

A Minton figure of Vintager with Basket in each Hand, base mottled green and brown, the figure with naturalistic polychrome colouring, impressed 'Minton'.
$1,600-2,800

Cf Victoria Cecil, Minton Majolica, 1982, No. 139, illustrated.

A Minton vase, modelled as a bamboo trunk with leafy bamboo shoots climbing up it, in yellow, green and brown, impressed Minton 1692 and date code for 1873, chip to base and minor glaze chips, 8in (19.5cm).
$4,000-6,800

A pair of Minton figures of 'Boy and Girl Resting on Basket', in naturalistic polychrome colouring, each figure impressed Minton the boy with date code for 1865 the girl for 1867, 10in (25cm).
$1,300-2,400

Cf Victoria Cecil, Minton Majolica, 1982, Nos. 23 and 24, *illustrated.*

A Minton teapot, the body modelled as a gourd, the cover surmounted by mushrooms forming the finial, pale green body with naturalistic polychrome colouring, impressed Minton 1710 and date code for 1861, 7in (17cm).
$4,000-7,500

A Minton majolica figure, 'Begging dog', in naturalistic polychrome colouring, impressed Minton and with date code for 1868, 6in (15cm).
$1,600-2,800

Cf Victoria Cecil, Minton Majolica, 1982, No. 55, *illustrated.*

A Minton Christmas Jug, the handle modelled as entwined holly branches, blue with green and yellow rim, pink interior and naturalistic polychrome colouring, impressed Minton 580, c1870, 9in (22.5cm).
$1,700-3,000

Cf Victoria Cecil, Minton Majolica, 1982, No. 32, *illustrated.*

A Minton majolica jug with silver rim, impressed marks, mid-19thC, 9½in (24.5cm).
$800-1,500

A Minton figural group, modelled as 2 long haired mermaids supporting a large shell, naturalistic polychrome colouring, impressed Minton 1182 and date code for 1868, 17in (43cm) long.
$1,700-3,000

Cf Victoria Cecil, Minton Majolica, 1982, No. 69, *illustrated.*

A Minton figural group, 'Lamp Stand', the urn decorated with a band of scrollwork and key pattern border, cobalt blue urn with pale blue interior, mottled green and brown base and naturalistic polychrome colouring, impressed Minton 1517 and with date code for 1881, 14½in (35.5cm).
$4,000-6,800

Cf Victoria Cecil, Minton Majolica, 1982, No. 67, *illustrated.*

A Minton majolica vase, modelled as a trunk of a tree, and with a bird, insects and oak leaves, impressed mark, 7in (17.5cm).
$1,200-2,100

A large Minton vase on stand, the turquoise vase with ochre pink interior, blue-black stand, impressed Minton and date code for 1866, 36½in (91cm).
$2,000-4,500

A pair of large Minton vases, the pale blue body with blue and white ornament, yellow bands and brown snakes, painted marks and indecipherable impressed marks, some restoration, c1870, 25in (62cm).
$8,000-15,000

Cf Victoria Cecil, Minton Majolica, 1982, No. 139, *illustrated.*

A pair of Meissen porcelain chestnut baskets, covers and stands, decorated in colours and gilt, with turquoise chequered banding to the borders, and with chestnut finials, the circular bases pierced with basket weave, scroll and oval motifs, within a border painted with scattered flower sprays and chequered banding in colours and gilt, one stand cracked, crossed swords mark in underglaze blue, baskets 7in (17cm) diam., stands 14in (35.5cm) diam.
$2,200-4,200

Bottles

A Worcester blue and white rosewater bottle, painted with an Oriental figure holding a bird by a pagoda on rockwork and trees, the reverse with children on a bridge, the garlic neck with a band of trellis and hatch pattern enclosing flower sprays, blue crescent mark, c1760, 10in (25cm).
$1,800-3,800

A pair of Sèvres-pattern square bottles and stoppers, decorated with portraits of Louis XIV and Me. de Lamballe, within gilt line cartouches enriched with ruby enamelled beading, the royal blue grounds enamelled in colours and gilt with elaborate jewelled ornament within turquoise bead borders, the shoulders and stoppers similarly decorated, imitation interlaced L marks, c1880, 6in (15.5cm).
$2,200-4,200

Bowls

A Bow blue and white flared bowl, the exterior with trailing vine, c1754, 3½in (9cm) diam.
$400-750

A Longton Hall bowl, painted in bright green, yellow and puce with flowering shrubs issuing from pierced rockwork, rim chips, c1755, 4½in (11.5cm) diam.
$400-900

A Meissen Kakiemon bowl, painted with chrysanthemum, bamboo and butterflies, the well with a dragon chasing a flaming pearl, his scales picked out in gold, blue crossed swords mark, c1730, 8in (19cm) diam.
$2,000-4,500

A pair of Coalbrookdale bowls and lids, encrusted with flowers, mid-19thC, 5in (12.5cm).
$2,000-4,500

A Furstenberg bowl, painted with sprays of full blown pink roses below a lightly feathered pink band entwined with a sinuous green foliate chain, the rim edged in gilt, blue F mark and incised numerals, late 18thC, 7in (17cm) diam.
$180-300

A Meissen pale blue ground bowl, reserved with shaped panels, one with a winter landscape, the other with an Italianate landscape, the interior with a Dutch river landscape en grisaille within a border of puce, gilt and iron red scrolls, restored, mark in blue, gilders number 10 and repairer's mark V, 6in (15cm).
$1,300-2,400

In perfect condition, **$4,500-9,000**

A Meissen powdered purple ground slop bowl, the interior with a circular panel of a sailing vessel with gilt rims, blue crossed swords mark, Pressnummer 3 and painter's mark in iron red V, c1740, 7½in (18cm) diam.
$3,200-6,000

A Pinxton sugar bowl and cover, painted in the Imari style with panels of flowering shrubs within blue edged cartouches divided by iron red trellis pattern on an iron red ground, c1800, 7in (17.5cm) wide.
$600-1,200

A Wedgwood Fairyland Lustre bowl, the exterior with a girl within arcades and bowers, the interior with a continuous scene of pixies and minarets, printed Portland vase mark in gold and pattern No. Z.4968T, c1925, 6½in (16cm) wide.
$1,600-2,800

A Wedgwood Fairyland Lustre bowl, printed in gilt and colours with imps and other little folk darting beneath spreading trees with cobwebs between, upon a ground of brilliant orange, printed Portland vase mark and Made in England, 8½in (20.5cm) diam.
$1,200-2,100

A Wedgwood Fairyland Lustre circular footed bowl, the exterior with a continuous scene, the interior similarly decorated with pixies in a radiating wooded landscape, the interior rubbed, printed Portland vase mark and pattern No. Z5360/2, c1925, 9½in (23cm).
$1,000-2,000

An early Worcester 'famille verte' bowl, the fluted sides painted with Chinese flowers and a butterfly, faint star crack, c1752-55, 4½in (11cm).
$1,000-2,000

A First Period Worcester cream jug and slop basin, painted with fruit by the 'Spotted fruit painter' on a ground of butterflies and scrolling tendrils in purple, pink, yellow, puce, red, green and gilt, with turquoise foliate diapered and gilt foliate scrolling borders, open crescent mark in underglaze blue, jug 5in (12cm), basin 6½in (16.5cm) diam.
$600-1,200

An English punch bowl, painted and gilt with a bold pattern of peony branches in colours and foliage and tendrils in dark blue and gilt in Chinese style, within a narrow blue and gilt foliage border, pattern No. 1361, 9in (23cm).
$300-600

A Worcester small flared bowl, transfer printed in black and coloured with The Red Bull Pattern, c1755, 4in (10.5cm).
$1,000-2,000

18th-CENTURY WORCESTER

★ founded in 1751
★ soft paste porcelain using soaprock (steatite)
★ c1751-53 a short experimental period. Sometimes difficult to differentiate between Lund's Bristol and Worcester
★ both blue and white and 'famille verte' polychrome wares produced
★ c1752-54 some wares marked with an incised cross or line
★ c1755-60 some finely painted and potted wares produced
★ painters marks, resembling Chinese letters, appear on base of wares
★ the underglaze blue is well controlled and of a good pale colour
★ polychrome decoration is crisp and clean
★ almost all patterns are based on Chinese prototypes
★ transfer printed wares appear c1754
★ from 1760-76 a consistently high standard of potting and decorating achieved though lacking spontaneity of earlier wares
★ most blue and white pieces now marked with a crescent
★ 1776-93 the Davis/Flight period
★ often difficult to differentiate from Caughley where open crescent mark also used

Boxes

A Meissen silver-mounted snuff box, the exterior with blue ribbons with pink roses at intervals, edged in gilding, the interior with a gentleman and 2 ladies standing before an extensive river landscape, with contemporary mount, blue crossed swords mark to the interior, c1755, 3in (7.5cm) wide.
$4,000-6,800

A Meissen bombé large snuff box, the interior to the cover with Harlequin and Pierrot beside ladies taking tea in a garden landscape, the gilt-metal mounts with flowers and foliage, c1745, 5in (12cm) wide.
$10,000-18,000

A Meissen bombé-shaped snuff box, the interior to the cover with further figures beside garden statuary and with contemporary silver mounts, scroll thumbpiece, the silver with French import marks, c1745, 3in (7cm) wide.
$3,200-6,000

A Volkstedt jagddose, the cover painted with a recumbent stag in an extensive landscape, the hinged silver-gilt mount with waved decoration, blue hayfork and M mark, c1760, 3½in (9cm) diam.
$12,000-21,000

The mark of the hayfork comes from the Prince of Schwarzburg-Rudolstadt and the M from the founder of the factory Georg Heinrich Macheleid. A soft-paste covered cup similarly marked is in the Kunstundgewerbe Museum, Hamburg.

A Meissen snuff box, the interior of the base gilt, with later English silver-gilt mounts, edge of cover damaged, the porcelain c1745, the silver London 1818, with maker's mark of Charles Rawlings, 3½in (9cm) wide.
$1,800-3,800

A Nymphenburg white scallop-shaped casket and cover, with whelk feet and finial naturally modelled and with copper-gilt mount, c1775, 6½in (16.5cm) wide, and another similar cover with copper-gilt mount, 6in (15.5cm) wide.
$3,200-6,000

A German box and cover, with silver-gilt mounts, possibly Furstenberg, finely painted with battle scenes and encampments in bright enamel colours, each within a gold and puce cartouche, 3in (7cm) wide.
$1,000-2,000

A Naples casket, the top and sides modelled in relief with the gods on Olympus, 19thC, 10½in (26.5cm).
$1,000-2,000

A German casket, painted with a group of putti with dead game, the sides with similar figures symbolic of the Seasons, the inside of the lid painted with a lady at her toilet, with numerous attendants, 19thC, 8in (19cm).
$1,000-2,000

An English porcelain snuff box in the form of a cat's head, with hinged brass lid and mount, its eyes in yellow enamel and its muzzle and nose touched in pink, 2in (5cm).
$300-600

Caddies

A Meissen tea caddy, painted in colours with Turkish and European merchants in extensive harbour landscapes, the long sides with iron red and gilt 'Laub und Bandelwerk' enclosing 'Böttger Lustre', blue crossed swords marks, gilder's mark 65, c1735, 3½in (9cm).
$1,800-3,800

A Meissen yellow ground tea caddy, painted in a Kakiemon palette with flowers issuing from rockwork and a bird in flight within shaped quatrefoil cartouche, blue crossed swords mark and former's mark of Seidel, c1730, 4in (10cm).
$1,800-3,800

A Frankenthal tea caddy, painted with peasant figures after Teniers, CT monogram in underglaze blue, incised B2, c1765-70, 4½in (11cm).
$1,800-3,800

A Worcester tea caddy and cover, of Lord Henry Thynne type, with a gilt line and turquoise foliage cartouche, flanked by loose bouquets and butterflies beneath a blue border edged in gilding, minute chips to finial, c1775, 7in (17.5cm).
$1,800-3,800

Provenance: A Trapnell.

A Nymphenburg tea caddy and domed cover, painted with wayfarers on paths carrying baskets and bundles in landscape vignettes, cover and finial repaired, blue hexagram mark, impressed Bavarian shield mark and incised mark, the cover with blue alchemical sign with the 4 elements and gilder's mark K, 1763-67, 5½in (14.5cm).
$1,300-2,400

A Kloster Veilsdorf tea caddy, painted with a gallant and companion beneath garden pergolas and with gilt bands, traces of blue mark on base, silver gilt cover, c1775, 4½in (11.5cm).
$1,300-2,400

Make the most of Miller's

Every care has been taken to ensure the accuracy of descriptions and estimated valuations. Price ranges in this book reflect what one should expect to pay for a similar example. When selling one can obviously expect a figure below. This will fluctuate according to a dealer's stock, saleability at a particular time, etc. It is always advisable to approach a reputable specialist dealer or an auction house which has specialist sales.

A Worcester tea caddy, decorated in gros bleu, with finely painted panels of flowers, cover missing, seal mark, c1765.
$600-1,200

With cover **$1,200-2,100**

NYMPHENBURG

★ factory founded in the late 1740's but the main production started in 1753
★ J J Ringler was employed as arcanist
★ from 1757 a fine milky-white porcelain was produced
★ the porcelain is of great quality and virtually flawless
★ F A Bustelli modelled some excellent figures from 1754-63 which perfectly expressed the German rococo movement
★ the models are the epitome of movement and crispness and are invariably set on sparingly moulded rococo pad bases
★ note light construction of the slip-cast figures
★ J P Melchior, previously at Frankenthal and Höchst, was chief modeller from 1797-1810
★ on finest pieces the mark is often incorporated as part of the design
★ the factory still exists

Candelabra

A Chelsea Birds-in-Branches chamber-candlestick group, the birds with yellow and puce plumage on a shaped oval base enriched in puce and applied with a dog, one bird with restoration to tail and wing, the other with minute restoration to one wing, flowers chipped, gold anchor mark, c1758, 7in (17.5cm).
$1,000-2,000

Gold anchor Chelsea is still undervalued by comparison with earlier wares. There are, however, signs of growth in the market for perfect pieces.

A pair of Bow figural and bocage candlesticks, with thick bocage beneath which stands a fox about to devour a chicken, and a spaniel with his bag of 2 partridge, all with decoration in overglaze enamels, both damaged, 11in (28cm).
$2,200-4,200

A pair of Royal Crown Derby candlesticks, on square moulded base supported by 4 gilt fish, painted with panels of iron red, blue and gilt foliage, printed mark, 10in (25cm).
$600-1,200

A pair of Derby candelabra groups emblematic of Liberty and Matrimony, on pierced scroll-moulded bases enriched in turquoise, puce and gilding, the balustrades supporting the foliage-moulded nozzles, Wm. Duesbury & Co., restorations to nozzles, plumes, his hand and one tree, chipping, c1770, 12in (30cm).
$2,600-5,300

A pair of Meissen candlesticks, painted in colours with 'deutsche Blumen' and with gilt foliage, tassels and rims, bases of nozzles repaired, blue crossed swords marks, c1745, 9½in (23.5cm).
$1,200-2,100

A pair of Meissen four-light candelabra, painted in colours and enriched with gilding, the shaped square bases painted with exotic birds and insects and moulded with shell scrolls, minor chips and one branch repaired, blue crossed swords marks and incised numerals, c1900, 19in (48cm).
$1,200-2,100

A Meissen five-light candelabrum, enriched in gilding and applied with coloured trailing flowers, restorations and some chipping, blue crossed swords mark, c1880, 19in (47cm).
$1,200-2,100

A pair of Meissen four-light candelabra, encrusted with brightly coloured flowers, minor chips, blue crossed swords mark and incised numerals, c1880, 21½in ((54cm).
$1,800-3,800

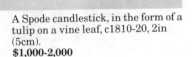

A Spode candlestick, in the form of a tulip on a vine leaf, c1810-20, 2in (5cm).
$1,000-2,000

A pair of Meissen candelabra stands, decorated with the figure of Ganymede being carried off by the God Zeus in the form of an eagle, slight chips to one base, incised crossed swords in a triangle, Nos. K49 and K50, 10½in (26.5cm).
$1,200-2,100

A Worcester blue and white chamber-candlestick, painted with carnations and trailing flowers within a crisply-moulded C-scroll border, with foliage-moulded nozzle and scroll handle with mask terminal, blue W mark, c1770, 6in (14.5cm).
$4,000-6,800

18thC English porcelain candlesticks are rare and keenly sought by collectors. Note the mask terminal on the handle.

A Spode taperstick in the form of a recumbent white elephant supporting the gilt sconce, with gilt ears and trunk, painted mark in red, c1815, 4in (10cm).
$300-600

A Royal Worcester chamber candlestick, as a small boy lying on a striped rug, balancing a drum on his right foot, his head resting on a bugle which forms the handle, oval base, impressed mark No. 3/18, 6½in (16cm) long.
$400-750

A Royal Worcester three-light candelabrum by James Hadley, moulded signature, 19in (47.5cm).
$1,700-3,000

Centrepieces

A Meissen table centre, modelled as an oval basket tied with pink ribbon supported on a foliage column, painted with 'deutsche Blumen' and moulded with pink, green and gilt rococo scrolls, minor repairs to foliage, blue crossed swords mark and impressed H, c1750, 18in (45cm) wide.
$4,000-6,800

A Meissen centrepiece, incised 1931, 42in (105cm).
$3,200-6,000

A Bow blue and white sweetmeat stand, painted in blue with a single large berried leaf against a shaded blue background, 1760's, 5½in (13.5cm).
$1,200-2,100

A large Sèvres centrepiece, signed 'Germain', within a border of stylised gilt scrolls and flowering vines on a dark blue ground, the whole with gilt metal mounts, 21in (52.5cm).
$1,800-3,800

A Royal Worcester 'ivory' mermaid and Nautilus centrepiece, decorated by Callowhill, the Nautilus-shell vase moulded with putti blowing trumpets, among foliage scrolls and gilt with entwined foliage, puce printed marks, c1878.
$2,200-4,200

A Worcester three-tier centrepiece, edged in pink surmounted by a bird with outstretched wings with predominantly puce and yellow plumage, on a pierced shell and coral encrusted base enriched in colours, some restoration to shells, c1770, 10in (25.5cm).
$3,200-6,000

An English porcelain and gilt metal table centre, probably Royal Worcester, damaged, c1860, 23in (58cm).
$1,200-2,100

A Royal Worcester centrepiece, the bowl supported by 3 Muses, heavily gilt and finely decorated, 9½in (23.5cm).
$900-1,700

A Continental comport encrusted with trailing foliage and roses, in natural colours, 15in (37.5cm).
$600-1,200

Clock Cases

A Dresden mantel clock, the whole encrusted with flowerheads and leaves, decorated in underglaze blue, black, flesh tones and gilt, some damage, cross swords mark in underglaze blue, 25in (63cm).
$1,300-2,400

A Meissen clock case, enriched with gilding, some minor chipping, blue crossed swords mark and incised numerals, c1880, the eight-day striking movement with enamel dial, chipped, 16½in (41.5cm).
$2,200-4,200

A Meissen (Teichert) clock case, moulded with foliage heightened in pink and turquoise, with 3 putti emblematic of Winter, Spring and Autumn, chips to flowers, blue Meissen mark, the movement by Lenzkirch, c1900, 20½in (51cm).
$1,600-2,800

A Sèvres-pattern porcelain and ormolu-mounted mantel clock, enriched with gilt and enamel spiral berried foliage, glass to circular dial cracked, imitation interlaced L and initial marks, c1880, 24½in (61.5cm).
$5,000-9,000

Cottages

A Staffordshire porcelain pastille burner, with detached brown roof, the walls painted with flowers and with pierced and gilt windows, on yellow base applied with coloured flowers, probably Spode, c1820, 4½in (11cm).
$1,300-2,400

A six-sided cottage pastille burner with pierced windows, probably by Thomas Parr, c1850, 6in (15cm).
$800-1,500

An English porcelain cottage pastille burner, with detachable roof, c1835, 5½in (13.5cm).
$1,200-2,100

An English porcelain cottage pastille burner, c1835, 4in (10cm).
$150-300

An English porcelain lilac cottage pastille burner, with detachable base, c1835, 4in (10cm).
$1,000-2,000

An English porcelain cottage pastille burner, c1835, 5½in (13.5cm).
$1,200-2,100

A porcelain cottage, with flower-encrusted front and roof, c1840, 4½in (11cm).
$600-1,100

An English porcelain cottage pastille burner, probably Coalport, c1835, 7in (17.5cm).
$1,800-3,800

A large porcelain pastille burner, flower-encrusted and gilt lined, c1835, 5½in (13.5cm).
$900-1,700

An English porcelain two-piece pastille burner in the form of Bladon church, 5in (12.5cm).
$800-1,500

An English porcelain pastille burner, in the form of a church, c1835, 6in (15cm).
$1,200-2,100

Cups

An Arras coffee cup and saucer, gilt with birds and floral garlands in scroll foliage cartouches reserved on blue ground and divided by white panels, blue AR marks, c1785.
$900-1,700

A Berlin cabinet cup and saucer, the cup painted in sepia and with lyres on iron red panels within gilt lozenge-shaped cartouches, reserved on lapis lazuli grounds, with gilt band rims, the centre to the saucer inscribed 'De par L'Amour on fait savoir à tous les coeurs qu'il faut aimer', blue sceptre mark, c1875.
$1,300-2,400

The inscription increases the value of this cup and saucer considerably.

A Berlin neo-classical cup and saucer, commemorating the Allied entry to Paris on 31 March 1814, the saucer with a map of Paris and inscription, blue sceptre mark, c1814.
$800-1,500

A Berlin neo-classical cup and saucer, painted with pink and white roses, the lilac borders gilt with anthemion between narrow green bands, blue sceptre marks and painter's marks, c1820.
$1,000-2,000

A Berlin neo-classical cup and saucer, painted with primulas and with gilt lozenge border, blue sceptre marks with painter's mark in puce, c1820
$1,000-2,000

A Berlin cabinet cup and saucer, painted in sepia with a named view of St. Marienkirche, within a gilt cartouche, the cup with blue sceptre mark, the saucer with blue sceptre and KPM marks, c1860.
$600-1,200

> ### BERLIN
>
> - ★ first factory started by W K Wegely in 1752
> - ★ body hard to distinguish from Meissen
> - ★ particularly close are the Cupids in Disguise and the Commedia dell'Arte figures
> - ★ closed in 1757 at the start of Seven Years War
> - ★ a second factory was started in 1761 by J E Gotzkowsky
> - ★ many artists came from Meissen, including F E Meyer
> - ★ porcelain has a distinctly creamy tone
> - ★ painting was in the restrained rococo manner
> - ★ pieces with puce scale borders and delicate flower painting
> - ★ derived from fashion for Sèvres – in common with most major German factories
> - ★ from 1770 the porcelain has a much colder more brilliant white tone
> - ★ the factory became influenced by the neo-classical movement in common with Fürstenburg and Meissen
> - ★ figure modelling was perfected by the brothers Friedrich Elias Meyer and Wilheim Christian Meyer – note the characteristic small heads and elongated bodies
> - ★ c1775 figure bases became more architectural in design, notably oval and square pedestals
> - ★ in the early 19thC the 'Empire' style of Sèvres and Vienna was copied
> - ★ as the 19thC progressed Berlin tended to follow the prevailing trends

A Berlin neo-classical cup and saucer, painted in colours with hyacinths, the gilt border with scroll motif, the interior gilt, blue sceptre marks and dash in iron red, c1821.
$800-1,500

A rare Bristol cup and trembleuse saucer, the borders with entwined scroll ornament in green enclosing pink foliage sprays within brown-edged rims, cup and saucer marked B6 in blue enamel.
$1,400-2,600

A Caughley blue and white wine taster with Fisherman pattern decoration, c1785, 1in high by 2in diam. (2.5 by 5cm).
$180-300

A Caughley blue and white tea bowl, c1785.
$60-120

A Chelsea teal bowl and saucer, of the raised anchor period, painted in Kakiemon style colours and exotic birds flying above blossoming shrubs issuing from banded hedges, raised anchor pad mark on saucer, c1750.
$5,000-9,000

A Coalport puce ground racing trophy and cover, gilt with the inscription 'Pains Lane Races Sepr. 27th, 1853', within gilt foliage and grass cartouches, the cover gilt with a band of trailing vine and with bunch of grapes finial, minute chip to handle, c1853, 11½in (28.5cm).
$1,400-2,600

A Derby stirrup cup, with 'Tally-Ho' on the collar, c1830, 5in (12.5cm) long.
$800-1,500

A Frankenthal 'bois simulé' cup and saucer, painted 'en grisaille' with landscapes imitating etchings and inscribed 'Braun und Leisser pinxit' and reserved on the simulated wood ground, minor frits to rim of saucer, blue crowned CT monogram mark, c1780.
$600-1,200

A Derby cabinet coffee can and saucer, finely painted in the manner of Banford, on a blue ground framed by simulated jewelling, on a ground of cornflowers and gilt stars, minor rubbing to gilding of saucer, crown, crossed batons and D mark and pattern no. 216 in puce, Wm. Duesbury & Co., c1790.
$4,000-6,800

Cf F Brayshaw Gilhespy, Crown Derby Porcelain, *pl 25, fig 44.*

Two Derby porcelain Named View coffee cans and saucers, the cups painted with views of Devernish Island and Kirkstall Abbey, and the saucers with Lock Gill (sic) and Borrowdale, reserved upon a deep cobalt ground decorated with groups of fronded leaves, all named on the base, 3 pieces with puce crown, crossed batons and D mark, one saucer marked in iron red.
$800-1,500

A Liverpool coffee cup and saucer, painted in an Imari palette with butterflies among flowering branches within an indented rim, minute chip to underside of saucer, Wm. Ball's Factory, c1764.
$800-1,500

LIMEHOUSE
(c1747-48)

(a re-attribution of some wares previously attributed to William Reid's Liverpool factory has taken place during the past year)

★ often a crude semi opaque body
★ glaze opacified by the use of tin outside
★ shell dishes and sauceboats are most commonly found
★ mainly blue and white
★ enamel colours are often vibrant and akin to saltglaze
★ some good landscapes, also fruit and roses in underglaze blue
★ identical motifs usually include imitation Chinese decoration – stylised peacock's feathers on handles and spouts
★ body of early phosphatic wares is often grey in colour

LIVERPOOL
Brownlow Hill
(c1755-68)

(It is now thought that wares previously attributed to William Ball were manufactured at Brownlow Hill, Liverpool, by William Reid, c1755-61, by his successor William Ball c1761-64 and by James Pennington from 1764-68. Ball may have been Reid's factory manager and could have continued in that capacity under James Pennington.)

★ underglaze blue is often bright and the glaze 'wet' and 'sticky' in appearance
★ shapes and style of decoration influenced by the Bow factory
★ decoration often resembles delft
★ paste often shows small turning tears. These show up as lighter flecks when held up to the light
★ polychrome wares are rare and collectable
★ polychrome transfer prints overpainted with enamels are sought after
★ elaborate rococo sauceboats were a factory speciality

A Liverpool blue and white miniature tea bowl and saucer, painted with a flock of birds above 2 wooded river islands, Richard Chaffers' Factory, c1762.
$1,200-2,100

LIVERPOOL
Richard Chaffers' Factory
(c1754-65)

★ early phosphatic wares have a greyish body
★ some fine polychrome wares are decorated with carefully drawn Chinese figures
★ attractive polychrome mugs are found in the phosphatic body
★ later steatitic wares are noticeably whiter in appearance
★ the underglaze blue of later wares is brighter and less grey
★ the 'Jumping Boy' pattern is particularly collectable
★ later chinoiseries are often peppered with dots. This decorative habit continues on Christians wares
★ potting based on Worcester shapes

A very rare Longton Hall blue and white coffee cup, with split-twig handle, painted with an Oriental gesturing towards a huge vase with a trailing flowering branch, the reverse with a flower spray, minute rim chip, c1755.
$1,600-2,800

Six Meissen tea bowls painted in Augsburg by E Auffenwerth in Eisenrot und Schwarzlot, the interiors with birds and further gilding, one cracked, c1725.
$3,200-6,000

Derived from prints by J E Ridinger, see S Ducret, Meissener Porzellan Bemalt in Augsburg, figs 100-02.

Cf R Rückert, Meissener Porzellan, no. 110 for a tea bowl with human figures, the interiors similarly decorated. See also Pazaurek Vol 1 Ch 2 for a discussion of this type of painting and gilding. ▷

A fine Meissen tea bowl and saucer, painted with Oriental figures, in the manner of J G Herold, c1725.
$4,500-9,000

A Meissen blue and white tea bowl and saucer, moulded with scrolls and painted in underglaze blue, the reverses similarly decorated, blue crossed swords marks and painter's marks, c1735.
$1,600-2,800

A Meissen blue and white tea bowl and saucer, after a Kangxi original, blue crossed swords marks and K of Kretzschmar, c1735.
$1,600-2,800

MEISSEN

★ in 1709 J F Böttger produced a white hard paste porcelain
★ wares often decorated by outside decorators (Hausmaler)
★ in 1720 kilnmaster Stozel came back to Meissen bringing with him J G Herold
★ from 1720-50 the enamelling on Meissen was unsurpassed – starting with the wares of *Lowenfinck* – bold, flamboyant chinoiserie or Japonnaise subjects, often derived from the engravings of Petruschenk, particularly on Augustus Rex wares, *J G Herold* – specialised in elaborate miniature chinoiserie figure subjects, *C F Herold* – noted for European and Levantine quay scenes
★ crossed swords factory mark started in 1723
★ marks, shapes and styles much copied
★ underside of wares on later body has somewhat greyish chalky appearance
★ in late 1720's a somewhat glassier, harder looking paste was introduced, different from the early ivory tones of the Böttger period
★ finest Meissen figures modelled by J J Kändler from 1731
★ best figures late 1730's and early 1740's – especially the great Commedia dell'Arte figures and groups
★ other distinguished modellers who often worked in association with Kändler were Paul Reinicke and J F Eberlein
★ cut-flower decoration (Schnittblumen) often associated with J G Klinger. The naturalistic flower subjects of the 1740's, epitomised by Klinger, gradually became less realistic and moved towards the so-called 'manier Blumen' of the 1750's and 1760's
★ early models had been mounted on simple flat pad bases, whereas from 1750's bases were lightly moulded rococo scrolls

A Meissen Kakiemon cup and saucer, painted in the Kakiemon palette with birds among flowering chrysanthemum and foliage, with chocolate rims, blue crossed swords marks, c1735.
$400-900

Provence: The Art Exchange.

A pair of Böttger porcelain tea bowls and saucers, with Augsburg Goldmalerei, the interiors to the bowls and the centres of the saucers gilt and engraved in the Seuter Workshop with chinoiserie figures above scrollwork supports, the porcelain 1720-25 and the decoration almost contemporary.
$4,000-6,800

A Meissen tea bowl and saucer, with powdered purple ground, painted with figures loading boats in harbour scenes, the saucer with quatrefoil lustre, puce and gold 'Laub-und-Bandelwerk' cartouche, blue crossed swords and K mark, c1735.
$1,800-3,800

A Meissen coffee cup and saucer, painted in puce monochrome and gold with 'indianische Blumen', with chocolate rims, blue crossed swords mark, c1735.
$1,000-2,000

A pair of Meissen powdered purple ground beakers and saucers, with purple cell-pattern and iron red foliage and with gilt scroll rims, 2 handles with minor cracks, blue crossed swords marks and gilder's number 15 to each piece, c1740.
$5,000-9,000

A pair of Meissen coffee cups and saucers, blue crossed swords marks, Pressnummern 2 and 24, gilder's number 67, c1745.
$2,600-5,300

A pair of Meissen yellow ground tea bowls and saucers, painted with merchants in river landscapes and wayfarers on horseback within chocolate and gilt quatrefoil cartouches, blue crossed swords marks and gilder's mark B. to each piece, various Pressnummern, c1740.
$4,000-6,800

A Meissen cabinet cup and cover with pine cone knop, snake handle and set on 3 paw feet, crossed swords mark, 4½in (11.5cm).
$500-900

A Le Nove chinoiserie tea bowl and saucer, painted with Chinese figures in landscape vignettes, iron red star marks, c1790.
$600-1,200

A pair of Sèvres tea cups and saucers, painted with birds in landscapes within gilt foliage cartouches on green grounds, tiny chip to footrim of one cup and rim of one saucer, blue interlaced L's enclosing the date letter I for 1761, painter's mark of Aloncle.
$1,700-3,000

l. A Meissen cup and saucer, probably painted by C F Herold, painted with shore scene with sailing boats within an elaborate scroll work border, the interior with a quay scene within double red lines, crossed swords mark in underglaze blue and no. 13 in gilt, c1740.
$4,000-7,500

r. A Meissen quatrefoil cup and saucer, painted with flowers, butterflies, dragonflies and other insects, having brown painted borders, crossed swords marked in underglaze blue, c1742.
$1,400-2,600

A Vincennes 'bleu lapis' coffee cup and saucer, gilt with 'ciselé' bunches of flowers, reserved on the bleu lapis ground and with gilt dentil rims, blue interlaced L marks, the cup enclosing the date letter A for 1753.
$2,000-4,500

A Sèvres apple green cup and saucer, painted with musical, amatory and floral trophies within 'ciselé' gilt scroll and foliage surrounds, on apple grounds with gilt dentil rims, blue interlaced L marks enclosing the date letter F for 1758, and painter's mark of Buteux aîné.
$2,600-5,300

SÈVRES

★ most decoration of these early years has a somewhat tentative appearance and few pieces show the sharpness of German contemporaries

★ the vases and other hollow wares including ice pails and flower holders epitomised the rococo style predominant at the court

★ Sèvres plaques were inset into furniture from 1760's

★ Sèvres managed to discover the secret of hard paste porcelain at the same time as Cookworthy at Plymouth in 1768

★ 'jewelled porcelain' was introduced in 1773, using a technique of fusing enamels over gilt or silver foil

A Sèvre hop-trellis fluted cup and saucer, painted with blue pilasters with entwined gilt scrolls between berried foliage and pink bands with further gilding and dentil rims, blue interlaced L marks enclosing the date letter L for 1764 and painter's mark of Thevenet, père, various incised marks.
$1,300-2,400

A Sèvres small cylindrical cup and saucer, painted with bands of blue trellis with flowers and bands of roses divided by gilt lines with gilt dentil rims, blue interlaced L marks enclosing date letter S for 1771 and painter's mark of Buteux aîné.
$600-1,100

A Sèvres small cylindrical cup and saucer, painted with panels of single roses with gilt cartouches on blue and gilt scale-pattern grounds, blue interlaced L marks enclosing the date letter Z for 1777 and painter's mark EL.
$1,400-2,600

A Sèvres 'bleu nouveau' trembleuse cup, cover and stand, reserved on the 'bleu nouveau' ground, further gilt with bands of C-scrolls enclosing seeding, rim of cover restored, blue interlaced L marks and painter's mark of Le Guay, c1775.
$1,700-3,000

VIENNA

★ factory founded by C I du Paquier in 1719 with the help of Stolzel and Hunger from Meissen

★ the body of du Paquier wares has a distinctive smoky tone

★ decoration tends to cover much of the body and can be more elaborate than Meissen

★ extensive use of trellis work or 'gitterwerk'

★ the 'State' period of the factory ran from 1744-84

★ the style of this period was 'baroque', with scrollwork and lattice-like gilding

★ plain bases were used from mid-1760's

★ excellent figure modelling was undertaken by J J Niedermayer from 1747-84

★ Konrad von Sorgenthal became director from 1784-1804

★ the style became far less based on rococo and much simpler in taste, but with good strong colours and raised gilding

★ factory closed in 1864

A Vienna Du Paquier chinoiserie beaker and trembleuse stand, painted with Chinamen standing with fans and seated at a table on terraces, with pierced gallery, one handle restored, c1735.
$4,000-7,500

A Sèvres 'bleu nouveau' cup and saucer, painted with brightly coloured birds in landscapes within gilt panels reserved on the 'bleu nouveau' ground with gilt 'ciselé' scrolling foliage, blue interlaced L marks enclosing the date letters AA for 1778 and painter's mark of Aloncle, gilder's mark of Chauveaux, the cup incised 27 and 36, the saucer 44.
$1,300-2,400

A Sèvres yellow ground trembleuse cup and saucer, painted with a band of symmetrical scrolls, ribbons and foliage between the lines, the yellow ground with trailing blue flowers and with gilt rims, blue interlaced L marks and the date letters KK for 1788, painter's mark of André Vincent Viellard, incised 37 to each piece, the cup with 3.
$1,800-3,800

A Sèvres hard paste coffee cup and saucer, painted with musical trophies in 'ciselé' gilt oval cartouches reserved in a pink ground of 'oeil-de-perdrix', the cartouches joined by floral garlands, minor chip to underside of saucer rim, iron red crowned interlaced marks and painter's mark DR perhaps of Drand and incised marks, c1780.
$1,400-2,600

l. A Spode tulip cup with green stalk handle, the overlapping petals striped in pink, the interior with yellow centre with black stamens, on a green octagonal base edged in gilding, 2 slight chips to underside, script mark in red, c1820, 3in (7cm).
$1,000-2,000

r. A Spode tulip cup, striped in red, slightly deformed in firing, red mark, c1820, 3in (7cm).
$800-1,500

A pair of Swansea fluted cups and saucers, probably painted by William Pollard, stencil marks in red, 1813-22 period.
$1,000-2,000

A Worcester cup, decorated in blue and white with floral sprays, blue crescent mark to base, 18thC.
$80-150

A Worcester porcelain tea bowl and saucer, Queen Charlotte's pattern, c1788.
$300-600

A Worcester chocolate cup and saucer, with pierced scroll handles edged in gilding, painted in dry blue with bouquets and scattered flower sprays within a gilt dentil rim, c1770.
$1,000-2,000

A Chamberlain's Worcester cup, cover and stand, with gilt ring handles, painted with named botanical specimens, the cover with chrysanthemum, the body with grape hyacinth and spear leaved geranium, the stand with wild rose, within gilt line rims, some minor rubbing to gilding, script mark in puce, c1800, 4½in (11.5cm).
$600-1,100

A Flight, Barr & Barr Worcester trio, comprising 2 tea cups and a saucer, with the Pagoda and Peony pattern, c1813-40.
$300-600

A Flight & Barr Worcester goblet, the grey marbled ground reserved with a shipping scene inscribed 'Dover' on a pale yellow ground within a gilt octagonal cartouche within gilt line rims, script mark and incised B, c1805, 5in (12.5cm).
$1,800-3,800

A Royal Worcester cabinet cup and saucer, painted with fruit, by Ricketts, signed.
$200-450

An English porcelain tankard, painted with colourful displays of garden flowers, restored, c1800-10, 5½in (13cm).
$180-300

A pair of Royal Worcester coffee cups and saucers painted with highland castle by J Stinton, and 4 other cups and saucers painted with various scenes by various artists in a brush fitted case.
$1,600-2,800

A Zurich tea bowl and saucer, painted in Schwarzlot with landscape vignettes and with gilt rims, blue Z marks with 2 dots on the saucer and incised marks, c1775.
$600-1,200

A pink pig, jumping through a drum, match strike.
$150-300

Two pigs smooching in the back of an open car, driven by a chauffeur.
$150-300

Two pink pigs accompanying themselves on a green piano, spill holder.
$150-300

A pink pig accompanying himself on a green piano.
$150-300

Figures – Animals

A pair of Bow white figures of a lion and lioness with fierce expressions, prowling on oval mound bases, lioness with crack to back right-hand thigh and left back foot, c1749, the lion 9in (22cm) wide, the lioness 9½in (23cm) wide.
$18,000-26,000

Cf Anton Gabszewicz and Geoffrey Freeman, op cit pl 251 for the pair in the Freeman Collection.

Lively modelling and early date make these figures highly collectable.

A pair of Bow white models of a lion and lioness, the lion with small firing crack to left forepaw and front of base, the lioness with extended fire crack through base and round her hind quarters, the rear part of the base restuck, some minute chipping to bases, c1750, 11½in (28cm) long.
$4,500-9,000

Cf George Savage, 18thC English Porcelain, pl 47b and another pair in the British Museum, R L Hobson, Catalogue of the Collection of English Porcelain, fig 4, no.I.11.

◁

A Bow white figure of an owl, his head pierced, perched on a tree stump applied with three flowers, extended firing crack round body, restuck to base, c1754, 7½in (19cm).
$2,600-5,300

Cf Untermyer Collection Catalogue, pl 78, fig 259 and Frank Stoner, Chelsea, Bow and Derby Porcelain Figures, pl 105 for similar examples.

BOW PORCELAIN
c1745-76

★ probably the first porcelain factory in England

★ early wares were mostly decorated in overglaze enamel colours

★ the body is of the phosphatic soft paste type as Lowestoft, early Chaffers and early Derby

★ it is sometimes difficult to differentiate between blue and white wares from Bow, Lowestoft, and Derby

★ painters numerals sometimes used on base or inside footrings as the Lowestoft (and occasionally Chaffers, Liverpool)

★ body heavy for its size

A Bow white figure of a standing pug, his incised collar with a florette standing on a rectangular mound base moulded with flowers, some minor staining, c1755, 3in (7.5cm) wide.
$1,800-3,800

A pair of Derby figures representing Autumn, both seated with baskets of grapes, coloured in pink and puce, with yellow hats, some restoration, c1760, 5in (12.5cm).
$1,800-3,800

A pair of Derby figures as Shepherd
and Shepherdess with musical
instruments, c1765, 9in (22.5cm).
$1,600-2,800

A Derby figure of a woodpecker,
with incised feather markings
enriched in green, yellow, iron red
and puce, chips to flowering foliage,
repair to tail and tree stump, c1765,
5in (12.5cm).
$1,300-2,400

A Derby group, Father Time
Clipping the Wings of Love, c1770.
$1,000-2,000

A Derby porcelain pug dog, c1768,
3in (7.5cm).
$500-900

A Derby porcelain cow figure,
c1768, 3½in (8.5cm).
$500-900

A pair of Derby porcelain sheep,
c1780, 3½in (8.5cm).
$800-1,500

A Derby porcelain cow and calf
group, c1770, 5½in (13.5cm).
$500-900

A black cow is unusual.

18th-CENTURY DERBY

★ some early white jugs
incised with the letter D
have been attributed to
the Derby factory under
the direction of John
Heath and Andrew
Planché, believed to start
c1750

★ early Derby is soft paste
and is generally lighter
than Bow and Chelsea

★ very rare to find crazing
on early Derby, the glaze
was tight fitting and
thinner than Chelsea

★ glaze often kept away
from the bottom edge or
edge was trimmed, hence
the term 'dry-edge'
(particularly applied to
figures)

★ c1755, three (or more)
pieces of clay put on
bottom of figure to keep it
clear of kiln furniture,
giving 'patch' or 'pad'
marks – which now have
darker appearance

★ Duesbury had joined
Heath and Planché in
1756

★ Duesbury's early works
display quite restrained
decoration, with much of
the body left plain,
following the Meissen
style

★ Derby can be regarded as
the English Meissen

★ the porcelain of this
period has an excellent
body, sometimes with
faintly bluish appearance

★ 1770-84 known as the
Chelsea-Derby period

★ Chelsea-Derby figures
almost always made at
Derby

★ 1770's saw the
introduction of unglazed
white biscuit Derby
figures

★ this points to the move
away from the academic
Meissen style towards the
more fashionable French
taste

★ in 1770's leading
exponent of the neo-
classical style, and
comparable to
contemporary wares of
Champion's Bristol

★ body of 1770's is
frequently of silky
appearance and of bluish-
white tone

★ 1780's Derby body very
smooth and glaze white,
the painting on such
pieces was superb,
particularly landscapes,
Jockey Hill and Zachariah
Boreman

★ 1780's and 1790's noted
for exceptional botanical
painting of the period
especially by 'Quaker'
Pegg and John Brewer

★ around 1800 the body
degenerated, was
somewhat thicker, the
glaze tended to crackle
and allow discolouration

PORCELAIN   FIGURES

A matched set of 4 Derby porcelain figures, representing the 4 continents, Africa, Asia, Europe and America, c1780, 9in (22.5cm).
$1,300-2,400

A pair of Dresden figures of King Charles Spaniels, blue printed Dresden Potschappel marks, 12in (30cm) long.
$1,300-2,400

A Meissen figure of a rhinoceros, modelled by J J Kändler after Albrecht Dürer, incised decorated in shades of brown with an armour-like skin, chips to ears and tail, 1735-40, 7in (17.5cm) long.
$4,000-7,500

A Derby biscuit group representing Music, c1790, 10in (25cm).
$1,000-2,000

A Dresden figure of a polar bear, the muzzle, eyes and claws picked out in blue, crossed swords mark in underglaze blue, 10in (25cm).
$1,700-3,000

A Kloster Veilsdorf figure of a crouching leopard, probably modelled by Pfränger Snr, with brown and black markings on brown mound base, c1775, 5in (12cm) long.
$1,000-2,000

A Longton Hall group of 2 putti with a goat, scantily draped in pink and yellow, on a scroll moulded base enriched in puce and green, restoration to goat's horns and base, c1755, 6in (15cm) wide.
$800-1,500

A Meissen pipe bowl, modelled as a recumbent sheep dog with hinged neck, incised and brown fur markings, one ear and forepaw restored, blue crossed swords mark on base, c1745, 3½in (8cm) long.
$1,800-3,800

A very rare Ludwigsburg figure of an elephant supporting an obelisk, naturally modelled with grey hair markings and pink ears, his puce saddle cloth lined in yellow and edged with gilding, the upper part of the obelisk and the elephant's tusks restored, blue crowned interlaced C mark, c1765, 11in (27cm).
$5,000-9,000

The modelling suggests it could possibly be that of Johann Christian Wilhelm Beyer, particularly the presence of the obelisk, a feature which appears in many of his known models.

LUDWIGSBURG

* porcelain factory was founded in 1758
* J J Ringler directed the factory from 1759-99
* best period was from 1765-75
* porcelain has a distinctly greyish tone which is generally poorer than contemporary German factories
* specialised in producing figures
* most desirable are the 'Venetian fair groups' produced by Jean-Jacob Louis
* in 1770's figures of a more classical nature were produced
* the later figures were of a much poorer quality
* quality of the flower painting is of a fairly undistinguished nature
* the factory closed in 1824

Two Meissen figures of seated cats, modelled by J J Kändler, with yellow, red and black facial markings and eyes and grey fur, on grassy mound bases, minor cracks, restoration to mouse and tail of one cat, blue crossed swords marks on base, c1740, 7in (17.5cm).
$14,000-24,000

First modelled by Kändler in September 1736 and others in January 1741, and according to Kändler's taxa between 1740-48.

Cf C Albiker: op cit no. 216 where he records the various entries.

A pair of Meissen figures of goldfinches, with incised feather markings enriched in yellow and grey, the tree stump enriched in brown and green, chips to beaks, one with chip to tree stump, blue crossed swords marks, c1745, 5½in (14cm).
$4,500-9,000

A Meissen figure of a mallard duck, with brown head and purple and brown breast, the tips of its wings and tail feathers enriched in black and purple, standing on turquoise water-weeds and on a circular green and yellow mound, cracks and repairs, blue crossed swords mark at back, c1740, 11½in (28cm).
$6,000-12,000

A Meissen bird nesting group, enriched in brown, green, yellow and flesh tints, one tail repaired, minor chips, c1750, 5½in (14cm) wide.
$800-1,500

Two Meissen figures of swans, ▷ naturally modelled by J J Kändler, their beaks, eyes and feet painted in black and iron red, blue crossed swords mark, c1745, 3in (7cm).
$4,500-9,000

A pair of Meissen figures of swans, with orange and black beaks, their white feathers with grey markings, firing cracks and some chipping, blue crossed swords marks and incised numerals, c1880, 12½in (30.5cm).
$2,600-5,300

A pair of Meissen pug dogs, modelled by J J Kändler and P Reinicke with belled orange and pink collars with green and blue ribbon ties, black and brown facial and fur markings, restoration and damages, one with blue crossed swords mark on base, c1745, 6in (15cm).
$8,000-15,000

First modelled by Kändler in 1741.

Kändler's taxa of June 1744 and December 1744 record the new models.

A Meissen Marcolini figure of a Chaffinch, blue crossed swords and star mark, c1790, 4in (10cm).
$800-1,500

In the Ceramics section if there is only one measurement it refers to the height of the piece.

A Meissen group of dogs and a kennel, modelled by J J Kändler, their fur naturally coloured in brown, grey and black, minor chips, blue crossed swords mark, c1750, 5½in (13cm).
$10,000-18,000

A large Meissen model of an elephant, naively modelled with large eyes and paw-like feet, some damage to trunk, 19thC, 17in (42.5cm) long.
$1,000-2,000

A Meissen figure of a monkey playing the cello, modelled by O Pielz, in white frock, blue jacket, and puce trousers, playing the cello blue crossed swords and dot mark, incised and impressed marks, 8in (20cm).
$1,300-2,400

A pair of Meissen small figures of pug dogs, after models by J J Kändler, with brown fur markings and black faces and paws, one with blue collar, the other with green, blue crossed swords marks, impressed marks, 3in (8cm) long.
$400-900

A Meissen figure of a frog, naturalistically modelled, enriched in green, black, yellow and flesh tones, blue crossed swords, impressed marks, 3in (7.5cm) long.
$600-1,200

A pair of porcelain figures, marked Rockingham, c1830, 5in (12.5cm).
$3,200-6,000

A pair of Meissen figures of mice, naturalistically modelled with brown hair markings on oval base, blue crossed swords, impressed ▷ marks, 2in (5cm) long.
$800-1,500

A Meissen group of 3 dogs, blue crossed swords, impressed and incised marks, 7in (17.5cm) wide.
$500-900

A Meissen figure of a squirrel, modelled after Kändler originals with incised hair markings enriched in brown, wearing a violet and gilt collar suspending a chain, blue crossed swords, incised and impressed marks, 8in (20cm).
$500-900

A seated brindled tabby cat with ginger colouring, Sitzendorf mark in underglaze blue, ears restored, c1870, 10in (25cm).
$800-1,500

A Staffordshire porcelain eagle, likely to be Lloyd Shelton factory, c1835, 7½in (18.5cm).
$400-750

A Samson figure of a partridge perched astride a tree stump applied with blue flowers, the bird's plumage in shades of brown and grey and with orange wattle and comb, blue cross mark, late 19thC, 6in (15cm).
$200-450

A Samson figure of a white rhinoceros, after the original by J J Kändler, naturally modelled, its nose and ears heightened with flesh tints and with yellow horn, blue cross mark, c1880, 9in (22.5cm) wide.
$1,000-2,000

A fine quality hand painted porcelain figure of a King Charles spaniel, sitting upon a mauve and gilt decorated cushion, early 19thC, 7½in (18cm).
$400-900

A Staffordshire porcelain dog group, c1835, 3in (7.5cm).
$1,000-2,000

A white porcelain bear, c1880, 9in (22.5cm).
$400-900

This is a late copy of the stoneware bears.

SAMSON, EDME ET CIE (PARIS)

★ factory opened in Paris in 1845
★ reproduced wares of virtually every other factory (both Continental and Oriental)
★ their fakes of Meissen and Chinese porcelain are excellent
★ their English soft-paste porcelain fakes are easier to detect, as they used a Continental hard-paste body
★ Samson claims that all wares have an S contained within the mark – however this can be easily removed by the unscrupulous
★ more pieces are attributed to Samson than they could possibly have made

---

Figures – People

A Bayeux, Langlois, figure of an Oriental spice-seller, one pot restored, c1835, 7½in (19cm) wide.
$1,000-2,000

Cf George Savage, Dictionary of 19thC Antiques, *col pl pp 84-5.*

A rare pair of Belleek female figures, wearing loose classical draperies in shades of iridescent mauve, one with a gold headband and armband, the other with a gold bead necklace, on circular bases, printed mark a hound, a harp and Belleek, 14½in (36cm).
$4,000-7,500

A Bow figure of Autumn, a girl sitting with a basket of grapes, square hole at the back, c1755, 4½in (11cm).
$1,400-2,600

A Bow figure of Spring, with lemon-yellow bodice, white apron and pink skirt, seated beside baskets of flowers on a circular mound base, minor chips, c1754, 5in (12.5cm).
$1,800-3,800

A Bow figure representing Smell, from a set of the Five Senses, with marble base, c1760, 10in (25cm).
$1,200-2,100

See George Savage, 18thC English Porcelain, *pl 43b.*

A Bow figure of a shepherdess, wearing a yellow bodice and puce decorated dress, slight damage, 18thC, 6½in (16cm).
$1,300-2,400

BOW FIGURES

★ the earliest Bow figures had simple pad bases in common with Chelsea and Derby
★ many figures left in the white
★ figures tend to be less sophisticated than those from the Chelsea factory
★ from 1750-54 many figures were modelled by the 'Muses modeller'
★ these figures have quite thick glaze and low square bases
★ best period runs from 1750-59
★ the influence of Meissen can be seen in the figures from c1755 on
★ rococo bases appeared in late 1750's, earlier bases of c1760 in common with Chelsea are relatively restrained
★ by 1760 'C & S' scroll decoration was in great demand as were large shell bases, which are often thought of as a trade mark of Bow (although other factories did use them)
★ by 1760's typical colours used are blue, emerald-green, yellow and a good red
★ from c1765 greater use of underglaze blue as a ground colour, like contemporaries at Longton Hall
★ late 1760's figures elevated on more elaborate and pierced bases, generally applied with flowers
★ figures with elaborate bocage are typical
★ figures tend now to copy Chelsea gold anchor groups
★ figures with an underglaze blue crescent tend to be Bow (Worcester produced very few figures)

A pair of Bow figures emblematic of Sight and Smell, wearing pale pink and yellow flowered clothes, Sight with firing crack to sides, some minute chipping, c1756, 6 and 5½in (15 and 13.5cm).
$3,200-6,000

A Bow figure of Autumn, modelled as a youth in yellow-lined pink jacket, dot-pattern waistcoat and flowered breeches, seated on a tree stump, on a four-footed scroll-moulded base enriched in puce and gilding, some minor chipping, c1762, 6in (15.5cm).
$1,400-2,600

A rare Bow figure of Summer from a set of Seasons taken from Meissen originals, probably modelled by Tebo, decorated in the Giles manner, sconce missing, c1760-65, 9in (22.5cm).
$1,600-2,800

A pair of Bow porcelain figures, The New Dancers, in mint condition, c1765, 10in (25cm).
$2,200-4,200

A Bow figure of a shepherd, wearing a colourful costume and green and primrose yellow-lined cape, on rococo base, 9in (22.5cm).
$1,200-2,100

A rare Coalbrookdale parian figure of the Duke of Wellington, modelled by G Abbott and issued by Daniell's, impressed Manufactured at Coalbrookdale and the name of sculptor and publisher, c1850, 10½in (26cm).
$600-1,100

◁ A Copeland parian group of a girl seated on a rock cradling a terrier on her lap, entitled 'Go to Sleep', impressed 'Art Union of London, J Durham Sc 1862', 17in (43cm).
$800-1,500

A Derby white figure of John Wilkes, minute chips to cloak and scroll, Wm. Duesbury & Co., c1765, 12in (29.5cm).
$800-1,500

A Copeland parian group of Cupid and another winged boy struggling for possession of a heart lying at their feet, on oval shaped base, 15½in (38.5cm).
$1,200-2,100

A Derby shepherdess, in yellow-lined pink jacket, the scroll moulded base enriched with turquoise and gilding, chips, Wm. Duesbury & Co., c1765, 10in (24.5cm).
$800-1,500

A pair of Derby figures emblematic of Summer, painted in the London studio of William Duesbury, he with restoration to hat and left arm, she to hat, arms and waist, Andrew Planché's period, c1753, 6½in (16.5cm).
$6,000-12,000

These early standing Seasons are each represented by a pair of contrasting figures for each Season.

William Duesbury's London Account Book refers specifically to Seasons thus:
'Joun 6 (1753) 1 Darbeyshire seson (sic) 1-0
August 3 pr of Darbishire sesons (sic) 0-6-0
and it seems highly likely that they were from this series rather than the seated Seasons of the same date, of which no coloured examples would seem to be recorded.

An early Derby figure of a girl with puce bodice and flowered skirt, 6in (15cm)
$1,000-2,000

An early Derby figure of a harvester, with pink jacket, gold and orange trousers, c1765, 7½in (18.5cm).
$1,400-2,600

A pair of Derby figures of a shepherd and shepherdess, both finely decorated in turquoise and yellow, minor chip on hat, c1760.
$2,200-4,200

A pair of Derby porcelain Mansion House dwarfs, c1780, 7in (17.5cm).
$1,600-2,800

A good pair of Bloor Derby figures of Shakespeare and Milton, Shakespeare modelled after the Scheemaker Memorial in Westminster Abbey, Milton probably modelled after John Cheere, both well decorated in bright enamels and gilt, slight chips, Milton with restored scroll, printed crowned banner marks in iron red, incised nos. 291 and 305, 9½in (23.5cm).
$900-1,700

A Derby figure of Andromache weeping over the ashes of Hector, c1800, 10½in (26cm).
$500-900

For the model see J Twitchett, Derby Porcelain, *plt 151. According to the Haslem and Bemrose lists the original cost 'Enamelled and Gilt' was $3.*

A pair of Derby porcelain figures of Billy Waters and African Sall, c1830, 3½in (8.5cm).
$800-1,500

A Derby porcelain figure of Edmund Keen as Richard III, c1800, 11in (27.5cm).
$1,200-2,100

A pair of Bloor Derby figures, c1830, 6in (15cm).
$1,200-2,100

A pair of Derby porcelain figures of children, raised on scrolled bases, damaged, incised no. 89 and crossed swords mark in underglaze blue, early 19thC, 4½in (11.5cm).
$500-900

A Frankenthal group of lovers emblematic of Autumn, her dress and apron decorated with puce flower sprigs, on low scroll moulded base picked out in puce and gilt, slight chips to branches and repair, his left hand restuck, blue rampant lion mark, impressed PH, c1750's, 11in (27cm).
$5,000-9,000

FRANKENTHAL

★ Paul A Hannong started producing porcelain in Frankenthal in 1755, under the patronage of the Elector Carl Theodor

★ glaze has a quite distinctive quality as it tends to 'soak in' the enamel colours

★ high quality porcelain produced under Modellmeister J W Lanz, was favoured striped gilt grounds and green and dark puce

★ K G Lück and his brother or cousin J F Lück came to Frankenthal from Meissen in 1758

★ K G Lück's work tends to be quite fussy and often on grassy mounds, with rococo edges picked out in gilding

★ in the late 18thC a fine range of figures produced by J P Melchoir and A Bauer

★ Melchoir also worked at Höchst

★ Frankenthal utility ware is noted for the quality of the painting, particularly flower painting

★ factory closed in 1799

★ moulds from the factory were used in many 19thC German factories

A Frankenthal figure of a young woman dancing, modelled by Joh Friedrich Lück, chips and repairs, blue lion rampant mark, and incised JH monogram, c1756-59, 9in (22cm).
$2,600-5,300

Cf Hoffman, Frankenthaler Porzellan, *Taf 57, no. 258.*

A Ludwigsburg miniature group of 3 figures rolling dice, in tricorn hats and coloured clothes, on green and black splashed rectangular base, blue interlaced C mark, c1775, 3in (8cm) wide.
$3,200-6,000

◁ A pair of Le Nove groups of putti, some repairs and damages, Antonibon's factory, c1780, 6in (14cm).
$600-1,200

Two Höchst figures of Das Weinende Mädchen and Jammernder Knabe, the girl in black headscarf, pale yellow bodice, grey skirt and puce underskirt, the boy in puce jacket, pale yellow breeches etched in gilding, and iron red shoes, her left hand repaired, blue crowned wheel marks, the boy incised 'Fohler', c1775, 6in (15cm).
$1,800-3,800

A Kloster Veilsdorf figure of Harlequin, modelled by Wenzel Neu, holding a yellow hat with black mask and multi-coloured harlequinade costume, on tree stump base, minor damage to his head, base repaired, 1764-65, 6in (14cm).
$4,500-9,000

A Kloster Veilsdorf figure of Dr Boloardo, modelled by Wenzel Neu, blue enamel crossed swords mark, 1764-65, 5in (13cm).
$4,500-9,000

Cf R S Soloweitschik, Thüringer Porzellan, *no. 29.*

A Höchst figure of a shepherdess, in white cap, chequered bodice and iron red striped skirt, iron red NB monogram and IH incised, c1775, 8in (20cm).
$3,200-6,000

A Limbach figure of Europe from the set of the Continents, enriched in puce, repair to his neck, both arms and sceptre, chips to fingers, c1775, 8in (20cm).
$1,200-2,100

Cf H Scherf, J Karpinski, Thüringer Porzellan, fig 233, where the figures of Asia and America in the Anger Museum of Erfurt are illustrated.

A Ludwigsburg figure of a Chinese musician, modelled by Joseph Weinmuller, his hat and coat lined in puce and edged in green and painted with florettes in iron red and green, on grassy rockwork base, restorations to arm, neck and instrument, c1767, 13in (32cm).
$6,000-12,000

HÖCHST

- ★ factory was founded in 1746 by the painter A F von Löwenfinck from Meissen
- ★ porcelain was produced from 1750
- ★ milk-white in colour, almost tin-glazed appearance
- ★ early wares tended to have poor translucency and be somewhat heavy
- ★ from 1758-65 the style reminiscent of the French 'Louis Seize' style came into fashion
- ★ this style was continued and developed by J P Melchior who was chief modeller 1767-79
- ★ the base of figures from 1765 tends to be in the form of a distinctive grassy mound, executed in dark café-au-lait and green stripes
- ★ the factory closed in 1796

A pair of Ludwigsburg figures of a river god and goddess, scantily draped in iron red and flowered cloths on grassy mound bases, extensively restored, one with incised FP mark, c1775, both 10in (24cm) long.
$6,000-12,000

A Meissen figure of Harlequin, modelled by J J Kändler, his black hat with red cockade, his jacket with chequer pattern and playing cards and his breeches turquoise, restoration to his hat and instrument, blue crossed swords mark under the base, c1742, 5in (13cm).
$1,800-3,800

A Meissen figure of a Dutch peasant, modelled by P. Reinicke, in pink hat and jerkin and turquoise trousers, hat rim and toe repaired, blue crossed swords mark at the back, c1745, 5½in (13.5cm).
$1,300-2,400

A Meissen group of Diana and attendants, she in black cape and flowered dress attended by a girl in a pink bodice and yellow dress, a man kissing her hand, and with Cupid seated on a stool in an ermine-lined pink cloak, extensively restored, blue crossed swords mark, c1745, 7½in (18.5cm).
$1,200-2,100

A Meissen group of Count Brühl's Tailor, modelled by J J Kändler, damage and repair to his scissors and one of the goat's horns, blue crossed swords mark, c1740, 10in (25cm).
$800-1,500

There are many later copies of this figure.

A Meissen figure of Harlequin disguised as a sailor, in puce-lined blue cloth cap, yellow jacket, gilt and flowered shirt, damage to his paddle and peak of his cap, blue crossed swords mark and impressed 10, c1750, 5½in (13.5cm).
$1,300-2,400

A Meissen figure of a pilgrim, modelled by J J Kändler, standing in black tricorn hat, black shelled cape, lilac jacket and white breeches, some restoration to hat, hands and extremities, blue crossed swords mark at back, c1745, 12in (29cm).
$1,800-3,800

Kändler's taxa of 1740 records that the pair of figures were originally made for Johanne Charlotte, Princess of Anhalt-Dessau who was abbess of the princely abbey of Herford.

A Meissen group of Harlequin beside a young woman, modelled by J J Kändler, Harlequin in harlequinade costume and she in flowered dress, Harlequin damaged through wrist and some damage to table and repairs to the tree, blue crossed swords mark, c1747, 7½in (18.5cm).
$6,000-12,000

A Meissen chinoiserie figure of a woman, modelled by P Reinicke, in white hat and flowered tunic on square base, blue crossed swords mark on the base, c1750, 5in (12cm).
$1,400-2,600

A Meissen figure of Justice, in white robe puce-lined yellow cloak, some repair to the sword, blue crossed swords mark at the back, c1750, 4½in (11.5cm).
$600-1,200

Three Meissen figures emblematic of Spring, Summer and Winter, after the models by J J Kändler, bases enriched with gilding, Spring's left hand lacking, some minor chipping, blue crossed swords marks, c1750, 9in (22.5cm).
$2,600-5,300

A pair of Meissen sweetmeat figures, painted with 'deutsche Blumen', the shaped bases edged with gilt scrolls, her bowl and left arm repaired, minor chips, blue crossed swords mark, c1750, 7in (18cm) long.
$1,600-2,800

A Meissen figural group of the Arts representing Music, slight damage to fingers and toes, crossed swords Pressnummer 16, c1755, 7½in (19cm).
$1,200-2,100

A Meissen figure of a bird-seller, from the cris de Paris series, standing in ermine-lined yellow hat, pale puce frock-coat and green breeches, chips and repairs, blue crossed swords mark at the back and incised 4, c1755, 5in (12cm).
$4,500-9,000

A Meissen figure of a trinket-seller, from the cris de Paris series, modelled by J J Kändler and P Reinicke, his hat and nose restored, blue crossed swords marks at back, incised no. 8, c1756, 6in (14cm).
$14,000-24,000

A Meissen pastoral group of children, minor damage to extremities, blue crossed swords, 19thC, 7in (18cm).
$1,000-2,000

A Meissen group of 3 figures under a tree, painted in bright enamel colours, slight chipping, mid-19thC, 10½in (26.5cm).
$1,000-2,000

A pair of Meissen groups of Cupid, decorated in colours and enriched with gilding, on oval gilt line bases, slight damage and minor restoration, blue crossed swords marks, c1850, 6½in (16cm).
$1,300-2,400

A Meissen musical group, decorated in colours and enriched with gilding, the shaped base edged with a gilt line, minor chips, blue crossed swords mark and incised numerals, c1860, 6½in (16cm).
$800-1,500

A pair of Meissen figures of a ▷ marksman and lady archer, both weapons and his arm and foot damaged, 19thC, 6in (15.5cm).
$300-600

A Meissen group of 2 putti emblematic of the Arts, the base moulded with scrolls and enriched with gilding, slight chip, one putto lacks wing, blue crossed swords mark and incised numerals, c1880, 6in (15.5cm).
$500-900

A Meissen group of Europa and 2 nymphs, painted in colours and enriched with gilding, minor chips, blue crossed swords mark and incised numerals, c1880, 9in (22.5cm).
$600-1,200

A Meissen group of Venus and Cupid, Venus in lavender drapery holding a gilt dish over the flames, Cupid scantily draped in purple, blue crossed swords mark and incised numerals, c1880, 14½in (36.5cm).
$1,800-3,800

A pair of Meissen figures of a man and woman in 18thC dress, their clothes decorated in colours and enriched with gilding, blue crossed swords marks and incised numerals, c1880, 8in (20cm).
$1,200-2,100

A late Meissen group of 2 freemasons, after the original model by J J Kändler, their blue and iron red jackets enriched with gilding and with black tricorn hats, hilts of swords lacking, chip to corner of one jacket and minor chips to flowers, cancelled blue crossed swords and incised numeral marks, c1880, 9in (22.5cm).
$800-1,500

A Meissen group of 2 scantily draped putti counting money, decorated in colours and enriched in gilding, the oval rockwork base moulded with scrolls and similarly gilt, blue crossed swords marks and incised numerals, c1880, 6in (14.5cm).
$600-1,200

A Meissen group of 3 children, decorated in colours and enriched with gilding, the fluted circular base with gilt and ochre decoration, chips and some restoration, blue crossed swords and incised numeral mark, early 20thC, 9in (22cm).
$800-1,500

A Meissen group of lovers, decorated in colours and enriched with gilding, chips to foliage, blue crossed swords mark and incised numerals, c1880, 6in (15cm).
$800-1,500

A late Meissen brightly coloured figure, modelled as a young lady, blue crossed swords mark, 6½in (16cm).
$600-1,200

A Meissen figure of a bass player, probably modelled by Paul Scheurich, blue crossed swords mark, incised P276 early 20thC, 14in (35cm).
$1,300-2,400

A Meissen group of Bacchus, the shaped oval base moulded with scrolls and enriched in gilding, minor chip, blue crossed swords mark and incised numerals, early 20thC, 8½in (21cm).
$600-1,200

A late Meissen articulated figure of a seated rotund Chinese woman, 6in (15cm).
$500-900

A Nymphenburg white figure of Capitano Spavento, modelled by Franz Anton Bustelli, chip to his sword, repair to dagger and tip of right foot, impressed Bavarian shield mark, c1765, 8in (19.5cm).
$2,600-5,300

A Nymphenburg white figure of Il Dottore, modelled by Franz Anton Bustelli, repair to his right arm, impressed Bavarian shield mark, c1760, 8in (20cm).
$2,600-5,300

A Minton parian figure of Child's Play, by John Bell, c1840, 14in (35cm).
$6,000-12,000

A parian bust of a young woman, unmarked, 28in (70cm).
$800-1,500

A parian standing female figure, probably Belleek but unmarked, 14½in (36.5cm).
$300-600

Cf C and D Shinn, Victorian Parian China, *pl 16, illustrates a Belleek catalogue of 1904 in which fig 20 shows an identical figure to the above.*

A rare Pfalz-Zweibrucken figure of a peasant woman, wearing white headscarf, lavender blouse, brown skirt and green overskirt, repair to duck, basket and one finger, W mark, incised i, c1770, 9in (23.5cm).
$3,200-6,000

A pair of Plymouth porcelain groups, The Gardener and his Companion, finished in white, slight damage to bocages, 10in (25cm).
$1,700-3,000

A large Royal Dux group with camel and Bedouin seated on its back, on oblong base with attendant, 20in (50cm).
$1,200-2,100

◁ A rare pair of Rockingham figures of Swiss girls, both with slight damage, one impressed griffin mark, Rockingham Works, Bramald, incised no. 18, the other impressed griffin mark, Rockingham Works, Bramald, incised no. 22, 7in (17.5cm).
$4,000-6,800

Cf D G Rice, Rockingham Pottery and Porcelain, *no. 18 'Paysanne du Canton du Zurich', no. 22 'Paysanne de Sagran en Tirol'.*

A pair of Royal Dux figures of a Middle Eastern man and companion, both wearing pink head-dresses and green costumes, dusted overall in gilt, impressed and raised numerals, and pink raised triangle mark, 15in (38cm).
$500-900

A pair of Mennecy white figures of a Sultan and Sultana, he repaired at neck, minor chips to both figures, incised D.V. marks on the mount bases, c1740, 9in (23cm).
$6,000-12,000

A pair of Volkstedt-Rudolstadt figures of a gallant and his lady, on naturalistic mound bases with scroll-mouldings picked out in pink, green and gilt, blue mark for H Greiner, late 19thC, 17in (42cm).
$500-900

A Sèvres white biscuit group of Le Valet de Chien, modelled by Blondeau after Oudry, restoration to his hat, one dog's foreleg, incised interlaced L mark, c1776, 12in (30.5cm) long.
$3,200-6,000

This is from the Surtout du Groupe des Chasses modelled by Blondeau after Oudry in 1776. There are two valents de chiens listed by Bourgeois but it is impossible to tell which this is.

A Sèvres bust of Napoleon as First Consul, the bust with green-bronzed patination on spreading green circular socle enriched with gilding, impressed Sèvres mark and incised 'Bonaparte 1. Consul' and with the dating for 1802, 12in (29cm).
$1,700-3,000

A Sèvres biscuit group of The Judgement of Paris, damages, incised interlaced L mark and numeral 54, incised modeller's monogram AB and a square, c1781, 16½in (41cm).
$3,200-6,000

Probably modelled by Alexandre Brachard after the original model by L-S Boizot.

Cf E Bourgeois, Le Biscuit de Sèvres, for the original model, still at Sèvres.

A Sèvres biscuit bust of Napoleon Bonaparte as First Consul, the square marble plinth inscribed 'Bonaparte 1er Consul 1800', the bust inscribed and with impressed Sèvres mark and date numeral 9 for 1802, 14½in (36cm).
$3,200-6,000

A Sèvres biscuit standing figure of Napoleon in uniform with the badge of the Légion d'Honneur, on later French porcelain base decorated with Napoleon at the Bridge of Arcole, chips to his hat, the figure c1810, 29in (72cm).
$8,000-15,000

A Thuringian figure of Provender for the monastery, the monk carrying a bundle of wheatsheaves concealing a young lady, chip to the back of his hood, c1775, 4½in (11.5cm).
$1,300-2,400

A Staffordshire porcelain figure of Byron, c1835, 6in (15cm).
$400-750

A Staffordshire porcelain figure of Maria Foote as Arinette, c1860, 6½in (16cm).
$300-600

A pair of Royal Worcester glazed parian figures of Paul and Virginia, standing before leaf-moulded tree stumps, painted in a pale palette, the rockwork bases applied with foliage, one with restoration to foliage, impressed marks, c1865, 13in (33cm).
$1,000-2,000

Cf Henry Sandon, Royal Worcester Porcelain, pl 9, for a group of Paul and Virginia.

A Strasbourg porcelain group of a seated young man and woman before a tree stump, in yellow hat, lime-green jacket and puce breeches, his companion in flowered blue and purple-lined dress on shaped mound base, his right hand restuck, other minor chips and repairs, impressed PH mark, c1755, 9in (23cm).
$4,000-7,500

A Royal Worcester figure of Karan Singh, from the Indian Craftsman Series, shape 1204, printed mark in puce and impressed, 1884, 5in (13cm).
$900-1,700

A Royal Worcester figure of a French fisher girl, by James Hadley, painted in pale enamel colours and gold, printed and impressed marks with the date code for 1888, 17in (43cm).
$1,000-2,000

A set of 6 Royal Worcester standing figures of John Bull, a Swiss man, a Chinese, an Indian, a Negro and an American, printed mark in puce for 1881 and impressed factory and registration marks.
$1,300-2,400

A Royal Worcester figure of John Bull, modelled by Hadley, coloured overall in green, bronze and ivory with dusted gilt highlights, printed date code for 1917, 7in (17.5cm).
$300-600

A Royal Worcester figure group of The Picnic, printed marks, no. 18 of a limited edition of 250, complete with certificate.
$600-1,200

A Royal Worcester standing figure of a lady, the circular base inscribed 'L'Allegro', printed mark in puce and impressed, 1890, 16½in (41.5cm).
$600-1,200

A Royal Worcester figural group in Kate Greenaway style, modelled by Hadley, coloured predominantly in shades of ivory and apricot with gilt highlights, damaged, printed factory marks and date code for 1892, incised artist's name, 9½in (24cm).
$500-900

A Royal Worcester standing figure of Munnasall, in shaded ivory, painted in soft colours and gilt, holding a vase, other vases on a low stool at his side, from the Indian Craftsman Series, shape 1222, printed mark in puce and impressed, 1890, 8in (20.5cm).
$600-1,200

A Caughley plate, decorated with powder blue ground and hand painted panels, c1775, 8in (20cm).
$300-600

A Chelsea silver shaped plate, finely painted with figures by a moored boat at a quayside, with a ruined turret to the left, the pale blue sky with birds in flight above, small rim restoration at 11 o'clock, c1752, 9in (22.5cm).
$8,000-15,000

A Chelsea leaf moulded dish, the basket work ground moulded in relief with large foliage enriched in tones of green, yellow, puce and turquoise, the rim with brown line, iron red anchor mark, c1760, 10in (25cm).
$3,200-6,000

A very rare Bristol spoon tray, with Meissen-type decoration in puce monochrome, c1775, 6½in (16cm) wide.
$1,200-2,100

A pair of Chelsea leaf dishes, moulded as cabbage leaves with puce stalks and veining and painted with bouquets, scattered flower sprays and insects, red anchor marks, c1756, 12in (29.5cm) wide.
$3,200-6,000

A pair of Bow leaf shaped pickle dishes, c1760, 3½in (8cm).
$1,300-2,400

Sometimes wrongly attributed to Longton Hall.

CAUGHLEY

* factory ran from 1772-99, when it was purchased by the Coalport management
* painted wares tend to be earlier than printed ones
* Caughley body of the soapstone type
* often shows orange to transmitted light, but in some cases can even show slightly greenish which adds to the confusion with Worcester
* glaze is good and close fitting, although when gathered in pools may have greeny-blue tint
* from 1780's many pieces heightened in gilding, some blue and white Chinese export wares were similarly gilded in England
* main marks: impressed 'Salopian', 'S' was painted on hand-painted designs, 'S' was printed in blue printed designs, although an 'X' or an 'O' was sometimes hand-painted beside it, one of the most common marks was the capital C. Hatched crescents never appear on Caughley, they were purely a Worcester mark
* Caughley is often confused with Worcester; they have many patterns in common, eg. The 'Cormorant and Fisherman' and 'Fence' patterns

A Chelsea plate, of silver shape, painted with sprays of flowers in green enamel, c1760, 8in (20cm).
$150-250

A Chelsea porcelain plate, painted in colours with scattered flower sprays, the border trimmed with feathered scrolls in brown and turquoise, brown anchor mark, c1760, 8½in (21cm).
$400-750

A Chelsea plate, boldly painted in bright enamel colours with sprigs and sprays of garden flowers, red anchor mark, mid 18thC, 8½in (21.5cm).
$400-900

A Coalport square shaped dessert dish, painted with a view of Tantallon Castle by A Perry, signed, on a rich blue ground, outlined with gilt trellis panels and foliage within a gilt gadroon rim, scroll handles, printed mark in green and impressed mark for 1908, 11½in (28.5cm).
$400-750

An H & R Daniel green ground crested dish from the Shrewsbury Service, the centre with the crest beneath an earl's coronet, c1827, 19½in (48cm) wide.
$1,300-2,400

A Derby botanical plate, pattern 141, Scorzeonera Tingitana, blue marking, c1790, 9in (22.5cm).
$1,200-2,100

A Derby dish with floral decoration, by the 'cotton-stalk' painter, c1756, 8½in (21cm).
$900-1,700

A pair of Derby botanical oval dishes, finely painted in colours with specimen flowers named on the reverse, one with 'Annual Lavatera, Large Flowered St. John's Wort & Scarlet Bizzare Carnation', the other with 'Tulip Oculus Solis, Campanula Coronatos & Evergreen Glaucum', with shaped gilt rims, iron red crown, crossed batons and D Marks, c1811-15, 10in (26cm) wide.
$4,500-9,000

A pair of Coalport circular dessert dishes, one painted with a view of Lake Maggiore by C Taylor, signed, the other with a view of Naworth Castle by H Perry, signed, on a rich blue ground, gilt with rococo scroll panels, flowers and scrolls, gilt gadroon borders, printed mark in green, 11½in (29.5cm).
$500-900

A Coalport dessert dish, c1805.
$400-750

A Derby plate, probably painted by William Cotton, hunting scene, red mark, c1810, 9in (22cm).
$1,800-3,800

A Derby plate, painted by William Billingsley, Love in the Mist, c1790, 8½in (21cm).
$600-1,200

Ex. Field Collection.

CHELSEA

★ some red anchor marks usually neat and very small and not in prominent position

★ later brown and gold anchor marks are larger and more thickly written

★ paste varies from white to greenish when seen by transmitted light

★ on red anchor ware, look out for 'moons' caused by frit in the kiln, also seen by transmitted light

★ three spur marks often found on the base, left by kiln supports, also a feature of Arita porcelain (not to be confused with Derby pad marks)

★ glaze on early pieces is reasonably opaque, this later becomes clearer and more glassy; later still it becomes thicker when it tends to craze

★ body on later gold anchor wares and figures often has a dry, brownish appearance

A Meissen blue and white plate, painted in the Kang Xi style, minute hairline crack from rim, blue crossed swords mark, c1728, 9in (23cm).
$800-1,500

A Meissen plate, painted by J E Stadler in bright colours and Böttger lustre, minor rim chip, blue crossed swords mark, c1730, 8½in (21.5cm).
$3,200-6,000

Two porcelain Presidential dinner service plates, Haviland and Co, Limoges 1877 or 1884; the other Tressemanes and Vogt, Limoges, c1900, the first enamelled with an eagle grasping a laurel branch and arrows, perched on an American shield above a banner inscribed E PLURIBUS UNUM, the rim with a dark puce band and gilt dots and 'alhambra' tracery, with erased mark and incised X, the second decorated with stars, marked, the first 9½ (23.5cm) diam. the second 8½ (21cm) diam.
$2,200-2,500

The first plate is probably one of the plates ordered by President Ulysses S. Grant in 1873 or President Chester H. Arthur in 1884 from the Washington D.C. retailers J.W. Boteler and Brothers to complete the original state service made for President Abraham Lincoln. The second plate is one of the plates ordered by President William McKinley to complete the original state service made for President Benjamin Harrison.

A Meissen saucer dish, painted with 'ombrierte Holzschnitt Blumen' and insects in a manner of Klinger and with gilt rim, blue crossed swords mark, 1735-40, 8in (21cm).
$1,600-2,800

A Liverpool blue and white shell moulded pickle dish, painted with trailing flowers and scattered insects, minute rim chip, c1755, 4½in (9.5cm) wide.
$1,300-2,400

A Meissen armorial plate from the Sulkowsky service, the large central armorial flanked by scattered Kakiemon flowers within ozier moulded border, blue crossed swords mark, c1738, 9½in (23.5cm).
$7,000-12,000

The arms are those of Graf Alexander Joseph von Sulkowski and his wife Maria Anna Franziska von Stein zu Jettingen. This is from a large service produced by 1735 and 1738 for Sulkowski who was Augustus III's minister. Numerous pieces from this service are illustrated by Rückert: figs. 487-90.

A Meissen Hausmalerei plate, painted by F F Mayer von Pressnitz, blue crossed swords mark, Pressnummer 14, the porcelain c1740, 9in (22.5cm).
$1,200-2,100

A Meissen shaped pentagonal teapot stand, painted with figures in a harbour scene within puce and gold 'Laub und Bandelwerk', the border with gilt scroll work, blue crossed swords and gilt 55 marks, c1735, 6in (15cm).
$1,300-2,400

A moulded Derby plate, with red mark, c1820, 10in (25cm).
$200-450

A pair of Meissen Hof service circular dishes, painted with a red dragon in iron red and gold, blue crossed swords mark, Pressnummer 16, puce K H C marks of K G L Hof-Conditorei, c1740, 12in (29.5cm).
$4,000-6,800

A Meissen Imari plate, painted with 'Brokatdekor' of a vase containing chrysanthemums, painted in underglaze blue and overglaze iron red, black, lustre and gilt, the reverse with trailing flowers, blue crossed swords mark and painter's mark for Kretzschmar, Pressnummer 22, c1740, 9in (22.5cm).
$6,000-12,000

Cf Rückert, No. 316.

A Meissen Marcolini plate from a Jagd service, gilt foliage border, small rim chip retouched, blue crossed swords and 4 mark, c1790, 9½in (24cm).
$600-1,200

A Meissen dish from the Christie Miller service, the centre painted with hunting figures and dogs, the 'Gitterwerk' well with 4 quatrefoil puce landscape panels, blue crossed swords mark and Pressnummer 22, c1742, 7in (17.5cm).
$14,000-24,000

A Meissen blue and white oval dish, blue crossed swords mark, Pressnummer 26, c1745, 9in (22.5cm).
$1,300-2,400

A Meissen armorial plate, from the St. Andrew service, painted with 'holzschnitt Blumen' and moulded with 'Gotzskowsky erhabene Blumen' and with gilt trellis rim, blue crossed swords mark and Pressnummer 16, red wax Hermitage inventory number, c1745, 9½in (24cm).
$6,000-12,000

A large Meissen dish from the series of 'Kinder a la Raphael', minor rim chips, blue crossed swords and dot mark, L mark, Pressnummer 95 and impressed Fromer's mark, c1770, 13in (33cm).
$800-1,500

A Meissen Marcolini dish, the centre painted with an entertainer before a crowd of people beside a tavern door, in gilt scroll borders, 14½in (36cm) wide.
$800-1,500

Twelve late Meissen pierced bordered plates, on blue, pink, yellow and claret grounds, blue crossed swords mark, 10in (25cm).
$8,000-15,000

A Meissen blue and white plate, painted in underglaze blue with a tiger and a dragon on rockwork with bamboo and prunus within shaped rim, the reverse with scrolling foliage, mock Chinese seal mark and Pressnummer 10, wax inventory number, c1740, 10½in (25.5cm).
$3,200-6,000

A Nantgarw plate, London decoration, impressed mark Nantgarw C.W., c1819, 9½in (23.5cm).
$1,400-2,600

A Nantgarw plate, London decoration, elaborate border gilding with central floral bouquet, impressed mark Nantgarw C.W., c1819, 8½in (21cm).
$1,200-2,100

A Nantgarw plate, painted by W H Pardoe, impressed mark, c1819.
$400-750

Possibly sold at the last public sale of Nantgarw in 1892.

A very good Nantgarw plate, painted with the typical Billingsley roses, impressed mark, 8½in (21cm) diam.
$1,200-2,100
Cf John's Nantgarw Porcelain, pl 43B.

Two porcelain Presidential dinner service plates by Edouard Honore, Champroux and Paris, 1846, the other c1853, one with the centre enamelled with a spray of sweet pea, the light green border centering an oval reserve of an American shield superimposed with a banner inscribed E PLURIBUS UNUM, marked, the second with stippled centre, the rim with alternate blue and gold bands, centering a stippled band, unmarked, the first 9in (22.5cm) diam. the second 9¼in (23cm) diam.
$2,500-3,000

The first plate was part of a state dessert service ordered by President James Polk from the New York firm of Alexander Stewart and Company in 1846. The second plate was part of a state dinner service ordered by President Franklin Pierce from the New York firm of Haughwot and Dailey in 1853.

A Sèvres soup plate from the Madame du Barry service, blue interlaced L marks enclosing the date letter S for 1771, and painter's mark of Bulidon, 9½in (24cm).
$3,200-6,000

From the service supplied to Madame du Barry on 29 August 1771, which was designed by Auguste de St. Aubin and consisted of 322 pieces.

A Nymphenburg dish, the centre painted with figures and merchants beside a ruin in a river landscape with sailing boats, impressed Bavarian shield mark and numeral 1, c1770, 9in (22cm).
$800-1,500

A Sèvres bleu celeste ground octagonal dish, painted in colours with exotic birds, minor wear to gilding, blue interlaced L mark enclosing the date letter for 1773, painter's mark, incised mark, 9in (23cm).
$600-1,200

A New Hall hard paste porcelain teapot stand, with chinoiserie painting, c1790, 8in (20cm) wide.
$200-450

SWANSEA PORCELAIN

★ factory produced high quality soft-paste porcelain from 1814-22
★ factory started by Dillwyn, Billingsley and Walker
★ superb translucent body, excellent glaze
★ in many ways one of the best porcelain bodies produced in the British Isles
★ also noted for delicacy of flower painting, usually attributed to Billingsley although much was obviously done by other decorators including Pollard and Morris
★ a close study of marked pieces will give one an idea of Billingsley's work but unless actually signed by him pieces should be marked 'possibly by Billingsley'
★ on pieces moulded with the floral cartouches the moulding can be detected on the other side of the rim, unlike the heavier Coalport wares which later utilised same moulds
★ especially notable are figure and bird paintings by T Baxter
★ the Swansea mark often faked, particularly on French porcelain at the end of the 19th, beginning of the 20thC
★ in 1816 Billingsley left to start up again at Nantgarw
★ many pieces were decorated in London studios

A Swansea square dish, with multiple floral decoration, unmarked, c1830, 8in (20cm).
$1,000-2,000

A rare pair of Swansea crested shell dishes, Mandarin pattern, painted in polychrome enamels, the borders with coloured bird on branch panels and various designs in rouge de fer, gilt, 8½in (20cm).
$3,200-6,000

Three Tournai ornithological plates, painted with brightly coloured birds in landscape vignettes, blue crossed swords and star marks and various incised marks, c1775, 9in (23cm).
$1,300-2,400

A Vienna cabinet plate, painted with a young girl attended by Cupid, inscribed in gilt, impressed mark Colln. Meissen, 9½in (25cm).
$200-450

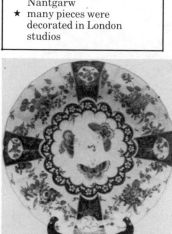

A Worcester fluted dish, the centre painted with 3 butterflies in colours, the fluted rim with trailing flowering plants divided by blue panels enriched in gilding, blue seal mark, c1760, 10in (25cm).
$1,300-2,400

A Worcester blue and white foliage moulded dish, rim chip to underside, c1765, 11in (27.5cm).
$1,800-3,800

A Worcester Blind Earl plate, enriched in green and puce and painted with scattered flower sprays, with scalloped gilt rim, c1765, 7½in (18cm).
$1,200-2,100

A fine Worcester dessert plate, transfer printed in black, washed in rich coloured enamels with 'Milking Scene No.1' by Robert Hancock, after an engraving by Luke Sullivan, the border enamelled with puce scrolls suspending gilt husks, the rim edged in gold, 7in (17.5cm).
$1,800-3,800

A Worcester apple green ground pierced oval footed dish, painted by the Spotted Fruit Painter, c1770, 12in (30cm).
$1,800-3,800

Three Royal Worcester dessert dishes, including an oval dish, a square shaped dish and a tazza, each piece painted with fruit and signed H H Price, printed mark.
$600-1,100

A Royal Worcester plate with pierced white and gilt border with 'jewelled pearls', painted by R F Perling after Herring, inscribed on the back 'after Herring by R F Perling', impressed mark, 9½in (23.5cm).
$200-450

A Royal Worcester circular dish, painted by C H C Baldwyn, signed, on a sky blue ground, printed mark in green for 1902 and Leadless Glaze, 12in (30cm).
$2,000-4,500

A Royal Worcester plate, painted, signed on the back 'D Perry', within a gilt dentil rim, mark in gold and Fine Bone China 1965, 11in (27cm).
$200-450

An English porcelain cabinet plate, with gilt scrolls on a blue ground, pattern 865 in puce, possibly Coalport, early 19thC, 9½in (24cm).
$150-250

A Chamberlain's Worcester two handled tray, finely painted with Buckingham Palace within a border encrusted with coloured shells and seaweed and a moulded gilt scroll rim, cracks to underside, script mark in puce, c1840, 13½in (33.5cm) wide.
$2,000-4,500

Cf Geoffrey A Godden, Chamberlain Worcester Porcelains, *pls 334 and 335.*

A First Period Worcester porcelain kidney shaped dish, painted in pink, blue, green, iron red and yellow and with gilt line borders, paint slightly worn, 11½in (28.5cm).
$400-750

A Royal Worcester cabinet plate, by E Barker, signed, within a tooled matt gilt border, printed mark, pattern Z1012, date code for 1935, 4½in (10.5cm).
$400-900

A large plate with cat and dog scene 'Oh Chase Me', signed 'Louis Wain'.
$300-600

A Victorian bone china cake stand, in green and gold with pink floral design, 9½in (23.5cm) diam.
$80-150

Three from a set of 7 Spode botanical decorated plates, with a yellow ground, c1810.
$4,500-9,000

A Continental porcelain circular dish, mounted in scrolling-foliate gilt-metal handles and rim, 19½in (48cm).
$300-600

A porcelain teapot stand, with relief moulding, c1825, 7in (17.5cm).
$80-180

Ice Pails

A pair of Berlin two handled ice pails of Antique Zierrath pattern, the angular handles enriched with gilding and with ribbon ties, blue sceptre mark and various impressed numbers, c1780, 6½in (16cm).
$3,200-6,000

A pair of Meissen ornithological two handled wine coolers, one handle with rim chips, blue crossed swords marks, one with star and numeral 4, mid 18thC, 8in (19.5cm).
$3,200-6,000

A Paris oviform ice pail, cover and liner, with gilt satyr's mask handles, handles damaged, c1810, 15in (37.5cm).
$500-900

Inkwells

A Caughley blue and white inkwell, c1780, 2in (5cm).
$900-1,700

A Sèvres porcelain ormolu mounted inkstand, with ormolu mounts and handle, standing on 3 scroll feet, 9in (23cm) diam.
$600-1,100

Jardinières

A large Worcester jardinière, with tin liner, slight chipping, printed and impressed marks, pattern no.1233, 20in (49cm) wide.
$1,600-2,800

A Sèvres pattern gilt bronze oval two handled jardinière of flared form, the gilt bronze mount to the rim joined to the pierced four footed base by berried foliage scroll handles with male mask terminals, c1860, 18in (44.5cm).
$1,700-3,000

A Royal Worcester circular jardinière, in apricot, outlined with gilding on a basket pattern ground, below a green and gilt basket work border, printed mark in green, 1902, 8in (18cm).
$300-600

A Royal Worcester jardinière, the handles modelled as gilt flowers on mock giltwood pierced stand, printed and impressed marks, 7in (17.5cm).
$300-600

A Chelsea fluted D shaped bough pot, with a yellow moulded band enriched with puce diamond pattern beneath a chocolate line rim, the top pierced, cracks to rim and base, red anchor mark and 21 c1755, 7½in (18.5cm).
$1,000-2,000

A Spode tub shaped jardinière and stand, with gilt dolphin mask and ring handles, wide gilt borders and bands of dentil pattern, marked Spode 1926 in red, 4½in (12cm).
$300-600

A large Royal Worcester jardinière painted by W Powell, signed, JH monogram, 10½in (26cm) diam. ▷
$600-1,100

A Belleek lustrous cream ground jardinière of lobed tapering shape, the shoulders with fine applied decoration, black transfer mark to base, 10in (25cm) diam.
$1,000-2,000

Jugs

A Caughley blue and white jug with Fisherman pattern decoration, c1785, 8½in (21cm).
$600-1,200

▷

◁

A lustre jug with Adam Buck decoration in burgundy, c1850, 4in (10cm).
$60-120

A Caughley blue and white jug with floral design, c1780, 6in (15cm).
$400-750

A Swansea 'duck egg' porcelain creamer, with gilded decoration and band of lavender blue surrounding body, unmarked, pattern 649, c1817.
$600-1,200

A porcelain pitcher, probably by the American China Manufactury, Philadelphia, Pennsylvania, each side enamelled in black with river scene, gilt decoration on rim, spout and handle, firing defect, c1826-38, 9½in (23.5cm).
$1,800-3,800

A Meissen octagonal jug and cover, painted in a bright palette, restored, blue caduceus mark and incised cross of J D Rehschuh, c1730, 6in (15cm).
$1,600-2,800

A Coalport Imari pattern jug, c1810, 8in (20cm).
$900-1,700

A porcelain pitcher by William Ellis Tucker, Philadelphia, 1882-1883, the base with moulded vertical reeding, the shoulder painted with a band of green and blue flowers with gilt leaves, the rim, handle and base with gilt borders, 9¼in (23cm) high.
$1,500-1,800

A Philip Christian's Liverpool porcelain helmet shaped cream jug, with flowers and sprigs, c1770, 4in (10cm).
$600-1,200

A Meissen yellow ground hot milk jug and cover, with contemporary French silver gilt mount, the hinged mount with foliate thumbpiece, blue crossed swords, décharge of Louis Robin, Fermier Général 1738-44, 5in (12.5cm).
$6,000-12,000

A very large early Worcester sparrow beak jug, with chinoiserie decoration, c1755, 8in (20cm).
$6,000-12,000

A Meissen jug with angled scroll handle, the scroll moulded lip and handle heightened in gilt, the rim with gilt fruiting branch design, blue crossed swords and dot mark, c1760's, 5½in (13.5cm).
$600-1,100

133

A Sèvres baluster jug and cover with quatrefoil basin, painted with spiralling bands of 'bleu nouveau' and gilt chain pattern with gilt laurel borders, basin cracked, c1780, jug 7½in (19cm).
$1,000-2,000

A Meissen baluster hot milk jug with fluted spout and shell and scroll handle, painted 'en camaïeu rose', blue crossed swords mark and gilder's mark Z, c1740, 5in (12cm).
$1,300-2,400

A Worcester blue and white baluster cream jug, painted with The Peony Pattern, painter's mark, c1758, 3in (7.5cm).
$600-1,100

A Grainger Worcester jug, the body superbly painted in the manner of Thomas Steel, unmarked, c1820, 3in (7.5cm).
$400-900

A Worcester blue and white cabbage leaf moulded jug, the bulbous body moulded with overlapping cabbage leaves and painted in blue, the cylindrical neck with stylised foliage, with loop handle, c1760, 8in (20cm).
$800-1,500

A large Dr Wall period Worcester mask head jug, painted with sprays of English flowers, c1770, 9in (23cm).
$9,000-15,000

A porcelain pitcher, attributed to the Tucker and Hemphill China, the body painted with polychrome floral bouquets, the rim, shoulder and footrim with gilt banding, spout with repaired crack, 9¼in (23cm) high.
$800-1,000

A First Period Worcester cabbage leaf jug, decorated in coloured enamels, with gilt line border and mask moulded spout, 7in (17.5cm).
$1,300-2,400

A Flight & Barr Worcester milk jug with scroll handle, incised B and script mark, c1800, 9in (23cm).
$300-600

Mugs

An English porcelain oviform jug with angular loop handle, inscribed in gilt 'T*WEBSTER 1821', flanked by a mock coat of arms with the inscription 'The Hand that reveals, & the Heart that conceals', the reverse with another coat of arms inscribed 'Success to Trade', some slight rubbing, c1821, 8½in (21.5cm).
$500-900

A porcelain cabbage leaf moulded mask jug, painted in 'famille rose' palette, with Orientals by a vase in a fenced garden, Baddeley & Fletcher's Factory, c1780, 5in (12cm).
$600-1,200

A Bow flared cylindrical mug with moulded loop handle, painted in 'famille rose' palette, c1752, 3½in (9cm).
$1,200-2,100

A Caughley outside decorated cylindrical mug, painted in sepia with the floral initial 'C' in blue and gold, star crack to base, c1795, 5½in (14cm).
$600-1,200

A very fine Dr Wall mug, transfer printed in black with a named portrait of Frederick the Great, the print signed 'R.H. Worcester' and dated 1757, known as the King of Prussia mug, 5in (12cm).
$1,800-3,800

A Worcester blue and white cylindrical mug, with grooved loop handle, blue crescent mark, c1765, 6in (15cm).
$1,300-2,400

A Worcester baluster mug, gilt with the monogram 'GG' with the motto 'Amity', minute crack to base of handle, c1770, 3½in(9cm).
$1,700-3,000

A Worcester Imari pattern armorial mug, painted with vertical panels of flowering shrubs divided by blue bands, gilt with scrolling foliage, reserved with a crest and arms, the interior with a gilt C scroll rim, blue square seal mark, c1770, 3½in (9cm).
$1,300-2,400

A Worcester blue and white cylindrical mug, transfer printed, with loop handle, blue crescent mark, c1765, 6in (15cm).
$600-1,100

A Worcester blue scale mug, painted with exotic birds among shrubs and trees and with butterflies and insects, between gilt vase and mirror shaped cartouches, between gilt line rims, blue square seal mark, c1770, 3½in (9cm).
$1,700-3,000

A Worcester blue scale mug, painted with exotic birds and butterflies, within gilt vase and mirror shaped cartouches, blue crescent mark, c1770, 5in (12cm). **$1,800-3,800**

A Worcester, Grainger Lee & Co., mug, painted with a view of Worcester Cathedral, within a gilt cartouche, script mark in iron red, c1815, 3in (8cm). **$600-1,100**

A First Period Worcester mug of tapering cylindrical form, printed in blue with La Promenade Chinoise and La Peche, grooved loop handle, crescent mark in blue, 4½in (12cm). **$400-750**

A porcelain bell shaped mug with grooved loop handle, painted in blue with an extensive chinoiserie landscape, diaper and foliate border, disguised numeral mark in blue, Brownlow Hill, c1756. **$1,600-2,800**

A Worcester mug of Lord Henry Thynne type, blue crescent mark, c1775, 5in (12.5cm). **$2,000-4,500**

A small First Period Worcester mug of cylindrical form, painted in blue and gilt, with grooved loop handle, 3½in (9cm). **$200-450**

Plaques

A Berlin rectangular plaque, painted after F Sturm, impressed sceptre and KPM marks, ebonised wood frame, c1880, 12 by 10in (31.5 by 25.5cm). **$1,200-2,100**

A KPM porcelain plaque, painted with a portrait of Ruth, named on reverse, impressed KPM and incised numerals, 13 by 8in (32.5 by 19cm). **$1,600-2,800**

A Berlin rectangular plaque, painted with The Penitent Magdalen after Battoni, by C A Lippold signed, the reverse inscribed in script, Die Magdalena des Battoni, Original copie von C A Lippold 1853, impressed sceptre, KPM and H mark, giltwood frame, 12 by 15in (30 by 38cm). **$2,000-4,500**

An English porcelain plaque painted with a brightly coloured bird perched on a branch in a river landscape, and another plaque painted with a cherub painting a portrait, both in wood frames, 4½in (11cm) and 5in (12.5cm). **$400-900**

A Dresden plaque, painted after Gerard Terborch, in carved and gilt frame, crossed swords mark in underglaze blue, 19thC, 17 by 15in (43 by 38cm).
$4,000-7,500

A pair of English porcelain plaques, c1835, 8½in (21cm).
$1,700-3,000

A Fürstenburg white biscuit oval plaque, modelled with a portrait bust of J H C v Selchow to the left with glazed border inscribed on the reverse with name and F. NO. 1, minor repair at back, c1782, 3in (7.5cm).
$180-300

A French plaque painted by Lucien Levy with an Eastern scene, signed, carved giltwood frame, late 19thC, 13 by 9in (32 by 22cm).
$1,000-2,000

A German porcelain plaque, painted after Randall with 2 cockatoos and a parrot perched on a knarled tree stump among foliage, c1880, 14½ by 12½in (36 by 30.5cm).
$1,300-2,400

A German porcelain allegorical plaque, painted after Shumann, with 'The Three Fates', framed, impressed numerals and signs of erasure, 12½ by 9½in (31.5 by 24cm) overall.
$1,000-2,000

A German porcelain plaque, painted with a classical scene, painted on the base K.P.M. under a star, 9½in (23cm).
$400-900

A Naples porcelain wall plaque, of domed form, the central panel moulded with classical mythological figures in a romantic landscape, within a border moulded with trophies of arms and musical items, heightened in colours and gilt, within moulded ebonised frame, crowned N in underglaze blue, 19½in (48cm).
$800-1,500

A Vienna pierced bordered rectangular tray, painted with Eleanor & King Edward I, 14½in (35cm).
$800-1,500

A Continental porcelain oval plaque, painted by Bergler after Rembrandt, with a woman wearing green plumed hat and red dress, with gilt surround, and blue porcelain border heightened with a raised gilt bird and spandrel design, gilt wood frame, porcelain border painted with blue Vienna beehive mark, 13½ by 10½in (33 by 26cm).
$1,700-3,000

A Royal Worcester oval plaque, painted by John Stinton, signed, with cattle watering at a river, printed mark in puce, 1906, 6½ by 9½in (16 by 24.5cm).
$1,800-3,800

A Vienna pierced bordered tray, painted with Cleopatra, Mark Antony and attendants, on various coloured grounds, painted blue beehive mark, 14in (35cm).
$800-1,500

A porcelain plaque, painted with an interior depicting Othello in the presence of the Doge, reserved within a shaped rectangular panel on a stippled gold ground with oval and diamond panels and scrolling foliage, complete with contemporary gold painted and plush frame, 20in (49cm).
$1,800-3,800

Pots

A very rare Caughley blue and white artichoke pot and lid, with Fisherman pattern decoration, 3½in (8.5cm).
$200-450

A pair of Derby D shaped bough pots, painted in the manner of Dodson, with scroll feet and handles, printed crown and circle marks, Robert Bloor & Co., one foot chipped, c1825, 7½in (18.5cm).
$1,000-2,000

A Doccia armorial pomade pot and cover, painted with accollé coats of arms within puce baroque scroll cartouches beneath a black lined purple mantling and gilt coronet, the reverse with a finely painted bouquet of flowers and with gilt foliage, the cover similarly decorated with flower finial, chips to flower, c1750, 6½in (16.5cm).
$8,000-15,000

Sauceboats

A very rare Derby cow creamer jug with floral decoration, slightly damaged, c1764, 3in (7.5cm).
$900-1,700

A rare small size New Hall helmet shaped cream jug with floral decoration, pattern 67, c1785, 4in (10cm).
$400-750

A Liverpool helmet shaped cream jug, with bridged scroll handle, the interior with iron red loop, dot and line pattern, on a circular domed foot, Philip Christian's factory, some minute chips and staining to rim, c1770, 4in (10cm).
$600-1,100

A Bow blue and white double lipped two-handled sauceboat, painted in a bright blue, c1750, 7½in (18cm) wide.
$800-1,500

A Bow blue and white peach-shaped butter boat, with tendril handle forming three short feet and painted with insects, flowers and leaves, c1765, 3in (7.5cm) wide.
$500-900

A Bow blue and white fluted oval sauceboat, painted within moulded flower and foliage cartouches, on a fluted oval foot, slight rim chips, crack beneath handle, impressed T mark, c1758, 7½in (18cm) wide.
$300-600

A Meissen pear-shaped cream pot and cover, with fluted ground and handle set to one side, painted with figures in an extensive harbour landscape, with silver chain attachment to cover, the pine cover finial restuck, blue crossed swords mark, c1740, 5½in (14cm).
$2,600-5,300

A pair of Worcester blue and white sauceboats, of silver shape, the exterior painted in the Oriental style, the interior with a boy fishing by a rock, the flaring rims with flowering foliage and insects, one damaged, c1755, 8in (19.5cm) long.
$1,000-2,000

A Worcester oval sauceboat of small size, painted with a bird in a fenced garden, the oval foot moulded with drapery swags, the interior with a flowering branch within a green diaper border, c1754, 6½in (16.5cm) wide.
$1,300-2,400

A Worcester blue and white faceted oval cream boat, with double scroll handle painted with The Root Pattern, painter's mark, c1758, 4in (10cm) wide.
$1,300-2,400

An early Worcester blue and white cream boat, moulded on each side with foliate scroll work enclosing chinoiserie landscape in underglaze blue, workman's mark, c1760, 4½in (11.5cm) wide.
$2,000-4,500

An almost identical cream boat is illustrated in Simon Spero's Price Guide to 18th Century Porcelain, *p. 122.*

A Worcester spirally moulded milk jug of flared form, painted in the 'famille rose' style with Orientals, minute blemishes to rim, c1770, 3½in (9cm).
$600-1,200

A First Period Worcester porcelain sauceboat, moulded with overlapping leaves, and with rustic loop handle, painted in colours on a white ground with green tinted borders, initialled P in red, c1760, 4in (10cm).
$500-900

A pair of Worcester diaper-moulded oval sauceboats, painted with brightly coloured aggravated birds, the interiors with scattered flower sprays, the gadrooned rims enriched in puce, c1765, 8½in (20.5cm) wide.
$5,000-9,000

Services

A New Hall bone china 26 piece tea service, complete and in mint condition, pattern no. 1542, c1815.
$2,000-4,500

An extensive Spode stone china dinner service, printed in blue with the Grasshopper pattern, including one deep platter, 2 others, 2 smaller, 2 of small size, 2 sauce tureens, covers and stands, 12 side plates, 24 dinner plates and 12 soup plates, blue mark Spode Stone China with pseudo Chinese seal mark, c1815.
$1,800-3,800

A good Copeland dessert service, decorated in 18thC Meissen style, with vignettes of Watteauesque lovers, including 15 plates, 3 tall circular tazze, and 5 low dishes, one plate cracked, one dish cracked, 2 tazze broken, printed green factory marks, third quarter 19thC.
$1,600-2,800

A Belleek white glazed coral ▷ moulded cabaret set, comprising: a teapot and cover, a milk jug, a sugar bowl, 3 teacups, 3 saucers, and an oval tray.
$1,200-2,100

A Coalport yellow ground supper set, comprising: a circular bowl and cover with knob finial, 4 trapezoidal dishes, c1820, 20in (51cm).
$1,200-2,100

A Coalport porcelain dessert service, comprising: 2 comports, 4 low stands and 12 plates, some damage, printed Salopian mark, c1875.
$800-1,500

A Chamberlain's type dessert service, decorated in Imari style with flowers, 18 plates, 4 oval dishes and one other larger, 7 plates cracked, one dish damaged, 19thC.
$1,700-3,000

◁ A Chelsea Derby Harlequin tea and coffee service, of 28 pieces, comprising: teapot on stand, lidded sucrier and cream jug, 2 shallow bowls, 8 teacups, 7 coffee cups and 8 saucers, some pieces damaged, 18 pieces marked with gold anchor and D mark for 1769-75 and 10 marked with blue painted Crown and Derby mark for 1770-82.
$1,600-2,800

Some pieces as found (a.f.)

A Davenport part dinner service, decorated in Imari colours, comprising: 2 vegetable dishes and 2 covers, a sauce tureen, cover and stand, a fruit dish, 2 oval dishes, 3 medium plates and 12 side plates, printed marks, pattern no. 51, c1850-70.
$1,600-2,800

A Davenport armorial part dessert service, comprising: 12 plates, 2 low comports, one high comport, 2 rectangular dishes and 2 preserve comports and covers, each raised on a gilded acanthus stem with triform base, 19thC.
$4,000-7,500

A Derby dinner service, painted in blue, ochre, green and gilt, comprising: oval soup tureen and cover, 3 square vegetable dishes, one lacking cover, sauce tureen and cover, 10 various oval meat dishes and stands, 25 10in (25cm) plates, 8 soup plates, 12 7in (17.5cm) plates, several pieces oven stained and some cracked, red crown over crossed batons over D mark.
$1,800-3,800

A Royal Crown Derby service for 12, including cups, saucers, 2 cake plates, teapot, cream jug and covered sugar basin, pattern no. 2451/L/M.
$800-1,500

A Meissen part tea service, comprising: a teapot and cover with silver chain attachment with branch handle and spout, chip to spout, 7½in (19cm) wide, a pear-shaped milk jug and cover, chip to finial, a sugar bowl and cover, a waste bowl, 6½in (16.5cm) diam., an octagonal small dish, 2 shaped oval spoon trays, 12 cups, 12 saucers, blue crossed swords and dot marks, Pressnummer 30, c1765.
$3,200-6,000

A Paris matt blue ground part coffee service, comprising: an oviform coffee pot and cover, a hot water jug, a sugar bowl and cover, 5 coffee cups, one damaged, one rubbed, and 5 saucers, one damaged, c1815.
$1,200-2,100

A Paris Faubourg St. Denis part tea service with gilt dentil rims, comprising: teapot and cover, a hot milk jug, a circular sugar bowl and cover with cherry finial, 6 cups and saucers, spout of teapot restuck, one cup handle restored, blue H marks of Pierre Antoine Hannong, 1771-6.
$1,600-2,800

A Ridgway pink ground part dessert service, comprising: an oval two-handled centre dish, chip to rim, 2 circular two-handled sauce tureens, covers and fixed stands, 2 oval two-handled dishes, 2 lozenge shaped two-handled dishes, 2 shaped square two-handled dishes, one repaired, 17 plates, 4 cracked, pattern no. 1321, 1825-30.
$2,600-5,300

A Sèvres 'feulle de choux' part dinner service, comprising: 3 seaux crenellés, 2 circular deep bowls, 4 shell shaped dishes with scroll handles, 3 shallow circular bowls, 3 slightly smaller shallow bowls, 72 dinner plates, 12 with rim chips, blue interlaced L marks enclosing various painter's and gilder's marks, 18thC.
$20,000-30,000

A Sèvres pattern royal blue ground part coffee service, comprising: a sugar bowl and cover, finial replaced, and 6 coffee cans and saucers, imitation interlaced L and initial marks, c1860.
$2,000-4,500

A Sèvres pattern gold ground tête à tête, painted with named French views, on a brilliant gold ground, comprising: an oviform coffee pot and cover, a sugar bowl and cover, a cream jug, 2 flared coffee cups and saucers and a circular tray, mock M. Imple. de Sèvres marks, c1900, the tray 14in (35cm) diam.
$900-1,700

A Sèvres dessert service, service fond blue lapis corbeille de fleurs, the 'blue lapis' border speckled with gilt and with gilt rims comprising: an oval sauce tureen, cover and fixed stand, 4 circular pedestal bowls on spreading gilt socles, the interiors with symmetrical trailing grape and vine leaves, 60 plates, blue printed interlacked L marks enclosing a fleur de lys, Sèvres and 23 for 1823, various incised marks, painted inside the foot rim in colours with an exact date, a painter's mark, a gilder's date and some with gilder's marks.
$60,000-100,000

Provenance: S.E.M. le Vicomte de Chateaubriand. The service was delivered upon the order of The Minister of the King's Household to the Vicomte de Chateaubriand, the Minister for Foreign Affairs on the 21st August 1823. The order was a supplement to the service previously ordered in two different batches whilst Chateaubriand was Ambassador to England. The previous orders were delivered on 15th April 1822 and 2nd May 1822.

A Staffordshire porcelain botanical part dessert service, comprising: a sauce tureen, cover and fixed stand, stained, cover riveted, 2 oval dishes, 2 quatrefoil dishes, 3 trefoil dishes, one cracked, a shaped oval dish, riveted, 17 plates, 7 damaged, each specimen named in iron red in script, perhaps Mayer and Newbold, c1820.
$1,600-2,800

A 'Vienna' gold ground tête à tête, decorated with scenes from Classical mythology reserved on gold ciselé grounds, comprising: a coffee pot and cover on 3 scroll feet, a hot milk jug and cover on 3 scroll feet, minor chip to spout, a circular sugar bowl and cover, finial repaired and chip to rim of cover, and 2 cylindrical cups and saucers, on an oblong octagonal tray, blue beehive marks, c1880, the tray 13in (13.5cm) wide.
$1,800-3,800

A Flight and Barr Worcester part tea service, swirl moulded in purple, green and gilt, comprising: a sucrier and cover, a saucer dish, 6 tea bowls, 4 coffee cups and 5 saucers, one saucer repaired, 2 tea bowls chipped, c1792-1800.
$800-1,500

A Royal Worcester dessert service, painted by Shuck, on dark blue and pink grounds, comprising: 2 square shaped dishes, 2 circular dishes, 2 oval shaped dishes and 12 dessert plates, printed marks, c1920.
$4,000-7,500

A Nantgarw part dessert service, painted with pink roses and scattered insects within a moulded border, with gilt dentil rims, comprising: a circular two-handled centre dish with gilt foliage bands to the foot, a pair of cushion-shaped dishes, 3 oval dishes, 21 plates, one riveted, 5 cracked, gilding rubbed, impressed Nant Garw C.W. marks, c1820.
$4,500-9,000

A First Period Worcester tea and coffee service, painted in Kakiemon style in mirror and vase shape panels with gilt scroll borders on a blue scale pattern ground, square seal mark in underglaze blue, comprising:
a teapot and cover with floral knop, 6½in (16.5cm). **$600-1,100**
a sugar basin and cover with floral knop, 5½in (13cm). **$400-750**
a bowl, 6½in (16.5cm). **$200-450**
a tea cup, coffee cup and saucer. **$400-750**
a tea cup, coffee cup and saucer. **$400-750**

A quartet of dessert serving dishes, from an important Flight, Barr & Barr Worcester service, with turquoise ground and finely burnished gilding, comprising:
a pair of plates **$800-1,500**
a square dish **$800-1,500**
a comport **$900-1,700**

A Chamberlain's Worcester part dessert service, on dark blue and gilt vermicule ground comprising: a sauce tureen, cover and stand, 3 pedestal dishes with pierced handles and 12 dessert plates, the stand with printed mark, c1845.
$1,200-2,100

Two Meissen cockerel teapots and covers, modelled with incised feather markings, enriched in a brilliant palette, blue crossed swords and incised marks, c1860, 6in (15cm) long.
$1,200-2,100

A Meissen teapot and cover in the form of a cockerel, modelled as a crouching cockerel, the head forming the spout and the tail feathers the handle, enriched in bright enamels and gilt, the cover with seated dog finial, repair to beak, finial and rim of cover, blue crossed swords mark, c1775, 7in (18.5cm) wide.
$2,000-4,500

Cf Rückert, Meissener Porzellan, fig. 1127, p. 277. Meissen models were repeated over many years. Early examples are almost invariably more valuable.

A Sèvres oviform teapot and cover, with flower finial, the handle gilt with stiff leaves and flowerheads, blue interlaced L marks enclosing the date letter 0 for 1767 and incised I, 6½in (16cm) wide.
$1,800-3,800

Tureens & Butter Tubs

A Berlin two-handled oval ornithological soup tureen and domed cover, blue sceptre marks and Pressnummer 35, c1760-70, 14½in (36cm) wide.
$3,200-6,000

A Chelsea apple tureen and a cover, naturally modelled and coloured in green and russet, the base modelled with a stalk with three green leaves, the cover with puce caterpillar finial, minute chips to two leaves, the base with red 3 mark, c1755, 4½in (10.5cm).
$8000-13,500

Cf The Cheyne Book of Chelsea, pl 15, nos. 307 and 308.

A pair of Derby pigeon tureens and covers, incised feather markings enriched in tones of brown, puce, green and iron red, seated on basket moulded nests, applied with grasses and feathers, enriched in yellow, puce and green, minor chips, c1765, 8in (20.5cm) long.
$4,000-7,500

A Sèvres écuelle, cover and stand, painted with blue panels encrusté with white dots and gilt cell pattern, the finial modelled as a berried branch, blue interlaced L marks enclosing the date letters, the stand with date letter K for 1763 and the écuelle with small q for 1769 and both with painter's mark S of P A Méreau, the écuelle with incised CZ, 8in (20cm).
$4,000-7,500

A Meissen partridge tureen, with incised feather markings enriched in tones of grey, brown and iron red, seated on a basket moulded nest, applied with grasses, enriched in green, minor chip to beak, traces of blue crossed swords mark, painter's mark Q to both pieces, c1745, 6½in (16cm) long.
$1,800-3,800

A Longton Hall cos lettuce tureen and cover, the overlapping leaves enriched in green with cauliflower sprig finial, firing cracks, minor repair to rim of cover, finial reglued, c1755, 9in (22.5cm).
$4,500-9,000

A Meissen blue and white butter tub and cover, with pierced tab handles, rim slightly reduced, Pressnummer 23, c1740.
$800-1,500

Cf R Rückert: op. cit., fig. 527.

A Meissen dolphin tureen and cover, with bared teeth, its tail curled over its back with grey scales and coral mouth, minor chip repaired to cover, blue crossed swords mark, c1750, 9½in (24cm) long.
$3,200-6,000

Vases

A pair of baluster shaped continental porcelain vases and covers, printed on an apple green ground, the shoulders and bases with gilt scale pattern, 18in (45cm).
$600-1,200

A pair of Berlin two-handled baluster vases and covers, painted in colours with lovers on landscapes after Watteau, with slightly domed covers and berried finials, KPM mark, 13in (32cm).
$600-1,100

A Coalport porcelain two-handled pedestal vase and cover of ovoid form, painted with a continuous river landscape at sunset, slight damage, printed mark, 10in (25cm).
$80-180

A garniture of 3 Coalbrookdale vases, painted in colours, on a scroll moulded ground enriched in turquoise and gilt, on scroll and foliage moulded feet and square bases, enriched in green and gilt, some repairs to applied flowerheads and foliage, blue crossed swords mark to one the centre vase with blue C.D. mark, c1820, the centre vase 12in (30cm).
$1,300-2,400

A pair of Derby rococo scroll moulded vases of asymmetrical form, painted with peacocks and a magpie in wooded river landscapes, within moulded green and puce foliage cartouches, Wm Duesbury & Co., c1765, 8in (19.5cm).
$1,000-2,000

A Coalport goblet vase, painted with three views of Loch Lomond, with three gilt scroll handles, on baluster stem and circular shaped domed foot, printed mark in green and impressed mark for January 1908, 9in (22cm).
$500-900

A pair of Derby pink ground pot pourri vases and covers, painted in colours with butterflies and moths, named to the base, within gilt foliage surrounds on the pink ground, the pierced covers, shell moulded handles and flaring feet enriched in gilding with foliage, stars and dots, one cover repaired, part of inner rim broken, blue crown, crossed batons and D marks, impressed No. 2, c1775, 8in (20cm).
$1,600-2,800

A Crown Derby porcelain vase and cover, of ovoid form, with pierced scroll handles and pierced knop, painted en grisaille with portrait heads, reserved in oval medallions, with swags of husks in colours, and raised on a square base, printed mark in red, date code for 1890, 9in (22.5cm).
$400-750

A garniture of 3 Derby blue ground tapering oviform vases, with gilt winged swan's neck handles, the bodies richly gilt with a band of trailing oak branches, printed crown and circle marks, Robt Bloor & Co., c1830, 10 to 12in (25 to 30cm).
$1,300-2,400

A Meissen Hausmalerei tall baluster vase, with garlic neck, compressed body and spreading circular foot, painted in the workshop of F F Mayer von Pressnitz, enriched with gilding, blue crossed swords mark and I overgilt with B, the vase c1725, the base and decoration c1745, 12in (29.5cm).
$2,000-4,500

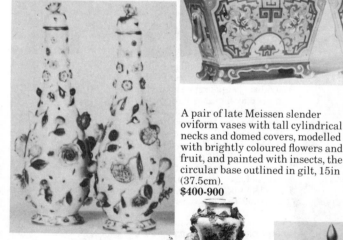

A pair of late Meissen slender oviform vases with tall cylindrical necks and domed covers, modelled with brightly coloured flowers and fruit, and painted with insects, the circular base outlined in gilt, 15in (37.5cm).
$400-900

A pair of Minton flared rectangular spill vases, with gilt fixed ring handles, enamelled and gilt in imitation of Chinese cloisonné, with dark blue, iron red and green geometric pattern cartouches on bright turquoise grounds, the brown glazed lower parts and scroll feet edged with gilding, one with impressed mark, c1880, 12in (30cm).
$2,000-4,500

A Meissen porcelain figural vase, painted with Watteauesque vignette and festooned with fruiting vine, on a naturalistic pedestal support and base, flanked by two cherubs, slight damage, blue crossed swords, impressed numerals, 19thC, 8½in (21cm).
$600-1,200

A pair of Meissen vases and covers, 19thC.
$1,000-2,000

147

A Samson copy of a Cantonese baluster vase and cover, in pinks and greens, c1820.
$3,200-6,000

A Meissen bullet shaped vase and cover on stand, in blue with decorated panels.
$800-1,500

A Sèvres pattern and gilt metal-mounted oviform pot pourri vase and cover, one handle partially detached, the decoration signed J Violet, late 19thC, 29½in (74cm).
$4,000-6,800

A Samson 'famille verte' baluster vase and cover.
$1,000-2,000

A Sèvres pattern and gilt metal-mounted garniture, comprising 2 oviform pot pourri vases and covers and an oval centre dish, with gilt metal winged caryatid handles, the royal blue grounds reserved and decorated with pairs of courtiers in 18thC dress, the shaped high domed covers with gilt metal pineapple finials, and on gilt metal circular 4 footed bases, the decoration signed 'Dr Dubuis', late 19thC, 30in (74cm).
$10,000-18,000

A Sèvres pattern pink ground gilt metal-mounted tapering oviform two-handled vase and cover, painted with a youth and companion in a garden, the flared neck with pendant jewelling and foliage, the circular base cast with berried foliage and with 4 square feet, late 19thC, 17½in (43.5cm).
$600-1,200

A massive pair of Sèvres pattern metal-mounted turquoise-ground oviform vases with flared necks, with metal caryatid and foliage scroll handles, the rims with metal mounts, the 4 footed circular bases applied with 2 putti flanking a vase, one with part of rim lacking, the other with damage to the stem, last quarter 19thC, 33½in (84cm).
$10,000-18,000

A pair of Sèvres pattern ormolu-mounted cylindrical urns, with applied cherub's mask handles, the bodies decorated in colours with equestrian hunting scenes, with ormolu mounts to the rims and lower parts, on shaped stems and square bases, last quarter 19thC, 8in (20cm).
$800-1,500

A Swansea ovoid vase,
1813-22, 9in (22.5cm).
$300-600

A pair of Spode urn shaped pot
pourri vases, pierced weights and
covers, with moulded arched
overhandles, painted in an Imari
palette, circular blue feet gilt with
foliage, one with iron red mark and
pattern no. 2214, c1820, 5½in
(13.5cm).
$1,600-2,800

A pair of Sèvres pattern gilt metal
slender oviform vases, the bodies
decorated with scantily draped
maidens and Cupid, imitation
Sèvres and Chateau des Tuileries
marks, c1900, 22½in (56cm).
$1,800-3,800

A fine garniture of Spode vases of
trumpet shape, with sprays of
flowers, all on paw feet, marked
Spode pattern no.2575 in iron red,
c1820, 5in and 6in (12.5 and 15cm).
$4,000-7,500

A Flight & Barr Worcester blue
ground spill vase, painted with a
band of coloured feathers above a
blue band gilt with foliage and
anthemion, c1805, 5in (12cm).
$800-1,500

A fine pair of Sèvres porcelain vases
and covers, the domed covers with
moulded ovoid finials, each with 4
pierced chain moulded handles,
beaded stems, fluted circular and
stepped square pedestal bases, each
painted with a half length portrait
of a lady in 18thC dress, in colours
within richly gilt border on a 'bleu
de ciel' ground, slight chips and
cracks, 18in (45cm).
$1,800-3,800

A Flight & Barr Worcester canary
yellow ground flared flower pot with
fixed gilt ring handles, painted in
sepia with a view of Worcester
Cathedral flanked by the Royal
China Manufactory, the base
inscribed 'A token of respect to the
Revd Mr Caradec. Barr Worcester
Porcelain Manufacturer to the
King', and with incised B mark,
c1805, 6½in (16cm).
$2,000-4,500

A pair of Dr Wall Period Worcester
vases, decorated upon a 'gros bleu'
ground with 2 panels enclosing
views of exotic birds in a landscape,
with tall buildings in the distance,
with elaborate gilt outlines, blue
open crescent mark, 6½in (16cm).
$3,200-6,000

149

A very fine and rare Flight, Barr & Barr vase, on a 'gros bleu' ground, the jewelled neck with cartouche of shells, c1815.
$4,500-9,000

A Graingers Worcester slender oviform vase and cover, painted with cattle in a country landscape by John Stinton, 12in (30cm).
$600-1,100

A Barr, Flight & Barr Worcester vase and cover, on triple dolphin supports, the bowl brightly painted with flowers on a ground of scrolling foliage, the beaded cover with matching decoration, and griffin knop, some damage, printed and impressed marks, early 19thC, 6½in (16cm).
$1,200-2,100

A Worcester vase, by H Davis, showing sheep in a highland setting, 6in (15cm).
$1,000-2,000

A Hadleys Worcester two handled quatrefoil oviform vase, painted with a view of Worcester Rowing Club by W Powell, reverse printed and painted with a coat of arms dated May 4th 1905, printed mark, 4½in (11cm).
$400-750

A pair of Royal Worcester vases and covers in Sèvres style, with turquoise ground, painted by Josiah Rushton, one inscribed 'Femme de Thebes', signed 'J. Rushton after Ch. Landelle', the other inscribed 'Tsigane Valaque', signed 'J. Rushton after E. Vernet Lecomte', on square bases with incuse corners, on a rich turquoise ground, printed mark in black and date letter for 1870, 16in (39cm).
$4,000-6,800

Cf Henry Sandon, Royal Worcester Porcelain, pl 56 illustrates a pair of vases with identical panels by Josiah Rushton.

A Royal Worcester shot enamel porcelain vase, of wrythen fluted squat baluster form, decorated with panels of fish by E Salter, in colours on an eggshell ground, with beaded collar to the fluted flared cylindrical neck, raised upon a domed circular pedestal foot, printed and numbered 1798 in puce, 11in (27cm).
$400-900

A Royal Worcester reticulated oviform vase by George Owen, enriched with gilding, incised signature, pattern no.1969, gilt marks and date code for 1912, 7in (17cm).
$4,000-6,800

A Royal Worcester 'bamboo' vase formed as a section of bamboo, applied with a flowering twig handle, coloured in green and toned ivory, heightened in gilt, date code for 1891, 8in (20cm).
$200-450

A Royal Worcester reticulated globular vase in the manner of George Owen, the sides pierced with a band of pale blue honeycomb decoration within ivory bands of stylised ornament, inscribed in gilt on the base 'January 4th 1895', gilt printed marks and date code for 1895, 4½in (11cm).
$1,000-2,000

A Royal Worcester large vase and cover, the oviform body painted by C H C Baldwyn, signed, printed mark in green, 1899, 17in (43cm).
$2,600-5,300

A Royal Worcester vase and cover, painted by C H C Baldwyn, signed, with scroll handles, printed mark in green for 1900, 8½in (21cm).
$2,000-4,500

A Royal Worcester cylindrical vase, with shaded ivory ground, printed mark in puce for 1919, 5½in (14cm).
$100-250

A Royal Worcester porcelain vase and cover, the domed cover with acanthus bud knop, painted in colours and gilt with flower sprays on a blushed ivory ground, printed mark in purple, number 2303, date code for 1907, 11in (28cm).
$300-600

A Royal Worcester two handled slender baluster vase and cover with griffin handles, painted by H Davies, printed marks, c1903, 17in (42.5cm).
$4,500-9,000

A Royal Worcester porcelain vase and cover, painted in colours and gilt with bouquets of summer flowers on a blushed ivory ground, gilt line borders, damaged, printed mark in purple, number 2249, date code for 1903, 11½in (28.5cm).
$300-600

A Royal Worcester vase with overhead handle and gilt lion masks in relief, painted by J Stinton, signed, with a pheasant among foliage, printed mark in puce for 1912, 5in (12.5cm).
$200-450

A Royal Worcester vase and cover, with pierced neck painted with sheep in a highland landscape by H Davis, printed marks, c1920, 13in (33cm).
$4,500-9,000

A pair of Royal Worcester vases, with pierced yellow ground handles and flared necks, painted with gilt flowering vines on a blue ground, printed mark, 10in (25cm).
$600-1,100

A Royal Worcester cylindrical vase, painted with sheep, by H Davis, signed, on pierced and gilt scroll foot, printed mark in puce, 6½in (16cm).
$600-1,100

A pair of Royal Worcester vases, painted with flowering vines outlined in gilt on a white ground, printed marks, 12in (30cm).
$400-900

A fine Royal Worcester pot pourri vase and cover, painted with highland cattle by John Stinton, c1930.
$1,700-3,000

An English porcelain pot pourri vase, slight damage, c1815, 12in (30cm).
$1,600-2,800

A Royal Worcester vase and cover by George Owen, the body pierced with a wide band of trellis pattern bordered with gilt scroll ornament and festoons, with pierced shoulders, neck, base and cover, griffin head and scroll handles, the square base with incuse corners, incised signature 'G. Owen' and printed mark in gold, 10½in (26.5cm).
$3,200-6,000

In the Ceramics section if there is only one measurement it refers to the height of the piece.

A pair of English porcelain blue ground campana vases, with gilt serpent handles painted within gilt octagonal cartouches flanked by gilt foliage and anthemion, pattern no.413, perhaps Ridgway, c1820, 6in (15cm).
$800-1,500

Lowestoft – *a brief history*

The Lowestoft factory commenced production by 1758 following earlier trials by 4 partners who had taken up the challenge after an earlier attempt by a local landowner, Hewlin Luson. The partners were Philip Walker, a tenant farmer on Luson's land, Obed Aldred, a bricklayer, Robert Browne the local blacksmith and James Richmond, merchant.

The partners converted Aldred's premises in Bell Lane, Lowestoft and ran some trials, apparently with a high failure rate. Browne, the manager of the fledgling factory appears to have taken employment at the Bow factory in order to gain experience and seems to have returned to Lowestoft in 1758 with both experience and a viable porcelain formula very similar to that in use at the Bow factory!

In January 1760 the partnership; trading as Walker and Co, took out their first newspaper advertisement and launched their wares on the open market.

It is possible, because of a number of dated pieces, to be reasonably accurate in dividing the Lowestoft output into various periods.

Early wares, c1759-60 are rare, popular and expensive. All are in blue and white as coloured wares were not introduced into general production until c1766. A similar date is hypothesised for the introduction of printed wares.

By 1761 the range of products had expanded enormously and encompassed most teawares, including rarities such as egg cups, salts and spoon trays. The wares of this first Middle Period, c1761-65, are generally well potted and painted in a crisp inky tone of blue with Chinese-style scenes.

In the latter half of the 1760s the amount of blue and white porcelain produced increased and both polychrome and printed wares were introduced. Again the patterns were usually based on Chinese originals or floral themes.

The period from 1770 to 1799 is known as the late period. The quality of painted blue and white patterns deteriorated and became stylised though some fine quality polychrome wares were produced.

Production ceased in 1799 though stock in hand continued to be sold for a year or 2 before the sale of factory equipment and buildings in 1802.

Specialist works on Lowestoft include: Lowestoft Wares *by Geoffrey Godden, Antique Collectors Club, Woodbridge,* $40; *and* Early Lowestoft *by Christopher Spencer – Order direct from Greystones, 29 Mostyn Road, Merton Park, London SW19,* $20.

An early guglet, decorated in underglaze blue with flowering plants and birds, c1760, 9in (22.5cm).
$4,000-7,500

The only early example recorded. Similar examples were produced in the middle period and these fetch **$1,200-2,100** *at auction.*

A rare basket, decorated in underglaze blue with a Chinese riverscape, some restoration, c1760, 6in (15cm) diam.
$3,200-6,000

One of 4 recorded examples.

l. A blue and white saucer, decorated with a Chinese riverscape, cracked and restored, c1762-64.
$80-150

c. A sparrow beak jug, decorated in runny underglaze blue with rocks and flowers, cracked, c1765.
$300-600

r. A saucer decorated in underglaze blue with the Boy on a Bridge pattern, c1763-65.
Perfect $200-450

The Boy on a Bridge pattern is attractive and popular with collectors. A similar saucer with a different pattern would be less expensive.

A large cider jug, moulded with flowers and leaves and painted with a continuous riverscape, cracked, c1765.
$800-1,500

A miniature tea bowl and saucer, painted in underglaze blue, 1770-75.
$500-900

A Lowestoft blue and white vase, the tall neck with a flared top, painted with flowering branches and scattered insects beneath a scroll pattern border, crack to shoulder, minute chip to rim, painter's numeral 5(?), c1768, 6in (14.5cm).
$1,600-2,800

Cf Sheena Smith, op. cit. no.647 and Geoffrey A. Godden, Lowestoft Porcelain, *pl.72.*

A Lowestoft polychrome bowl, decorated in underglaze blue and overglaze iron red and gilt with the Dolls House pattern, unmarked, c1780, 6in (15cm) diam.
$150-300

A rare Lowestoft saucer dish, painted in underglaze blue, cracked, c1775, 7½in (18.5cm) diam.
$400-750

A rare butter dish, decorated in overglaze polychrome enamels with flower sprays, some restoration, c1768.
$600-1,200

An early example of polychrome decoration.

A Lowestoft blue and white miniature globular teapot and cover, painted with pagodas on river islands beneath a loop and dot pattern border, painter's numeral 13(?), c1768, 3in (8cm).
$1,700-3,000

Cf Sheena Smith, Lowestoft Porcelain in Norwich Castle Museum, *no.572.*

Lowestoft – a guide to identification
Early Period *c1757-61*

Style of Decorations: A limited range of motifs, including flowers, birds, trees, boats and houses in Chinese-style, delicately outlined and shaded in 2 tones of underglaze blue.

Potting: The body often displays a pinkish or pinkish-brown tone and is not always translucent. Wares are thickly potted in the first few years but some very finely potted pieces with white translucency were introduced c1760-61.

Glaze: Before 1760 the glaze is frequently clouded by tin oxide or myriad bubbles. By 1760 a very successful clear 'wet' glaze had been developed.

Underglaze blue: A pale grey-blue is found on some early wares. By 1760 a darker blue was used. Wares were generally marked with a painters number inside the footring. For a fuller consideration of early wares see 'Early Lowestoft' by Christopher Spencer.

Middle Period *c1761-70*

Style of Decoration: The early decorative themes were soon developed into standard patterns but these can lack the vigour of the early designs. Painters numerals used to mark the base: these are generally from one to 14. Both transfer printing and polychrome decoration were introduced in about 1766. Lowestoft transfer prints are often outlined in a hesitant way, to use a phrase coined by a well known expert, 'as if with a failing ball-point pen'.

Potting: During the early part of the middle period great care was taken with potting. Shapes continued to be well finished. Gradually shapes became simplified and the finish of moulded parts, such as handles, was given less emphasis. After 1765 a more open body showing a yellow, rather than white, translucency was used.

Glaze: Often thick, shiny and more glassy then in the early period. The glaze is prone to bubbling and can show a green hue in gathers around the footrim, under handles or around mouldings.

Underglaze blue: An inky blue was used throughout the period, though sometimes a paler colour is found. Transfer printed pieces are generally dark in tone.

Late Period *c1770-99*

Style of Decoration: The quality of blue and white patterns gradually declines. Chinoiseries tend to be heavily shaded and quickly executed. Floral patterns are highly stylised. By 1775 a brighter blue had been introduced. In contrast some excellent polychrome patterns were introduced and these are highly collectable, particularly those which include Chinese figures or tulips.

Potting: The quality of potting remains robust and utilitarian in concept. A large number of shapes were made and some of these are of great interest to collectors, particularly eye baths, egg cups and other unusual domestic wares. A few figures and animals were made. These are highly popular.

Glaze: A clear glaze which gives the body a creamy appearance was developed about 1775. Polychrome decoration can look particularly pleasing against this warm background.

A Lowestoft blue and white tea caddy, painted with trailing peony, minute chip to shoulder, blue crescent mark, c1775, 4in (10cm).
$400-750

A moulded cream boat, minor chips, c1770, 3½in (8.5cm).
$300-600

A Lowestoft patty pan, decorated in blue and white with outcurved sides, some damage, c1770, 3in (7.5cm) diam.
$150-300

A Lowestoft blue and white Robert Browne pattern part tea service, comprising: a teapot and cover, handle repaired, finial lacking, a pear-shaped milk jug, minute cracks to lip, a tea caddy, rim chip, a slop basin, 8 tea bowls, 2 cracked, and 8 saucers, one cracked, many pieces with blue crescent marks, some with painter's numeral 17, c1780.
$1,800-3,800

Cf Sheena Smith, op. cit. no.589.

A Lowestoft scallop-shaped shell dish, painted with flowers in underglaze blue, c1775, 4½in (11cm) diam.
$300-600

A rare Lowestoft blue and white inkwell, inscribed with the owner's name and dated 1798.
$2,600-5,300

A Lowestoft crested coffee cup and saucer from the Ludlow service, c1785.
$1,600-2,800

Cf Geoffrey A. Godden, Lowestoft Porcelain, pl.175 and col. pl. V.

A Lowestoft blue and white eye bath, lightly moulded with scrolls and painted with 2 flower sprays, c1780, 2in (5cm).
$1,200-2,100

A rare Lowestoft blue and white inscribed and dated mug, cracked.
$2,000-4,500

A rare Lowestoft milk jug and cover, painted in underglaze blue with the Dragon pattern, c1780-85, 5in (13cm).
$1,200-2,100

W. H. Goss China

Illustrated in this section are examples of Goss porcelain made by the Goss factory in Stoke-on-Trent between 1858 and 1939. The range is wide and varied, and to indicate age items are numbered (1), (2) or (3):

(1) First period 1858-87
(2) Second period 1881-1934
(3) Third period 1930-39

Throughout the years of manufacture the standards were high, and reproduction of the buildings, Roman urns etc they were modelled after is amazingly accurate. The hand painted coats-of-arms were exact, and the recipes for the brilliant enamels and parian body were developed by Mr William Henry Goss himself. Their quality surpassed that of most other potteries.

Over 1,500 different shapes bearing some 7,000 different decorations and coats-of-arms were produced. For further information, collectors are recommended to *The Price Guide to Goss China* and *Goss China, Arms Decorations and Their Values* by Nicholas Pine, Milestone Publications, Murray Road, Horndean, Hants.

A parian bust of Napoleon, (1/2). $200

'Married Bliss', comedy piece, (3). $150

A Weston-Super-Mare clock, in garish coloured surround, (3). $200

Cenotaph (2/3) **$80**, Blackpool Tower (2) **$100** Richmond Market Cross (2) **$100** Big Ben (3) **$100**

The Lucerne Lion, (2). $100

A Swiss milk pot and lid, (2). $30

A selection of large named models, all with inscriptions on their bases. (2). **$16-40**

A Seaford Roman urn, with butterfly transfer, (1/2). $100

Windsor Castle, (3). $150

A range of models, (2), from smalls at **$8** to the Egyptian Pyramid at $150

GOSS AND CRESTED WARE

Damage considerably affects the value of porcelain. Haircracks, chips and faded crests can halve the values recorded here. Full prices can only be obtained for perfection. Minor firing flaws can be ignored. Goss china shrank up to 10% in the firing processes so manufacturing flaws and minor differences in size are common

DIFFERENTIATING MING AND QING WARES

In order to distinguish Ming porcelain from the later Qing wares it is necessary to appreciate the technical rather than the decorative differences between the 2. The Qing decorators frequently copied ancestral designs with great accuracy and at first sight it is sometimes difficult to attribute certain pieces.

A good example of this is the Doucai (contrasting colours) category. The originals were produced during the Ming reign of Chenghua (1465-87) and the copies were made in the reign of the Qing emperor Kangxi. Were it not for the characteristic smoky ivory appearance of the Ming glaze one might well be at a loss to differentiate early from late.

In the first place, with certain exceptions, Ming porcelain is more heavily glazed and the depth of glaze effects a bluish or greenish tint. The glaze is rarely evenly applied and if carefully examined one can detect runs and dribbles of excess glaze. Most Qing wares are covered in a glaze of uniform thickness. Particularly characteristic is the pure white appearance achieved by the Kangxi potters by only coating the vessel or dish in a thin and even wash. The reigns of Yongzheng and Qianlong did witness some pieces (non-export) which were deliberately covered in a thick glaze in order to emulate the early 15thC porcelains.

As far as potting is concerned there are more obvious idiosyncracies enabling easier identification.

For example, Ming vases if of sufficient size to warrant being made in 2 or more pieces are generally luted horizontally even on vessels which it would appear to be simpler to make in 2 vertical sections, Yongle and Xuande 'moon' or 'pilgrim' bottles are a case in point. Qing pilgrim bottles would invariably be made by joining 2 vertical halves.

The footrims on Ming wares are generally knife-pared and little effort made to remove the facets left by the blade. Most, if not all, Qing pieces are smoothed after the trimming. The feet on Ming dishes or bowls are for the most part higher than Qing examples. They are frequently undercut immediately indicating that they have been thrown by hand and not as many Qing pieces which have been moulded by a mechanical process utilising a profile cutter. A further point concerning the footrim on Ming wares – it will generally manifest a narrow orange zone abutting the edge of the glaze. This is due to the presence of iron in the body of the porcelain which appears to oxidise more strongly in the kiln in the area most closely in contact with the glaze.

This section is alphabetically arranged by object: bowl, box, censer, etc. In each group the wares are firstly divided into Chinese followed by Japanese and then ordered chronologically.

Bowls

A large Jian Yao brown-glazed 'hare's fur' bowl, the mottled and lightly-streaked glaze thinning to matt around the rim and pooling darkly in the well and stopping irregularly around the dark shallowly-cut foot, chip restored, glaze tears around the foot polished, Song Dynasty, 5in (13cm) diam., fitted box.
$1,000-2,000

A Jun Yao shallow bowl, covered in a pale blue glaze thinning to a pale translucent brown at the rim, small foot chip and minor restoration, Yuan Dynasty, 4½in (11.5cm) diam.
$1,000-2,000

A bulb bowl covered with a crackled celadon glaze, not reaching the centre, on 3 feet, Ming, 12in (30.5cm).
$900-1,700

A Transitional Wucai fish bowl, painted with 4 fish amongst water weeds below a band of iron red breaking waves, chipped, 17thC, 9in (22.5cm) diam.
$1,000-2,000

A Chun Yao bowl, with a rich sky blue mottled glaze falling from the brownish rim, with a purple splash, the outside with a deeper shade of mottled blue, Sung, 8in (19.5cm).
$1,800-3,800

A dated blue and white small bowl, the exterior with 4 auspicious characters in star-shaped panels against a floral meander below cell pattern at the neck, engraved collectors' marks, the base with an encircled four-character mark including a cyclical date, 4½in (11cm) diam.
$2,600-5,300

The cyclical date dingsi year probably corresponds to A.D. 1617.

A blue and white bowl painted on the exterior in a vivid blue, the centre of the interior with a pine in a jardinière reserved on a trellis-pattern ground, below a band of hexagonal cell-pattern reserved with cartouches of pine, prunus, bamboo and peony at the rim, minute rim chips, areas of rim polished, encircled Chenghua six-character mark, Kangxi, 8in (19.5cm) diam.
$1,600-2,800

A pair of bowls decorated in 'famille verte' enamels, the narrow borders of scrolls in iron red, the insides each with a flowerhead medallion, fang-shêng mark, Kangxi, 6in (15cm).
$2,600-5,300

An ormolu-mounted 'famille rose' bowl, restored, the porcelain Qianlong, the ormolu 19thC, 12½in (31cm) wide.
$600-1,200

A 'famille verte' bowl, the interior painted with flowers below a cell-pattern border reserved with cartouches of peach, prunus and finger citrus, the exterior below a cell-pattern border reserved with cartouches of ribboned emblems, chipped, cracked, pieces restuck, Kangxi, 12in (30.5cm) diam.
$1,400-2,600

A 'famille rose' punch bowl, painted with 2 large panels of a family group, on a ground of gilt scrolls reserved with puce monochrome and larger polychrome floral panels, Qianlong, 10in (26cm) diam.
$1,700-3,000

A Chinese export porcelain punch bowl, decorated with European figures in landscapes separated by prunus blossom sprays, 10in (25cm) diam.
$600-1,100

A pair of Chinese blue and white shallow bowls and domed covers, Kangxi, 7in (17.5cm) wide.
$1,700-3,000

A 'famille verte' punch bowl, painted on the exterior with figures below a band of animal cartouches, reserved on a floral seeded green ground at the rim, restored, Kangxi, 14in (35cm) diam.
$2,200-4,200

A Chinese export porcelain bowl, enamelled with figures within a landscape and 4 male figures with a girl at a window, small rim chips, slight wear to enamels, 10in (26cm).
$300-600

A Qianlong bowl, with a red enamel scroll border above 3 cartouches, surrounded by a blue ground, of birds sitting in a peony tree, damaged.
$150-300

A bowl and cover enamelled in 'famille verte' palette, with borders of green 'cracked ice' with flowerheads in iron red, the handles issuing from masks, Kangxi, 8in (19.5cm).
$2,200-4,200

A Qianlong 'famille rose' barber's bowl painted in colours, 12½in (31cm) wide.
$1,400-2,600

A Chinese export porcelain bowl, enamelled with a family at a window and with 3 figures with a bird, both groups with colourful leafage and within blue, shaped cartouches, 10in (25.5cm).
$400-900

An unusual large Chinese blue and white circular shallow basin, the everted rim with wave pattern and the exterior with 4 groups of peony, chrysanthemum, plum and lotus, c1800, 27in (67.5cm) diam.
$7,000-12,000

A Chinese export porcelain bowl, enamelled in the 'famille rose' palette with bouquets and sprigs of large blooms, restored, 12in (29cm).
$600-1,100

A Cantonese bowl, decorated with panels of flowers and figures, 19thC, 14in (35cm).
$900-1,700

A large Cantonese porcelain punch bowl, in 'famille rose' and 'famille verte' enamels and gilt, 16in (40cm) diam.
$1,000-2,000

A fine large Cantonese bowl, painted on the exterior with panels of figures before pavilions, 22in (55cm) diam.
$10,000-18,000

A Cantonese fish tank, 19thC, 10in (25cm).
$600-1,200

A massive blue and white fish bowl, painted with a wide band of 2 four-clawed dragons striding in pursuit of a flaming pearl amongst cloud scrolls above breaking waves and below roundels and cloud scrolls at the rim, cracked, 19thC, 24½in (62cm) wide.
$2,200-4,200

A Chinese circular fish bowl, painted in coloured enamels on a yellow ground, applied with 2 'shi-shi' blue glazed handles, 19thC, 14in (35cm).
$2,600-5,300

A fine large 'famille rose' fish bowl, the inside decorated with carp swimming amongst weeds and lily, 18in (45cm).
$3,200-6,000

A large deep Imari bowl and domed cover, decorated in iron red, black, green enamels and gilt on underglaze blue, the brass acorn finial of later date, late 17thC, 19½in (48cm).
$3,200-6,000

A Raku chawan with mixed black and chestnut brown glaze stopping short of the foot, 18thC, 4½in (11cm) diam., with box.
$2,600-5,300

The chawan shows the influence of the fourth generation Raku potter Ichinyu (1640-96), who is said to have initiated the addition of a dash of red to the typical black Raku glaze.

An Imari barber's bowl, painted in the interior with flowering and fruiting trees, the border with iron red and gilt scrolling flowers and panels of stylised foliage, early 18thC, 11in (27.5cm) diam.
$1,000-2,000

A deep Imari bowl and cover, decorated in iron red, enamel and gilt on an underglaze blue ground, Genroku period, 8½in (21.5cm) diam.
$1,700-3,000

A shallow Imari bowl, painted with 'ho-o' among pine and plum, divided by underglaze blue floral lappets, finial chipped, c1700, 8½in (21cm) diam.
$1,600-2,800

An Imari shaving dish, decorated in underglaze blue, iron red and gilt, a narrow band of underglaze blue and gilt with 4 cartouches containing stylised foliage separating the wide rim decorated with stylised flowers and foliage, the reverse with sprays of plum blossom, gilt rim, repair to rim, Genroku period, 11in (28cm) wide.
$900-1,700

A Satsuma bowl, 5in (12cm) diam.
$600-1,200

A pair of earthenware bowls and covers, supported on 3 feet modelled as children, 7in (18cm) diam.
$600-1,100

An Imari bowl, the centre painted with a fabulous beast, set with 3 foliate medallions of chrysanthemums, the exterior similarly painted, mid-19thC, 10in (25cm) diam.
$600-1,100

A Japanese Imari reeded round bowl, decorated in blue, gilt and iron red flowers, 19thC, 9½in (23.5cm).
$900-1,700

An Imari shaving bowl, decorated in iron red, dark green and light green, aubergine and black enamels and gilt, on an underglaze blue ground, Genroku period, 10½in (26cm) diam.
$1,000-2,000

A Satsuma baluster-shaped bowl, the body enamelled and gilt, with men working in a garden setting, the lid decorated with a sitting figure, mid-19thC, 6in (15cm) diam.
$2,000-4,500

A Kyoto chrysanthemum-shaped deep bowl, decorated in colours and gilt, signed on the base 'Kizan kore o tsukuru', late 19thC, 12in (30cm) diam.
$2,200-4,200

An Imari bowl, 19thC, 13½in (33.5cm) diam.
$900-1,700

An Imari boat-shaped and pierced pedestal stand.
$200-450

A large Imari bowl, decorated in underglaze blue, iron red, green, yellow enamels and gilt, the exterior with a wide band of flowers and foliage, 19thC, 16in (40cm) diam.
$2,000-4,500

Bottles

A pair of Chinese Imari slender square bottles, Kangxi, 9½in (23.5cm).
$2,000-4,500

A pair of Imari bottles, painted with broad bands of pine, bamboo and plum, early 18thC, 9in (23cm).
$1,700-3,000

A Chinese blue and white bottle with flared foot, Kangxi, 9in (23cm).
$900-1,700

A pair of Imari slender pear-shaped bottles, the moulded collared shoulders and necks with alternate underglaze blue and gilt bands, early 18thC, 9in (22.5cm).
$2,600-5,300

Cups

A Chinese underglaze blue and copper red decorated bottle, painted with a coiled dragon pursuing a flaming pearl among clouds, 18thC, 17½in (44cm).
$1,200-2,100

A Kakiemon-type cylindrical sake bottle (tokkuri), decorated in iron red and coloured enamels, fitted with a European gilt metal finial surmounted by a hawk attached to a link chain, 18thC/early 19thC, 9in (23cm).
$7,000-12,000

A pair of blue and white semi-eggshell beakers and saucers, painted with a design derived from a European print, the interior of the beakers and saucer reverses with 4 fish swimming in mutual pursuit, below leaf-pattern bands at the rims, encircled stork marks, Kangxi.
$900-1,700

This is an example of the so-called Cuckoo in the House design.

161

Eight 'famille rose' coffee cups and saucers, each enamelled in colours and gilt, Qianlong.
$1,300-2,400

Six export tea cups and saucers for the American market, each enamelled and gilt with an eagle, 19thC.
$1,600-2,800

CHINESE PORCELAIN – VALUE POINTS

★ about 80% of the marks that appear on Chinese porcelain are retrospective

★ if a piece bears a correct, as opposed to a retrospective, reign mark then its value compared to an unmarked but comparable specimen would probably be of the magnitude of 3 to 4 times more

★ a piece of a known date but bearing the mark of an earlier reign would be adversely affected and could possibly fetch less than an unmarked piece of the same vintage

★ as a rule condition will adversely affect a readily available type of ware more than a very rare or early type

★ original covers or lids can raise the price considerably – especially if the vessel appears more complete with it. Hence a baluster vase, for example, would be less affected than a wine ewer

Ewers

A Transitional blue and white silver-mounted oviform ewer, the handle restuck, c1640, 10in (25cm).
$1,600-2,800

The mounts are Dutch bearing the hall marks for 1856.

An Arita blue and white broad oviform ewer, handle cracked, c1670, 10in (24cm).
$900-1,700

A 'famille rose' standing duck, with multi-coloured wing feathers, the body primarily painted with sepia plumage, astride a green and blue plinth, neck luting repaired, Qianlong, 7in (17cm).
$2,200-4,200

Figures – Animal

A red-painted grey pottery horse's head, modelled with bulbous eyes, flared nostrils and open mouth, Han Dynasty, 6in (15cm).
$2,200-4,200

The result of a thermoluminescence test, Oxford, 366L19, is consistent with the dating of this piece.

An unglazed grey pottery figure of a standing caparisoned horse, with areas of green and white pigment remaining under earth encrustation, repaired, 6th/7thC A.D., 11in (27.5cm), with stand, fitted box.
$2,200-4,200

An export figure of a recumbent dog, its fur painted in brown and gilt and the mouth in pink, the sconce with a band of green below iron red and gold, chipped, sconce reduced, Qianlong, 6½in (16cm) wide.
$1,000-2,000

An ochre-glazed pottery figure of a recumbent dog, with a vivid glaze, Tang Dynasty, 4in (9.5cm) long.
$4,000-7,500

A pair of biscuit figures of Dogs of Fo, seated, their coats green with tufts in yellow and aubergine, Kangxi, 18in (44cm).
$1,300-2,400

A pair of 'famille rose' figures of standing cranes, the white bodies incised and moulded with feather markings, the eyes, beaks, tail feathers and legs in black and with pink crests, chipped beak, 19thC, 8in (20cm).
$1,800-3,800

An export figure of a hound, the eyes and mouth picked out in brown, traces of cold-enamel decoration, fritted, Qianlong, 6in (14.5cm).
$3,200-6,000

An aubergine and green-glazed cat night light, the body incised with short fur markings and dappled in apple green on the rich aubergine-brown ground, cracked, c1800, 8in (20.5cm) wide, wood stand.
$4,000-6,800

A pair of Chinese porcelain cockerels decorated with pink, green, blue and yellow plumage on pale green bases, one comb damaged, 19thC, 10½in (26cm).
$1,800-3,800

A Fukagawa white glazed model of a goat, with black-painted eye pupils, Hirado style, signed on the base 'Dai Nihon Imara Fukagawa sei', c1875, 7½in (19cm) long.
$800-1,500

Figures – People

An unglazed buff pottery figure of a court lady, wearing an orange painted jacket and brown striped dress, Tang Dynasty, 10in (25cm).
$1,300-2,400

The result of a thermoluminescence test, Oxford, 366L22, is consistent with the dating of this piece.

A late Japanese Imari recumbent cat, with a blue and gilt bow on its neck, the fur iron red, 8½in (21cm) long.
$1,000-2,000

A Ming tilemaker's pottery equestrian group, the ochre-robed dignitary turning to his right, on a green domed base, surface chips and minor repair, 17thC, 16in (39cm).
$1,300-2,400

An unglazed red pottery figure of an equestrian lady, restoration to legs and tail, ears chipped, Tang Dynasty, 15in (37cm).
$5,000-9,000

The result of thermoluminescence test, Oxford, 366h26, is consistent with the dating of this piece.

A blanc-de-Chine Buddhist group, formed as Guanyin, with a small acolyte, repaired at her right wrist, small chips, Kangxi, 10in (25cm).
$800-1,500

A pair of 'famille verte' figures of the Laughing Twins, Hehe Erxian, painted with iron red aprons over white robes, the bases with 4 large peony heads, one repaired, Kangxi, 11in (27cm).
$1,700-3,000

A 'famille verte' 'egg-and-spinach' figure of Guanyin, wearing a green cowl, white robe and splashed undergarments, chipped, Kangxi, 8in (20cm).
$800-1,500

A 'famille verte' figure of Guanyin, wearing a green-ground yellow floral robe, some restoration, Kangxi, 14in (34.5cm).
$900-1,700

A Japanese porcelain figure of a standing lady, Kwannon, with painted, enamel and gilt decoration, late 19thC, 22½ (56cm).
$200-450

A blanc-de-Chine figure of Pu-Tai, standing on his bag of happiness, Kangxi, 13in (32.5cm).
$800-1,500

Flatware

A crackled celadon hexafoil dish of Guan yao type, the pale blue widely crackled glaze pooling in the recesses and stopping around the neatly cut orange-fired foot, slight glaze degradation, Southern Song Dynasty, 6in (15.5cm).
$2,000-4,500

Make the most of Miller's

Miller's is completely different each year. Each edition contains completely NEW photographs. This is not an updated publication. We never repeat the same photograph.

A blue and white late Ming Kraak porselein dish, hair crack, fritted, early 17thC, 12½in (31.5cm).
$1,000-2,000

A Zhejiang celadon dish, delicately carved with a crane in flight, under an olive glaze pooling on the shallowly-cut grey biscuit foot, Song Dynasty, Li Shui type, 11in (27.5cm).
$1,600-2,800

A large late Ming blue and white Kraak porselein dish, fritted, late 16th/early 17thC, 20in (50.5cm).
$2,200-4,200

A Kraak porselein blue and white dish, the centre painted with deer in a landscape, Transitional, 11in (27cm).
$600-1,100

A 'famille verte' saucer dish, chipped, encircled Chenghua mark, Kangxi, 14in (34.5cm).
$1,000-2,000

A 'famille verte' plate, Kangxi, 8½in (21cm).
$1,300-2,400

A late Ming blue and white blue-ground saucer dish, 16thC, 12in (30cm).
$600-1,200

A deep circular dish, decorated in 'famille verte' enamels, shop seal mark, Kangxi, 14½in (36.5cm).
$6,000-12,000

A large Kangxi blue and white plate, small chip, Chia Ching mark, c1710, 14in (35cm).
$800-1,500

An unusual saucer dish with everted rim, Kangxi, 9½in (23.5cm).
$800-1,500

A 'famille verte' saucer dish, painted with an audience scene around a tented building, small rim chips, 3 patches of blue glaze flaked, Kangxi, 14in (35cm).
$3,200-6,000

TRANSITIONAL WARES

★ these wares are readily identifiable both by their form and by their style of decoration

★ Forms: sleeve vases, oviform jars with domed lids, cylindrical brushpots and bottle vases are particularly common

★ the cobalt used is a brilliant purplish blue, rarely misfired

★ the ground colour is of a definite bluish tone, probably because the glaze is slightly thicker than that of the wares produced in the subsequent reigns of Kangxi and Yongzheng

★ the decoration is executed in a rather formal academic style, often with scholars and sages with attendants in idyllic cloud-lapped mountain landscapes

★ other characteristics include the horizontal 'contoured' clouds, banana plantain used to interrupt scenes, and the method of drawing grass by means of short 'V' shaped brush strokes

★ in addition, borders are decorated with narrow bands of scrolling foliage, so lightly incised as to be almost invisible or secret (anhua)

★ these pieces were rarely marked although they sometimes copied earlier Ming marks

A pair of Chinese blue and white plates, Kangxi six-character marks and of the period, 8in (20cm).
$600-1,100

A pair of 'famille verte' basins, the exteriors with further birds amongst pine and chrysanthemum, restored, Kangxi, 14in (34.5cm).
$2,200-4,200

A Qianlong plate, decorated in 'famille rose' enamels with the Judgment of Paris, gilt shell and scroll border, 9in (22.5cm).
$1,400-2,600

A 'famille verte' fluted saucer dish, Kangxi, 11½in (29cm).
$900-1,700

A pair of Chinese saucer dishes, each painted in iron red and gilt, outlined in underglaze blue, Kangxi, 8½in (21cm).
$800-1,500

A Qianlong 'famille rose' plate, c1740, 9in (22.5cm).
$200-450

A 'famille rose' Valentine pattern plate, centrally painted with a long-tailed bird in flight approaching 2 seated dogs with 3 puppies, with iron red and gilt shell and scroll border, chipped, Qianlong, 9in (23cm).
$600-1,100

A pair of 'famille rose' plates, the wells with grisaille foliage and blue enamel dragons, the borders with iron red and gilt trailing flowers, Yongzheng/early Qianlong, 9in (22.5cm).
$1,000-2,000

A set of 3 Chinese 'famille rose' plates, the outer border decorated in iron red with dominoes, 2 cracked, Qianlong, 9in (22.5cm).
$500-900

A 'famille rose' ship saucer dish, painted in the centre in iron red, black and green with a full-masted European vessel flying a Scandinavian flag, beneath puce scale panels, c1790, 8in (20cm).
$1,400-2,600

A pair of large 'famille rose' circular dishes, Qianlong, 15in (37.5cm).
$3,200-6,000

A pair of Chinese 'famille rose' plates, one cracked, one chipped, Qianlong, 9in (22.5cm).
$400-750

A pair of blue and white plates, centrally painted with leaping Buddhistic lions above 'lingzhi' sprays within elaborate scroll, pomegranate, cell-pattern and foliage-spray borders, chipped, Qianlong, 10in (24cm).
$900-1,700

A Chinese export porcelain plate, the central panel painted with a woman and a boy seated beneath trees on the seashore, in coloured enamels, within a puce diapered border, with pierced rim and gilt outer rim, 8in (20cm).
$500-900

A pair of large 'famille rose' dishes, small hairline, minor chips, Qianlong, 14in (35cm).
$600-1,100

A pair of Chinese export Herculaneum pierced oval stands, painted in iron red, white, blue and green enamels, late Qianlong, 11in (27.5cm) wide.
$1,600-2,800

A pair of Chinese Imari dishes, painted with a lady and a child on a fenced terrace, Qianlong, 15in (38cm) wide.
$3,200-6,000

An Imari dish, 17thC, 17½in (44cm).
$1,700-3,000

A rare European subject grisaille plate, painted in shades of grey and flesh tones, grisaille possibly strengthened, small rim chip, mid-Qianlong, 9in (23cm).
$1,400-2,600

An Imari dish, painted in underglaze blue, yellow, green, turquoise enamels, iron red and gilt, late 17thC, 14in (35cm).
$1,800-3,800

A set of 4 rare Arita blue and white plates, each painted with The Hall of One Hundred Children, late 17thC, 8in (20cm).
$2,600-5,300

Cf. Catalogue Japanese Blue and White Porcelain Exhibition in Leeuwarden, February 1981.

A large Imari deep dish, with iron red and gilt petals, the border with 4 gold-ground panels of flowers on a ground of scrolling pomegranate, flowers and leaves, c1700, 21½in (54cm).
$3,200-6,000

A Kyoto dish, painted in colours and gilt with 3 ladies at leisure among flowers in a riverside garden, 6in (15cm) wide.
$800-1,500

A pair of Arita Kakiemon style saucer dishes, the porcelain early 18thC, the decoration later and probably Dutch, 8in (20cm).
$900-1,700

A pair of Japanese porcelain dishes, finely painted with figures of ladies and actors in extensive landscapes, with elaborate floral borders, 19in (47.5cm).
$1,700-3,000

An Imari dish, 18thC, 21in (54cm).
$2,600-5,300

A Kaga thickly-potted saucer dish, painted in iron red and richly gilt, 14in (35cm).
$600-1,100

JAPANESE ART PERIODS

★ *Prehistory and Protohistory*
c7000 B.C. Jomon culture; first recorded pottery with simple design.
c300 B.C. Yayoi culture; bronzes and more sophisticated pottery.
1st to 4thC A.D. Haniwa culture. Bronzes and distinctive red pottery.
A.D. 220; first influence from Korea

★ *Asuka Period* – 552-645

★ *Hahuko Period* – 672-85

★ *Nara Period* – 710-94

★ *Heian Period* – 794-1185

★ *Kamakura Period* – 1185-1333

★ *Muromachi (Ahikaga) Period* – 1338-1573

★ *Momoyama Period* – 1573-1615
1598: immigrant Korean potters begin kilns at Kyushu, producing the first glazed pottery

★ *Edo (Tokugawa) Period* – 1615-1867
1616: first porcelain made by Ninsei (1596-1666)
1661-73: great age of porcelain; Arita, Nabeshima, Kutani and Kakiemon
1716-36: popularity of lacquering and netsuke as art forms

★ *Meiji Period* – (1868-1912)
Strong influence of Western cultures developing and growing. Japanese art appears to decline in many respects. Much trading with the West

Make the most of Miller's
When a large specialist well-publicised collection comes on the market, it tends to increase prices. Immediately after this, prices can fall slightly due to the main buyers having large stocks and the market being 'flooded'. This is usually temporary and does not affect very high quality items.

A large Ao-Kutani saucer dish, decorated in iron red, coloured enamels and gilt, rim repaired, signed on the base 'Dai Nihon Kutani sei, Fukuriken', 19thC, 24in (60cm).
$1,400-2,600

A Japanese Imari charger, in underglaze blue, iron red, green and gilt, early 19thC, 13½in (34cm).
$600-1,100

Garden Seats

A pair of Chinese garden seats, freely painted and enamelled with peony and prunus boughs on a celadon green glazed ground, late 19thC, 19in (48cm).
$1,700-3,000

A Canton 'famille rose' garden seat, with turquoise grounds enriched with foliage and fruit sprays, early 19thC, 19in (48cm).
$2,600-5,300

A blue and white barrel-shaped garden seat, painted with birds perched and in flight amongst rockwork and peony within bands of fruit and flower sprays, 19thC, 18½in (46.5cm).
$1,700-3,000

Jardinières

A large Imari jardinière, interior body crack, mid-19thC, 19in (48cm).
$4,000-6,800

A blue and white jardinière, decorated with panels of the Hundred Antiques and Shou characters, Kangxi, 8½in (21cm) diam.
$900-1,700

A Chinese 'famille rose' jardinière, with reserved panels on black ground, early 19thC, 16in (40cm).
$1,000-2,000

A 'famille rose' jardinière, painted with a procession before a pavilion set out for tea, late 19thC, 9½in (23.5cm) wide.
$600-1,100

A blue and white jardinière, painted in the 15thC style, 18thC, 9½in (23.5cm).
$1,400-2,600

A 'famille verte' jardinière, rim chip, 19thC, 11in (27.5cm) wide.
$600-1,100

A Canton jardinière, the exterior painted in 'famille rose' enamels, cracked, mid-19thC, 10in (25cm).
$900-1,700

A large Imari jardinière, painted in underglaze blue, iron red, colours and gilt, late 19thC, 21in (53cm) diam.
$4,000-7,500

Jars

A Yue Yao four-handled jar, the thin translucent glaze stopping above the foot with concave base, restored, 3rd/4thC A.D., 6in (14.5cm) diam.
$500-900

A Henan black-glazed ribbed jar, the globular body below a short unglazed rim, covered with a fine lustrous glaze, the glaze stopping irregularly around the cut buff stoneware foot, Song Dynasty, 5½in (13.5cm) diam.
$4,000-7,500

A large Cizhou jar, loosely painted in brown with bands of leaf scrolls on a cream ground, Ming Dynasty, 25in (62.5cm).
$1,700-3,000

A potiche and cover, enamelled with 2 dragons, green and yellow, Ming, 16in (40cm).
$1,800-3,800

A pair of late Ming blue and white jars and covers, painted in a blackish blue, one rim chipped, early 17thC, 5½in (14cm).
$1,000-2,000

A large late Ming blue and white oviform jar, painted with floral lappets on the shoulder and ruyi above the foot, neck cracked, early 17thC, 17in (42cm).
$2,600-5,300

A 'famille verte' broad baluster jar and cover, the neck with a band of cracked-ice and ribboned emblems, restoration to cover and finial, Kangxi, 16in (40cm).
$2,600-5,300

A pair of Chinese blue and white square tea jars, one with cover, the shoulders and necks mounted in bronze, minor frits, cover chipped, the porcelain Kangxi, 11½in (29cm).
$2,600-5,300

A Transitional blue and white jar and domed cover, delicately painted in a linear style filled-in with contrasting pale and dark washes, c1643, 12½in (31cm).
$1,600-2,800

A baluster jar, together with similar cover, slight damage, Transitional, 8in (20.5cm).
$1,600-2,800

A large Chinese blue and white broad baluster jar and domed cover, Kangxi, 22½in (56cm).
$5,000-9,000

A Chinese jar incised and decorated in underglaze blue, with flowers issuing from celadon rockwork and with copper red peonies and a flying bird in blue and copper red, six-character Kangxi mark and of the period, 8in (20cm) diam.
$1,000-2,000

A small Chinese blue and white jar and domed cover, Kangxi, 3½in (9cm).
$400-750

A blue and white jar, small neck chip, c1800, 11in (28cm).
$2,200-4,200

A Chinese green-dragon jar, pencilled in underglaze blue with 2 dragons in pursuit of flaming pearls, the shoulders with the 'Ba Jixiang' decoration, all picked out in translucent green enamel of pale emerald colour, seal mark and period of Qianlong, 8in (20cm).
$5,000-9,000

A Chinese Imari jar, the top painted with 2 underglaze blue 'qilin', early Qianlong, 25in (62cm).
$1,400-2,600

A 'famille jeune' jar, decorated with birds amongst prunus, 19thC, 9in (22.5cm).
$150-300

A Satsuma jar, decorated in coloured enamels and gilt on a finely crackled off-white ground, signed on the base 'Dai Nihon Satsuma yaki Tachibana Yoshinobu Isshuin' below a blue Shimazu 'mon', 19thC, 'sentoku' domed cover with 'kiku' finial, decorated in relief with the 'Takaramono' and flowers, 10in (25cm) high overall.
$4,000-7,500

A fine Arita blue and white jar, painted with 2 'ho-o' among paulownia, peony and rocks, late 17thC, 21in (53cm), wood cover.
$7,000-12,000

A Kyoto compressed globular koro, decorated in colours and gilt with figures among buildings and trees in a mountainous river landscape, signed on the base 'Kinzan', Meiji period, 3½in (8.5cm) diam., pierced silvered metal cover.
$1,700-3,000

A large Satsuma jar and domed cover, boldly decorated in iron red, colours and gilt with Tokugawa (aoi) 'mon', rim with some restoration, finial with some gilt rubbed off, body with restored crack, signed on the base in a rectangular reserve 'Kintozan', 19thC, 19in (48cm).
$1,000-2,000

Tea & Coffee Pots

A 'famille verte' teapot and cover, painted with birds perched on peony branches, restoration to handle and spout, Kangxi, 8in (20.5cm) wide.
$600-1,100

A Chinese export polychrome coffee pot and cover, painted on each side with a pair of European lovers, handle repaired, body crack, Qianlong, 10½in (26cm).
$1,000-2,000

A Kakiemon type Mokkogata teapot, vividly decorated in iron red and coloured enamels, handle cracked, spout with gold lacquer repair, cover repaired and chipped, 18th/19thC, 8in (19cm) long.
$2,000-4,500

An earthenware teapot, with gilt mark, 3½in (9cm) diam.
$200-450

A Chinese 'famille verte' wine pot and cover, c1700.
$800-1,500

A Satsuma wine pot and cover, slight chip to spout, 5in (12cm) diam.
$600-1,200

A blue and white teapot, Qianlong, c1760, 4½in (11cm).
$600-1,100

A large Cantonese baluster teapot and domed cover, Jiaqing, 9½in (23.5cm).
$800-1,500

A Chinese part tea set, painted in blue and white with gilding, c1790.
$400-750

Tureens

A Chinese 'famille rose' tureen and cover, the base with iron red animal head handles, star crack to base, crack to lid, Qianlong, 11in (28cm) diam.
$2,200-4,200

A 'famille rose' tureen, cover and under-dish, handles chipped, Qianlong, the stand 14in (35.5cm) wide.
$2,200-4,200

A pair of 'famille rose' shallow vegetable tureens, covers and stands, within iron red and black cell-pattern bands, the iron red and black trellis-pattern borders reserved with panels of gilt emblems, one tureen restored, late Qianlong, the stands 10in (25cm) long.
$5,000-9,000

Vases

A Yingqing oviform vase, the spreading foot with a band of key pattern, the glaze stopping around the neatly cut concave base, minor chip, Song Dynasty, 4½in (11.5cm).
$600-1,200

A rare Longquan celadon vase, modelled after a bronze of broad 'gu' shaped form, under a semi-translucent thick glaze filling the interior and the underside of the spreading hollow foot and stopping neatly around the orange-fired grey biscuit foot rim, cracks in foot and small rim crack, Southern Song/ Yuan Dynasty, 9½in (23.5cm).
$3,200-6,000

Two late Ming blue and white vases, meiping, both tops leaning to one side, glaze cracks, Wanli, 10½in (26cm).
$2,200-4,200

A pair of Chinese blue and white sauce tureens, Qianlong, the stands 7in (17cm) wide.
$1,600-2,800

A Transitional blue and white double-gourd vase, c1640, 13½in (33.5cm).
$4,000-7,500

A late Ming blue and white baluster vase, painted with a Buddhistic lion amongst scrolling peony, reserved on a scale-pattern ground at the shoulder, neck made up, Wanli, 12in (29cm).
$900-1,700

A large Ming blue and white slender meiping, painted with 3 pairs of scholars and attendants, neck damaged, long body crack, Wanli six-character mark on the shoulder and of the period, 23in (57.5cm).
$1,200-2,100

A polychrome goose tureen and cover, the webbed feet yellow and the tail feathers in shaded tones of russet, brown, black and grey, extensive restoration and repaint to cover, late Qianlong, c1780, 15in (37cm) long.
$7,000-12,000

A pair of Chinese Transitional period vases, c1650.
$9,000-15,000

A pair of bottle-shaped vases, covered with a rich blue glaze, Kangxi, 20½in (52.5cm).
$4,000-7,500

A Chinese blue and white tapering sleeve vase, Transitional, 7in (18cm).
$2,600-5,300

A Transitional blue and white sleeve vase, the waisted neck with stiff leaves, the neck and base with incised lines, c1640, 17½in (43.5cm).
$7,000-12,000

A vase of octagonal baluster form, painted in underglaze blue with figures outside a walled city in a hilly landscape between borders of formal flower branches, Kangxi, 12in (31cm).
$1,700-3,000

A large Transitional blue and white cylindrical brush pot, painted in a vivid colour with 3 quail, extended firing crack from rim, c1640, 10½in (26.5cm).
$2,200-4,200

A large vase of almost cylindrical form with trumpet neck, painted in underglaze blue, artemisia leaf mark, Kangxi, 21in (53cm).
$3,200-6,000

◁

A blue and white baluster vase, painted in a vivid blue on the panels with birds amongst chrysanthemum, encircled 'lingzhi' mark, Kangxi, 17½in (44cm).
$3,200-6,000

A Chinese Imari baluster vase and domed cover, painted in iron red, underglaze blue and gilt, cover similarly painted, cover restored and with replacement blanc-de-chine Buddhistic lion finial, late 17th/early 18thC, 25½in (64cm).
$3,200-6,000

▷

A pair of blue and white baluster vases and covers, painted all over with lotus in dense inky blue leafy scroll, one body and covers with old damage, Kangxi, 16½in (41cm).
$2,200-4,200

VALUE POINTS FOR CHINESE PORCELAIN

★ condition – this is always an important factor when dealing with porcelain. Some collectors will only buy perfect pieces – this is particularly the case with Far Eastern buyers. They will pay high prices for excellent condition. This affects the price considerably as a very good piece with a hair line crack or small chip can reduce the value by up to two thirds

★ rarity – as with most aspects of antiques, rare items fetch substantially more than common counterparts. This is also important when thinking of damage, as damage to a common piece is much more likely to affect the price dramatically than a similar damage to a rare piece

★ imperial v. export – most of the high prices for Chinese porcelain seem to come from the Hong Kong salerooms. The Far Eastern buyers tend to collect the pieces made by the Chinese potters for their own market rather than exportware. Hence prices are higher

A rare 'famille rose' European subject square baluster vase, painted almost certainly after a Dutch special commission, the domed base with a band of turquoise trellis such as one finds on wares decorated after designs by Cornelis Pronk, rim frits, edge and one foot corner chips, c1735, 12in (29.5cm).
$4,000-7,500

There is considerable controversy as to whether this design is from the Pronk workshop, or whether it just forms part of the distinctively European 'special commission' range of designs and vessels which have not been attributed to a particular source; see Howard and Ayres, op.cit. p.304, and Jorg, op.cit. The design comes from a Merian source book of botanical drawings.

A pair of vases, originally blue and white, now 'clobbered', decorated with jardinières of flowers and circular medallions within borders of petal ornament, on iron red and green grounds, Kangxi, 19in (48cm).
$3,200-6,000

Two blue and white baluster vases and domed covers, painted with a fisherman steering his craft, scholars playing a board game, restorations to covers and one neck, Qianlong, 17in (43cm).
$3,200-6,000

Two blue and white baluster vases, painted in a vivid colour with a phoenix in flight beside hydrangea sprays, Kangxi, 9in (22.5cm), wood covers.
$1,800-3,800

A pair of Chinese export porcelain vases and covers, in dark pink palette with brocade borders and rouge-de-fer bases, one cover restored, the other cover with restored lion dog, 12½in (31cm).
$3,200-6,000

A large 'famille rose' baluster vase and domed cover, with gilt Buddhistic lion finial, cover restored, Qianlong, 20in (50cm).
$1,800-3,800

A blue and white 'yen yen', decorated with 2 figures in a river landscape, foot chipped, Kangxi, 18in (45cm), with pierced wood stand.
$1,800-3,800

Two large 'famille verte' vases, one chipped, encircled iron red Wanli four-character mark, late Qing Dynasty, 25in (62.5cm).
$3,200-6,000

A pair of gourd-shape blue and white vases, one converted to a lamp, one with silver collar, as tops are missing, c1810, 14in (35cm).
$2,200-4,200

A pair of baluster shape vases, enriched with gilt, 17in (42.5cm).
$1,200-2,100

A pair of Canton vases, painted in 'famille rose' enamels with figures and panels of text between bands of flowers and insects, mid-19thC, 18in (45cm).
$1,200-2,100

An Imari vase, decorated in underglaze blue and overglaze red and gilt, late 19thC, 14½in (36cm).
$500-900

A Kyoto slender oviform vase, decorated in coloured enamels and gilt, signed on the base 'Kinkozan zo', late 19thC, 10½in (25.5cm).
$4,000-6,800

A Kyoto tapering rectangular vase, gilt slightly rubbed, signed in a square reserve 'Nihon Yozan', Meiji period, 5in (12.5cm).
$1,300-2,400

A large Canton vase, complete with carved wood stand, 26½in (66.5cm) high overall.
$1,200-2,100

A 'famille rose' butterflies bottle vase vividly painted, Guangxu four-character mark and of the period, 15½in (38.5cm).
$4,000-6,800

A pair of large Arita slender baluster vases, decorated in iron red, coloured enamels and gilt, on a red lacquered ground decorated in 'hiramakie', both with hairline cracks to neck, 19thC, 33½in (83.5cm).
$2,600-5,300

A pair of Imari double gourd vases, one rim chipped, early 19thC, 12in (30.5cm).
$1,600-2,800

A pair of Japanese Kutani porcelain vases and covers, with domed covers and 'Fo' dog finials in iron red, green, brown and gilt, 14½in (36cm).
$2,600-5,300

An Imari baluster vase and cover, the jar with an internal lid, 13in (33cm).
$800-1,500

A large Japanese Imari vase and cover, with alternating vertical bands of red and blue, 19thC, 19in (47.5cm).
$800-1,500

A gilded Imari ovoid vase and domed cover with dog of Fo knop, 19thC, 19in (47.5cm).
$1,000-2,000

A pair of Satsuma oviform vases, painted in colours and richly gilt, 9½in (23.5cm).
$1,300-2,400

Miscellaneous

A pair of Chinese export polychrome candlesticks, painted predominantly in 'famille verte' enamels, Qianlong, 7½in ((18.5cm).
$4,000-6,800

A Transitional blue and white candlestick after a European bronze original, short neck crack, c1640, 13in (32cm).
$600-1,200

A Dehua blanc-de-chine pierced cylindrical brush holder, the sides with an elaborately reticulated design, Kangxi, 5in (13cm).
$1,300-2,400

A gilt-metal mounted 'famille rose' rectangular snuff box and cover, moulded in shallow relief to resemble basketwork, slightly chipped and restoration to base, Qianlong, 3in (7cm) wide.
$4,000-6,800

A rare 'famille rose' wall sconce, restoration to extremities and hinge section, Qianlong, 8½ by 5½in (21 by 14cm).
$2,600-5,300

177

Chinese dynasties and marks

Earlier Dynasties

Shang Yin, c.1532-1027 B.C.
Western Zhou (Chou) 1027-770 B.C.
Spring and Autumn Annals 770-480 B.C.
Warring States 484-221 B.C.
Qin (Ch'in) 221-206 B.C.
Western Han 206 BC-24 AD
Eastern Han 25-220
Three Kingdoms 221-265
Six Dynasties 265-589
Wei 386-557

Sui 589-617
Tang (T'ang) 618-906
Five Dynasties 907-960
Liao 907-1125
Sung 960-1280
Chin 1115-1260
Yüan 1280-1368

Ming Dynasty

Hongwu (Hung Wu)
1368-1398

Yongle (Yung Lo)
1403-1424

Xuande (Hsüan Té)
1426-1435

Chenghua (Ch'éng Hua)
1465-1487

Hongzhi
(Hung Chih)
1488-1505)

Zhengde
(Chéng Té)
1506-1521

Jiajing
(Chia Ching)
1522-1566

Longqing
(Lung Ching)
1567-1572

Wanli (Wan Li)
1573-1620

Tianqi
(Tien Chi)
1621-1627

Chongzhen
(Ch'ung Chêng)
1628-1644

Qing (Ch'ing) Dynasty

Shunzhi
(Shun Chih)
1644-1661

Kangxi (K'ang Hsi)
1662-1722

Yongzheng (Yung Chêng)
1723-1735

Qianlong (Ch'ien Lung)
1736-1795'

Jiaqing (Chia Ch'ing)
1796-1820

Daoguang (Tao Kuang)
1821-1850

Xianfeng (Hsien Féng)
1851-1861

Tongzhi (T'ung Chih)
1862-1874

Guangxu (Kuang Hsu)
1875-1908

Xuantong
(Hsuan T'ung)
1909-1911

Hongxian
(Hung Hsien)
1916

178

An Irish bowl of fine colour and unusual form, c1790, 15in (37cm) long.
$1,600-2,800

A very rare Irish circular glass bowl of double ogee shape, entirely moulded with fine horizontal flutes, on plain stem with centre triple rings and square foot, of fine colour and in extremely fine condition, c1795, 9in (22cm).
$1,200-2,100

A heavy dark metal, double ogee, circular fruit bowl, with strawberry diamond- and facet-cut bowl, heavy ball knop stem with air-tear, plain conical foot, c1810, 9½in (24cm).
$600-1,200

A cut-crystal punch bowl, on separate base with 11 punch glasses, 6 liquor glasses and ladle.
$300-600

A set of 3 English shallow boat-shaped bowls, comprising: a pair and one slightly larger, with scalloped borders and cut swags and stars, on knopped stems and fluted feet, c1800, large bowl 6in (15cm) high.
$2,200-4,200

A pair of Georgian glass fruit bowls of rare form, with brilliant diamond and step cutting and silver-plated mounts, c1820, 9in (22.5cm).
$2,600-5,300

These were made in two parts in order to take ice.

A group of octagonal step-cut dessert dishes, c1820.
$200-450

A pink frosted bowl, with frilled and dimpled border painted with flowering foliage, on gilt metal stand, 13in (32.5cm) wide.
$400-750

A sugar basin of opaque white pressed glass, moulded with a portrait head of Benjamin Disraeli, Earl of Beaconsfield, registered by Henry Greener, Wear Flint Glass Works, Sunderland, 31st August 1878, 5½in (14cm).
$80-150

Candelabra

A baluster candlestick, the stem with true baluster section above a beaded knop and triple annulated basal knop, on a domed and terraced foot, c1745, 8in (19.5cm).
$1,300-2,400

An air-twist candlestick, the inverted baluster stem filled with spirals and base knop, on a domed and terraced foot, c1750, 8in (20cm).
$1,200-2,100

A candlestick, the pan-topped sconce with a double collar above a stem with a single cable air-twist, base collar and air-beaded knop, domed plain foot, c1745, 8in (20.5cm).
$900-1,700

A pair of candlesticks, with moulded pedestal stems, c1750.
$1,800-3,800

A pair of candlesticks, with facet-cut stems, c1770.
$1,800-3,800

A pair of Regency two-light candelabra, with ormolu mounts, hung with icicle drops, c1820.
$4,500-9,000

A Sowerby 'Queen Anne' pressed-glass candlestick, in 'Patent Ivory Queen's Ware', marked 'Queen Anne candlestick, J. Mortlock & Co., Oxford Street and Orchard Street, London' and bearing the Sowerby trade mark of a peacock's head, c1886, 10in (26cm).
$150-250

A pair of Regency cut-crystal and ormolu table candelabra, 16½in (41cm).
$6,000-12,000

A pair of Georgian ormolu-mounted, cut and coloured glass candlesticks, with blue and white jasper porcelain pedestals and beaded spreading bases, 13½in (34cm).
$3,200-6,000

▷ A pair of Regency diamond-cut candlesticks, with ormolu mounts, hung with icicle drops, c1820.
$1,700-3,000

◁ A pair of brass and glass candelabra, with hanging chains and drops, 19thC, 28in (70cm).
$1,200-2,100

Decanters

A rare pair of Lynn decanters, the tapered bodies with horizontal moulded bands, cut spire stoppers, c1750, 9in (22.5cm).
$1,600-2,800

A pair of Victorian pink opaque glass lustres under domes, in white and blue enamel and gilt, hung with 14 crystal drops, c1860, 14in (35cm).
$800-1,500

A pair of shouldered decanters and lozenge stoppers, engraved with 'Port' and 'White Wine' in quatrefoil labels, bordered with flowers and fruiting vine, c1755-60, 12in (29.5cm).
$1,700-3,000

A rare pair of decanters, the bodies cut all over with hollow diamond pattern, with steeple stoppers, c1765.
$1,700-3,000

A tapered decanter with cut base fluting and lunar-cut lozenge stopper, the body engraved with egg-and-tulip looped band, c1770, 10in (24.5cm).
$400-750

A Bristol blue carafe, engraved with grapes and vine leaves, with a Sheffield plate stopper, c1830.
$400-750

An Irish decanter of club shape with base fluting, scale cut neck, engraved with intertwined bands of laurel leaves with cut stars, cut lozenge stopper, c1780, 9in (23cm).
$400-750

l. A tapered decanter, the body engraved with rose sprays, cut lozenge stopper, c1780, 10in (25cm).
$400-900

r. A fine tapered decanter, the body mould fluted at base, engraved with sunflowers and looped husk decoration, facet-cut neck, cut lozenge stopper, c1780, 10in (24.5cm).
$400-900

A pair of Georgian wine decanters, documented as having been the property of William Wordsworth, mallet-shaped and panel-cut with facet-cut ringed-necks with disc stopper and replacement faceted ball stopper and red lacquer coasters, 14½in (36cm).
$600-1,200

A fine pair of Irish club-shaped decanters, with base and neck fluting, the bodies cut with a band of shallow diamonds, heart-shaped cut lozenge stoppers, c1780, 9½in (23.5cm).
$1,000-2,000

Miller's is a price Guide not a price List
The price ranges given reflect the average price a purchaser should pay for similar items. Condition, rarity of design or pattern, size, colour, pedigree, restoration and many other factors must be taken into account when assessing values.

A pair of tapering magnum decanters, with hobnail-cut bodies, panelled necks and shallow swag-cut shoulders and star bases, with lozenge stoppers, one neck chipped, late 18thC, 13½in (34cm).
$600-1,100

An Irish Cork decanter, the ovoid body with moulded fluting and cut-star decoration, 3 feathered neck rings, radially-cut lozenge stoppers, marked underneath Cork Glass Co., c1800, 9in (22cm).
$900-1,700

A good tapered decanter, the base and neck flute-cut, band of tulip and printy decoration, cut lunar stopper, c1780, 10in (25cm).
$500-900

An amber-tinted wine decanter, with single loop handle, plated mount to neck and matching stopper, 8½in (21cm).
$80-180

A pair of very fine prismatic step-cut and pillar-moulded Georgian decanters, c1830.
$600-1,100

A pair of very good quality decanters, the ovoid bodies cut with broad flutes and sprig decoration, 3 cut neck rings and cut mushroom stoppers, c1825, 9in (22cm).
$1,000-2,000

A most unusual heavy baluster glass, the trumpet bowl with pouring lip and folded rim, on a stem with inverted baluster knop with air-tear and base knop, domed folded foot, c1700, 6in (15cm).
$1,600-2,800

A calligraphic baluster goblet, attributed to Bastiaan Boers or François Crama, engraved in diamond point with the calligraphic inscription 'sine vulnere laedo', the inverted baluster stem enclosing a small tear above a folded conical foot, c1700, 7in (17.5cm).
$12,000-21,000

A fine quality Victorian cut glass decanter, c1880, 11½in (29.5cm).
$200-450

Drinking Glasses

An early baluster goblet, the large round funnel bowl with thickened base, set on a wide flattened knop and base knop with tears, conical folded foot, c1690-1700, 8in (19.5cm).
$2,200-4,200

Three 'heavy' baluster wine glasses, c1700-15, 5½in (14cm).
$1,200-2,100 each

A composite-stem Jacobite wine glass, the trumpet bowl engraved with a rose and one bud, on a stem with a beaded knop, central and base ball knops, domed and folded foot, c1750, 7in (17cm).
$1,600-2,800

A plain-stemmed landscape wine glass by David Wolff, on a plain stem and conical foot, The Hague, 1790, 6in (15cm).
$12,000-21,000

The stippled landscape is somewhat reminiscent of an arcadian scene painted by Paulus Constantijn La Fargue in 1778, Rijksmuseum, Amsterdam, depicting the Scheveningsche Boschjes situated between The Hague and the sea, at that time (and still) a very popular recreational area, ideal for promenading. The dunes seen in the distance on the glass would seem to confirm that location.

An armorial wine glass, by David Wolff, decorated with the crowned arms of Prussia, for Princess Frederika Sophia Wilhelmina, the wild men supporters standing on a broad-rimmed shaped solid base suspending a floral swag, on a plain stem and foot, The Hague, c1790, 6in (15cm).
$4,500-9,000

Although there are approximately 2 dozen recorded glasses stippled with the arms of the Princess's husband, Prince Willem V, and some 15 Alliance glasses with the arms of both the Prince and Princess, apart from the present example only 3 other glasses are known stipple-engraved with the arms of Princess Wilhelmina.

A rare Jacobite glass with a portrait of the Young Pretender, c1745.
$10,000-18,000

This glass has a particularly important inscription and portrait which adds considerably to its value.

l. A wine glass, the round funnel bowl with a band of engraved fruiting vine, on a stem with shoulder and base knopped multiple-spiral air-twist stem, plain conical foot, c1745, 5½in (14cm).
$300-600

r. A wine glass, the ogee bowl on a stem with centre cushion knop and multiple-spiral air-twist, plain conical foot, c1745, 6½in (14cm).
$400-750

A wine glass, with trumpet bowl on a drawn mercury-twist stem and domed foot, c1745, 7in (18cm).
$500-900

A plain-stemmed Jacobite wine glass, the funnel bowl with a seven-petalled rose and a bud, on a conical foot, c1750, 6in (15cm).
$600-1,200

A green wine glass, the cup-shaped bowl on a plain stem, conical foot, c1760, 5in (12.5cm).
$300-600

Three trumpet wine glasses with drawn air-twist stems, the centre glass with folded foot, c1740-50.
$300-600 each

l. A wine glass, the round funnel bowl with base moulding on a stem with cable air-twist, plain conical foot, c1750, 6½in (16cm).
$500-900

r. A wine glass, the round funnel bowl on a stem with single-corkscrew air-twist, plain conical foot, c1740, 6in (15cm).
$300-600

A lead wine glass, the round funnel bowl on a stem with a coarse incised twist, c1750, 6½in (16cm).
$800-1,500

This has an extremely rare folded conical foot for this type of glass.

l. A wine glass, the bell bowl on a stem with multiple-spiral air-twist, the twist starting in the base of the bowl, plain conical foot, c1745, 6½in (16cm).
$300-600

r. A wine glass, the waisted bowl on a stem similar to above, but with a vermicular collar round stem, c1745, 6½in (16cm).
$400-750

A wine glass, the round funnel bowl on a multiple-spiral air-twist stem with shoulder and central knops, plain conical foot, c1750, 6in (15cm).
$300-600

A fine cordial, the small fluted-trumpet bowl engraved with a floral rose band, on a stem with corkscrew mercury air-twist, folded conical foot, c1750, 6½in (16cm).
$900-1,700

A Jacobite wine glass, the bell bowl engraved with a rose, 2 buds and moth, double knopped multi-spiral air-twist stem, conical foot, c1750, 7in (17.5cm).
$900-1,700

A Jacobite wine glass, the bell bowl engraved with Jacobite rose and one bud, on a stem with multiple-spiral air-twist and vermicular collar, plain conical foot, c1750, 7in (17.5cm).
$1,300-2,400

Two unusual opaque-twist wine glasses, the ribbed round funnel bowls set on a double series opaque-twist stem, conical foot, c1760, 6in (15cm).
$300-600

A good mixed-twist wine glass, the bell bowl on a stem with central air-twist gauze and pair of outer opaque spiralling tapes, very rare folded foot, c1770, 6½in (16.5cm).
$600-1,200

Ex Horridge collection.

An incised-twist wine glass, the generous bell bowl with honeycomb-moulded lower part, on a conical foot, c1760, 7in (17.5cm).
$600-1,100

An ale glass, the extended funnel bowl engraved with hops and barley, on a double series air-twist stem, conical foot, c1750, 8in (19cm).
$600-1,100

A cordial glass, the bowl diamond-engraved by an amateur hand with a sailing ship, churches, a house and a lighthouse, inscribed 'Success to the Ellen Snow Monday Poole drew this glass', English, c1770, 6½in (15.5cm).
$600-1,100

A cordial glass, the small round funnel bowl set on a thick stem enclosing a single series opaque-twist, conical foot, c1760, 7in (16.5cm).
$600-1,100

A group of 18thC opaque-twist wine glasses, c1760.
$200-450 each

A wine glass, the ogee bowl engraved with a good hunting scene ▷ below a band of cross hatching, double series opaque-twist stem, plain conical foot, c1760, 5½in (14cm).
$800-1,500

Two 'Lynn' wine glasses.

l. A Beilby opaque-twist wine, the bowl decorated in white enamel with a border scroll, traces of gilding to rim, c1770, 5½in (14cm).
$1,800-3,800

r. A Beilby opaque-twist wine, the bowl decorated in white enamel with a border of fruiting vine, traces of gilding to rim, c1770, 6in (15cm).
$2,000-4,500

l. The rounded funnel bowl with horizontal moulded bands on lower half of bowl, on a double series opaque-twist stem, conical foot, c1760, 6in (15cm).
$600-1,100

r. The rounded funnel bowl with typical horizontal moulded bands, on a double series opaque-twist stem, conical foot, c1760, 5in (13cm).
$600-1,100

Three good-quality opaque-twist wine glasses, c1760.
$300-600 each

A tartan-twist wine glass with bell bowl, the stem with an opaque corkscrew core, edged with brick red and translucent green threads and entwined by 2 opaque threads, on a conical foot, c1760, 7in (17cm).
$4,000-7,500

A set of 3 ale glasses, the deep round funnel bowls engraved with hops and barley, on double-series opaque-twist stems, plain conical feet, c1760, 7½in (19cm).
$1,300-2,400

A ratafia glass, the slim funnel bowl engraved with a band of stylised decoration, moulded vertical ribs, on a double-series opaque-twist stem, conical foot, c1765, 8in (19cm).
$900-1,700

A 'Beilby' wine glass, the round funnel bowl enamelled in white with a temple and fir trees, on a stem with a double-series opaque-twist, plain conical foot, c1770, 5½in (14cm).
$900-1,700

This glass has all the stylistic decoration and enamel of a Beilby, but the decoration is on the front only. It may possibly have been a trial piece.

A facet-stemmed portrait wine glass by David Wolff, the ovoid bowl decorated with a portrait of Cornelus de Witt, the stem cut with hexagonal facets and on a conical foot, The Hague, 1780-85, 6in (15cm).
$11,000-20,000

In Dutch history the year 1672 is known as the disaster year. The plight of the country had become so desperate that finally the populace turned to the young Prince Willem III of Orange, the future King of England, whose talents and courage eventually saved the Republic from the dire effects of gross injustice inflicted by France and England.

There were, however, opponents of Orangist strategy, among whom were two renowned statesmen, the brothers de Witt: Cornelus (1623-72) and Johan (1625-72). At the height of their careers both were most brutally lynched by a pro-Orange mob in The Hague on August 27, 1672.

Memories of these events were stirred in 1755 by the publication of the volume of Wagenaar's Dutch History in which that era is dealt with. Between the years 1757 and 1758 a 'de Witt's war' on paper ensued between the Orangists and Patriots about the role the brothers de Witt had played in political history. The brothers were again brought to prominence in 1781 when they were hailed as paragons in an inciting Patriotic pamphlet.

A dram glass, the ogee bowl on a double series opaque-twist stem, c1760, 4in (10cm).
$300-600

A sweetmeat, the double ogee bowl with a dentillated rim, on a knopped stem with multiple-spiral opaque-twist, ribbed conical foot, c1760, 3in (7.5cm).
$400-750

A green wine glass, the rounded cup-shaped bowl set on a hollow ball, knopped stem and folded foot, c1760, 4in (10cm).
$600-1,100

Paperweights

A Baccarat garlanded white double-clematis weight, 3in (7.5cm) diam.
$1,400-2,600

A Clichy swirl weight, with alternate turquoise and white staves radiating from a central claret, green and white cane, 3½in (8.5cm) diam.
$1,300-2,400

A Bacchus close-concentric-millefiori weight, the central pale pink and white cane enclosed within 4 circles in pale shades of green, white, pink and blue, 4in (9.5cm) diam.
$1,400-2,600

Scent Bottles

Four clear scent bottles, probably by Apsley Pellatt, 3 with alternate diamond-cut gadrooned panels and plain shoulder, the 4th with plain gadrooning and diamond-cut shoulder, silver-gilt screw mounts, hallmarked 'T & J Phipps', London 1820.
$1,400-2,600

A cameo glass salts bottle, carved with flowers and ferns in opaque white on a satin ochre ground with silver screw top, in case, 19thC, 4in (10cm) long.   ▷
$400-900

A pear-shaped apothecaries bottle and stopper, impressed and over-gilt with the name 'Fortnum & Mason Parfumerie Bond Street London, by app to HRM Queen Victoria 1860'.
$300-600

A Thomas Webb & Son cameo glass swan's-head scent bottle, silver-gilt mount, reg'd mark no.11109, London 1884.
$1,600-2,800

Vases

A pair of Irish urn-shaped vases, with lemon squeezer feet, c1790.
$1,600-2,800

An opaque pale blue pressed-glass 'swan' vase, unmarked, c1870, 7in (17.5cm).
$80-150

A pair of French cut-glass vases, with ormolu mounts, c1820.
$1,800-3,800

TURNED TABLE LEGS OF THE SEVENTEENTH CENTURY

MONARCH CHRONOLOGY

Dates	Monarchs	Period
1558-1603	Elizabeth I	Elizabethan
1603-1625	James I	Jacobean
1625-1649	Charles I	Carolean
1649-1660	Commonwealth	Cromwellian
1660-1685	Charles II	Restoration
1685-1689	James II	Restoration
1689-1694	William & Mary	William & Mary
1694-1702	William III	William III
1702-1714	Anne	Queen Anne
1714-1727	George I	Early Georgian
1727-1760	George II	Georgian
1760-1812	George III	Late Georgian
1812-1820	George III	Regency
1820-1830	George IV	Late Regency
1830-1837	William IV	William IV
1837-1860	Victoria	Early Victorian
1860-1901	Victoria	Late Victorian
1901-1910	Edward VII	Edwardian

Beds

An oak bedstead of Elizabethan design, with plain double arched back and heavily carved border decoration, 72 by 54in (180 by 135cm).
$3,200-6,000

A carved oak tester bed, the whole carved in relief with guilloche and foliate friezes, on 2 turned and bulbous cup and cover supports, on block feet, parts 17thC, 103 by 70in (260 by 175cm).
$6,000-12,000

An Elizabethan oak full tester bedstead, some carving replaced, 85 by 54in (215 by 135cm).
$14,000-24,000

A Federal carved maple high post bedstead, with tapering square headposts, and later rails, Massachusetts, c1790-1810, 86 by 57in (218 by 143cm).
$11,000-20,000

A Federal maple high post bedstead, with baluster and ring turned headposts centering a rectangular headboard, the conforming footposts on inverted baluster and ring turned feet, New England c1800-1820, 86 by 54in (218 by 135cm).
$11,000-20,000

An oak tester bed, the footboard carved with panels of foliate strapwork and the motto 'Lord have mercy upon me', part early 17thC, 82 by 62in (208 by 156cm).
$6,000-12,000

A late Federal figured maple bedstead, with panelled and scrolled headboard, 4 old rails and modern tester, probably Pennsylvania, 80 by 61in (203 by 153cm).
$3,200-6,000

A fine oak and stained pine four poster bed, the bases replacements, late Elizabethan and later, the crewel-work bed cover and valance with bold designs of scrolling foliage, 102 by 74in (257 by 188cm).
$14,000-24,000

An oak four poster bed, the panelled headboard dated 1611, with carved canopy and posts, geometric ring-turned collars, boxspring and mattress, 17thC and later, 93 by 64in (235 by 160cm).
$6,000-12,000

Bookcases

A Chippendale cherrywood secretaire bookcase, rear feet restored, various small patches, Connecticut, c1765-1780, 90 by 38in (229 by 95cm).
$18,000-26,000

A Georgian oak bureau bookcase, with fitted interior and 4 long drawers beneath, with original brass handles and on bracket feet, 87 by 42in (222 by 107cm).
$2,200-4,200

A Victorian carved dark oak bookcase, with 2 glazed doors, 2 drawers and cupboards under, 42in (105cm).
$6,000-12,000

A Georgian oak bureau bookcase, with a shaped and fitted interior with well, repairs and some restorations, 80 by 36in (203 by 90cm).
$4,500-9,000

A Georgian oak bureau bookcase.
$2,200-4,200

A Victorian pollard oak inverted breakfront library bookcase, 108 by 190in (273 by 478cm).
$6,000-12,000

A Queen Anne oak bookcase, 70 by 48in (175 by 120cm).
$1,800-3,800

Bureaux

An early Georgian oak bureau, the fall front enclosing a fitted interior, with later bracket feet, with restorations, 38in (97cm).
$2,200-4,200

A George II oak bureau, with later added inlaid banding and bracket feet, 33in (83cm).
$1,800-3,800

A Queen Anne oak bureau, the fall flap with book rest, well fitted interior, on bracket feet, 36in (90cm).
$1,800-3,800

A very small two-part padoukwood bureau, with original carrying handles, stepped interior and well, c1720, 30in (75cm).
$12,000-21,000

A Queen Anne solid walnut kneehole bureau of fine colour and patina, stepped interior and a well.
$10,000-18,000

A yew veneered bureau, the fall flap crossbanded, cedar lined, with replacement old pierced brass plate handles and escutcheons, on replacement bracket feet, old restoration, early 18thC, 40in (100cm).
$1,800-3,800

A good example with well fitted interior would make substantially more in yew wood.

A fine George I star-inlaid elm bureau of good colour and patina, 36in (90cm).
$6,000-12,000

A Queen Anne walnut bureau, crossbanded and feather banded, with fitted interior, on later bun feet, 39in (98cm).
$18,000-26,000

A George II period red walnut bureau, with fitted interior, on replacement bracket feet, 37in (93cm).
$3,200-6,000

A Dutch bombé oak bureau, inlaid with marquetry, with brass grip handles, 18thC, 47in (118cm).
$2,600-5,300

A small oak bureau, with oak lined interior, 4 long drawers, on bracket feet, 18thC, 36in (90cm).
$1,300-2,400

A small faded oak bureau, with oak lined interior, mahogany crossbanded, on bracket feet, 18thC.
$2,200-4,200

An oak bureau, with fitted interior and 3 graduated drawers, on bracket feet, late 18thC, 35in (88cm).
$1,300-2,400

A good Georgian oak bureau, with chequered inlay and mahogany crossbanding, pressed plate handles, back needing restoration, c1780, 39in (98cm).
$3,200-6,000

An oak bureau, crossbanded in walnut, on bracket feet, 18thC, 34in (85cm).
$2,000-4,500

An English oak bureau, c1770, 36in (90cm).
$2,000-4,500

A George III oak bureau, with narrow mahogany crossbandings, the fall flap enclosing a fitted interior and with 4 graduated long drawers, on bracket feet, 36in (92cm).
$2,000-4,500

Cabinets

A good George I oak bureau cabinet of small proportions.
$6,000-12,000

A George II inlaid oak spice cabinet, with boxwood and ebony herringbone crossbanding, the fielded panel door inlaid with a spice plant, enclosing a fitted interior, top replaced, 28 by 22in (70 by 55cm).
$1,000-2,000

A Louis XV provincial oak and walnut side cabinet, with moulded rounded top and a pair of shaped panelled cupboard doors, enclosing a later shelf, on scrolled feet, 41in (104cm).
$1,800-3,800

A Dutch oak display cabinet, 19thC, 90in (228cm) high.
$1,800-3,800

Chairs

A Charles II oak wainscot chair, Leeds, c1680.
$4,000-7,500

A good Stuart period oak wainscot chair.
$4,000-7,500

A Charles I style oak armchair with arched scroll crest rail and panelled back, carved with scrolled strapwork, wood seat and on turned front legs and plain stretcher rails.
$1,200-2,100

A closely matched set of 8 highback fruitwood, ash and elm wheelback chairs, c1800.
$8000-13,500

A rare beechwood X-framed open armchair, the scrolled shaped back and squab seat covered in fragments of contemporary associated tapestry, 17thC.
$8,000-15,000

An English Hepplewhite elm chair, c1780.
$1,600-2,800

A set of 6 spindle-back elbow chairs, each with a triple row of spindles, rush seat and turned underframe, late 18thC.
$5,000-9,000

A fine Charles I beech open armchair, stretchers and rails with restorations, the finials later.
$3,200-6,000

A set of 10 and 2 similar yew and elm smokers bow armchairs.
$13,000-22,000

A closely matched set of 6 Macclesfield ladderback chairs, plus 2 armchairs, c1820.
$8000-13,500

A massive oak armchair, carved on a stamped ground, the rectangular back with a crenellated top and carved in deep relief with Daniel in the lions' den, inscribed 'My God hath sent his Angel and hath shut the lions' mouths', the open arms formed of scrolling winged beasts, the solid seat carved with flowerheads, on square legs, 19thC.
$1,200-2,100

A harlequin set of 6 Cromwellian dining chairs.
$10,000-18,000

A Queen Anne maple corner chair, with stepped horseshoe-shaped back over 3 tapering columnar supports above a rush seat, the front leg block and baluster-turned with pad foot, the legs joined by double stretchers, New England, 1735-1765, 27½in (68cm).
$1,800-3,800

A Chippendale period pierced splat chair, English, c1765.
$1,800-3,800

A rare and bold solid yew turners chair, 17thC.
$11,000-20,000

A set of 4 oak country Chippendale dining chairs, the backs having carved top rail above pierced splat, drop-in seats raised on chamfered square legs, first half 19thC.
$1,700-3,000

A set of 6 Cromwellian period oak dining chairs, the seats covered in floral Turkey needlework, the turned front legs with bobbin foot rails and stretcher rails, old restoration.
$10,000-18,000

A set of 8 George III country oak Hepplewhite chairs, c1800.
$6,000-12,000

A rare matching set of 10 walnut dining chairs, 8 singles and 2 armchairs, c1670
$20,000-30,000

Eight matching embossed leather dining chairs, Portuguese, late 17thC.
$8,000-15,000

A set of 6 carved oak dining chairs, 19thC.
$1,300-2,400

A pair of William and Mary walnut side chairs, now with Flemish floral verdure tapestry and mustard velvet squab cushions.
$3,200-6,000

A set of 8 Victorian dark carved oak dining chairs, with red hide seats and barley twist columns.
$2,000-4,500

A set of 4 Swiss oak hall chairs, with pierced shaped moulded backs, carved with wolves heads, with shaped and moulded solid seats.
$1,200-2,100

An unusual pair of yew Windsor armchairs, 18thC.
$1,800-3,800

A harlequin set of 10 Derbyshire/South Yorks. oak dining chairs, late 17thC.
$20,000-30,000

A closely matched set of 6 Billinge Wigan ladderback chairs, plus 2 armchairs, c1800.
$8000-13,500

A set of 4 Macclesfield ladderback chairs, with turned top rail, rush seats with turned front legs and stretcher.
$3,200-6,000

A rare set of 5 Charles II side chairs, c1675.
$12,000-21,000

Seven ash ladderback chairs, including one with arms, all with shaped ladderbacks, rush seats and turned underframes, 19thC.
$5,500-9,000

A harlequin set of 8 Lancashire carved panel back chairs, c1680.
$14,000-24,000

An elm and beech Windsor armchair with arched toprail and railed splats, the back possibly reduced, 18thC.
$1,300-2,400

A closely matched set of 6 spindleback chairs with Chippendale ears, plus 2 armchairs, c1800.
$6,000-12,000

A good set of 8 single elm and ash spindleback chairs with unusual spade cresting rails, c1800.
$6,000-12,000

A William and Mary maple bannister-back side chair, with shaped crest flanked by turned finials above 4 half-baluster supports, minor patch to stile pendants, New England, 1720-40, 41in (103cm) high.
$800-1,500

A set of 12 ash and elm spindleback chairs, the tops of the uprights stamped P.C. and W.C.
$1,800-3,800

An oak chair, the back with 2 arched and foliate carved horizontal stretchers, on turned and stretchered legs, restorations, 17thC.
$600-1,200

Four Lancashire spindle-back chairs, including 2 armchairs, with bun feet and stretchers, 19thC.
$2,000-4,500

An ash spindle back armchair with a pierced splat back, shaped seat, standing on turned supports with hoop form stretcher.
$1,000-2,000

A pair of yew-wood Windsor elbow chairs, with bow backs and pierced splats, dished elm seats and crinoline stretchers joining the turned supports, early 19thC.
$2,600-5,300

△ A good composed set of 8 Windsor high-back elbow chairs, in yew and elm, with pierced splats, mid-19thC.
$26,000-45,000

A walnut Windsor armchair, with an arched cresting rail and outscrolled arms with spindle supports, damaged arm, mid-18thC.
$2,000-4,500

A Georgian beech and elm Windsor chair, and a beech and elm Mendlesham chair, with curved arms above a solid seat on turned legs and stretchers, 19thC.
$800-1,500 each

A yew and elm Windsor armchair, with pierced vase-shaped splat, first half 19thC, 35in (87.5cm) high.
$1,300-2,400

A set of 6 ash and elm Windsor chairs, including 2 armchairs, the arched backs with pierced baluster vertical splat flanked by stick splats, late 18thC.
$7,000-12,000

A rare set of 8 Robert Pryor design yew Windsor armchairs, c1800.
$12,000-21,000 ▷

A fine harlequin set of 8 yew-wood Windsor armchairs, with decorative splats, early 19thC.
$18,000-26,000

A set of 6 yew wood Windsor style chairs with crinoline stretchers pierced and stick backs.
$12,000-21,000

An oak settle, the base with a row of 2 fine raised fielded panels, the front with 2 long raised and fielded panels, shaped arms on turned baluster supports, previously with end drawers, solid seat, c1700, 66in (165cm).
$1,300-2,400

A Gothic Revival oak stall, the solid back filled with tracery with hinged seat and linenfold panelled sides, with silk and metal thread squab cushion, 96 by 26in (242.5 by 65cm).
$2,000-4,500

A fine roundel carved oak coffer, late 16thC.
$4,000-7,500

A James I particularly well-carved and moulded oak coffer.
$4,000-6,800

Chests

A small coffer with unusual carving, late 16thC.
$4,000-7,500

A late Stuart oak chest faced with ebony and walnut veneers, the upper portion with one narrow and one deep drawer, the lower part with 2 panel doors enclosing 3 drawers, on stile feet, 48in (120cm).
$1,700-3,000

An oak coffer with plain cover, with panel sides and front, the central panel also inlaid with 2 small shields with initials AC and date 1604 in vermilion, with moulded stiles and muntins with stop fluting, with repairs, 17thC, 55in (139cm).
$4,000-7,500

A rare chestnut and walnut coffer with outstanding carving, Spanish origin, 16thC.
$14,000-24,000

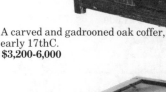

A carved and gadrooned oak coffer, early 17thC.
$3,200-6,000

A Continental oak coffer, the top a replacement, 16thC, 70in (175cm).
$4,000-7,500

A small oak coffer, early 17thC.
$2,600-5,300

A rare well-carved oak coffer, dated 1627, by repute from the Penn family, initialled I.P.
$4,500-9,000

A Continental walnut chest with beech top, fitted drawers and cupboards below, all with deeply moulded panels with iron lockplates, the plain panelled sides with iron carrying handles, 17thC, 43in (107.5cm).
$3,200-6,000

A small William and Mary oak chest-on-stand, c1695.
$10,000-18,000

A Jacobean walnut chest, fitted with 3 long drawers, with geometric moulded panels, 43in (107.5cm).
$3,200-6,000

A fine Charles I block fronted oak mule chest, c1640.
$3,200-6,000

A William and Mary birch high chest of drawers, in 2 sections, one rear ball foot restored, 44in (110cm).
$18,000-26,000

Provenance: Historic Deerfield Inc.

A Jacobean oak chest with brass oval loop handles and geometric moulded drawer fronts, 41in (102.5cm).
$1,300-2,400

A fine and unusual William and Mary oak mule chest, crossbanded with end grain oak, c1695.
$3,200-6,000

An English oak carved panelled coffer, good colour and patination, 17thC.
$1,600-2,800 ▷

A Commonwealth oak coffer, the plank top above a foliate and S-scroll carved frieze flanked by the initials T.D. and dated 1650, the front with a central panel of raised geometric mouldings, 51in (127cm).
$1,800-3,800

A well carved Charles II oak coffer.
$2,200-4,200

A Charles II oak chest, the top with moulded edge above 4 long drawers with thin geometrically panelled fronts flanked by split baluster turnings, 40½in (101cm).
$1,300-2,400

A William and Mary oyster-veneered chest with oak-lined drawers, the top with small roundel and half-round inlay and crossbanding, standing on 4 bun feet, not original, 37in (92.5cm).
$20,000-30,000

A Chippendale maple chest-on-chest, minor patches, New England, c1770-1785, 38in (95cm).
$7,000-12,000

A West Country painted oak coffer, late 17thC.
$1,800-3,800

A William and Mary walnut chest, the moulded top with an oval panel and banding of wavy chevron design in holly and walnut, with brass drop handles, on later turned feet, 37in (92.5cm).
$8,000-15,000

A mid-Georgian oak tallboy, crossbanded in fruitwood with fluted pilaster angles, the base with 2 long drawers, chamfered angles and ogee bracket feet, 46in (115cm).
$2,000-4,500

A cedarwood, fruitwood and oak chest in 2 sections, late 17thC, 41in (102.5cm).
$4,500-9,000

A rare William and Mary burr yew crossbanded chest of drawers, of good colour and patina, 36in (90cm).
$10,000-18,000

A mid-Georgian oak and mahogany crossbanded mule chest, 58in (145cm).
$1,000-2,000

An oak dower chest, the top with thumb mould edge, 3 fielded panels to the front with date, the drawers fitted with brass swan neck loop handles, on ogee bracket supports, 61in (152.5cm).
$800-1,500

A rare William and Mary solid yew carved coffer with bold carving to the front panels, good moulding, 2 drawers below, fine colour and patina, 50in (125cm).
$8,000-15,000

Cupboards

A rare small late Elizabethan inlaid oak court cupboard, of very fine colour and patina.
$12,000-21,000

A painted oak food cupboard, with rectangular top and one cupboard door, flanked by panels with pierced tracery on plank feet, early 16thC, 44in (110cm).
$14,000-24,000

A late Stuart cupboard, carved with foliate scrolls and strapwork designs, later back and handles, 60 by 58in (150 by 145cm).
$4,500-9,000

A good small James I three-tier standing or court cupboard, with fine carving, colour and patina.
$18,000-26,000

A Gothic hutch with pierced tracery, restored and lower door later, 15thC, 44 by 42in (110 by 105cm).
$20,000+

A rare oak Cromwellian hanging cupboard, with very good punched decoration, dated 1650.
$2,600-5,300

A rare carved and inlaid oak marriage cupboard, late 16th/early 17thC.
$18,000-26,000

A Flemish oak low cupboard, geometrically moulded and panelled doors inset with rosewood and ebony, flanked by lion mask corbels, on bun feet, c1680, 65in (162cm).
$4,500-9,000

An oak hall cupboard with pine top and back, mid-17thC. $8,000-15,000

An early Charles II arcaded oak press cupboard, dated 1665. $11,000-20,000

An early Georgian oak court cupboard, with moulded canopy with pendant finials above 3 panelled doors, the base with frieze drawers and panel doors on block feet, 58in (145cm). $4,000-6,800

A rare spindle-fronted wall hutch, with enclosed stepped cupboard below, c1680. $8,000-15,000

A fine early Georgian oak double corner cupboard, of excellent colour and patina. $4,000-7,500

A Flemish oak cupboard in 2 sections, with strapwork carved doors, on bun feet, constructed using some 17thC components, 49in (123cm). $1,700-3,000

A good William and Mary oak court cupbord in 2 stages, the upper having a carved scrollwork frieze with ownership triad w^{s}i and dated 1689, the lower having carved stiles and borders, with flute-moulded panelled doors, the interior having a single shelf, c1689, 63 by 72in (157 by 180cm). $4,000-6,800

This cupboard now has an added Victorian lightly-attached egg-and-dart mould which could be easily removed to restore the piece to virtually original condition; the lower hinges are Georgian replacements.

A French Provincial oak cupboard, with moulded cornice above a pair of panelled and carved cupboard doors, above a pair of panelled frieze drawers and a pair of cupboards, on scrolled feet, mid-18thC, 94 by 47in (237.5 by 117.5cm). $4,500-9,000

A good small carved oak livery cupboard, mid-17thC. $13,000-22,000

A fine carved oak livery cupboard, early 17thC.
$18,000-26,000

An oak cupboard with a pair of fielded panelled doors and a pair of drawers under, 17thC, 54in (135cm).
$2,200-4,200

An oak corner wall cupboard, with panelled door and pine interior, 18thC.
$400-750

A good small oak court cupboard of fine colour and patina, early 17thC.
$8,000-15,000

A large Georgian oak standing corner cupboard, the upper section enclosing shelves to the interior, over a single dummy drawer and double panelled cupboard below, all with brass H-shaped hinges, 49in (123cm).
$1,800-3,800

A carved oak food cupboard, on block feet, early 17thC.
$8,000-15,000

A rare spindle-fronted wall cupboard with spoon rack, 17thC.
$4,500-9,000

A carved oak livery cupboard, the rectangular top containing a cupboard enclosed by a pair of panelled doors with central fielded panel, on ring-turned baluster front supports united by an undertier with undulating frieze, on block feet, 52½in (131cm).
$4,000-6,800

A Charles II well carved oak court cupboard, good colour, patina and originality.
$10,000-18,000

A Georgian oak wall cupboard with 3 drawers below, good colour and patina.
$3,200-6,000

An oak hanging glass cupboard, the lower section with bobbin-turned spindle cupboards, part 17thC, 56½in (141cm).
$1,700-3,000

An oak livery cupboard, 18thC, 66in (165cm).
$2,000-4,500

A George II oak tallboy with pierced bracket feet, c1750.
$2,000-4,500

A rare small carved oak standing cupboard of good colour and patina, early 17thC.
$18,000-26,000

A yew hanging cupboard, 18thC, 78 by 42in (197.5 by 105cm).
$7,000-12,000

An unusual fruitwood corner cupboard of excellent colour and patina, mid-18thC.
$1,300-2,400

An oak cupboard on low stand, with a moulded cornice above 2 doors with arched shaped panels enclosing shelves, the stand with 3 drawers in a waved apron and with moulded block feet, 18thC, later backed, 79 by 51in (200 by 127.5cm).
$1,300-2,400

A good Charles II carved oak court cupboard.
$6,000-12,000

An oak cupboard, with fall-front and the interior now fitted with pigeon holes and shaped drawers, all with arched panels and mahogany crossbandings throughout, on bracket feet, partly 18thC, 61 by 62in (152.5 by 155cm).
$4,500-9,000

A two-door oak cupboard, early 18thC, 48 by 52in (120 by 130cm). $4,000-7,500

A small rare English oak bacon seat and table with drawer, panelled on all sides, 18thC. $8,000-15,000

A Louis XVI oak armoire with shaped panelled and fielded cupboard doors, on scrolled feet, 89 by 61in (225 by 152.5cm). $4,500-9,000

A good small carved oak court cupboard, dated 1704. $6,000-12,000

A French oak armoire, the moulded cornice with foliate carved frieze, with 2 similarly carved panelled doors on cabriole legs, Breton, late 18thC, 63in (158cm) $4,000-7,500

A Federal poplar and cherrywood corner cupboard, mid-Atlantic States, 1790-1810, 85 by 38in (215 by 95cm). $6,000-12,000

A George II oak hanging cupboard, c1745. $2,600-5,300

A Louis XV Provincial armoire, on scrolled feet, 95 by 57in (240 by 142.5cm). $4,000-6,800

An oak food hutch, 19thC, 36½in (90cm). $600-1,200

A Federal tiger-maple cupboard probably Virginia, feet restored, 1800-1810, 85 by 54½in (215 by 136cm). $8,000-15,000

An oak court cupboard, the top section with a projecting cornice hung with 2 finials above 3 ogee-arched fielded panelled doors, the base fitted with 3 drawers above 2 panelled doors, on block feet, 60in (150cm). $4,500-9,000

A late George III oak cupboard on base of 4 drawers, c1820.
$2,600-5,300

A Welsh oak deudarn, 2 doors with ogee-arched panels, 3 frieze drawers, 2 panelled doors below and on stile feet, 69 by 53in (172.5 by 132.5cm).
$2,200-4,200

A rare oak dresser with original lozenge carved panels, well shaped rack, good colour and patina, late 17thC.
$18,000-26,000

Dressers

A fine oak moulded dresser base of excellent quality, late 17thC, 32 by 102in (80 by 257.5cm).
$18,000-26,000

A good William and Mary oak dresser with moulded plank top above 4 drawers with moulded facings, shaped frieze on 3 turned front supports, 97in (245cm).
$6,000-12,000

An oak and elm dresser, with 3 plate shelves and 2 spice cupboards enclosed by arched doors, the base fitted with 3 drawers on square chamfered legs, 18thC, 80in (202.5cm).
$3,200-6,000

A Georgian oak dresser, with 3 mahogany crossbanded drawers on 4 square supports and 3 open shelves over, 74in (187.5cm).
$3,200-6,000

A rare Charles II dresser base with 3 barley twist front legs, fine colour and patina, 34 by 84in (85 by 212.5cm).
$11,000-20,000

◁ A Georgian oak dresser with plate rack.
$4,000-7,500

A Charles II oak dresser, ▷ the low raised back with 4 indented panels, fitted 4 drawers with double geometric panel fronts, engraved brass escutcheons and swan neck handles, 108in (272.5cm).
$18,000-26,000

A large Georgian oak Welsh dresser, with delft rack and 6 small drawers, 3 deep drawers, all with brass handles and lock escutcheons, shaped frieze, cabriole legs ending in pad feet, parts possibly of later date, 91in (230cm).
$6,000-12,000

A particularly fine oak dresser of excellent colour and patina, early 18thC.
$12,000-21,000

An unusually small oak canopy dresser, early 18thC, 50in (125cm).
$10,000-18,000

A small oak dresser base, fitted 3 short drawers with brass bail handles and escutcheons, on rectangular supports with potboard, 18thC, 51½in (128cm).
$6,000-12,000

A George I oak dresser base, good colour and patination, original brasses, c1720.
$8000-13,500

A fine Queen Anne walnut crossbanded cabriole-legged dresser base.
$10,000-18,000

A good oak dresser base of fine colour and patina, North Wales, early 18thC, 74in (187.5cm).
$12,000-21,000

A good North Wales oak dresser and rack with raised fielding, fine colour and patina, early 18thC, 72in (180cm).
$12,000-21,000

An oak Welsh dresser, with 5 baluster turned front legs and pot board, later brass handles and escutcheons, early 18thC, 98in (247.5cm).
$18,000-26,000

A small walnut potboard dresser and rack, early 18thC, 60in (150cm).
$18,000-26,000

An oak and fruitwood dresser base, with moulded rectangular top and 3 drawers with waved apron on cabriole legs, the drawers partly re-supported, early 18thC, 79in (200cm).
$6,000-12,000

An early Georgian oak dresser with moulded top, the frieze with 3 drawers and a waved apron on turned tapering legs with pad feet, 73½in (186cm).
$5,000-9,000

An oak dresser base, with 3 drawers with shaped apron on cabriole front legs with pad feet, 86in (217.5cm).
$6,000-12,000 ▷

A good potboard dresser and rack, mid-18thC.
$6,000-12,000

An oak potboard dresser base, North Wales, c1750.
$6,000-12,000

An oak 3-drawer dresser, the drawers crossbanded and edged with quadrant mould and period escutcheons, panelled ends and ogee moulding surround, 3 baluster turned front legs, c1700, 75in (190cm).
$8000-13,500

An oak dresser, the plate rack with shaped frieze, shelves and 2 cupboard doors, the base with 3 drawers and shaped apron raised on well shaped cabriole supports, the whole inlaid and crossbanded in mahogany, early 18thC, 74in (187.5cm).
$8,000-15,000

A solid yew dresser base, mid-18thC, 84in (212.5cm).
$18,000-26,000

A rare and bold oak dresser of unusual detail, early 18thC.
$12,000-21,000

◁ An outstanding inlaid and crossbanded oak dresser of very fine form, good colour and patina, mid-18thC.
$18,000-26,000

A fine George I ▷ crossbanded oak dresser base with breakfront and vertical reeding, 84in (212.5cm).
$14,000-24,000

A George II oak cupboard dresser, crossbanded with oak, c1740.
$8,000-15,000

An oak dresser with 4 moulded drawers with brass drop handles and escutcheons, shaped beaded apron with turned pendants and turned legs with block feet, one leg broken, handles old replacements, 98in (247.5cm).
$8,000-15,000

An oak dresser with spice drawers, excellent colour and patina, mid-18thC, 74in (187.5cm).
$10,000-18,000

A fine oak cupboard dresser base, crossbanded in burr elm, c1750.
$8,000-15,000

A good oak cupboard dresser with spice drawers, mid-18thC.
$12,000-21,000

An early George III oak cupboard dresser base, crossbanded with mahogany, c1760.
$8,000-15,000

A French Provincial dresser or buffet a deux corps in oak and chestnut, with original brass hinges and escutcheons, late 18thC, 90 by 54in (228 by 137cm).
$4,000-6,800

An oak low dresser with a crossbanded top and front with 3 drawers and a shaped apron, on tapering turned legs, with pointed pad feet, 33 by 76½in (82.5 by 193cm).
$4,500-9,000

An oak dresser base with later delft rack, with moulded cornice, shaped frieze and 3 shelves, flanked by 2 cupboards, mid-18thC, 69in (172.5cm).
$2,000-4,500

A fine Montgomery oak dresser and rack of excellent colour and patina, mid-18thC.
$12,000-21,000

A George III low oak dresser with 3 frieze drawers with bevelled panels above 2 cupboard doors, flanking a central panel, on stile feet, with restorations, 35 by 82in (87.5 by 207.5cm).
$3,200-6,000

A George III oak dresser with 3 drawers to the base and open shelves above, 63in (157.5cm).
$3,200-6,000

A fine George III oak Montgomeryshire pot boarded dresser, the lower section with 4 cockbeaded and crossbanded drawers, 81½ by 88in (206 by 222cm).
$14,000-24,000

A small oak dresser, 18thC.
$1,800-3,800

An oak dresser with 3 drawers in base and potboard under, the square top fitted with 3 plate shelves, 84 by 45in (212.5 by 112.5cm).
$2,600-5,300

A George III oak low dresser with the stiles forming the feet, some repairs, 32 by 73½in (80 by 186cm).
$6,000-12,000

An oak and inlaid Welsh dresser, the base having 3 top drawers and 3 dummy drawers, flanked by cupboards, with later moulded glass handles, 76 by 67in (192.5 by 167.5cm).
$2,600-5,300

A George III oak Welsh dresser base, with 4 mahogany crossbanded drawers with brass bail handles, on cabriole legs, 18thC, 29½ by 86½in (73 by 218cm).
$8,000-15,000

An oak mahogany-banded 9 drawer dresser base, with quarter fluted columns and 4 ogee feet, pierced plate handles and escutcheons, low gallery back, late 18thC, 84in (212.5cm).
$4,000-6,800

Stools

A small oak dresser.
$2,600-5,300

A good bold Charles I oak joint stool, in original order.
$4,000-6,800

A Charles II oak joint stool, with oblong moulded plank top on bobbin-turned supports and plain stretcher rails, one foot replaced, 16in (40cm).
$1,800-3,800

A good matching pair of oak joint stools, 17thC.
$8,000-15,000

A rare stool table, the flaps raised on lopers, 17thC.
$6,000-12,000

A good oak joint stool, the plank top raised above 4 turned legs, united by a stretcher at the base, 17thC.
$1,700-3,000

An oak joint stool, with moulded rectangular top and ring-turned legs joined by plain stretchers, with label initialled FMT, 17thC, 17in (42.5cm).
$2,000-4,500

A good oak box stool, early 17thC.
$6,000-12,000

l. A fine Charles II bobbin-turned oak joint stool
r. A bold oak joint stool, early 17thC.
$3,200-6,000 each

A William and Mary walnut stool, the padded top upholstered with a fragment of early 17thC tapestry, the scrolled legs with arched front stretchers and bobbin-turned H-shaped stretcher, 17in (42.5cm).
$4,500-9,000

Tables

A fine Charles II ▷
10-seater oak gateleg table, with exceptional turnings.
$20,000-45,000

An oak gateleg dining table, with oval twin-flap top on turned spreading knopped legs, joined by moulded stretchers, the top with minor replacements, 17thC, 75in (190cm) open.
$4,500-9,000

A large 10-seater oak gateleg table, the top French polished but of good originality, 17thC, 74in (187.5cm).
$6,000-12,000

A bold and fine Charles II oak double gateleg dining table with refined turnings, good colour and patina, seating 10-12.
$30,000-50,000

A fine walnut 6-seater gateleg table, late 17thC.
$10,000-18,000

An oak gateleg dining table, with oval twin-flap top and a later frieze drawer with bobbin turned frame, the frame partly reinforced, 17thC, 70in (175cm) open.
$6,000-12,000

A rare yew lowboy, the burr yew top with crossbanded edge and re-entrant corners above 3 drawers and raised upon turned legs with overlapping knees and pad feet, early 18thC.
$8,000-15,000

A small oak oval top gateleg table, fitted with a drawer, and flat section gates and turned legs, late 17thC, 36½ by 30in (91 by 75cm).
$2,000-4,500

An oak gateleg dining table, 19thC, extending to 60in (150cm).
$4,000-6,800

An important and large oak gateleg table, raised on bobbin and vase-shaped legs, joined by solid square stretchers, 66 by 72in (165 by 180cm) open.
$18,000-26,000

A solid yew 6-seater gateleg table, late 17thC.
$10,000-18,000

A good oak gateleg dining table with well turned under-frame, late 17thC.
$10,000-18,000

A yew and cedar gateleg table, fitted with 2 drawers, with baluster turned gates and supports, united by stretchers, late 17thC, 62in (155cm).
$24,000-50,000

A George II oak drop-leaf dining table of large size with deep elliptical leaves, on plain turned tapered legs with pad feet, 55 by 67in (138 by 167cm).
$2,600-5,300

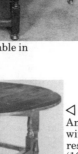

A very bold oak refectory table, early 17thC.
$24,000-42,000

◁ A large oak gateleg dining table, with twin-flap rectangular top, the double gateleg action with spirally turned legs and stretchers, re-supported, 66in (165cm) open.
$6,000-12,000

An oak 8-seater gateleg table in sound order, late 17thC.
$8,000-15,000

◁ An oak gateleg dining table with oval twin-flap top, minor restorations, 17thC, 67in (167.5cm) open.
$10,000-18,000

▷ A Charles II walnut side table, with later oak feet, 35in (87.5cm).
$5,500-9,000

A Jacobean oak refectory table, the triple plank top with clamped end, 94½in (238cm).
$6,000-12,000

▷

An oak dining table, the top with moulded edge, a small drawer one end and raised on 4 baluster turned supports, joined by H-stretchers, added block feet, 18thC, 30 by 70½in (75 by 175cm).
$4,500-9,000

A Chippendale cherrywood drop-leaf table, on moulded square legs, probably New Hampshire, tiny patch to edge of top, 1770-1790, 48in (120cm).
$3,200-6,000

Provenance: Josiah Bartlett, signatory of the Declaration of Independence from New Hampshire

An oak refectory table, dated 1667, good colour and patina, 102in (257.5cm).
$14,000-24,000 ▷

An oak lowboy, late 18thC.
$800-1,500

A fruitwood side table with drawer, 17thC, 33in (82.5cm).
$1,800-3,800 ▷

◁ A William and Mary oak side or refectory table, with a 3-plank top, the front frieze carved with a band of foliate scrolls and triad initials GWM and date 1691, on modified bulbous supports, 30 by 83½in (75 by 211cm).
$4,500-9,000

A good oak refectory table of bold
proportions, mid-17thC, 150in
(377cm).
$20,000-45,000

An oak refectory table, 17thC,
156in (392cm).
$20,000-45,000

A William and Mary side table, the
moulded top parquetry inlaid in
green-dyed ivory and various
woods, raised on barley sugar twist
elm legs with curved cross
stretchers uniting in an oval
parquetry panel, replacement
turned feet, 31in (77.5cm).
$20,000-30,000

A particularly fine oak refectory
table of good colour and patina, in
very original order, 17thC, 138in
(345cm).
$25,000-54,000

A George III oak refectory table, the
four-plank top with cleated ends,
lacking drawer, 115in (290cm).
$4,000-6,800

A Queen Anne cherrywood
candlestand, with a single drawer
over a cylindrical tapering pedestal
with a compressed ball turning, on
arched cabriole legs with shod
slipper feet, Pennsylvania, 1740-60,
17in (42.5cm).
$3,200-6,000

A Flemish oak side table, with
rectangular top and one panelled
frieze drawer with waved apron and
bulbous ring-turned tapering legs
with moulded waved stretchers,
with minor restorations, 17thC,
57in (142.5cm).
$4,500-9,000

A William and Mary oak side table
with rectangular top on slender
turned baluster and knopped legs,
joined by an X-shaped stretcher,
with bun feet, 18½in (46cm).
$6,000-12,000

A rare Flemish oak
side table, the
folding oval top
resting on a split
bobbin turned gate,
61½in (153cm).
$6,000-12,000

A Charles II oak side table, the top
with moulded edge above a panel
front frieze drawer, on baluster
turned legs, 27in (68cm).
$1,800-3,800

An oak cricket table with an octagonal top, on bobbin-turned legs joined by moulded square stretchers, some restoration, 17thC, 27 by 31½in (67.5 by 77.5cm).
$1,800-3,800

A Dutch oak rent table, the sliding top enclosing a frieze compartment, on ring-turned columns and dentil-arched apron united by stretchers, bearing an autograph note discussing his acquisition, signed H. Rider-Haggard, 1920, 17thC, 39in (98cm).
$2,000-4,500

A Federal birch and maple stand, with square top above a through-sliding drawer, New England, 1790-1810, 16in (40cm).
$2,200-4,200

A Charles II oak table settle with pivoting top, the base with hinged lid, carved lunette frieze, indented front and side panels, within moulded stiles, 60in (150cm).
$6,000-12,000

A Chippendale cherrywood serpentine-top tea table, Massachusetts, 1760-1790, 33in (82.5cm).
$3,200-6,000

A fine late Elizabethan oak drawleaf table with bold cup and cover legs, gadrooned frieze, in sound order, 168in (422.5cm) open.
$30,000-60,000

▷

A good oak farmhouse table with well chamfered legs, 18thC, 132in (332cm).
$10,000-18,000

An unusual early Georgian oak serving table, the hinged rectangular top enclosing a flap with 2 shelves and a lift-out tray beneath, with 3 frieze drawers, the cabriole legs joined by a concave-sided platform with pointed pad feet, 36in (90cm).
$6,000-12,000

A 3-plank oak trestle table, 79½in (201cm).
$3,200-6,000

Miscellaneous

◁ A rare oak bench table in sound original order, late 16thC, 72in (182.5cm).
$10,000-18,000

▷

An oak dough bin, 45in (112.5cm).
$800-1,500

Above: A rare small Charles II oak inlaid chest of drawers.
$18,000-26,000

Left: A rare and unusually small late Elizabethan carved oak 3-tier buffet.
$30,000-60,000

Provenance: Littlecote House

Above: A fine James I oak refectory table, with 6 well turned baluster legs, moulded stretchers, serpent carved front frieze, 132in (332cm).
$24,000-45,000

Left: A rare Charles II cushion moulded oak dresser base with 4 barley twist legs and split balusters between the drawers and blind fretwork centres.
$18,000-26,000

Provenance: Snitterton Hall, Derbyshire

The Private Dining Room…

English cooking and fresh food are the main principles of Chilston's excellent Dining Room. Breakfast, for instance, might include porridge, kidneys, bacon, scrambled and coddled eggs, kippers, kedgeree and muffins. A baron of beef, roast saddle of lamb, game, hams…and a variety of proper puddings feature on the menu.

The Reception Hall…

Atmosphere, warmth and light flickering from chandeliers welcome you to Chilston. Gleaming wood, bright with the patina of age, sets off a gathering of family portraits…dogs doze in front of a blazing log fire…and your hosts wait to receive you.

The Drawing Room…

With an emphasis placed upon comfort, the Drawing Room provides a quiet retreat. Somewhere to rest after a journey or a day's entertainment…to take tea in the afternoon or foregather with friends for a drink before dinner…and to relax completely at the end of the day.

The Bedrooms…

There are 25 bedrooms at Chilston, all of which have private bathrooms en suite. All are luxuriously appointed and delightfully furnished and guests are quite likely to find themselves in a four-poster bed. A special degree of personal comfort is provided by traditional hot-water bottles, complete with hand-knitted woollen covers.

A rare Regency black and gold lacquer side cabinet, decorated in raised gilt, 2 doors enclosing 20 drawers, 92in (234cm). **$70,000-120,000**

Above A Sheraton period satinwood and tortoise-shell cabinet on stand, with tulipwood crossbanding, serpentine apron, on square tapered legs ending with brass cappings.
$14,000-24,000

Left A Charles II black and gold lacquer cabinet on stand, the doors decorated with chased gilt metal, the interior with various-sized drawers, very heavily carved silvered stand, 45in (113cm) wide.
$24,000-45,000

Above A Queen Anne walnut secretaire cabinet, with brass carrying handles, the upper part fitted with shelves, the fall enclosing a fitted interior, 42in (106cm).
$12,000-21,000

Below A pair of mid Victorian ormolu mounted and walnut side cabinets, with three-quarter pierced galleries above cupboard doors centred by oval porcelain plaques, 26½in (66cm).
$18,000-26,000

A William III walnut veneered cabinet on stand with fitted interior, raised on an open stand with 5 barleysugar twist supports, some restoration.
$6,000-12,000

An ormolu-mounted scarlet boulle side cabinet, mid-19thC, 51in (129.5cm). **$2,600-5,300**

A William and Mary burr-yew bureau, inlaid crossbanded flap, stepped fitted interior with secret drawer, front legs with gateleg action, 32in (80cm).
$6,000-12,000

Left: A William III mulberry veneered bureau bookcase, sides banded in yewwood, interior with pigeonholes and 17 drawers, doors with yewwood and brass banding, fall flap revealing a well-fitted interior, on later bracket feet, 38in (95cm).
$140,000-220,000

Above left: A George III mahogany secretaire-cabinet, centre door enclosing pigeonholes, 11 small drawers, 5 drawers with silver plaques inscribed 'Bills Paid' etc., surrounding 2 doors inlaid with chequered lines, central drawer with baize-lined slide, 43in (109cm).
$160,000-250,000

Right: A Schleswig Holstein walnut and parcel gilt secretaire cabinet, upper part with shelves and drawers enclosed by a slightly arched door inset with a mirror, the fall to the bombé lower part enclosing fitted interior, late 18thC, 93in (232cm) high.
$12,000-21,000

Left: A George III mahogany and satinwood cylinder bureau, the solid sliding cylinder enclosing a fitted interior, 45in (114.5cm).
$12,000-21,000

A Chippendale cherrywood desk and bookcase, the upper part with scrolled pediment and 3 spiral-turned and leaf-carved finials, the lower section with thumb moulded lid, opening to a fitted interior, over 4 long drawers, 41½in (103cm).
$24,000-45,000

A Chippendale mahogany chest on chest, by James Bartram, the upper part moulded with swan's neck pediment, on ogee bracket feet, tip of cartouche missing, Philadelphia, c1750-70, 44½in (110cm).
$160,000-250,000

A Queen Anne walnut bureau cabinet.
$74,000-120,000

An Italian walnut and ivory marquetry bureau cabinet, inlaid with rosewood, mulberry and fruitwood, 18thC, 49in (122cm).
$20,000-30,000

Below A Dutch burr walnut veneered bureau cabinet, with fitted interior, the base with oak lined drawers, 18thC, 50in (126cm).
$18,000-26,000

Above An important William and Mary seaweed marquetry bureau cabinet, attributable to Gerrit Jensen, decorated overall with geometric panels of stylised foliate and arabesque inlay, the sloping section enclosing a fitted interior and rosewood veneered slide, all on later bracket feet, 39in (97cm).
$20,000-30,000

222

Lakeside Antiques

All work undertaken in our own large workshops by a group of highly skilled craftsmen.

Customers commissions gladly undertaken.

Large stock of good quality, mahogany and walnut furniture in most popular styles.

A set of 11 George III mahogany dining chairs, including an open armchair, the panelled solid toprails with fluted tapering splats, turned tapering legs with ribbed collars, later blocks, some replaced seat rails, and a later open armchair.
$30,000-54,000

A set of 4 George III mahogany dining chairs, a pair of armchairs and a pair of side chairs *en suite*, of later date.
$10,000-18,000

A pair of mahogany deep seat elbow chairs, with curved backs and moulded frames, scroll arms with ball terminals, padded seats, reeded frames, on sabre legs, English, c1805.
$14,000-24,000

A rare set of 6 Queen Anne walnut side chairs, on cabriole legs with pad and disc feet, 3 seat frames original, Annapolis, Maryland, 1740-60, 37½in (92.5cm).
$40,000-66,000

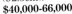

A set of 18 Regency dining side chairs, each with incurved tablet back and horizontal bar splat, stamped Gillows, Lancaster, early 19thC.
$18,000-26,000

A set of 4 Victorian rosewood dining chairs, the moulded pierced balloon backs carved with foliage, ribbon-tied strapwork and flowerheads with grotesque masks, the shaped padded seats with foliate centres to the seat rails on mask and husk cabriole legs with gilt metal rams head sabots.
$6,000-12,000

An unusual pair of walnut folding chairs, with suede upholstered seats and backs, the frames carved to simulate bamboo, with carrying handles, mid-19thC.
$6,000-12,000

A pair of Regency painted satinwood open armchairs, with pierced heart-shaped backs, one replaced front rail.
$18,000-26,000

A fine set of 6 George III painted open armchairs, the pierced shield-shaped backs painted in pastel shades with ribbon-tied feathers and summer flowers, with later caned bowed seats and ivory damask squab cushions, turned tapering legs, with similar decoration.
$36,000-60,000

A set of 6 Regency simulated rosewood and parcel gilt dining chairs, 3 seat frames inscribed 'Boxall'.
$30,000-50,000

A set of 12 George IV oak dining chairs in the manner of Morel and Seddon, the backs with octagonal finials and panelled friezes carved with quatrefoils.
$30,000-50,000

A George IV mahogany reading chair, attributed to Morgan and Saunders, spliced back foot.
$6,000-12,000

A fine Adam period carved giltwood settee in the manner of John Linnell, with carved and moulded serpentine back, 91in (230cm).
$12,000-21,000

A Regency brass-mounted mahogany tub bergère, with moulded arm supports.
$11,000-20,000

A rare pair of William and Mary scarlet and gold lacquer x-frame open armchairs, 26½in (65cm) wide.
$60,000-100,000

A George III giltwood sofa in the manner of John Linnell, 69in (172.5cm).
$12,000-21,000

A fine George I mahogany twin-back settee, the back with solid baluster splats with scroll and shell crestings, shepherd's crook arm supports, claw-and-ball feet, 55in (137.5cm).
$56,000-90,000

A Charles II oak sleeping armchair.
$6,000-12,000

Right A pair of George IV gilt-wood open arm chairs, attributed to Gillows of Lancaster. **$24,000-45,000**

A set of 6 George II giltwood side chairs, with slightly arched padded backs and upholstered seats, the hipped legs carved with lion masks with bared teeth, 27in (68cm).
$250,000-380,000

Right A William and Mary walnut armchair, with arched padded back, scrolled arm supports and upholstered seat, the cabriole legs joined by a scrolled stretcher. **$20,000-30,000**

A pair of mid 18thC mahogany library armchairs with padded backs, armrests and seats, on strapwork cabriole legs and pad feet.
$36,000-60,000

Right A pair of William and Mary walnut and beechwood side chairs, on moulded scrolled shaped legs with X-shaped stretchers. **$10,000-18,000**

A fine Charles II walnut stool with caned seat, on S-scroll legs.
$14,000-24,000

A George I gilt gesso stool with moulded frame, 24½in (60cm) wide.
$44,000-69,000

A pair of George II giltwood open armchairs, on imbricated cabriole legs.
$190,000-300,000

A Regency mahogany window seat of horseshoe shape, with caned seat and leather squab cushion, stamped IF twice, 63in (157.5cm).
$14,000-24,000

A pair of Regency mahogany metamorphic library armchairs, attributed to Morgan & Saunders, 23in (57.5cm).
£12,000-14,000   C

A pair of William IV oak throne armchairs, in the Gothic style, with quatrefoil roundels centred by the Wyndham crest, 53in (132.5cm) high.
$14,000-24,000

A Queen Anne oyster-veneered walnut chest, with geometric fruitwood stringing.
$10,000-18,000

A George I burr yew wood, laburnum crossbanded and inlaid coffer on stand, 49in (122cm).
$6,000-12,000

A George III mahogany secretaire chest, the chamfered top with hinged flap, 60in (150cm).
$10,000-18,000

A George III satinwood and mahogany serpentine chest, the top inlaid with a batswing oval, 41in (102cm).
$10,000-18,000

A Queen Anne burr walnut and featherstrung banded secretaire on chest, the crossbanded fall enclosing a fitted interior, on bracket feet.
$8,000-15,000

Above A Genoese kingwood and tulipwood crossbanded bombé commode surmounted by a serpentine moulded top, with gilt bronze rococo handle pulls and keyplates, 18thC, 54in (135cm).
$10,000-18,000

Right A walnut and crossbanded tallboy chest, 18thC, 40in (100cm).
$6,000-12,000

A George II mahogany commode, with rocaille handles and lockplates, 42in (105cm).
$30,000-60,000

A William and Mary black and gold lacquer cabinet on chest, 33½in (83cm) wide.
$20,000-30,000

A Louis XVI mahogany, kingwood, ormolu-mounted and inlaid demi-lune commode, with a drawer in the simulated fluted frieze, 2 crossbanded drawers below, with a similarly inlaid enclosed compartment to either side, stamped 'I.P. Dusautoy' and 'JME', 50in (125cm).
$24,000-45,000

A Louis XV French Provincial walnut commode of serpentine shape, the 3 drawers with incised moulded lines above a shaped apron carved with leafage design, continuing to hoof feet and with gilt brass handles formed from leafage swags and ribbon bows, 50in (125cm).
$10,000-18,000

Below A pair of George III satinwood, sycamore and marquetry commodes, cross-banded top with rosewood and inlaid with demi-patera and radiating flutes, the scalloped borders with fan lunettes and foliate scrolls outlined with boxwood lines, 46in (115cm).
$46,000-75,000

An early Louis XV rosewood, crossbanded and ormolu mounted serpentine commode, applied with rococo cartouche keyplate and foliate handles, pierced scroll sabot bracket feet, marble top defective, 51in (127cm).
$8,000-15,000

A fine Queen Anne giltwood and blue and gold verre eglomisé overmantel, with bevelled divided plate, 24 by 52½ (60 by 134cm).
$20,000-30,000

Above A fine George I giltwood mirror with rectangular bevelled plate with scrolling broken pediment, lacking cresting, and imbricated convex frieze, the sides with strapwork and foliate Corinthian pilasters, the pierced apron centred by a shell flanked by flowerheads and profile masks, 35in (87cm).
$20,000-30,000

Right A fine Charles II carved limewood mirror with later rectangular plate and overlapping foliage slip, the frame crisply carved with Royal arms and motto flanked by foliage and cherubs, the side with putti climbing amid trailing flowerheads and fruit, the base carved with shells, a crab, a lobster and sea serpents, applied to later rounded back with gilt border, some restoration, 64 by 48in (160 by 120cm).
$24,000-40,000

An Irish George III giltwood overmantel, 59 by 60in (147.5 by 150cm).
$30,000-50,000

A George II walnut mirror bevelled plate, 60 by 33in (150 by 84cm).
$13,000-22,000

A Regency burr yew breakfront bookcase, by Marsh & Tatham, inscribed, stencilled and branded with VR monogram, crown and 1866, 74in (188cm) wide.
$300,000-460,000

A pair of Regency rosewood card tables, the baize-lined tops inlaid with brass bands and dots, on tapering stepped shafts, 36in (90cm).
$10,000-18,000

Top A George I walnut bureau cabinet, the moulded cornice and later glazed arched cupboard door enclosing a fitted interior, the sloping flap enclosing a fitted interior, the sides with candle slides, the base with hinged writing flap and 4 long drawers, the top fitted with later cedar liners on later bracket feet, 21½in (53cm).
$36,000-60,000

Above A fine Regency and parcel gilt plum pudding mahogany centre table, the circular top banded and crossbanded in rosewood with fluted frieze on moulded tripartite fluted S-scroll shaft, arched waved, concave side plinth centred by a turned step finial, scrolled claw feet, 50½in (126cm) diam.
$14,000-24,000

Cf. a table illustrated in R. Edwards and P. Macquoid, The Dictionary of English Furniture, rev. edn., 1954, Vol III, p. 317, fig 35.

A Regency rosewood card table with leather and brass inlaid top, 37in (94cm).
$18,000-26,000

A Victorian satinwood, ebony and marquetry centre table, with waved frieze and a drawer at each end, on quadruple spirally turned shafts, 42in (105cm) wide.
$6,000-12,000

A fine Italian specimen marble circular table, in a variety of coloured marbles and hardstones, on a carved mahogany base, 19thC, 40in (101cm).
$20,000-30,000

A William and Mary padoukwood and oak gateleg dining table, 56in (140cm) wide, open.
$6,000-12,000

A rare Sheraton satinwood and mahogany oval library table with inset green tooled leather top, late 18thC, 72in (182.5cm).
$40,000-66,000

A fine George III mahogany four-pedestal dining table, with lion's paw brass casters, early 19thC, 174in (442cm).
$90,000-150,000

Left An early Victorian mahogany dining table, circular top divided into wedges to accommodate 16 leaves, baluster turned stop-fluted stem on quadruped base with lion's paw and scrolled feet, signed 'Johnstone and Jeaves Patentees', mid 19thC, 60in (152cm) diam.
$40,000-75,000

A Regency rosewood occasional table, 31in
(77.5cm).
$6,000-12,000

A Regency mahogany library table with leather-lined
swivelling circular top, fitted with 4 drawers, 36in
(90cm) diam.
$20,000-30,000

A George III walnut and mahogany
Pembroke table.
$12,000-21,000

A pair of gilt gesso centre tables, each with later inset
honey-coloured marble tops, 21in (52.5cm).
$12,000-21,000

An oak side table, with one frieze
drawer, 17thC, 37½in (94cm).
$9,000-15,000

A fine George II mahogany side table with rounded
rectangular Portor marble top, the panelled gadrooned
frieze crisply carved with scrolling foliage, 43½in
(108cm).
$24,000-40,000

Left An oak side table, mid-17thC, 28in (70cm).
$24,000-42,000

Above A pair of mahogany side tables, 78in (198cm) wide.
$22,000-40,000

A Milanese ebonised and ivory marquetry Blackamoor console table, with D-shaped top, raised on a crouching sculptured figure on a plinth base with bun feet, 19thC, 40in (100cm).
$6,000-12,000

A George II parcel gilt side table, 80in. **$50,000-90,000**

A Regency rosewood and brass inlaid sofa table, with well figured rectangular twin flap top bordered and inlaid with brass foliate scrolls, the baluster turned stem on outcurved quadruped base, 59in (147.5cm), extended.
$10,000-18,000

A pair of George III satinwood pier tables, with crossbanded D-shaped tops and fluted tapering legs with spade feet, 23in (57.5cm).
$20,000-30,000

A fine Irish mid-Georgian mahogany gateleg table with oval twin-flap top on cabriole legs, on hairy claw-and-ball feet, 58½in (145cm) wide.
$14,000-24,000

A Victorian mahogany specimen marble and semi-precious stone centre table, 27in (67.5cm) diam.
$10,000-18,000

A Regency parcel gilt and burr maple centre table, the circular top inlaid with foliate ebony banding with spreading gadrooned foliate shaft and concave sided tripartite platform base, with scrolled foliate feet, 52in (132.5cm) diam.
$20,000-30,000

A Regency faded rosewood drum table with crossbanded circular top, 36in (90cm) diam.
$12,000-21,000

An unusual Regency rosewood card table, with rounded baize-lined top inlaid with scrolling brass lines, on lotus leaf ormolu feet, 36in (90cm).
$18,000-26,000

A fine William and Mary burr walnut card table, with crossbanded semi-elliptical folding top, fitted with 3 drawers and 2 candle slides, 30in (75cm).
$34,000-57,000

A George III mahogany writing table with leather-lined top, and 3 frieze drawers either side, on square tapering legs, joined by plain stretchers, 59½in (151cm).
$14,000-24,000

A George III satinwood and rosewood tripod table, 26½in (67cm).
$18,000-26,000

A Regency rosewood and gilt metal mounted writing table, with leather inset three-quarter pierced galleried top, on lyre-form trestle ends, brass casters, 19thC, 44in (110cm).
$50,000-100,000

A Federal mahogany and bird's eye maple sewing table.
$70,000-130,000

Above A French kingwood crossbanded ormolu and porcelain mounted bureau plat in Louis XV taste, stamped EHR, 19thC, 38in (95cm).
$12,000-21,000

Right A Regency brass mounted mahogany wine cooler, 29½in (73cm).
$28,000-48,000

A George III mahogany davenport with carrying handle and pierced gallery, 15½in (38cm).
$13,000-22,000

An early George III mahogany tea and games table, 32½in (80cm).
$18,000-26,000

A fine William and Mary walnut writing or card table, the bun feet with restorations, 30in (75cm).
$18,000-26,000

A Regency mahogany library globe with Cary's terrestrial globe depicting 'the tracks and discoveries made by Captain Cook etc. dated March 1, 1815, additions and corrections to 1841', the stand with shaped ribbed tapering legs with foliate baluster collars joined by plain stretchers, centred by a glazed compass, 28in (70cm) diam.
$32,000-50,000

Left A Regency burr walnut and giltwood torchere, with concave-sided top on tapering foliate leopard's head supports, joined by a circular platform and claw feet, 17in (42.5cm).
$7,000-12,000

239

A pair of George III
chinoiserie japanned lacquer
pole screens.
$2,000-4,500

Right A pair of George III
mahogany urns and pedestals,
the vases with spirally turned
shaped lids, the bodies with
grotesque masks joined by
ribbon-tied drapery swags, the
socles with egg-and-oval collars
with gadrooned bases and square
plinths, 64in (160cm) high.
$36,000-60,000

A Regency mahogany three-tier
étagère, 24in (60cm) wide.
$20,000-30,000

A pair of Regency parcel gilt and tôle peinte
pole screens, early 19thC, 44in (110cm) high.
$12,000-21,000

A Regency scarlet and gold lacquered papier
mâché tray, stamped 'Clay, King Street, Covt.
Garden', on later red-painted and gilded bamboo
stand, 26in (65cm) wide.
$7,000-12,000

Right A marquetry boudoir grand piano by
Steinway & Sons, the case lid inscribed 'C Mellier
of London INV ET FECIT', 57 by 86in (142 by
218cm).
$18,000-26,000

BRITISH ANTIQUE EXPORTERS LTD

WHOLESALERS, EXPORTERS   PACKERS   SHIPPERS

HEAD OFFICE: QUEEN ELIZABETH AVENUE, BURGESS HILL, WEST SUSSEX, RH15 9RX   ENGLAND

TELEPHONE BURGESS HILL (04446) 45577   TELEX 87688 ANTIQE G

To: Auctioneers, Wholesalers and Retailers of
      antique furniture, porcelain and decorative items.

Dear Sirs

We offer the most comprehensive service available in the UK.

As wholesalers we sell 20ft and 40ft container-loads of
antique furniture, porcelain and decorative items of the
Georgian, Victorian, Edwardian and 1930's periods. Our
buyers are strategically placed throughout the UK in order
to take full advantage of regional pricing.

You can purchase a container from us for as little as £5,000.
This would be filled with mostly 1880's to 1930's furniture.
You could expect to pay approximately £7,000 to £10,000 for
a shipment of Victorian and Edwardian furniture and porcelain.
£10,000 to £25,000 would buy a Georgian, Queen Anne and
Chippendale style container.

Containers can be tailored to your exact requirements - for
example, you may deal only in office furniture and therefore
only buy desks, file cabinets and related office items.

Our terms are £1,500 deposit, the balance at time of arrival
of the container. If the merchandise should not be to your
liking for any reason whatsoever, we offer you your money
back in full, less one-way freight.

We have now opened a large showroom where you can purchase
individual items.

If you wish to visit the UK yourself and purchase individually
from your own sources, we will collect, pack and ship your
merchandise with speed and efficiency. Our rates are competi-
tive and our packing is the finest available anywhere in the
world. Our courier-finder service is second to none and we
have experienced couriers who are equipped with a car and the
knowledge of where to find the best buys.

If your business is buying English antiques, we are your contact.
We assure you of our best attention at all times.

Yours faithfully
BRITISH ANTIQUE EXPORTERS LTD

Norman Lefton
Chairman & Managing Director

DIRECTORS: N. LEFTON (Chairman & Managing),   P. V. LEFTON,   THE RT. HON. THE VISCOUNT EXMOUTH,   A. FIELD, MSC FBOA DCLP FSMC FAAO.
REGISTERED OFFICE: 12/13 SHIP STREET, BRIGHTON   REGISTERED No. 893406 ENGLAND
BANKERS: NATIONAL WESTMINSTER BANK LTD. 155 NORTH STREET, BRIGHTON, SUSSEX   THE CHASE MANHATTAN BANK, N.A., 410 PARK AVENUE, NEW YORK

THERE ARE A GREAT MANY ANTIQUE SHIPPERS IN BRITAIN

but few, if any, who are as quality conscious as Norman Lefton, Chairman and Managing Director of British Antique Exporters Ltd. of Burgess Hill, Nr. Brighton, Sussex. Twenty-four years' experience of shipping goods to all parts of the globe have confirmed his original belief that the way to build clients' confidence in his services is to supply them only with goods which are in first class saleable condition. To this end, he employs a cottage industry staff of over 50, from highly skilled, antique restorers, polishers and packers to representative buyers and executives. Through their knowledgeable hands passes each piece of furniture before it leaves the B.A.E. warehouses, ensuring that the overseas buyer will only receive the best and most saleable merchandise for their particular market. This attention to detail is obvious on a visit to the Burgess Hill showrooms where potential customers can view what must be the most varied assortment of Georgian, Victorian, Edwardian and 1930s furniture in the UK. One cannot fail to be impressed by, not only the varied range of merchandise but also the fact that each piece is in showroom condition awaiting shipment.

As one would expect, packing is considered somewhat of an art at B.A.E. and the manager in charge of the works ensures that each piece will reach its final destination in the condition a customer would wish. B.A.E. set a very high standard and, as a further means of improving each container load their customer/container liaison dept. invites each customer to return detailed information on the saleability of each piece in the container, thereby ensuring successful future shipments. This feedback of information is the all important factor which guarantees the profitability of future containers. "By this method" Mr. Lefton explains, "we have established that an average £7000 container will immediately it is unpacked at its final destination realise in the region of £10000 to £14000 for our clients selling the goods on a quick wholesale turnover basis". When visiting the warehouses various container loads can be seen in the course of completion. The intending buyer can then judge for himself which type of container load would best be suited to his market. In an average 20-foot container B.A.E. put approximately 75 to 150 pieces carefully selected to suit the particular destination. There are always at least 10 outstanding or unusual items in each shipment, but every piece included looks as though it has something special about it.

Based at Burgess Hill 7 miles from Brighton and on a direct rail link with London 39 miles (only 40 minutes journey) the Company is ideally situated to ship containers to all parts of the world. The showrooms, restoration and packing departments are open to overseas buyers and no visit to purchase antiques for re-sale in other countries is complete without a visit to their Burgess Hill premises where a welcome is always found.

BRITISH ANTIQUE EXPORTERS LTD

QUEEN ELIZABETH AVENUE   Member of L.A.P.A.D.A.
BURGESS HILL   Guild of Master Craftsmen
WEST SUSSEX, RH15 9RX, ENGLAND
Telex 87688
Cables BRITISH ANTIQUES BURGESS HILL

Telephone BURGESS HILL 011-44-446-45577

243

One of the more interesting trends within the furniture market, and one that is gaining increasing momentum has, on the surface at least, little to do with furniture.

In recent years, the major auction houses have made genuine and praiseworthy efforts to humanise their image, encouraging members of the general public to seek advice, to sell individual items, and to buy against the bids of dealers. And auctioneers throughout the length and breadth of the country are reporting increasing numbers of private buyers chancing their arms and buying direct from the saleroom instead of seeking the security afforded by buying from the High Street dealer. In

consequence, sales are well-attended, and bidding tends to be vigorous – particularly for middle-range furniture of good, usable quality.

Despite the fact that the quantity of goods passing through the salerooms is not particularly large, quality is normally consistently good. This is a factor which particularly affects the largest pieces of all – the mammoth library bookcases, for example, and massive oak refectory tables. Such pieces, when (and only when) of superb quality continue to rise to astronomical heights despite constant assurances that they have at last reached their limits.

In general terms, Southern buyers favour smaller pieces from the later Georgian and Regency periods, paying particular attention to usability rather than mere decoration, while Scottish salerooms are finding it comparatively easy to sell larger pieces such as partners' desks, breakfront bookcases and large dining tables with sets of eight to twelve chairs – with good repro items fetching notable sums.

In the longer term, such a trend bodes well for a buoyant market in which even the most hardened dealers will find themselves paying higher and higher prices for good, stock pieces, while items in need of restoration are likely to fall still further behind.

Beds

An Irish Chippendale four-poster bedstead, 96 by 54in (240 by 135cm), mid-18thC.
$11,000-20,000

This bed has been lengthened to take an interior box spring and mattress.

A walnut four-poster bed, the canopy carved with egg-and-dart ornament, the headboard carved with blind fretwork, with shaped footrest, 82in (208cm) wide.
$4,500-9,000

A painted four-poster bed, the canopy with pierced foliage, with shaped moulded headboard centred by a scallop and confronting foliate C-scrolls, with 2 moulded pillars, mattress and hangings, 103 by 88in (261.5 by 222.5cm).
$6,000-12,000

BEDS

Beds have invariably been altered. The most common change being in length – we are simply much taller now. This is regarded as acceptable generally if the bed is to be used. Size can account for considerable differences in price – a good Charles II four poster of, say, 4ft 7in wide by 6ft long might well be less desirable than a less good bed measuring 5ft 6in wide and 7ft long. Most bed buyers *do* want to use their 'fantasy' furniture while retaining 20thC comfort.

An Empire grain-painted and stenciled maple bed, New England, possibly Maine, 1830-1845, with a red and black grain-painted headboard and footboard, flanked by ring and vase turned posts, each with a ball finial, one post repaired, some chips, 56in (140cm) wide overall.
$2,000-3,000

A mahogany four-poster bed, the 2 cluster columns with foliate baluster bases with box-spring and mattress, one distressed leg, George III and later, 93 by 60in (236 by 152.5cm).
$6,000-12,000

A mahogany cradle, early 19thC, 34in (85cm).
$800-1,500

A late Federal mahogany 4 post tester bedstead, North Shore, Massachusetts, 1800-1820, 2 modern rails and 4 modern tester rails, foot posts 87in (220cm) high.
$3,500-4,500

A mahogany four-poster bed, the scrolled backboard headed by a shell and cartouche on reeded spreading posts, claw-and-ball feet headed by shells, with flame-pattern hangings in shades of brown outlined in beige, 94in (239cm) wide.
$8,000-15,000

Bonheur du jour

A George III mahogany bonheur du jour, the superstructure with 2 oval inlaid doors, pigeonholes and short drawers, 36½in (92cm) wide.
$8,000-13,500

A rare George III mahogany bonheur du jour the raised superstructure with bobbin-turned gallery, the lower part with secretaire drawer also containing compartments for inkwells, quills etc., 30in (75cm).
$5,000-9,000

A Regency mahogany bonheur du jour, inlaid with geometric ebonised lines, 33in (82.5cm).
$1,800-3,800

A Regency calamanderwood bonheur du jour, the base with hinged flap enclosing 2 wells, decorated later with an oval of summer flowers framed by trailing foliage above a cedar-lined drawer and a material-lined work-basket, on satinwood inlaid tapering legs, 26in (66cm) wide.
$6,000-12,000

A William IV flamed mahogany bonheur du jour with writing slope, set in a secretaire drawer.
$4,000-7,500

A Victorian inlaid walnut bonheur du jour, in the French style, 43in (107.5cm) wide.
$3,200-6,000

An Edwardian mahogany and satinwood crossbanded bonheur du jour, by T Willson of London, incised on drawer T Willson, 68 Great Queen Street, London, 45in (112.5cm) wide.
$1,700-3,000

A small mahogany breakfront bookcase, the lower part beneath a fluted chair rail with a pair of central fielded panelled doors flanked by glazed doors, on bracket feet, c1840, 92 by 72in (232.5 by 182.5cm).
$13,000-22,000

A mahogany breakfront bookcase, the moulded cornice above a boxwood inlaid frieze and trellis astragal glazed doors, 85in (215cm) wide.
$4,000-6,800

Bureau Bookcases

A late Georgian mahogany bureau bookcase, banded in satinwood and inlaid with boxwood lines, rippled fan ovals and angles, and leafy garlands, 47in (117.5cm).
$5,000-9,000

A Victorian mahogany breakfront bookcase, 94 by 114in (237.5 by 287.5cm).
$4,000-7,500

A Victorian mahogany breakfront three-tier bookcase, 110 by 142in (277.5 by 357.5cm).
$6,000-12,000

A gilt and pale green lacquered architectural breakfront bookcase, 73 by 100in (185 by 252.5cm).
$3,200-6,000

A walnut and feather banded bureau bookcase, early 18thC, 88 by 38in (222.5 by 95cm).
$10,000-18,000

A mahogany breakfront library bookcase, on plinth base, 19thC 101 by 132in (256 by 336cm).
$7,000-12,000

A Victorian mahogany breakfront library bookcase, 95 by 77in (240 b 195cm).
$4,500-9,000

A George III style breakfront library bookcase, banded and inlaid with boxwood lines, the top section with a dentilled cornice and broken swan-neck pediment applied with satinwood fanned roundels, 100 by 140in (252.5 by 352cm).
$12,000-21,000

It is interesting to note the strong price paid for this later reproduction. This is due to the high quality of the piece.

◁ A walnut bureau cabinet, the fall-flap enclosing a fitted interior abov 5 drawers, on later bracket feet, partly early 18thC, 22in (56cm) wide.
$14,000-24,000

Provenance: by repute Welbeck Abbey.

A figured walnut bureau bookcase, early 18thC, 83 by 39in (210 by 97.5cm).
$9,000-15,000

A Georgian mahogany bureau bookcase, 43in (107.5cm).
$4,000-7,500

An early George III mahogany bureau bookcase, the bureau with fitted interior above 4 graduated long drawers with original brass handles and escutcheons and side carrying handles (part missing), and on later turned feet, 78 by 40in (198 by 102cm).
$6,000-12,000

An exceptional Queen Anne period bureau bookcase, in finely figured walnut veneers, the cornice unusually with cushion frieze above a single bevelled mirrored door enclosing an interior with adjustable shelves and small fitted drawers, with good quality replaced brasswork, c1710, 80 by 26½in (202.5 by 66cm).
$32,000-60,000

The plate, brasswork and feet are good early replacements to this fine piece.

A George III mahogany bureau bookcase with associated upper section, the sloping fall front later inlaid with a shell medallion, quadrants and boxwood and ebony stringing, restored, 85 by 39½in (215 by 98.5cm).
$3,200-6,000

An early George III period mahogany bureau bookcase, having finely fret carved broken pediment and cornice, the fall-front enclosing drawers, pigeonholes, central cupboard, and secret compartments, some damage to pediment, 42½in (106cm) wide.
$36,000-60,000

A walnut, crossbanded and featherstrung bureau bookcase, the upper part with rosewood fitted interior with chequerstrung drawers and open compartments, the sloping fall enclosing a similarly decorated interior about an enclosed cupboard with sliding compartment concealing 2 drawers, early 18thC, 41in (102cm).
$20,000-30,000

A Georgian mahogany bureau, with later bookcase over, 34in (85cm) wide.
$2,200-4,200

A 'marriage' is perfectly acceptable, especially if well matched, if the price reflects it.

A mahogany bureau bookcase, the crossbanded fall enclosing a fitted interior of drawers and pigeonholes the two sections associated, basically late 18thC, 39½in (99cm) wide.
$2,200-4,200

A Queen Anne style bureau bookcase in walnut, the domed top with panelled door enclosing shelves above a candle slide, 66 by 21½in (165 by 53.5cm).
$5,000-9,000

A mid-Victorian mahogany bureau bookcase, 96 by 43in (242.5 by 107.5cm).
$1,000-2,000

A neo-classical style cylinder bureau bookcase, inlaid with boxwood lines and rosewood bands, 31½in (78.5cm).
$5,500-9,000

A Victorian mahogany cylinder bookcase, 47in (117.5cm) wide.
$2,200-4,200

A small Italian ebonised bureau bookcase, extensively decorated with etched ivory panels in the classical style, late 18thC, 32in (80cm) wide.
$2,200-4,200

Dwarf Bookcases

A pair of George III small open bookcases, decorated in gilt, grey and claret, c1800, 49 by 21½in (122.5 by 53.5cm).
$5,000-9,000

The decoration has been restored.

A Regency mahogany open bookcase, 34½in (87.5cm) wide.
$3,200-6,000

An Edwardian satinwood bureau bookcase, banded in rosewood and inlaid with boxwood and ebony lines, 31½in (78.5cm) wide.
$3,200-6,000

A George IV mahogany bookstand, with gadrooned and bobbin and reel applied moulded borders, 46in (115cm).
$1,700-3,000

A late Regency rosewood dwarf breakfront bookcase, 84in (212.5cm).
$3,200-6,000

A good pair of George III mahogany open bookshelves.
$8,000-15,000

A Regency mahogany and gilt metal mounted breakfront dwarf open bookcase, the flowerhead decorated frieze fitted with a central drawer, 85in (215cm).
$7,000-12,000

A small Regency bookcase, having graduated shelves flanked by original brass carrying handles, with original brass casters, the whole decorated in simulated rosewood with fine gilt stringing, c1815, 46 by 24in (115 by 60cm).
$4,000-6,800

A Victorian breakfront walnut bookcase, decorated with parquetry bands and ormolu mounts, 85in (215cm) wide.
$1,300-2,400

An Edwardian satinwood revolving bookcase, 56in (140cm) high.
$4,000-6,800

Library Bookcases

An Edwardian mahogany and satinwood banded low bookcase, the crossbanded top above a ribbon and bellflower swag frieze, 50½in (126cm) wide.
$900-1,700

Make the most of Miller's

Miller's is completely different each year. Each edition contains completely NEW photographs. This is not an updated publication. We never repeat the same photograph.

A George III mahogany bookcase or display cabinet, the upper part with moulded cornice and blind fret frieze, c1780, 74½ by 35in (188.5 by 87.5cm).
$6,000-12,000

A George III mahogany bookcase, 99in (250cm).
$6,000-12,000

BOOKCASES

★ Check that the glazing bars match the rest of the bookcase in quality, timber and age. Breakfront wardrobes of the mid to late 19thC can be turned into bookcases by removing the solid panels to the doors and glazing the frames

★ during the late 19thC many old glazed door cabinets were removed from their bureau or cupboard bases to have feet added and the tops fitted in to make 'Georgian' display or bookcases. This was not an 18thC form; the correct version was much taller and often had drawers to the frieze base. The low 'dwarf' bookcases without doors became popular during the late 18thC

★ the earliest form of adjustable shelf on the better quality bookcases was achieved by cutting rabbets into the sides of the cabinet into which the shelves could slide. Next came a toothed ladder at each side, the removable rungs forming the shelf rests. Finally, by the end of the 18thC, came movable pegs fitting into holes. Regency examples were often made of gilt metal or brass

★ check when a bookcase sits on a bureau or cupboard base that it is slightly smaller than the base, and it is preferable that the retaining moulding is fixed to the base not the top; also, it is unlikely that the top surface to such a base would have been veneered originally

★ a bureau made to take a bookcase on top will have a steeper angle to the fall front to create a greater depth to accommodate the case or cabinet

A George III mahogany bookcase, 79½ by 36½in (202 by 93cm). **$5,500-9,000**

A George III mahogany bookcase, 50in (125cm) wide. **$3,200-6,000**

A Georgian mahogany bookcase, 110 by 63½in (277.5 by 158.5cm). **$3,200-6,000**

A Regency mahogany library bookcase, with inlaid ebony and boxwood lined doors, 102 by 88in (257.5 by 222.5cm). **$8,000-13,500**

A George III mahogany bookcase, inlaid with ebony stringing, relined drawers, c1810, 38½in (96cm) wide. **$2,200-4,200**

A George III mahogany bookcase of Gothic style, designed for an alcove, 82½ by 37in (209.5 by 93.5cm). **$4,000-7,500**

A George III mahogany bookcase, with moulded dentilled cornice, 98 by 59½in (249 by 151cm). **$4,000-7,500**

A George III mahogany bookcase-on-stand, the base with blind fretwork frieze and pierced angle brackets on moulded square supports joined by moulded cross stretchers, 47in (117.5cm) wide. **$3,200-6,000**

In the Furniture section if there is only one measurement it usually refers to the width of the piece.

A Regency mahogany library alcove bookcase, with an oak carcase, the mahogany front with a domed moulded cornice above a pair of glazed tracery doors, the sides later infilled, 100 by 87in (252.5 by 220cm). **$7,000-12,000**

An oak book press of the Pepys model. **$9,000-15,000**

The celebrated 12 bookcases commissioned by Samuel Pepys, secretary to the Navy, in the late 1660s from 'Sympson the joyner' were bequeathed to Magdalene College Cambridge. Pepys is credited with the invention of the free standing case book press.

A Regency mahogany bookcase inlaid with ebonised lines, 52½in (131cm).
$4,000-7,500

A bookcase, veneered in walnut with marquetry and ebonised inlay, 19thC, 47in (117.5cm).
$3,200-6,000

A Victorian rosewood bookcase, 53in (133cm) wide.
$1,800-3,800

An early Victorian mahogany bookcase, 45½in (113.5cm).
$1,600-2,800

A mahogany bookcase, on matched contemporary base, early 19thC, 51½in (128.5cm) wide.
$2,200-4,200

A pair of George IV mahogany standing pedestal bookcases, 23½in (58.5cm).
$3,200-6,000

A Victorian mahogany and ebonised library bookcase, 90 by 115in (225 by 288cm).
$2,000-4,500

A set of four oak double sided library bookcases, 113 by 102in (285 by 257.5cm).
$14,000-24,000

A Victorian mahogany bookcase, 61in (152.5cm) wide.
$1,700-3,000

A large Victorian pollard oak breakfront bookcase cabinet, 108 by 84in (272.5 by 212.5cm). ▷
$5,500-9,000

A mahogany bookcase, c1920, 90in (227.5cm) high. ▷
$1,300-2,400

A large Victorian mahogany
bookcase, 78in (197.5cm).
$1,700-3,000

A mahogany bookcase cupboard,
19thC, 76½ by 43in (194 by 109cm).
$4,000-6,800

A Victorian mahogany library
bookcase, 98 by 34in (247.5 by
85cm).
$800-1,500

Secretaire Bookcases

A pair of Edwardian satinwood
bookcases, inlaid in various woods,
the bases banded in coromandel, the
tops centred by ovals inlaid with a
satyr leading a goat, above 2
drawers centred by trophies, on
square tapering legs hung with
pendant bellflowers, 97in (245cm).
$6,000-12,000

A George III mahogany secretaire
bookcase, the pull-out secretaire
drawer below with fall-flap opening
to reveal a fitted interior of
pigeonholes and drawers, 91 by
43in (230 by 107.5cm).
$2,600-5,300

An Edwardian bookcase, inlaid
with parquetry and boxwood
stringing, 47in (117.5cm) wide.
$900-1,700

A small George III mahogany
secretaire bookcase, the moulded
coved cornice with satinwood
banding above a pair of doors with
arched astragal glazing bars and
mainly original glass, c1800, 86 by
34in (217.5 by 85cm).
$10,000-18,000

A George III mahogany secretaire
bookcase, 37in (93cm) wide.
$5,000-9,000

A George III breakfront secretaire
library bookcase.
$11,000-20,000

A George III mahogany and satinwood secretaire bookcase, 100 by 39½in (252.5 by 100.5cm).
$5,000-9,000

A mahogany secretaire bookcase, c1800, 46in (115cm) wide.
$2,200-4,200

A late George III mahogany secretaire bookcase, 92 by 54in (232.5 by 135cm).
$2,000-4,500

A Georgian mahogany secretaire bookcase, the lower section having dummy top drawer, revealing a secretaire base fitted with writing slide concealing 6 filing drawers and 2 secret drawers, 87in (220cm) high.
$8,000-15,000

A mahogany secretaire bookcase, the secretaire drawer fitted with satinwood faced small drawers and pigeonholes, early 19thC, 40in (100cm) wide.
$9,000-15,000

A Chippendale walnut secretary bookcase, Pennsylvania, c1760-85, the upper with a molded swan's neck pediment ending in carved rosettes above a pair of panelled doors opening to a shelved interior, the lower section with a slant front opening to a fitted interior, prospect door probably restored, restorations to feet, 96¼in (243cm) high.
$16,000-19,000

A Federal mahogany veneer desk and bookcase, Salem, 1780-1800, the upper case with a scrolled pediment with carved flower rosettes centering a plinth with an urn finial, the lower case serpentine, with drawer opening to form a writing surface and fitted with small drawers, the center drawer fan-carved and with a hidden compartment, the fitted drawer above 3 graduated long drawers, on ogee bracket feet, 92in (232cm) high.
$15,000-17,000

Alfred M. Frankfurter, 'The Furniture of Samuel McIntire, Master Carver', The Antiquarian (November 1930) pp41-45, illustration p44.

A Georgian mahogany secretaire bookcase, 45in (112.5cm).
$4,500-9,000

A Regency mahogany secretaire bookcase, 87 by 37½in (221 by 95cm).
$7,000-12,000

A late George III mahogany secretaire bookcase, decorated with inlaid boxwood stringing, 89 by 43in (225 by 107.5cm).
$7,000-12,000

A Regency mahogany secretaire bookcase, the secretaire drawer with satinwood faced small drawers, apron drawers and pigeonholes, 48½in (121cm) wide.
$3,200-6,000

A Regency mahogany secretaire bookcase, the lower part a secretaire with good interior containing a tambour cupboard, small drawers and pigeonholes, c1810, 91 by 42½in (230 by 106cm).
$14,000-24,000

A William IV mahogany secretaire bookcase, decorated with gadrooned and beaded mouldings, 44in (110cm) wide.
$4,000-7,500

A William IV mahogany secretaire bookcase, applied with ebonised beadings and fitted with brass mounts, 56in (140cm).
$3,200-6,000

A late Regency mahogany and ebony moulded secretaire bookcase, 100 by 61in (252 by 152cm).
$8,000-13,500

A Federal mahogany secretary, Boston area, 1800-1815, in 3 sections, the pediment centering 2 C-scroll bracketed plinths with urn finials, the bookcase section with double round-arched and reeded mullion glazed doors, the lower section with hinged writing flap, small chips, 80in (202cm) high.
$9,000-11,000

A Victorian painted and decorated pine secretary bookcase, Heywood Brothers, Gardner Massachusetts, painting attributed to Edward and Thomas Hill, c1860, the middle section with a slant front and an elliptical painted scene, opening to a fitted interior, above a beaded long drawer with gilt scroll decoration and floral sprays, some restoration to paint, feet reduced, 87½in (221cm) high.
$18,000-22,000

This secretary is closely related to a painted bedstead made for the president of Heywood Brothers, now in the collection of the Museum of Fine Arts, Boston. These pieces represent the highest quality in so-called cottage furniture because of their fine painting by the English-trained ornamental painter Edward Hill (1843-1923) and his brother Thomas Hill (1829-1908) who were employed by the Heywood factory before becoming landscape painters in their late careers. The bedstead is illustrated in Jonathan L. Fairbanks, 'A Decade of Collecting . . . at the Museum of Fine Arts, Boston', Antiques (September 1981), pl XXVIII, p614.

An early Victorian mahogany secretaire bookcase, on bun feet, 48in (120cm).
$2,600-5,300

A Victorian satinwood secretaire bookcase, of neo-classical design, inlaid with masks, amaranth cornucopiae and harewood foliate marquetry arabesques, 44½in (111cm).
$8,000-15,000

A Victorian mahogany secretaire bookcase, 34in (85cm).
$2,200-4,200

Bureaux

A William and Mary walnut table bureau, the fall-flap enclosing a fitted interior, 22½in (56cm) wide.
$2,200-4,200

A Queen Anne walnut bureau, with a quarter veneered flap decorated with feather banding, 40 by 36in (100 by 90cm).
$6,000-12,000

A small Queen Anne walnut bureau, the figured herringbone inlaid crossbanded surface with slight gallery, the fall including a book rest opening to reveal a well fitted interior with a well, pigeonholes and small stepped drawers, all with good quality replaced brasswork, the veneers to the feet restored, c1710, 35½ by 30in (88.5 by 75cm).
$26,000-45,000

A Queen Anne walnut slant front desk, Pennsylvania, 1735-1770, the interior with 8 valanced pigeonholes and 4 short drawers above a board with slides to reveal a storage well, 30½in (76cm) wide.
$13,000-16,000

A walnut bureau, crossbanded and feather inlaid with burr veneer to the fall-flap enclosing a fitted interior with 2 sliding panels to the well, small drawers and central cupboard, early 18thC, 39in (97.5cm) wide.
$5,000-9,000

A George III mahogany bureau, the flap enclosing a fitted interior, 28in (70cm).
$4,000-7,500

A George III mahogany and inlaid bureau, the satinwood banded fall inlaid with an oval swagged urn medallion, 45in (112cm) wide. **$2,600-5,300**

An early Georgian walnut bureau, the flap enclosing a stepped and shaped fitted interior, on later bun feet with later back, restored, 37in (94cm) wide.
$11,000-18,000

A walnut bureau, the fall-front enclosing fitted interior, with centre cupboard, secret drawers, small drawers and pigeonholes, 18thC, 35½in (88.5cm).
$1,600-2,800

A George III mahogany bureau, the fall enclosing a well fitted interior of drawers and pigeonholes flanking a star inlaid cupboard with blind fret borders, 36½in (91cm) wide.
$2,600-5,300

BUREAUX

- ★ Bureaux were not made in this country until after the reign of Charles II
- ★ this writing box on stand was initially produced in oak and then in walnut
- ★ these were originally on turned or straight legs but cabriole legs became popular in the last decade of the 17thC
- ★ note the quality and proportion of the cabriole legs – good carving is another plus factor
- ★ always more valuable if containing an *original* stepped interior and well
- ★ also the more complex the interior – the more expensive
- ★ from about 1680 most bureaux made from walnut, many with beautiful marquetry and inlay
- ★ from about 1740 mahogany became the most favoured wood, although walnut was still used
- ★ the 'key' size for a bureau is 3ft 2in, as the width diminishes so the price increases dramatically
- ★ original patination, colour and original brass handles are obviously important features for assessing any piece of furniture, but these are crucial when valuing bureaux and chests

A George III mahogany bureau, having fitted interior with 6 small drawers, 6 pigeonholes, 2 secret drawers and centre cupboard, 38in (95cm).
$1,800-3,800

A fine Federal inlaid mahogany ladies tambour desk, attributed to the shop of John and Thomas Seymour, Boston, Massachusetts, 1794-1810, in 2 sections, the upper with chevron-inlaid top edge above swag husk inlaid tambour doors centered by pilasters and enclosing a compartmented interior, the lower case with hinged writing flap above 2 line-inlaid long drawers flanked by inlaid pilasters, several minor patches, backboard of top, drawer bottom and brackets restored, 37in (92cm) wide.
$85,000-95,000

This desk, descended in the Hutchinson family of Lynnfield, Massachusetts, is almost identical to the one in the Bayou Bend Collection of the Museum of Fine Arts, Houston, illustrated in David B. Warren, American Furniture, Paintings and Silver from the Bayou Bend Collection (Houston 1975) p87, No.168. They are closely related to an example at Winterthur, discussed in Charles Montgomery, American Furniture in the Henry Francis du Pont Winterthur Museum: The Federal Period (New York, 1966), pp228-29, No.184, which bears the label of John Seymour and Son. The Hutchinson desk shows evidence of original circular enamel pulls similar to those on the Bayou Bend and Winterthur desks.

A mahogany bureau, with fitted interior, late 18thC, 36in (90cm) wide.
$1,400-2,600

A Chippendale carved mahogany slant front desk, Rhode Island, 1765-1785, the compartmented interior comprised of a central concave shell-carved prospect door opening to a vertical bank of 3 drawers, flanked by 6 pigeonholes headed by concave-front valance drawers over 2 blockfront drawers flanked by 2 vertical banks of 3 concave-blocked short drawers, some restorations, 41½in (103cm) wide.
$8,000-9,000

BUREAUX

Points to look for:
* ★ originality and condition
* ★ good colour and patination
* ★ good proportions
* ★ quality of construction
* ★ original handles and escutcheons
* ★ original feet
* ★ small size (3ft is about average)
* ★ stepped interior and a central cupboard
* ★ fitted 'well' with a slide
* ★ oak drawer linings
* ★ secret compartments

A Georgian mahogany bureau, with fitted interior, 36in (90cm).
$1,800-3,800

An Edwardian mahogany satinwood, boxwood and ebony strung bureau, 29½in (73.5cm) wide.
$900-1,700

A Victorian mahogany cylinder top fitted bureau, 48in (120cm).
$1,000-2,000

A Chippendale maple slant front desk, Eastern Connecticut or Rhode Island, 1760-1785, the compartmented interior comprised of 8 valanced pigeonholes above 4 short drawers centering a prospect door, patch to one foot, various repairs 36in (90cm) wide.
$3,000-4,000

An Edwardian mahogany and marquetry bureau of small proportions, the top and sides with satinwood stringing, bearing retailers plaque for Simkin, Upholstery and Furnishing Expert, Colchester, 24in (60cm) wide.
$1,600-2,800

A William and Mary style walnut bureau-on-stand, 33in (82.5cm).
$1,800-3,800

A late Georgian mahogany bureau, the oak lined drawers with later brass handles, raised on bracket feet, 45in (112.5cm) wide.
$1,200-2,100

A mahogany child's bureau, 19thC, 22in (55cm).
$800-1,500

An Edwardian Sheraton style rosewood cylinder front bureau.
$1,400-2,600

A Dutch walnut and marquetry cylinder bureau, with interior pigeonholes and drawers, 19thC, 36in (90cm) wide.
$2,600-5,300

A French mahogany and brass-mounted cylinder bureau, 19thC, 34½in (86cm).
$1,400-2,600

A Dutch mahogany and floral marquetry cylinder bureau, reduced, early 19thC, 50in (125cm).
$6,000-12,000

A French bureau, the fall-flap enclosing a fitted interior of tiered short drawers and pigeonhole, late 18thC, 29½in (73.5cm).
$2,600-5,300

A Dutch mahogany and rosewood cylinder bureau, the rosewood crossbanded top and fall inlaid with boxwood stringing, enclosing a fitted interior of pigeonholes, c1820, 47½in (118cm) wide.
$1,700-3,000

A French inlaid rosewood bureau-de-dame, with marquetry decorated fall, the fitted interior with well and 2 small drawers, 26in (65cm).
$1,600-2,800

NOTES ON DUTCH MARQUETRY BUREAUX

★ beware badly split flaps and sides
★ marquetry on walnut fetches more than marquetry on mahogany, which in turn fetches more than marquetry on oak
★ cylinder bureaux as a general rule fetch less than fall front bureaux
★ always look out for marquetry which includes bone and/or mother-of-pearl
★ marquetry including birds and insects is slightly rarer than the usual floral marquetry

---

A Dutch rosewood cylinder bureau, distressed, early 19thC, 48in (120cm) wide.
$1,800-3,800

An Empire mahogany and ormolu mounted bureau à cylindre, the black fossil marble slab above a superstructure of 3 drawers divided by ormolu lyre mounts, the bird's eye maple interior fitted with 3 drawers above a slide, the kneehole surrounded by an arrangement of drawers and a secure compartment, 58in (144cm) wide.
$8,000-13,500

An Italian walnut bureau, inlaid with ivory, late 17thC, 46in (115cm) wide.
$10,000-18,000

Bureau Cabinets

A tulipwood and purple heart Italian cylinder bureau, highly polished and with walnut linings. $8,000-15,000

A Queen Anne walnut bureau cabinet, with later moulded cornice and reduced bracket feet, 81½ by 43in (207 by 109.5cm). $20,000-30,000

A Queen Anne cabinet-on-chest, in figured walnut veneers, the moulded cornice with frieze drawer above a pair of herringbone crossbanded doors concealing drawers and a cupboard of similar decoration, with early replaced turned bun feet and brass drawer pulls, c1710. $18,000-26,000

An early George III mahogany bureau cabinet, 82 by 39in (208 by 98cm). $7,000-12,000

A Queen Anne walnut cabinet-on-chest, the base with a fitted secretaire drawer and 2 deep long drawers, on later bracket feet, bearing a label inscribed in ink in a 19thC hand '. . . iam Dashwood Bart Kertleton Oxfordshire', 66 by 39½in (167.5 by 100cm). $11,000-20,000

A Queen Anne walnut bureau cabinet, the moulded cornice above a pair of later glazed arched bevelled cupboard doors and 2 candle-slides, on later bun feet, 78½ by 39in (199.5 by 99cm). $11,000-20,000

◁ A late George III mahogany secretaire cabinet, 86 by 46in (219 by 117cm). $3,200-6,000

An early Georgian walnut bureau cabinet, the associated top with moulded cornice above a pair of glazed cupboard doors, the sloping flap enclosing a fitted interior above 4 graduated long drawers on later bracket feet, later back, 83 by 37½in (211 by 95cm). $9,000-15,000

A George III mahogany secretaire cabinet, with moulded tear-drop cornice, a fitted secretaire drawer above a pair of panelled doors, enclosing slides, 91½ by 49in (232.5 by 124.5cm). $8,000-15,000

259

A George III mahogany bureau cabinet, the fall enclosing an interior of drawers and pigeonholes flanking a cupboard and blind fret pilaster drawers, 40in (99cm) wide. **$1,800-3,800**

With a 1945 invoice from Waring & Gillow for $180

A late George III mahogany cabinet on chest. **$3,200-6,000**

A George III mahogany bureau cabinet, the crossbanded lower section with a fall enclosing an interior of drawers and pigeonholes flanking a cupboard, the 2 sections associated, 40in (100cm) wide. **$2,600-5,300**

A walnut, crossbanded and feather-strung bureau cabinet, the lower part with a sloping fall enclosing a fitted interior with a central cupboard, fluted pilaster secret compartments, drawers and pigeonholes having a well with slide below, 18thC, 37in (92cm). **$9,000-15,000**

A mahogany bureau cabinet, a sloping fall-front enclosing a stepped fitted interior with a well, the base 18thC, altered, 77 by 32in (195 by 80cm). **$5,000-9,000**

A George III mahogany secretaire cabinet, in the Sheraton style, c1800. **$5,500-9,000**

A George III satinwood and rosewood secretaire cabinet, the baize-lined fall-flap enclosing a fitted interior, 36in (91.5cm). **$20,000-30,000**

A figured mahogany bureau cabinet, the recessed cabinet with concealed sliding pillars enclosed by twin panelled doors crossbanded in walnut, the base having fall-front revealing stepped interior with pigeonholes, drawers, well and concealed section, early 19thC, 38in (95cm). **$5,000-9,000**

A mid-Georgian mahogany bureau cabinet, the scrolled pediment with flowerhead ends centred by a shell cartouche, partly re-supported, 97 by 45in (246.5 by 114cm). **$13,000-22,000**

An early Victorian mahogany secretaire cabinet, 42in (105cm) wide.
$2,000-4,500

A Regency mahogany cabinet, 65½ by 20½in (166 by 52cm).
$4,500-9,000

A Louis XVI tulipwood secretaire abattant.
$6,000-12,000

A French kingwood and walnut marquetry inlaid bombé secretaire à abattant, rouge marble top, all with ormolu mounts, 19thC.
$1,600-2,800

A fine Victorian walnut dentists cabinet, in Elizabethan taste, with cylinder front and 12 narrow panelled drawers, fitted with 2 veined black marble panels, brass fittings, c1880, 83 by 36½in (210 by 90cm).
$5,000-9,000

A figured mahogany escritoire in the Biedermeier style, the interior with compartments, drawers and central cupboard, 60 by 40½in (150 by 100cm).
$1,400-2,600

Make the most of Miller's

Every care has been taken to ensure the accuracy of descriptions and estimated valuations. Price ranges in this book reflect what one should expect to pay for a similar example. When selling one can obviously expect a figure below. This will fluctuate according to a dealer's stock, saleability at a particular time, etc. It is always advisable to approach a reputable specialist dealer or an auction house which has specialist sales.

A south German walnut bureau cabinet, the upper section with frieze drawer and monogrammed beneath a crown amongst marquetry foliage, inlaid with marquetry, the centre with a queen sitting upon a throne holding a sceptre, the centre section with a marquetry and crossbanded fall, early 18thC, 50in (125cm) wide.
$34,000-60,000

A north Italian walnut veneered bureau cabinet, the fall-front revealing 7 drawers, late 18thC, 88 by 52in (222.5 by 130cm).
$8,000-15,000

Cabinets-on-stands

A walnut and mahogany writing cabinet-on-stand, the later stand with square tapering legs with carrying handles, the cabinet early 18thC, 20in (50cm) wide.
$5,500-9,000

A Carolean jewel casket, veneered in walnut with yewwood banding, the front hinging down to reveal 2 secret drawers, the interior lined with rosewood, with brass strapwork bands and hinges, terminating in fleur-de-lis and a fine steel pierced key, the original stand with frieze drawer, casket 18in (45cm) wide, stand 29in (72cm) high.
$18,000-26,000

A William and Mary oyster-veneered walnut cabinet-on-stand, the cupboard doors inlaid with concentric circles enclosing 8 various sized drawers and a central cupboard door with 3 further drawers, with later stand, 36½in (93cm) wide.
$10,000-18,000

An unusual George III mahogany secretaire cabinet, the projecting lower part with a hinged writing surface and 5 crossbanded drawers on turned reeded legs matching the pilasters, c1800, 79 by 31in (200 by 77.5cm).
$11,000-20,000

An Edwards & Roberts Italianate ebonised cabinet-on-stand inlaid with ivory, 70 by 41in (175 by 102.5cm).
$1,400-2,600

A William and Mary walnut cabinet-on-stand, on mid-Georgian stand with foliate and bellflower cabriole legs and claw-and-ball feet, 44½in (113cm) wide.
$6,000-12,000

A good George III satinwood small secretaire cabinet, crossbanded in harewood, the square tapering legs decorated with boxwood lines, 63 by 31in (157.5 by 77.5cm).
$26,000-45,000

A Chinese black and gold lacquer cabinet-on-stand, of Charles II style, 41½in (105.5cm) wide.
$7,000-12,000

A late Victorian carved black oak cabinet, having 3 leaded stained glass doors enclosing adjustable shelves, 80 by 72in (202.5 by 180cm).
$400-750

An Edwardian inlaid satinwood Bijouterie cabinet, 24in (60cm) wide.
$1,600-2,800

A Flemish tortoiseshell and ebony cabinet-on-stand, the associated stand with 3 frieze drawers on spirally turned legs, stretchers and squashed bun feet, basically 17thC, 53in (134.5cm) wide.
$7,000-12,000

In the Furniture section if there is only one measurement it usually refers to the width of the piece.

A Chinese Chippendale Edwardian mahogany Bijouterie cabinet, 30in (75cm) wide.
$600-1,100

A Dutch walnut and marquetry cabinet-on-stand, 65 by 43in (165 by 109cm).
$5,500-9,000

A French ormolu mounted bombé fronted kingwood cabinet, in 2 sections, all drawers and cupboard door are fronted with Vernis Martin panels, late 19thC, 65 by 36in (162.5 by 90cm).
$6,000-12,000

An ebonised and brass mounted vitrine cabinet, the base in the form of vitrine table with a hinged glazed lid, 36in (90cm).
$2,200-4,200

A Dutch ebonised, walnut and oak 17thC style cabinet-on-stand, inlaid with tortoiseshell panels, tulipwood and rosewood bands in chequer bone borders, enclosing a parquetry and mirror lined interior above a small frieze drawer, on square tapering legs, 27½in (68.5cm).
$2,000-4,500

An Indo-Portuguese cabinet-on-stand, probably in nadum wood, with chased brass mounts, 18th/19thC, 60 by 39in (153 by 99cm).
$1,800-3,800

A good late Victorian mahogany display cabinet, with inlaid satinwood panels above a pair of glazed cupboard doors flanked by shelves, on cabriole legs, 55in (138cm).
$900-1,700

An Edwardian mahogany china display cabinet, with boxwood and ebony chequer banding, on square tapering supports with shaped spandrels, 54in (135cm) wide.
$1,200-2,100

An Edwardian mahogany display cabinet, with satinwood stringing and chequered banding, 44in (110cm) wide.
$1,400-2,600

An Edwardian mahogany display cabinet, 64½in (161cm).
$1,000-2,000

A mahogany Chinese Chippendale design free standing display cabinet, late 19thC, 84in (212.5cm).
$7,000-12,000

A Georgian-style carved mahogany display side cabinet, 78in (197.5cm).
$3,200-6,000

An Edwardian mahogany inlaid display cupboard, 42in (105cm).
$600-1,200

An Edwardian satinwood display cabinet, the whole crossbanded and painted in the classical style and on square tapering supports with block feet, 69 by 42in (176 by 107cm).
$1,800-3,800

A pair of Edwardian mahogany and satinwood banded display cabinets, inlaid in the neo-classical taste with urns, foliate swags, bellflowers and paterae, 28½in (71cm).
$4,000-7,500

An Edwardian inlaid mahogany display cabinet, the centre panel with marquetry, ribbon and musical trophy inlays on square tapering supports and spade feet, 50in (125cm) wide.
$2,000-4,500

An Edwardian rosewood, serpentine front display cabinet, bone inlaid.
$2,600-5,300

A pair of Edwardian mahogany kidney-shaped miniature display cabinets, inlaid with boxwood and ebonised stringing, on outswept legs, 22½in (56cm) wide.
$1,800-3,800

An Edwardian Sheraton-style inlaid mahogany display cabinet, 36in (90cm).
$2,200-4,200

◁ An Edwardian inlaid mahogany display cabinet, 75in (190cm) high.
$1,200-2,100

▷ An Edwardian inlaid mahogany display cabinet, 41in (102.5cm) wide.
$900-1,700

An Edwardian inlaid mahogany vitrine, inlaid panel doors decorated with musical instruments, sabre supports, 76in (192.5cm) high.
$2,200-4,200

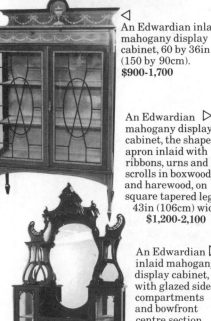

◁ An Edwardian inlaid mahogany display cabinet, 60 by 36in (150 by 90cm).
$900-1,700

An Edwardian ▷ mahogany display cabinet, the shaped apron inlaid with ribbons, urns and scrolls in boxwood and harewood, on square tapered legs, 43in (106cm) wide.
$1,200-2,100

An Edwardian ▷ inlaid mahogany display cabinet, with glazed side compartments and bowfront centre section having painted panel.
$600-1,100

An Edwardian mahogany and marquetry display cabinet, inlaid throughout with sprays of summer flowers and foliage, 86in (217.5cm) high.
$1,800-3,800

An Edwardian mahogany display cabinet.
$800-1,500

An Edwardian mahogany display cabinet, 38in (95cm) wide.
$900-1,700

A Dutch marquetry shaped domed top display cabinet, some damage, 48½in (121cm) wide.
$4,000-7,500

A Dutch oak small cabinet, 18thC, 32 by 32½in (80 by 81cm).
$1,300-2,400

A Dutch walnut and marquetry china cabinet, with boxwood and ebony chequer stringing with carved paw feet, late 18thC, 74 by 37in (187.5 by 92.5cm).
$5,000-9,000

A Dutch carved mahogany china cabinet, late 18th/early 19thC, 95in (241cm).
$8,000-15,000

A Dutch walnut and marquetry veneered display cabinet, 70 by 46in (175 by 115cm).
$5,000-9,000

A Scandinavian satinbirch display cabinet, 39in (97cm) wide.
$1,000-2,000

A Dutch walnut and marquetry display cabinet, early 19thC, 90 by 68in (227.5 by 170cm).
$5,000-9,000

A French kingwood, parquetry and marquetry display cabinet in the Louis XV/XVI transitional taste of bowed outline, 19thC, 65½in (164cm).
$8,000-15,000

A gilt display cabinet, in the Venetian style, 19thC, 85 by 31in (216 by 79cm).
$2,200-4,200

Side Cabinets – Chiffoniers

A George III mahogany side cabinet, on later turned tapering legs, 68in (170cm).
$4,000-7,500

A Regency pollard oak and burr yew dwarf cabinet, 26in (65cm) wide.
$1,800-3,800

A Regency mahogany chiffonier, 31½in (78cm).
$3,200-6,000

A Regency chiffonier, in figured rosewood veneers, the lower part a cabinet with brass grillework backed by pleated green satin, c1820, 48 by 30in (120 by 75cm).
$5,000-9,000

A Regency rosewood side cabinet, 48 by 54in (120 by 135cm).
$1,800-3,800

A pair of Regency brass bound and inlaid rosewood side cabinets, 29in (72.5cm).
$5,000-9,000

A Regency mahogany secretaire chiffonier, inlaid with chequered bands and applied with gilt metal mounts, 42in (105cm).
$11,000-18,000

A fine Regency rosewood chiffonier, the mirrored superstructure with an urn finial, the whole applied with beaded and bobbin mouldings and with baluster turnings and pierced X-shaped supports to the sides, 22in (55cm) wide.
$5,500-9,000

A Regency satinwood veneered chiffonier, the pair of rosewood veneered solid panel doors with kingwood crossbanding and centred with oval satinwood floret motifs, 36in (90cm) wide.
$2,200-4,200

A Regency inlaid and crossbanded mahogany side cabinet, 41in (102cm).
$4,000-6,800

A Regency rosewood chiffonier, 60 by 57in (150 by 142cm).
$3,200-6,000

A Regency mahogany side cabinet, with crossbanded top, the frieze applied with giltmetal anthemions and roundels, 27in (68cm) wide.
$7,000-12,000

A Regency rosewood and maple chiffonier, 45 by 31in (112.5 by 77.5cm).
$2,600-5,300

A mahogany cabinet, 50in (125cm) wide.
$4,500-9,000

A Regency rosewood chiffonier, 36in (90cm).
$1,400-2,600

A Regency rosewood chiffonier, 33in (82cm) wide.
$6,000-12,000

A William IV rosewood chiffonier, 37in (92cm) wide.
$1,000-2,000

An early Victorian rosewood chiffonier cabinet, fitted with 2 long and 4 short penwork drawers, decorated with classical motifs, above 5 similarly decorated drawers, 36in (90cm).
$3,200-6,000

A William IV rosewood breakfront dining room cabinet, 66in (165cm) wide.
$1,200-2,100

A William IV figured mahogany chiffonier, 46in (115cm) wide.
$1,300-2,400

An early Victorian mahogany chiffonier, 41in (102.5cm) wide.
$500-900

A Victorian satinwood side cabinet, the top with rosewood banding within satinwood stringing, 73in (182cm) wide.
$2,200-4,200

A small Victorian mahogany chiffonier.
$400-750

A Victorian figured mahogany chiffonier, 47in (117cm) wide.
$800-1,500

A Victorian boulle dwarf cabinet, with extensive ormolu decoration and single panel door, 34in (85cm).
$1,300-2,400

A mid-Victorian walnut and inlaid side cabinet with scrolling leaf inlaid frieze, with gilt metal capitals and burr walnut inlay, 43½ by 34½in (108 by 85cm).
$1,000-2,000

A William IV carved walnut and marquetry chiffonier, 50in (125cm) wide.
$1,000-2,000

A Victorian inlaid walnut and gilt metal mounted side cabinet, 32in (80cm) wide.
$1,000-2,000

A Victorian satinwood white painted and gilt side cabinet, in the gothic taste, 47in (117.5cm).
$2,200-4,200

A Regency small rosewood chiffonier, 49 by 30in (122.5 by 75cm).
$2,000-4,500

A Victorian inlaid and marquetry panelled cabinet with fitted ormolu mounts.
$500-900

A Victorian rosewood serpentine front marble top chiffonier.
$900-1,700

A north Italian crossbanded walnut and marquetry inlaid dwarf cabinet, feet probably later, 44in (110cm) wide.
$1,400-2,600

A French chiffonier, 19thC.
$1,000-2,000

A Dutch crossbanded walnut dwarf cabinet, early 19thC, 23in (58cm) wide.
$600-1,200

A French ebonised, ebony, boulle and pewter meuble d'appui, mid-19thC, 34in (85cm).
$1,600-2,800

Side Cabinets – Credenzas

A mid-Victorian amboyna, purpleheart and marquetry breakfront side cabinet, 72in (180cm) wide.
$4,000-7,500

A Victorian ebonised and amboyna marquetry breakfront credenza, 72in (180cm).
$800-1,500

A Victorian burr walnut breakfront side cabinet, inlaid with marquetry and geometric boxwood lines and applied with gilt metal mounts, 60in (150cm).
$2,200-4,200

A Victorian walnut veneered credenza, the polished top with cast floral scroll brass mounts, the front with floral marquetry, 50in (125cm) wide.
$4,000-7,500

A Victorian burr walnut and ebonised credenza, banded in amboyna and inlaid with bone arabesques and fitted with gilt metal beading, 72in (180cm).
$1,400-2,600

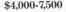

A Victorian walnut veneered side cabinet, applied with gilt brass mouldings, 46 by 60in (115 by 150cm).
$1,700-3,000

A Victorian burr walnut breakfront credenza, decorated with inlaid and marquetry panels having original white marble top and cast ormolu mounts, 78in (195cm) wide.
$2,600-5,300

A Victorian ebonised and marquetry side cabinet, applied throughout with gilt brass mounts and caryatids, 43 by 72 (107 by 180cm).
$2,600-5,300

A Victorian marquetry inlaid walnut credenza, 42 by 88in (105 by 220cm).
$2,600-5,300

A Victorian walnut serpentine front credenza, 48in (120cm) wide.
$600-1,100

◁

A Victorian walnut and marquetry inlaid breakfront credenza, 72in (180cm) wide.
$1,400-2,600

A mid-Victorian walnut and inlaid credenza, 42 by 72in (105 by 180cm).
$2,200-4,200

CREDENZAS

★ side cabinets are often known as credenzas
★ a credenza normally implies the more ornate pieces, in the French or Italian taste
★ some of these pieces display the over elaborate decoration and lack of craftsmanship which would decrease their desirability
★ serpentine shaped front and sides is always a good feature

Canterburies

A George III mahogany canterbury, 20in (49cm) wide.
$1,600-2,800

CANTERBURIES

★ name denotes a piece of movable equipment usually used for sheet music
★ first music canterburies appeared c1800
★ round tapered legs appeared in c1810
★ the canterbury shows quite well the stylistic development of the 19thC – from the quite straight, slender severe to the bulbous and heavily carved later examples
★ many Victorian examples with good carving fetch more than the earlier examples
★ elegance is one of the major criteria in this small expensive piece of furniture
★ note that some are made from the base of a whatnot or étagère but even more are modern reproductions

A George III mahogany canterbury, 18in (45cm) wide.
$1,600-2,800

A Regency mahogany canterbury with 3 dividers headed by turned finials, on original castors, c1810, 20 by 20½in (50 by 50.5cm).
$4,000-6,800

An early Victorian rosewood x-frame canterbury, with wreath carved decoration, 20in (50cm) wide.
$900-1,700

A late Victorian walnut canterbury, raised on pierced double C scroll end standards, 25½in (64cm) wide.
$1,200-2,100

271

Chairs – Open Armchairs

A Victorian rosewood canterbury, raised on spindle supports with fretwork panels, 23in (57.5cm) wide.
$1,000-2,000

A Victorian figured walnut canterbury, the later two-handled tray top lifting off to reveal 2 divisions, 26in (66cm) wide.
$800-1,500

A pair of walnut open armchairs, upholstered in gros point foliate needlework, one with reinforced backrail, the other with partly reinforced seat, late 17thC.
$4,500-9,000

A George I walnut wing armchair, the front feet spliced.
$5,000-9,000

A Queen Anne walnut armchair.
$13,000-22,000

A George I red walnut library armchair.
$7,000-12,000

An early Georgian walnut open armchair.
$1,600-2,800

A George I walnut open armchair, the bowed drop-in seat with shepherd's crook arms on shell cabriole legs and claw-and-ball feet.
$10,000-18,000

A George II walnut armchair, altered from a single chair.
$600-1,200

A George I walnut open armchair, with shell-and-husk cabriole legs, pad feet, later blocks.
$9,000-15,000

A pair of George III polished beechwood open armchairs, covered in gros and petit point needle work.
$4,000-7,500

A Queen Anne walnut armchair, Pennsylvania, 1740-1770, with serpentine crest-rail centering a carved shell motif and ending in flared ears, 41½in (103cm) high.
$23,000-26,000

A pair of George III mahogany open
armchairs.
$10,000-18,000

A pair of early George III mahogany
open armchairs.
$9,000-15,000

A fine set of 4 early George III
mahogany library armchairs.
$60,000-120,000

A pair of black and gold lacquer
open armchairs, the rectangular
backs with pierced lyre splats
decorated with geometric designs,
possible redecorated, late 18thC.
$8,000-15,000

A George III green-painted open
armchair, with shield-shaped back
with pierced splat decorated with
flowers and foliage.
$1,000-2,000

A fine set of 8 George III painted
armchairs.
$42,000-70,000

A pair of George III giltwood open
armchairs.
$12,000-21,000

A Chippendale painted maple
armchair, Massachusetts or Rhode
Island, 1755-1775, with serpentine
shaped crest above a pierced vase-
shaped splat, on block and short
vase turned legs joined by double
ball- and ring-turned side
stretchers, painted with a
mahogany finish, 40½in (101cm)
high.
$1,500-2,000

A mahogany elbow chair, in the
French Hepplewhite style, with
repairs, late 18thC, 34in (87cm)
high.
$1,000-2,000

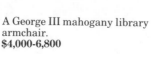

A good pair of George III gilt
armchairs.
$8,000-13,500

A George III mahogany library
armchair.
$4,000-6,800

A pair of George III elbow chairs, in the Chinese Chippendale manner, the crest rails carved with C scrolls and pagodas, interlaced fret backs with leaf carving, fret arms and stuffed seats on plain straight legs with stretchers.
$14,000-24,000

A Windsor writing armchair, New England, 1780-1800, the scrolled arm and shaped writing surface above 4 baluster-turned supports and 16 swelled spindles above a shaped seat, formerly a rocker, repairs to feet, drawer now missing, 48½in (121cm) high.
$3,000-3,500

A good pair of Georgian wheel-back cross-frame armchairs, carved with foliate bosses to the front rails, veneered in mahogany.
$28,000-50,000

A Regency beechwood tub armchair.
$2,200-4,200

A mahogany open armchair in the Regency style, the square tapering sabre legs headed by foliate collars, 19thC.
$9,000-15,000

Cf. a design for 'Library Fauteuils in Profile' included as pl.48 in George Smith, A Collection of Designs for Household Furniture, 1808.

A Windsor sack-back armchair, Rhode Island, 1780-1800, the curved back enclosing 7 tapering spindles which pierce the U-shaped, slightly peaked seat, on vase-and-reel turned legs joined by bulbous stretchers, 39in (97cm) high.
$1,500-2,000

A pair of Regency simulated rosewood tub bergeres, on sabre legs.
$7,000-12,000

The continued demand for Regency furniture leads to higher prices.

A fine pair of late Regency mahogany tub armchairs, ending in brass capped feet and castors.
$8,000-15,000

Make the most of Miller's

Miller's is completely different each year. Each edition contains completely NEW photographs. This is not an updated publication. We never repeat the same photograph.

Six Regency painted elbow chairs, the beech frames with rectangular and canted openwork backs, with renewed seat rails and some repairs.
$8,000-15,000

A Regency metamorphic library armchair, attributed to Morgan and Saunders, the padded seat opening to reveal 4 baize-lined treads on sabre legs with reinforced seat rails.
$8,000-15,000

A metamorphic library armchair of identical design by Morgan and Saunders is at Trinity College, Oxford and is illustrated in R Edwards and P Macquoid, The Dictionary of English Furniture, *rev. ed., 1954, vol. 11., p.291. fig. 15. A chair of this type was published in Ackerman's Repository in July 1811 and was captioned 'This ingenious piece of furniture is manufactured at Messrs. Morgan and Saunders's. Catherine-St Strand' (P Agius,* Ackerman's Regency Furniture & Interior, *1984, fig. 29).*

A mahogany open armchair, the seat rails with pierced X-framed base, early 19thC.
$5,000-9,000

A pair of Regency parcel-gilt and black painted open armchairs, repainted, partly re-supported, later blocks.
$9,000-15,000

A Regency painted and decorated beechwood armchair, on faceted simulated bamboo sabre legs.
$1,600-2,800

A pair of Regency mahogany open armchairs, with ribbed top rails and pierced foliate vertical splats, the later caned seats with leather squab cushions.
$11,000-18,000

A pair of Federal style armchairs, probably by Ernest Hagen, New York, c1880, each with leaf carved crest rail tablet flanked by reeded stiles continuing to scroll arms, over reeded baluster supports, 32½in (80cm) high.
$3,000-4,000

These chairs are believed to be part of the set of a 'Dozen of Phyfes Dining Armchairs' made for Frederic Bronson Jr. by Ernest Hagen.

A Regency mahogany floral marquetry carver chair.
$800-1,500

A pair of Regency painted open armchairs, with gothic arcaded backs, pierced with quatrefoils and crocket finials, the later solid seats with squab cushions.
$4,500-9,000

A pair of Regency ebonized, parcel-gilt and caned open armchairs, early 19thC.
$11,000-20,000

An early Victorian mahogany ladies chair.
$300-600

A Regency mahogany armchair, with brass inlaid top rail above lyre splat.
$1,000-2,000

A rare and historical carved oak armchair, Bembe and Kimbel, New York, c1857, 38in (95cm) high.
$6,500-8,500

This chair belonged to a group of 262 chairs commissioned by Congress in 1857 for the House of Representatives.

Thomas U. Walter, architect of the U.S. Capitol from 1851 to 1865, extended the Capitol exterior, adding the present dome and wings, and renovated the interior, including the design of new desks and chairs for the chamber of the House of Representatives. This armchair, from the 1857 order, was one of 131 chairs manufactured by Bembe and Kimbel in New York according to Walter's drawings which survive today in the collection of the Capitol. The other 131 chairs, which are of lesser quality, were supplied at the same time by Hammitt Desk Mfg. Co. of Philadelphia.

A Victorian walnut framed spoon-back open arm easy chair, with carved floral cresting.
$1,600-2,800

A mid-Victorian mahogany easy armchair.
$4,000-7,500

A rare pair of late Federal armchairs, New York, early 19thC.
$20,000-23,000

A pair of late Regency mahogany armchairs.
$1,000-2,000

A pair of Victorian dining chairs, some damage to seats.
$4,000-6,800

A Victorian rosewood open armchair.
$1,800-3,800

A Victorian walnut open armchair.
$1,000-2,000

An Edwardian mahogany bergere chair.
$1,400-2,600

An early Louis XV carved giltwood fauteuil.
$6,000-12,000

A Louis Quinze carved and gilded wood fauteuil, covered in contemporary tapestry.
$1,200-2,100

A Louis XV walnut armchair, covered in gros point and petit point needlework.
$8,000-15,000

A pair of French Empire mahogany elbow chairs, early 19thC.
$4,500-9,000

A Flemish walnut open armchair, re-railed, 17thC and later.
$1,800-3,800

A walnut armchair, of French design, 19thC.
$2,000-4,500

A pair of Restauration mahogany fauteuils, with scrolling arms terminating in lotuses.
$2,600-5,300

A Dutch walnut and marquetry elbow chair with spoon back, 19thC.
$6,000-12,000

A set of 3 Continental carved giltwood and cream-painted elbow chairs, in the Louis XVI taste, late 18thC, probably Dutch.
$4,000-7,500

A Harlequin set of 10 Spanish walnut open armchairs.
$12,000-21,000

A Venetian carved giltwood open armchair, in the manner of Bustolon, 18thC.
$2,200-4,200

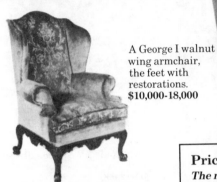

A George I walnut wing armchair, the feet with restorations.
$10,000-18,000

A pair of mid-Georgian style mahogany wing armchairs, on cabochon headed cabriole legs and knob feet.
$1,400-2,600

Upholstered Armchairs

A Queen Anne walnut wing armchair, re-railed.
$10,000-18,000

A fine Queen Anne walnut easy chair, Massachusetts, 1730-50, on cabriole legs with pad feet joined by block and arrow-turned stretchers, front right foot pierced, rear stretcher replaced, some repairs to frame, 48in (120cm) high.
$15,000-17,000

A pair of armchairs on walnut frames, 19thC.
$600-1,100

Prices

The never-ending problem of fixing prices for antiques! A price can be affected by so many factors, for example:
- *condition*
- *desirability*
- *rarity*
- *size*
- *colour*
- *provenance*
- *restoration*
- *the sale of a prestigious collection*
- *collection label*
- *appearance of a new reference book*
- *new specialist sale at major auction house*
- *mentioned on television*
- *the fact that two people present at auction are determined to have the piece*
- *where you buy it*

One also has to contend with the fact that an antique is not only a 'thing of beauty' but a commodity. The price can again be affected by:
- *supply and demand*
- *international finance – currency fluctuation*
- *fashion*
- *inflation*
- *the fact that a museum has vast sums of money to spend*

A George II mahogany wing armchair, raised upon square reeded front legs with outward splayed back legs, united by an H stretcher.
$800-1,500

A fine Chippendale mahogany easy chair, New York, 1750-80, the bow seat frame above cabriole legs with claw-and-ball feet, 44in (110cm) high.
$23,000-26,000

An early Georgian walnut wing armchair, with restorations, later blocks.
$7,000-12,000

A mid-Georgian mahogany wing armchair with claw-and-ball feet, the rails re-supported, the back rail replaced.
$6,000-12,000

A George III mahogany wing armchair, on square chamfered legs joined by an H-stretcher and stepped feet, front rail reinforced.
$4,000-7,500

Two George III stained beechwood bergères of Louis XVI style, with spirally turned arm supports on fluted tapering legs, later blocks.
$14,000-24,000

A Regency mahogany tub armchair, with fluted frame and ribbed arm supports and sabre legs.
$7,000-12,000

A pair of George III upholstered armchairs, on 4 cabriole legs moulded with scrolls and ending in scroll feet, 38½in (96cm).
$10,000-18,000

A mid-Georgian elm wing armchair, outscrolled arms and seat on cabriole legs joined by turned stretchers and pad feet.
$4,500-9,000

Provenance: by repute Blair Castle, Perthshire.

A Victorian mahogany spoon backed chair, with shaped cabriole legs.
$600-1,100

A pair of Regency mahogany bergères with scrolled backs and reeded arm supports, with distressed upholstery in ribbed frames on ribbed ring turned tapering legs.
$8,000-13,500

A Victorian mahogany Regency Revival Grecian-style armchair, the close nailed scroll adjustable panel back, seat and armpads, upholstered in leather cloth above graduated leaf and anthemion carved side panels and apron, on lappeted turned tapering front legs.
$800-1,500

A French blue painted bergère with curved caned back and seat in moulded frame on cabriole legs.
$1,400-2,600

A pair of Louis XVI style bergères, on turned and fluted tapering legs.
$1,200-2,100

A giltwood bergère with shaped back and sides ending in dolphin heads, on club legs and paw feet, c1840.
$5,000-9,000

A late Regency mahogany bergère, the scoop shaped caned back with lappet carved arms continuing to turned and lobed tapering legs. ▷
$2,000-4,500

A mid-Victorian easy armchair.
$8,000-13,500

A Victorian walnut framed upholstered armchair. ▷
$800-1,500

A William IV rosewood armchair, with scrolled arm supports on ring turned ribbed, tapering legs, formerly caned.
$4,000-7,500

A pair of Louis XVI-style cream painted and gilt bergères, on fluted tapering legs headed by scroll capitals, stencilled Jansen, Paris.
$4,000-7,500

Chairs – Dining

A rare set of 8 Federal inlaid mahogany dining chairs, branded 'Anderson', New York, 1790-1810, comprising 2 armchairs and 6 side chairs, the stepped crest rail of each centered by bellflower, swag and spandrel motifs, above 2 open vertical lozenges suspended by simple latticework, the arm supports with inlaid bellflowers, on square tapering legs decorated with stringing and cuffs, 2 with ended feet, minor repairs, each 37 by 20½in (94 by 52cm).
$100,000+

An identical chair, also branded 'ANDERSON', and originally from this set, is discussed in Roderic H. Blackburn, 'Branded and Stamped New York Furniture', Antiques (May 1981), p.1134, fig. 8. For an article on a related group of inlaid furniture, which includes an illustration of a side chair originally from this set, see Barry A. Greenlaw, 'A New York Sideboard in the Colonial Williamsburg Collection', Antiques (May 1974), pp.1155-1161. In the article, Greenlaw explains that 'ANDERSON' may refer to one of several New York City furniture makers working at the turn of the 19thC. Their names include Elbert Anderson Sr. and Jr., Andrew Anderson, Alexander Anderson Sr. and Jr., Samuel Anderson, John B. Anderson and Walter Anderson.

A fine and rare set of 12 dining chairs, Rhode Island, 1785-1810, comprising 2 arm and 10 side chairs, each with modified shield back centering a splat of vertical shaped ribs and centering a leaf-carved urn above a trapezoidal over-upholstered leather seat, 38in (95cm) high.
$50,000-65,000

For an illustration of a similar Rhode Island armchair, see The Rhode Island Historical Society, John Brown House Loan Exhibition of Rhode Island Furniture (1965) pp.15-16, No.15.

A set of 8 George III stained beechwood dining chairs, the pierced backs filled with trellis-work and pilasters, later blocks, and a set of 4 en suite of a later date with leather seats.
$14,000-24,000

The form of these chairs is related to some of designs for 'Gothick' and 'Chinese' chairs in Robert Manwaring, The Cabinet and Chair-Maker's Real Friend and Companion, 1765, figs, 10, 12, 14, 15 and 31.

A set of 4 Irish George II mahogany chairs, the dished toprails with scroll ears, the vitruvian scroll seat rails on shell and acanthus carved cabriole legs, c1740.
$4,500-9,000

A set of 14 George III mahogany ladderback dining chairs, including a pair of armchairs with waved backs, some splats replaced, some partly re-railed and with later blocks.
$20,000-30,000

A pair of walnut veneered dining chairs with drop-in seats, on cabriole legs, early 18thC.
$4,000-6,800

A set of 5 early George III mahogany dining chairs, second quarter 18thC.
$10,000-18,000

A set of 4 George III mahogany dining chairs.
$1,800-3,800

A set of 6 George III mahogany dining chairs, including two open armchairs, some re-railed.
$3,200-6,000

A set of 6 Irish mid-Georgian dining chairs, the seat rails replaced.
$5,000-9,000

A set of 6 George III mahogany dining chairs, the shaped eared toprails above pierced vase splats.
$6,000-12,000

A set of 8 mahogany dining chairs.
$5,000-9,000

A red walnut chair, with pierced vertical splat back, mid-18thC.
$1,700-3,000

A set of 8 late Georgian mahogany dining chairs, including 2 with arms, with restorations.
$12,000-21,000

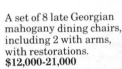

A set of 4 George III cream and green painted dining chairs, the shield shaped backs with arched splats with rush seats.
$3,200-6,000

A set of 8 George III mahogany dining chairs, including two armchairs, 7 with backrails reinforced, one with reinforced front and side rails, one armchair with drop-in seat and later blocks.
$14,000-24,000

A set of 13 late George III mahogany dining chairs, including a pair of armchairs, the shield shaped backs with pierced vase shaped splats, carved with paterae and foliage, one of the armchairs with later arms.
$18,000-26,000

A set of 6 Georgian mahogany dining chairs, in Hepplewhite style, with pierced vase shaped back splats.
$3,200-6,000

A set of 6 George III mahogany dining chairs, 19thC.
$2,600-5,300 ▷

A set of 3 George III walnut dining chairs, including an armchair.
$2,600-5,300

A set of 8 George III mahogany dining chairs, including a pair of armchairs, the shield shaped backs with pierced interlaced splats carved with wheatears and husks and inlaid with fan medallions.
$14,000-24,000

The design of these chairs is based on a design in George Hepplewhite, The Cabinet Maker's and Upholsterer's Guide, 1788, pl.4.

◁ A set of 6 George III mahogany dining chairs, the shield shape backs with wheatsheaf and husk crestings.
$6,000-12,000

A set of 6 mid-Georgian mahogany △ dining chairs, the waved toprails and pierced splats carved with flowerheads and foliage, the seatrails reinforced.
$13,000-22,000

A George III mahogany dining chair, the geometrically pierced splat with conforming rockwork and C-scrolls, later blocks.
$1,700-3,000

Three George III mahogany dining chairs, each with a channelled arched back with pierced palmette and waisted splat, later blocks and restorations.
$1,700-3,000

A set of 8 George III carved mahogany dining chairs, in the Sheraton taste, the backs with reeded curved uprights, satinwood and ebony strung panel backs and horizontal splats with ball ornament, including a pair of elbow chairs.
$9,000-15,000

A set of 10 George III mahogany dining chairs, repairs, late 18thC.
$14,000-24,000

A set of 8 Sheraton mahogany dining chairs, with inlaid rails within reeded uprights, the carvers with reeded outswept arms on turned reeded uprights, upholstery replaced, c1800.
$10,000-18,000

A set of 8 Sheraton mahogany dining chairs, including 2 carvers, the backs with pierced plume splats and serpentine oval line inlaid crests.
$6,000-12,000

A set of 8 Sheraton mahogany dining chairs, with bar and lozenge shaped paterae decorated backs, 2 elbow, 6 standard.
$8,000-15,000

A set of 6 Sheraton carved mahogany dining chairs, including an elbow chair, the moulded arched backs with foliate headed Gothic arched and reeded vertical splats.
$5,000-9,000

A set of 8 George III Hepplewhite mahogany dining chairs, including 2 carvers.
$12,000-21,000

Cf. George Hepplewhite, The Cabinet Maker and Upholsterers Guide, *1794, plates 6 and 11.*

A set of 10 late George III mahogany dining chairs, each with a curved and incised cresting rail above an X-shape splat and reeded uprights, 4 reduced in height.
$8,000-13,500

A set of 8 Regency dining chairs, decorated in black and gilt with reeded frames, with padded seats and backs, carved in gilt with leaves, tendrils and patera, on turned legs with carved gilt leaves and brass terminals, c1805.
$30,000-60,000

In the manner of chairs supplied by Marsh and Tatham for Southill, Bedfordshire.

A set of 8 Regency mahogany dining chairs, including a pair of armchairs with curved rope twist toprails, re-caned.
$9,000-15,000

A set of 10 Regency rosewood dining chairs, including a pair of armchairs, with curved toprails, centred by rosettes, rope twist supports and bar splats.
$14,000-24,000

A set of 4 George III mahogany dining chairs.
$1,800-3,800

A set of 12 Regency mahogany dining chairs, including 2 armchairs, some repairs.
$13,000-22,000

A set of 6 Regency ebonised dining chairs, including a pair of armchairs, with turned shaped toprails and pierced lattice-work splats, 4 stamped SG.
$4,500-9,000

A set of 6 Regency mahogany dining chairs.
$4,000-6,800

Make the most of Miller's

Every care has been taken to ensure the accuracy of descriptions and estimated valuations. Where an attribution is made within inverted commas (e.g. 'Chippendale') or is followed by the word 'style' (e.g. early Georgian style) it is intended to convey that, in the opinion of the publishers, the piece concerned is a later – though probably still antique – reproduction of the style so designated. Unless otherwise stated, any description which refers to 'a set', or 'a pair' includes a valuation for the entire set or the pair, even though the illustration may show only a single item.

A good set of 8 Regency mahogany dining chairs.
$10,000-18,000

A set of 9 Regency sabre-leg brass inlaid dining chairs.
$11,000-20,000

◁ A set of 13 Regency mahogany dining chairs, including a pair of armchairs, with moulded tablet toprails, the horizontal splats filled with balls.
$18,000-26,000

A set of 12 Regency mahogany dining chairs, including 2 armchairs, the carved and yoked toprails above anthemions and curved horizontal splats.
$12,000-21,000

A set of 6 Regency mahogany
dining chairs, including one
armchair, with brass inlaid
backrails.
$2,200-4,200

A set of 12 Regency mahogany and
brass inlaid dining chairs, several
with some brass missing.
$14,000-24,000

A set of 4 Regency
rosewood dining
chairs on sabre legs.
$1,600-2,800

A set of 4 Regency ebonised and gilt
dining chairs, with turned and
reeded toprails on scroll supports
above caned seats, and a similar
open armchair.
$2,600-5,300

A set of 7 Regency mahogany
dining chairs, including 2 elbow
chairs, with panelled oversailing
cresting rails and reeded frames,
one with rails lacking, c1800.
$4,500-9,000

A set of 6 late Regency simulated
rosewood dining chairs, including a
pair of elbow chairs.
$2,200-4,200

A set of 6 Georgian mahogany
dining chairs, including an
armchair.
$6,000-12,000

A set of 6 Regency simulated
rosewood dining chairs, with
ropetwist cresting rails above drop
in Trafalgar seats, raised on sabre
legs.
$2,200-4,200

A set of 6 simulated rosewood
dining chairs, including 2
armchairs, early 19thC.
$2,200-4,200

A set of 6 Regency
mahogany dining
chairs.
$2,000-4,500

A set of 8 Regency mahogany
dining chairs, inlaid with ebonised
lines, including 2 armchairs.
$10,000-18,000

A set of 6 Regency mahogany
dining chairs, including one
armchair.
$2,600-5,300

A set of 11 rosewood grained and
parcel-gilt chairs, including a pair
of armchairs.
$8,000-13,500

A set of 3 Irish Regency oak dining
chairs, including a pair of
armchairs, stamped AH.
$5,000-9,000

A set of 6 Regency rosewood brass-
inlaid dining chairs, early 19thC.
$4,500-9,000

A set of 6 William IV rosewood
dining chairs.
$1,800-3,800

A Harlequin set of 11 mahogany
dining chairs, including one
armchair, early 19thC.
$4,000-7,500

A set of 6 William IV dining chairs
in mahogany, c1830.
$3,200-6,000

A set of 5 George IV rosewood
dining chairs.
$1,700-3,000

A set of 12 William IV mahogany
dining chairs.
$9,000-15,000

A set of 8 William IV mahogany
dining chairs, including 2
armchairs.
$5,000-9,000

A set of mahogany dining chairs,
including 2 armchairs, mid-19thC.
$3,200-6,000

A set of 8 William IV mahogany
dining chairs, including one
armchair.
$2,000-4,500

A set of 6 William IV mahogany
dining chairs, with a seventh
matching chair which requires
restoration.
$1,800-3,800

A set of 8 William IV rosewood
dining chairs.
$2,600-5,300

A set of 6 late Victorian walnut
framed dining chairs, the hoop
backs with carved garlands.
$2,200-4,200

A set of 4 Victorian rosewood
chairs.
$1,000-2,000

A set of 6 William IV rosewood
dining chairs, on ring-turned
shaped tapering legs, later blocks.
$5,000-9,000

A set of 8 rosewood dining chairs,
mid-19thC.
$5,000-9,000

A set of 8 rosewood dining chairs,
early 19thC.
$2,600-5,300

A set of 8 Victorian mahogany dining chairs, some repairs.
$3,200-6,000

A set of 6 early Victorian mahogany dining chairs.
$1,700-3,000

A set of 6 rosewood dining chairs, early 19thC.
$1,800-3,800

△ A set of 6 Victorian mahogany chairs, c1860.
$3,200-6,000

A set of 6 Victorian balloon-back rosewood dining chairs.
$2,200-4,200

A set of 6 Victorian walnut balloon-back chairs.
$1,800-3,800

△ A set of 6 Victorian walnut oval balloon-back dining chairs, c1860.
$2,200-4,200

A set of 10 Victorian mahogany dining chairs.
$3,200-6,000

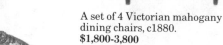

A set of 4 Victorian mahogany dining chairs, c1880.
$1,800-3,800

A set of 4 Victorian mahogany chairs, c1870.
$1,200-2,100

A set of 6 Victorian mahogany chairs, c1860.
$1,800-3,800

A set of 6 Victorian rosewood dining chairs, carved decoration to vase splat and shaped fronts.
$2,200-4,200

A set of 6 mahogany Victorian balloon-back chairs, c1850.
$1,600-2,800

A set of 6 Victorian walnut
balloon- back chairs.
$1,800-3,800

A set of 7 early
Victorian rosewood
dining chairs.
$2,000-4,500

A set of 8 Renaissance style oak
dining chairs, late 19thC.
$1,400-2,600

A set of 6 Edwardian walnut dining
chairs, c1910.
$2,200-4,200

A set of 10 Edwardian mahogany
dining chairs, including 2 carvers,
c1910.
$2,000-4,500

A set of ▷
6 mahogany
Edwardian
dining chairs,
c1910.
$1,600-2,800

A set of 6
Victorian
rosewood dining
chairs.
$2,200-4,200

A set of 6 mid-Victorian mahogany
dining chairs.
$1,700-3,000

A set of 6 early Victorian
rosewood balloon-back
dining chairs, stamped
Hughes & Co., makers,
47 Bold Street, Liverpool
$1,800-3,800

◁
A set of 6 Edwardian
walnut chairs, c1910.
$1,200-2,100

A set of 6 late Victorian mahogany
dining chairs.
$1,000-2,000

A set of 6 Queen Anne style walnut
dining chairs, with carved shell
cresting rails.
$1,800-3,800

▷

A set of 6 Victorian mahogany
dining chairs, c1850.
$2,000-4,500

A set of 8 walnut Queen Anne style dining chairs, including 2 armchairs, c1900.
$8,000-15,000

A set of 6 George I style mahogany dining chairs, the baluster splat headed by a carved shell and pendant bell flowers.
$2,200-4,200

A set of 8 early George III style ▷ mahogany dining chairs, including 2 armchairs, each back having shaped and pierced splat with simulated interlaced loopings, with ball and claw feet, c1910.
$5,000-9,000

The backs of these chairs are not dissimilar to illustration No. 122 page 148, of Edwards Dictionary of English Furniture.

A set of 8 George II style mahogany dining chairs.
$4,000-7,500

A set of 6 Hepplewhite design mahogany camel-back dining chairs.
$1,200-2,100

A set of 6 mahogany dining chairs, including 2 with arms, in the Georgian style.
$1,700-3,000

A set of 8 Georgian style mahogany dining chairs.
$4,500-9,000

A set of 8 Chippendale style mahogany dining chairs, including 2 elbow chairs.
$6,000-12,000

A set of 5 Chippendale style mahogany dining chairs, including one armchair, 19thC.
$1,700-3,000

A set of 8 Chippendale design mahogany dining chairs, including 2 armchairs, 19thC.
$5,500-9,000

Twelve mahogany Chippendale style dining chairs, including 2 armchairs.
$9,000-15,000

A set of 8 mahogany dining chairs, including 2 armchairs, in the Chippendale manner, c1920.
$9,000-15,000

A set of 8 George III style mahogany dining chairs, including 2 armchairs, the serpentine cresting and pierced vase shaped splat backs applied with anthemions.
$6,000-12,000

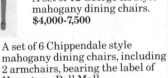

A set of 8 mahogany Hepplewhite style shield-back dining chairs, including 2 armchairs.
$3,200-6,000

A set of 12 George III style mahogany dining chairs.
$4,000-7,500

A set of 6 Chippendale style mahogany dining chairs, including 2 armchairs, bearing the label of Hamptons, Pall Mall.
$4,000-7,500

A set of 12 Hepplewhite style mahogany dining chairs.
$3,200-6,000

A pair of English provincial Chippendale style ladderback chairs.
$800-1,500

A set of 8 Hepplewhite style mahogany dining chairs, including 2 armchairs, the shield shaped backs with foliage and drapery carved pierced splats.
$2,600-5,300

A set of 6 Georgian mahogany dining chairs, including one carver.
$6,000-12,000

A set of 3 Dutch walnut and floral marquetry dining chairs, in the Queen Anne taste, 18thC.
$3,200-6,000

A pair of Dutch marquetry veneered single chairs, late 19thC.
$800-1,500

Chairs – Hall

A set of 12 late Empire style mahogany dining chairs, inlaid with urns, acanthus arabesques and geometric boxwood lines, one stamped Newman Gilbey.
$3,200-6,000

A pair of Queen Anne scarlet painted hall chairs, now lightly gilded, 44in (110cm) high.
$10,000-18,000

△
A pair of George III mahogany hall chairs, the backs with central ovals, painted with coat-of-arms, repairs.
$1,800-3,800

A set of 4 George III grained hall chairs.
$3,200-6,000

A fine pair of Regency mahogany hall chairs.
$10,000-18,000

A set of 6 Regency mahogany hall chairs, each painted with a lion.
$3,200-6,000

A set of 4 late Georgian mahogany hall chairs.
$1,000-2,000

Chairs – Side

A set of 7 Gothic style hall chairs with 'bamboo' column supports, 19thC.
$28,000-50,000

A beechwood side chair, late 17thC, re-railed.
$2,200-4,200

A George III mahogany child's high chair, late 18thC, 36½in (91cm) high.
$1,200-2,100

A set of 4 oak framed Gothic chairs, in the manner of Pugin, one damaged, 19thC.
$800-1,500

A mahogany child's miniature rocking commode chair, 18thC.
$1,000-2,000

A Burgomaster chair on 6 cabriole legs, top of the arms surmounted with carved clergymen heads, c1750.
$4,000-7,500

A George III mahogany folding campaign chair, the folding frame mounted with brass.
$1,700-3,000

A George III painted side chair, with pierced and interlaced oval back and anthemion centre, painted with red and blue harebells on a stone coloured ground, with the trade label of M. Butler Ltd., Dublin.
$2,600-5,300

A George III mahogany side chair.
$2,200-4,200 ▷

A walnut ▷ side chair, in the manner of David Marot.
$1,400-2,600

A fine pair of Queen Anne carved walnut side chairs, Philadelphia, 1745-1765, each with a shaped and arched crest with scrolled volutes centering a carved scallop shell, above a pierced and scrolled splat flanked by reverse-curved stiles with a bead-molded edge, over a balloon seat, on cabriole legs, each carved with a scallop shell, a pendant husk, and scrolls at the knee, on ball-and-claw feet, 42in (105cm) high.
$112,000-115,000

A set of 8 classical mahogany side chairs, New York, 1810-1830, each Klismos shaped, with curved crest rail and carved tablet slat, above removable padded seat, on sabre legs, 32½in (83cm) high.
$4,000-5,000

A Queen Anne walnut side chair, Pennsylvania, 1740-1770, the serpentine crest-rail with scrolled ears over a shaped splat above a slip-in seat, on cabriole legs joined by shaped flat stretchers and with panelled pad feet, 41in (102cm) high.
$9,000-11,000

A pair of Queen Anne walnut side chairs, probably Massachusetts, 1745-1775, each with a shaped crest rail ending in molded, slightly flared ears, the base-shaped splat above a slip-in seat, 38in (95cm) high.
$5,000-6,000

A pair of Chippendale carved walnut side chairs, Philadelphia, 1765-1785, each with serpentine crest rail centering carved leafage above a gothic-pattern pierced splat flanked by molded stiles over a trapezoidal slipseat, on cabriole legs with ball-and-claw feet, 38in (95cm) high.
$15,000-17,000

A set of 4 Queen Anne maple and walnut side chairs, New England, 1740-1770, each with a yoked crest-rail and vase-shaped splat with pierced heart motif, the back of each chair is spliced, with screw reinforcement, minor repairs to some feet and stretchers, 41in (102cm) high.
$5,500-6,500

Miller's Antiques Price Guide builds up year by year to form the most comprehensive photo-reference system available. The first six volumes contain over 50,000 completely different photographs.

A set of 4 George III
side chairs,
with restorations.
$1,700-3,000

A Regency rosewood music chair,
the adjustable seat on reeded and
turned tapering splayed legs united
by cross stretchers.
$1,300-2,400

A Regency mahogany
correction chair.
$1,300-2,400

A set of 7 Regency period mahogany
side chairs.
$7,000-12,000

*These could easily come under the
heading of dining chairs – these
chairs were used as both.*

A set of 6 orange painted and
polychrome decorated plank seat
side chairs, Pennsylvania, c1830-
1850, each with a shaped crest rail
centered by a painted and stenciled
double rose motif, above a pierced
vase-shaped splat, the seat with a
line and rose decoration and
supported by ring-turned legs
supported by stretchers, 33½in
(85cm) high.
$1,800-2,200

A Regency simulated bamboo side
chair in the Brighton Pavilion
taste, the panelled divided splat
painted with Chinese characters,
the cane-filled seat on turned
tapering legs joined by conforming
stretchers, branded No.139.
$4,000-6,800

*An identical chair, but of black
lacquer, is illustrated in the King's
bedroom at the Royal Pavilion,
Brighton, in M. Jourdain and R.
Fastnedge,* Regency Furniture, *rev.
edn., 1955, pl.1.*

ENGLISH CHAIRS

★ c1630 backs of chairs were
like panelled sides from a
coffer
★ early 17thC chairs very
square and made of oak
★ in Charles II period
principal wood walnut –
such chairs tend to break
as walnut splits easily and
is relatively soft
★ chairs have carved top
rails, often with a crown,
the stretcher will then be
similarly carved, the legs
are either turned or plain
and simple spirals –
sometimes called barley
sugar twists; the caning in
the backs is usually
rectangular – any chair
with oval caning is highly
desirable
★ by the end of the 17thC
backs were covered in
needlework, the cabriole
leg made its appearance,
now stretchers have
subtle curves
★ the beginning of the
18thC – the Queen Anne
spoon back chair – with
upright shaped splat,
plain cabriole front legs,
pad feet
★ George I – carved knees
and ball-and-claw feet,
solid splats were walnut
or veneered, often in burr-
walnut
★ William Kent –
introduced heavy carved
mouldings – greatly
influenced by Italian
baroque
★ from this time on chairs
became lighter in design
through the work mainly
of Chippendale and
Hepplewhite
★ splats now pierced, legs
square or tapered
★ the square legs were also
much cheaper than the
cabriole legs, so they
appealed to the large and
growing middle class
★ many of the designs came
from France
★ Hepplewhite, in
particular, developed the
chair with tapered legs, no
stretchers and very plain
splats
★ during the 19thC the taste
was once again for heavier
more substantial
furniture

A Victorian button backed armchair, c1890, 32in (80cm).
$500-900

A late Victorian Prie-dieu mahogany chair, with barley twist sides and front legs, 37in (93cm) high.
$300-600

A Regency mahogany chair with curved toprail inlaid with flowerheads and ebony lines on reeded uprights, bearing a brass plaque inscribed 'This chair, the last which Napoleon Bonaparte sat on, was at his bedside when he died and was brought home by Gov'nr. Chas. Dallas of St. Helena' with details of an 1883 sale pasted beneath, with 2 authenticating documents.
$14,000-24,000

A pair of Edwardian inlaid mahogany side chairs, c1910, 23in (58cm).
$600-1,100

A Regency burr maple chair.
$1,700-3,000

A set of 6 Victorian carved salon chairs.
$1,800-3,800

A pair of German Biedermeier salon chairs, framed in rosewood, early 19thC.
$800-1,500

A set of 4 Victorian walnut side chairs, with acanthus carved top- and back-rails on French cabriole front supports.
$1,300-2,400

A set of 6 Victorian walnut side chairs.
$2,200-4,200

A late Victorian mahogany grandmother chair, with button back.
$600-1,200

A fine set of 6 Chippendale mahogany side chairs, New York, 1760-1780, each with serpentine crest-rail with shaped ears centering a fan-curved shell above a pierced splat flanked by stiles, on cabriole legs with shell-carved knees and ball-and-claw feet, various minor breaks, 38in (95cm) high.
$36,000-40,000

An almost identical side chair is in the collection of the New Haven Colony Historical Society. See John T. Kirk, American Chairs, Queen Anne Chippendale (New York, 1082), fig. 141.

A Queen Anne walnut side chair, Newport, Rhode Island, 1745-1765, the arched crest-rail centering a carved scallop shell over a solid vase-shaped splat with in-cut ears, flanked by curving stiles, over a compass seat, 39½in (99cm) high.
$10,000-12,000

A Queen Anne walnut side chair, Pennsylvania, 1740-1765, the serpentine crest-rail with beaded edge and scrolled ears centering a rocaille motif, above a shaped solid splat over a trapezoidal slip seat, 41½in (103cm) high.
$6,500-7,500

A set of 4 classical mahogany Klismos side chairs, possibly by Charles Bouvier, Philadelphia, c1805-1825, each with a curved, molded flame grained crest-rail, upholstered seat cushion and sabre legs, 31in (79cm) high.
$3,000-4,000

A fine pair of Federal inlaid mahogany side chairs, attributed to the Shop of John and Thomas Seymour, Boston, 1794-1810, each wth stepped and narrow-panelled crest rail above a reeded stile square back centering 3 reeded vertical bars forming gothic arches at the top, 36½in (92cm) high.
$14,000-16,000

A Federal inlaid mahogany side chair, Massachusetts, 1790-1810, with shield back centering 5 curving molded vertical bars radiating from an inlaid fan, 37½in (94cm) high.
$1,000-1,300

A set of 4 Victorian walnut salon chairs.
$800-1,500

A pair of Victorian ebonised low chairs.
$4,000-6,800

A Victorian button back mahogany nursing chair, c1870, 41in (103cm) high.
$800-1,500

A Victorian walnut nursing chair.
$4,000-6,800

A Victorian rosewood framed nursing chair.
$400-750

A Victorian carved walnut nursing chair, with foliate scroll carved and pierced cresting.
$300-600

A Baroque Revival parcel-gilt ceremonial chair or sleigh, with acanthus, scallop shell and scroll carving, seat replaced, 38 by 53½in (95 by 134cm).
$1,300-2,400

An Edwardian mahogany drawing room suite of 7 pieces, with satinwood panel and boxwood string inlay.
$1,000-2,000

A black painted ladderback high chair, probably Delaware, 1770-1800, with 4 graduated shaped splats flanked by turned stiles with acorn finials above turned arms with swelled grips over baluster supports, 38in (95cm) high.
$2,200-2,500

In the Furniture section if there is only one measurement it usually refers to the width of the piece.

A set of 4 Dutch marquetry inlaid dining chairs.
$1,800-3,800

An Anglo Indian padoukwood planter's chair, 2nd quarter of 19thC.
$2,200-4,200

A set of 4 Dutch rococo inlaid walnut side chairs, restorations, second quarter 18thC.
$6,000-12,000

A German cowhorn armchair, with twin splat back, late 19thC.
$600-1,200

A set of 4 Italian walnut and painted side chairs, later blocks, mid-18thC.
$2,200-4,200

Furniture – Chests

l. An infant's American rocking chair, late 19thC.
$200-450

r. An American rocking chair, late 19thC.
$200-450

A set of 4 Régence painted and carved salon chairs.
$4,000-7,500

A William and Mary oyster-veneered walnut and olivewood chest, on later bun feet, 34½in (87.5cm).
$12,000-21,000

A walnut bachelor's chest, 31½in (79cm).
$28,000-50,000

A walnut bachelor's chest, with crossbanded hinged top, the sides with carrying handles, 30in (76cm).
$14,000-24,000

A Queen Anne walnut bachelor's chest, 33½in (85cm).
$25,000-45,000

A Queen Anne burr walnut chest, the rectangular quartered crossbanded top with re-entrant front corners and a slide, on later bracket feet, 30in (76cm).
$10,000-18,000

A Queen Anne period walnut chest, the faded top quarter veneered with cross and herringbone banding, 33½in (83.5cm).
$11,000-20,000

A pair of miniature mahogany chest of drawers, American, early 19thC, each with rectangular top above 4 graduated drawers over a scalloped skirt, on straight bracket feet, right rear legs off, right skirt on one chest missing, 15in (38cm) wide.
$2,000-2,500

A Federal walnut chest of drawers, Delaware or Pennsylvania, 1790-1810, the case with 4 thumb-molded and graduated long drawers flanked by fluted quarter columns, on French feet, small chip to one drawer, patch to left front foot, 41in (101cm) wide.
$2,800-3,500

A Queen Anne cedar blanket chest on frame, Bermuda, 1740-1780, the lift-top with molded edge, opening to a till above a dovetailed case with molded plinth over a scalloped skirt, on short cabriole legs with ring-turned pad feet, top now unattached, old breaks to rear leg, 37½in (95cm) wide.
$6,500-7,500

This red cedar chest on frame is typical of a group of similar pieces from Bermuda which have elaborate dovetailing. Several related chests-on-frames are illustrated in Bryden B. Hyde, Bermuda's Antique Furniture & Silver (Bermuda, 1971), figs. 322-330. This piece is of a rare small size.

A Chippendale cherrywood chest of drawers, Connecticut, 1770-1790, small piece of left rear foot restored, 35 by 41in (89 by 101cm).
$4,000-5,000

A Federal inlaid walnut serpentine chest of drawers, probably Virginia, 1795-1815, the serpentine front edge with stringing and banding, the line inlaid drawers flanked by chamfered columns with vine and urn inlay over a shaped skirt, on French feet, feet reduced, some inlay loss, 39½in (100cm) wide.
$5,000-6,000

A fine Chippendale cherrywood reverse-serpentine chest of drawers, Connecticut River Valley, probably Hartford area, 1775-1795, the rectangular molded-edge top with reverse-serpentine front above a conforming case with 4 cockbead molded and graduated long drawers flanked by fluted quarter columns, on ogee bracket feet, 43in (109cm) wide.
$25,000-28,000

While the design of this chest of drawers related to the work of Eliphalet and Aaron Chapin and their students George Belden and Erastus Grant, the construction differs significantly from pieces attributable to this school. Nevertheless, the style of this chest, with its blocked reverse-serpentine front, engaged quarter columns and ogee bracket feet places it in the Hartford County area. A chest-on-chest by Eliphalet or Aaron Chapin with a base relating to this piece is illustrated in Gerald W.R. Ward and William N. Hosley, eds. The Great River: Art & Society of the Connecticut Valley, 1635-1820, (Hardford, 1985), fig. 112, p.321.

A Federal cherrywood and maple bowfront chest of drawers, Massachusetts or New Hampshire, 1800-1815, with pattern-inlaid bowfront and outset turned front corners above a conforming case with 4 cockbead-molded long drawers, each drawer with central oval panel flanked by rectangular panels, outlined with stringing and mahogany banking, 45in (114cm) wide.
$3,800-4,400

A small Queen Anne walnut chest on later stand, the top crossbanded and inlaid with geometric stringing, 31in (78cm).
$9,000-15,000

A Queen Anne chest in figured walnut veneers, of a finely faded colour, the book-matched surface boxwood strung and crossbanded, replacement brasswork, standing on restored feet, c1710, 38in (95cm).
$7,000-12,000

An early Georgian burr yew chest, on reinforced bracket feet, 37in (92.5cm).
$10,000-18,000

A small George I walnut and herringbone banded chest, with quartered top and 4 long graduated drawers with brass handles on bracket feet, original condition but in need of some restoration, 31 by 29in (77.5 by 72cm).
$34,000-60,000

A walnut chest, with oak top, early 18thC, 38in (95cm).
$1,800-3,800

A George I chest, in figured walnut veneers, the surface with herringbone inlay and crossbanding, with replaced brasswork, and fretted bracket feet, c1720, 40½in (101cm).
$11,000-20,000

A bachelor's chest, early 18thC.
$4,000-7,500

A mahogany bachelor's chest, with writing slide, 31in (77.5cm).
$4,000-7,500

Make the most of Miller's

Unless otherwise stated, any description which refers to 'a set' or 'a pair' includes a valuation for the entire set or the pair, even though the illustration may show only a single item.

An early Georgian walnut crossbanded chest, 38in (95cm).
$1,700-3,000

An early George III mahogany chest, with good quality replaced rocaille brasswork, c1770, 41in (102.5cm).
$6,000-12,000

A figured walnut chest, with later ornate brass handles and escutcheons, early 18thC, 39½in (98.5cm).
$2,600-5,300

An early George III mahogany serpentine chest, the figured satinwood strung surface with moulded edge, with original lions' mask brasswork, c1760, 42in (105cm).
$10,000-18,000

An early Georgian walnut chest, on later bracket feet, 40½in (101cm).
$4,500-9,000

A George III mahogany serpentine front chest of drawers, 47in (117.5cm).
$4,500-9,000

A George III mahogany chest, with partly replaced ogee bracket feet, the back partly replaced, 42in (105cm).
$8,000-15,000

A George III mahogany serpentine chest, crossbanded and inlaid with stringing, 43in (107.5cm).
$4,500-9,000

A George III mahogany serpentine front chest, 38in (95cm).
$6,000-12,000

A Georgian walnut veneered dwarf chest, with writing slide, crossbanded and inlaid with ebony and boxwood stringing, 32in (80cm).
$9,000-15,000

A walnut and banded chest, in need of restoration, early 18thC, 36in (90cm).
$1,700-3,000

A fine George III mahogany serpentine dressing chest.
$11,000-18,000

A good George III mahogany and inlaid secretaire chest, c1750.
$5,000-9,000

A George III mahogany serpentine chest, inlaid with stringing, 42½ (105cm).
$1,800-3,800

An early George III mahogany chest, of rare small size, the good quality fretted brass drawer-pulls are replacements for the original turned wood examples, c1770, 21in (52.5cm).
$5,500-9,000

A George III mahogany chest of drawers, with a brushing slide, restorations to feet, 31in (77cm).
$1,800-3,800

A good George III mahogany mule chest, the broadly crossbanded top above a frieze inlaid with shell and ostrich plume medallions, 65in (162cm).
$2,200-4,200

An unusual George III mahogany dressing chest, 49in (123cm).
$3,200-6,000

A George III mahogany dressing and secretaire chest, the uppermost drawer containing sliding baize-covered writing surface and book rest with compartments beneath, the second drawer unusually flanked by supporting lopers, c1770, 36in (90cm).
$5,000-9,000

A George III mahogany serpentine chest, the top banded in satinwood and yew wood and with a central oval fan inlay, 44in (110cm).
$6,000-12,000

A George III mahogany serpentine chest, 45in (111cm).
$4,500-9,000

A George III mahogany small chest, 36in (90cm).
$1,700-3,000

A George III satinwood chest, tulipwood banded, boxwood and ebony inlay, 46in (115cm).
$6,000-12,000

A George III crossbanded mahogany chest of drawers, the top warped, 36in (90cm).
$1,800-3,800

Chests

- ★ 17thC oak coffers were made in sufficient numbers to allow a reasonable supply today
- ★ still expect to find original wire or plate hinges; original lock and hasp; original candle box; reasonably tall feet
- ★ the *best* English chest of drawers of the walnut period will be veneered on to pine or other cheaper timber, the drawer linings will be oak, but the interior of the drawer front wil not be; only the top surface visible when the drawer is open will have a slip of oak attached
- ★ an oak drawer front veneered with walnut suggests either Continental provenance or an early oak chest veneered at a later date; check that holes for handles are compatible inside and out for further evidence of this
- ★ feet on William and Mary chests were either formed by the stile continuing down to the floor or by large turned 'buns'. The former were often retained and used as blocks to be encased by the later more fashionable bracket feet; the 'buns' were often removed in the same cause. To ascertain this, remove the bottom drawer and a hole in each front corner will be present, if bun feet were originally used
- ★ by the end of the 18thC, turned wood knobs were fashionable. They were at first fine and small, but soon became the flat bulbous mushrooms so popular on most bedroom and staff quarters furniture. If these are original, it is better to resist the temptation of removing them and applying reproduction brass handles
- ★ accept proper restoration but avoid improvements

A Georgian inlaid mahogany bowfronted chest, 36in (90cm).
$1,600-2,800

A Regency mahogany serpentine chest, the top with banded boxwood line borders, 38in (95cm).
$8,000-15,000

A burr walnut chest of drawers, 19thC, 40in (100cm).
$1.000-2,000

A George IV mahogany secretaire, having boxwood and ebony inlaid decoration, 48in (120cm).
$1,700-3,000

A mahogany bowfront chest of drawers, early 19thC.
$1,000-2,000

A fine Regency mahogany military secretaire chest, the top drawer opening to reveal secretaire comprising small cupboard, 3 drawers and pigeonholes, 42in (105cm).
$2,200-4,200

A Regency mahogany chest.
$600-1,100

An unusual pale oak chest of graduated drawers, below a line of 3 inlaid mahogany faced accessory drawers, c1830.
$1,800-3,800

A pale mahogany campaign chest.
$2,200-4,200

A small Regency inlaid satinwood bowfront chest of drawers, 31in (77.5cm).
$1,300-2,400

A mahogany serpentine chest of drawers, with crossbanded front, the top drawer with divided interior, early 19thC, 44in (110cm).
$3,200-6,000

A Victorian mahogany artists material storage chest, having glazed and sloping lid, 60in (150cm).
$800-1,500

A mahogany secretaire chest, 19thC, 25½in (63.5cm).
$800-1,500

A Dutch walnut veneered chest of drawers, inlaid with elm(?) bands, 18thC, 36in (90cm).
$6,000-12,000

A Colonial rosewood chest of drawers, with parquetry top, c1740.
$6,000-12,000

A mid-Georgian style mahogany dwarf serpentine chest, inlaid with satinwood fanned ovals, spandrels and chevron boxwood lined borders, 30in (75cm).
$3,200-6,000

A Dutch floral marquetry bombé chest of drawers, late 18thC, 34in (85cm).
$4,000-6,800

A continental rosewood dressing chest, probably German, mid-19thC, 51in (127.5cm).
$800-1,500

A William and Mary style chest, inlaid with scrolling foliate marquetry, the sides inlaid with ebonised boxwood stars, 39in (97.5cm).
$3,200-6,000

A Dutch walnut and marquetry bombé chest, the serpentine top inlaid, supported by later feet, mid-18thC, 56in (140cm).
$9,000-15,000

A Venetian green painted and parcel-gilt chest, late 18th/early 19thC, 49in (122cm).
$4,000-6,800

Chests-on-Chests

A Queen Anne/George I feather banded walnut chest-on-chest, 39in (97.5cm) wide.
$10,000-18,000

A Queen Anne walnut tallboy, the angles inlaid with lines, on bracket feet, 69 by 44in (172 by 110cm).
$8,000-15,000

A George II walnut veneered tallboy, some restoration, 76 by 47in (192.5 by 117.5cm).
$7,000-12,000

A George III mahogany secretaire tallboy, with dentilled broken pediment, 82 by 45 (208 by 112.5cm).
$10,000-18,000

A Queen Anne cabinet-on-chest, the cornice with later acorn vase finials above a pair of cupboard doors enclosing 11 drawers, below 2 fall-flaps with a slide beneath, the associated base with a fitted secretaire drawer and 3 graduated long drawers on later elongated bun feet, 82 by 41 (207.5 by 102.5cm).
$26,000-45,000

A Fine Chippendale mahogany block-front chest-on-chest, Boston, 1750-1785, in 2 sections, the upper with 2 flame finials, a molded swan's neck pediment centering a shaped pendant and gilt pine phoenix, the 2 short drawers centering a blocked and fan-carved center drawer, with 4 graduated long drawers below, all flanked by fluted pilasters; the lower section with 4 blocked long drawers, all drawers surrounded by cockbeaded dividers, the molded plinth centered by a drop pendant, on bracket feet, brasses appear to be original, side handles probably of English origin, 80 by 38 by 22in (202.5 by 95 by 55cm).
$300,000+

A walnut and herringbone banded tallboy, early 18thC, 41in (102.5cm) wide.
$8,000-15,000

A George I walnut chest-on-chest, with crossbanded herringbone inlaid drawers, on restored bracket feet, the brasswork an early replacement, c1720, 75 by 42 (190 by 105cm).
$18,000-26,000

◁A George III mahogany tallboy, the top section with a dentil moulded cornice above a blind fret carved frieze, 44in (110cm) wide.
$3,200-6,000

An early Georgian oak tallboy, of small size, 56½ by 34½in (140 by 86cm).
$10,000-18,000

A George I walnut chest-on-chest, the crossbanded cockbeaded drawers all with fretted brasswork, the feet and back are old replacements, c1720, 67½ by 40in (168 by 100cm).
$18,000-26,000

A George III mahogany tallboy, on ogee bracket feet, c1780.
$4,000-7,500

A George III mahogany tallboy, with original brass fittings, 44in (109cm) wide.
$2,000-4,500

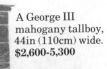

A George III mahogany tallboy, 44in (110cm) wide.
$2,600-5,300

A Georgian walnut inlaid tallboy, 70 by 39in (175 by 97.5cm).
$4,500-9,000

A mahogany chest-on-chest, in the Chippendale style, the upper section with acanthus carved broken swan neck pediment, pierced with diapering, with blind fret carved frieze, 18thC.
$20,000-30,000

A fine George III bowfront chest-on-chest, in flamed mahogany veneers, the moulded cornice above cockbeaded drawers with rocaille brasswork, c1790, 73 by 42½in (185 by 106cm).
$6,000-12,000

A late Georgian mahogany tallboy chest, 42in (105cm) wide.
$1,600-2,800

A Regency mahogany bowfront tallboy, the arched cornice inlaid with geometric ebony lines, 44½in (111cm) wide.
$2,200-4,200

Chests-on-Stands

A Georgian mahogany tallboy, with fitted secretaire drawer, 39in (97.5cm) wide.
$4,500-9,000

A William and Mary walnut chest-on-stand, 61 by 42in (152.5 by 105cm).
$7,000-12,000

A William and Mary walnut and burr yew chest-on-stand, restored, the stand renewed in part, 62½ by 40in (156 by 100cm).
$4,000-7,500

A fine Queen Anne maple high chest of drawers, Newbury, Massachusetts area, 1750-1770, in 2 sections, the upper with cover-molded cornice above 2 short thumb-molded drawers over 4 long graduated drawers, the lower case with applied mid-band molding over a single thumb-molded long drawer above 3 short deep drawers, the brasses appear to be original and retain evidence of original gilt, the chest has an overall mahoganizing finish, a few minor drawer corner repairs, 73 by 40in (185 by 110cm).
$22,000-25,000

This high chest is nearly identical to 2 chests with Newbury histories, which are discussed in Brock Jobe and Myrna Kaye, New England Furniture: The Colonial Era, *Boston 1984, pp.208-210, No.39. All 3 pieces share distinctive construction features as well as obvious stylistic similarities.*

A Queen Anne oyster veneered walnut chest-on-stand, inlaid with concentric roundels above 2 short and 3 graduated long drawers, the stand with partly re-lined drawer and oak bun feet, later back, adapted, 36in (90cm).
$14,000-24,000

A Queen Anne walnut chest-on-stand, with feather banding and on later cabriole supports with pointed pad feet, 68 by 38½in (170 by 96cm).
$6,000-12,000

A Chippendale walnut high chest of drawers, Pennsylvania, 1760-1790, the upper section with a removable molded cornice with blind fretwork above a frieze of 3 short drawers over 4 graduated long drawers, each thumb-molded, flanked by fluted quarter columns, 45½in (130cm) wide at cornice.
$20,000-25,000

This high chest of drawers descended in the Bringhurst-Lea family of Wilmington. A copy of John Lea's will, dated 1803, was found with other family documents in one of the drawers. In this will John Lea left to his wife 'all of the household furniture that I delivered to her in the year one thousand seven hundred and seventy-one . . . consisting of our featherbed and furniture, walnut chairs, tables, chest of drawers and other articles'.

A Chippendale carved walnut high chest of drawers, Massachusetts, 1760-1780, in 2 sections, the upper with cove-molded bonnet pediment, the lower case with long single drawer over 3 short drawers, the center one shell-carved above a shaped apron, on cabriole legs with ball and claw feet, brasses appear to be original, right front leg restored, restoration to pediment, 40½in (105cm) wide.
$14,000-18,000

A George II red walnut chest-on-stand, 48½in (121cm) wide.
$3,200-6,000

A Chippendale walnut high chest of drawers, Philadelphia, 1760-1790, in 2 sections, the upper with dentilled cornice above a case with 3 short thumb-molded drawers over 2 similar short drawers over 3 graduated long drawers, flanked by fluted quarter columns, the lower case with applied mid-molding over 3 short drawers above one long drawer over a shaped apron, a few minor drawer edge chips and one small patch on rear of side, 44½in (125cm) wide.
$10,000-14,000

A fine Chippendale carved cherrywood high chest of drawers, East Windsor, Connecticut area, 1780-1800, in 2 sections, the upper with molded swan's-neck and pierced latticework pediment centering 3 finials above a case with 3 thumb-molded short drawers, the center one relief-carved with crossed scrolled tendrils, the lower case with single thumb-molded long drawer over 3 short drawers, the center one carved as above, 41in (105cm) wide.
$28,000-30,000

This high chest is similar in design, materials and construction to a dressing table and a chest-on-chest attributed to the two Chapins by Gerald W.R. Ward and William N. Hosley Jr., eds., The Great River: Art & Society of the Connecticut Valley, 1635-1820 (Hartford, 1985), Nos.111 and 112, pp.230-232. The Philadelphia-inspired design features of this high chest, especially the interlocking foliage on 2 drawers, the swirled termini in the pediment, the well-shaped cabriole legs, the deep skirt and its distinctive profile, and the basket-weave pediment, reflect Eliphalet Chapin's training in that city in the late 1760s. The drawer supports on this high chest are tenoned through the backboards, a typical Chapin feature found on the dressing table mentioned above and on a Chapin-attributed high chest of drawers at the Wadsworth Athenaeum. The Wadsworth high chest is stylistically a virtual mate to this high chest, except for its use of fluted quarter columns, see the colour illustration in Philip Johnston 'Eighteenth and Nineteenth Century American Furniture in the Wadsworth Athenaeum,' Antiques (May, 1979), pl. IV, p.1018.

A Chippendale walnut tall chest of drawers, Pennsylvania, 1760-1780, now on casters, minor patches, break to one drawer front, 43in (120cm) wide.
$8,500-10,500

A Queen Anne walnut chest on frame, Pennsylvania, 1750-1780, some re-shaping to front of skirt, 70 by 41in (178 by 120cm).
$14,000-16,000

A fine diminutive William and Mary burl walnut veneer and maple high chest of drawers, Boston, Massachusetts, 1700-1740, in 2 sections, the upper with a molded cornice and 2 short drawers above 3 graduated long drawers, the lower with 2 deep short drawers centered by a short drawer, the shaped and valenced apron on partially ebonized trumpet and ring-turned legs, with small turnip-shaped feet, upper back boards and right stretcher restored, 39in (99cm) wide.
$43,000-45,000

A fine Chippendale carved walnut high chest of drawers, Salem, Massachusetts, 1765-1785, in 2 sections, the upper with a molded bonnet pediment centering 3 plinths with flame finials above a case with short fan-carved central drawer flanked by 2 shallow short drawers over 4 long drawers, the lower section with single long drawer over 3 short drawers, the central one with conforming carved fan, brasses appear to be original, 42in (115cm) wide.
$60,000-80,000

An old note in the top drawer of the lower case read: "This highboy was the property of Reverand Brom Emerson of Salem Massachusetts, (b. Ashby, Mass. 1778, d. Salem 1872) Mar. Oct. 29-1806 Mary Hopkins Emerson." He was pastor of South Church of Salem for 67 years. The chest came to his daughter Harriet A. Emerson Latting in 1872 at New York and was willed by her son Charles P. Latting to Emerson Latting (great grandson of Brom Emerson).

A fine Chippendale mahogany high chest of drawers, Massachusetts, 1760-1780, the upper section with a scrolled pediment surmounted by 3 'corkscrew' finials over a fan-carved drawer flanked by 2 short drawers, the lower section with a molded waist over a long drawer above a frieze of 3 short drawers, the center drawer fan-carved and blocked, 42in (115cm) wide.
$30,000-40,000

Wellington Chests

A William IV rosewood secretaire wellington chest, the 6 long drawers with beaded edge flanking a central secretaire drawer, 40in (100cm) wide.
$2,200-4,200

A Victorian burr maplewood wellington chest, with locking bar, 52 by 26in (130 by 65cm).
$1,800-3,800

Coffers

A walnut four-panelled coffer with mitred decorations, 19thC.
$1,800-3,800

A Queen Anne ▷ walnut coffer, the moulded top inlaid with geometric feather banding, with later bun feet, 38in (96cm) wide.
$9,000-15,000

An Italian walnut cassone, 17thC, 70in (175cm).
$1,000-2,000

A German oak Renaissance chest, 16thC, 46in (115cm).
$4,500-9,000

◁ A North Italian or South German walnut and marquetry small coffer, the domed top inlaid with a monogram, strapwork, flowers and star motifs, 18thC, 15½ by 31in (37.5 by 77.5cm).
$1,200-2,100

△ A North Italian cedarwood chest, 17thC, 22 by 72in (55 by 180cm).
$1,600-2,800

An Anglo–Indian green leather covered travelling chest, early 19thC. 37in (92.5cm).
$800-1,500

▷

A Spanish walnut coffer, 17thC, 66½in (166cm) wide.
$1,700-3,000

Commodes

A mahogany pedestal commode, with brass side carrying handles, the locker enclosed by 2 crossbanded doors, the lower pull-out section converted to a drawer, 19in (47.5cm) wide.
$1,200-2,100

A George III gentleman's mahogany commode, of serpentine form with cross banded top, the top drawer well fitted with lidded and open compartments, ratchetted mirror and enclosed by a baize-lined slide, 41in (102.5cm).
$3,200-6,000

A George III mahogany tray top commode, with converted drawer and cupboard doors.
$3,200-6,000

A Hepplewhite style mahogany commode, serpentine front with tambour shutter, late 18thC, 28 by 22½in (70 by 55cm).
$1,000-2,000

An Italian olivewood and walnut commode, converted to a cabinet, the broadly crossbanded top, with a central panel inlaid with lapping boxwood circles, the 2 fruitwood-banded long drawers now forming a fall-front on short cabriole legs, 41in (102cm) wide.
$900-1,700

A George III mahogany tray-top commode, with ebony stringing, 21in (52.5cm) wide.
$1,200-2,100

A Georgian bowfront satinwood commode, decorated with rosewood crossbanding and painted floral bands, 45 by 60in (112.5 by 150cm).
$4,000-6,800

A mahogany, rosewood, sycamore and marquetry commode, with crossbanded serpentine top, with adapted interior, third quarter 18thC, 33½ by 52in (83 by 130cm).
$4,500-9,000

The inlaid decoration on this commode has possible links with the work of Swedish marqueteurs working in England in the 1770s, particularly for John Linnell. A commode at Castle Howard made by Christian Furlohg in 1767 while in the Linnell's employ is inlaid with similar urns (H. Hayward and P. Kirkham, William and John Linnell, 1980, vol. II, fig.109).

An Empire mahogany commode, with grey fossil marble top, 34½ by 51½in (86 by 128cm).
$5,000-9,000

A Georgian mahogany bedside commode, having inlaid decoration, 18in (45cm).
$800-1,500

A Danish rosewood and parcel gilt commode, with later shaped eared mottled white marble top, restorations, mid-18thC, 28in (70cm).
$4,500-9,000

An Anglo–Dutch mahogany serpentine commode, inlaid with swags and ribbons, the front with a pair of tambour cupboards flanked by fluted canted corners, c1800, 40in (101cm) wide.
$2,000-4,500

A Louis XV style serpentine commode, in kingwood veneers with moulded rouge marble surface, with rocaille ormolu mounts, c1870, 32 by 24in (80 by 60cm).
$4,500-9,000

An ormolu mounted kingwood and floral marquetry bombe commode, of Louis XV style, 51½in (128cm) wide.
$4,500-9,000

A South German walnut commode, with parquetry decorated serpentine front and sides, 18thC, 46in (115cm).
$6,000-12,000

A South German walnut and parquetry serpentine commode, 18thC, 51in (128cm).
$4,500-9,000

Cupboards – Armoires

A high Victorian dark oak court cupboard, 82in (207cm) wide.
$2,200-4,200

A Flemish rosewood oak ebonised and tortoiseshell cupboard, on later bun feet, minor restorations, 17thC, 67 by 64in (167.5 by 160cm).
$6,000-12,000

A fine Dutch walnut and marquetry secretaire armoire.
$22,000-40,000

A French chestnut armoire, carved with a central basket of flowers and ribbon tied bouquets, Breton, late 18thC, 63in (157.5cm).
$4,500-9,000 ▷

A carved oak, two-door cabinet on cupboard base, 19thC, 45in (112.5cm).
$600-1,200

A French red walnut small armoire, with boxwood and ebony inlay.
$4,500-9,000

A Louis XV provincial chestnut armoire, 97 by 60in (245 by 150cm).
$2,000-4,500

A German ebonised beech armoire, with classical corner brackets in the form of male guards with tortoiseshell plaques and strung with ebony, c1770.
$10,000-18,000

A Flemish oak buffet, carved throughout with fruit and foliage, 19thC, 125 by 86in (314.5 by 217.5cm).
$2,200-4,200

A German painted, marblised and parcel-gilt pine armoire, mid-18thC, 70in (175cm).
$4,500-9,000

A small Chippendale walnut cupboard, Pennsylvania 1750-1785, the molded cornice above a panelled door opening to an interior with 2 short drawers over one long drawer each fitted with original engraved brasses, with a molded long drawer below, feet restored, 25½in (63cm).
$5,000-6,000

A Chippendale poplar hanging cupboard, Pennsylvania 1750-1785, the molded cornice above a door with raised panel and wrought iron rat-tail hinges above scrolled side boards and a shallow shelf, 27½in (68cm).
$5,000-6,000

Cupboards – Bedside

A Georgian mahogany pedestal toilet cupboard, 14in (35cm).
$600-1,100

An Empire mahogany cupboard, with an ormolu plaque of Orpheus, 63 by 27in (157.5 by 67.5cm).
$1,300-2,400

A pair of Biedermeier mahogany bedside cupboards, 33 by 22in (82.5 by 55cm).
$26,000-45,000

Cupboards – Corner

A Queen Anne black japanned corner cupboard, 22½in (56cm).
$1,300-2,400

A George III oak two-stage corner cupboard, no back, 86 by 59in (217.5 by 147.5cm).
$2,600-5,300

A George III mahogany bow front corner cupboard, outlined with boxwood stringing, 31in (78cm).
$1,600-2,800

CORNER CUPBOARDS

★ these cupboards were made right through the 18thC in various woods including walnut and mahogany, as well as oak
★ examples in oak are usually 'country' versions of the more sophisticated pieces made in walnut or mahogany
★ corner cupboards with glazed doors, that are suitable for the display of porcelain or other objects, are the most sought after type. They are, however, far more difficult to find and are consequently more expensive
★ bow fronted examples are usually considered the most desirable, especially if they are fitted inside with two or three small drawers and the shelves are shaped
★ these cupboards are usually constructed in two parts; 'marriages' do exist and whilst these may be acceptable, it should be reflected in a lower price. Check that the backboards of the two parts match and that the quality of timber and style of construction correspond

A George III mahogany corner cupboard, flanked by canted sides inlaid with boxwood, 34in (85cm). **$800-1,500**

A Georgian red lacquered standing corner cupboard, decorated in chinoiserie, 36in (90cm). **$2,600-5,300**

A Chippendale walnut corner cupboard, Delaware Valley, 1760-1790, the upper section with a cove-molded and broken cornice above arched and glazed cupboard doors, flanked by fielded panels in the spandrels and by fluted pilasters, the lower section with a molded waist over 2 panelled cupboard doors flanked by fluted pilasters, on a coved molding, on ogee bracket feet, 50in (125cm) wide. **$20,000-25,000**

A good George III mahogany bow front corner cupboard, 31in (77cm). **$1,800-3,800**

◁ A mahogany cylinder front corner cupboard with moulded cornice and brass H hinges, 43 by 29in (107.5 by 72.5cm). **$1,200-2,100**

◁ A Georgian walnut standing corner cupboard, probably veneered, 82 by 44in (207.5 by 110cm). **$1,800-3,800**

A George IV fruitwood corner cupboard, c1820, 85 by 41in (215 by 102.5cm). **$6,000-12,000**

A Dutch walnut and marquetry corner cupboard, the top inset with a clock, the painted dial signed A Brugger, 79 High Holborn, London, 99 by 30in (250 by 75cm). **$5,500-9,000**

A mahogany double bow front corner cupboard, 87 by 38in (220 by 95cm). **$1,600-2,800**

A satinwood and ▷ rosewood banded standing corner cabinet, inlaid with ebonised lines, basically 19thC, 26in (65cm). **$1,600-2,800**

A George III mahogany corner ▷ cupboard with fielded panel doors, c1810. **$3,200-6,000**

Cupboards – Linen Presses

A George III mahogany plain clothes press.
$2,200-4,200

A George III mahogany linen press, the dentil cornice above a pair of doors veneered in oval panels with chequer inlay, c1790, 73 by 51½in (185 by 128cm).
$6,000-12,000

A rare diminutive Queen Anne maple linen press, Middle Atlantic States, possibly Delaware Valley, 1750-1785, in 2 sections, the upper with a molded overhanging cornice above a pair of panelled doors flanked by fluted chamfered corners and opening to a shelved interior; the lower section with 3 graduated molded long drawers above 3 molded short drawers, the shaped apron with center pendant, retains its original brasses, 42½in (105cm).
$30,000-40,000

An early George III secretaire clothes press, 74½ by 45½in (187.5 by 114cm).
$4,500-9,000

A small Regency mahogany clothes press, 59½ by 36in (147.5 by 90cm).
$10,000-18,000

A good George III mahogany bow front linen press, c1810, 50½in (126cm).
$3,200-6,000

A George III design mahogany serpentine fronted linen press, the frieze inlaid with oval shell panels and tied laurel leaves, 48in (120cm).
$4,500-9,000

△

A George III mahogany press with moulded and dentilled cornice, the doors with oval satinwood banding, 78 by 49in (197.5 by 122.5cm).
$2,000-4,500

A George III satinwood clothes press, 82 by 49½in (207.5 by 112.5cm).
$8,000-15,000

Cupboards –
Wardrobes

An Edwardian figured
walnut wardrobe
chest, 81in (205cm).
$600-1,200

An inlaid mahogany linen press,
early 19thC, 50in (125cm).
$2,000-4,500

A Sheraton mahogany inlaid
gentleman's press cupboard, c1795.
$4,500-9,000

An Italian walnut wardrobe, late
17thC, 69in (172.5cm).
$2,200-4,200

A Victorian mahogany wardrobe,
inlaid with a marquetry satinwood
panel and geometric boxwood lines,
53in (132.5cm).
$1,200-2,100

A massive walnut cupboard,
possibly German, 19thC, 96 by 66in
(242.5 by 165cm).
$1,000-2,000

A Regency mahogany linen press,
inlaid with ebony stringing and
fleurs-de-lys to the corners, 53in
(132cm).
$3,200-6,000

Davenports

A mahogany
davenport, early
19thC, 36 by 20in
$2,200-4,200

A George IV
mahogany davenport,
with a pierced brass
gallery, 34½
by 21½in (86 by 53cm).
$2,600-5,300

An early Victorian rosewood piano-
top davenport, with well fitted
interior, pen and ink compartments
and slides and with a secret pull
button in one of the drawers
activating the pop-up document top
with pigeon holes and small
drawers.
$3,200-6,000

A Continental oak hanging
cupboard, late 17thC, 83in (210cm).
$1,300-2,400

DAVENPORTS

★ the name derives from Gillow's cost book where an illustration of this piece of furniture appeared for the first time. Beside the illustration was written 'Captain Davenport – a desk'

★ first examples date from the late 1790s

★ they were extremely popular during the Regency and well into Victoria's reign

★ there are two quite distinct types of davenport – the quite severe Regency as opposed to the more generous and often highly carved Victorian

★ they are bought by a quite different market – at the moment the walnut well carved Victorian can be said to be selling much better than the earlier Regency

★ points to look out for: burr-walnut, satinwood, secret drawers or complex interior arrangement, good quality carving and cabriole legs, galleried top

★ unless stated all davenports in this section are fitted with 4 real opposed by 4 dummy drawers.

A Victorian rosewood davenport, 22in (55cm).
$1,400-2,600

A William IV rosewood davenport with gallery to the top, sloping writing surface with leather insert 33in (82.5cm).
$1,800-3,800

A Victorian walnut davenport, with hinged stationery compartment, 31in (77.5cm).
$1,000-2,000

A Victorian walnut davenport, inlaid with foliate marquetry and boxwood lines, 23in (57.5cm).
$3,200-6,000

A Victorian burr walnut davenport, stamped T Willson, 58 Great Queen Street, London.
$4,000-6,800

A Victorian walnut serpentine fronted davenport, with a pierced and carved gallery to the raised stationery compartment, 37 by 23in (92.5 by 57.5cm).
$1,400-2,600

A Victorian burr walnut piano-front davenport, with pop-up top section.
$1,800-3,800

A Victorian figured walnut davenport, with boxwood string inlay, on a shaped plateau base, 21in (52.5cm).
$1,300-2,400

A mahogany davenport desk, c1920, 32 by 21in (80 by 53cm).
$600-1,200

A George III mahogany kneehole desk, 42½in (106cm).
$11,000-20,000

A George III mahogany kneehole desk, 38in (95cm).
$4,000-6,800

A mahogany kneehole desk, the whole inlaid with chevron bandings, 37in (93cm).
$1,200-2,100

A George III mahogany kneehole desk, later added castors and some repairs, 36½in (91cm).
$4,000-7,500

A George III mahogany kneehole secretaire, in the manner of Gillows, with fitted secretaire drawer, 49½in (123cm).
$8000-13,500

A walnut and feather banded kneehole desk, 29½in (74cm).
$9,000-15,000

A small mahogany and satinwood crossbanded Carlton House desk, 19thC, 48in (120cm).
$2,600-5,300

An Edwardian mahogany kneehole pedestal desk, inlaid with satinwood bands and chequered boxwood line borders, 48in (120cm).
$1,800-3,800

A mid-Georgian padouk wood kneehole desk, 43½in (108cm).
$5,500-9,000

A small Chippendale mahogany kneehole desk, with a small restored patch on the surface, c1770, 29 by 33in (72.5 by 82.5cm).
$9,000-15,000

A George III mahogany desk, the top crossbanded, 33in (82.5cm).
$2,600-5,300

A Hepplewhite style mahogany partners' kneehole pedestal desk, 46 by 71in (115 by 177.5cm).
$14,000-24,000

A George III flamed mahogany bow fronted kneehole desk, c1790.
$4,000-7,500

A mahogany pedestal desk of serpentine outline, 60in (150cm).
$2,600-5,300

A mahogany roll top desk, the S-shape tambour fall enclosing fitted interior, lacking pull-out surface, 50in (125cm).
$1,400-2,600

A bamboo framed desk, late 19thC, 46 by 27in (115 by 67.5cm).
$800-1,500

An unusual George III mahogany clerk's desk, the upper part with raised gallery, with lid lifting to reveal simple interior with 2 drawers, c1775, 37 by 23in (92.5 by 57.5cm).
$4,500-9,000

Dressers

A mahogany crossbanded oak dresser, early 19thC, 73in (185cm).
$3,200-6,000

A Victorian walnut writing desk, in the French style, late 19thC, 42 by 32in (105 by 80cm).
$1,700-3,000

A Victorian mahogany automatic action cabinet desk, 45in (112.5cm).
$1,000-2,000

Dumb Waiters

A mahogany crossbanded oak dresser, early 19thC, 73in (185cm).

A Flemish oak dresser, 18thC, 62in (155cm).
$1,700-3,000

An unusual walnut Swiss buffet, on later bun feet, restoration, 18thC, incorporating a complete pewter wall cistern with tray, Swiss, late 18thC, 87in (220cm) high.
$12,000-21,000

A George III mahogany two-tier dumb waiter, inlaid with brass lines, 36in (90cm).
$11,000-20,000

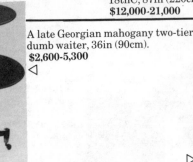

A late Georgian mahogany two-tier dumb waiter, 36in (90cm).
$2,600-5,300
◁

A George III ▷ mahogany dumb waiter, 24in (60cm) diam.
$2,200-4,200

▷

An early Victorian circular three-tier dumb waiter, 40in (100cm).
$1,300-2,400

DUMB WAITERS

★ there is some controversy about when dumb waiters made an appearance

★ they were certainly produced in the 1720s but are rare until the 1750s

★ defined by Sheraton (Cabinet Dictionary 1803) as 'a useful piece of furniture, to serve in some respects the place of a waiter, whence it is so named'

★ 18thC dumb waiters *generally* consist of three tiers

★ made usually from mahogany

★ in Chippendale period supports often carved with foliage, acanthus leaves, broken scrolls, etc

★ Robert Adam's neo-classical style radically changed the design

★ the pillars now tended to become plainly cylindrical with turned collars at top and bottom

★ the late 18thC and early 19thC saw the introduction of pierced galleries often made of brass

★ during the Regency period some dumb waiters made from rosewood

★ marriages are around so beware
 – differing turning on 3 trays
 – two-tier examples (they can be right but are often 'naughty')

◁ A mahogany two-tiered collapsible dumb waiter, c1820.
$4,000-6,800

▷ A George III mahogany three-tier dumb waiter, 46in (115cm).
$3,200-6,000

Fireplaces

A parcel gilt and blue painted fireplace, 53½in (134cm) high.
$2,600-5,300

An early Victorian cast iron insert, stamped Carron, with a decorative shell design border.
$600-1,200

A St. Annes Chimneypiece, with full pink columns, c1870, with an arched cast iron interior, c1880.
$1,700-3,000

▷

◁ A fine George III Carrara marble chimneypiece.
$22,000-40,000

A good George III period mantelpiece in pine with classical gesso decoration, c1780, 54½in (136cm) high.
$6,000-12,000

An Art Nouveau tiled fireplace, with Art Nouveau design to canopy, 38in (95cm) square.
$500-900

Lowboys

A Queen Anne walnut lowboy, 30in (75cm).
$14,000-24,000

A Georgian oak lowboy, 30½in (76cm).
$2,600-5,300

A George II walnut and elm lowboy, the figured quartered herringbone inlaid crossbanded surface with moulded edge, with good quality replacement brasswork above fretted apron and 4 legs on pad feet, c1740, 28 by 32in (70 by 82.5cm).
$4,500-9,000

A small George I lowboy, c1725, 26in (65cm).
$6,000-12,000

A walnut lowboy, with quarter veneered top, early 18thC, some damage, 30 by 19in (75 by 47cm).
$7,000-12,000

This piece was painted.

A mahogany lowboy, crossbanded and satinwood inlaid to the rim, late 18thC, 29½in (74cm).
$1,000-2,000

A lowboy, late 19thC, 34½in (86cm).
$600-1,200

A George I figured oak lowboy, the surface unusually crossbanded in walnut and inlaid with boxwood, with replaced brasswork, c1720, 29in (72.5cm).
$7,000-12,000

Mirrors

A George I walnut lowboy, the quartered surface inlaid and crossbanded, with replaced brasswork, c1730, 28in (70cm).
$8000-13,500

A William and Mary walnut, oyster veneer and marquetry cushion frame wall mirror, inset with a later bevelled plate, 45 by 29in (112 by 73cm).
$8,000-15,000

A George II mahogany and parcel-gilt mirror, with later rectangular plate, re-gilded, 37 by 22½in (92.5 by 56cm).
$2,200-4,200

A walnut framed △
landscape mirror,
early 18thC, 53½ by
18in (134 by 45cm).
$2,200-4,200

A George I wall mirror,
54 by 24in (135 by 60cm).
$8,000-15,000

An early George III painted wood
looking glass, 32 by 25in (80 by
62.5cm).
$6,000-12,000

A George II pier glass, with original
plate, within gilt slip and figured
walnut frame, c1740, 42½in
(106cm).
$6,000-12,000

An English carved giltwood and
painted overmantel frame, 18thC,
54 by 49in (135 by 122.5cm).
$1,000-2,000

A George I walnut and parcel-gilt
mirror, 37 by 17in (92.5 by 42.5cm).
$8000-13,500

A George III gilt wall mirror,   ▷
repairs, 52 by 34in (130 by 85cm).
$10,000-18,000

◁ A Chippendale period carved pine
frame, in the manner of Matthias
Locke, inset with a later plate, 83
by 62in (210 by 155cm).
$7,000-12,000

A pair of early George III carved
giltwood mirrors, 25 by 30in (62.5
by 75cm).
$32,000-54,000

MIRRORS

★ until 1773, 18thC English
looking glass plates were
produced from blown
cylinders of glass. This
restricted the size and so
large mirrors of the period
were made up of more
than one plate. In 1773, a
new process enabled the
production of the large
single piece mirrors which
became fashionable
thereafter

★ 18thC carved and gilded
mirror frames will be of
wood covered with gesso,
or occasionally of carton
pierre

★ in the 19thC, cheaper and
greater production was
achieved by the use of
plaster 'stucco' or
composition 'carved'
decoration built up on a
wire frame. This has
tended to crack and is
thus detectable. Stucco
work cannot be pierced
with a needle. Carved
wood can

★ do not have the old mirror
plate re-silvered if it has
deteriorated, carefully
remove and store; replace
it with a new specialist
made plate. This
particularly applies to
toilet and dressing
mirrors

★ store original mirror
upright, never flat, using
8 batons slightly larger
than the plate – 6 upright
and 2 across to crate the
mirror around bubble
paper

A North Italian carved giltwood running pattern frame, 37 by 35in (92.5 by 87.5cm).
$1,800-3,800

A William IV giltwood overmantel, with moulded rope twist and concave channelled frame with foliate top corners, branded VR below a crown, 65½ by 42in (162.5 by 105cm).
$8,000-15,000

A Louis XV carved giltwood pierced and swept frame, 11 by 8in (27.5 by 20cm).
$1,000-2,000

Provenance: H.R.H. the late Princess Alice, Countess of Athlone, Kensington Palace.

The overmantel was originally at Claremont, near Esher, rebuilt by Capability Brown and Henry Holland, 1769–72, for Clive of India, near the site of the original Vanbrugh House. In 1816 Parliament purchased the house for the newly wed Princess Charlotte, only child of the Prince of Wales, later George IV, and Prince Leopold. After the 1848 revolution King Louis Philippe lived at Claremont until his death in 1850, his widow died there in 1866. Sixteen years later Queen Victoria settled the estate on her youngest son Leopold Duke of Albany, upon his marriage to Princess Helen of Waldeck, the parents of Princess Alice.

The overmantel bears Queen Victoria's cypher and probably formed part of one of the refurnishings of Claremont, perhaps after the death of Queen Marie-Amelie of France, and may have come from another Royal residence.

A finely carved Louis XV giltwood frame, 39 by 49in (97.5 by 120cm).
$8,000-15,000

A William and Mary dressing mirror, in figured walnut veneers, the later plate within a moulded frame crested by a pediment fretted in the form of a coronet, the base herringbone inlaid and crossbanded with shaped drawers, c1700, 32½ by 16½in (81 by 41cm).
$3,200-6,000

A German stained oak mirror, mid-18thC, 62 by 41in (155 by 102.5cm).
$4,500-9,000

An Empire giltwood frame, with later rectangular mirror plate, 27½ by 40½in (67.5 by 100cm).
$7,000-12,000
Provenance: One of a set of 6 frames reputedly presented by Napoleon to Marshal Bernadotte, later King of Sweden.

A George II mahogany toilet mirror, 17in (42.5cm).
$1,000-2,000

A giltwood toilet mirror, of George II style, 32½in (81cm).
$9,000-15,000

A Swedish walnut veneered cushion frame wall mirror, early 18thC, 37 by 23in (92.5 by 57.5cm).
$1,800-3,800

An early George III mahogany toilet mirror, 19in (48cm).
$1,000-2,000

A small Chippendale walnut mirror, American, 1750-1780, the scrolled pediment above a shaped rectangular mirror frame with a molded edge, over a scrolled pendant, 25 by 14in (62 by 35cm).
$1,200-1,500

A Chippendale mahogany mirror, American, 1760-1780, the scalloped and pierced pediment centering a gilt eagle flanked by shaped ears above a rectangular mirror with molded frame flanked by shaped ears above a scalloped pendant, partial loss to eagle wings, 35in (87cm).
$900-1,100

A French Empire mahogany cheval mirror, ormolu mounted, c1810.
$4,000-7,500

A birchwood toilet mirror, with oval plate in Gothic arched frame, decorated with lines, second quarter 19thC, 29in (72.5cm).
$1,600-2,800

Screens

A pair of George III mahogany polescreens, with later silk floral sprays, one slightly reduced, 14½in (36cm).
$800-1,500

A painted and gilded cheval firescreen of Empire design, with a panel of early 19thC Lyons cut velvet in shades of purple and gold, 27in (67.5cm).
$6,000-12,000

A mahogany needlework pole screen, 19thC.
$400-750

A pair of Regency parcel gilt and cream painted firescreens, with later glazed adjustable rectangular panels in moulded beaded frames, 18in (45cm).
$900-1,700

A Charles X fruitwood and ebonised firescreen, with glazed needlework panel, 53½in (134cm).
$3,200-6,000

A painted three-fold screen in a moulded mahogany frame, the wooden panels painted with exotic birds in flowering branchwork on a turquoise ground in Chinese style, each panel 69½ by 22in (175 by 52.5cm).
$1,300-2,400

A Dutch leather four-fold screen, painted with naive figures, buildings, animals, trees, insects, etc, on yellow ground, early 18thC, 76 by 70in (192.5 by 175cm).
$1,000-2,000

A Dutch painted and gilded leather six-leaf screen, decorated in bright colours in imitation of coromandel lacquer, the leather panels 18thC, each leaf 108 by 21in (272.5 by 52.5cm).
$8,000-13,500

Settees

◁ An early Georgian walnut settee, the seat rail centred by a partly ebonised shell with moulded cabriole legs and pad feet, later blocks, 58in (147cm).
$6,000-12,000

An early George II mahogany sofa, in the French taste, 61in (152.5cm).
$7,000-12,000

A Regency satinwood chaise longue, the scrolled back crossbanded with rosewood and framed by ebonised and boxwood lines, 67in (167.5cm).
$10,000-18,000

A pair of George III simulated rosewood window seats, 46in (115cm).
$20,000-30,000

A George III mahogany small humpback sofa, 63in (157.5cm).
$12,000-21,000

A classical carved and veneered mahogany sofa, New York, 1820-1845, with a rolled, veneered crest rail flanked by carved stylized eagle heads, the cornucopia and leaf-carved curved arm supports flanking the partially upholstered back and upholstered seat, on leaf and animal paw carved feet, 77½in (180cm) wide.
$1,500-1,800

A George III mahogany sofa, 66in (165cm).
$5,000-9,000

A suite of Edwardian mahogany ▷
seat furniture, inlaid with boxwood
and bone arabesques with rosewood
plaques, comprising: a two-seat
settee, a pair of open armchairs, a
pair of occasional chairs and a pair
of squat chairs.
$1,800-3,800

◁ A cream painted wood verandah
seat, 60in (150cm).
$1,200-2,100

A suite of American cast iron
garden furniture, partly signed
Lister and Fee, Brooklyn, New
York, late 19thC, the settees 46in
(115cm).
$14,000-24,000

A carved mahogany bergere lounge
suite of 5 pieces, comprising a
settee, 2 easy arm-chairs and 2 side
chairs.
$3,200-6,000

Shelves

A pair of mahogany hanging
shelves, of Gothic style, the sides
with interlaced trellis-work with
cluster columns and scrolling
foliate bases, 34in (85cm) high.
$10,000-18,000

A set of George III mahogany
hanging shelves, 36in (90cm).
$8,000-15,000

A pair of Victorian walnut hanging
brackets each with 3 shelves,
crossbanded and with satinwood
line inlay, 18in (45cm).
$1,800-3,800

Sideboards

A Georgian mahogany serpentine
fronted sideboard, with one lead-
lined cellaret drawer and 2 others,
66in (165cm).
$10,000-18,000

△
A George III mahogany
serpentine sideboard,
crossbanded and inlaid with
narrow bands, flowerheads
and stringing, the brass rail
missing, 67in (167.5cm).
$18,000-26,000

▷
A George III mahogany bow front
sideboard, inlaid with satinwood
bands and boxwood lines, with
cellaret drawer and side fall-flap,
72in (180cm).
$4,000-6,800

A George III mahogany sideboard,
the figured overhanging surface
with satinwood stringing, the
tambour door cupboard flanked on
one side by a lead lined cellaret and
on the other a pair of drawers,
c1800, 74in (187.5cm).
$6,000-12,000

A mahogany inlaid and crossbanded sideboard, with cellaret and 3 drawers, 18thC, 52in (130cm).
$3,200-6,000

A late Georgian mahogany sweep front sideboard, 55in (137.5cm).
$3,200-6,000

A Sheraton period mahogany sideboard, inlaid with satinwood and ebony herringbone stringing, housing a cupboard at each side with a fitted cellaret, 68in (170cm).
$3,200-6,000

A Georgian mahogany sideboard, with satinwood stringing and inlay, the bowed doors with batswing inlay and satinwood crossbanding, 82in (207.5cm).
$2,600-5,300

A Federal carved mahogany sideboard, Salem, Massachusetts, 1810-1820, the set-back gallery with concave center, on tapering reeded legs with ball-turned feet, 44½in (110cm) high.
$2,800-3,800

A Georgian inlaid mahogany bowfront sideboard, 48in (120cm).
$2,200-4,200

An Irish mahogany cottage sideboard, c1820, 54in (135cm).
$1,600-2,800

A fine quality George III mahogany sideboard, the upper part with original brass gallery and superstructure with tambour doors, the lower part breaking forward with central crossbanded drawer above a further pair of tambour doors, flanked on both sides by further drawers, cupboards, and a cellaret all of similar decoration on square taper inlaid legs with mahogany collared feet, Scottish, c1780, 66in (165cm).
$10,000-18,000

An unusual late Georgian mahogany pedestal sideboard, the bow fronted pedestals with 2 cellaret drawers, one fitted for bottles, 75in (190cm).
◁ **$7,000-12,000**

A mahogany secretaire serpentine sideboard, early 19thC, 57in (142.5cm).
$3,200-6,000

A mahogany sideboard, of inverted breakfront outline on front spirally turned legs with paw feet, early 19thC, 85in (215cm).
$600-1,200

A Regency Scottish mahogany sideboard, ebony line inlaid, 91in (230cm).
$5,000-9,000

Stands

A Victorian feathered mahogany pedestal sideboard, 84in (212.5cm).
$900-1,700

A George III style mahogany sideboard, the crossbanded top above a central bowed frieze drawer and napery drawer flanked by 2 cupboard doors faced with 4 mock short drawers, inlaid with barber's-pole stringing, 57in (143cm).
$1,800-3,800

A French provincial oak breakfront sideboard, 19thC, 68in (170cm).
$2,600-5,300

A Sheraton style mahogany sideboard with satinwood crossbanding and boxwood inlaid.
$6,000-12,000

A Regency rosewood music stand, with carved double lyre and on adjustable column and platform base, ormolu scroll feet, 15in (37.5cm) wide.
$3,200-6,000

A George III mahogany music stand, with adjustable rounded rectangular top, 18in (45cm).
$2,000-4,500

◁ A George III mahogany music stand, fitted with a mirror and urn finial, 56in (140cm).
$3,200-6,000

A carved Black Forest bear hall/stick stand, 19thC, 84in (212.5cm) high.
$2,600-5,300

A Regency rosewood duet music stand.
$1,400-2,600

Two Regency rosewood tripod jardinieres, one bearing the label of Richard Henry Masters, furnishing warerooms no. 1, Pitville Street, Cheltenham, possibly Anglo–Indian, 34in (85cm).
$10,000-18,000

An unusual pair of mahogany and satinwood urns and pedestals, early 19thC, 52in (130cm).
$7,000-12,000

A pair of Venetian polychrome blackamoors, 19thC, 82in (207.5cm) high.
$8,000-15,000

A carved and ▷
giltwood folio
stand,
mid-19thC.
$300-600

An early Victorian mahogany folio
stand, 27in (67.5cm).
$3,200-6,000

△
A pollard oak font, in the Gothic
style, now converted to a
washstand, early 19thC, 23½in
(58cm).
$1,200-2,100

Steps

A set of George III mahogany
library steps, 30in (75cm).
$6,000-12,000

A Japonnaiserie bamboo and △
porcelain hat-and-coat stand,
84in (212.5cm).
$3,200-6,000

A pair of Spanish scarlet and green
painted parcel-gilt torcheres, with
later bun feet, 18thC, 44in (110cm).
$2,200-4,200

A George III mahogany library
steps/table, 28in (70cm) wide.
$4,500-9,000

Stools

A William and Mary stool, 64in
(160cm).
$5,000-9,000

◁ A George II mahogany stool,
possible Irish, 20½in (51cm).
$4,000-6,800

A pair of George III black lacquer
stools, 24½in (61cm).
$4,500-9,000

A Regency mahogany hall bench,
the scrolled sabre legs with turned
baluster carrying handles, stamped
James Winter 101 Wardour St, 47in
(117.5cm).
$12,000-21,000

A pair of Regency beechframed
window seats, 34in (85cm).
$9,000-15,000

A pair of Regency mahogany music stools.
$4,000-7,500

⊲ A pair of oak stools, possible Liberty & Co., late 19thC, 13½ by 14½in (33 by 36cm).
$1,000-2,000

An Edwardian inlaid mahogany △ kidney shape dressing stool.
$300-600

A George III mahogany stool, 36in (90cm).
$4,000-7,500

⊲ An early Victorian mahogany octagonal seat, 21in (52.5cm) wide.
$6,000-12,000

STOOLS

★ until the middle of the 17thC stools were virtually the only form of seat for one person

★ many 17thC 'joint' or 'joyned' stools have been reproduced

★ look for good patination, colour and carving on oak examples. Yew-wood examples with good turning are highly desirable

★ by the end of the 17thC the chair was taking over and the oak stool became less popular, walnut stealing the show from about 1670

★ stools now tend to follow the style of chairs of the period, they also tend to be upholstered

★ many Queen Anne stools have stretchers

★ these have usually disappeared by George I

★ when mahogany was introduced from 1730–40, stools became simpler, the cabriole leg being replaced with the straight leg, often with stretchers

★ mid-18thC the 'drop-in' seat became fashionable

★ some stools made from chairs (this can increase the value of the chair 20 times)

★ check for hessian under the seat – never used until 1840 (often conceals some alterations)

Tables – Architects

A George II mahogany architect's table, with single ratchet slope and hinged side flaps, c1750.
$4,500-9,000

A George III mahogany artist's table, labelled 'Geo D Pooley, 4 Great Queen Street, Queensway, West Central 2.' 39½in (100cm).
$4,500-9,000

An early George III mahogany architect's table, the rectangular moulded easel top with re-entrant corners, the partly fitted interior including an inkslide to the right, 2 candle sconces, 33in (84cm).
$7,000-12,000

A George III mahogany architect's table, 37½in (94cm).
$6,000-12,000

An early Victorian mahogany breakfast table, 57in (143cm).
$900-1,700

A Federal carved mahogany drop-leaf breakfast table, attributed to the Duncan Phyfe Shop, New York, 1805-1815, with shaped drop leaves flanking a rectangular top above an apron with single drawer and turned drops over 4 ring-end baluster-turned columns centering a carved pineapple on a fluted platform, patch to hinge area of one leaf, 29in (72cm) high.
$5,000-8,000

Tables – Card

A Federal inlaid mahogany card table, Massachusetts, 1790-1810, with hinged serpentine bow-front top with pattern-inlaid edge above a conforming apron centering a lightwood veneered rectangular panel, some inlay missing and inlay restorations, 29in (72cm) high.
$1,500-1,800

A George II mahogany card table, the baize-lined surface with corner candle stands and counter wells, 36in (90cm).
$5,000-9,000

A George III satinwood card table, crossbanded with rosewood and edged with amaranth, 36in (91cm).
$3,200-6,000

A George II walnut card table, the fold-over top crossbanded and featherbanded with eared corners and opening to reveal candle stands and counter wells with concertina action, 32½in (83cm).
$20,000-30,000

A George III mahogany and satinwood card table, the crossbanded D-shaped top with a band of trailing berries and foliage, 36in (91cm).
$6,000-12,000

CARD TABLES

★ the commonest 18thC form has the fold-over top supported on one back leg hinged to wing out at 90 degrees. Better is the model with both back legs hinged, each opening to 45 degrees from the frame

★ best of all is the 'concertina' or folding frame

★ popular during the early 19thC and thereafter was the swivel top allowing use of the central column support

★ the swivel top was also used on French Revival models after 1827, particularly those decorated with Boulle marquetry

★ 19thC Boulle work, revived in 1815 in London by Le Gaigneur, was thinner than the 18thC original. Can be spotted by the brass being prone to lift and the tortoiseshell to bubble. Presence of this plus a swivel top eliminates 18thC origin. The four flap 'envelope' or bridge table was a development of the Edwardian period Sheraton Revival. The best examples are of rosewood with a degree of fine inlay. In view of comparatively recent age, condition should be excellent to command a high price

★ many plain Sheraton period card tables were inlaid during the Edwardian period. To spot, view obliquely against the light; original inlays will conform perfectly with the rest of the surface; new inlay will not, unless completely resurfaced, when shallow colour and high polish will be evident

★ all carving to English cabriole legs should stand proud of the outline of the curve; such decoration within the outline indicates recarving

An early Georgian mahogany combined tea, card and writing table, the semi-circular top with 3 flaps, the baize-lined card top with guinea wells, the hinged baize-lined writing surface enclosing a mirror-backed compartment with pen slide and inkwell, possibly Irish, 32½in (83cm).
$10,000-18,000

A George III satinwood, demi-lune card table, with kingwood, partridgewood and boxwood crossbanding.
$4,000-6,800

A fine pair of George III gilt demi-lune side tables, the later Carrara marble slabs above guilloche friezes, centred by an urn of wheatears tablet, 51½in (129cm).
$30,000-60,000

Provenance: The Pepys Cockerell Collection, the most famous piece being the gaming table given by Charles II to Samuel Pepys now in the Victoria and Albert Museum. These tables have been handed down through the Pepys Cockerell family.

A George III sycamore and inlaid serpentine card table, the crossbanded top inlaid, 37in (93cm).
$3,200-6,000

A George III satinwood card table, inlaid radially and crossbanded in faded rosewood, with a later baized playing surface, the square tapering ebony-strung legs headed by inlaid panels and terminating in small spade feet, c1790, 36in (91cm).
$4,500-9,000

A Dutch marquetry card table, 32½in (81cm).
$1,800-3,800

A pair of George III mahogany tables, one for cards, the other for tea, the card table having been re-baized, c1800, 38in (95cm).
$12,000-21,000

A George III kingwood and satinwood card table, 36½in (92cm).
$2,000-4,500

A pair of Federal flame-birch veneered mahogany serpentine-front card tables, Boston area, 1800-1815, 29in (72cm) high.
$25,000-27,000

A Regency rosewood and parcel gilt fold-over top card table, with bobbin and bead mouldings to the top and frieze, 36in (91cm).
$1,400-2,600

A pair of Regency card tables, in figured burr elm veneers, inlaid with ebony stringing and symmetrically placed stars, c1820, 39in (98cm).
$12,000-21,000

An unusual Regency D-shaped card table, banded and inlaid with satinwood lines on ring-turned simulated rosewood legs 35in (89cm).
$4,000-7,500

An unusual Regency rosewood brass-inlaid patent card table, the top inlaid with brass line and fleur-de-lys and with dished money wells on the reversed baized side, the mechanical scissor action operated by the push plaques beneath the frieze to extend the legs to take the foldover top, profusely decorated in applied ormolu mounts, lotus leaf feet and brass casters, 36in (91cm).
$13,000-22,000

There is a pair of similar card tables with the same scissor action in the music room at Buckingham Palace.

A carved rosewood fold-over top card table, early 19thC, 37in (93cm).
$1,800-3,800

A good Regency rosewood and brass-inlaid card table, inlaid with borders of stars and quatrefoils, 36in (91cm).
$4,000-6,800

A Federal inlaid mahogany card table, Eastern Massachusetts, 1795-1815, the foldover top with serpentine sides, above a conforming frieze centered by an inlaid astragal shaped flame birch tablet, 29½in (73cm) high.
$4,000-4,500

A late Victorian burr walnut and ebonised banded card table, inlaid with amboyna bands, Vitruvian scrolls and boxwood lines, stamped Gillow & Company and numbered 3079, 36in (91cm).
$4,000-6,800

A pair of classical mahogany card tables, Boston 19thC, each with hinged rectangular top with canted corners swivelling above a conforming skirt with an applied brass rope molding, over a trestle base with 4 reeded supports, one with repaired cracks to feet, 30in (75cm) high.
$5,500-6,500

A George I style walnut card table, with crossbanded top, 32½in (81cm).
$1,600-2,800

A Federal inlaid mahogany card table, Middle Atlantic States, 1800-1815, the foldover top with broad rounded corners, 28½in (71cm) high..
$3,000-3,500

Tables – Centre

A Queen Anne giltwood centre table, 30in (76cm).
$8,000-15,000

A George III satinwood centre table, the circular tip-up top crossbanded with rosewood, inscribed in ink 'From Drawing Room', 41in (104cm) diam.
$18,000-26,000

A Regency mahogany centre table, in a pale figured mahogany, the top with coromandel crossbanding, c1815, 45in (113cm).
$10,000-18,000

An Empire rosewood marble-top center table, New York, 1825-1835, with a circular white marble-top over a veneered skirt, on 3 columnar supports, each with a carved and gilt capital, feet restored, 30in (75cm) high.
$5,000-5,500

A Regency cast-iron, gilt-metal centre table, surmounted by a circular specimen marble top, radiating segments in a variety of coloured marbles and hardstones including lapis lazuli, malachite, porphyry, sarrancolin, brocatelle and poxtor, on a white ground, with a verde antico outer band, 40½in (101cm) diam.
$20,000-30,000

A Regency rosewood centre table, the top inlaid with brass banding with anthemion spandrels, 45in (114cm).
$5,000-9,000

A Regency brass-inlaid rosewood centre table, with crossbanded tip-up top and spreading gadrooned shaft, 50½in (128cm) diam.
$6,000-12,000

A gilt-gesso centre table, 32in (81cm).
$3,200-6,000

A Victorian walnut centre table, the top inlaid in various woods with birds, butterflies, flowers and scrolling foliage on a quartered ground, 53in (133cm).
$4,000-7,500

A Victorian massive giltwood centre table, with marble top.
$10,000-18,000

Provenance: His Grace the Duke of Westminster.

A Victorian circular top table, inset in a radiating design with specimen marbles and hardstones including lapis lazuli, malachite and onyx, 34in (86cm) diam.
$12,000-21,000

A marquetry and parquetry centre table, in the French manner, the top finely inlaid with various trophies, the spandrels inlaid with various woods and ivory in a classical style, attached paper label inscribed 'Howard & Sons, 22 & 26 Berners Street, London', late 19thC, 43in (108cm).
$4,500-9,000

A Queen Anne cherrywood tavern table, New England, 1740-80, the top above a flat arched apron, on tapering cylindrical legs with pad and disc feet, 26in (65cm) high.
$14,000-15,000

An important white marble conservatory table, the circular top with broad Grecian key pattern border and graduated segmented centre, originally inlaid with coloured mosaic, probably Italian, early 19thC, 38in (96cm) high.
$34,000-60,000

Tables – Console

A pair of Regency rosewood and parcel-gilt console tables, with white marble tops, 54in (137cm).
$12,000-21,000

An Italian marble topped centre table, the top inlaid in coloured marbles, 18thC, 63in (158cm).
$6,000-12,000

A grained and parcel-gilt centre table, in the early Georgian style, with massive breche violette top, stamped 'J. Seglie, fecit 1914', 69in (175cm).
$6,000-12,000

A Dutch walnut centre table, with marquetry inlaid and a frieze drawer, c1790.
$4,500-9,000

A Spanish walnut centre table, with turned iron flying stretchers, 17thC and later, 51in (129cm).
$4,000-7,500

A pair of Louis XV giltwood console tables, with shaped breccia marble tops, re-gilded, 23½in (60cm).
$6,000-12,000

A Louis XVI mahogany console desserte, with brass mounts and grey veined marble top, 34in ▷ (85cm).
$3,200-6,000

Tables – Dining

A Cuban mahogany twin-flap top dining table, early 18thC, 49in (123cm).
$7,000-12,000

A Regency mahogany dining table, 125in (318cm).
$18,000-26,000

A mahogany three-pedestal dining table, the rounded rectangular end sections with fluted borders on ring-turned spreading shaft and quadripartite bases with gilt-metal anthemion feet, 101½in (255cm) including 2 extra leaves.
$14,000-24,000

A Louis XVI carved giltwood petite console table, surmounted by a moulded D-shaped marble top, 26in (64cm).
$2,600-5,300

A George III mahogany banqueting table, in 5 parts, of good originality, brass stamped S. Dobbins & Co. Patent, Bristol, extending in various sections up to 192in (480cm).
$30,000-54,000

An extremely fine George III mahogany dining table, c1790, 120in (300cm).
$40,000-75,000

A Regency mahogany D-ended dining table, with replacement clips, c1820, 113in (283cm).
$14,000-24,000

A three-pillar mahogany dining table, part Georgian and part later, 142in (359cm) fully extended.
$12,000-21,000

A George III mahogany extending dining table with 5 pillar supports, 2 pillars and 2 leaves probably later additions, 183in (460cm) wide, fully extended.
$70,000-130,000

A fine Regency mahogany patent Imperial dining table, in the manner of Gillows, 174½in (449cm) extended.
$24,000-42,000

A Regency mahogany D-ended dining table, in 3 sections, the casters stamped S. Dobbins & Company, Patent, Bristol, 125in (313cm) fully extended.
$8,000-15,000

A George III style mahogany 3 pillar dining table, together with a pair of shallow D-shaped flaps for use on a pillar as a breakfast table, 51in (128cm) extended.
$8,000-13,500

An early Victorian mahogany extending banqueting table, 176in (440cm) long, including 7 leaves.
$5,500-9,000

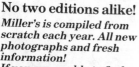

A Victorian mahogany extending dining table, 166in (422cm) including 4 various-sized leaves.
$20,000-30,000

A George IV mahogany ▷ extending dining table, the rounded rectangular top with concertina action, 118in (295cm) extended, including 3 extra leaves.
$11,000-20,000

◁ A Victorian walnut and marquetry pedestal dining table, with casters, 52in (130cm).
$4,000-6,800

A George IV mahogany △ twin pedestal dining table, with 2 later leaves, 91in (228cm) extended.
$4,500-9,000

Tables – Drop-Leaf

A late George II mahogany two-flap table, 59in (150cm) extended.
$4,000-7,500

A mahogany drop-leaf table, late 18thC, 36in (91cm).
$800-1,500

A Queen Anne maple drop-leaf table, New England, 1735-1765, with double hinged-leaf top over a scalloped bolection apron, apron possibly reshaped, 27½in (68cm) high.
$6,000-6,500

Tables – Drum

A George III mahogany drum table, with leather-lined revolving circular top and 4 frieze drawers, 2 divided, with the ivory letters A to D, 38½in (98cm) diam.
$10,000-18,000

A George III mahogany drum table, with revolving top, 44in (110cm).
$18,000-26,000

A Victorian mahogany drum top table, 47in (120cm) diam.
$1,200-2,100

Tables – Games

A George II mahogany demi-lune triple fold-over top tea/games table, having money wells and compartment, 33in (83cm).
$1,800-3,800

A George II mahogany games table, the top enclosing a backgammon well with candle slides and guinea trays, 36in (91cm).
$4,500-9,000

A late George II mahogany triple top table, with concertina action, 34in (86cm).
$9,000-15,000

A Regency mahogany combined games and work table, 19in (48cm).
$8,000-13,500

A Regency rosewood games table, 35in (89cm).
$4,000-7,500

> In the Furniture section if there is only one measurement it usually refers to the width of the piece.

A parcel-gilt and calamander games table, the instepped top with reversible slide with chess squares and backgammon board, with 2 small drawers enclosing a few ivory chessmen, trestles re-gilded, 28½in (72cm).
$4,500-9,000

Tables – Gateleg

A George II mahogany gateleg dining table, 59in (150cm) wide, open.
$4,500-9,000

An unusual mid-Georgian mahogany gateleg table, 48½in (123cm) wide, open.
$7,000-12,000

An early George III walnut gateleg table, 48½in (123cm).
$1,700-3,000

Tables – Library

A George IV ormolu-mounted parcel-gilt and fruitwood library table, the top with egg-and-dart border, 56in (142cm) diam.
$20,000-30,000

A Regency mahogany library table, 32½ by 48in (81 by 120cm).
$7,000-12,000

A Regency mahogany library table with crossbanded top, one of the drawers fitted with a baize-lined hinged writing surface crossbanded in faded rosewood, 51½in (128cm).
$6,000-12,000

A George III Chippendale style rectangular library table, with 6 drawers and gadrooned all round, c1770.
$10,000-18,000

A William IV mahogany library table, the top with gadrooned border and 4 frieze drawers, flanked by 4 small pivoted drawers on foliate baluster shaft, possibly Irish, 35½in (90cm) diam.
$5,000-9,000

A William IV pollard oak library table, with inset top and canted panelled corners with brass mounts and satinwood mouldings, the ends and one side with open shelves, the front with 2 doors set with calf tooled book-spines with concealed locking mechanism, on casters, 57in (144cm).
$10,000-18,000

Tables – Loo

A George IV oak library table, with leather-lined top and 2 drawers, on turned baluster stem and tripod base, 42½in (107cm).
$4,000-7,500

A William IV rosewood library or centre table, fitted with 2 drawers, 54in (138cm).
$2,000-4,500

A George IV rosewood library table, the top inset with green leather, on moulded scroll cabriole legs, with scroll feet, 62in (155cm).
$4,000-7,500

A figured walnut oval loo table, c1850, 58in (145cm).
$3,200-6,000

Tables – Needlework

A Victorian inlaid figured walnut loo table, with centre pillar and 4 turned supports and 4 carved feet, 46in (115cm).
$400-900

A small Victorian burr walnut oval loo table, on carved quadruped base.
$800-1,500

△ A good quality Regency period mahogany needlework table, c1820, 25in (63cm).
$4,500-9,000

A Regency period needlework table, with a figured satinwood rosewood crossbanded lid, above an ebonised gilt decorated octagonal frieze, c1810, 17in (43cm).
$4,000-7,500

Nests of Tables

A Regency period nest of 3 occasional tables in rosewood veneers, originally a nest of 4 tables, c1820, 19in (48cm).
$4,000-7,500

A set of 4 satinwood quartetto tables, the tops with ebony stringings on ring-turned twinned trestle ends and shaped feet, 14in to 19½in (35.5 to 49.5cm).
$6,000-12,000

A nest of 3 rosewood and mahogany quartetto tables, the centre table inlaid with maple and rosewood chessboard, the largest 19½in (49cm).
$1,700-3,000

Tables – Occasional

▷ A George IV occasional table, made from the willow growing over Napoleon's grave, the rectangular top edged with reed ornament, on ebonised bun feet, 26in (66cm).
$2,000-4,500

A Queen Anne red walnut pad foot occasional table.
$5,000-9,000

◁ A George III satinwood cheveret, the detachable superstructure with carrying handle, the folding cloth-lined writing slide and one frieze drawer formerly with a work basket beneath, on square tapering legs, 22in (56cm).
$6,000-12,000

A parquetry table, the hexagonal tip-up top on a tapering pillar, inlaid overall in cube patterns, with rosewood, mahogany and satinwood, 19thC, 27in (68cm).
$1,000-2,000

Tables – Pedestal

A Regency rosewood pedestal table, the octagonal top with an Italian inlaid marble panel, framed by specimen marbles, 24½in (62cm).
$2,000-4,500

A George IV ebonised and gilded pedestal table, the beaded rounded rectangular top with a painting on glass, 24in (61cm).
$1,700-3,000

Tables – Pembroke

A Chippendale mahogany Pembroke, Pennsylvania, 1760-1785, the top flanked by 2 shallow rectangular leaves, above a skirt with one drawer fitted with a brass pull, the drawer retains its original rococo brass handle, 29in (72cm) high.
$4,500-5,000

A Federal inlaid mahogany Pembroke table, Middle Atlantic States, 1795-1815, with top flanked by leaves with rounded inset corners, the frieze fitted with one drawer, 28½in (71cm) high.
$4,500-5,000

A George III oval mahogany Pembroke table, on square tapered supports.
$1,300-2,400

A George III mahogany Pembroke table, the satinwood crossbanded top with elliptical leaves above a similarly banded bowed drawer, on square tapered legs, 33½in (84cm).
$1,800-3,800

A George III mahogany Pembroke table, the oval two-flap top crossbanded, inlaid with stringing, with a central large oval fan motif, 39in (99cm) extended.
$2,600-5,300

A George III period small Pembroke table in mahogany, with figured hinged surface above single cockbeaded drawer and fluted square taper legs, c1800, 33½in (84cm) open.
$4,500-9,000

PEMBROKE TABLES

★ became popular in the mid to late 18thC, possibly designed and ordered by Henry Herbert, the Earl of Pembroke (1693-1751)

★ on early examples the legs were square which are by far the most desirable

★ later tables had turned legs

★ the turned and reeded legs are much less popular

★ those with oval or serpentine tops more desirable

★ flaps should have three hinges

★ rounded flaps and marquetry again increase desirability

★ satinwood was greatly favoured, particularly with much crossbanding and inlay

★ many 18thC Pembroke tables have chamfering on the insides of the legs

★ the Edwardians made many fine Pembroke tables which have been known to appear wrongly catalogued at auction

★ Edwardian tables now in great demand

A George III period Pembroke table in mahogany, with satinwood crossbanding above cockbeaded dummy and working drawers with original brasswork, with good quality replaced brass casters, c1800, 35½in (90cm).
$6,000-12,000

A Regency mahogany Pembroke table, with most unusual banded umbrella understretchers.
$2,600-5,300

A fine quality Irish Regency period mahogany Pembroke table, c1820, 45in (113cm) wide, open.
$4,000-7,500

Tables – Pier

A Regency satinwood Pembroke table of unusual form, with banded rounded rectangular twin-flap top and one frieze drawer opening to each side, on splayed square tapering legs, 44in (112cm) wide, open.
$7,000-12,000

A late Regency mahogany Pembroke table, with a rosewood crossbanded two-flap top, fitted with 3 drawers opposite 3 dummy drawers, the frieze with stylised ebony inlay, on 4 spiral twist tapering supports, 32in (82cm) extended.
$2,000-4,500

A classical mahogany and gilt-stencilled pier table, New York, 1820-1830, with white marble top above a bolection frieze stencilled with leafage and fruit and a patterned border, on columns with gilt and carved capitals resting on a shaped shelf with stencilled border and a rectangular mirror plate, on gilt cornucopia and leaf carved animal paw feet, top replaced, 28½in (71cm) high.
$1,800-2,400

A classical mahogany and marble top pier table, New York, 1820-1830, with white marble top above a frieze centering a cornucopia ormolu mount, on marble columns with ormolu capitals resting on a shaped shelf with a rectangular mirror plate flanked by marble pilasters, on carved and gilt acanthus leaf and animal paw feet, some chips to veneer and gilt, 36in (90cm) high.
$1,800-2,000

Tables – Reading

A Georgian mahogany reading table, with lift-up top with adjustable support, 2 drawers in the frieze and 2 candle slides, 19in (48cm).
$5,000-9,000

A pair of early Victorian mahogany pedestal reading tables, the adjustable tops on lotus leaf lappeted turned tapering columns, the triform platform base with bun feet, 18in (45cm), and a centre table, en suite, 28in (70cm).
$4,000-7,500

Tables – Serving

A George III carved mahogany serpentine serving table, with a bevelled ledge, the fluted frieze with 2 concave drawers, on square tapered legs headed with oval beaded paterae medallions and terminating in block feet, 92in (231cm).
$8,000-13,500

A George III mahogany serpentine serving table, with brass rail at the back, the top and frieze crossbanded and inlaid with stringing, with figured panels, 97in (244cm).
$18,000-26,000

A George III mahogany serving table, the serpentine top with a three-quarter gallery centred by a plum-pudding mahogany tablet, the whole inlaid with boxwood stringing, restorations, 46in (115cm).
$5,000-9,000

A George III mahogany serpentine front serving table, with plain top above 3 frieze drawers, on 4 square tapering supports, 72in (183cm).
$3,200-6,000

Tables – Side

A fine George II giltwood side table, with carved rectangular brown jasper-veneered top on fluted shell-centred frieze hung with oak swags, on partly imbricated scrolled legs carved with entrelacs and foliage, 52½in (134cm).
$24,000-45,000

A Regency bird's-eye maple and ebonised side table, the top inlaid with a rosewood band above a frieze drawer, on ring-turned tapering legs, 20in (50cm).
$1,600-2,800

An early Georgian walnut side table, on foliate cabriole legs and shaped pad feet, formerly a card table, 33in (84cm).
$1,800-3,800

A Georgian mahogany side table, with a grey and white mottled marble top, 36in (91cm).
$4,000-7,500

A Spanish walnut side table with moulded top, on fluted baluster legs with moulded stretchers and bun feet, late 16thC and later, 65in (165cm).
$3,200-6,000

A Federal mahogany and bird's eye maple veneer dressing table, Salem, Massachusetts, 1790-1810, the top with molded edge, on baluster and reeded tapering legs, now missing dressing mirror, minor beading loss, 35½in (88cm) high.
$4,900-5,200

A free standing side table in rosewood, profusely inlaid with brass, with 3 frieze drawers, c1830.
$5,000-9,000

A George III mahogany side table, crossbanded with satinwood, 56in (143cm).
$6,000-12,000

A rare Chippendale walnut chamber table, Pennsylvania, 1760-1790, with molded-edge rectangular top above a case with single thumb-molded long drawer flanked by fluted quarter columns over a scrolled and shaped apron, on cabriole legs with claw-and-ball feet, small strip replaced on back edge of top, 31in (77cm) high.
$8,000-9,000

A Regency mahogany bow front side table, with arched and moulded three-quarter galleried top, 58in (145cm).
$2,000-4,500

A Georgian mahogany side table, with marble inset top, supported on boldly carved cabriole legs decorated at the knees with acanthus and scrollwork, ending in claw-and-ball feet, 64in (160cm).
$14,000-24,000

Tables – Silver

A George III style mahogany silver table, the top with an arcaded and scrolling foliate pierced gallery, 36½in (91cm).
$2,000-4,500

A George III mahogany serpentine silver table, the spindle gallery with shaped corners, on turned column, with birdcage and carved tripod support, 24in (60cm).
$5,000-9,000

Tables – Sofa

A mahogany sofa table, the two-flap top with a wide yewwood band edged with stringing, 60in (152cm) extended.
$2,000-4,500

A George III mahogany sofa table, the 2 drop leaves above 2 shallow drawers with ebony edge, 51in (128cm) wide, open.
$3,200-6,000

A late Regency rosewood sofa table, with foliate marquetry panels and crossbanding, 60in (150cm).
$4,000-7,500

A Regency partridgewood sofa table, 47½in (125cm) wide, open.
$4,500-9,000

SOFA TABLES

★ an elegant feminine writing table, usually with two shallow drawers
★ genuine ones are rarer than it might appear
★ either had two vertical supports or a central pillar
★ many fine examples made in mahogany with satinwood or rosewood stringing and crossbanding
★ rosewood examples can be of exceptional quality
★ examples with stretchers tend to be later
★ lyre end supports, particularly with a brass strip, are likely to increase value
★ many sofa tables have been made from old cheval mirrors
★ if the stretcher rail is turned and has a square block in the centre – it could be from a converted cheval mirror
★ many good sofa tables have been carved with Egyptian heads in the manner of Thomas Hope
★ long drawers are undesirable but many have been cut down

344

A Regency mahogany sofa table, inlaid with ebonised lines in geometric style, 59in (150cm) extended.
$4,500-9,000

A Regency fruitwood and mahogany crossbanded sofa table, 60in (150cm) wide, open.
$2,000-4,500

A George IV mahogany sofa table, with rounded rectangular twin-flap top and 2 panelled frieze drawers, with solid scrolled trestle ends, moulded splayed feet and lions paws, bearing the trade label R. Snowdon Cabinet Maker and Appraiser Northallerton, 62in (153cm) wide, open.
$4,000-7,500

A Regency mahogany sofa table, inlaid with ebony lines, 60in (150cm).
$4,500-9,000

A Regency rosewood and boxwood line inlay sofa table.
$12,000-21,000

A Regency rosewood sofa table, extensively inlaid with brass in stylised foliate design and plain lines, 59in (150cm) extended.
$4,000-6,800

Tables – Sutherland

An Edwardian painted satinwood sofa table, the rounded rectangular twin-flap top painted with rustic scene, the 2 frieze drawers with oval silvered handles, 67½in (170cm) wide, open.
$5,500-9,000

A Victorian figured walnut oval gateleg Sutherland/occasional table, with fluted bulbous supports, on shaped legs and casters, 42in (105cm) extended.
$900-1,700

Tables – Tea

A Queen Anne walnut tea table, Pennsylvania, 1730-1775, the top above a shaped skirt fitted with one drawer, on round tapering legs with pad feet, 27in (67cm) high.
$7,000-8,000

A Chippendale mahogany tilt-top tea table, possibly Lancaster, Pennsylvania 1760-80, on acanthus leaf-carved legs with claw-and-ball feet, the top may not be original to base, 29in (72cm) high.
$20,000-25,000

A George II mahogany tea table with shaped fold-over top, single drawer with brass drop handle and turned tapered legs, on pad feet, 28½in (71cm).
$2,200-4,200

A Georgian demi-lune mahogany folding top tea table, on square tapering legs, 35in (88cm).
$1,700-3,000

An inlaid mahogany half round fold-over tea table, with oval satinwood and marquetry panel, 18thC.
$1,700-3,000

A Chippendale cherrywood tilt-top tea table, Connecticut, 1760-1790, on tripod arched cabriole legs with pad feet, 28in (70cm) high.
$1,500-1,700

A rare and important Chippendale carved mahogany tea-table, Philadelphia, 1760-1780, with molded and scalloped-edge top comprised of 8 plain and 8 serpentine alternating segments tilting and turning above a baluster-turned birdcage support over a fluted columnar pedestal with compressed scrolling-leafage carved ball and ribbon and rosette-carved collar, on leafage-carved tripod arched legs with claw-and-ball feet centering blind fret-carved panels and C-scrolls on the pedestal base, the feet hollowed and fitted with casters, 27½in (67cm) high.
$200,000-400,000

A George IV brass-inlaid mahogany tea table, with bold scroll supports and brass casters, 39in (99cm).
$1,700-3,000

Tables – Tripod

A George II mahogany tripod table, the moulded circular top with deep pierced fretwork gallery, 15in (38cm) diam.
$4,000-7,500

A fine and rare George III mahogany round table, with raised border, attributed to Ince & Mayhew, 22in (55cm) diam.
$46,000-75,000

A George II mahogany tripod table, with pie-crust top, 10in (25cm) diam.
$4,000-7,500

A George III padoukwood tripod table, with moulded circular tip-up top, birdcage action, 23in (59cm) diam.
$6,000-12,000

A Queen Anne walnut tilt-top bird-cage candlestand, Pennsylvania, 1740-1765, with circular dish top tilting above a bird cage support and ring-turned standard with compressed ball, 27½in (67cm) high.
$12,500-13,000

A Chippendale walnut birdcage stand, middle Atlantic Colonies, 1760-1780, the dished circular top tilting and turning above a column-and-vase pedestal, minor old repair to pedestal base, top re-glued, 28½in (71cm) high.
$6,000-6,500

A Federal tilt-top mahogany candlestand, probably Massachusetts, 1780-1810, the oval top with swirled grain, tilting above a ring-and-urn turned pedestal, one foot replaced, 27in (67cm) high.
$1,800-2,000

A George III mahogany tripod table, with octagonal tip-up top with lightly raised edge, on an unusual triform support formed as C-scrolls, on a base shaped as opposing C-scrolls, with original leather casters, 28in (71cm).
$20,000-30,000

The stem and base of this table is most unusual, but compares to an example by John Linnell, illustrated in Ward-Jackson, fig. 191, and another illustration in The Norman Adams Collection, *by Stevens and Whittington, page 297.*

A Federal inlaid cherrywood tilt-top candlestand, Connecticut, 1780-1800, the square top inlaid at center with two-tone star motif and wide stringing, above a reeded urn-turned post, 28in (70cm) high.
$3,700-4,000

A George III mahogany tripod table, 34in (87cm) diam.
$2,000-4,500

A circular Regency rosewood tip-up library table, the top inlaid with brass scroll band, 54½in (136cm) diam.
$2,000-4,500

A mid-Georgian burr yew tripod table, with circular tray tip-up top and spreading vase-shaped shaft, the arched base with shaped pad feet, 23in (58cm) diam.
$6,000-12,000

Tables – Wake

A rare George II mahogany double gateleg wake table, with rectangular top on 8 cannon barrel legs linked by powerful mahogany-veneered oak plain stretchers above outset feet, 36 by 58in (90 by 145cm) extended.
$2,200-4,200

Tables – Wine/Lamp

A Georgian style walnut wine table raised on turned column, with 2 tiers of revolving open book racks raised on tripod supports, 30in (75cm) high.
$1,300-2,400

Tables – Work

A Regency ebonised lamp table, with rectangular hinged lacquer top on turned stem mounted with stamped giltmetal, 18in (46.5cm).
$2,200-4,200

An unusual George III mahogany work table, with revolving square easel top, the frieze fitted with 4 drawers and 2 candle stands, the panelled pedestal with a cupboard door, 25in (63cm).
$5,000-9,000

A late Regency rosewood work table, with brass line inlays, 25in (63cm).
$1,800-3,800

A William IV ▷
rosewood work
table, the
rectangular top
with canted
corners above a
reel-mouled frieze
drawer and pleated
silk work basket,
23in (56cm).
$500-1,100

A George III mahogany and inlaid
oval work table, the figured top
inlaid with musical trophies, 26in
(64cm).
$1,700-3,000

A Regency mahogany sewing table,
with 2 graduated and 2 dummy
drawers, velvet covered sliding
pouch on lyre form supports and
leaf carved scroll feet with brass
casters, 22 by 19in (55 by 48cm).
$1,600-2,800

A Regency ▷
rosewood work
table,
inlaid with brass
lines and foliate
motifs, with fitted
interior and work
bag, 30 by 16in
(75 by 40cm).
$6,000-12,000

◁
A small Regency
period mahogany
work table.
$1,700-3,000

A Victorian burr walnut folding top
card/work table on twin carved
supports with stretcher, having
chessboard top, 3 drawers and
sliding work box under, 29in
(72.5cm).
$1,800-3,800

◁
A George IV rosewood rectangular
work table, inlaid with stringings
one fitted drawer with
compartments and a work-well
covered with pleated sateen, 20 by
16in (50 by 40cm).
$1,300-2,400

A Victorian
mahogany work
table, with convex
front, the quarter-
veneered top
enclosing
compartments,
19in (48cm).
$1,300-2,400

A Victorian walnut tripod base
work box, with marquetry and
parquetry games top.
$800-1,500
▷

An early Victorian mahogany
Pembroke work table, with
fall-leaves, 2 drawers and false
drawers over a mahogany sliding
well, 19in (48cm).
$1,700-3,000

A Federal mahogany sewing table,
attributed to the shop of Duncan
Phyfe, New York, c1810, the
astragal shaped flamed-grained
mahogany top with reeded edge and
opening to a fitted interior and a
felt-covered adjustable writing
board, the tambour-covered case
inlaid and fitted with 3 false
drawers and one working drawer,
above a reeded plinth; the ring and
urn turned standard on 4 reeded
sabre legs ending in brass animal
paw feet and brass casters, 30in
(75cm) high.
$25,000-30,000

Tables – Writing

A rare Hepplewhite mahogany kidney-shaped ladies' writing table, the top with a narrow crossbanding and inset tooled leather, 18thC, 54in (135cm).
$44,000-69,000

A George III mahogany writing table, with leather-lined top, the carcase possibly reduced, on square tapering legs, 42in (105.5cm).
$7,000-12,000

An unusual Regency mahogany writing table, with 2 oval moulded drop leaves, the top fitted for writing, all with ebony line inlay on simulated bamboo turned splay supports and brass castors, 22in (55cm).
$10,000-18,000

A George III inlaid mahogany secretaire, with shaped tray top, with baize-lined ratchet adjustable writing slope, brass ring handles, concave undertier, on square tapered supports, 17in (42.5cm).
$8,000-15,000

A fine George III mahogany bookshelf writing table.
$8,000-13,500

An Edwardian satinwood kidney shape writing desk, with gilt-tooled leather panel, 48in (120cm).
$5,500-9,000

A transitional parquetry kingwood and bois-satiné table à ecrire by J. P. Dusantoy, with leather lined top, stamped 'I.P. Du Sautoy JME', 15in (37.5cm).
$7,000-12,000

Jean-Pierre Dusantoy, maître in 1779.

An Italian ebony veneered and pietra dura writing table, the top with inset writing surface within a gilt bronze moulding, 19thC, 43in (107.5cm).
$5,000-9,000

Washstands

Teapoys

A Regency mahogany teapoy, the eared rectangular hinged top enclosing a divided interior with later tin liners, the front and sides with ormolu banding, 20in (51cm).
$4,500-9,000

Provenance: Quebec House, Westerham, Kent.

◁

A Regency brass inlaid rosewood teapoy, the chamfered top inlaid, enclosing a fitted interior, 2 lidded compartments lacking mixing bowls, with Bramah lock and carrying handles, 18in (45cm).
$4,500-9,000

A George III mahogany enclosed washstand, inlaid with boxwood stringing and enclosing a later mirror and apertures for bowls, c1800, 24in (61cm).
$1,300-2,400

A Georgian mahogany enclosed washstand, with fold-over top, rising mirror and fitted compartments and basin with drainage hole, the front with 2 small cupboard doors, one drawer and the pull-out base with original pewter pot, 18in (46cm).
$1,800-3,800

Whatnots

A late Georgian birds'-eye maple four-tier étagère with turned column supports, 24in (61cm).
$6,000-12,000

Wine Coolers

A George III brass-bound mahogany cellaret, the hexagonal top crossbanded in satinwood enclosing lead-lined interior retaining tap beneath, the slightly tapering body with carrying handles, the stand with square tapering legs, 19in (48cm).
$5,500-9,000

A rosewood four-tier free standing whatnot, with barley twist supports and fitted drawer, c1840.
$1,800-3,800

A small late Regency mahogany whatnot, c1830, 20in (50cm).
$2,600-5,300

A Regency rosewood whatnot of four tiers, on slender baluster turned columns, the third tier fitted with a drawer, 19in (47cm).
$1,700-3,000

A rare mahogany free standing three-tier dumb waiter, c1830.
$2,600-5,300

A Regency mahogany serving side buffet, on baluster column supports with turned tapering legs, 36in (90cm).
$1,700-3,000

WINE COOLERS

★ cisterns for cooling wines were noted back in the 15thC and as objects of furniture became popular after about 1730. The cellaret is basically a cooler with a lid and fitted with a lock

★ there are two main types: those made to stand on a pedestal or sideboard and those with legs or separate stands to stand on the floor

★ octagonal, hexagonal, round or oval, the commonest form is of coopered construction with a number of brass bands

★ a cooler made to stand on a pedestal will often have the lowest brass band as near to the base as possible; a cooler made to fit into a stand will have the band slightly up the body to allow a snug fit

★ it is important that all mounts are original and condition should be good, but the absence of the old lead lining is not serious. An octagonal cooler or cellaret on stand may command a slightly higher price than a hexagonal model, but both are much in demand

★ after 1800, the sarcophagus shape became popular and later Regency models were made with highly figured mahogany veneers and large carved paw feet

★ there were not many new designs after the 1850s

A George III mahogany and brass bound oval wine cooler or jardinière, with brass loop handles and zinc liner, 24 by 18in (60 by 45cm).
$4,500-9,000

A Regency mahogany wine cooler, in the manner of Gillows, with oval tin-liner and slightly tapering body, with giltmetal lion-mask handles, 29in (73cm).
$8,000-15,000

An Italian parcel-gilt and blue-green painted headboard of scrolled foliate shape, with two putto crestings, 72 by 69in (183 by 175cm).
$1,700-3,000

A late George III mahogany wine cooler, with carved decoration, the hinged lid opening to reveal a lead-lined interior, raised on paw feet, 30in (75cm).
$4,000-7,500

Miscellaneous

A mahogany waste-paper basket, the slightly tapering octagonal body filled with pierced trellis work with paper liner, on bracket feet, 14in (35cm).
$5,000-9,000

A set of
William IV style
brass fire tools
and stand, 27in
(68cm) high.
$800-1,500

A Regency mahogany oval wine cooler, in the manner of Gillows, with lead-lined interior and tapering body with baluster ribbed pilasters on turned tapering feet, 28in (69cm).
$8,000-13,500

A pair of Regency painted coal boxes, each with slightly domed lid and tapering body, decorated in blue on a beige ground with trailing foliage, on gilt paw feet, 21in (52cm).
$2,000-4,500

A mahogany urn table, the waved square top with pierced fretwork gallery, the plain frieze edged with cabochon-and-rosette with a slide, on moulded legs edged with bead-and-reel and joined by an arched pierced cross-stretcher, 13in (33cm) square.
$3,200-6,000

A Regency mahogany wine cooler, with tapering rectangular body with tin-liner and gadrooned border, 34in (86cm).
$4,500-9,000

A Burroughs & Watts full size oak-framed snooker table, raised on 8 supports, each turned and fluted, recently recovered and maintained to a high standard, with white cotton cover, lighting canopy, counter balanced brass fittings and rails for playing billiards.
$8,000-13,500

Possibly the most interesting feature of the clocks market at present is the difference in buying trends between northern and southern areas of the country. Although there is a universal demand for high quality and originality throughout – with such virtues being well rewarded in terms of prices – it is in the matter of taste that the divide is seen.

A consensus of Scottish auctioneers and dealers shows the northern trend to be toward simplicity, with soberly-styled English bracket and mantel clocks being in greatest demand along with early mahogany longcase clocks. Boulle, less-than-superb ormolu, painted faces and other embellishments are regarded by many northern and Scottish buyers as minus points.

Buyers in southern parts, conversely, seem universally to be looking for distinctly decorative qualities. That is not to suggest that less emphasis is placed on quality and originality, however, for even relatively minor defects in either department will be found to have a disastrous effect on price.

Still at the low end of the market are the Victorian marble 'lumps', which many people consider to be seriously underpriced through lack of demand. This particularly applies to those with black marble cases. In view of the fact that there are, if anything, fewer clocks appearing on the market than in years past, it is quite possible that these long-ignored pieces will begin to pick up, particularly since many have excellent movements which will give years of reliable use.

In general terms, the clock market is extremely buoyant, with many dealer/restorers finding less time to devote to dealing through pressure of repair work.

Clocks – Longcase

A George III dark green japanned longcase clock, the dial signed Thomas Allen Deptford, with strike/silent ring above the silvered chapter ring enclosing sunken seconds and calendar aperture, the 5-pillar movement with rack strike and anchor escapement, 90in (230cm).
$4,000-7,500

A 30-hour longcase ▷ clock, of exceptional quality, maker Matthew Bold of Bold, in original oak case, crossbanded also in oak, c1740, 90in (227.5cm).
$2,200-4,200

◁ An 8-day painted dial longcase clock, maker Edward Bell, Uttoxeter, in original oak case with mahogany trim, c1785, 92in (232.5cm).
$2,600-5,300

A mahogany longcase clock by William Barnish of Rochdale, the arch with calendar and lunar aperture painted with faces of the moon and figures in rural and coastal scenes, inscribed 'I am Moving Whilst thou art Sleeping', the 3-train movement with later comb and cylinder strike on 6 graduated bells, and with anchor escapement, late 18thC, 89in (225cm).
$4,500-9,000

An 8-day longcase clock with white dial, maker William Bellman of Broughton, in original oak case with mahogany trim, c1790, 78in (197.5cm).
$1,800-3,800

A chinoiserie black lacquered 8-day longcase clock, the brass dial with silvered chapter ring by John Blake, London, 18thC, 90in (227.5cm).
$2,000-4,500

◁A Regency mahogany longcase clock, the 11in (27.5cm) painted dial with subsidiary seconds, signed Barrauds, Cornhill, London 1140, the 5-pillared movement with signed, shaped plates, maintaining power, and deadbeat escapement, the wood rod pendulum with calibrated rating nut, 76in (192cm).
$12,000-21,000

A mahogany longcase clock, 13in (32.5cm) dial with painted rolling moon in the arch, signed Nathaniel Brown, Manchester, centre sweep seconds and date pointer, 8-day 4-pillar rack striking movement with dead beat escapement, c1780, 95½in (241cm).
$600-1,200

A walnut and marquetry longcase clock, the 8-day 5-pillar movement rack striking, signed Claudius de Chesne, Londini, the marquetry door, which is not original, inlaid with panels of flowers and birds, 89in (225cm).
$3,200-6,000

A mahogany longcase clock, with 12in (30cm) brass dial, calendar aperture, seconds hand, strike and silent dial, the 2-train 8-day movement with anchor escapement, by John Berry, London, 18thC, 84in (213cm).
$4,500-9,000

A 30-hour longcase clock, oak with mahogany crossbanding, by H. Blake of Appleby, c1830.
$900-1,700

An 8-day pine longcase clock, the 12in (30cm) brass dial with subsidiary seconds and dated aperture, signed John Carne, Penzance, 84in (212.5cm).
$1,000-2,000

An 8-day brass dial longcase clock with moon dial, maker Nathaniel Brown of Manchester, original case in dark Cuban mahogany, c1750, 97in (245cm).
$6,000-12,000

IMPORTANT NOTES TO CLOCKS
by Brian Loomes

Originality is of paramount importance; any alterations, modifications or marriages of any kind cause prices to fall drastically. In longcase clocks originality of the case to the clock is vitally important and often difficult for the inexperienced to establish. One would expect to pay more for such an item from a specialist dealer who will guarantee his goods than when buying at auction where normally no such guarantee is given.

Auction estimates are useful as a vague guide only; actual prices realised may vary widely from the auctioneer's estimates.

A clock in unrestored condition is very difficult for the inexperienced to value as a great deal depends on the amount of restoration needed and, in extreme cases, even whether such restoration can be done. It is very easy to spend $400 or $600 on straightforward cleaning of a clock. Consequently with a clock of low value it is quite possible that restoration could prove more costly than the clock's total worth.

High quality of workmanship in clocks puts such examples at a premium. The beginner may well be unable to distinguish which features are indicative of high quality and which are conventional for the period.

Features of a rare or unusual nature add considerably to the value of a clock, as does greater complexity of the movement. The inexperienced may not be able to recognise an exceptionally rare feature from a commonplace one.

In longcase clocks small height is a very important plus feature, provided the clock has not been shortened in some way or otherwise reduced in size – whether recently or long ago is not important. A very tall clock is often difficult to sell and will usually be held down in price by this feature. Because of this a great many have been reduced in height over the years and the ability to recognise this is vital.

A Federal inlaid mahogany tall-case clock, by Stephen Taber, New Bedford, Massachusetts, and Providence, R.I. c1790, the arched line inlaid door opening to an arched white painted brass dial with painted lunar dial and day indicator and 2 celestial globes flanked by floral and gilt spandrels, with inscription 'S. Taber' flanked by fluted colonettes with brass stop-fluting and capitals, above a waisted case over a rectangular line and quarter fan inlaid cupboard door with molded edge flanked by stop-fluted quarter columns above a line and quarter fan inlaid box base, on flaring French feet, fretwork, right front and rear feet restored, minor inpainting on dial, 89in (225cm).
$15,000-17,000

A Federal inlaid and carved walnut tall-case clock, dial signed by Eli Bentley, Tawney Town, Maryland, c1790, the hood with molded and rosette-carved swan's neck pediment centering 3 urn-turned finials above 2 inlaid rosettes over an arched and glazed door flanked by colonnettes enclosing an enamelled dial with calendar aperture, seconds dial, and painted moon dial, the works marked 'WILSON BIRMm'; the case with door flanked by fluted quarter columns over a base with fluted quarter columns, on short ogee bracket feet, minor damage to finial tips and a few other small chips, 95in (240cm) high.
$9,000-12,000

A Chippendale mahogany tall-case clock, dial signed by Joseph and John Hollingshead, Burlington, New Jersey, c1780, the hood with molded swan's neck pediment centering 3 urn-shaped finials above an arched glazed door opening to a brass dial with calendar aperture, seconds dial and painted moon dial, flanked by gilt spandrels, the dial inscribed 'Jos. & John Hollingshead, Burlington' flanked by columns over a waisted case with cupboard door flanked by fluted quarter columns above a box base with applied molding, on ogee bracket feet, 98in (247cm) high.
$13,000-15,000

A rare Queen Anne walnut tall-case clock, dial signed by Peter Stretch, Philadelphia, 1715-1725, the coffered-bonnet hood, above an arched and door flanked by colonettes opening to an engraved brass dial with applied dolphin and mask spandrels, a day-of-the-month aperture, and a seconds dial, the case with molded-edge arched door over a base with molded bracket foot base, finials and one small piece of molding missing, minor loss to fret carving, 96½in (243cm) high.
$34,000-36,000

A Federal mahogany veneered cherrywood tall-case clock, Conrad Selig, Reading, Pennsylvania, 1800-1825, the bonnet with swan's neck pediment centering the fluted plinths with urn finials above an arched door opening to an enamelled dial, inscribed 'Conrad Selig/Reading' and with a revolving lunar aperture above second, minute and hour hands and day of the month indicator, flanked by colonettes, over a cove molding and waisted case with a beaded and banded door, above a banded box case with scalloped apron and French feet, 101½in (256cm) high.
$6,000-7,000

A Federal inlaid mahogany tall case clock, dial signed by Aaron Willard, Boston, c1800-1810, the hood with 3 ball and steeple brass finials between pierced fretwork above a molded cornice over a glazed arched door opening to a white painted dial with a lunar dial over a seconds dial and calendar day aperture flanked by gilt spandrels and over cartouches, the dial signed in script 'Aaron Willard, Boston' flanked by reeded colonettes above a waisted case with molded inlaid door with maple banding flanked by reeded quarter columns over a box base edged with maple banding, on French feet, fretwork restored, 94½in (238cm) high.
$17,000-20,000

A mahogany veneered longcase clock, the 8-day movement rack striking, subsidiary seconds dial and signed Cottell, Crewkerne, 92½in (233cm).
$1,400-2,600

A mahogany longcase clock, the 12in (30cm) brass dial, signed Thos. Bruton, Bow, Midlx., with subsidiaries for seconds and for date and with strike/silent in the arch, the 5-pillared movement with anchor escapement, 18thC, 102in (257.5cm).
$9,000-15,000

A black lacquered and chinoiserie decorated longcase clock, with 12in (30cm) brass dial, recessed subsidiary seconds, and date aperture, signed Joseph Cayre St. Neots, and with strike/silent in the arch, the 5-pillared movement with anchor escapement, 18thC, 99in (250cm).
$3,200-6,000

A fine month longcase clock with 11in (27.5cm) brass dial, having second and date indicators, by Richard Colston, London (apprenticed 1637, member of the Clockmakers Co. 1646-1697), in walnut veneered and marquetry inlaid case, 86in (217.5cm).
$18,000-26,000

A fine oak and crossbanded longcase clock, by David Collier, Gatley, with painted frieze bearing the initials E.M. 1768, 13in (32.5cm) brass dial, with rolling moon to the arch, 4-pillar 8-day rack striking movement striking on a bell, late 18thC, 80in (202.5cm).
$3,200-6,000

A walnut longcase clock, the 12in (30cm) brass dial signed William Clark, Stalbridge with subsidiary seconds and date aperture, the 5-pillared movement of month duration now with deadbeat escapement striking on a gong, 18thC, 95in (240cm).
$600-1,200

A 30-hour longcase clock with painted dial, prestigious maker Samuel Deacon, with original bill of sale, in original oak case with mahogany trim, c1800, 88in (222.5cm).
$1,600-2,800

A Victorian mahogany longcase clock, with 8-day movement by J. Galloway, Leeds.
$1,300-2,400

A walnut longcase clock, the 8-day movement with anchor escapement, rack striking, with 13in (32.5cm) painted dial, subsidiary seconds and calendar dials, signed W. Donald, Glasgow, 85½in (215cm).
$1,800-3,800

A 30-hour longcase clock, maker Fothergill of Knaresborough, original oak case crossbanded and trimmed with mahogany, c1825, 90in (230cm).
$800-1,500

An 8-day painted dial longcase clock, with moonwork in arch, maker Thomas Holmes, Cheadle, in original mahogany case, c1800, 87in (220cm).
$1,800-3,800

A George III mahogany and boxwood strung longcase clock, the 13in (32.5cm) arched brass dial with silvered chapter ring, centre date (the hand missing) and subsidiary seconds, signed Finney, Liverpool, the twin-train movement with anchor escapement, 94in (237.5cm).
$3,200-6,000

An oak longcase ◁ clock, the 8-day movement rack striking, with 12in (30cm) brass dial, with subsidiary seconds dial and date aperture, signed James Green, Nantwich, 84in (212.5cm).
$2,600-5,300

A walnut, boxwood and ebony strung longcase clock, with 12in (30cm) brass dial, signed Benj. Heeley, Deptford, with strike/silent in the arch the 5-pillared movement with anchor escapement, the pagoda-topped hood reduced, 18thC, 96in (244cm).
$5,000-9,000

◁ A Georgian mahogany longcase clock, the 12in (30cm) painted dial with subsidiaries for seconds and for date, signed C.W. Hooke, London, the 5-pillared movement with anchor escapement, 92in (232.5cm).
$7,000-12,000

An 8-day oak and mahogany crossbanded longcase clock by Ebenezer Fisler of Ellesmere, the dial with rolling moon, by Wright, Birmingham, c1835.
$1,300-2,400

An Irish 8-day ▷ mahogany longcase clock, the 13in (32.5cm) brass dial signed John Knox, Larne, No. 156, date aperture, subsidiary dial for age of the moon and concentric tidal dial, the 4-pillar movement with semi dead beat escapement and maintaining power to the going train, c1775, 92in (232.5cm).
$3,200-6,000

An 8-day brass dial longcase clock, maker Hampson, Bolton, in original case of dark mahogany, c1780, 94in (237.5cm).
$6,000-12,000

A Federal inlaid mahogany dwarf tall-case clock, dial signed by Edmund Currier, Salem, Massachusetts, 1820-1830, the hood with 3 molded plinths and urn-turned finials centering pierced fretwork above an arched line inlaid door opening to a white painted dial with a gilt Masonic eye and symbols, minute registers, gilt and painted fans, inscribed 'E. Currier' over a rectangular plinth, the case inlaid with an oval birch panel above the box base centering an octagonal inlaid birch panel flanked by outset reeded columns over a shaped skirt, on baluster and ring-turned legs, 30in (75cm) high.
$27,000-29,000

A Federal cherrywood tall-case clock, dial signed by Christian Winters, Easton, Pennsylvania, c1800, the hood with a spherical brass finial above brass volutes over an arched glazed door opening to a white painted dial with calendar aperture, seconds dial, and painted moon dial flanked by painted floral spandrels, signed 'Christian Winters Easton', flanked by turned columns above a waisted case with arched shell-carved cupboard door flanked by fluted quarter columns over a box base with applied moldings and fluted quarter columns, restorations to base, case and seconds hand, 97in (245cm) high.
$5,000-6,000

A Federal cherrywood tall-case clock, dial signed by Samuel Shourds, Bordentown, New Jersey, c1770, the hood with molded swan's-neck pediment above an arched glazed door opening to an arched brass dial with an engraved circular medallion inscribed 'Samuel Shourds', the dial with sweep seconds dial and calendar day aperture flanked by brass spandrels and ring-turned colonnettes, above a waisted case with rectangular cock-beaded cupboard door flanked by chamfered sides over a box-base with cock-beaded panel, 89in (225cm) high.
$3,000-4,000

A Federal inlaid mahogany tall-case clock, dial signed Alex J. Willard, New Jersey, early 19thC, the hood now with a carved eagle above an arched door opening to a white painted wooden dial with floral spandrels inscribed 'Alex J. Villard/Ashby, works probably not original to case, 86in (217cm) high..
$4,000-5,000

A Federal inlaid mahogany tall-case clock, dial signed by Aaron Willard, Boston, c1805-1810, the hood with 3 plinths centering pierced fretwork above a molded cornice over an arched glazed door with patterned stringing opening to a white painted dial with a rocking ship movement above the dial with sweep seconds dial flanked by floral spandrels, inscribed 'Aaron Willard, Boston' flanked by colonnettes with brass stop-fluted bases above a waisted case, the rectangular line-inlaid and banded cupboard door with applied molding flanked by fluted quarter columns with brass stop-fluted bases over a box base above a valanced skirt, on flared French feet, partial loss to fretwork, feet cut but includes original lower sections, 88in (222cm) high.
$25,000-30,000

◁ A George III figured mahogany longcase clock, with 8-day movement by James Lomax of Blackburn, having additional musical movement, 88in (222.5cm). **$2,200-4,200**

A carved walnut quarter chiming longcase clock, the movement with massive pillars, anchor escapement, and quarter chiming on 8 bells and 4 gongs, signed Maple & Co., London. ▷ **$3,200-6,000**

◁ A Regency mahogany longcase clock, with 8-day chiming movement, anchor escapement by J.A. Paterson, Edinburgh. **$2,200-4,200**

An 8-day brass dial longcase clock with centre calendar and fixed arch landscape scene, dated 1777, maker Thomas Shaw of Lancaster, in original case of bookmatched mahogany, case attributed to Gillows of Lancaster, 90in (227.5cm). **$6,000-12,000**

◁ An 8-day mahogany longcase clock, the 14in (35cm) brass dial signed William Lawson, Newton, around a rolling moon, the 4-pillar movement with rack striking and anchor escapement, 89in (225cm). **$2,600-5,300**

◁ A green stained and chinoiserie 8- day longcase clock by Rich Rayment, Bury, early 18thC, 90in (227.5cm). **$2,200-4,200**

An 8-day painted dial longcase clock with moonwork and centre seconds feature, maker Roberts of Otley, in original mahogany case, c1790, 92in (232.5cm). **$2,600-5,300**

HINTS TO DATING LONGCASE CLOCKS

Dials

8in square	to c1669	Carolean
10in square	from c1665-1800	
11in square	from 1690-1800	
12in square	from c1700	from Queen Anne
14in square	from c1740	from early Georgian
Broken-arch dial	from c1715	from early Georgian
Round dial	from c1760	from early Georgian
Silvered dial	from c1760	from early Georgian
Painted dial	from c1770	from early Georgian
Hour hand only	to 1820	
Minute hand introduced	c1663	
Second hand	from 1675	post-Restoration
Matching hands	from c1775	George III or later

Case finish

Ebony veneer	up to c1725	Carolean to early Georgian
Walnut veneer	from c1670 to c1770	Carolean to mid-Georgian
Lacquer	from c1700 to c1790	Queen Anne to mid-Georgian
Mahogany	from 1730	from early Georgian
Softwood	from c1690	from mid-Georgian
Mahogany inlay	from c1750	from mid-Georgian
Marquetry	from c1680 to c1760	from Carolean to mid-Georgian
Oak	always	

A George III mahogany longcase clock with brass dial, with phases of the moon, the 8-day striking movement with anchor escapement by Standring of Bolton, c1790, 90in (227.5cm).
$600-1,200

◁ A Georgian mahogany longcase clock, the 12in (30cm) arched silvered dial with subsidiary seconds and date aperture, signed James Thwaites, London, and with strike/silent subsidiary in the arch, the 5-pillared movement with anchor escapement, 90in (227.5cm).
$2,200-4,200

A month longcase clock with 12in (30cm) brass dial, inscribed James West, London, in figured mahogany case, 18thC, trunk 13½in (33cm) wide.
$5,000-9,000

An 8-day brass dial longcase clock with lunar and universal tidal dials in arch, maker prestigious William Stumbels, Totnes, in original oak case with walnut trim, c1740, 96in (242.5cm).
$4,500-9,000

A walnut and floral marquetry longcase clock, the 12in (30cm) brass dial signed John Wainwright, Wellingboro, No. 1132, with subsidiary seconds and date aperture, the 5-pillared movement with anchor escapement, 84in (212.5cm).
$6,000-12,000

▷ A month going 8-day longcase clock, with 14½in (36cm) brass dial, signed 'Samll Young, Nant Wich', the 4-pillar movement with latched plates and anchor escapement, in pollard oak and crossbanded case, case reduced, movement repaired, 85in (214cm).
$600-1,200

A walnut and marquetry longcase clock, the 12in (30cm) brass dial signed Wm. Wright, Londini Fecit, with subsidiary seconds and date aperture, the 5-ringed pillared movement with latched dial feet and plates, with anchor escapement and inside countwheel strike, the base with replaced skirting, early 18thC, 98in (247.5cm).
$20,000-30,000

A walnut longcase clock, makers name Windmills, London, with 11in (27.5cm) brass face, the 8-day 2-train movement with anchor escapement, with later marquetry, 18thC, 91in (230cm).
$1,800-3,800

A George III △ mahogany longcase clock with brass inlaid reeded columns and quarter columns, W. Yardley of Bishops Stortford, 96in (242.5cm).
$3,200-6,000

Clocks – Regulators

A Victorian mahogany longcase regulator, with brass glazed bezel to 12in (30cm) dial, signed P.G. Dodd & Son From Cornhill London, dust cover to movement of high count with Harrison's maintaining power, jewelled dead beat escapement and cranked roller crutch, 75in (190cm). $4,000-7,500

A Federal cherrywood tallcase clock, probably New Jersey, seatboard replaced 1810-30. $4,000-6,800

Provenance: A brass plate inside the door of the case indicates the first owner was Lieutenant Samuel Cutler, and gives the line of descent in the Cutler family.

A Continental walnut longcase clock and polyphon, with a winding handle to the side, complete with 26 polyphon discs, and original receipt dated 21st March, 1901, for £33. 10s. 0d. $8000-13,500

A George III mahogany longcase regulator case, now fitted with a single train movement, the 10in (25cm) square silvered dial signed for Fras. Perigal, Bond Street, the shaped plates with 5 pillars and anchor escapement, stamped on the front I. Thwaites, and numbered with the dial and seatboard 1080, 72in (183cm). $6,000-12,000

A rosewood striking longcase regulator, the 12in (30cm) dial signed W. C. Shaw, Glasgow, the going train with dead beat escapement and maintaining power, 83in (210cm). $4,500-9,000

A Regency mahogany longcase regulator, the 11in (27.5cm) dial signed Thwaites & Reed London, high count train with screwed depthed end caps throughout, Harrison's maintaining power, jewelled dead beat escapement with micrometer beat setting to stem of pallet bow and compensated pendulum, now silver plated, 73in (185cm). $20,000-30,000

This pendulum compensation presumably a development from that in Ritchie's patent (see Rees, Clocks, Watches and Chronometers, 1819-20, republished extracts 1970, p.343, fig.9.).

Clocks – Bracket

A George I ebonised striking bracket clock, the dial signed Ed. Bayley, London, twin fusee movement with verge escapement, the scroll engraved backplate with securing brackets to the case, 19in (48cm). $3,200-6,000

An early Georgian bracket clock, with single train movement, anchor escapement by George Elliot, 14in (35cm). $3,200-6,000

A mid-Georgian ebonised striking bracket clock, the dial signed John Fladgate London, the twin fusee movement with verge escapement and profusely engraved backplate with pendulum hook, 18½in (46cm).
$3,200-6,000

HINTS TO DATING BRACKET CLOCKS		
Dials		
Square dial	to c1770	pre-George III
Broken arch dial	from c1720	George I or later
Round/painted/silvered	from c1760	George III or later
Case finish		
Ebony veneer	from c1660 to c1850	Carolean to mid-Victorian
Walnut	from c1670 to c1870	Carolean to Victorian
Marquetry	from c1680 to c1740	Carolean to early Georgian
Rosewood	from c1790	from mid-Georgian
Lacquered	from c1700 to c1760	Queen Anne to early Georgian
Mahogany	from c1730	from early Georgian

A double fusee bracket clock, with strike/silent feature, prestigious maker, Frodsham, London, anchor escapement, c1820, 20in (50cm).
$2,200-4,200

An ebony bracket clock by Christopher Gould, Little Moorfields, London, with double fusee movement and verge escapement, pull repeat on 6 bells, c1720-25, 18½in (46cm).
$1,800-3,800

◁ A walnut cased bracket clock, having brass and silvered dial, inscribed Thomas Harrison, Liverpool, with chain fusee movement.
$1,300-2,400

An ebony veneered quarter repeating bracket clock, the 2-train 5-pillar fusee movement with verge escapement, signed Henry Fish, Royal Exchange, London, contained in a bell top case with glazed side panels, 17½in (43cm).
$6,000-12,000

Henry Fish, 4 Sweetings Alley, Royal Exchange, c1730. Britten says, probably the son of Henri Poisson.

A Charles II ebonised striking transitional bracket clock, twin fusee movement with outside countwheel strike, the backplate signed Henry Jones in the Strand, converted to anchor escapement but retaining original pendulum securing clip, and pull quarter repeat train removed, 12½in (31cm).
$12,000-21,000

An ebonised bracket timepiece, the 5-pillared movement with verge escapement, signed Jeffery Harris, London, 18thC, 17in (42.5cm).
$3,200-6,000

361

A mahogany bracket clock, signed Edwd. Moore, Oxford, the movement converted to anchor escapement with engraved backplate, late 18thC, 20½in (51cm), together with a later mahogany wall bracket.
$2,600-5,300

A George III mahogany bracket clock, the silvered dial inscribed John Skinner, Exon, 8-day striking fusee movement converted to anchor escapement, 21in (52.5cm) overall.
$1,800-3,800

John Skinner of Exeter, recorded working around 1780, died in 1818.

A rosewood bracket clock by Benjamin Lautier of Bath, the 8-day movement having double fusee, early 19thC, 17½in (43cm).
$4,000-7,500

An ebonised bracket clock, inscribed Philip Lloyd, Bristol, the bell striking repeating movement with anchor escapement, 18thC, 21in (52.5cm).
$1,700-3,000

A Regency brass mounted mahogany bracket clock, the painted dial signed James Murray, Royal Exchange, London, the movement with anchor escapement, 19½in (49cm).
$2,600-5,300

A single fusee mahogany bracket clock, maker John Nicholls, London, converted to anchor escapement, c1770, 15in (37.5cm).
$1,800-3,800

An ebony and gilt brass mounted bracket clock, the 7in (17.5cm) brass dial signed J. Mondehare, Londini Fecit, the 5-tulip pillared movement with latched dial and plates, with replaced verge escapement and pull quarter repeating on 3 bells, 18thC, 15in (37.5cm).
$8,000-15,000

An ebonised bracket clock, with brass dial engraved Jasper Taylor, Holbourn, London, the 5-pillar movement with verge escapement, hour strike and engraved backplate, 18thC, 16in (41cm).
$4,000-6,800

A mahogany and brass decorated Regency bracket clock, the 7in (17.5cm) painted dial signed Thomas Pace, London, unusual twin fusee movement with circular plates, 4-pillar rack striking movement, 19in (47.5cm) overall.
$1,800-3,800

A George III ebonised bracket clock, with brass dial, having 3-train movement striking on 2 bells, engraved brass movement by Justin Vulliamy, London, 12in (30cm).
$1,700-3,000

A Victorian bracket clock, with rosewood case and ormolu mountings, chime on bells and Westminster, c1880, 30in (75cm).
$2,200-4,200

A musical ormolu mounted mahogany bracket clock, the 3 train chain fusee movement with anchor escapement and chiming on 9 bells and 9 hammers, signed S. Williams, London, with chime selector in the arch for 'Song', 'Minuet', 'Cotillon' and 'Air', 20in (50cm).
$5,500-9,000

A mahogany veneered bracket clock, the movement with verge escapement, signed in the arch Richd. Ward, Winchester, with restorations, 18½in (46cm).
$4,000-6,800

Richard Ward is recorded in Winchester c1795.

A miniature ebony bracket clock by Samuel Watson, London, with pull repeat, 14-day duration, c1680, 13in (33cm).
$34,000-60,000

A large Victorian oak bracket clock, the double chain fusee movement with Westminster chimes striking on 8 bells and 5 gongs, 23in (58cm).
$1,200-2,100

A Regency mahogany and brass inlaid bracket clock, the white enamel dial inscribed J. Wells, 15 Hanway St, Oxford St, W.C., wire gong striking movement, 25in (62.5cm).
$1,800-3,800

A repeater musical bracket clock, fitted 8-day movement chiming on 8 bells and Westminster, late 19thC, 23in (57.5cm).
$2,600-5,300

Make the most of Miller's

Every care has been taken to ensure the accuracy of descriptions and estimated valuations. Where an attribution is made within inverted commas (e.g. 'Chippendale') or is followed by the word 'style' (e.g. early Georgian style) it is intended to convey that, in the opinion of the publishers, the piece concerned is a later – though probably still antique – reproduction of the style so designated. Unless otherwise stated, any description which refers to 'a set', or 'a pair' includes a valuation for the entire set or the pair, even though the illustration may show only a single item.

A Regency ebony and brass mounted quarter chiming bracket clock, the painted dial with strike/silent, signed Wm. Wright, Ongar, with triple fusee movement, and anchor escapement striking the quarters on 8 bells, 25½in (64cm).
$3,200-6,000

A brass mounted mahogany table or bracket clock, the French 8-day movement having half-hour striking on gongs, late 19thC, 17½in (43cm).
$600-1,100

A late Victorian 3-train brass inlaid rosewood clock and matching bracket, the fusee movement chiming the quarters on 8 bells and striking the hours on a gong, with Cambridge/Westminster selector, the clock 30in (75cm), 43in (108cm) overall.
$2,600-5,300

A Victorian walnut quarter chiming bracket clock, with subsidiaries at the top for chime/silent, regulation and for Westminster or 8 bells, the triple fusee movement with anchor escapement, 31in (77.5cm).
$1,600-2,800

A Neuchatel black lacquered quarter striking bracket clock, the twin-train movement striking on 2 gongs, with enamel dial, with the matching wall bracket, 19thC, 37in (92.5cm).
$1,600-2,800

Clocks – Carriage

A French tortoiseshell, cut brass inlaid and ormolu mounted bracket clock, the 5-tulip pillared movement converted to anchor escapement, with rectangular plates and countwheel strike, with matching wall bracket, 18thC, 48in (122cm) overall.
$3,200-6,000

A Victorian ormolu mounted mahogany bracket clock, the strike/silent and chime selection with anchor movement, 27in (67.5cm).
$2,600-5,300

A tortoiseshell and silver carriage timepiece, with lever movement, the dial signed for Mappin & Webb, London, the silver marked London 1910, 5in (12.5cm).
$1,300-2,400

A repeating carriage clock, with 3in (7.5cm) white enamelled dial signed Müller/Twickenham, the 8-day movement with compensated balance wheel, and lever escapement, 8in (20cm), with carrying case and key.
$800-1,500

A French repeater carriage clock, retailed by A. E. Halfhide, Wimbledon, 19thC, 7in (17.5cm).
$1,800-3,800

A French gilt brass carriage clock, the lever movement striking on a gong with push repeat, the side panels and dial of pietra dura, 7in (18cm).
$3,200-6,000

A French brass carriage clock, the lever movement striking on a gong, with alarm and push repeat and bearing the trademark B in a circle, 19thC, 7½in (19cm).
$1,000-2,000

A gilt brass enamel mounted carriage clock, the movement with lever escapement, compensated balance, gong striking and repeating at will, with outer carrying case, 8in (20cm).
$1,600-2,800

A fine French striking and repeating carriage clock, with original lever escapement, by Henri Jacot, Paris, c1880, 7½in (19cm), with travelling case and key.
$2,200-4,200

A French carriage clock, by Francois-Arsene Margaine, Paris, with half-hour repeater movement, the dial inscribed Hamilton & Co., Calcutta and Bombay, 6in (15cm), with morocco travelling case and key.
$900-1,700

A French brass carriage clock, 5in (12cm).
$300-600

A brass carriage clock, the movement with replaced lever escapement, now striking on a gong, with alarm and push repeat, 19thC, 7in (18cm).
$600-1,200

An engraved oval alarum carriage clock, the enamel dial signed Tiffany & Co., New York, the striking movement with later lever platform, 6in (15cm).
$1,300-2,400

A French grande-sonnerie repeating carriage clock, the white enamel dial having numerals replaced by names 'Margaret' and 'Kate', having day, date and alarm subsidiary dials, the backplate stamped 'W.T. & Co.', 19thC, 6in (15cm), with original red morocco leather travelling case and key.
$2,600-5,300

A French gilt brass carriage clock, the movement with replaced lever platform, striking on a bell, with push repeat and alarm, 19thC, 6in (15cm).
$1,000-2,000

A gilt brass striking carriage clock, with uncut bi-metallic balance to silvered lever platform, strike/repeat on gong, stamp of Henri Jacot, 5½in (14cm).
$1,400-2,600

A rare ivory and marquetry panelled timepiece carriage clock, with platform escapement, the top panel signed with monogram FD, Bte, 5in (12cm).
$1,600-2,800

An Austrian gilt metal carriage clock, the lever movement with grande-sonnerie striking on 2 gongs, with alarm and push repeat, 19thC, 6in (15cm).
$1,300-2,400

Clocks – Mantel

A calendar carriage timepiece, the movement with cylinder platform, 5in (12cm).
$800-1,500

A French repeating alarum carriage clock, with the inscription 'Chedel, Paris', over a subsidiary alarm dial, striking the hours and half-hours on a single bell, with repeat mechanism, 7in (17.5cm), in leather covered carrying case.
$1,800-3,800

A Regency black slate and gilt bronze mantel timepiece, the fuse movement signed on the backplate Grimalde & Johnson, 431 Strand, London, 11in (28cm).
$1,800-3,800

A black slate, bronze and gilt metal mounted mantel timepiece, the fusee movement with anchor escapement and rise and fall regulation, signed Vulliamy, London, 510, 19thC, 12½in (32cm).
$7,000-12,000

A gilt bronze mantel clock, the twin fusee movement with anchor escapement, signed Payne, 163 New Bond Street, 19thC, 13½in (33cm).
$1,800-3,800

A Federal cherrywood shelf clock, dial signed by David Wood, Newburyport, Massachusetts, c1800, in 2 parts: the upper case with shaped pediment and 2 brass urn finials centering an eagle finial above a glazed door with applied arched molding flanked by applied pilasters opening to a white painted dial with painted floral spandrels, the dial inscribed 'David Wood, on a molded base; the lower section with molded top above a rectangular door with applied fluted pilasters encasing the front corners and rear edges on a cover-molded base; the weight-driven movement strikes once on the hour, restorations to some applied molding, finials, seatboard and backboard replaced, 32½in (81cm) high.
$8,000-9,000

A French Louis XV black boule clock, 39in (97.5cm).
$4,000-7,500

A slate cased regulator mantel clock, signed Howell & Co., 19thC, 15½in (39cm).
$1,000-2,000

A Louis XVI marble and ormolu mantel clock, the circular movement mounted between two Ionic pilasters, the movement with countwheel strike, 28in (70cm).
$5,000-9,000

A French boulle mantel clock, the 2-train movement with embossed gilt dial and white enamel numeral reserves, 23in (57.5cm).
$1,300-2,400

A Victorian carved oak mantel clock, 3-train spring driven movement, quarter striking and repeating on 8 gongs, 23in (57.5cm).
$600-1,200

A French tortoiseshell and cut brass inlaid mantel clock, the gilt dial with enamel numerals, signed Gaudron A Paris, the movement with anchor escapement and square plates signed on the back, 18thC, 20in (50cm).
$3,200-6,000

An ormolu mantel timepiece, containing a calendar verge watch movement with Continental bridge cock and diamond endstone, 12in (30cm).
$900-1,700

A rare and important Federal inlaid mahogany shelf clock, by David Wood, Newburyport, Massachusetts, c1800, the hood with molded arched pediment with 3 shield-inlaid plinths and brass flame finials centering a gilt pewter fretwork above an arched cross-banded inlaid door opening to a white painted iron dial with gilt foliate spandrels, minute registers, inscribed 'D. Wood, Newburyport', the case with cross banded and line-inlaid hinged door with applied ogee molding, on ogee bracket feet, with original brass carrying handles; the brass weight driven movement strikes the bell once on the hour, 34in (85cm) high.
$57,000-60,000

A late Empire bronze, ormolu and griotte marble mantel clock, 31in (77cm).
$2,600-5,300

A French red marble perpetual calendar mantel clock and barometer, the movement with Brocot type suspension, and bell striking, 2 thermometers, both tubes defective, 18½in (46cm).
$1,600-2,800

A French mantel clock, the striking skeleton movement by J. Valery, Paris, 19thC.
$300-600

A French Empire striking clock, the 4in (10cm) enamel face having exposed escapement wheel, the movement with outside countwheel, 21in (52.5cm).
$1,200-2,100

A French red marble and bronze mantel clock, the case of Louis XVI style, in the form of an urn surmounted by a pineapple finial, 19thC, 33in (82.5cm).
$6,000-12,000

A French green boulle mantel clock, with ormolu mounts, countwheel striking on a bell, 13in (33cm).
$1,300-2,400

A French mantel clock, with 3in (7.5cm) diam. white enamelled dial inscribed Engler à Bordeaux, 8-day movement by Pons (De-Paul) with outside countwheel, striking the hours and half-hours on a bell, dial cracked, glazed door cracked, 16in (40cm).
$900-1,700

A Federal mahogany shelf clock, by Aaron Willard, Boston, Massachusetts, c1800, with fluted plinth and brass ball finial above a door opening to a kidney-shaped white painted dial with inscription 'Aaron Willard, Boston', over a coved molding above a box base with rosewood banding over a shaped skirt, on bracket feet, lacks pediment, weight, pendulum, feet reduced; together with a modern wall bracket, 33in (82cm) high.
$6,500-7,000

An ornate metal elephant clock, with 8-day chiming movement, outside countweel, 21in (52.5cm).
$1,300-2,400

A gilt metal mantel clock, in the form of an elaborate Gothic tower, the works with outside countwheel and maker Raingo, Paris, mid-19thC, 28in (70cm).
$1,400-2,600

A gilt metal striking mantel clock, with outside countwheel in the form of a Gothic arch, mid-19thC, 20½in (51cm).
$1,400-2,600

A French alabaster and gilt metal mantel clock, the movement winding through the face and striking on a single bell, numbered 5754, 19thC.
$600-1,200

A French porcelain mantel clock, with 8-day striking movement, the dial inscribed Raingo Freres, Paris, 19thC, 15in (37 5cm).
$500-900

A French mantel clock, in white marble ormolu mounted case, late 19thC.
$900-1,700

A South German negro automaton clock, the brass octagonal movement with twin resting bells, basically mid-17thC, 11½in (28cm).
$8,000-15,000

A Louis XV style mantel clock, with white enamelled dial signed Meunier à Paris, having an 8-day spring-driven striking movement, 19thC, 22½in (56cm).
$2,600-5,300

Clocks – Lantern

A Charles II brass cased lantern clock with 30-hour striking verge movement, inscribed Jos. Norris Abingdon, c1670.
$3,200-6,000

An English lantern clock, unsigned, with original verge escapement and original alarmwork, c1700, 16in (40cm).
$1,800-3,800

Clocks – Skeleton

An English skeletonised fusee clock, with anchor escapement.
$1,000-2,000

l. A brass skeleton timepiece with strike and chain drive under dome, 15in (37.5cm).
$500-900
r. An Orrery clock under glass dome, limited edition numbered 259.
$500-900

A small Victorian brass skeleton clock, with fusee movement.
$900-1,700

A massive brass 3-train 'Westminster Abbey' skeleton clock, striking on gong and nest of 8 bells having mercury pendulum, by W.F. Evans and Sons, Soho Clock Factory, Handsworth, under oval dome, 24in (60cm).
$9,000-15,000

A brass skeleton clock, the ▷ twin chain and fusee movement with anchor escapement striking on a bell above, with wood rod pendulum, on oval wooden stand and glass dome, 19½in (49cm).
$1,800-3,800

◁ A brass skeleton clock, 8-day movement with 'one at the hour' strike on a steel bell, 17½in (44cm).
$800-1,500

Clocks – Wall

A mid-Georgian black japanned tavern or Act of Parliament clock, signed Robert Allam London on the 30in (75cm) dial, the timepiece movement with tapered plates and anchor escapement, 59in (147.5cm).
$8000-13,500

An adapted George III brass ▷ mounted mahogany wall clock, with anchor escapement and rack strike to the fusee movement, signed Dutton London 3 on backplate, the 14in (35cm) dial signed Mattw. & Willm. Dutton London, 38in (95cm).
$3,200-6,000

The cast brass foliate volute mounts have parallels with the mounts on various barometers by Tompion

An Act of Parliament clock, decorated in red and gilt in a chinoiserie landscape, with 8-day movement, 18thC, 54in (134cm).
$1,300-2,400

A drop dial wall clock by Birkle ▷ Bros. Commercial Rd, London, with fusee movement, in mahogany case, c1870, 19in (48cm).
$600-1,100

Make the most of Miller's

When a large specialist well-publicised collection comes on the market, it tends to increase prices. Immediately after this, prices can fall slightly due to the main buyers having large stocks and the market being 'flooded'. This is usually temporary and does not affect very high quality items.

l A walnut and ebonised 8-day weight-driven 2-train Vienna regulator, 'The Farringdon Regulator', 48in (122cm).
$1,000-2,000
c A Continental 8-day mahogany weight-driven 2-train Vienna regulator, 58in (145cm).
$600-1,200
r A walnut and ebonised 8-day weight-driven 2-train Vienna regulator, 42in (107.5cm).
$800-1.500

A Dutch walnut Zaanklok, decorated with the motto Nu Elck Syn Sin, the brass movement with decorative 3-spoked wheels, Dutch striking and verge escapement, and alarm, 18thC, 29in (72.5cm).
$4,500-9,000

◁An ash and maple double weight Vienna regulator, with architectural pediment, c1840.
$3,200-6,000

A late Biedermeier rosewood Vienna regulator, stamped Crot Berlin 302, with weight-driven movement with deadbeat escapement, 39½in (98cm).
$1,700-3,000

△
A triple-weight Vienna regulator wall clock, in a walnut case, with grande sonnerie striking, c1870, 51in (129cm).
$2,600-5,300

A cartel clock in the Louis XV style, the 2-train movement with
▽ countwheel strike on a bell, some damage to chapters, late 19thC, 30in (75cm).
$1,200-2,100

A walnut cased Vienna regulator, signed H. Samuel, Manchester, c1860, 48in (120cm).
$900-1,700

A Louis XVI ormolu cartel timepiece, the movement with pull quarter repeating work, incomplete, the enamel dial signed Hans A Paris, 18in (45cm).
$600-1,200

A Black Forest automaton wall clock, an aperture above revealing 3 jacks quarter-chiming on bells, mounted above a red roofed building, the 3-train movement of traditional form, with restorations, 19thC, 20½in (50cm).
$4,000-7,500

A Dutch East Friesland wall clock.
$2,600-5,300

A Continental striking cartel clock, 25½in (63cm).
$1,200-2,100

A Dutch marquetry Staartklok, with 11in (27.5cm) painted dial, now fitted with an English 8-day longcase clock movement, case deepened to accommodate movement, 52in (130cm).
$4,000-6,800

Clocks – Garniture

◁ A French gilt brass and enamel clock garniture, the lever movement striking on a gong, numbered 5752, 19thC, 10½in (26cm), together with a matching pair of side urns.
$1,300-2,400

A white marble and gilt metal 3-piece clock set, the French movement chiming on a gong, makers J. Marti and Cie, 23in (57.5cm).
$1,800-3,800

A French ormolu and bronze clock garniture, 19thC, 17in (42.5cm), with matching pair of side urns.
$2,000-4,500

A French porcelain mounted mantel clock garniture, 2-train movement by Japy Freres, 18in (45cm), with a pair of associated gilt metal urns, 13½in (33cm).
$1,000-2,000

An English quarter chiming gilt brass clock garniture, the 3-train chain fusee movement with anchor escapement, chiming the quarters on 8 bells and striking the hours on a coiled steel gong, signed on the backplate J.C. Jennens & Son, 25-26 Great Sutton St. London, 18in (45cm).
$1,300-2,400

Make the most of Miller's

Miller's is completely different each year. Each edition contains completely NEW photographs. This is not an updated publication. We never repeat the same photograph.

A French ormolu mounted tortoiseshell clock set of Louis XV design, retailed by R & W Sorley, Paris, the clock 23in (57.5cm).
$2,200-4,200

A pale royal rouge marble and ormolu 3-piece clock set, 34in (85cm).
$13,000-22,000

A French silver plated brass 3-piece clock garniture, 19thC.
$1,000-2,000

A French bronze and ormolu 3-piece clock garniture, the bell striking movement inscribed Charpentier, Ft. de Bronzes, 283 à Paris, 19thC, 35½in (88cm), the side pieces inscribed with the initials V.P. beneath a crown, 37in (92.5cm).
$8,000-15,000

Clocks – Table

A gilt brass strut timepiece, the dial signed for Carrington & Co, 130 Regent St, the movement with lever escapement with compensated balance and overcoil spring, the reverse engraved W.V. (probably Wilhelm Vasel) 19thC, 8in (20cm).
$1,200-2,100

Clocks – Miscellaneous

A gilt brass strut timepiece in the manner of Thomas Cole, the dial signed for Hunt & Roskell, London, the movement with lever escapement and plain gold 3-arm balance, 19thC, 6in (15cm).
$1,000-2,000

A German gilt brass octagonal table clock, the movement with chain fusee for the going and resting barrel for the rack strike and repeat, verge escapement with spring balance, eared pierced cock and foot on top plate signed L. Petitot, Berlin, early 18thC, 4in (11cm) diam.
$600-1,200

L. Letitot, a Huguenot émigré to Germany, working 1700-1725 (see Abeler).

A French musical automata clock, the base mounted with a clock movement, containing a Swiss musical movement, 19thC, 34in (85cm).
$4,000-7,500

A three-dimensional wood model picture clock showing French Chateau, windmill and farmhouse with bridge in centre, complete with music box revolving windmill, 21½in (53cm).
$2,600-5,300

A London and North Western Railways signal box timepiece in mahogany case, 6in (15cm).
$400-750

A British Railways dial clock, with fusee movement, in a mahogany case.
$300-600

A Japanese pillar clock, the weight-driven movement with verge and balance wheel escapement, movement with replacement wheel and case lacking drawer at base of trunk, 20in (50cm).
$1,200-2,100

A George III large turret clock movement by Aynsworth and John Thwaites, London for Lees Court, Kent, with anchor escapement, 3-train, ting tang quarter and hour strike, 2 winding cranks, 4 leading off rods and a box of pulleys, 46in (115cm).
$4,000-6,800

Originally made for Hon. Lewis Thomas Watson, later 2nd Baron Sondes, Lees Court, Faversham, Kent, with photocopy of Thwaites's day book entry relating to this clock (original deposited at Guildhall Library, London).

An Edwardian novelty timepiece, modelled as a ship's steering wheel, with easel back, Chester, 1909.
$300-600

A fine rosewood clock, inlaid with various fruitwoods, late 19thC, 18in (45cm).
$900-1,700

An English dial, the 14in (35cm) brass dial signed John Neve, Hingham, the verge escapement in tapering plates, 16½in (41cm) diam.
$3,200-6,000

A French 'Reims' cathedral clock, the movement with Brocot type suspension and gong striking, 21½in (53cm).
$3,200-6,000

A rare German 'talking clock' movement by Gustav Becker, with plated cast plates and train, the massive spring barrel, train and diaphragm geared to the roller mechanism with fragment of original tape giving the time in German every half hour, the vertically mounted horn of papier mâché.
$1,300-2,400

Stick

A mahogany stick barometer, the silvered brass plate signed J. Patrick, London, mounted with a thermometer the silvered plate with scale engraved Extream Cold/Extream Hot, restored, early 18thC, 39in (97.5cm).
$4,000-7,500

A Georgian mahogany stick barometer, the brass plate signed Wisker York, 36in (90cm).
$900-1,700

A mahogany ships barometer, the ivory plates unsigned, 36in (90cm).
$1,700-3,000

A mahogany wheel barometer, the 12in (30cm) silvered dial engraved with scrolls, with level signed Pastorelli, No. 156 Holborn, London, Timepiece, Thermometer, hygrometer, mid-19thC, 48in (121cm).
$2,000-4,500

A mahogany stick barometer, the silvered brass plate signed Palmer, London, the boxwood and ebony strung case inset with boxwood paterae, the case with hydrometer and swan neck pediment, 19thC, 42in (105cm).
$3,200-6,000

Wheel

A George III mahogany clock barometer, with boxwood edging and inlaid with shell motifs, signed Wm. Ticadell(?) Glasgow, the 10in (25cm) silvered registered dial of 'regulator' pattern, signed W. Cooper Hamilton with subsidiary clock and date of month dials, the clock movement of Sedan type with verge escapement, plain steel balance and signed Jas. Jarvis, London No.709, 44in (110cm).
$6,000-12,000

A rosewood wheel barometer, with unusual 6in (15cm) dial, level signed Limbach, Hull, with thermometer, hygrometer, 19thC, 38½in (96cm).
$600-1,200

A bird's-eye maple wheel barometer, with silvered 8in (20cm) dial level signed J. Cetta, Stroudwater, mirror, thermometer, and hygrometer, 39in (97.5cm).
$1,000-2,000

Chronometers

A rare two-day Victorian marine Chronometer with 'Hartnup's Balance', the silvered dial signed Thos. Russell & Son, Makers to the Queen, 30 & 32 Slater Street, Liverpool, No.6626, 10.5cm diam. of dial.
$9,000-15,000

The Hartnup balance, unique in design and construction, was invented by John Hartnup, the Liverpool Observatory's first director, appointed in 1843. As distinct from the Chronometer Department at Greenwich, primarily concerned with rating and purchase of chronometers for Government service, one of Hartnup's chief tasks was the rating of chronometers for merchant ships and he soon became concerned with the problem of 'middle temperature error'. The

Liverpool maker, William Shepherd, made the prototype of Hartnup's balance probably in 1847. After very successful trials at Liverpool, Hartnup contacted Airy, the Astronomer Royal, at Greenwich. Three Shepherd chronometers with Hartnup's balance were tried there in 1848. The Greenwich trials were not as favourable as those at Liverpool and Hartnup then questioned the mode of testing at Greenwich. Airy, no stranger to disputes, hotly defended Greenwich, enlisting Sheepshanks's aid in the Notices of the R.A.S. Sheepshanks's editorial comments contributed to the commercial failure of Hartnup's balance. As confirmed by Gould, it was never generally used, and therefore extant examples are very rare.

An eight-day Marine Chronometer, by Victor Kullberg, the spotted movement with Earnshaw type spring detent escapement, the freesprung balance with Kullberg's auxiliary compensation.
$18,000-26,000

A two-day Marine Chronometer, the movement with Earnshaw type spring detent escapement, signed William Farquhar, Tower Hill, London, Q/7, in a brass bowl.
$2,000-4,500

Dials

An unusual Italian brass azimuth compass dial, late 17th/early 18thC, 9in (23cm) square.
$2,000-4,500

A brass universal equinoctial ring dial by R. Glynne, London, 4½in (12cm) diam., in chamois lined leather covered case with gilt tooled decoration to the lid.
$5,500-9,000

A brass universal equinoctial ring dial, unsigned, late 18thC, 3in (8cm) diam.
$800-1,500

A brass universal equinoctial ring dial, 3½in (9.2cm) diam., in a gold galloon edged chamois lined leather case, blind stamped with rocaille.
$14,000-24,000

Possibly from the circle of Brander bearing his fleur-de-lys mark and the mark(?) of another maker.

A brass mechanical equinoctial dial, by Thomas Wright, 18thC.
$5,000-9,000

A ?German Planispheric Astrolabe, not signed or dated, gilt brass and silver, diam. 6.7cm, ?c1600, The Rete of silver, for 35 stars, two plates, for latitudes 46°, 49°, 52° and 55°, the alidade, rule, bolt and nut appear to be original.
$26,000-48,000

Considering its small size, this astrolabe is well engraved and detailed. It closely resembles a gilt brass and silver astrolabe not signed or dated, in the Museum of the History of Science, Oxford, of which the wider limb increases the diameter to 6.9cm (C.C.A.no.275; see Robert G. Gunther, Astrolabes of the World, 2 vols, Oxford, 1932, repr. London, 1976, vol.II, no.275 & illus.). Both instruments may be attributed to the workshop which produced the astrolabes and other instruments signed by Johann Anton Lynden, a citizen and goldsmith of Heilbronn. The dated instruments signed by Lynden are sun dials and range from 1594 to 1606.

Globes

An 18in (45cm) terrestrial globe, by W. & A. K. Johnson, dated 1888, 26in (66cm) high.
$3,200-6,000

A German 12¾in terrestrial globe, by J. G. Klinger, with engraved brass meridian, globe defective, 18thC.
$1,700-3,000

A pair of 18in Dudley Adams terrestrial and celestial globes, signed 'D. Adams, 60 Fleet St., London, 1809', printed with Latin and English names, and the routes of explorers, lacks equatorial zodiac ring, 41½in (107cm) high overall, early-19thC.
$18,000-26,000

Surveying

A library 12in terrestrial globe, signed by Bardin, London, with label of Bate, London, pasted over, 1802, the globe bearing a cartouche with the following inscription: 'The new 12in British Terrestrial Globe, representing the accurate positions of the principal known places of the earth, from the discoveries of CAPTAIN COOK and subsequent circumnavigators to the present period, 1802'. The globe is corrected with the additions to the year 1807. 30in (76cm) high, 12in (31cm) diam. of globe, 17in (43cm) diam. of globe with horizon ring.

$600-1,200

Thomas M. Bardin was a globe maker who flourished between the years 1806–1827. His address is given by E. G. R. Taylor as 16 Salisbury Square, Fleet Street, London. Robert Brettell Bate is listed as being at 20–21 Poultry, London. In 1807 Bate was apprenticed and must have started in business about 1815. Bate was a well-known instrument maker and was famous for his nautical instruments; he made an artificial horizon, which could be attached to any sextant. See E. G. R. Taylor, Mathematical Practitioners of Hanoverian England, p.355.

A fine theodolite-stand and ▷ compass-table, signed 'G. F. Brander fecit Aug. Vind.', calibrated with three scales for Cathetus, Basis and Gradius, the limb traversing the 360° horizontal scale with vernier scale and micrometer adjustment screw and clamp, 9in (23cm) diam. of table.

$10,000-18,000

No similar theodolite compass-table is recorded in Brachner.

A black enamelled and lacquered brass theodolite, signed 'J. Casartelli Manchester', 13in (34cm) high.

$900-1,700

A fine part theodolite, signed 'G.F. Brander fecit Aug. Vind', with rare or unique mahogany barrelled telescope of square section with brass endpieces, mounted with bubble level, and with unusual facility for removing the lens units via latches to one side, 13in (33cm) length of scope.

$14,000-24,000

A surveyor's lacquered brass level attributed to the Brander workshop, unsigned, 11¼in (29cm) wide.

$3,200-6,000

Although unsigned, the construction of this instrument and decoration of the case suggest it being a product of the Brander workshop.

A lacquered brass level, signed 'Hyde, Bristol', with rack and pinion focusing, level and cross bubble, ray shade and dust cap, with trade label for Henry Husband and a mirror in the original mahogany case, 14in (36cm) wide.

$300-600

An ebony framed octant, with inset ivory scale and unsigned makers cartouche, in mahogany case, early 19thC, index arm radius 9½in (24cm).

$600-1,200

A brass sextant with telescope, five shades, mirror and detachable rosewood handle, signed 'Northen Hull', 6in (15cm) across the index arm with vernier, lacks magnifier, 3½in (9cm) radius, with one telescope, in mahogany case, early 19thC, 7in (18cm) wide.

$1,700-3,000

A rare lacquered brass distance measuring instrument, the drum-type tubular body signed 'G.F. Brander fecit Aug Vind', with a surviving glass micrometer, the eye-piece protected by a red glass shade, in the original fruitwood case, 11¼in (28.5cm) high.

$4,000-7,500

It has been suggested that only one other micrometer glass survives in a distance meter of this type. Although principally a distance finder, this instrument was designed to be used also as a camera obscura and lucida.

An oxydised brass three circled frame sextant, signed 'Cox & Coombs, Devenport, Plymouth, No.3460', with four index glass and three horizon glass coloured shades, sun inverting and star telescopes, in mahogany box with trade label of George Lee, 33 The Hard, Portsea, index arm radius 6¼in (16cm).
$600-1,200

A rare surveyors set of brass plane-table triangulation dividers, signed and dated 'I. De Cranendonck M.F.A. 1607', 15½in (39cm) wide, fully opened.
$8,000-15,000

Microscopes

A brass dissecting microscope, signed Carl Zeiss, Jena 12670, with swivel mirror, the stage fitted with 2 leather covered rests, in original case, 19thC, 6¾in (17cm) high.
$400-750

Telescopes

A rare lacquered brass miniature refracting telescope, signed 'Dollond, London', the 1¼in (3cm) lens covered with a screw on dust cap, 4in (9.8cm) long body tube with single graduated draw tube, the eye-piece with rotating wheel of four lens powers, in the original fishskin covered card case, late 18thC, 5in (12.5cm) long.
$3,200-6,000

A brass microscope by Smith, Beck & Beck, complete with lenses, in mahogany case, late 19thC.
$600-1,100

A lacquered brass 'Martin' type drum microscope, the draw tube signed Gogerty 72 Fleet St. London, with a set of 6 numbered objectives, slides, forceps and bull's-eye condenser, case 11in (28cm) wide.
$500-900

A lacquered brass 3in (7.5cm) refracting telescope by Clarkson's, Holborn, the 36½in (92.5cm) long body tube with rack and pinion focusing, with sighting accessories in the original case, late 19thC, 40in (102cm) wide.
$1,000-2,000

A brass simple microscope, unsigned, with 3 objectives, 18thC, the case 5in (13cm) wide.
$400-900

POINTERS FOR TELESCOPES

* first telescopes developed from 1605 to 1608
* 17thC refracting models made of vellum with horn binding
* 1758 Dolland developed lens for day and night vision
* 18thC has greatest appeal for collectors as everything was hand made
* 18thC barrels made of mahogany, brass for metal parts
* 19thC plainer style, machine produced
* Instruments still widely available. Currently excellent investment potential for 18thC and good 19thC examples

A brass reflecting telescope, in the manner of G.F. Brander, unsigned, the 1¾in (4.5cm) diam. body tube 8¼in (21cm) long, with screw rod focusing, in original walnut case, 11½in (29cm) wide, the interior lined with Augsburg red marbled finished paper as used by G.F. Brander.
$5,500-9,000

A Jones 'Most Improved' type compound monocular microscope in brass, signed Adams, LONDON. with various accessories, late 18thC.
$3,200-6,000

379

SCIENTIFIC INSTRUMENTS

MICROSCOPES

A 'Culpeper' type microscope, unsigned, early 19thC, base 3¼in (8cm) diam.
$1,000-2,000

It appears that this small size of 'Culpeper' type microscope was introduced by W. & S. Jones in about 1798. See G. L'E. Turner, Collecting Microscopes, p.42.

A Victorian lacquered brass binocular microscope, probably by Smith and Beck, with the trade plaque of Hesketh Walker, Liverpool, objectives, oculars and live box, in fitted case, c1890, 23in (58cm) high.
$1,200-2,100

A brass compound monocular microscope, signed J.B. Dancer Optician Manchester, with bull's-eye condenser, 8 objectives, 2 Watson illuminators, 3 eye-pieces, other accessories and items in the original mahogany case, 19thC, 16in (41cm) high.
$1,000-2,000

A Victorian brass binocular microscope by C. Coleman, 77 Great Titchfield Street, London, with 2 oculars, 2 object lenses, 2 prismatic attachments, in a fitted mahogany case, 19in (48cm) high overall.
$1,300-2,400

A pocket monocular microscope, the limb signed Cary, London, with accessories in mahogany case, early 19thC, 3¾in (9.5cm) wide, inset with mounting thread.
$500-900

A lacquered and oxydised brass compound binocular microscope, by J. Swift, University St, London, with 4 eye pieces, 4 objectives and a bull's-eye condenser, in original case, 14in (35.5cm) high.
$600-1,200

Medical Instruments

A Smellie's perforator, signed S. Moore & Son & Thompson, London, c1870, 14in (36cm).
$1,000-2,000

A plaster relief anatomical model of the head, coloured and with numbered labels for the organs, veins and muscles, 13in (33cm) high, and a companion model similarly mounted.
$1,000-2,000

A Georgian mahogany domestic medicine chest, the lid rising to reveal compartments with 4 large jars having brass caps, a pewter double measure and funnel, a spatular, a cautery iron and a balance, the rear door enclosing a poison compartment with 8 glass bottles with stoppers, 10in (26cm) wide.
$1,000-2,000

A walnut homoeopathic domestic medicine chest, by Allshorn, 51 Edgware Road, 19thC, the chest 8½in (21cm) wide.
$500-900

A demonstration model head, originally with a glass dome over the model, now lacking, the model consisting of a human cranium with all the vessels, main arteries; nerves being replaced using coloured wax, the eyes made of glass, the teeth natural, the right side of the cranium being hinged in order to allow a view of the blood vessels, the nerves and tissues, the eyes, nose, mouth, etc, Paris, late 19thC, 17in (43cm) high maximum, the base 9in (23cm).
$3,200-6,000

A walnut homoeopathic domestic medicine chest, by Thompson & Capper, with 50 medicine bottles, 2 small powder compartments and a copy of Ruddock: Homoeopathic Vade Mecum Medical & Surgical; the 2 drawers below containing a collection of bottles with original labels, late 19thC.
$600-1,200

A surgeon's travelling instrument case, signed Evans of Old Fish Street, London, with 3 sections of surgeon's instruments, c1855.
$4,500-9,000

A pair of Murphy's craniotomy forceps in steel with ebony grips, signed Wood, c1850, 13in (33cm) long.
$900-1,700

A mahogany and brass mounted domestic medicine chest, applied with a label for William R. Hoare, Successor to Squire, 121 Cornwall Rd, Bayswater, 19thC, the chest 10in (26cm) wide.
$1,700-3,000

A fine set of surgeon's amputation knives and accessories by Evans & Wormall, 31 Stamford St, Blackfriars, London, with 6 Liston knives, 4 trocar and connulae in fitted case, the lid with a brass plaque engraved B.W. Vince, Saffron Walden, England, late 19thC, 17in (43cm) wide.
$1,400-2,600

A monaural stethoscope of ebonised wood, late 19thC. 2⅛in by 6⅜in (5.5 by 16cm).
$400-750

A Staffordshire jar for Leeches, inscribed in gilt over dark pink decoration, 10½in (26cm) high.
$2,600-5,300

An amputation set, including a large Liston's knife and a double-edged Lisfranc's knife, a hook, a saw, a metacarpal saw and Petit's screw tourniquet, each knife stamped Blackwell, of 3 Bedford Court, London, mid-19thC, in a fitted case, 17in (43cm) wide.
$600-1,200

An inhaler, with a pressed copper label with the inscription 'Alformant R.L.P. The Formalin Hygienic Company Limited', c1900, 10in (25cm) high.
$150-300

A brass fountain enema, embossed brass maker's plate and coat-of-arms, Salt & Son, Cutlers to the Queen, Surgical Instrument Manufacturers, Birmingham, mid-19thC, 10in (24.5cm) high.
$300-600

1. An unusual pair of blued steel framed 'D' folding sides clear glass 'railway' spectacles, in a later case.
$200-450

2. A good pair of tortoiseshell 'D' folding sides spectacles with blue and blue-green shades and silver turnpin sides, in a later case, 19thC.
$600-1,200

3. An unusual pair of prismatic reading spectacles, in original case.
$60-120

4. A pair of Chinese brass rimless spectacles, with ornamental double hinged folding sides, pale brown quartz lenses, in a later case.
$400-750

An ear trumpet, signed F.C. Rein & Son Sole Inventor and Patentees 108 Strand, London, the trumpet silver-plated with a turned ivory earpiece, in original leather case with velvet and silk lining, c1860, 4 by 2½in (10 by 6cm).
$1,600-2,800

A cast metal inhaler, together with the original bottle of fluid called Cresolene made by the Vapo-Cresolene Company of 180 Fulton Street, New York, U.S.A., c1900, 7 by 2½in (18 by 7cm).
$180-300

The front of the bottle bears a label 'POISON' and advises those who have taken an accidental dose to take a large glass of whisky or brandy, vinegar or alcohol. If it falls on the skin, apply the same.

Dental Instruments

A set of dental instruments, signed C. Ash & Sons, England, including a selection of probes and scalers with smooth handles, silver ferrules and steel implements, an ebony-handled mirror, a tooth key, 2 pairs of molar forceps, 3 stump elevators and a pocket knife with various scalpels, c1870.
$2,600-5,300

A dental scaling kit, comprising 6 steel instruments with tortoiseshell handles, and a pair of scissors in the form of a stork, early 19thC.
$600-1,100

A selection of demonstration wax teeth in 2 glazed cases, c1900, each measuring 10 by 12in (25 by 30cm).
$1,700-3,000

Miscellaneous

A fine lacquered brass gyroscope, signed Newton & Co Opticians & Globe Makers to the Queen. 3 Fleet St, Temple Bar London, 19thC, 9½in (24cm) wide.
$900-1,700

A brass and steel drawing compendium comprising dividers, tripod dividers, double-pen, dividers scale rules, pens, a protractor, square, proportional dividers and sector signed Baradelle A Paris, in original simulated fishskin cover case, 90% complete, 18thC, 9in (23cm) wide.
$3,200-6,000

An Edwardian period barograph of unusually large size by J. Hicks, 8, 9 & 10 Hatton Garden London, the card drawer containing cards and correspondence, 22in (56cm) wide.
$2,200-4,200

A brass sector, unsigned, 17thC, each arm 12in (30cm) long.
$1,400-2,600

A rare boxwood plane table frame or ruler, by Henry Sutton, signed H. Sutton fecit 1655, 17in (43cm) wide by 13in (33cm) high extended.
$4,500-9,000

An electrostatic generator, signed Abraham, Liverpool, with original black silk screens, slightly torn, c1825, 18in (46cm) high.
$4,000-7,500

A rare lacquered brass voluter, ▷ signed 'The Voluter H. Johnson's Patent 1857' on the triangular section beam graduated 0-6in, mid-19thC, the case 13in (33cm) wide.
$1,800-3,800

Invented by Henry Johnson, 39 Crutched Friars, and manufactured by F Hoffmann, 39 Wilmington Square, Clerkenwell, the voluter was designed for tracing spiral curves; deep-sea pressure gauges; for recording the density of sea-water at various depths and deep-sea thermometers.

An unusual ophthalmoscope by ▷ Edward Messter, Berlin, late 19thC, the case 10in (26cm) wide.
$1,200-2,100

A kaleidoscope demonstration apparatus, late 19thC, 10in (25cm) high.
$900-1,700

A rare money scale, by S Henry, London, for weighing a guinea, half and quarter, the brass beam, pans missing, with spring-loaded locking mounted on the oval base, stamped S. Henry Inventor by Royal Patent, in the original fishskin covered case, with instruction label, the lid arranged to hold the scales in 2 grooves when in use, 18thC, the case 5in (13cm) wide.
$900-1,700

A brass chondrometer, unsigned, with beam engraved 24-80, the weight lbs per Bushel with accessories and instruction label, in fitted mahogany case, 19thC, 11½in (29cm) wide.
$400-750

An acoustic siren, signed Becker, London, the brass wind chest supported on a mahogany circular base, the speed of rotation indicated on 2 dials, one marked 0-100 the other 0-5000, c1910, 8½in (21cm) high.
$800-1,500

A similar instrument is illustrated in Philip Harris & Co, Catalogue of Scientific Instruments, 1905, p383. This type of siren is fully described, with its history, in G. L'E. Turner, 19th Century Scientific Instruments, pp136-7.

A fine money scale, by John William Herberts, the steel beam with brass pans, pillar and weights, 30dram weight missing, contained in the original fitted mahogany case, with original trade label dated 1772 and inscribed JOHN WILLM. HERBERTZ, 18thC, 7½in (19cm) wide.
$1,200-2,100

Johann Wilhelm Herbertz (fl 1763-1779) moved from Solingen and took up residence c1763 in Stidwell (Steedwell) St London, later renamed New Compton St. Soho.

A gilt-brass letter balance modelled in the form of a bacchante holding a vine supporting the beam, engraved ¼-16, the counter poise in the manner of 2 baskets of grapes, late 19thC, 6½in (16cm) wide.
$2,200-4,200

Cameras

A good Contax III camera outfit, camera No. D.60875 with 3 Sonnar lenses comprising: 5cm.f 1.5 – No. 1909655, 8.5cm. f 2 – No.1493169 and 13.5cm. f 4 – No.2253846, the latter two with hoods and caps, Zeiss Universal viewfinder, Universal sports finder, Contameter set, various filters, Zeiss quick-tilt head, five film cassettes, Zeiss film trimming template, e.r.c., maker's carton. $600-1,200

A rare Wide-Angle Rolleiflex twin-lens reflex camera, No.W.2490454 with Distagon 55mm. f 4 lens in Synchro-Compur shutter, standard and pentaprism finders, lens-hood, Rolleinar 2 attachment, spare focusing screen, three filters, pistol grip and carrying case. $2,200-4,200

A rare Thornton-Pickard F 2 Ruby Speed camera, no.123705, Ermanox-copy with Taylor-Hobson Cooke Anastigmat 3in. Series 0 f 2 lens in helical focusing mount, focal-plane shutter, folding sports finder, three d.d.s. and box of plates, in maker's leather carrying case. $4,500-9,000

A Houghton's 45mm by 107mm Royal Mail Stereolette camera, with lenses in spring-cocked guillotine shutter, prismatic viewfinder and focusing screen. $1,200-2,100

A 6cm by 13cm Rolleidoscop reflex stereoscope roll-film camera, by Frank Heidecke, No. 3852, with Tessar 7.5cm. f 4.5 lenses in shaped leather case. $1,200-2,100

A Brun's Detective Camera, with luxury varnished wooden body, and Anastigmat lens. $2,200-4,200

A fine 35mm. mahogany hand crank cine camera, by Zollinger of Turin, Tipo A No.34, with F. Koristka Zeiss Tessar f 3.5 50mm lens, in fitted case. $1,200-2,100

A London Stereoscopic Co.'s stereoscopic changing-box camera, with 16 plate holders and dealer's plaque on front panel. $1,000-2,000

A quarter-plate Redding's Luzo box-form roll-film camera in ever-ready case. $1,200-2,100

A 4.5cm by 6cm Ernemann Miniature-Ernoflex folding Reflex camera, with Ernon 7.5cm f 3.5 lens in helical mount, film pack adapter, 11 s.m.s., 3 cut film sheaths and French instructions, in maker's leather carrying case.
$1,000-2,000

A quarter-plate box-form mahogany survey camera by J.H. Dallmeyer, London.
$900-1,700

A fine Rolleiflex 2.8 f gold-plated Aurum twin-lens reflex camera, by Rollei Fototechnic GmbH, with Xenotar 8mm f2.8 taking-lens and neck strap.
$1,800-3,800

A four-lens multiple-exposure camera, probably by J. Lancaster & Sons, taking four 2 by 1½in exposures on one quarter plate, lacking ground glass and plate holders.
$2,600-5,300

A rare 1930s The Ensign 'Sanderson' 'Regular Model' quarter-plate camera, with Aldis-Butcher f6.3 5.25in.lens in Compur shutter, and Dallmeyer f6.5 3¼in wide angle lens, with matching lens cap, with three d.d.s. and film pack back, in Ensign case.
$400-900

An original-model 9cm by 12cm Goerz Anschutz focal-plane box-form camera, with Goerz, Extra-Rapid Lynkeioskop Serie C. No.1, brass-bound lens and folding sports finder.
$2,000-4,500

A rare Adams & Co. Tropical Vaido mahogany and brass half-plate camera, lacking viewfinder.
$1,000-2,000

l A 15cm by 10cm Ica Tropical folding plate camera in metal reinforced teak casing, with Tessar 13.5cm f 4.5 lens in dial-set Compur shutter, folding sports finder, film pack adapter and three d.d.s.
$300-600

c A quarter-plate Gandolfi hand-and-stand camera in mahogany casing with screw-reinforced joints, with Aldis Anastigmat 5¾in f 6 lens in Universal diaphragm shutter and one d.d.s.
$600-1,200

r A 9cm by 12cm Tropical Goerz Tenax folding plate camera in brass-reinforced teak casing with Xenar 13.5cm f 4.5 lens in Compur shutter, red leather bellows and film pack adapter, in leather case.
$400-750

A 3¼ by 6½ Lancaster's stereoscopic camera, with matched pair of Dallmeyer landscape lenses nos. 18003 and 18004, stereo roller-blind shutter and one d.d.s.
$600-1,200

A rare 2¼ by 2¼ Redding's Luzo roll-film camera in brass-reinforced mahogany casing, Patent No.17328, camera no.878, with lens behind spring-activated sector shutter.
$1,000-2,000

A rare Dickinson's Patent 'The Radial' quarter-plate magazine detective camera, by Marion & Co.
$600-1,200

A prototype 2 by 2 miniature changing-magazine camera, apparently by Alexander Rogers, Optician, Croydon.
$150-300

A good Stirn's Waistcoat detective camera, No.5065, in nickel-plated brass casing taking six circular exposures on circular plate with button-hole lens.
$1,000-2,000

Viewers

A Murray & Heath, 43 Piccadilly, London, Registered, stereo viewer, with sliding removable eyepiece lens and folding light diffuser, 1850s.
$200-450

A Cibis hand-cranked 35mm cinematograph projector, with film reels mounted side by side beneath, 35in (89cm) high.
$1,700-3,000

An unusual rosewood pedestal stereoscope with Knight's Cosmorama-style mirror arrangement, on telescopic brass column with lead-weighted base.
$1,800-3,800

A rare London Stereoscopic Company's Patent leather-covered Brewster pattern stereoscope, in fitted rosewood box, opening to sectioned compartment containing 17 stereo cards, 13in (33cm) wide.
$800-1,500

A Claudet-type stereo viewer, the brass eyepieces with assymetric lenses, mid-1850s.
$800-1,500

A Zoetrope with revolving metal cylinder, mounted on a turned mahogany base, together with a collection of comic strips, late 19thC, 14in (35.5cm) high.
$400-750

Art Nouveau – Carpets

A wool hanging designed and embroidered by Mary Newill, The Garden of Adonis, 77 by 48in (192 by 121cm).
$2,600-5,300

The embroidery is one of a set of three commissioned by the architect E. Butler for his own house, the other two now being in the Worcester Museum. This panel was exhibited at the Paris International Exhibition of 1900 and is illustrated in colour in the Studio Special Number 1901.

A large Art Nouveau hand-tufted woollen carpet, designed in the manner of C.F.A. Voysey, woven in rich reds, greens, yellow and blue, with faults, 208 by 146in (519 by 366cm).
$1,400-2,600

Ceramics

A Bretby pottery 'Egyptianesque' jardinière, in the manner of Christopher Dresser, covered overall with an amber glaze shading to olive, impressed marks, 9in (22.5cm).
$300-600

A Carlton ware lustre china coffee service of 15 pieces, with gilded and enamelled sunflower and hollyhock decoration, comprising: coffee pot and cover, cream jug and sugar basin, 6 cups and saucers, coffee pot 8in (20cm) high.
$600-1,200

A Copeland comport, with green and gilt decoration, printed Copeland, England, late 19thC, 17in (43cm).
$500-900

An unusual Elton pottery ewer, with incised linear decoration beneath a bright blue and green glaze revealing patches of reddish brown, signed 'Elton', 13½in (34cm).
$600-1,100

A Foley 'Intarsio' earthenware clock case, with painted underglaze polychrome decoration, printed marks The Foley 'Intarsio' England, Rd.No.337999, c1900, 13in (33cm).
$1,000-2,000

A Della Robbia vase, decorated in coloured slip over a terracotta ground, incised DR mark with sailing ship and painted mark 'ENID', 11in (27cm).
$400-750

A Della Robbia pottery vase, with incised ship mark and marks of Charles Collis, potter and sgraffito artist and Gertrude Russell, painter, some damage, c1903-06, 11in (28cm).
$200-450

A late Foley Shelley 'Intarsio' ware vase, probably designed by Walter Slater, decorated in green, blue and pink, reserved against a brown ground, printed factory marks No.'3624, 379', 9in (22.5cm).
$300-600

A pair of Foley 'Intarsio' circular wall plates, designed by Frederick Rhead, printed factory marks and Rd Nos. 330399 for 1898-99, 12in (31cm) diam.
$1,400-2,600

A Gallé yellow ground cat, c1900, 13½in (33.5cm).
$1,700-3,000

A terracotta bust of a lady, signed 'Lefevre', c1900.
$500-900

A Gallé cat in tartan garb, c1900, 13in (33cm).
$1,800-3,800

In the Ceramics section if there is only one measurement it usually refers to the height of the piece.

A large Ault pottery vase, designed by Christopher Dresser, the magnolia-coloured body painted in colours possibly by Clarica Ault, impressed facsimile Dresser signature and number '247', 27½in (69.5cm).
$1,200-2,100

A Linthorpe pottery ewer, designed by Christopher Dresser, with linear decoration beneath a streaked honey, green, blue and grey glaze, factory marks, facsimile signature and 'HT' for Henry Tooth, 9in (22cm).
$300-600

A Christopher Dresser Linthorpe pottery pot pourri vase and cover, silver mounted with blue glazed underside, the pierced silver cover with fluted dome and ball finial, impressed marks and no.277, c1900, 9½in (23.5cm) diam.
$800-1,500

A Linthorpe pottery tobacco jar, the brown glazed body having electro-plated rim and swing handle, impressed mark, Henry Tooth monogram and shape no.913, late 19thC, 5in (12.5cm).
$100-250

A Christopher Dresser Linthorpe vase, decorated in plum and green crackle effect glaze, impressed marks and shape no.875, late 19thC, 12in (30cm).
$200-450

A globular green glazed bowl, designed by Christopher Dresser, impressed with facsimile signature 'Ch. Dresser', 5½in (14.5cm).
$1,200-2,100

A pair of William de Morgan tiles with Isnik style decoration of stylised flowerheads, green, yellow and purple on a pale green ground, framed together, 8in (20.5cm) square.
$600-1,200

A Linthorpe pottery pouring vessel, designed by Christopher Dresser, the brown body streaked milky-green with yellow speckling, 'Linthorpe Chr. Dresser' mark, 'HT' for Henry Tooth and '267', 5½in (14cm).
$900-1,700

A Pilkington 'Royal Lancastrian' oviform vase, by William Salter Mycock, painted in golden and ruby lustres, against a shaded blue ground, impressed rosette mark, incised 'E.T.R.' for E T Radford the potter, artist's monogram and date code for 1933, 8½in (21cm).
$600-1,100

A Mintons 'Secessionist' ware garden stool, decorated in raised outline against a printed ground of flowers and foliage, glazed in turquoise, green, brown and yellow against a cream ground, indistinct impressed marks, date code for 1908, 21in (54cm).
$800-1,500

A Mintons 'Secessionist' jardinière and stand, probably designed by John Wadsworth and Leon Solon, in pinks, reds and yellows against a ground of block-printed foliage in greens, the cylindrical stand similarly decorated, printed marks and date code for 1902 on stand, 42in (105cm) total height.
$1,400-2,600

A Maw & Co. oviform vase, designed by Walter Crane, painted in olive green, signed with designer's device on base, 13in (32.5cm).
$800-1,500

A Mintons 'Secessionist' ware jardinière, decorated in green slip-trailing with cream-amber stylised buds on blue stems, reserved against a purple ground, stamped marks and printed mark 'NO.1', 10½in (26.5cm).
$6,000-12,000

A Minton's art studio pottery twin-handled moon flask, the design in the manner of Christopher Dresser, decorated in 2 tones of grey, white and gilt, with leaves against a chocolate-brown ground, circular 'Kensington Gore' marks, impressed 'Minton' with date code for 1872, printed marks 'S.122' and 'K92', 13in (33cm).
$400-750

Four William de Morgan tiles, ruby lustre on a cream ground, c1890, 6in (15cm) square.
$1,800-3,800

A William de Morgan ruby lustre charger, c1900, 14in (36cm).
$1,200-2,100

A fine monumental earthenware vase, by Grueby, executed by Ruth Erikson, the elongated ovoid form body moulded with long petals in a textured cucumber matte glaze, inscribed 'RE', 30½in (76cm) high.
$23,000-25,000

A pair of earthenware bookends, by Pewabic, moulded with fanciful monkey-like creatures bordered by an iridescent cobalt and crimson glaze, both impressed PEWABIC DETROIT, 5in (12cm) high.
$350-400

An earthenware vase, by Newcomb College, executed by Joseph Meyer and decorated by Sadie Irvine, the ovoid body modelled with blue and green trees, with smaller blue trees in the background, on a green, violet and pink matte ground, impressed with firm's, potter's and artist's marks and '240 JV 57', 1918, 3in (8cm) high.
$650-750

A fine earthenware vase, by Frederick E. Walrath, decorated with small red flowers and long sinuous olive stems and broad leaves on a mottled green matte ground, inscribed 'Walrath Pottery', 6in (15cm).
$3,200-3,500

An earthenware vase, by Marblehead, executed by Arthur E. Baggs, the cylindrical matte green body decorated with incised dark olive trees, inscribed with a ship and 'MP AB T', 4½in (11cm) high.
$1,100-1,300

A silver-overlaid earthenware vase by Rookwood and Gorham, decorated by Matthew A. Daly, the body with twin handles, with yellow roses and green and brown leaves in a 'Standard' glaze, and overlaid with chased silver in an ornate design, impressed with firm's mark and '292C G' and inscribed 'MAD/L', the silver impressed 'Gorham Mfg. Co. R296', 1889, 10in (26cm) high.
$3,500-4,000

An earthenware vase, by Marblehead, executed by Hanna Tutt, the oviform body decorated with black outlined stylised blue-tan trees on a matte dark blue ground, impressed with a ship and MP, painted HT, 7in (17cm) high.
$800-1,000

An earthenware vase, by Rookwood, decorated by Fred Rothenbusch, the body with bare light blue, navy and violet trees in a 'Vellum' glaze, impressed with firm's mark, and '892C V' and inscribed with artist's monogram, 1911, 9in (23cm) high.
$650-700

A large earthenware vase, by Van Briggle, moulded with flowering yucca plants in a sky blue and green speckled powder blue matte glaze, inscribed with firm's mark and Van Briggle 1905 V, 17in (43cm) high.
$1,000-1,200

A set of 6 earthenware tiles, by Grueby, forming an off-white polar bear in relief on a crazed blue-green ground, unsigned, with some chips at edges, 24 by 21in (60 by 52.5cm).
$1,000-1,300

A set of 10 William de Morgan 'Poppy' tiles, painted with aubergine coloured stylised flowers on green leafy stems, reserved against an off-white ground, impressed 'Merton Abbey' mark, 5in (13cm) square.
$1,000-2,000

A German rectangular tile, in bright colours, 6½ by 11in (16 by 27.5cm).
$800-1,500

A Royal Dux conch shell group with 3 water nymphs in relief, on natural ground, 17½in (44cm).
$1,000-2,000

A Van Briggle baluster vase, 'Despondency', the vessel all beneath a matt turquoise glaze, signed with double 'A' mark and 'Van Briggle Colo Spgs Co.', 16in (40.5cm).
$500-900

A Sevres stoneware jug, with Gustave Keller gilt metal mounts and cover.
$4,000-7,500

A French inlaid mantel clock, with lever escapement, c1910, 12in (30cm).
$180-300

Clocks

A Liberty pewter and enamel table clock designed by Archibald Knox, the mottled turquoise enamel face with red enamel decoration and gilt numerals, stamped 'English Pewter made by Liberty and Co. 0608', c1900, 5½in (14.5cm) high.
$2,600-5,300

Cf. Adrian J. Tilbrook, The Designs of Archibald Knox for Liberty & Co. fig. no. 93.

A 'Jaeger Le Coultre' timepiece, fashioned in gilded metal, marked 'Jaeger Le Coultre', with original fitted box, 8½in (21.5cm) high.
$600-1,100

A Dutch Art Nouveau table pendulum clock, carved walnut with circular copper face and hands, 19in (47.5cm) high.
$6,000-12,000

An Arnhem clock set, with hand-painted Art Nouveau stylised plant-form decoration in blues, greens and browns on a cream ground, with painted Arnhem mark with cockerel, c1900, clock 15½in (38.5cm) high.
$2,000-4,500

A Liberty & Co. pewter, copper and turquoise enamel clock, the copper face with embossed Roman numerals set with a round turquoise enamel plaque, the pewter partly hammered, marked 'Tudric 0150', c1900, 13in (33cm) high.
$1,200-2,100

A Liberty pewter and enamel clock, designed by Archibald Knox, the rectangular case incorporating carriage clock movement, the turquoise enamel face with red enamel design, stamped '0608 RD 426015', 5½in (14cm) high.
$1,800-3,800

A Gallé mahogany and marquetry cabinet, signature 'Gallé Nancy' and cross of Lorraine, c1910, 30in (76cm).
$2,000-4,500

Furniture

An Arts and Crafts oak settle, possibly American, by Stickley, 51in (128cm).
$800-1,500

An Art Nouveau mahogany breakfront cabinet, probably made by Liberty's, c1898, 55in (139cm) wide.
$1,200-2,100

See item seven in The Liberty Style, published by Academy Editions, London.

A set of 6 Finmar stained birch chairs, designed by Alvar Aalto, with Finmar Ltd. label.
$900-1,700

In the Furniture section if there is only one measurement it usually refers to the width of the piece.

A small Art Nouveau oak cupboard, 12in (30cm).
$150-300

An oak sideboard, by Gustav Stickley, with red decal mark and paper label on reverse, model no.817, c1902, 74½in (187cm).
$2,000-4,500

A Scottish Arts and Crafts oak cabinet, 45½in (114cm).
$3,200-6,000

An English Arts and Crafts brass-mounted mahogany, sycamore and walnut marquetry partners' desk, 51½in (129.5cm).
$4,500-9,000

A mahogany, ebonised and marquetry jardinière in the style of Charles Bevan, with 9 marquetry panels inlaid in various fruitwoods, with zinc liner and later burr-walnut chamfered cover, 29in (73.5cm).
$600-1,200

A Glasgow School mahogany and inlaid corner cupboard, 68in (170cm) high.
$1,400-2,600

A Sidney Barnsley oak bureau with a fitted interior, 34½in (86cm).
$4,500-9,000

An Emile Gallé oak and marquetry table à deux plateaux, signed in the marquetry 'Gallé', 21in (53cm).
$1,400-2,600

A Wylie and Lochhead mahogany display cabinet designed by E. A. Taylor, inlaid with brass, pewter, mother-of-pearl in a stylised floral motif, mounted with pewter lockplates and drop loop handles on square-sectioned railed trestle ends joined by platform shelf and turned stretchers, 35in (88cm).
$4,000-6,800

An Emile Gallé walnut and marquetry music stand, 23in (57.5cm).
$2,200-4,200

A mirror attributed to Bugatti, decorated with beaten copperwork and copper and pewter inlay, c1900, 26 by 24in (66 by 61cm).
$3,200-6,000

A Heal's oak linen press designed by Ambrose Heal, c1910, 37in (93cm).
$1,400-2,600

Cf Simple Bedroom Furniture in Oak Chestnut and Colonial Mahogany, designed by Ambrose Heal, Junior, Heal and Son catalogue, no. 432.

An Art Nouveau mahogany plant stand, 46in (115cm) high.
$200-450

An oak and leather 3-panel screen, by Gustav Stickley, each panel with inset leather panels above on front and back, unsigned, model No.91, c1909, 68½in (171cm) high.
$4,000-5,000

An oak single door bookcase, by Gustav Stickley, the door with 16 panes, triangular hardware, with red decal and brown 'Craftsman' paper label bearing the model No.715, c1909, 35in (87.5cm) wide.
$2,500-3,000

Price

Prices vary from auction to auction – from dealer to dealer. The price paid in a dealer's shop will depend on:
1) what he paid for the item
2) what he thinks he can get for it
3) the extent of his knowledge
4) awareness of market trends
It is a mistake to think that you will automatically pay more in a specialist dealer's shop. He is more likely to know the 'right' price for a piece. A general dealer may undercharge but he could also overcharge.

An oak library table, by Gustav Stickley, of trestle form with through tenons and keys, with red decal Stickley outlined, model No.437, c1904, 48in (122cm) wide.
$1,400-1,600

An oak settle, by Gustav Stickley, the slatted sides joined by a horizontal member, with original cushion, model No.225, c1910, 78in (197cm) wide.
$5,000-6,000

An oak chalet desk, by Gustav Stickley, with panelled back and dark finish, unsigned, c1901, 46in (115cm) high.
$1,100-1,500

An oak slatted flat arm Morris chair, by Gustav Stickley, with light brown finish and original blue leather laced cushions and rope seat, with red decal, Stickley outlined, model No.2342, c1903.
$3,000-4,000

A rare oak tabouret, by Charles Rohlfs, the 8 sides reticulated and each panel further decorated with an outline of pegs, 2 panels hinged to form a door to the storage area below with finely carved key to hold the latch, with maker's logo, c1901, 32in (80cm) diam.
$11,000-14,000

An oak telephone table, by Gustav Stickley, of narrow vertical form with an undershelf, unsigned, model No.605, c1910, 14in (35cm) square.
$600-700

An oak lunch table, by Gustav
Stickley, with medial stretcher
terminating in through tenons and
keys, a red decal, the logo outlined,
stencilled with model No. SB 424,
c1901, 40in (100cm) wide.
$1,200-1,500

An oak magazine stand, by Gustav
Stickley, with 4 shelves above a
curved apron, branded signature
and paper label, model No.79,
c1912, 14in (35cm) wide.
$1,500-2,000

A maple reclining chair, designed
by Frank Lloyd Wright for the
Arthur Heurtley House, Oak Park,
Illinois, the back with inset plank,
the arms tapering outward to a
triangular form and supported by
uprights set on an angle with wood
band detailing, c1902, 37in (93cm)
high.
$20,000-22,000

A set of 6 oak side chairs, by Gustav
Stickley, the backs with 4
horizontals, the top with a curve,
with red decal, the logo outlined
and Cobb-Eastman paper labels,
model No.1297, c1903, 37in
(92.5cm) high.
$3,000-3,500

A willow armchair, by Gustav
Stickley, with square cut-outs
below each arm, model No.60,
c1910, 39½in (100cm) high.
$800-1,000

An oak footstool, by Gustav
Stickley, the 4 legs joined by crossed
stretchers, with original fabricoid
seat and tacks, model No.725,
c1902, 17in (42.5cm) high.
$1,700-2,000

MAKE THE MOST
OF MILLER'S
*Price ranges in this book
reflect what one should
expect to pay for a similar
example. When selling one
can obviously expect a
figure below. This will
fluctuate according to a
dealer's stock, saleability
at a particular time, etc. It
is always advisable to
approach a reputable
specialist dealer or an
auction house which has
specialist sales.*

A rare oak armchair, by Gustav Stickley, of massive broad form, the top of the two horizontal rails with an inverted 'V' and a reverse taper to legs, the seat of reddish brown leather, unsigned, model No.2612, c1901, 24in (60cm) wide.
$1,000-1,200

A rare and fine inlaid Honduras mahogany armchair, designed by Greene & Greene, executed in the workshop of Peter Hall for the dining room of the Robert R Blacker House, Pasadena, California, the crest rail featuring ebony splines and pegs above a vertical splat carved in an undulating motif and repeated with inlay of silver vine and stylised florettes of abalone, copper, pewter and exotic woods, a drop-in trapezoidal seat, the arms stepped to form handrest with ebony pegging, the side stretchers lightly carved with cloud lift design and joined by a medial stretcher, the chair frame stamped 'I', the seat stamped 'I', 1907-09, 42in (105cm) high.
$42,000-45,000

An oak and leather side chair, by Gustav Stickley, with original leather upholstery and tacks, red decal with logo outlined, model No.1295, c1902, 19in (47.5cm) wide.
$300-400

A rare oak side chair, by Gustav Stickley, the low back with 3 vertical slats below a curving crest rail and flanked by 2 spandrels, with original fabricoid covered seat, a red decal with Stickley outlined, model 2610, c1901, 33in (82.5cm) high.
$300-400

An oak 'banded' chest, by Gustav Stickley, the 6 drawers with conforming backplates for the ring pulls, branded signature, model No.906, c1912, 41in (102.5cm) wide.
$5,000-6,000

An oak plantstand, by Gustav Stickley, with splayed legs under a broad top, unsigned, model No.660, c1910, 18in (45cm) square.
$600-800

An oak bent arm spindle Morris chair, possibly Gustav Stickley, with canvas sling seat and webbing, unsigned, c1905.
$3,000-3,500

An oak tabouret, by Gustav Stickley, branded signature, model No.602, c1912, 18in (45cm) high.
$600-700

Glass

A small Daum Nancy vase, signed in gilt 'Daum/Nancy' with croix de Lorraine, 4in (10cm).
$600-1,100

A D'Argental cameo glass vase, with deep turquoise sides overlaid in navy, signed in cameo 'd'Argental', 6in (15cm) high.
$800-1,500

A Gallé enamelled and green glass jug, enamelled in white, blue and red, inscribed 'E. Gallé Nancy', 8½in (21cm) high.
$400-900

A Daum cameo glass vase, the matt streaked yellow ground overlaid in shades of purple, cameo signature 'Daum Nancy France' and with retailer's paper label, 19in (48cm).
$1,700-3,000

A small Daum cameo glass vase, with pale blue acid-etched body, signed 'Daum Nancy', 6½in (17cm) high.
$800-1,500

A green cameo glass vase, etched by De Vez.
$800-1,500

A good enamelled Gallé enamelled jardinière of green glass, marked on base with acid-etched mushroom and signed 'Emile Gallé delt, Serie C, ft' and 'depose' in fine red script, 13in (33cm) across.
$2,600-5,300

A Gallé oviform vase, overlaid and etched in amber, red and green with daffodils among grasses, cameo signature 'Gallé', bearing label, 13in (33cm) high.
$2,000-4,500

A Gallé cameo glass vase, tinged with yellow and pink overlaid in deep amber and decorated with acid-etched and carved decoration of anemones, 'Gallé' cameo signature, c1905, 10in (26cm) high.
$2,000-4,500

A Gallé cameo glass vase, the frosted white and lemon sides overlaid with deep purple, signed in cameo 'Gallé', 7½in (18.5cm).
$800-1,500

A fine quality cameo glass vase, by Gallé, with rich brown ochre overlaid on an amber ground with a design of tiger lilies, signed 'Gallé', 8in (20cm) high.
$2,600-5,300

A Gallé cameo footed glass vase, the frosted white and light green sides overlaid with deep purple, signed in cameo 'Gallé', 4in (9.5cm).
$800-1,500

A Gallé cameo glass vase, overlaid in deep mauve with sprays of laburnum, cameo mark 'Gallé', c1900, 12½in (31.5cm).
$1,400-2,600

A large Gallé enamelled glass vase, the clear sepia glass enamelled in tones of mustard, pink, turquoise and grey, details highlighted in gilt, etched 'Gallé', c1885, 11½in (29cm).
$1,800-3,800

A small Gallé cameo glass vase, the frosted white sides overlaid in lime green, signed in cameo 'Gallé', 3½in (8.5cm).
$500-900

A Legras glass garniture, the 2 oviform vases with tall extended necks, all of white glass cased in a rich red glass and decorated with gilded stylised bell-shaped flowers, gilt mark 'L & Cie St. Denis – Paris', the tall vase 18in (45.5cm) high.
$800-1,500

A Gallé cameo glass vase, with cameo signature 'Gallé', 14in (34.5cm).
$1,800-3,800

A Gallé glass vase, with overlaid ruby decoration of flowers, signed, 5in (12.5cm).
$800-1,500

A Gallé green ground overlay vase, 12in (30cm) high, with brown floral decoration, and line of verse:
    Béni soit le coin sombre
      où s'isolent nos coeurs
from French symbolist poetess, Marceline Desbordes-Valmore.
$4,500-9,000

A Gallé cameo glass vase, with amber-tinted body overlaid with 2 tones of ruby glass, signed in cameo 'Gallé', 5½in (14cm) high.
$900-1,700

A glass dish attributed to Heckart Petersdorfer Glashütte, with enamel painted decoration of a purple clematis bloom, 9½in (23.5cm).
$400-750

A Loetz vase in iridescent pink and gold glass, c1900, 6in (15.5cm) high.
$1,700-3,000

A Müller Frères cameo glass vase, with mottled orange, ochre and deep violet sides overlaid with turquoise, signed in relief 'Müller Fres/Luneville', 5in (12.5cm).
$2,000-4,500

A set of 4 stained glass panels, designed in the Scottish taste, clearly showing the influence of E.A. Taylor and Oscar Paterson, each 46½ by 18in (116 by 46cm) approx.
$1,400-2,600

These were at one time installed in a house belonging to Barratts, the shoe manufacturers in Northampton, the town having obvious Scottish connections with the work of designer Charles Rennie Mackintosh for Bassett-Lowke at Derngate.

A Meyr's Neffe wine goblet, the design attributed to Otto Prutscher, with green over clear glass, c1900, 8in (20cm).
$1,300-2,400

A small Loetz iridescent glass vase, the peacock-blue green lustrous surface applied with a silver spray of flowers with chased detailing and silver collar, 4½in (11.5cm).
$300-600

A Wiener Werkstätte amethyst glass vase and cover, designed by Josef Hoffmann, etched 'WW' monogram, 7in (17cm) high.
$1,600-2,800

A Muller Croismaire cameo glass vase, the shaded orange and amber ground overlaid with darker orange, cameo mark on the base with butterfly and 'H. Muller Croismaire près Nancy', c1900, 14in (35cm).
$1,400-2,600

A large Müller Frères early glass vase with pale green sides, etched in shades of green and ochre, signed in enamel 'Müller, Croismare', 14in (35cm).
$800-1,500

A Tiffany Favrile glass bottle, with gilt metal stopper on a chain, the glass iridescent gold, the metal ring with chain attached stamped 'Tiffany & Co.', the glass engraved 'W8565', c1900, 9½in (24cm).
$6,000-12,000

Miller's is a price Guide not a price List

The price ranges given reflect the average price a purchaser should pay for similar items. Condition, rarity of design or pattern, size, colour, pedigree, restoration and many other factors must be taken into account when assessing values.

A Tiffany Favrile iridescent glass dessert set, comprising a large bowl, 11 smaller similar bowls and 10 saucer dishes, en suite, all exhibiting a golden iridescence with shades of blue, red and mauve, signed 'L.C.T.Favrile' or 'L.C.T.', large bowl 8½in (21cm) diam.
$3,200-6,000

Jewellery

An unusual Argentinian bracelet, stamped 'Axel Giorno'? – 'Buenos Aires', 8in (20cm) long.
$150-300

An Art Nouveau plique-à-jour brooch, stamped 'Deposé' and '900', 1½in (3cm) wide.
$800-1,500

A Boucheron powder compact and 2 lipstick holders, the compact marked 'Boucheron, London, NO.875012. Made in France' and the lipstick holders marked, one – 'Boucheron Paris' and the other – 'Boucheron, London 875012', compact 3 by 2¼in (7.6 by 5.7cm).
$400-900

An Unger Brothers Art Nouveau brooch, stamped with maker's monogram, 'Sterling' and '925 fine', 2¼in (5.5cm) across.
$400-750

An Omar Ramsden silver and enamel circular brooch, signed 'Omar Ramsden Me fecit' London silvermarks, 2¼in (5.5cm) diam.
$800-1,500

An unusual Arts and Crafts pendant brooch, 2½in (7cm) long.
$600-1,100

An Art Nouveau enamelled pendant, the sliding front revealing a mirror, stamped '900', 'Deposé' and dragonfly maker's mark, probably Austrian, 1½in (3.5cm).
$200-450

An Art Nouveau necklace, 21½in (54cm) long.
$200-450

An Arts and Crafts enamelled pendant, painted in naturalistic enamelled colours, signed on reverse 'Pegram', 2¼in (5.7cm) across.
$300-600

A Liberty & Co. 'ship' pendant, designed by Bernard Cuzner, the hull set with a pale blue tourmaline cabochon, unmarked, 2in (4.5cm).
$400-750

A Liberty & Co. enamelled silver pendant, designed by Jessie M. King, marks for W.H. Haseler and 'Silver', 2in (4.5cm).
$300-600

A German Art Nouveau pendant of red and green paste, stamped '900' and wolf's head and 'W' maker's mark, 2¼in (5.5cm).
$200-450

A Murrle Bennett & Co. gold and mother-of-pearl pendant, designed in the manner of Knox, stamped 'MB&Co.' monogram and '15ct', 2¼in (5.5cm).
$300-600

A Murrle Bennett gold Art Nouveau brooch, enclosing a speckled turquoise-coloured cabochon, marked 'MB&Co' and '15ct', 1¼in (3cm) with fitted box.
$300-600

A German Art Nouveau pendant necklace, stamped 'sterling silber', 2¼in (5.5cm).
$150-300 ▷

A Lalique Art Nouveau medallion, signed 'R. Lalique' on both sides, partially converted for use as a buckle, 2in (4.75cm).
$800-1,500

An Art Nouveau diamond-set pendant on chain spaced with pearls, 2in (5cm).
$800-1,500

An Art Nouveau bronze oil lamp base with jewelled brass shade and glass funnel, cast after a model by G. Leleu, converted for electricity, signed in the bronze 'G.Leleu', c1900, 23in (57cm) without funnel.
$1,300-2,400

Lamps

A W.A.S. Benson chandelier.
$4,000-7,500

An unusual figural brass lamp, fitted with lamp fitments, 21½in (54.5cm).
$600-1,200

A Tiffany Studios Favrile glass and bronze ten-light lily lamp, some damage, 19½in (48.5cm) high.
$10,000-18,000

Miller's Antiques Price Guide builds up year by year to form the most comprehensive photo-reference system available. The first six volumes contain over 50,000 completely different photographs.

A Gallé table lamp in lemon glass, double overlaid with two-tone russet cameo, c1898, 25in (62.5cm) high.
$18,000-26,000 ▷

An unusual Austrian bronze hanging lampshade, with removable frosted glass oval centre as shade, 26in (65cm) wide.
$600-1,200

401

An earthenware and leaded glass table lamp, base by Grueby, shade possibly by Bigelow and Kennard, the shade with yellow-centred pink apple blossoms amongst green leaves on a white-streaked green ground, unsigned, with partial Grueby paper label, the base executed by Ruth Erikson, enclosing an electrified fuel canister, ovoid and modelled with broad petals in a matte cucumber glaze, impressed Grueby Pottery Boston U.S.A. and inscribed RE, base with 2 paper labels and canister with one, 18in (45cm) high.
$6,000-6,500

A rare and important leaded glass table lamp, designed by Frank Lloyd Wright, for an unknown commission, the pyramidal shade cantilevered on an adjustable arm on an upright bronze stantion rising from square stepped base, the shade with colonial caming of iridescent, opaque, semi-opaque and clear glass, c1904, 17in (42.5cm) high.
$50,000-53,000

A copper and mica table lamp by Roycroft, the copper shade, with 3 inset rectangular sections, on a hammered copper base with tapered cylindrical column and circular foot, impressed with firm's mark, 15½in (38cm) high.
$1,100-1,500

A copper and mica table lamp, by Dirk Van Erp, the shade, with 3 mica sections set in a riveted hammered copper frame, supported by 3 arms riveted to a hammered copper base with a central riveted band, impressed with a windmill and 'Dirk Van Erp San Francisco', 23in (57.5cm) high.
$7,500-8,000

A copper and mica table lamp, by Dirk Van Erp, the shade of 4 panels encasing a copper floral design and separated by riveted hammered copper columns, raised on an ovoid hammered copper base, impressed with a windmill and 'San Francisco Dirk Van Erp', c1915, 11in (27.5cm) high, in a broken box.
$3,000-3,500

A glass and bronze table lamp, by Handel, the shade of opalescent glass painted with orange flowers and berries amongst green-speckled white leaves on a blue-green, olive and mauve ground, painted 'Handel 6628' and impressed 'Handel Pat'd No.979664,' the ribbed bronze base, raised on rectangular feet, impressed Handel, 23½in (58cm) high.
$2,100-2,500

Price

Prices vary from auction to auction – from dealer to dealer. The price paid in a dealer's shop will depend on:
1) *what he paid for the item*
2) *what he thinks he can get for it*
3) *the extent of his knowledge*
4) *awareness of market trends*
It is a mistake to think that you will automatically pay more in a specialist dealer's shop. He is more likely to know the 'right' price for a piece. A general dealer may undercharge but he could also overcharge.

A Tiffany shade in milk glass on a contemporary base, signed 'L.C.Tiffany', 17in (43cm) high.
$1,400-2,600

Martin Bros

A Martin Brothers stoneware hanging bowl, painted in white, brown and green with the frieze reserved against a brown ground, the centre incised and heightened in brown and cream and reserved against a buff ground, incised 'R.W.Martin & Brothers, London & Southall', 7.1890, 11½in (28.5cm).
$1,200-2,100

A Martin Brothers stoneware model of a grotesque bird, its plumage glazed in green, blue, beige and brown, signed 'R.W.Martin & Bros. London and Southall', head dated 15.1.1907, base 19.1.1907, 9in (22.5cm).
$4,500-9,000

A Martinware gourd pottery jug, the ribs separating vertical bands of dark olive filled incised crescents on a cream ground, incised 'Martin Bros. London, Southall', c1900, 10in (25cm) high.
$800-1,500

A Martinware jug incised with birds perched on flowering branches, incised marks, 5½in (13.5cm) high.
$600-1,200

▷

A Martin Brothers stoneware vase, glazed in blue and black, reserved against a beige ground, signed 'R.W. Martin, London & Southall, 9.7.81', 9in (22.5cm) high.
$200-450

△

A Martin Brothers stoneware grotesque double faced jug, in brown mottled matt glaze, with white glazed eyes, incised 'Martin Bros. London and Southall 4–1897', 9in (22.5cm) high.
$2,600-5,300

A Martin Brothers stoneware tile, incised and decorated in brown, white and green against a stippled brown and cream ground, signed around the edge 'Martin Bros., London, Southall, 3-1895', 6¼in (15.5cm) square.
$150-300

l. A Martinware grotesque spoon warmer of dragon form, impressed 'R W Martin, London & Southall' and '58', 8in (20cm).
$2,600-5,300

c. A Martinware owl with large beak and sardonic expression, on wood socle, head and base both impressed 'R W Martin & Bros., London & Southall 8.6.1905', 11in (27.5cm).
$4,500-9,000

r. A Martinware grotesque spoon warmer in the form of a bearded animal, impressed '27 R W Martin, London & Southall 11–79', 5½in (13.5cm).
$4,000-6,800

A rare Martinware plaque of the interior of the pottery titled 'Southall Pottery, Middlesex, 1882 R. W. Martin Sc', showing named and identified figures 'Wheel boy, Tom Cox (?)', 'Bench boy, Elvin Kelford' and 'Thrower, Edwin Bruce Martin', 16 by 7in (40 by 17.5cm).
$4,000-7,500

A Martin Brothers stoneware vase, with incised decoration in green, brown and white tones on a buff coloured ground, incised 'Martin Bros. London & Southall 18.7.84', 8in (20.5cm) high.
$800-1,500

A good Martin Brothers stoneware oviform vase, incised with brown and white detailing reserved against a bronze-coloured metallic ground, signed 'Martin Bros., London & Southall', and dated '4–1899', 7in (18cm) high.
$800-1,500

A Martin Brothers stoneware vase, with incised decoration in dark brown glazes over a buff ground, incised 'R.W.Martin Bros. London Southall, 1889', 13in (33cm).
$600-1,200

A Martin Brothers vase, decorated with sea creatures, signed and dated 1909.
$1,300-2,400

Metal

A bronze table lamp in the form of a frog, with red glass eyes, red tasselled fringe, 15in (38cm).
$3,200-6,000

See Miller's Guide *1981, p.475 for a similar example.*

A bronze bust of the 'Genie of the Dance' by Carpeaux.
$3,200-6,000

A gilt bronze figure of Loie Fuller by Raoul-Francois Larche, with 2 light fittings, base inscribed 'Raoul Larche' numbered K809, stamped founder's mark, Siot Decauville Fondeur, Paris, 18in (45.5cm) high.
$800-1,500

A bronze figure of Diana Wounded, by Bertram MacKennal, with good patina but with patches of verdigris across her breasts and right thigh, 16½in (41.5cm).
$20,000-30,000

A bronze figure of a woman by Bertram MacKennal.
$10,000-18,000

A seven-branch brass candlestick, the design attributed to Bernhard Pankok, raised circular base and central column on which the arms pivot, with cast decoration of concentric rings, 12in (29.5cm) high.
$2,600-5,300

An important and rare copper urn, designed by Frank Lloyd Wright, probably executed by James A Miller, for the Susan Lawrence Dana House, Springfield, Illinois, of large spherical form set on a 4-part foot, the vessel finely worked in repoussé with 4 circular designs, with thumb print detailing, within an elaborate Gothic frame, unsigned, c1903, 18in (45cm) high.
$85,000-90,000

A Tiffany Studios bronze and iridescent glass candlestick, with separate pendant snuffer, having overall greeny-brown patination, stamped 'Tiffany Studios New York 1212', 10in (25cm) high.
$1,200-2,100

A bronze bowl with swing-handle, cast after a model by Gustav Gurschner, signed in the bronze 'Gurschner' and stamped with foundry mark K.K.K.F. Wien 1246, c1900, 6in (15.5cm).
$1,000-2,000

A pair of WMF Art Nouveau pewter vases, stamped marks, 14½in (37cm).
$1,000-2,000

A Hukin & Heath plated soup tureen and cover, designed by Christopher Dresser, maker's marks, design lozenge for 28th July 1880, numbered '2123' and 'Designed by Dr. C. Dresser', retail mark on cover for 'W. Thornhill & Co. New Bond St. W.', 8½in (21cm) high.
$3,200-6,000

An Arts and Crafts plated metal cross, in the manner of Omar Ramsden, engraved with a memorial to 'Frederic Wilkins, Preist', dated '10th January 1937', 22in (56cm) high.
$1,000-2,000

A Guild of Handicraft Ltd. silver spoon with circular bowl, and ivory handle, the bowl stamped G of H Ltd. with London hallmarks for 1900, 8½in (21cm).
$1,700-3,000

A WMF electroplated pewter drinking set, comprising a lidded decanter, 6 goblets and a tray, all pieces with usual impressed marks, c1900, tray 19 by 13½in (48 by 34cm).
$1,400-2,600

A set of 6 H.M. silver Art Nouveau teaspoons in fitted case, Birmingham 1900.
$300-600

A brass chamberstick, by Robert Jarvie, the neck, encircling a removable bobeche, continuing to a handled trumpet-shaped body, incised Jarvie, 6in (15cm) high.
$450-550

An unusual Liberty & Co. Tudric-Moorcroft cake tray, stamped 'Tudric Pewter 0357', 12in (30cm).
$600-1,100

A Barnard Aesthetic Movement silver gilt christening set, comprising: a tankard, a knife, fork and spoon, all engraved and gilded, stamped W.B.J., maker's marks for London 1879, 9oz, in original Goldsmith & Silversmith Company box, tankard 3½in (9.5cm) high.
$1,200-2,100

A Georg Jensen silver tazza, stamped marks, 7½in (19cm).
$1,400-2,600

A copper tray, by Dirk Van Erp, with hammered texture, recessed centre and twin oval handles with raised ovals, impressed with a windmill and 'Dirk Van Erp', 13½in (34cm) diam.
$700-900

A Heath & Middleton silver and glass claret jug, in the manner of Christopher Dresser, maker's marks JTH/JHM and Birmingham 1892, 15in (38cm).
$600-1,100

A set of 12 silver goblets, by Kalo, each with hammered finishes, folded rims and trumpet-shaped bases, impressed 'Sterling Kalo P95', 6½in (17cm) high, 60 troy oz net weight.
$2,600-2,900

A Hukin & Heath silver-mounted claret jug, designed by Dr. Christopher Dresser, with ebony handle, stamped with maker's monogram JWH & JTH and London hallmarks for 1884, 9in (23cm).
$1,800-3,800

A set of 4 Hukin & Heath silver salts with salt-spoons, decorated in silver, copper and silver gilt, marked H & H and with Birmingham hallmarks for 1879, 6oz 4dwt, 1½in (3.5cm).
$1,700-3,000

An Art Nouveau silver and enamelled garniture of 3 vases by Hutton & Sons, with blue/green enamelled motif, London 1902/3.
$500-900

A copper humidore, by Roycroft, with hammered texture, the cover with a large poppy blossom, impressed with firm's mark, 5½in (13cm) diam, with glass liner.
$500-600

A William Hutton and Co. 5-piece silver tea-set, comprising a teapot, coffee pot, milk jug, sugar basin and sugar tongs, the teapot and coffee-pot with ebony handles, all pieces en suite, each piece stamped with maker's marks WH & Co and London hallmarks for 1904, teapot 6½in (17cm) high, 57ozs 11dwts gross weight.
$3,200-6,000

A Liberty & Co. Cymric silver vase, the design attributed to Archibald Knox, marked L & Co, Cymric, Birmingham hallmarks for 1903 and numbered 2020, 5½in (14cm) high.
$600-1,200

An unusual Tiffany & Co. cup and saucer, embellished against a copper ground, marked Tiffany & Co, Sterling Silver and other metals, pattern numbers 5623, c1879–1880, cup 2½in (6.5cm) high.
$900-1,700

A Liberty & Co. silver biscuit box, marked Cymric and L & Co, and with Birmingham hallmarks for 1902, 20oz 14dwt, 5½in (14cm).
$1,000-2,000

A Tiffany & Co. hammered white metal and parcel-gilt 3 piece tea-set, comprising a tea pot, milk jug and sugar bowl, engraved Tiffany & Co maker's mark, sterling silver and other metals and various numbers, c1890, tea pot 6½in (17cm) high.
$8000-13,500

A rare enamelled silver box, by Elizabeth E. Copeland, Boston, raised on 4 padded feet, the hinged cover with bosses around the edges and enamelled with a simple floral motif in yellow, violet, navy, white, green and dark pink, with applied silver monogram 'ec' and impressed 'sterling', 4½in (12cm) wide, 16 troy oz.
$5,000-5,200

A pair of cast iron door escutcheons, door knobs and keys, designed by Louis H. Sullivan, executed by the Yale and Towne Manufacturing Co., for the Guaranty Building, Buffalo, New York, cast with an ornate scrolled and stylised floral design and 'GUA NTY' cast 'Y & T', 1894-95, 14in (35cm) long.
$2,100-2,300

An Art Nouveau dressing table tray, maker's mark, R.P., Birmingham 1902, 14in (36cm) long, 13.5ozs (420gms).
$1,200-2,100

A silver box, with inserted miniature on ivory, signed, hallmarked 1904.
$400-750

A German four-light candelabra, stamped with crown, crescent and 800, maker's marks for probably Bruckmann and retail mark for M. Stumpf & Sohn, 17½in (44cm).
$1,600-2,800

An Art Nouveau silver condiment set, all with green liners.
$400-750

A white metal and enamel box with parcel gilt interior, circular shape, the polychrome enamelled decoration depicting a maiden with long hair, in profile, against a background of flowers and leaves, c1900, 4in (10cm).
$1,200-2,100

A Perry and Co red enamelled chamber candlestick, designed by Christopher Dresser, the base with brass fitments and curved wooden handle, trade mark for maker, registration mark for 30th October 1883 and Dr. Dresser Design, 5½in (14cm).
$600-1,200

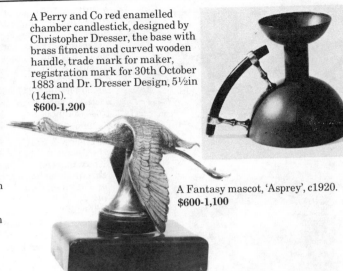

A Fantasy mascot, 'Asprey', c1920.
$600-1,100

A bronze-plated cast iron baluster, designed by Louis H. Sullivan, executed by the Yale and Towne Manufacturing Co., for the Guaranty Building, Buffalo, New York, the central shield within an ellipse bordered by ornate scrollwork and surmounted by stylised foliage, unsigned, 1894-95, 34in (85cm) high.
$3,700-4,000

Three pairs of escutcheon plates and door knobs, designed by Burnham and Root, executed by the Yale and Towne Manufacturing Co., for the Reliance Building, Chicago, cast with scrolled ends, one plate cast with 'Reliance', the scalloped door knobs cast with radiating curved lines, all cast 'Y & T', 4 impressed '401½ IN.S' and 2 impressed '0409', c1895, 2 pairs 9½in (22.5cm) long and one pair 6½in (15cm) long, with shafts and 2 mortice door locks.
$1,000-1,200

Moorcroft

William Moorcroft Wares

William Moorcroft was born in Burslem in 1872. He studied at the Burslem School of Art, the National Art School (now the Royal College) and in Paris. In 1897 he joined James Macintyre and Co as a designer in their new Art Pottery department. In 1898 Moorcroft designed and produced a range known as Florian Ware. Moorcroft had total control of production and was able to experiment with a variety of glazes and decorating methods. Moorcroft used a white porcellaneous body of great strength. Wares were generally thrown rather than moulded and Moorcroft drew the original designs for every shape and size of pot himself. These were generally taken from nature, particularly plant forms, and were outlined on the pot using a thick slip which also served to prevent the metallic infill glazes from merging during firing.

Macintyre's Art Pottery closed in 1913 and Moorcroft established his own company at Cobridge, continuing with designs produced at Macintyre's as well as developing new ones. In 1928 Moorcroft gained the Royal Warrant and his company flourished on an international reputation built on the foundations of quality and style. During the late 1930s many Art Potteries were forced to close but Moorcroft soldiered on thanks to the continued support of a thriving American market. In 1945 William's son Walter took over the Cobridge works and continued to produce a wide range of designs mostly sold to an appreciative American public.

A Moorcroft pottery squat-shaped vase, painted with green trees on yellow to blue ground, impressed marks and signed in blue, 5½in (14cm).
$500-900

A Moorcroft pottery vase, painted in red and purple on a dark blue ground, impressed Burslem mark, signed 'W. Moorcroft' in blue, 13in (31cm).
$400-900

A Moorcroft Claremont vase, decorated in yellows, reds, olive-green and blue against a streaked green-blue ground, marked 'Moorcroft Made in England' and signed 'WM', 7in (17cm).
$500-900

A Moorcroft bowl, painted with red and green toadstools on a mottled green ground, printed marks and signed in green, 8in (20cm).
$1,000-2,000

A Moorcroft Florian ware vase, with black stylised foliage on a white and black ground, printed marks, signed in green, 12½in (32cm).
$600-1,100

A pair of Moorcroft dawn pattern vases, painted in deep blue against a pale blue sky, between chevron borders of blue and cream, painted initials in blue, impressed Moorcroft, Made in England, 8in (19cm).
$800-1,500

An important two-handled trumpet-shaped vase, on matt blue ground, full signature, des., c1898-1900, 10in (25cm).
$500-900

A Moorcroft-Macintyre tobacco jar, decorated in reds, blues, browns and greens and apricot, Macintyre marks and signed 'WM', 4½in (11cm).
$600-1,200

A Moorcroft 'Brown Cornflower' vase, decorated in reds, dark blue and orange against a shaded beige-blue ground, impressed 'Moorcroft Burslem' and signed 'W. Moorcroft', 8in (20cm).
$400-900

> ### MACINTYRE/ MOORCROFT
>
> ★ first Art Pottery produced in 1897. Early wares marked Macintyre and/or W. Moorcroft des.
> ★ William Moorcroft established his own works in 1913
> ★ 1913-21 wares impressed MOORCROFT BURSLEM with painted W.Moorcroft signature
> ★ after 1916 impressed ENGLAND
> ★ 1921-1930 impressed MADE IN ENGLAND
> ★ 1930-1949 paper label, BY APPOINTMENT, POTTER TO H.M. THE QUEEN used
> ★ 1949-1973 label states BY APPOINTMENT TO THE LATE QUEEN MARY
> ★ rivals copied patterns and colours

A Moorcroft Claremont pattern vase, decorated on a greeny-blue ground, base chipped, impressed Moorcroft Burslem England 1440 and with green painted 'W. Moorcroft' signature, 8in (22cm).
$800-1,500

A Moorcroft Macintyre vase, Florian-style decoration, full signature, des., c1900, 7in (18cm).
$300-600

A Moorcroft Macintyre baluster vase, decorated in bluey-green and gold against olive green, Macintyre marks signed 'W.M. des.,' and Rd. No. '404017', 12½in (31cm).
$800-1,500

A Moorcroft Claremont bowl, decorated in greens, blues, reds and yellows against a shaded olive green and blue ground, 'Made for Liberty' and 'W. Moorcroft', 10in (26cm) diam.
$1,000-2,000

Miscellaneous

A Moorcroft Macintyre two-handled vase, painted with peacock feathers in green and blue, design number 360574, signed in green 'W. Moorcroft, des.', 7½in (19cm).
$600-1,200

Alphonse Mucha: 4 unusual menus for Moet & Chandon, lithographic prints, signed in the block, c1900, 8½ by 6in (22 by 15cm).
$800-1,500

A cartoon for a stained glass window, depicting 'Winter' as an allegorical figure wearing a holly wreath and carrying a bundle of wood, charcoal and gouache on paper, framed, c1890, 48 by 24in (121 by 62cm).
$300-600

A Moorcroft bulbous pottery jug, painted in cream and pastel shades on a bluish ground, impressed Moorcroft marks, initialled WM in blue, 8in (21cm).
$400-900

A set of 6 Guild of Handicraft Ltd. buttons, each embellished with a heart-shaped leaf on a berried stem, unmarked but in fitted case for Brook St., with the 'works' in Chipping Camden, ½in (1.5cm) diam.
$400-900

Use the Index!

Because certain items might fit easily into any of a number of categories, the quickest and surest method of locating any entry is by reference to the index at the back of the book.
This has been fully cross-referenced for absolute simplicity.

Posters

A pair of silk-embroidered panels attributed to Morris & Co in coloured silks on a cream ground, 55 by 23in (89 by 59cm).
$600-1,200

An unusual walnut and gold-painted 'Puzzle', in a shaped case, the sliding covers emblematic of Yin and Yang, enclosing segments in jig-saw fashion of the entwined bodies, heads and hair of woman, reminiscent of the designs of Jan Toorop, 15½in (39cm) across.
$600-1,200

Jessie M. King: 'The Story of Rosalynde' – pen and ink, watercolour and gilding on vellum, signed bottom left 'Jessie M. King. Invt. Del', 9 by 6in (23 by 14cm).
$1,600-2,800

This was designed for the front cover of The Story of Rosalynde *by Thomas Lodge with illustrations by Edmund J. Sullivan, of which there were twenty-five copies published by Cedric Chivers Ltd., Bath.*

An unusual Austrian figural cigar-cutter by C. Kauba, modelled as the silver-patinated figure of a partially-clad girl, the cutter operated by the movement of her legs (wince!), signed on girl's head, 'C. Kauba', 8½in (22cm).
$600-1,100

Doulton

A Doulton siliconware owl by J A Milne.
$800-1,500

A Doulton Lambeth stoneware Queen Victoria Jubilee commemorative jug, silver mounted neck, 7½in (19cm).
$300-600

A pair of Doulton ivory earthenware 'Galleon' jugs, each inverted ovoid body printed with 6 galleons in choppy seas, dolphin lower frieze, c1885, 7in (18cm).
$300-600

A group modelled as two frogs attacking two mice, on an oval mound base, entitled 'The Combat', by George Tinworth, 4in (10cm).
$1,700-3,000

A Doulton Lambeth vase, decorated with leaves and pâte-sur-pâte birds on brown ground, by Florence E. Barlow.
$200-450

DOULTON

★ Doulton & Watts pottery established by John Doulton at Lambeth, London in 1815–specialised in stoneware sanitary, laboratory and other utilitarian items – known by this name until 1858

★ 1860 began reviving earlier types of stoneware, for example copies of 18thC brown ware

★ from 1862 produced blue-decorated salt-glazed wares

★ 1866 onwards closely associated with Lambeth School of Art where Martin brothers and George Tinworth trained

★ Tinworth joined Doulton but, although they undertook work for Doulton, the Martins did not join the company

★ J-C Cazin joined the firm in 1870 and introduced sgraffiato. This technique taken up by Hannah and Florence Barlow whose 'Barlow Wares' decorated with animals and scenes became very popular

★ continental collectors as well as museums began buying Doulton 'artistic' wares by early 1870s and an increasing number of 'art potters' – from six in 1873 to 345 in 1890 – were employed

★ during this period the range of wares widened – earthenware decorated with enamel colours (1873), 'silicon' ware (1879), 'marquetry' ware (1887)

★ porcelain factory opened at Burslem, Staffordshire in 1884

★ notable tile panels by W J Neatby produced c1900

DOULTON WARES

Doulton marks – abbreviations

o.u.m.	– oval updated mark
o.m.	– oval mark, dated
c.m.	– circular mark
r.m.	– rosette mark
r.m.& e.	– rosette mark and England
d.l.e.	– Doulton Lambeth England
d.s.l.	– Doulton Silicon Lambeth
d.s.p.	– Doulton & Slaters Patent
c.m.l.& c.	– circle mark, lion & crown
c.m.& l.	– circle mark and lion
r.d.e.	– Royal Doulton England
s.c.m.	– slip-cast mark
i.c.f.m.	– impressed circular faience mark
r.d.f.	– Royal Doulton Flambé
b.r.m.& c.	– Burslem rosette mark & crown

A Doulton Lambeth stoneware bowl by Frank A. Butler, in green, pink and blue beneath a beaded band, with gilt metal rim, impressed Doulton mark, incised monogram FAB, dated 1882, 9½in (24cm) diam.
$200-450

A Doulton Lambeth stoneware figure, attributed to John Broad, impressed 'Doulton' on base, 18in (46cm).
$600-1,200

l. A pair of inverted baluster form salt-glazed stoneware vases, initials of Florence E. Barlow, assistant Eleaner Tosen, one rim chipped, c1902-5, 10½in (26.5cm).
$400-750

r. A pair of tall salt glazed stoneware vases, coloured grey-green with blue and ochre details, initials of Bessie Newbery, a supervisor at Doultons from 1911, c1912-18, 12in (31cm).
$180-300

A Lambeth vase, with incised panels of deer, by Hannah Barlow and assistant Annie Jentle, date 1887, 11in (28cm).
$300-600

An unusual Doulton Lambeth stoneware commemorative vase by George Tinworth, glazed in shades of brown, green and blue, incised 'GT' monogram, o.m. 9in (23cm).
$1,000-2,000

A Lambeth vase finely decorated in Art Nouveau style with mauve flowers on green ground, by Eliza Simmance, 14in (36cm).
$400-750

Royal Doulton – Figures

◁ A set of 'The Four Seasons', 2nd version, 'Spring' HN2085, 'Summer' HN2086, 'Autumn' HN2087, 'Winter' HN2088, designer Margaret Davies, introduced 1952, withdrawn 1959, 6in–8in (15cm–20cm).
$1,700-3,000

◁ 'Spring flowers', HN1945, designer L. Harradine, introduced 1940, withdrawn by 1949, 7in (18cm).
$400-900

A Royal Doulton china group, 'Afternoon Tea', HN1747, 5½in (14cm).
$200-450

ROYAL DOULTON FIGURES

★ since 1913 2,000 different models have been produced by the Royal Doulton factory
★ basically thought of as a modern day Staffordshire figure revival
★ since 1920's figures mainly designed by Peggy Davies, Leslie Harradine and Mary Nicoll
★ the HN numbering sequence was introduced with Charles Vyse 'Darling' HN 1 (which is still in production today)
★ since 1938 new figures are introduced only to replace ones which are to be withdrawn and so at any one time there are only 200-300 figures in production
★ any figure which is unsuccessful is withdrawn – and those are the ones most sought after by collectors

'Veronica', no number, should be HN1943, designer L. Harradine, introduced 1940, withdrawn by 1949.
$200-450

'The Awakening', HN1927, 1st version, designer L. Harradine, introduced 1940, withdrawn by 1949.
$2,600-5,300

'Top O' The Hill', HN1834, designer L. Harradine, introduced 1937, 7in (18cm).
$200-450

◁ 'The Bather', no number, model as HN1708 but with different decoration, with black and white check robe, black costume and blue base, designer L. Harradine, withdrawn 1938, 7½in (19cm).
$400-900

◁ 'Mantilla', HN2712, designer E.J. Griffiths, introduced 1974, withdrawn 1979, 12in (30cm).
$300-600

'The Mask', HN733, designer L. Harradine, introduced 1925, withdrawn by 1938, 7in (18cm).
$1,800-3,800

A charming pilot Royal Doulton figure of a boy carrying a lantern, in red coat and tricorn, not produced, 6½in (17cm).
$1,700-3,000

◁ 'Sea Sprite', HN2191, designer Margaret Davies, introduced 1958, withdrawn 1962, 7½in (19cm).
$300-600

'Ellen Terry as Queen Catherine', HN379, designer C.J. Noke, introduced 1920, withdrawn by 1949, 12½in (32cm).
$1,700-3,000

'Spring', a Doulton figure designed ▷ by Richard Garbe, modelled as a partially draped maiden holding flowers to her bosom as she is swept upwards, her drapery resting on a circular plinth above a stepped square section base, cream-coloured glaze, in two sections with original screw and nut fixing, hand painted signature 'Potted by Doulton & Co. Edition Limited to 100, No. 61 'Spring' by Richard Garbe ARA' and with moulded artist's signature and date 1932 on the plinth, 21½in (54cm) including plinth.
$5,500-9,000

'Gladys', HN1740, designer L. Harradine, introduced 1935, withdrawn by 1949, 5in (13cm).
$600-1,200

'Carmen', HN1267, designer L. Harradine, introduced 1928, withdrawn 1938, 7in (18cm).
$900-1,700

'Henry Lytton as Jack Point', HN610, designer C.J. Noke, introduced 1924, withdrawn 1949, 6½in (17cm).
$600-1,200

'Angela', HN1204, designer L. Harradine, introduced 1926, withdrawn 1938, hairline crack to base, 7½in (19cm).
$600-1,100

◁ 'Coppelia', HN2115, designer Margaret Davies, introduced 1953, withdrawn 1959, 7½in (19cm).
$1,000-2,000

A Royal Doulton figure, The Mendicant, depicting figure wearing draped costume and turban holding a tambourine and seated on a heap of red bricks, HN1365, printed Doulton mark, withdrawn from production 1969, 8½in (22cm).
$200-450

'A Yeoman of the Guard', HN2122, designer L. Harradine, introduced 1954, withdrawn 1959, 6in (15cm).
$900-1,700

'Moorish Piper Minstrel', on plinth, no number, should be HN301, designer C.J. Noke, withdrawn 1938, 13½in (34cm).
$1,300-2,400

'Lady Jester', HN1222, designer L. Harradine, introduced 1927, withdrawn by 1938. ▷
$2,000-4,500

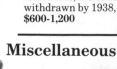

'Mask Seller', HN1361, designer L. Harradine, introduced 1929, withdrawn by 1938, 8½in (22cm).
$600-1,200

Three rare miniatures, 'One of the Forty', decorated in gilt, no number, should be HN423, designer H. Tittensor, 2½in, 2in, 3in (6cm, 5cm, 8cm).
$1,800-3,800

Miscellaneous

A porcelain group of Spooks modelled as two elderly gentlemen wearing long turquoise coloured cloaks and black caps, HN88 by C.J. Noke, printed and painted Royal Doulton, England and Doulton & Co. marks, 7in (18cm).
$1,800-3,800

'Fox in red coat', seated, HN100, 6½in (17cm).
$500-900

A Royal Doulton stoneware garden ornament, impressed C.M. & I., 11½in (29cm).
$800-1,500

A Royal Doulton Limited Edition loving cup to commemorate the reign of Edward VIII, modelled by H. Fenton, edition No. 699 of 2000, printed inscription and factory mark, and a certificate signed by Charles J. Noke, 10in (25cm).
$400-900

A Royal Doulton pottery 'Nelson' loving cup, inscribed 'I Was In Trafalgar Bay' and 'England Expects', decorated in colours and incised Fenton, the base with printed inscription in green, printed mark in green, limited edition number 579 of 600, 10½in (27cm).
$1,000-2,000

'Old Charley', a Royal Doulton character teapot and cover, c.m.l. & c., date code for 1939, introduced 1939, withdrawn 1960, 7in (18cm).
$2,000-4,500

'Mephistopheles', a Royal Doulton character jug, designed by C.J. Noke and H. Fenton, c.m.l. & c., introduced 1937, withdrawn 1948, 6in (15cm).
$1,800-3,800

'Sairey Gamp', a Royal Doulton character teapot and cover, c.m.l. & c., date code for 1939, introduced 1939, withdrawn 1960, 7in (18cm).
$1,700-3,000

A Royal Doulton Golfing series ware mug, decorated in relief with figures in period costume, glazed in colours, c.m.l. & c. D5716, 6in (15cm).
$300-600

A Kingsware whisky flask and stopper, printed Royal Doulton, England Marks, 8in (20cm).
$200-450

A Doulton flambé figure by Noke, with pagoda-like red silk and cream braid shade with metal mounted faceted glass drops, printed Royal Doulton Flambé mark and original printed label, c1930, 22½in (58cm).
$1,700-3,000

'Santa Claus' and 'Lambeth Walk', a Royal Doulton 'Bunnykins' candleholder with loop handle, designed by Barbara Vernon, made between 1940 and 1949, c.m.l. & c., Bunnykins back stamp, 7in (18cm).
$300-600

A pottery character jug modelled as Santa Claus, D6690, printed Royal Doulton England marks, 7½in (19cm).
$150-300

Make the most of Miller's

Every care has been taken to ensure the accuracy of descriptions and estimated valuations. Where an attribution is made within inverted commas (e.g. 'Chippendale') or is followed by the word 'style' (e.g. early Georgian style) it is intended to convey that, in the opinion of the publishers, the piece concerned is a later – though probably still antique – reproduction of the style so designated. Unless otherwise stated, any description which refers to 'a set', or 'a pair' includes a valuation for the entire set or the pair, even though the illustration may show only a single item.

Lalique Glass

RENÉ LALIQUE

The work of René Lalique spans both the Art Nouveau and Art Deco periods. He began his career as a designer of jewellery and was an innovator among goldsmiths in the 1890s, being more concerned with the craftsmanship and decorative elements of the work than its intrinsic value. His pieces of this time are recognised as the finest examples of Art Nouveau jewellery.

By the 1900 Paris Exposition – 'the triumph of Art Nouveau' – the movement was actually on the wane. This, combined with the fact that he had more commissions than he cope with and that numerous imitations of his work were appearing, made him turn elsewhere for inspiration. He found it in glass and exhibited some pieces at the Salon in 1902. In the same year he designed a new studio and set up a workshop where his most notable cire-perdue and glass panels were produced.

He was introduced to commercial glass production around 1907 when François Coty asked him to design labels for perfume bottles. In fact, Lalique designed the bottles as well. These were manufactured by Legras et Cie, until he opened his own small glassworks at Combs in 1909 to cope with the demands of this and other work. After the First World War he opened a larger glassworks which was responsible for the bulk of his output.

Just as Lalique had triumphed at the 1900 Paris Exposition with his Art Nouveau jewellery, so he dominated the 1925 Exposition, establishing him as the leading exponent of mass-produced glassware. His designs by now were in the Art Deco style but the earlier Art Nouveau influence was still apparent in some of the decorative elements.

He was very much concerned with the commercial mass-production of his designs and it is as much as a pioneer of mass-produced art glass that he should be remembered as for his earlier imaginative jewellery.

A frosted glass bottle and domed stopper, 'Enfants', base rim ground and polished, Mk. no. 1, 4in (9cm).
$400-900

A frosted clear and black enamelled box, 'Roger'.
$800-1,500

A clear scent bottle, 'Imprudence', designed for Worth, formed as a series of graduated discs, including the stopper, Mk. no. 1 with 'France', base with paper label printed with 'Fatice', 3in (7.5cm).
$400-900

This bottle contains its original contents and is sealed.

An opalescent Bruce parfum bottle, 'Papillons', Mk. no. 10, 7½in (19cm).
$1,000-2,000

A rare set of 3 Lalique scent bottles, made for D'Orsay, heightened with brown staining, each moulded 'R. Lalique', having paper labels for 'Fleurs de France', 'Charme D'Orsay' and 'La Flambe-D'Orsay', original fitted case, each bottle 3½in (9cm) high.
$600-1,100

A stylish and rare frosted and enamelled scent bottle, designed for Lucien Lelong, heightened with black enamel, Mk. no. 10 with 'France', with original chromed and enamelled metal case, echoing the design of the bottle, the base with 'Lucien Lelong' in stylish script and 'VDA 1876 1931', 4½in (11.5cm) overall.
$1,600-2,800

An opalescent and frosted glass encrier, '4 Sirenes', heightened with turquoise stain, Mk. no. 6, 6½in (16cm).
$1,700-3,000

A rare perfume bottle and stopper, 'Althea', base moulded with rare 'RL' mark and 'Brevete', 4in (10cm).
$800-1,500

A clear glass scent bottle, 'Palerme', Mk. no. 10, 5in (12cm).
$500-900

A frosted clear and black-stained hexagonal-sectioned box, 'Saint Nectaire', Mk. no. 10, 3½in (8.5cm).
$600-1,200

A frosted and clear glass encrier, '3 Papillons', formed as 3 insects, Mk. no. 2, traces of turquoise stain, 4in (10cm).
$600-1,200

An opalescent circular glass box, 'Cleones', the cover moulded on the underside in relief with beetles upon pinnated foliage, Mk. no. 10, 6½in (17cm).
$900-1,700

This box has a card from Marlborough House inscribed with 'A gift from Queen Mary, Bazaar at Durham'.

A Lalique blue opalescent circular box and cover, 'Three Dahlias', moulded signature R. Lalique, 8in (21cm).
$600-1,200

An opalescent circular glass box, 'Deux Sirens', the cover moulded in relief with two sea nymphs, Mk. no. 10, 10in (25cm).
$2,600-5,300

An opalescent glass vase, Mk. no. 1, 6in (15cm).
$900-1,700

A fine and rare frosted and siena-stained circular box and cover, Mk. no. 1 with 'France', 5in (12cm).
$2,600-5,300

A frosted, clear and turquoise-stained circular box, 'Amour Assis', the cover formed as a cherub, Mk. no. 6 with 'France' in script, 5in (12cm).
$1,700-3,000

A green, frosted glass vase, 'Languedoc', of strong hue, Mk. no. 1, two rim chips and fracture to body, 9in (23cm).
$800-1,500

A good green-cased, frosted glass vase, 'Alicante', Mk. no. 2, with 'France No. 998' in script, 10in (25.5cm).
$12,000-21,000

An opalescent and frosted glass vase, 'Laurier', Mk. no. 3 on side at foot, etched 'No. 947' on base, rim ground, 7in (18cm).
$600-1,200

A frosted and clear glass vase, 'Pierrefonds', one handle slightly ground on top, Mk. no. 3, 6in (15cm).
$1,800-3,800

A frosted glass vase and stopper, '12 Figurines avec Bouchon', Mk. no. 2 with 'France' in script, 11½in (29.5cm).
$2,000-4,500

A frosted glass statuette, 'Source de la Fontaine', heightened with siena stain, Mk. no. 3 with 'France', 28in (71cm).
$5,500-9,000

A frosted and clear glass vase, 'Bellecour', small internal fissure beneath one bird, Mk. no. 2, with 'France No. 9**', indistinct, 11in (29cm).
$1,700-3,000

A fine and rare frosted and black-stained glass peacock lamp, Mk. no. 10, 16in (41cm).
$20,000-30,000

A frosted and clear glass bowl, moulded in relief with a design of hounds, Mk. no. 12 with 'France', 9½in (24cm).
$400-750

A grey frosted glass vase and cover, 'Tourterelles', Mk. no. 2, 11½in (29cm).
$4,000-7,500

A Lalique opalescent deep circular bowl, 'Ondine Ouverte', moulded with a frieze of sirens, acid etched R. Lalique, France, 12in (30cm).
$1,200-2,100

An opalescent glass bowl, Mk. no. 3 with 'France', 11in (28cm).
$1,000-2,000

A frosted, opalescent and turquoise-stained vase, 'Ceylan', Mk. no. 3, and a period lamp fitting with clear celluloid shade painted with similar parakeets, 18½in (47cm) overall.
$2,600-5,300

A Lalique frosted and clear glass oval dish, etched R. Lalique, etched script mark France, slight reduction at rim, 17in (43cm).
$1,300-2,400'

An R. Lalique car mascot, c1920.
$4,000-7,500

A frosted and blue-stained nightlight, 'Hygenie', Mk. no. 10, with original bronze base, 6½in (16cm).
$1,600-2,800

A frosted glass clock, electric movement by ATO, enamelled chapter ring, Mk. no. 3 with 'France', 7in (18cm).
$800-1,500

A clear and frosted glass car mascot of pale amethyst hue, 'Faucon', Mk. no. 10 with wheel-cut 'France', beak ground, 6½in (16cm).
$800-1,500

A Lalique car mascot, 'Levrier', clear and satin finished glass moulded in intaglio, moulded signature R. Lalique, France, 2½in (7.5cm).
$2,600-5,300

Cf Catalogue des Verreries de René Lalique, *1982, pl.77, no.1141.*

A frosted and clear glass clock, electric movement marked ATO, Mk. no. 10, without 'R', 4½in (11cm).
$800-1,500

A frosted glass clock, electric movement marked ATO, Mk. no. 3, with 'France', 8½in (22cm).
$800-1,500

A large frosted glass ceiling dome, 'Charmille', minor chips and a small hole, 13½in (34cm).
$500-900

Miller's is a price Guide not a price List

The price ranges given reflect the average price a purchaser should pay for similar items. Condition, rarity of design or pattern, size, colour, provenance, restoration and many other factors must be taken into account when assessing values.
When buying or selling, it must always be remembered that prices can be greatly affected by the condition of any piece. Unless otherwise stated, all goods shown in Miller's are of good merchantable quality, and the valuations given reflect this fact. Pieces offered for sale in exceptionally fine condition or in poor condition may reasonably be expected to be priced considerably higher or lower respectively than the estimates given herein.

Art Deco – Ceramics

A Foley Art China coffee set, designed by George Logan, comprising: 6 cups and saucers, 6 side plates and a sandwich platter, in green and lilac on white ground, printed mark Foley Art China Peacock Pottery.
$800-1,500

A Shelley 23 piece tea service, 1930's.
$500-900

A Foley china part tea service, designed by Paul Nash, comprising: 5 cups and saucers, a milk jug, a slop bowl, 5 side plates and a cake plate, each piece painted in green, brown, yellow and red, factory marks and facsimile signature, cake plate 9in (23cm) diam.
$300-600

A Foley 'Intarsio' character teapot, designed by Frederick Rhead, no.3359, late Foley mark, Rd. no. 363131, 4½in (11.5cm).
$1,300-2,400

A Foley china 'Dainty white' shape part teaset comprising: 12 cups and saucers, 12 plates, 2 cake plates, milk jug and slop bowl, each piece decorated in pink, red, green, blue and butterscotch with a white ground, printed factory marks, Rd.no. 272101, 1896.
$400-900

A Shelley 'Mode' shape 'sunray' pattern coffee set, comprising: coffee pot and cover, 6½in (17cm), 6 cups and saucers, milk jug and sugar bowl, each piece decorated in beige, yellow and black against a white ground, printed factory marks, Rd.no. 756533.
$800-1,500

A Foley 'Intarsio' vase, designed by Frederick Rhead, in brown, with 4 yellow 'scaled' panels with mauve irises below against a green ground, factory marks and numbered 3003, 8½in (21.5cm).
$400-900

A Foley 'Intarsio' vase, decorated in blue, white, pink, green and brown, printed factory marks, no 3469, 9in (23cm).
$400-750

A Foley 'Intarsio' tapering cylindrical vase, printed marks, 8½in (21.5cm).
$400-900

A Shelley 'Mode' shape 'Butterfly Wing' pattern part teaset, comprising: 6 cups and saucers, 6 plates, a cake plate, milk jug and sugar bowl, each piece decorated in green, black and grey against a white ground, printed factory marks, Rd. no. 756533.
$1,000-2,000

A Carlton ware coffee service, glazed in pale primrose, comprising: coffee pot, cream jug, covered sugar bowl and 6 cups and saucers, printed marks.
$200-450

A Shelley 22 piece teaset, comprising: teapot, milk jug, sugar basin, 6 cups, saucers and plates and a cake plate, with orange, silver and black geometric decoration.
$1,000-2,000

A set of 6 Carlton Ware cups and saucers, in mottled red and black lustre, printed marks Carlton Ware Made in England Trade Mark, c1930.
$800-1,500

A Carlton ware 'Egyptianesque' ginger jar and cover, decorated in colours and gilding, against a powder-blue ground, factory marks on base, 15½in (39cm).
$4,000-6,800

l. A Carlton Ware rouge royale vase, in enamels and gold, 6in (15.5cm).
$150-250

r. A Carlton Ware rouge royale tulip form vase, in enamels and gold, 5½in (14cm).
$40-75

c. A Carlton Ware rouge royale diamond shaped dish, in enamels and gold, 12in (30.5cm).
$40-75

An earthenware vase, by George Ohr, with twin serpentine handles, the obverse incised with an eagle upon a shield, the reverse incised with a sailing ship, encircled by leafy branches in a green mottled olive brown glaze, impresed 'G.E. Ohr, Biloxi, Miss.', 8½in (21cm) high.
$5,000-5,500

A Carlton Ware vase, decorated on mottled purple and white ground, enriched with gilding, marked Carlton Ware, Made in England, 'Trade Mark', c1930, 10½in (26.5cm).
$500-900

An earthenware vase, by Charles F. Binns, with flared rim, in a chestnut glaze shading to a brown with gold-brown crystalline highlights, inscribed 'CFB 1930', 9in (22.5cm) high.
$4,000-4,500

A large Louis Wain pottery vase, decorated in green, black and red on a cream ground, moulded signature 'Louis Wain', 10in (25.5cm).
$2,000-4,500

A Royal Worcester porcelain horse's head vase, glazed white, 10½in (26.5cm).
$200-450

An English brown glazed stoneware wall mask, modelled as Comedy, 24in (61cm).
$300-600

A Lenci figure of a rooster, painted with black and green spots against a white and black ground, orange painted 'comb', painted marks Lenci, 1936 S.P., 11½in (29cm).
$2,000-4,500

A Lenci pottery wall mask modelled as a young girl wearing a multi-coloured head scarf, printed marks, 11½in (29cm) wide.
$400-900

A Goldscheider pottery mask of a girl looking down, the polychrome decoration highlighted with vivid orange for wavy hair and lips, printed Goldscheider Wien mark, Made in Austria, and impressed with artist's monogram B, c1925, 9in (23cm).
$600-1,200

A Goldscheider terracotta head of a young lady, with orange hair and lips, printed marks, 9½in (24cm).
$300-600

A large Goldscheider terracotta bust, printed marks and incised 'Goebel', 14½in (36.5cm).
$800-1,500

A Rosenthal ceramic sculpture by Gerhard Schliepstein, pale buff coloured crackle glaze, with impressed Rosenthal mark and impressed 'Schliepstein', c1930, 19½in (50.5cm).
$3,200-6,000

A Lallemant vase, the polychrome hand-painted decoration illustrating the French nursery rhyme, 'Il Pleut, Il Pleut Bergère', painted signature, 'T. Lallemant France', c1925, 11in (28cm).
$1,000-2,000

A Theodore Haviland porcelain cruet set to a design by Edouard Marcel Sandoz, with factory marks and facsimile of designer's signature, large frog 4in (10.5cm).
$600-1,100

A Haviland porcelain ashtray, commissioned by the Compagnie Generale Transatlantique for the oceanliner 'Normandie', CGT monogram in relief and printed marks, c1935, 8in (20.5cm) wide.
$300-600

A large Ruskin high-fired transmutation glaze vase and matching circular stepped stand, with cloudy deep purple glaze with green mottling and speckling over a mottled pale grey ground, vase and stand impressed Ruskin England, c1930, 14½in (36cm), including stand.
$600-1,200

A KPM white porcelain mask by Hubatsch, blue printed KPM device and moulded signature 'Hubatsch 1930', 9½in (25cm).
$600-1,200

A Sèvres porcelain lantern with bronze tassel, designed by Henri Rapin, glazed in dark celadon and amber on a cream ground and embellished with gilding, circular red printed Manufacture Nationale Décoré a Sèvre 1923, and black rectangular S 1923DN marks, 20in (51.5cm).
$1,300-2,400

A Berlin 'KPM' porcelain box and cover, in colours and gilding, and embellished with oval intaglio panels of birds and flowers, sceptre mark and KPM and orb inside cover, SR on base, 8½in (22.5cm).
$4,000-7,500

A vase of cylindrical shape attributed to Venini and the design of Carlo Scarpa, of deep amethyst colour with a random pattern of white dashes, the surface partly iridescent and partly polished, c1958, 8in (20cm).
$1,000-2,000

A Brannan green glazed model of a dragon, with yellow and blue markings, incised marks, 8in (20cm).
$200-450

A Rosenthal ginger jar designed by Kurt Wendler, with abstract design in blues, red and green heightened with gilding on a white ground, printed Rosenthal Selb Bavaria mark and artist's signature 'Kurt Wendler', c1925, 8½in (21cm).
$600-1,200

An Amphora vase, polychrome on a white porcelain ground, enriched with gilding, impressed Amphora and printed Turn Teplitz R. St. K. with maker's device and D.464, c1930, 7½in (18.5cm).
$1,800-3,800

A Limoges porcelain box and cover designed by Sandoz, with white and yellow plumage and blue beak, 6½in (16cm) and another similar 2in (5cm), both with printed marks, signed Sandoz.
$400-900

A Fraureuth porcelain box and cover, blue and white with black and gilt stylised foliate hand-painted decoration, printed mark Fraureuth Kunstabteilung, c1920, 8½in (21cm).
$400-900

A Fornasetti porcelain circular rack plate, printed in black against white, 'eye' mark, Tema E. Variazioni, Fornasetti-Milano, Made in Italy, numbered 94, 10½in (26.5cm).
$150-300

A Clarice Cliff Fantasque Lotus jug, in orange, purple, green and blue, gilt printed on base Lawley's Norfolk Pottery Stoke, and Fantasque by Clarice Cliff, 11½in (29cm).
$800-1,500

A Clarice Cliff Bizarre Inspiration two-handled vase painted with bands of yellow, blue and turquoise stylised foliage outlined in brown on a turquoise ground, printed marks, 10in (25cm).
$6,000-12,000

A Clarice Cliff Bizarre oviform jug, painted in yellow and black, printed marks, 7in (18cm).
$600-1,200

A fine example of a Brangwyn plaque, decorated by Clarice Cliff, 17in (43cm) diam.
$4,000-7,500

A Clarice Cliff Fantasque single handed Isis vase, painted with blue, purple and orange blossoms amid green and black foliage between yellow rim, printed marks, 9½in (24.5cm).
$600-1,100

A Clarice Cliff Bizarre part dinner service, each piece gaily decorated, comprising: 2 tureens and covers, a gravy boat, a pair of graduated oval dishes and 6 plates.
$500-900

A Clarice Cliff Bizarre ginger jar and cover, painted with bright colours, signed with factory marks on base, 8in (20cm).
$600-1,200

A Clarice Cliff Lotus shape jug, painted in bright colours, reserved against a cream ground with coloured banded borders, printed facsimile signature, factory marks, Newport, 11½in (29cm).
$1,000-2,000

A Clarice Cliff Fantasque baluster shaped vase, painted with bands of yellow, blue, orange and green, outlined in black between horizontal bands of orange, black, blue and green, printed marks, 16in (40.5cm).
$2,000-4,500

A Clarice Cliff Bizarre crocus pattern tea service, comprising: teapot, milk jug, sugar basin, 2 bread and butter plates, 10 cups, 12 saucers and 12 side plates.
$500-900

A Clarice Cliff Lotus shape jug, painted in bright colours, reserved against a cream ground with orange borders, printed facsimile signature and factory marks, Newport, 11½in (29cm).
$1,200-2,100

A Clarice Cliff Lotus vase with twin handles, painted with yellow trees on tall green trunks, with red buildings, further black and mauve trees against blustery white clouds, printed signature and 'Fantasque' marks, 11½in (28.5cm).
$1,700-3,000

A Clarice Cliff Bizarre part breakfast set, painted in bright colours, comprising: a teapot and cover, a milk jug, a sugar bowl, 2 teacups, 2 saucers, a side plate, a two-handled shaped bowl and cover and a rectangular shaped dish, all with printed marks.
$1,300-2,400

Bronze figures

A bronze figure by Karl Perl, on marble base, inscribed 'Karl Perl', 24½in (61cm).
$2,000-4,500

A bronze figure by Barbara MacDonald, of a young woman standing with naked torso and hands held closely to her body on a tall hexagonal base, inscribed 'Barbara MacDonald, 1936', 27in (68.5cm) overall.
$1,300-2,400

A green painted metal figure by Le Verrier supporting a red glass lamp, adapted for electricity, 23½in (60cm).
$1,300-2,400

A mechanical bronze figure cast after a model by C. Kauba, on bronze base, signed in the bronze 'C. Kauba', c1920, 8½in (21cm).
$1,600-2,800

A bronze figure cast after a model by C.J.R. Colinet, on marble base, dull gold patina highlighted with cold-painted colouring, signed in the bronze 'C.J.R. Colinet', c1925, 18½in (47cm).
$3,200-6,000

A bronze, marble and glass lamp, cast after a model by M. Le Verrier, signed 'M. Le Verrier' in the bronze, c1925, 34in (86cm).
$3,200-6,000

A bronze figure of a naked maiden, cast after a model by D.H. Chiparus, dull gold patina on black and brown marble base, signed in the marble 'D. H. Chiparus', c1925, 21½in (54.5cm) including base.
$1,200-2,100

An unusual bronze figure of a naked woman, mounted on marble base, inscribed 'Gergel S', 12½in (31cm).
$600-1,200

A bronze figure, 'Thoughts', cast after a model by M. Geraud Rivière, on marble plinth, c1930, 7in (17.5cm).
$1,200-2,100

A bronze figure, 'Nocturne', cast after a model by Edward-Louis Collet, inscribed in the bronze 'Collet Scpt' stamped foundry mark E Colin & Co. Paris, 18in (45.5cm).
$1,300-2,400

A bronze figure cast after a model by Hugo Lederer, dark brown patina, on stepped circular speckled grey marble base, signed in the bronze 'Hugo Lederer', c1925, 17in (43cm).
$1,600-2,800

A painted bronze figure by Molins, on black marble base, 19in (48cm).
$1,200-2,100

A Guiraud Riviere bronze figure, 'Stella', inscribed on star 'Guiraud Riviere', 'Etling Paris' and 'Bronze France', 11½in (28.5cm).
$2,600-5,300

A cold-painted gilt bronze figure in the style of Bruno Zack, on green onyx base, 12in (30.5cm).
$1,200-2,100

A bronzed electric table lamp with a mottled glass globular shade, on oval base with onyx stand, 20in (51cm).
$600-1,200

A Chiparus bronze figure, 'Dancer of Olynthus', signed on base 'Chiparus', 15in (38cm).
$1,300-2,400

A Laurel silvered bronze figure, signed 'Pierre Laurel' and stamped 'Marcel Guillemard 14', 17½in (44cm).
$1,700-3,000

A silvered bronze figure by Le Faguays, 'Vestal', each hand holding an onyx cup, inscribed 'Le Faguays', 14½in (36.5cm).
$2,000-4,500

A German gilt bronze figure, by Schmidt-Hofer, inscribed 'Schmidt-Hofer', 16in (41cm).
$1,000-2,000

A pair of cold painted bronze figural bookends, 'Chinese Students', by H.M. White, on marble bases, signed 'H.M. White', 8½in (22cm).
$600-1,200

An amusing bronze candleholder, possibly by Gurschner, 2½in (7cm).
$400-750

An Ouline green patinated model of a panther, signed on the base 'Ouline', 26½in (67cm) long.
$1,700-3,000

A large pewter and gilt metal simulated gem set bust, 'Salammbô', cast from a model by Louis Auguste Moreau, inscribed Salammbô and L. Moreau, 31in (79cm).
$4,500-9,000

A bronze model of a young bull elephant, 'Young Elephant', with short ivory tusks, signed 'C. Wollek Fec', and dated 'MCMXI' (1911), 11in (28cm).
$1,200-2,100

A bronze figure, 'The Skater', c1930, 9in (23cm).
$500-900

A bronze figure of a flamingo, cast after a model by Rochard, dull gold patina, on black marble base, the base signed 'Rochard', c1925, 18½in (47.5cm).
$3,200-6,000

Ceramic Figures

A Goldscheider pottery figure, impressed marks, 14in (34cm).
$900-1,700

A Guiraud Rivière crackled white pottery figure, inscribed 'Guiraud Rivière', 22in (56cm).
$800-1,500

◁

An amusing Lenci figure modelled as a girl wearing a black and white dress, a black and red hat and scarf, signed 'Lenci, Made in Italy, Torino', 17in (43.5cm).
$1,300-2,400

A Lenci pottery figure, painted marks, 9½in (24cm).
$900-1,700

▷

A Lenci pottery figure, painted marks, 14in (35.5cm).
$900-1,700

A Royal Dux model of a bathing belle, painted in pale enamel colours and gold, 18½in (47.5cm).
$800-1,500

A Goldscheider pottery figure, impressed marks, 14in (34cm).
$800-1,500

An R. Philippe white glazed pottery group, impressed 'R. Philippe', 15in (38cm).
$150-300

An Ochies pottery figure designed by Dax, printed and painted marks, 13in (33cm).
$200-450

A Lenci figure 'Giovane Negra con Anfore' designed by Scavini, on green circular moulded base, printed marks, 21in (53cm).
$1,700-3,000

A Rosenthal porcelain figure designed by Gerhard Schliepstein, white and flesh tones, printed mark Rosenthal Germany and impressed 'G. Schliepstein', c1930, 13½in (33.5cm).
$1,200-2,100

A figure of a dancer by Royal Dux, 13in (33cm).
$400-750

A Hermann Kähler figure, blue and brown on a cream ground, incised monogram, HAK, c1915, 18½in (47.5cm).
$800-1,500

Bronze and Ivory figures

A Preiss painted bronze and ivory figure, 'Champagne Dancer', on red marble base, marked on bronze 'F Preiss', 16½in (42cm).
$4,500-9,000

An ivory and bronze figure, 'Syrian Dancer', carved and cast from a model by Demêtre Chiparus on a brown striated marble base set with a bronze plaque of a similar figure, and intaglio signed 'D.H. Chiparus', slight restoration, 14in (35cm).
$3,200-6,000
Ref. 'Art Deco and other Figures' *by Brian Catley, p.80 for illustration of similar.*

A Preiss bronze and ivory figure, 'Con Brio', the young girl wearing silver and green tinted bikini with matching skull cap, on circular green marble dish, 12in (30.5cm) high.
$600-1,200

A Preiss painted bronze and ivory figure, 'The Torch Dancer', modelled as a girl, naked except for silvered and red flowered bloomers, on black and green onyx base, signed 'F. Preiss', replacement flames, 16in (41.5cm).
$600-1,200

A Preiss painted bronze and ivory figure, 'Little Cricketer', modelled as a young boy wearing pale brown short trousers, a silvered short sleeved shirt, signed 'F. Preiss' on base, 7in (18.5cm).
$1,600-2,800

A bronze and ivory figure by Montini of Henry Fielding playing Dante, robes cold-painted in bronze red, on black marble plinth base, one thumb missing, 1930's, 16in (41cm) overall.
$1,800-3,800

A bronze and ivory figure by Chiparus, 'The Fan Dancer', the base inscribed 'D. H. Chiparus', 15in (38cm).
$10,000-18,000

A gilt bronze and ivory figure, 'Priestess', cast and carved from a model by Demêtre Chiparus, with enamelled blue and green simulated jewellery, inscribed in the bronze 'Chiparus', 17in (43cm).
$6,000-12,000

A gilt bronze and ivory figure of a girl, 'Innocence', cast and carved from a model by D. H. Chiparus, inscribed, on cream onyx base, 15in (38cm).
$5,000-9,000

A bronze and ivory figure, a dancer, cast and carved from a model by Demêtre Chiparus, inscribed 'D. Chiparus', 21½in (54.5cm).
$4,000-7,500

A carved ivory and marble figure, by Ernst Seger, signed 'E. Seger', 11½in (29.5cm).
$2,200-4,200

Furniture

A wrought iron and zebra wood cabinet, the base with a pair of parquetry cupboard doors, each centred by marquetry cartouches inlaid in various fruitwoods and mother-of-pearl with stylised floral motifs, on plinth base, carved signature 'J. Cayette, Nancy', c1925, 32½in (82cm).
$2,600-5,300

A burr-maple cocktail cabinet of semi-circular section, the upper section enclosing mirrored and fitted interior above overhanging bar fitted with 3 mirrored slides, the lower section enclosing fitted interior on platform base, fitted for electricity, 62in (153.5cm).
$1,300-2,400

A satinwood cabinet on chest, designed by Betty Joel, printed paper label, 'Token' Hand Made Furniture designed by Betty Joel, made by E.O. Miller, H. R. Green, May 1938, 30in (76cm).
$1,000-2,000

A Peter Waals oak bedside cabinet, the rectangular moulded top and panelled frieze drawer with bronze drop handles above plain rectangular shelf on square moulded legs, executed by Peter Waals, assisted by P. Burchett, 1928, 16½in (41.5cm).
$2,000-4,500

Make the most of Miller's

Unless otherwise stated, any description which refers to 'a set' or 'a pair' includes a valuation for the entire set or the pair, even though the illustration may show only a single item.

A Hille ash and cream lacquered dining room suite, designed by Robin Day, comprising: a rectangular dining table, 88in (223cm) extended, and 6 cream lacquered chairs with brown and white upholstery, and an ash sideboard raised on cream lacquered supports, 73in (185cm), stamped on drawer 'Hille of London'.
$2,000-4,500

A pair of mahogany and oak upholstered armchairs, by André Sornay, unsigned, c1935, 25in (63.5cm) wide.
$2,000-4,500

A walnut cabinet on chest, designed by Betty Joel, printed paper label, 'Token' Hand Made Furniture designed by Betty Joel, Manufactured by G. Butcher, C. M. Fox, September 1935, 30in (76cm).
$400-750

A Heal's sideboard, designed for the Paris Exhibition 1914, this example made 1926.
$3,200-6,000

A sofa designed by Serge Chermayeff, in brown velvet with cream piping on stained wooden platform base.
$2,000-4,500

This sofa was removed from the Mendelssohn House at 64, Old Church Street, Chelsea, the house for which Serge Chermayeff originally designed it.

A decanter and stopper, engraved and decorated in black with triangles and segments of circles, 11in (28cm).
$300-600

A black bakelite and chrome necklace, German.
$100-250

Jewellery

A Lacloche Frères patterned silver and red gold minaudiere, set with 5 sapphires, fitted with compartments inside and mirror inside lid, in suede case, stamped with maker's monogram and silver and gold import marks for 1935, 5 by 3½in (13 by 8.5cm), 13oz. 14 dwt. gross weight.
$2,000-4,500

An Art Deco style platinum cocktail watch.
$1,300-2,400

A two-coloured bracelet, the band formed of basket-weave design, with faceted and buckle design clasp, stamped 750.18ct.
$1,800-3,800

A black bakelite and chrome dress clip, French.
$80-150

A brooch, yellow metal set with diamonds and formed as a triple bow, 1940's, 7cm long.
$600-1,200

A brooch, fashioned in abstract form as an owl, stamped 'sterling' and mark of 2 R's back-to-back in monogram, 4.5cm, and a 'fish' brooch, silver-coloured metal with 'W.W' and Polish marks, 4cm.
$300-600

A pair of paste red cabochon dress clips, American.
$100-250

Clocks

A silver and enamel desk clock, enamelled in shades of green on a rich green ground, with easel support, stamped maker's mark C & A. London hallmark for 1930, 9cm high.
$200-450

An Art Deco timepiece, the green marble rectangle centred with a square dial with blue enamelled back, 7½ by 8½in (19.5 by 22cm).
$400-900

A mottled rouge marble and silvered bronze clock garniture, the clock striking movement by F. Martin, Paris, 24in (61cm) wide, 2 side ornaments en suite with applied silvered bronze geometric decoration, 9in (22.5cm) high.
$1,300-2,400

A David Anderson pink-enamelled timepiece, stamped 'David Anderson' and '925S', 13.75cm high.
$600-1,200

A pair of Arts and Crafts brass hinges, 6½in (16.5cm) long.
$600-1,200

A bronze dish, cast after a model by Gazan Chiparus, signed in the bronze 'Gazan Chiparus', c1920, 12½in (31.5cm).
$600-1,200

A German cocktail shaker, the multi-coloured vanes being containers for various spirits, the red body containing the shaker and measures, 10½in (27cm) overall.
$400-750

A Georg Jensen 64-piece Chess pattern table service, stamped Georg Jensen, Sterling, Denmark, comprising: 8 table forks, 8 dessert forks, 8 dessert spoons, 8 tea spoons, 8 table knives with steel blades, 8 cheese knives with steel blades, 50oz 12dwt weight not including knives.
$4,000-7,500

A set of 10 Ernst Treusch metal, wood and glass modernist tea cups, with flat rounded wooden handles, stamped Ernst Treusch Leipzig and with continental silver marks, c1930, 3in (7.4cm).
$1,300-2,400

A stylised 'Deco' enamelled cigarette case, French.
$150-250

An Art Deco table lighter in the form of a cocktail bar with negro barman, 7in (18cm) high.
$200-450

A Dunhill gold and enamelled combined lighter, cigarette case and watch, with black enamelled banding, marked 'AD' and 9ct. hallmarks for London 1929, 4in (10.5cm) wide.
$1,800-3,800

A bronze vase, 'Fisherman', cast from a model by J. Öfner, inscribed 'J. Öfner', 7in (18cm).
$1,000-2,000

A Georg Jensen silver tazza, stamped with maker's marks, Georg Jensen, Denmark, Sterling, 263B and London import marks for 1928, (design introduced 1918), 7½in (18.5cm), 18oz.
$2,000-4,500

Cf. Georg Jensen Silversmithy, 77 Artists, 75 years, Renwick Gallery, Smithsonian Institution, Washington D.C. 1980, p.168, similar tazza illustrated.

◁ A Georg Jensen silver teapot and cover, with ivory handle at right angles to it and a domed cover with ivory finial, Danish maker's mark, numbered 80A and with London import marks for 1938, 5½in (13.5cm).
$1,000-2,000

A plated coffee set, comprising: a coffee pot, hot milk jug, cold milk jug and sugar bowl, G.W.S. maker's marks, pots 6½in (17cm) high.
$600-1,100

Miscellaneous

A celluloid life-size mask, c1930.
$200-450

An ivory bakelite telephone in working order, c1938.
$200-450

A sheet alabaster leaded ceiling lamp shade, with stylized floral motifs, wreath border, 24in (61cm) diam.
$200-450

An illustration design showing a group of ladies and gentlemen in evening dress gathered round a Bugatti motor car, 9½ by 12½in (23 by 32.5cm).
$1,700-3,000

A carved wooden panel, 'Speed', partially gilded, with oak frame, 28½ by 45in (73 by 113cm).
$800-1,500

A carved rosewood figure, possibly by Nicholson Babb, 21in (53.5cm).
$600-1,200

A large carved stone circular plaque, by Alan Lydiat Durst, signed 'Alan Durst' and dated '1923', 32in (81cm) diam.
$1,300-2,400

A J.J. Adnet wool pile carpet, of russet, black, brown and beige, monogram JJA woven into right-hand bottom corner, c1930, 62½ by 57½in (156.5 by 144.5cm).
$1,800-3,800

A James Woolford plaster figure, patina-like grey painted finish, slight restoration and some chips, incised monogram JW, c1930, 23in (59cm) high.
$400-900

A chromolithograph, Leo Putz, 'Moderne Galerie -Edke Theatiner- u. Maffeistrasse Arcopalais', signed en block centre, left 'Leo Putz', published by Reichhold & Lang Munchen, image area 43½ by 32in (108.5 by 81.5cm) framed and glazed.
$400-900

A stone carving in 2 sections, depicting a bust of a maiden with streaming hair gazing at a sphere held in her hand, c1930, 16in (42cm) high.
$1,300-2,400

Four cover illustrations for 'Die Dame', 14 by 10½in (35 by 27cm) approx.
$1,700-3,000

Post war

A refrigerator, decorated by Piero Fornasetti, printed in black on white, 37in (94cm) high.
$1,800-3,800

A laminated birchwood chaise longue, designed by Bruno Mathsson, with interlaced russet-coloured webbing, with designer's printed label, rubber stamped, Made in Sweden, 60in (151cm) long.
$1,000-2,000

A KPM modernist teapot, designed by Georg Schutz, white porcelain with a brass handle, with impressed manufacturer's mark and monogram MR, c1960.
$400-900

A white leather upholstered sofa bed, 'Anfibio', designed by Alessandro Becchi, 95in (240cm) wide.
$1,800-3,800

An Italian teak and glass executive desk, 1950's, 78in (198cm) wide.
$1,200-2,100

A 'Lips' sofa, after a design by Salvador Dali, upholstered in red nylon stretch fabric, 83in (209cm) wide.
$3,200-6,000

An upholstered chaise longue, 'Djinn series' designed by Olivier Mourgue, c1965, 68in (170cm) long.
$1,700-3,000

Cf. Kathryn B. Heisingen/George H. Marcus Design since 1945, *cover illustration.*

An enamelled oval plaque, converted to brooch, after a design by Salvador Dali, various marks on reverse with '25th Decembre, 1950, New York', 4.5cm high.
$150-300

A Christofle electro-plated 4-piece modernist tea set, 'Como', designed by Lino Sabattini, comprising: a tea pot, coffee pot, milk jug and sugar basin, each piece stamped Gallia France Pro. Christofle, c1955, teapot 8½in (22cm) high.
$7,000-12,000

Cf. Museum Villa Stuck, Die Fünfziger, Stilkonturen eines Jahrzehnts 1984, *colour pl.14, similar set illustrated.*

An unusual white painted metal lamp, 'Rimorchiatore', designed by Gae Aulenti, with lamp, a night lamp, vase and a vide-poche, 14½in (37cm) high.
$600-1,200

A pair of upholstered lounge chair 'Djinn series', designed by Olivier Mourgue, c1965.
$1,700-3,000

A Gio Ponti table lamp, in original carton marked with manufacturer's monogram and 'Designer Gio Ponti', 17½in (45cm) high.
$600-1,200

Silver – Baskets

A George II oval cake basket, the base engraved with a central coat-of-arms within a rococo cartouche, maker Peter Archambo, London 1742, 11½in (29cm), 52oz 5dwt.
$4,500-9,000

A George III swing handle oval sweetmeat basket, maker's mark, probably that of Edward Aldridge, London 1767, 6in (15cm) long, 3.1oz. (97gm).
$400-900

A fine George III shaped oval cake basket by John Houle, London, finely engraved with coat-of-arms superscribed from 'IFF to PP', dated 1815, 15in (38cm) wide.
$18,000-26,000

A George II shaped oval cake basket, by Edward Aldridge, two shell feet later replacements, probably 1746, 14½in (36.5cm) long, 56oz.
$4,500-9,000

A shaped oval swing handle cake basket, engraved at the centre with coat-of-arms, marks worn, maker's mark J.M. Dublin, c1780, 29.9oz (930gm).
$1,700-3,000

A pair of George III oval dessert baskets, with a crest and coronet, by William Pitts and Joseph Preedy, one maker's mark overstruck with another, I.P. in an oval, with later plain liners with scalloped borders, engraved with the Lascelles crest and Garter motto, 1799, 11in (28cm) long, 119oz.
$9,000-15,000

A sugar basket, by William Garret Forbes, New York, with a bail handle and an oval footrim, the rim with bright cut engraved border, and the body with a bright cut engraved wreath, name touch struck twice on base, monogram removed, c1810, 6in (15cm) high, 8oz.
$450-700

An early George III basket weave pattern fruit or bread basket, by Parker and Wakelin, the Royal Goldsmiths, 1780, 10½in (26.5cm), 39oz.
$11,000-20,000

An important George III cake basket, belonging to Admiral Lord Nelson and reputedly used by him before the Battle of Trafalgar, by William Summers, London 1798, with accompanying letter written in 1939 by the daughter of Lady Mary Duncan in which she states the cake basket had been handed down through her family from Nicholas Duncan, one of the midshipmen of the 'Victory' in 1805.
$4,000-7,500

Exhibited at the Trafalgar Centenary Exhibition, item no. 21426. Exhibited at the Victory Exhibition, 1910.

A George III sugar basket, engraved with an initial within shield, by Abraham Peterson, 1795, 6½in (17cm) wide.
$800-1,500

A George III Irish cake basket, the centre engraved with a crest above script initials, by John Graham, no date letter otherwise fully marked, Dublin c1765, 13in (32.5cm), 38oz.
$5,000-9,000

A large Irish cake basket, centre inscription, Dublin 1801, 15in (38cm), 28oz.
$1,300-2,400

A William IV circular panelled cake basket, by Charles Fox, London 1832, 11in (28cm) diam, 27oz.
$800-1,500

A cake basket, by Dominick & Haff, New York and Newark, the serpentine pierced rim with cast applied decoration simulating wood lattice with blackberries, vines and blossoms, the handle similarly decorated, marked on base, 1903, 12in (30cm) diam, 45oz.
$1,900-2,200

A William Comyns oval cake basket, with pierced scroll and quatrefoil panels, London 1912, 14½in (37cm).
$2,000-4,500

A William IV pedestal cake basket by the Barnards, London 1836, 13in (33cm) diam, 934gm.
$800-1,500

A pair of Victorian swing handled shaped oval baskets, in 18thC style, on pierced bases, C.S. Harris, London 1900, 9½in (24cm), 23.1oz (721gm).
$800-1,500

A rare parcel-gilt campaign beaker, probably by an unidentified Pennsylvania or Maryland maker, the seamed rim silver-gilt, marked with 'DK' initial touch and an eagle pseudo-hallmark on bottom, c1800, 3in (8cm) high, 3oz 10dwt.
$650-750

The bottom is engraved with the later inscription 'Margaret Washington McClelland nee Cabell 1805'. Margaret Cabell McClelland was born on November 24, 1785 at 'Union Hall', Nelson County, Virginia, and married Thomas Stanhope McClelland in 1803. McClelland was born near Gettysburg in 1777, and moved to Virginia after 1795, when he graduated from Dickinson College in Carlisle, Pennsylvania.

A pair of Daniel Pontifex goblets, the rims engraved 'As a Token of Gratitude, John Crickitt, Marshall of the Admiralty to James Henry Arnold LLD for his disinterested Assistance as Counsel', London 1797, 6¾in (17cm), 16oz.
$1,300-2,400

Beakers

A set of 6 water goblets, by Georg Jensen, U.S.A., of tulip form, on pedestal base, monogrammed, 5½in (13cm), 42oz.
$500-600

Compotes

A dessert compote, by Ball, Black & Co., with figural stem of a Grecian maiden loosely draped with outstretched arms supporting the shallow circular bowl, flanked with a pair of winged putti at each side, monogrammed, c1865, 11in (27.5cm) high, 41oz.
$950-1,200

A Charles I style pierced compote, with a scalloped brim of foliage, scrolls, and winged cherubs' masks, the bowl with pierced sides of griffins, snails and winged cherubs' masks centering a boss chased with a wreath surrounding a shield, on a pierced fluted flaring cylindrical foot, marked 'E.F. Caldwell & Co', New York, mark engraved on foot with word 'sterling', mid/late 19thC, 11in (27.5cm) diam, 24oz.
$650-750

A pair of compotes, by Gorham Manufacturing Company, Providence, each with an everted scalloped brim repoussé and chased with flowers and scrolls, on a spreading circular foot also repoussé and chased, marked on base, c1900, 4½in (11cm) high, 38oz.
$750-850

A fruit compote, by Ball, Black & Co., the baluster pedestal on circular base, flanked with a pair of leaf and hoof supports terminating with Etruscan masks below faceted glass bowl, c1868, 14in (35cm) high, 27oz.
$1,200-1,400

Bowls

A sugar bowl and cream pitcher, by Gorham Manufacturing Company, Providence, each spherical, on 3 tall ostrich legs with talon feet; the sugar bowl with a bail handle and the bowl repoussé and chased with leaves and scrolls; the cream pitcher with a cast foliate spout and a ring handle, the bowl with engine turned and bright cut ornament, each with 2 reserves engraved with matching initials and date 'Sept. 25th 1861', each with gilt interior, marked on base, c1861, sugar bowl 6½in (16cm) high overall, 10oz 10dwt.
$600-800

A large silver-rimmed cut glass punch bowl, by Redlich, with multi-faceted glass, the everted silver rim pierced chased and repoussé with foliate clusters; together with a double lipped punch ladle, 17in (43cm) high.
$1,900-2,100

A covered sugar bowl, by Richard Humphreys, Philadelphia, of inverted pyriform, the lid with a spirally-fluted finial, on a domed circular foot repoussé and chased with a gadrooned moulding, the rim with a cast applied gadrooned moulding, one side engraved with foliate script initials 'MC', marked on base, c1785, 8in (20cm), 13oz.
$3,000-3,500

A covered sugar bowl, a waste bowl and a cream pitcher, by Joseph Anthony Jr, Philadelphia, the sugar bowl and creamer each double pyriform, with an applied gadrooned rim and a spreading circular foot with a repoussé and chased gadrooned border; the sugar bowl with a domed lid with a cast pineapple finial, and a cast gadrooned rim, on a cast moulded circular foot; each piece struck twice with script initial mark, c1785-1790, sugar bowl 6½in (16cm) high, 37oz 10dwt.
$3,000-4,000

A set of 8 George V circular fruit bowls with frosted glass liners, on spreading bases, in fitted case, with 8 spoons, Mappin and Webb, Sheffield, 1926–8, extensive damage to glass liners, bowls 4½in (11.5cm) diam, 42.9oz (1,336gm).
$1,200-2,100

Boxes

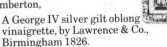

A George IV hunting scene snuff box, the cover cast and chased with 'The Kill', by John Jones III, 1824, 3½in (8.8cm).
$1,000-2,000

A George III 'goldstone' mounted vinaigrette, with a panel of 'goldstone' (aventurine glass), by John Shaw, Birmingham 1809, 2.9cm.
$200-450

A George III oblong vinaigrette, engraved with a border of oak leaves around the name 'M.G. Binnie', by Samuel Pemberton, Birmingham 1810.
$300-600

A George IV silver gilt oblong vinaigrette, by Lawrence & Co., Birmingham 1826.
$1,000-2,000

A William IV silver gilt vinaigrette, the cover engraved on a matted ground, pierced grille, by Taylor and Perry, Birmingham 1833, 2.1cm.
$180-300

An unusual George III flat oblong vinaigrette, engraved with a tiger, by Thropp & Taylor, Birmingham 1812.
$400-900

A Victorian silver gilt shaped oblong vinaigrette, engraved with foliate scrolls and flowers, by Eliezer Nash, 1853.
$500-900

A George IV vinaigrette in the form of a purse, with gilt interior and pierced scroll foliage grille, by Lawrence & Co., Birmingham 1821, 3cm.
$400-750

A George IV rectangular vinaigrette, the cover engraved with script initials, with gilt interior, by John Bettridge, Birmingham 1825, 3cm.
$180-300

A George IV rectangular vinaigrette, the cover chased with roses on a matted ground, with gilt interior, by Thomas Newbold, Birmingham 1821, 3.2cm.
$400-750

A George IV silver snuff box, London 1825, 3in (8cm) wide, 5oz.
$600-1,100

A George III silver mounted cowrie shell snuff box, the lid engraved with a crest, inscribed 'E.N. Parole Jevis' and with a leaf scroll monogram, by Phipps & Robinson, c1800, 3 by 2in (7.5 by 5cm).
$400-750

A Victorian serpentine vinaigrette with engraved decoration, by Nathanial Mills, Birmingham 1845, 1¾in.
$400-900

A Victorian oblong table snuff box with chased floral borders, engine-turned surfaces and vacant reserve, by Edward Edwards 1846, 3½in (9cm) long, 6oz.
$500-900

A Victorian silver tobacco box, Birmingham 1900, 3½in (8.5cm) high, 10oz.
$600-1,100

A George III oval nutmeg grater, by Phipps & Robinson, 1793, 5.4cm long.
$400-750

An Austrian cigarette and match case combined, with 2 hinged lids, each with a cabochon sapphire clasp, end strike, maker's mark J.R. for Scharwg and Steiner, 3½ by 2in (9 by 5cm), 3oz.
$200-450

An unusual Edwardian commemorative vesta case, the cover enamelled in green with an inscription in yellow beneath a white panel, the inscription reading 'Inauguration of the New Shortest & Quickest route from New York to London, via Fishguard, by the Great Western Railway, August 30th, 1909', the interior of the cover inscribed with facsimile signature, 'From Churchill, Xmas 1909', by Sampson Mordan & Co., 1909, 5.5 by 4.5cm.
$800-1,500

A cigar case, initialled G.K. Moscow 1879, assayer's mark AK.
$400-750

An engraved cigarette case, 1924.
$300-600

A George III oval nutmeg grater engraved with cartouche and floral swags and with chased borders, by Phipps & Robinson, London 1800, 2 by 1in (5 by 2.5cm).
$300-600

A George IV gadrooned nutmeg grater, with shell and foliate handle, engraved with a monogram, I.R. London 1825, 4in (10cm).
$800-1,500

A George IV silver gilt engine-turned rectangular toothpick box, engraved with an earl's coronet above a unicorn crest, by Mary & Charles Reily, 1827, 3½in (8.5cm).
$400-750

A Victorian litmus paper case engraved with foliate scrolls and inscribed on an oval cartouche, 'Dr. Barton', by Hilliard & Thomason, Birmingham 1889.
$300-600

A Queen Anne oval tobacco box, the cover elaborately engraved, at a slightly later date, engraved with EB monogram above the date 1736, Britannia Standard 1708 maker's mark rubbed, possibly AS, 4in (10cm).

$800-1,500

The only new standard maker's mark AS recorded is that of Thomas Ash, though an attribution to Ash seems unlikely as there is evidence that Ash was a specialist maker of candlesticks.

An Edwardian trinket box, with piquet work hinged lid, guilloche border, raised on pierced trefoil feet, 4in (10cm) wide.
$400-750

A George III rectangular toothpick box, the base with rayed prick dot decoration, by Samuel Pemberton, Birmingham 1795.
$200-450

A George III silver tobacco box, marks rubbed, 4½in (11.5cm) wide, 4oz.
$400-750

A Continental box, presumably to hold a small pack of cards, the panel signed 'Hovander', one mark only on the rim, rubbed, mid 19thC.
$400-750

A Victorian novelty box modelled as a valise with two buckled straps, by William Summers, 1875, 2in (5cm) long.
$200-450

A decorative combined purse and note pad with pencil, by Davis, Moss & Co., Birmingham 1911.
$400-900

A Dutch toilet box, with engraved decoration, the cover with English armorials, by Jesayas Engouw, The Hague, 1725, 5½ by 4½in (14 by 10.5cm), 15oz.
$1,700-3,000

A George III rectangular toothpick box with rounded ends engraved on cover with rayed prick dot decoration, the base with navette cartouche, by Samuel Pemberton, Birmingham 1796, 7.3cm long.
$400-750

An unusual Victorian silver mounted octagonal oak jewel casket, heavily carved, the domed hinged cover with two applied shield-shaped cartouches, one engraved with a coat-of-arms, two inlaid monograms, and a crest finial in the form of a whelk on seaweed base, the mounts by John S Hunt, 1856, 10in (25.5cm) high.
$2,200-4,200

The arms are those of Shelley.

A George III ivory toothpick box, with Highland scene in ivory on a blue background, behind glass panel in a gold frame, c1800.
$300-600

A George III circular patch box with bright-cut borders and monogram, by Joseph Taylor, Birmingham 1799, ¾in (2cm) diam.
$180-300

A silver and silver-gilt Freedom casket, 'City of Bristol', with enamelled City of Bristol crest, makers Walker and Hall, Sheffield 1921, approx 116oz.
$1,600-2,800

A Victorian card case chased in relief with the Scott Memorial, by Nathaniel Mills, Birmingham, date letter unclear.
$300-600

A contemporary silver three-branch candelabrum, No. 159 of a limited edition of 250, London 1977, 11in (28cm), 25oz.
$300-600

Candelabra

Four important Louis XV four-light candelabra, femier-general Hubert Louvet, maker's mark perhaps PH for Pierre Hannier, Paris, 1732, 13½in (34cm), 217oz.
$100,000-200,000

A pair of German two-light candelabra, the branches date letter 'L', the columns date letter 'G' by a different maker to the branches, Augsburg, c1820, 15½in (40cm), 51.5oz.
$1,800-3,800

A Victorian cast four-light candelabrum, by the Barnards, 1873, 25½in (65cm), 90oz.
$2,600-5,300

Two George IV three-light candelabra, the central light with flame finial, by John Watson, Sheffield, 1823, one branch 1820, one nozzle defective, 25½in (64.5cm), weight of branches 99oz.
$6,000-12,000

A pair of German five-light candelabra, by Johann Georg Christoph Neuss, Augsburg, c1830, date letter 'O', 28in (71cm), loaded, weight of branches 107.5oz.
$7,000-12,000

A pair of Victorian five-light Corinthian column candelabra, engraved with inscription dated 1886, maker's mark, 26½in (67cm) high overall, weight of branches 116oz.
$10,000-18,000

A Victorian cast six-light candelabrum centrepiece, by E & J Barnard, 1852, 27½in (70cm) high, 194oz.
$6,000-12,000

A set of 4 candlesticks and matching candelabrum, Sheffield 1898–1900, weight of branches 64oz.
$6,000-12,000

A pair of silver gilt three-light candelabra, in the style of the 1730's, by the Goldsmiths and Silversmiths Company Ltd., 1911, 33.2oz.
$3,200-6,000

Candlesticks

A pair of early George I cast candlesticks, maker Thomas Ash, London, 1714, 6½in (16.5cm), 25oz 7dwt.
$10,000-18,000

A set of 4 Queen Anne silver candlesticks, maker's mark M.E. probably Lewis Mettayer, 1711, 7½in (19cm), about 78oz.
$200,000+

A pair of George II cast table candlesticks, John Cafe, London, 1754, nozzles apparently unmarked, 9in (23cm), 36.3oz (1,131gm).
$2,600-5,300

A pair of George II cast silver candlesticks with detachable nozzles, maker John Cafe London, 1752, 8½in (22cm), 37oz.
$2,000-4,500

A pair of shell-cornered candlesticks, by Samuel Courtauld, London 1751, 9in (23cm), 44oz.
$7,000-12,000

A pair of German cast table candlesticks, maker's mark IWV, Osnabrück, c1750, 6½in (16.5cm), 12oz.
$7,000-12,000

A pair of early George III cast table candlesticks, by William Cafe, the sockets with standard marks, one nozzle only with standard mark, 1760, 8½in (22.5cm), 30oz.
$2,000-4,500

A pair of George II cast silver candlesticks, with detachable nozzles, maker William Cafe, London, 1758, 10in (25.5cm), 41½oz.
$6,000-12,000

A pair of Frederick Kandler candlesticks, the cast shaped hexafoil bases with gadroon borders, London, 1765, 10½in (26.5cm), 44oz.
$4,500-9,000

A pair of George II cast table candlesticks, with detachable nozzles, by John Preist, 1754, the nozzles unmarked, 8in (20cm), 27.3oz.
$2,600-5,300

A set of 4 early George III cast candlesticks, by William Cafe, the detachable nozzles marked with a French control mark, London, 1761, 10½in (25.5cm), 76.5oz.
$18,000-26,000

A set of 4 George III cluster-column candlesticks, engraved with crests, by Ebenezer Coker, 1766, 12in (30.5cm).
$7,000-12,000

A matched pair of early George III cast table candlesticks, 1762 maker's mark DM over a star and 1763 by Ebenezer Coker, the sockets with standard marks and the nozzles unmarked, 10½in (26cm), 42oz.
$3,200-6,000

A rare pair of candlesticks, by William B. Heyer, New York, each baluster form, with an urn-shaped candlecup with a square bobeche, on a domed square foot, the bobeche and foot with gadrooned borders, the foot engraved in script 'RMW', each filled and both on a wood base, marked on bobeche, c1810, 8in (20cm), 19oz gross, excluding wood bases.
$7,000-10,000

Provenance: Richard and Maria (Roosevelt) Varick, married 1789.

A pair of George III coffee house candlesticks, each engraved New Hummums Coffee House, with detachable nozzles engraved with a crest, 1765 by Ebenezer Coker, one candlestick with maker's mark only, 11½in (28.6cm), 29oz.
$2,600-5,300

Tavern Anecdotes, *a work published c1825, mentions two houses so named, The Old and The New, both situated in Covent Garden 'affording excellent accommodation to gentlemen and families and where there are commodious hot and cold baths'. Hummums being a corruption of Hammum, the Arabic term for bath or bagnio.*

A matched pair of George II cast table candlesticks, with detachable conforming nozzles, 1758 by William Gould and 1760 maker's mark indistinct, perhaps that of John Cafe, the sockets with standard marks and the nozzles unmarked, 9in (22.5cm), 34oz.
$2,000-4,500

A pair of early George III cast candlesticks, with detachable nozzles, the bases engraved with a contemporary coat-of-arms, Ebenezer Coker, London 1766, 10in (25cm), 38.5oz. **$9,000-15,000**

A pair of Regency chamber candlesticks, by William Burwash, marked on bases and extinguishers, London 1818, 6in (15cm) long, 27oz. **$4,000-7,500**

A Victorian silver gilt cast Harlequin taperstick, by S Crespell, 1838, 7in (17.5cm), 10oz. **$1,200-2,100**

A pair of George III table candlesticks, by John Green & Co., Sheffield 1804, 13in (32cm), loaded bases, scratch weight 30oz 16dwt. **$3,200-6,000**

A matched set of 5 George IV and William IV rococo style candlesticks, maker John Watson, Sheffield 1824, 1827 and 1836, and a matched plated three-branch candelabrum insert with snuffer, 17½in (45cm) wide overall. **$3,200-6,000**

An early Victorian chamber candlestick, by Charles T and George Fox, crested, London 1842, 7in (18cm), 10.5oz. **$1,800-3,800**

A pair of George III table candlesticks, John Rowbotham & Co., Sheffield 1814, 7in (18cm), loaded. **$1,400-2,600**

A pair of Victorian embossed table candlesticks, on square bases, Sheffield 1844, 9½in (24cm). **$1,400-2,600**

A set of 4 Portuguese cast candlesticks, maker's mark FIF or PIF, Lisbon, c1830, 18in (46cm) high, 239.25oz. **$7,000-12,000**

A pair of William IV circular table candlesticks, Mathew Boulton, Birmingham 1830, 9in (23cm) high, loaded. **1,400-2,600**

A set of 4 late Victorian cast table candlesticks, in the style of the mid-18thC, by W Gibson and J Langman of The Goldsmiths and Silversmiths Company Ltd., 1896, 11in (27cm), 95oz. **$9,000-15,000**

A pair of Victorian Corinthian column candlesticks, by Heath & Middleton, 1898, 16½in (42cm). **$2,600-5,300**

A set of 4 William IV candlesticks, makers T J and N Creswick, Sheffield 1832, 11in (28cm) loaded.
$2,600-5,300

A pair of late Victorian candlesticks, maker's mark HW, Sheffield 1899, 8½in (21.5cm), loaded.
$800-1,500

A pair of George V table candlesticks in 18thC style, Mappin & Webb, Sheffield 1908, 9in (23cm), loaded.
$900-1,700

A pair of George V table candlesticks in 18thC style, J. Round and Son, Sheffield 1919, 11in (28cm), loaded.
$900-1,700

A pair of late Victorian table candlesticks, with a pair of plated three-light candelabra branches en suite, maker's mark J & T, Sheffield 1894, 18in (46cm), loaded.
$1,200-2,100

Casters

A caster, by Stephen Emery, Boston, of baluster form, the domed cover with an urn-turned finial above 6 pierced and engraved panels, the body with a bead-moulded midband above engraved initials 'DIS', marked 'SE', on base, the interior bearing unidentified touchmark 'IB', lid torn, c1780, 5½in (13cm) high, 3oz.
$600-900

A Warwick cruet, comprising 3 shakers and 2 full height faceted clear glass bottles with caps, with a matched stand with central carrying handle and 4 scrolled legs with scallop shell feet, bottles probably by Mordecai Fox, 1754, stand probably by Samuel Wood, 1759, 8½in (21cm), 40oz.
$3,200-6,000

A fine and rare caster, by Simeon Soumaine, New York, the domed lid pierced and engraved, with a knop finial and moulded rim fitted with bayonet mounts, above the baluster-shaped body with a moulded midrib, on a moulded circular foot, the base engraved with initial 'W', now almost completely erased, struck with maker's mark on side, 1730-50, 7in (17cm) high, 8oz.
$28,000-30,000

Centrepieces

A George III centrepiece, pierced and shaped with leaf, floral and fruit decoration, comprising central four-footed stand with shaped oval basket surrounded by 4 similar smaller baskets on detachable scroll supports, William Pitts, London 1764, 10½in (26.5cm) high, 17in (43cm) wide, 81oz.
$9,000-15,000

A table centrepiece, the base with lion mask and claw corners, cut glass bowl on a contemporary old Sheffield plate mirrored plateau base, Sheffield 1818.
$5,000-9,000

A Victorian oval-shaped centrepiece, in the Egyptian taste, by Elkington & Co., Birmingham 1884, 11½in (29cm) high overall, 122oz net, together with a similarly bordered Victorian oval shaped mirror plateau, by Elkington & Co., Birmingham 1889, 21½in (54cm) wide.
$600-1,200

Provenance: Charles Littlewood Hill Collection.

Coffee Pots

A pair of Victorian comports, by Smith & Nicholson, one glass liner missing, 1864, 12in (30.5cm) weighable silver 74.5oz.
$1,800-3,800

A fine silver coffee pot, by Christian Wiltberger, Philadelphia, the domed hinged lid with a spirally fluted finial and a gadrooned rim, the acanthus-carved wood handle attached by applied scrolled joins, the S-shaped spout case with foliage and a ruffled cartouche, the foot flaring cylindrical, with a repoussé and chased gadrooned border, repaired crack to wood handle, name touch struck twice on base, one mark double-struck, c1785-90, 14in (35cm) , 51oz gross weight.
$18,000-25,000

An Edwardian epergne, London 1907, 13in (33cm), 46oz gross, weighted.
$400-750

◁ A George I coffee pot and stand, by John East, 1714, 10in (25cm), 33oz gross.
$52,000-87,000

A George II baluster silver coffee pot.
$1,600-2,800

A Queen Anne coffee pot, engraved with a baroque cartouche enclosing a later coat-of-arms, by Edward Yorke, 1711, 9in (23cm), 20oz gross.
$5,000-9,000

The arms are those of Forbes.

▷ A George II coffee pot and cover, engraved with an armorial shield, by Peter Archambo, London 1732, 838gm gross.
$2,600-5,300

A George II pear shaped coffee pot, with stepped cover, by Jas. Morrison, London 1746, 22oz.
$2,600-5,300

A George I coffee pot, by Simon Pantin, 1714, 10½in (26cm), 29oz.
$8000-13,500

A George II chocolate pot, maker's mark IB coronet above, probably a variation of John Burdon's mark, Exeter, 1736, 10in (25cm), 28oz gross.
$7,000-12,000

A George II coffee pot, with a contemporary engraved crest within a baroque cartouche, maker Edward Feline, London 1740, 9in (23cm), 26oz 10dwt.
$2,600-5,300

A George II coffee pot, engraved with a crest, by John Cafe, c1750, 9in (23cm), 25oz gross.
$3,200-6,000

A George V coffee pot, Birmingham 1922, 847gm gross.
$500-900

A French baluster shaped chocolate pot, Paris, c1776, 20½oz.
$1,800-3,800
◁

A George II pear-shaped coffee pot, engraved with a coat-of-arms and crest within chased rococo cartouches, by Isaac Cookson, Newcastle 1748, 9in (23cm), 26oz gross.
$3,200-6,000

A George II coffee pot, chased in the contemporary rocaille manner, by John Swift, 1748, 10in (25cm), 30oz.
$5,000-9,000

A George III baluster coffee pot by Hester Bateman, London 1781, 12½in (32cm), 857gm gross.
$4,000-7,500
◁

A George IV coffee jug, by William Eaton, London 1824, 30oz.
$900-1,700
◁

An early George III Irish coffee pot, with embossed ornament of later date, fruitwood handle, repair to body, Dublin hallmarks indistinct, 12in (30.5cm), 37oz.
$1,300-2,400

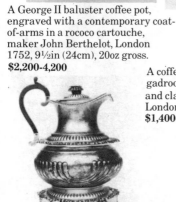

A George II baluster coffee pot, engraved with a contemporary coat-of-arms in a rococo cartouche, maker John Berthelot, London 1752, 9½in (24cm), 20oz gross.
$2,200-4,200

An Empire coffee pot, by Thomas-Michel Bary, Paris, 1798–1809, 8½in (21.5cm), 15oz gross.
$3,200-6,000
▷

A coffee biggin, part fluted, shaped gadroon edge, crested, on heavy leaf and claw feet, Joseph Angell, London 1815, 41oz.
$1,400-2,600

A Victorian baluster coffee pot, by C & G Fox, London 1847, 9½in (24cm), 31.1oz (968gm).
$900-1,700

A George V baluster coffee pot with matching hot water jug, in Queen Anne style, London 1910–14, 8in (21cm), 43.1oz (1,341gm) gross.
$800-1,500

Cups

A pair of footed cups, by John Sayre, New York, each with an engraved rim, above a foliate script monogram 'JEB' within a wreath, on a flaring cylindrical stem, on a circular foot, with gilt interior, one with splits and tears to rim, marked on foot, c1800, 6in (15cm) high, 10oz.
$1,500-2,500

A New York Yacht Club Trophy by Tiffany & Co., New York, with 2 open scroll handles, on a domed circular foot, the surface repoussé and chased with ocean waves, seaweed and 2 stylised dolphins, the front with cast aplied mermaid blowing a seashell trumpet, the rim with an etched stylised inscription 'Won by Sasca Autumn Sweepstakes New York Yacht Club Sept 15th, 1892 2nd Prize', the interior gilt and the rim with cast applied seaweed, small dents to rim, marked bottom, 1892, 15in (37.5cm) high overall, 82oz.
$8,000-9,000

A George III cup and cover, by William Holmes, 1789, 12½in (32cm), 32oz.
$1,000-2,000

A George III trophy cup and cover, raised on a circular foot, slightly damaged cover with canopic finial, maker John Emes, London 1803, 1,873gm.
$1,000-2,000

A French two-handled chocolate cup, cover and trembleuse stand, maker Francois Joubert, Paris 1772 hallmarks, also later Paris hallmark for 950 quality silver, 13oz.
$1,000-2,000

A William IV campana shape cup and cover, by E, E J and W Barnard, with Jack Tar finial with rope and anchor, cast leaf border, London 1834, 13in (33cm), 40oz.
$1,400-2,600

▷

◁ A matching pair of Victorian parcel gilt covered cups in the Gothic style, by D & C Hands, one 1862, the other 1860, with cover 1874, 10½in (27cm), 36oz.
$1,200-2,100

A French silver cup of inverted bell shape, maker's mark I.B., early 19thC.
$80-180

A Victorian floral embossed and chased two-handled Theseus cup, Sheffield 1898, 35oz.
$5,000-9,000

A lidded trophy cup, inscribed 'The Gift of Mrs. Cordeux In Memory of Lt. E.H.N. Cordeux Killed In Action at The Bluff, Ypres. September 1915', maker John Marshall for Messrs. Spink, London 1911, 1,033gm.
$600-1,100

An M.T.E. Rosyth Adam design two-handled boxing trophy and cover, Birmingham 1920, 13½oz.
$150-300

A Charles Boyton regatta trophy and cover, London, 1937, 7oz.
$80-180

A Victorian yachting trophy, with a presentation inscription, by Stephen Smith, 1867, 16in (41cm), 77oz.
$2,000-4,500

The inscription relates to the 'Royal Cornwall Yacht Club'.

Cutlery

cl). A William III Provincial ascribed Norwich trefid, the back of the cleft terminal pricked SS/SA/1703 with below later initials B.B., by Elizabeth Haselwood, Norwich, 1697, 8in (20cm).
$1,000-2,000

l). A rare William III Provincial ascribed Hull trefid, part lace back, cut with the initials AH, punched twice with the Hull mark (the treble crowns) and the maker's mark TH three pellets above and one below for Thomas Hebden, c1690.
$600-1,100

cr). A Charles II Provincial unascribed trefid, struck with 3 marks, a leopard's head, the second indistinguishable, and a third resembling a figure, c1680, 8in (20cm).
$300-600
There are various attributions to the leopard's head, outside London. Ellis, p69 suggests possibly Great Yarmouth(?), Jackson, pp.446–447 illustrates and states Shrewsbury.

r. A Charles II Provincial ascribed Plymouth (Exeter) trefid, the back of the pronounced cleft terminal pricked FY/P/TE/1687, punched twice with the Exeter crowned 'X', the third overstamped with script R for Row of Plymouth, 8½in (21cm).
$400-750

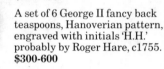

A William III trefid, the back of the cleft terminal prick-dotted 1709/LS, maker's mark NG in a heart-shaped shield, possibly for Nathaniel Greene(?), 1695, 8in (20.5cm).
$400-750

A set of 6 George II fancy back teaspoons, Hanoverian pattern, engraved with initials 'H.H.' probably by Roger Hare, c1755.
$300-600

A George III cheese scoop, the blade crested, with green stained ivory handle, maker's mark obliterated, 1790.
$500-900

A rare George II Irish soup ladle, engraved with a crest, initial and Baron's coronet, date letter and maker's mark lacking, Dublin, c1745, 15in (38cm), 12oz 19dwt, on fitted wooden stand.
$1,800-3,800

A pair of George III Irish table spoons, now converted to berry spoons and a sifter spoon, of Celtic taper pattern, by John Nicolson, Cork c1790, 182gm total, cased.
$400-750

A large part service of George III Old English and Thread pattern cutlery, comprising: 20 table forks, 12 table spoons, 12 dessert forks, 12 dessert spoons, 13 teaspoons, a gravy spoon, a salad fork and an Old English pattern gravy spoon, 1784, 1790 and 1795 by Richard Crossley, except the table forks and salad fork, 1776, 1777 and 1781 by William Sumner I and Richard Crossley, the teaspoons 1804 by George Creak and the gravy spoon 1767 by Paul Crespin, 139oz.
$600-1,200

A set of Regency Coburg pattern cutlery, comprising: 6 table spoons, 12 table forks, 12 dessert spoons and a pair of sauce ladles, makers William Eley and William Fearn, London 1819, 88oz, and a set of 12 steel blade dinner knives, maker George W. Adams, London 1864.
$1,800-3,800

A composite table service, Georgian and Victorian, mostly Irish, various dates and makers, comprising: 28 table spoons, 74 table forks, 30 dessert spoons, 15 dessert forks, 29 teaspoons, 6 egg spoons, 4 sugar shovels, a pair of sugar tongs, a sauce ladle, a soup ladle, 4 basting spoons, a strainer spoon, 34 table knives with steel blades, 12 fruit knives with silver blades, 352oz.
$7,000-12,000

A Victorian silver gilt travelling canteen of cutlery, W.W. & F.D., London 1867.
$1,000-2,000

A Queens pattern table service, comprising: 42 table spoons, 48 table forks, 36 dessert spoons, 24 dessert forks, 14 teaspoons, 4 sauce ladles, a soup ladle, 3 condiment spoons, 2 sifting spoons, a pickle fork, a butter knife and a fish slice and fork, c1830, 445oz.
$10,000-18,000

◁ A Victorian silver gilt Christening set, the terminals cast with a Russian double eagle displaying the Moscow Imperial arms, the spoon by George Adams, 1845, the fork and knife by Nikols Karland Plinke, St. Petersburg, 1847, 5.25oz weighable silver.
$400-900

A William IV King's pattern doll's knife with silver blade, Birmingham 1835, 4in (10cm), and a matching three-pronged fork, 4in (9.5cm), unmarked.
$80-180

A set of 6 pairs of Russian silver gilt and niello fruit knives and forks, by Antip Kusmitshev, Moscow, 1886, 26oz gross.
$1,600-2,800

A gilt Bacchanalian pattern dessert service, comprising: 18 dessert forks, 18 dessert knives, 18 dessert spoons, 6 serving spoons, a pair of grape scissors, a pair of sifter spoons, a serving knife and fork, London 1888.
$10,000-18,000

A 12 piece setting of Victorian cutlery, consisting of 12 table forks, 12 table spoons, 12 dessert forks, 6 dessert spoons, London 1850, 6 dessert spoons, London 1874, maker George Angell, engraved with lion rampant crest, 117oz.
$4,500-9,000

A French Christening set, comprising: a beaker, an egg cup, a napkin ring, a rattle with whistle, a table knife, fork and spoon, and an egg spoon, French post 1838 guarantee and purity 950/1000 marks for large items, and with maker's mark of Veyrat of Paris, 8.8oz weighable silver.
$800-1,500
◁

A Victorian 3 piece Christening set, George Adams, London 1859–61, 4.6oz (144gm.) gross.
$300-600

A set of 6 Victorian cast salt spoons, silver gilt, by Francis Higgins 1880, 4½in (10.5cm).
$400-750

A 235-piece Olympian pattern flatware service, by Tiffany & Co., New York, comprising 24 lunch knives; 18 each of soup spoons, bouillon spoons, fish knives with sterling blades, salad forks and fruit knives; 17 butter knives with sterling blades; 12 each of dinner forks, dinner knives, teaspoons, orange spoons, oyster forks, ice teaspoons, and coffee spoons; 11 lunch forks; 4 carving pieces, (one large and one small pair); 2 salad servers, (a fork and a spoon); 1 serving fork; 1 serving spoon; 1 cake slice, with various monograms, variously dated 1878-1907, 280oz 10dwt excluding knives.
$12,000-15,000

A tablespoon, by Simeon Soumaine, New York, the oval bowl with a rat-tail, the upturned handle with a midrib, engraved on back with initials 'M*C', marked, 1730-50, 8in (20cm) long, 1oz 10dwt.
$500-600

A chrysanthemum pattern ladle, by Tiffany & Co., New York, with a scalloped and spirally fluted bowl and a chrysanthemum handle engraved on the front with script initials and the date '1890' on the reverse, 12in (30cm) long, 11oz.
$1,000-1,200

A group of Tiffany flatware, comprising: A kidney-shaped strawberry spoon; a tomato vine pattern ice cream server; a set of 8 eggplant vine pattern dessert spoons; small slice Richelieu pattern; and a Gorham kidney-shaped pierced holly pattern spoon, monogrammed, 16oz.
$900-1,100

A set of 7 souvenir spoons, comprising an Iroquois spoon with Indian mask, the reverse depicting Niagara Falls; cat-o'-nine tails, S. Dakota; crouching Indian, La Grande, Ore; Masonic Temple, Chicago; standing Indian, Kansas City; 'On Prospect', Colorado; California state spoon, 5.5oz.
$250-300

A 132-piece Richelieu pattern flatware service, by Tiffany & Co., New York, comprising 12 each of dinner forks, dinner knives, lunch forks, lunch knives, butter knives with sterling blades, fish forks, fish knives with sterling blades, seafood forks, teaspoons, tablespoons and dessert spoons, with an engraved script monogram, each marked, 9 pieces of later date and with no monogram, 1892-1902, 135oz 10dwt excluding knives, in a fitted mahogany case with brass hardware.
$8,000-9,000

HOW TO USE MILLER'S

Unless otherwise stated, any description which refers to 'a set' or 'a pair' includes a valuation for the entire set or the pair, even though the illustration may show only a single item.

A canteen of cutlery, the mahogany box fitted with 2 trays containing various Old English pattern flatware including: 6 soup spoons, 7 table spoons, one soup ladle, 2 sauce ladles, sugar tongs, 12 table knives, 9 dessert knives, carving set, 12 teaspoons, 12 dessert forks, 12 table forks, 103oz approx.
$1,700-3,000

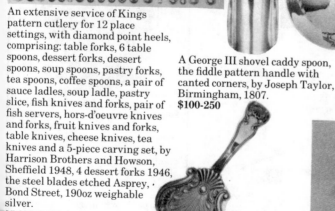

An extensive service of Kings pattern cutlery for 12 place settings, with diamond point heels, comprising: table forks, 6 table spoons, dessert forks, dessert spoons, soup spoons, pastry forks, tea spoons, coffee spoons, a pair of sauce ladles, soup ladle, pastry slice, fish knives and forks, pair of fish servers, hors-d'oeuvre knives and forks, fruit knives and forks, table knives, cheese knives, tea knives and a 5-piece carving set, by Harrison Brothers and Howson, Sheffield 1948, 4 dessert forks 1946, the steel blades etched Asprey, Bond Street, 190oz weighable silver.
$5,000-9,000

A George IV caddy spoon, by Joseph Taylor, Birmingham, 1826.
$200-450

A service of Hanoverian pattern cutlery for 12 place settings, comprising: 12 table forks, 6 table spoons, 12 dessert forks, 12 dessert spoons, 12 soup spoons, 12 tea spoons, 12 coffee spoons, a pair of sauce ladles, 12 pairs of fish knives and forks, a pair of fish servers, and the following with stainless steel blades, 12 table knives, 12 cheese knives and a 5-piece carving set, all contained in a floor standing bow front mahogany veneered canteen, with trade label of Harrods Ltd., Knightsbridge, SW., maker's mark G & H, Sheffield 1960-63, 169oz excluding steel-mounted items.
$7,000-12,000

◁A Victorian Adelaide pattern table service, mostly by George Adams, comprising: 23 table forks, 12 table spoons, 22 dessert forks, 24 dessert spoons, 18 teaspoons, 4 sauce ladles, a pair of basting spoons, 2 meat skewers, 7 condiment spoons, a soup ladle, a sifting spoon, a butter knife and a pair of sugar tongs, 1858, 273oz.
$18,000-26,000

A George III shovel caddy spoon, the fiddle pattern handle with canted corners, by Joseph Taylor, Birmingham, 1807.
$100-250

Four various foreign silver caddy spoons.
$400-750

Spoons – Caddy

A George III feather edge caddy spoon, with scalloped bowl, maker's mark T(?), c1770.
$100-250

A George III caddy spoon, with scalloped bowl and short handle engraved with petal motifs, no maker's mark, 1791.
$100-250

A Continental caddy spoon, with ribbed back to oval bowl and with bifurcated volute handle, engraved with owl crest, possibly Italian, late 18th or early 19thC.
$100-250

A good George III caddy spoon, the stem and oval bowl engraved with Greek key decoration, the centre of the bowl pierced with an oval filigree panel, by Samuel Pemberton, Birmingham, 1807.
$200-450

l). A George III leaf caddy spoon, the bowl chased with veins, and with coiled tendril handle, King's head and sterling lion marks only, c1810.
$200-450

c). A George IV fiddle pattern caddy spoon with oval bowl engraved with acorns, by William Traies, 1825.
$150-300

r). A Victorian Irish fiddle pattern caddy spoon, with scalloped bowl, maker's mark J.S., Dublin, 1884.
$150-300

An American parcel gilt fancy spoon, by Tiffany & Co., c1890, 4½in (12cm).
$150-300

Dishes

A rare George I Plymouth tazza by Pentecost Symonds, with an elaborate contemporary coat-of-arms, either Nanphant, Cornwall or Penpons, Treswithian, Cornwall, raised on a plain trumpet foot, fully marked to top and foot, Exeter 1721, 8in (20cm) diam, 10oz.
$1,700-3,000

A Victorian covered dish, by J. Mortimer & S. Hunt, 1840, 8in (20cm) high, 69oz.
$2,600-5,300

A fine set of 12 George II plates by Edward Feline, engraved contemporary coat-of-arms, within gadroon borders, London 1747, 9½in (24cm) diam, 227oz.
$22,000-40,000

Four George II circular strawberry dishes, engraved with a coat-of-arms in a rococo cartouche, three by Charles F. Kandler, 1747, one by S. Herbert & Co., 1753, 10in (25.5cm), 81oz.
$28,000-48,000

A set of 12 butter plates, by Heer-Schofield Company, Baltimore, each with a hammer-faceted surface, the brim engraved with a stylised monogram within an oval reserve, marked on back, 1905-1928, 6in (15cm) diam, 48oz.
$600-800

A set of 6 Timothy Renou dinner plates, with engraved leaf of Arms and motto, London 1800, 9½in (24cm), 114oz.
$3,200-6,000

A set of George III style plates, American, each with a five-lobed brim with an applied gadrooned moulding, the brim engraved with a crest and motto, marked 'Sterling' on reverse, 20thC, 11in (27cm) diam, 228oz 10dwt.
$5,000-6,000

A pair of George III oval meat dishes, with armorial bearings, possibly Thomas Heming, London 1763, 12in (30.5cm), 38oz.
$1,400-2,600

A pair of Victorian shaped circular entree dishes and covers and matching serving dish and cover, London 1895, 5,750gm weighable silver.
$4,500-9,000

A set of 4 graduated circular silver trays or waiters, maker's mark C.B. & S., Sheffield 1925–6, 88.75oz.
$1,400-2,600

A George V shaped oval dish with matching smaller dish, Birmingham 1913, 14in (36cm) and 10in (26cm) long, 56.3oz (1,754gm).
$1,700-3,000

A pair of Edward VII rococo style oval fruit dishes, with presentation inscription dated 1908, Birmingham 1906, 12in (30.5cm) wide, 31oz.
$600-1,200

◁

A set of 4 William IV butter shells, on cast whelk feet, by Richard Sibley, London 1831.
$4,500-9,000

Inkstands

A George IV rectangular inkstand, fitted central taperstick and snuffer, and two cut glass ink bottles, maker Matthew Boulton, Birmingham 1826, 11in (28cm) wide, 33oz 10dwt weighable silver.
$2,600-5,300

A large George IV inkstand with ▷ three cut glass cubic fittings, with silver covers, the centre with fitted taperstick and snuffer, engraved with crest and inscribed 'Presented by my friend Thomas Roberts Esqr, Novr 1 1823', by William Elliott, 1821, 13in (33cm) wide, 60oz weighable silver.
$5,000-9,000

A rectangular late Victorian double inkstand, by W J Barnard, London 1894, 11in (28cm), 25oz.
$1,000-2,000

A George III oval inkstand with French gadroon mounts to the rim, on 4 reeded panel feet, with oval lidded box at centre, by John Emes, London 1804, 9 by 4in (23 by 10cm) with cut glass and silver mounted pounce pot and a later inkwell for same, 10oz weighable silver.
$800-1,500

An early Victorian portrait bust inkstand on plinth of The Duke of Wellington, by Charles T. & George Fox, interior with a glass liner and pierced cover, London 1846, 8in (20.5cm), loaded.
$2,000-4,500

A ewer and matching salver, by Jones, Ball & Co., Boston, the ewer on spreading circular foot, the rims with beaded borders, the surface repoussé and chased with oak leaves and acorns, enclosing an engraved inscription 'M.W.S. Sept. 29 1858', marked on base, 15in (37.5cm) high; the salver on 3 beaded scroll feet, the moulded rim with a beaded border, the border engraved with foliage and scrolls, enclosing a matching engraved inscription, with matching mark on base, 1852-58, 11in (27.5cm) diam, 56oz 10dwt.
$1,400-1,600

A Masonic covered pitcher, by Wood and Hughes, New York, retailed by Hyde and Goodrich, New Orleans, Louisiana, of baluster form, with a curved spout and a domed hinged lid with a foliate finial, and an S-shaped handle with a mask terminus, the body repoussé and chased with Grecian figures bearing libations centering an engraved eye above the inscription 'Presented by the Members of Hope Lodge No.14 to William G. Latham', marked on bottom, c1860-1866, 7in (17.5cm) high, 12oz.
$1,100-1,300

A cream pitcher, by Josiah Austin, Charlestown or Boston, Massachusetts, with a moulded rim, the curved spout with an applied drop, the spout S-scrolled, on 3 scroll legs with trifid feet, the body engraved with a contemporary crest surrounded by a later engraved presentation inscription dated 1845, marked 'I. Austin' on base, c1745-65, 3½in (8cm) high, 3oz.
$1,000-1,500

The inscription reads 'Presented to Thomas Hitchcock in remembrance of his great great Grandfather William Abrams who died Spt. 27 1845 Aged 101 years 8 mos. 11 days'.

A cream pitcher, by Samuel Tingley, New York, with a scalloped rim, and a spurred double scroll handle, on 3 scroll legs with fluted shell knees and stepped hoof feet, base engraved with block initials 'IMS', initial mark, Belden touch c, struck twice on base, c1765, 4in (10cm) high, 3oz 10dwt.
$3,500-4,500

A water pitcher, by Baldwin Gardiner, New York, with a scroll handle and foliate handle joins, a circular footrim, and beaded borders on rim, shoulder and foot, marked on base, 1827-35, 10in (25cm) high, 32oz 10dwt.
$1,300-1,500

A cream pitcher, by Samuel Bartlett, Concord or Cambridge, Massachusetts, with a scalloped edge, and a scrolled handle, on 3 scroll legs with trifid feet, the body engraved with block letter initials 'WBN', marked 'SB' in script on base, c1775, 4in (10cm) high, 3oz.
$1,800-2,000

A cream pitcher, by Joseph Richardson, Jr., Philadelphia, with a spurred strap handle and a flaring cylindrical stem over a square foot, the body partly reeded, the rim and foot with beaded borders, one side engraved with script initials 'JMS', the other engraved with a later coat-of-arms and motto, initial mark struck twice on base, c1785-1810, 7in (17cm) high, 5oz 10dwt.
$1,200-1,400

A Victorian foliate pierced gadrooned oblong gallery inkstand on scroll feet, E & J Barnard, London 1853, 28.75oz, free.
$1,800-3,800

An early George III pear shaped silver cream jug, with scroll handle and foot, by James Waters, London 1763.
$200-450

A George III claret or hot water jug, engraved with a shield of arms, and on the other side script initials below a crest, by Henry Chawner, 1791, 12½in (31cm), 23oz gross.
$2,600-5,300

Jugs

 A rare George I sparrow beak cream jug, engraved with a crest, maker's mark G(?), 1727, 8cm, 2.5oz.
$800-1,500

A William IV fluted inverted pear shaped claret jug with domed hinged cover, with presentation inscription, Messrs. Barnard, London 1836, 12in (30.5cm), 29.25oz.
$1,300-2,400

A George II sparrow beak cream jug, engraved with armorials, the underbase with the contemporary inscription, 'Mrs Elizth Edwards at Ye King & Queen', by Benjamin Sanders, 1737, 3½in (9cm), 3oz.
$1,000-2,000

A George IV claret jug, maker's mark rubbed, but probably that of Joseph Angell, 1829, 11½in (29cm), 31oz.
$3,200-6,000

An unusual Victorian cream jug formed as a nanny goat, with hinged cover, gilt lined, Joseph and John Angell, London 1840, 5in (12.5cm), 8.25oz.
$4,000-7,500

A Victorian glass claret jug, the tapering body etched on oval panel of monkeys imbibing, with a bead drape border, maker W.E., London 1873, 12in (30.5cm).
$2,000-4,500

An American jug, chased with water lilies, made by the Moore Company for Tiffany & Co., c1853, 9½in (24cm), 27.25oz.
$3,200-6,000

Marks as page 247, No.5, Tiffany Silver by C.H. & M.G. Carpenter.

Models

A French silver gilt statuette of an angel, loop on back for attachment, hands possibly replaced, reddish marble base, 15thC, 8.3cm.
$3,200-6,000

A statuette of a knight, with shield and sword, ivory carved head, his belt set with semi-precious stones, import marked, 14in (35.5cm) high.
$2,600-5,300

A French silver gilt statuette of Napoleon, standing in uniform with his right hand tucked inside his coat, 19thC, 12in (30.5cm).
$1,400-2,600

A Continental model of a coach and horses, the coach with detachable cover, import mark for London 1902, 11in (28cm) long, 11.7oz (365gm).
$1,000-2,000

A pair of silver pheasants, 1970, about 23oz, and a pair of chicks, about 5oz.
$900-1,700

A silver gilt statuette of an angel holding a reliquary, in the Gothic manner, the wings separately attached, standing on an octagonal base, 19in (48cm) high.
$4,000-6,800

Mugs

An early Victorian silver goblet, presentation inscription dated 1866, maker's mark I.H. and R.R. surmounted by a crown, Hunt & Roskell, London 1865, 8oz 15dwt.
$800-1,500

A George II silver half pint mug, with engraved armorial, maker possibly Thomas Whipham, London 1744, 5in (12cm), 12oz.
$600-1,200

An early George II mug, the tapering body engraved with script initials below the everted moulded rim and on a tuck-in base, with a spreading foot rim, scroll handle, the underside engraved with initials, by Francis Spilsbury I, 1735, 4½in (11cm).
$1,000-2,000

A George II silver mug, the scroll handle with initials I.H., maker John Langlands, Newcastle 1756, 5in (12.5cm), 9½oz.
$800-1,500

◁

A George II mug, by Richard Bayley, London 1747, 4in (10cm), 7oz.
$500-900

A large Chinese Export mug, by Hung Chong of Canton & Shanghai, c1880, 5½in (14cm), 13.5oz.
$1,000-2,000

Salts

A set of 4 George III plain circular salt cellars, by Paul Storr, 1798, 3in (8cm), 15oz 5dwt.
$2,600-5,300

The crest and coronet are those of the Dukes of Bedford.

A pair of George II circular silver salt cellars, each with 3 feet, maker's mark I.M., London 1757.
$300-600

A set of 4 George III silver two-handled boat shaped salts, on rectangular bases, maker's mark J.W. (John Wren), London 1791, one 1790, 14oz 12dwt.
$800-1,500

A pair of William IV circular fluted salts, crested, maker William Eaton, London 1837, 4in (10cm) diam, 12oz.
$800-1,500

A William IV circular mustard pot, with blue glass liner, by Charles Fox, London 1837, 9oz, and a cast salt spoon, London 1831.
$900-1,700

A pair of George I plain circular salvers, each on central spreading foot, with moulded borders, engraved with a coat-of-arms in a baroque cartouche, by Robert Timbrell and Joseph Bell I, 1714, 10in (25cm) diam, 33oz.
$12,000-21,000

The arms are those of Winston impaling another.

A fine and heavy pair of French salt cellars, the well chased and gilded shell bowls supported on two fighting dragons, by Lebrun, Paris, c1860.
$3,200-6,000

A Victorian H.M. silver matching set of 6 open salt cellars and spoons in fitted case, maker Richard Sibley, London 1868.
$300-600

A George II waiter, monogrammed, maker probably William Justus, London 1752, 6in (15cm) diam, 6½oz.
$400-750

Salvers

A George II circular salver, initialled to reverse, maker Francis Pages, London 1736, 9in (23cm) diam, 15oz.
$1,000-2,000

A pair of George III salvers, David Whyte and William Holmes, London 1762, 8in (20cm) diam, 24.6oz.
$1,700-3,000

A George I rare silver gilt fifteen-sided salver, on 3 cast pad feet, with moulded border, engraved with a coat-of-arms in a baroque cartouche, by Augustin Courtauld, 1723, 11in (28cm), 35oz.
$50,000-100,000

The arms are those of Willmot of Stodham, Co. Oxford, impaling Mann.

An early George III salver, by John Crouch, 1772, 12in (30.5cm), 30oz.
$1,400-2,600

Twelve George III shaped circular dinner plates, by Paul De Lamerie, 1741, 9½in (24cm) diam, 233oz.
$60,000-100,000

A fine pair of George II salvers, London 1730, 5½in (14.5cm), 443gm gross, and a fine pair of George II salvers, London 1735 and 1736, 6½in (17cm), 567gm gross.
$1,000-2,000

A George II plain octafoil salver, by John Robinson II, 1738, 13½in (34cm) diam, 30oz.
$4,500-9,000

A large Ebenezer Coker waiter, on well cast shell feet, engraved full coat-of-arms in floral cartouche, London 1772, 14in (35.5cm).
$3,200-6,000

A George III salver, on 4 claw and ball feet, by Richard Rugg, 1775, 14in (35.5cm) diam, 42oz.
$2,000-4,500

A small salver, by Gorham Manufacturing Company, Providence, with moulded rim with applied Greek key border, the centre engraved with a grapevine surrounding a stylized monogram, on 3 scroll feet, moulded on back, also with retailer's mark, c1865, 8in (20cm) diam, 11oz.
$250-300

A George III salver, on 4 ball and claw supports, the underside engraved with triad initials, by John Crouch, 1774, 13½in (34.5cm), 42oz.
$1,600-2,800

While there is no record of Crouch's mark alone, only in partnership with Thomas Hannam, it is known he worked alone between 1774 and 1784.

A George III salver, on 4 tapering cast panel feet, by William Fountain and Daniel Pontifax, London 1793, 13in (33cm) diam, 34oz.
$1,400-2,600

A small salver, by Marquand & Co., New York, with moulded and beaded rim, the centre engraved with script initials 'OEH', on 3 foliate feet, marked on back, c1850, 8in (20cm) diam, 9oz.
$300-350

A William IV salver, on 3 leaf scroll feet, makers Samuel Roberts & Co., Sheffield 1833, 18in (46cm) diam, 70oz.
$2,000-4,500

A pair of George III salvers, by William Bruce, 1817, 12in (30.5cm), 52oz.
$5,000-9,000

A silver salver, maker's mark W.B., London 1824, 9in (23cm), 18.75oz.
$500-900

A pair of George III Irish salvers, on 3 anthemion and paw supports, by John Laughlin Jnr, Dublin 1782, 8½in (21.5cm), 26oz.
$1,600-2,800

A late Victorian silver salver, maker's mark W.J.B. (Messrs. Barnard), London 1894, 27oz approx.
$800-1,500

A salver, with shaped and moulded border embossed with scrolled foliage, Sheffield 1943, 14½in (37cm) diam, 45oz.
$800-1,500

A George III tray, by Thomas Hannam and John Crouch, 1800, 21in (52cm), 53oz.
$4,000-7,500

A salver, with cast Chippendale style border, Sheffield 1973, 15in (38cm) diam, 54oz.
$1,200-2,100

An early Victorian salver, maker William K. Reid, London mark 1837, 19½in (49cm), 98oz.
$1,800-3,800

Sauceboats

A George II style silver sauceboat, mark rubbed.
$200-450

A George II silver sauceboat, 1755, 5oz.
$600-1,200

A pair of George II plain sauceboats, with serpent scroll handles, by Robert Brown, 1743, 24oz.
$4,500-9,000

A rare pair of side-handled sauceboats, by Samuel Blachford, Exeter 1732, 4½in (35cm), 11oz.
$11,000-20,000

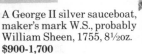

A pair of George II sauceboats, by John Pollock, London 1749, 7in (18cm) long, 21oz 10dwt.
$3,200-6,000

A George II silver sauceboat, maker's mark W.S., probably William Sheen, 1755, 8½oz.
$900-1,700

A pair of George II sauceboats, by
William Robertson, London 1755,
808gm.
$3,200-6,000

A pair of Georgian oval
sauceboats, rubbed
marks, London 1759,
22oz.
$1,200-2,100

An early George III
sauceboat, maker's mark
G.S., London 1764,
6oz 10dwt.
$900-1,700

Four George II plain sauceboats, by
Edward Wakelin, 1757, 74oz.
$10,000-18,000

A matched pair of George III/IV cast
sauceboats, one by Paul Storr, 1812,
the other by Robert Garrard, 1825,
59oz.
$20,000-30,000

A pair of large George IV
sauceboats, by I.H. and G. Lias,
London 1824, 28oz.
$2,600-5,300

Scent bottles

A Victorian silver gilt
double-ended scent flask,
maker E.M.S. London
1884, 5in (12.5cm).
$1,400-2,600

A George IV silver gilt scent bottle
stand, hexagonal, William Eaton,
London 1829, 10oz, and cut glass
scent bottle.
$600-1,200

A pair of George III helmet shaped
pedestal sauceboats, by William
Pitts, London 1784, 710gm.
$3,200-6,000

A set of 4 mint condition
sauceboats, by Edward, Edward,
James and William Barnard,
London 1835, 9in (22.5cm) 79oz.
$18,000-26,000

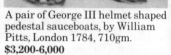

A Victorian silver gilt and ruby
glass scent bottle and vinaigrette,
by S. Mordan, London 1866, 4in
(10cm).
$400-750

A scent bottle with silver collar,
1937.
$500-900

◁ A Victorian cut glass perfume
bottle, with a silver top,
Birmingham 1892.
$200-450

A Victorian silver scent phial,
Birmingham 1892, 8in (20cm) long,
5oz, in case.
$500-900

Services

A five-piece tea and coffee service, by Redlich & Co., Canterbury pattern, comprising: teapot, coffee pot, covered sugar bowl, cream jug and waste, vase shaped on spreading shaped oval base, the partly fluted body repoussé with shells, foliage and scrolls enclosing scalework, the domed cover surmounted with urn finial, monogrammed, teapot 11in (27.5cm) high, 105oz.
$2,000-2,500

A George I style eight-piece tea and coffee service by Gorham & Co., comprising a tea kettle on stand, teapot, coffee pot, covered sugar bowl, cream jug, sugar tongs and shaped oval two-handled tray, the pear-shaped teapot on moulded foot, with domed cover surmounted with knop finial, wood scroll handle and faceted scroll spout, monogrammed, tray 25in (62.5cm) wide, 267oz.
$5,000-6,000

A George IV silver tea service.
$2,600-5,300

A George III silver teapot, maker C.P., London 1817, 21oz.
$500-900

A George IV silver sugar bowl, maker Edward John and William Barnard, London 1829, and a matching William IV cream jug, London 1830, 23½oz.
$600-1,100

A George IV and William IV three-piece tea service, maker R. Pearce and G. Burrows, London 1828 and Joseph and John Angell, London 1833, 43oz gross.
$1,000-2,000

A Victorian four-piece tea and coffee service, Dublin 1845–6, 82oz.
$3,200-6,000

A William IV tea and coffee service, by Charles Fox, London 1835, 90oz gross.
$6,000-12,000

A Victorian tea service, Louis XV pattern, by Joseph and Albert Savory, London 1850, 41oz.
$1,000-2,000

◁ A William IV silver tea and coffee set, makers E.J. and E.W. Barnard, 1833–4, 77oz.
$4,000-7,500

A five-piece tea and coffee service, by Shreve Brown & Co., Boston, with die-rolled guilloche borders and engraved at the neck with banding, the handles scrolled, the feet circular, with lobed rims, the sides fluted, each marked, 1857-60, 11½in (29.5cm), 114oz 10dwt.
$2,000-2,200

A three-piece tea service, by Monell & Williams, New York, comprising: a teapot, a covered two-handled sugar bowl and a cream pitcher, each with broadly reeded sides and a wide shoulder with a die-rolled foliate border, on a moulded oval foot, the lids each domed, with a flowerbasket finial and repoussé and chased with a floral band, the teapot with a scrolled spout and a handle with ivory insulating rings, each marked on base, c1825, 9½in (24cm), 54oz gross weight.
$1,400-1,800

A three-piece demi-tasse service, by Tiffany & Co., New York, comprising: a coffee pot, a cream pitcher and an open sugar bowl, each urn shaped, with reeded borders, on spreading circular foot, marked, 1928-1947, coffee pot 9in (22.5cm) high, 30oz 10dwt gross weight.
$800-900

A six-piece child's service in fitted case, by Gorham & Co., comprising: mug, plate, cereal bowl, knife, fork and spoon, with band of applied sycamore leaves separated by spring flowers, monogrammed, c1910, plate 7in (18cm) diam, 22oz.
$800-1,000

An assembled seven-piece tea and coffee service, the teapot, sugar bowl and cream pitcher probably Philadelphia, c1815, the other pieces Tiffany & Co., New York, 1907-47, comprising: a kettle on stand, a coffee pot, a teapot, a hot milk pitcher, a covered sugar bowl, a cream pitcher and a waste bowl, each square, the shoulders with die-rolled oak leaf and acorn borders, the sugar and creamer with serpent handles, each with engraved script initials, teapot, sugar bowl and creamer unmarked, the other pieces marked, tea kettle on stand 14in (35cm) high, 201oz gross weight.
$5,000-7,000

A three-piece tea service, by William Thomson, New York, comprising: a teapot, a covered sugar bowl and a cream pitcher, each oval, with broadly reeded sides, on spreading oval feet, with die-rolled egg-and-dart borders, the lids each domed with a berry finial, the handles and spout scrolled, with script monograms, c1815-20, teapot 9in (22.5cm) high, 65oz.
$1,900-2,100

A George III three-piece silver teaset, maker's mark W.H., London 1818–19, 41oz.
$1,200-2,100

An early Victorian tea and coffee service, by William Eaton, 1838 and 1839, coffee pot 8½in (21.5cm) high, 75oz.
$2,600-5,300

A Victorian four-piece silver tea service, Sheffield 1883, 118oz 16dwt.
$2,000-4,500

A Victorian eight-sided silver tray to match, Sheffield 1884, 24in (61cm) wide, 147oz.
$2,000-4,500

A William IV coffee pot, teapot and milk jug, by Henry Wilkinson & Co., Sheffield 1832, coffee pot 9½in (24cm) high, 62oz.
$1,600-2,800

A Victorian tea and coffee service, by J. Whipple & Co., Exeter, 1877 and 1879, 90oz gross.
£2,000-2,500   C

A Victorian four-piece engraved tea set, maker's mark J D & S, 1867, 71.75oz.
$4,000-6,800

An Edward VII tea and coffee service, Mappin & Webb Sheffield 1901, and a pair of sugar tongs, 65.5oz.
$1,800-3,800

A Victorian five-piece tea and coffee service, with tray, Holland, Son and Slater, London 1881–2, 127.7oz.
$3,200-6,000

A Victorian tea and coffee service, by John Edward Terrey, 1844, coffee pot 10½in (26.5cm) high, 73oz.
$2,600-5,300

A Victorian three-piece teaset and coffee ewer, by Martin & Hall, Sheffield 1868, the ewer London 1879, 75.5oz weighable silver, cream jug loaded.
$4,000-6,800

A Victorian tea and coffee service,
by Thomas Smiley, 1865, coffee pot
8½in (21.5cm) high, 68oz.
$2,200-4,200

A South American four-piece teaset
on tray, 113oz.
$1,200-2,100
▷

A Danish silver coffee service by
Georg Jensen,   23oz.
$2,200-4,200
▽

A Victorian silver tea/coffee service,
makers Martin Hall & Co., London
1869–70, 110oz, in a fitted oak case.
$5,000-9,000

An Edward VII three-piece coffee
set, in the neo-classical style,
Sheffield 1909, 1,400gm gross.
$1,000-2,000

An Edward VII five-piece tea and
coffee service, Birmingham 1902,
81oz 4dwt.
$1,200-2,100

An oriental
three-piece silver
teaset, 44oz.
$800-1,500

A William IV tea service, the teapot
and milk jug by Marshall & Sons,
Edinburgh 1836, the sugar basin by
George Hunter II, London 1835,
48oz gross.
$900-1,700

A four-piece silver tea set.
$800-1,500

A modern five-piece tea and coffee
service, maker's mark C.J.V Ltd.,
London, 1961, 127.3oz (3,960gm).
$2,600-5,300

A Victorian four-piece silver tea
and coffee set, maker's mark
F.B.M., London 1886, 57.25oz.
$1,400-2,600

Tankards

A George II silver engraved tankard, 1747, 13oz.
$500-900

A Charles II tankard and cover, maker's mark EG, 1671, 6½in (16.5cm), 21oz.
$7,000-12,000

A Queen Anne silver tankard by S. Holaday, London 1709, 7in (18cm)
$8000-13,500

A George II silver engraved tankard, maker's mark J.P., John Payne, 1754, 7oz.
$600-1,100

A James II tankard and cover, maker's mark IO a device between, perhaps for John Oliver, York 1686, 7in (18cm), 21oz.
$7,000-12,000

A George I tankard, by Christopher Canner II, fully marked Britannia Standard 1719, 6½in (17cm), 22oz.
$3,200-6,000

A George II tankard, by Francis Crump, London 1755.
$2,000-4,500

A George II silver tankard, London 1759, 5in (12.5cm), 10oz 12dwt.
$600-1,100

A George II silver tankard, maker's mark I.S., Joseph Smith, 1730, 8oz.
$600-1,200

A William III tankard, engraved with later armorials, 1730, the handle with contemporary initials R*I, by John Gibbons, 1701, 7½in (18.5cm), 26oz.
$4,000-6,800

A George III tankard, maker Thomas Watson, Newcastle 1795, 5in (12.5cm), 10.25oz.
$300-600

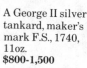

A George III tankard, by John Payne, 1768, the handle with maker's mark, 8in (20cm), 26oz.
$2,000-4,500

A cann, by Joseph Loring, Boston, with a double scroll handle and a moulded rim, on a moulded circular foot, the base engraved with contemporary initials 'WNM', marked with Belden initial touch c or e on base, 1760-80, 5½in (13cm), 13oz.
$1,500-1,800

A George II silver tankard, maker's mark F.S., 1740, 11oz.
$800-1,500

A late Victorian large tankard trophy, the base inscribed 'The Gift of Her Most Gracious Majesty Queen Victoria, Cowes Regatta, 1888', by Robert Allan Roskell & John Mortimer Hunt, 1887, 14in (35cm) high, 96oz.
$8000-13,500

A Scandinavian silver gilt tankard, maker's mark P.K.I., possibly for Peder Knudsen of Oslo, c1660.
$10,000-18,000

A German tankard, inscribed around the rim 'Ludwich Pruszycky Anno 1677', by Abraham Wilde, Königsberg, Prussia, c1675, 8½in (22cm), 32.5oz.
$5,000-9,000

A Norwegian peg tankard, dated 1666, 9in (23cm), 26oz 12dwt.
$7,000-12,000

An Indian tankard, with inscription 'AMA, shot for at the Maroon Club of H.M. 14th Regiment, Berhampore 1813–14. Won by Lieut. Colnl. Watson', by Robert Hamilton, Calcutta, c1812, 6in (15cm), 19oz 8dwt.
$5,000-9,000

Tea Caddies

A pair of George III tea caddies, oval, straight sides, reeded upper mount, pull-off covers, London 1783.
$1,000-2,000

A George III tea caddy, by John Denziloe, London 1787, 6in (15cm), 13oz.
$1,800-3,800

A Queen Anne tea caddy, by Thomas Ash, London 1702, 4½in (11.5cm), 5.75oz.
$900-1,700

A set of George II tea caddies and ▷ sugar box, by Peze Pilleau, 1743, in a fitted velvet lined shagreen box, with lockplate, key and handle, 4in (10cm), 38oz.
$6,000-12,000

◁ A pair of caddies, chased with leaves, flowers and shells, by Joseph Angell, London 1821, 4½in (11cm), 34.75oz.
$4,000-7,500

Three Pierre Gillois tea caddies, London 1760-65, 33oz.
$3,200-6,000

A George III tea caddy, maker Hester Bateman, London 1788, 6in (15cm) wide, 14oz gross.
$900-1,700

A George III tea caddy, by John Robins, 1790, 6in (15cm), 16oz.
$6,000-12,000

Tea Kettles

A George II baluster tea kettle on stand, maker John Payne, London 1754, 15in (38cm).
$5,000-9,000

Teapots

A George III teapot on stand, by Henry Chawner, 1796, the stand 1795, teapot 10½in (26cm) wide, 19.2oz gross.
$1,600-2,800

A George III teapot, by John Emes, 1801, 10½in (27cm) wide, 16.7oz gross.
$400-750

A fine copper-applied tea kettle on stand, by Tiffany & Co., New York, the tea kettle with a bail handle and a flat lid with a copper finial, marked, the stand on 4 cabriole legs joined by a ring base to hold lamp fluid and with an ivory knob to adjust the wick, marked, the teapot and stand each with applied copper clouds in the Japanese taste, 1889-91, 9in (22.5cm), 33oz 10dwt gross weight.
$3,000-3,500

This tea kettle was designed for the Paris Exposition of 1878, where Tiffany's exhibit featured an entire collection of silver in the Japanese taste and the famous 1,250-piece Mackay table service

A 'bright cut' teapot and stand, the former by Robert Hennell, London 1791, the latter by Edward Jay, 1792, both engraved with the letter 'B' for Luke Baker of Roxbury of Connecticut, whose name is engraved on the base of the stand, 18oz.
$4,000-6,800

A George IV teapot and a similar cream jug.
$1,000-2,000

A hot water kettle on stand, by John C. Moore & Son for Tiffany & Co., New York, the kettle with 2 open handles and a foliate spigot, the domed lid with an ivy finial, on a pierced stand held by 2 ivory knobs, on 4 legs with lion's paw feet, the burner and kettle handles decorated with cast ivy leaves, one side of kettle with stylized engraved initials, marked on base, c1865-70, burner later, 16in (40cm), 79oz 10dwt.
$2,000-2,500

A George III biggin, stand and lamp, engraved with armorials, by William Frisbee, 1802, 12½in (31cm) high overall, 59oz.
$3,200-6,000

A George IV small coffee pot, by William Bateman, 1827, 7½in (19.5cm) high, 34oz.
$1,200-2,100

A teapot, by Samuel Richards, Philadelphia, the domed lid with a flame finial, the handle with ivory insulating rings, the S-scroll spout squared, on a spreading rounded rectangular base, on 4 cast lion's paw feet, marked twice on base, c1810, 11in (27.5cm), 42oz 10dwt gross weight.
$800-900

A teapot with a sugar bowl and a cream pitcher, the teapot by Gorham Manufacturing Company, Providence, 1874, the sugar and creamer by Peter L Krider, Philadelphia, c1860, the teapot square, with bowed sides, a flat circular lid with a reeded finial, a straight tapering cylindrical spout, and a bamboo handle with ivory insulating rings and leafage applied at the handle join, on 4 bracket feet, with a band of engraved foliage around the sides, marked, the covered sugar and creamer each vase-shaped, with engraved strapwork centering inscription 'Cook', marked, teapot 6in (15cm) high, sugar bowl 4in (10cm), creamer 5in (12.5cm), 30oz 10dwt gross weight.
$900-1,100

A presentation teapot, by Conrad Bard & Son, Philadelphia, with a domed lid with an urn finial, a scrolled spout and a scrolled handle with insulating rings, on a spreading circular foot, the entire surface repoussé and chased with flowers and leaves against a stippled punchwork ground with 2 cartouche reserves with the engraved inscription 'To Hon. Neal Dow, By his friends in Penna', marked on base, 1850-59, 11in (27.5cm), 36oz gross weight.
$1,300-1,800

Neal Dow, 1804-97, was born in Portland, Maine, of Quaker parents. A major temperance reformer, Mr. Dow is known as 'the father of the Maine Law' which drove the illegal liquor traffic from the City of Portland. Dow served two terms as Mayor of Portland, 1851 and 1855, and ran for President of the U.S. in 1880 as a candidate of the Prohibition party, receiving 10,305 votes.

A teapot, by Christian Wiltberger, Philadelphia, with a domed rectangular lid with an urn finial, a scroll spout, a carved wood handle with an acanthus grip, on a stepped rounded rectangular foot, the rim and footrim with applied gadrooned borders, one side engraved with script initials 'HM', the underside of base with later engraved family names, marked on base, c1825, 10in (25cm), 40oz gross weight.
$900-1,100

An Indian Colonial silver pear-shaped teapot, by Hamilton & Co., Calcutta, c1830, 5½in (14cm) high, 18.5oz.
$600-1,100

An Indian oval teapot, by Hamilton & Co., Calcutta, c1822, 7in (17.5cm), 29oz gross.
$4,000-6,800

Trays

A tea tray by William Stroud, London 1802, 23in (58cm) overall, 84oz.
$4,000-7,500

A tea tray, maker's mark rubbed, 1906, 27in (70cm), 145oz.
$2,200-4,200

An oval tea tray by Walker and Hall, Sheffield 1914, 24½in (62.5cm), 92oz.
$1,600-2,800

A George III tray by John Crouch, 1807, 26in (66cm) long, 102oz.
$8000-13,500

A tea tray by Walker and Hall, Sheffield 1910, 29in (74cm) across handles, 131oz.
$2,200-4,200

A William IV card tray, London 1833, 8½in (21.5cm) diam, 11.5oz.
$400-750

A tea tray, maker's mark JS, Sheffield 1927, 26in (66cm) across handles, 104oz.
$1,700-3,000

Tureens

A soup tureen, by Tiffany & Co., New York, with 2 open handles and a stepped oval lid with an open ring finial, on a spreading oval foot, the lid, rim and foot with die-rolled Greek key borders, one side with engraved initials 'M.A.R.', marked by Tiffany, Young and Ellis, 1860-65, 12in (30cm) high, 69oz.
$2,000-2,500

A George IV tray by William Elliot, 1822, 24½in (62cm) long, 138oz.
$4,000-7,500

A George III soup tureen, by Paul Storr, 1807, 18in (45cm) long, 207.5oz.
$36,000-57,000

A pair of George III Regency two-handled oval sauce tureens and covers, by Thomas Robins, 1810, 9in (23cm), 74oz.
$7,000-12,000

A soup tureen, by Tiffany & Co., New York, with a domed lid engraved with foliage and surmounted by a cast sheep finial, the bowl with cast steer's head handles and an oval foot, the rim and footrim with applied die-rolled guilloche borders, marked on base, 1870-75, 13in (32.5cm) high, 86oz.
$2,700-3,200

A set of four George III sauce tureens and covers, by R. Sibley and W. Burwash, 1807–1808, 8¼in (21cm), 112oz.
$7,000-12,000

A double vase on stand, by The Sweetser Co., New York, the 2 squared vases shaped at the neck and conjoined at the corner edge, all sides acid-etched with foliage in the Japanese taste, one side engraved with stylized monogram 'SFC', the rim, shoulder and base with applied 14ct. gold borders, the stand of copper, marked on base of vase, 1900-15, 11½in (28cm), 20oz 10dwt gross weight of vase.
$1,700-2,000

A bud vase, by Theodore B. Starr, New York, with a flaring rim, the sides applied with 4 Grecian figures, above a circular foot, 1900-15, 7in (17.5cm), 8oz.
$400-500

A vase, by Gorham Manufacturing Company, Providence, with a moulded rim above repoussé and chased flowers, on a moulded footrim, marked on base, 1917, 12in (30cm), 24oz.
$2,000-2,500

A two-handled flower vase, by Whiting Div., repoussé at each corner with scrolling acanthus, the scroll handles in conforming design, monogrammed, 10in (25cm), 36oz.
$550-650

Spirit Flasks

A spirit flask, by Tiffany & Co., the obverse chased with a cowboy on a bucking horse with lasso in hand, the reverse monogrammed, the border and cap chased with prickly cactus, 1891-1902, 5½in (13cm), 8oz gross weight.
$1,900-2,100

An Art Nouveau hip flask, by Tiffany & Co., the obverse with scene of a nymph loosely clad amidst scroll, garland and love birds, 1891-1902, 6in (15cm), 6oz.
$1,500-2,000

A spirit flask, by Tiffany & Co., the obverse chased with a gunman dressed in shooting attire, accompanied by retrievers within woodland, the reverse monogrammed in the Art Nouveau style and chased above with a grouse perched on wooden fence, the border decorated with stylized wheat, 1891-1902, 7in (18cm), 12.5oz gross weight, in a fitted leather case.
$1,800-2,000

A brass and steel bladed worm corkscrew.
$60-120

A peg and worm or serpentine corkscrew, 4½in (11.4cm) long when closed.
$180-300

A German corkscrew with wire spring barrel and hinged flange to assist in the removal of the cork.
$150-250

A rare George III Provincial cartouche wine label, by Richard Richardson, Chester, c1765.
$300-600

A George III wine label, by Hester Bateman, c1765.
$300-600

Four George III wine labels, by Matthew Boulton and John Fothergill, Birmingham, two with replaced chains, two 1774 and two 1776, 2oz.
$1,200-2,100

A George III scroll wine label, pierced 'Claret', by Susanna Barker, c1785.
$600-1,100

A George III wine label, incised 'Claret', by John Steward, c1790, 2in (5cm) long.
$180-300

A George III Scottish Provincial plain eye-shaped wine label, incised 'Gin', by John Ewen, Aberdeen, c1790.
$150-300

A rare George III Provincial wine label, incised 'Lisbon', by Langlands & Robertson, Newcastle, c1790.
$600-1,100

A George III wine label, maker's mark overstruck by that of Richard Evans of Shrewsbury, 1791.
$500-900

A George III crescent-shaped wine label, probably by Crespin Fuller, 1800.
$400-750

A George III disc wine label, by Robert Barker, 1794, 1½in (3.5cm).
$400-750

A very rare George III fouled anchor wine label, incised 'Madeira', by Phipps & Robinson 1799, 2in (5cm) high.
$2,200-4,200

A George IV Irish wine label, in the late 18thC style, incised 'Burgundy' by James Fray, Dublin, c1820, also bearing retailer's name of West, and a similar label incised 'White', by Susanna Barker, 1784–5.
$100-250

A George IV oval wine label, by John Reily, 1824, 2½in (6.5cm) long.
$500-900

A George III/IV Scottish wine label, incised 'Cape-Madeira', by Francis Howden, Edinburgh, c1820.
$180-300

This design is unusual for a Scottish label.

A George IV wine label, pierced 'Calcavella' by Emes & Barnard, 1825.
$300-600

A rare Irish wine label, incised 'Ennishowen', maker's mark only H.F., untraced, but almost certainly an alternative mark of Henry Flavelle of Dublin, c1825.
$600-1,100

A George IV Scottish vine leaf wine label, pierced 'Madeira', maker's mark Edinburgh, c1825, 3½in (9.5cm) long.
$80-150

A George IV Provincial wine label, with a disc surmount engraved with a Blackamoor's head crest within a garter, inscribed 'Gang Forward', the crest of Stirling, incised 'Rum', by Joseph Hicks, Exeter, 1825.
$300-600

A rare George IV armorial wine label, a dragon's head raised between two wings, by I.E. Terry, 1828.
$1,000-2,000

A George IV Irish wine label, incised 'Port', by Henry Flavelle, Dublin, 1829, 2in (5cm) long.
$180-300

A George IV cast wine label, pierced 'Sherry' and surmounted by the coronet of the Earl of Eglington, by Rawlings & Summers, c1829.
$900-1,700

An early Victorian architectural wine label, on an unusual chain, by Robert Garrard, 1839, 2½in (6cm) long.
$500-900

A rare and large Victorian fern leaf wine label, with applied title 'Port', apparently no maker's mark, 1845, 3½in (9cm).
$1,600-2,800

A Victorian cast cartouche shaped label, with border of raised scrolls, pierced 'Madeira', by John S. Hunt, 1849.
$300-600

A pair of Victorian pierced wine labels, enamelled in blue and red, 'Burgundy' and 'Sherry', W.S. London, 1886.
$600-1,100

A Victorian silver gilt label, in the Gothic style, incised 'Maraschino', by Robert Garrard, 1846.
$300-600

A cast silver gilt decanter label, hallmarked London.
$300-600

A Victorian electroplated wine label, chased with a 'flying fox', 3½in (8cm) long.
$150-250

A composite set of 6 cast bacchanalian wine labels, some unmarked.
$600-1,100

An Indian silver wine label or bottle ticket, marked 'Orr' on the reverse.
$100-250

A pair of George III coasters, with wood bases and silver buttons, by S. C. Younge & Co., Sheffield 1817, 6in (15cm).
$1,600-2,800

Two early Victorian decanter stands, by Charles Fox and Charles T and George Fox, London 1839–41.
$2,600-5,300

◁ An unusual pair of George IV brass bound mahogany wine coasters, 12½in (31.5cm) high.
$4,000-7,500

A pair of Sheffield plate coasters, 7½in (18.5cm).
$300-600

▷

A pair of Sheffield plate coasters, 6in (15cm) diam.
$400-750

A pair of double coasters as carriages, with turned wooden bases, and turned ivory handles.
$600-1,200

A pair of plated circular bottle stands, 4½in (11.5cm).
$200-450

A George III H.M. silver wine funnel and stand, no date letter, but marks for Ann Robertson, Newcastle 1801.
$800-1,500

A George III silver wine funnel, maker's mark P.B.A.B, Peter and Ann Bateman, London 1793, approx 4oz 10dwt.
$800-1,500

◁ A Hannah Northcote wine funnel, London 1811.
$600-1,200

▷

A pair of Sheffield wine coolers by James and Thomas Settle, 1817, 10in (25cm), 136oz.
$26,000-45,000

A fine pair of Victorian wine coolers, engraved with armorials and presentation inscription, by Messrs. Barnard, 1838, 10½in (26.5cm), 237oz.
$26,000-45,000

The inscription reads: 'To Sir James Gibson Craig Baronet, from his Countrymen and Fellow Citizens, December 1838'.

An American ovoid wine ewer, the body chased overall in the Chinese style, by Samuel Kirk, Baltimore, c1830, 16in (41cm) high, 48oz.
$3,200-6,000

A Victorian electroplate and cut glass claret jug, engraved with coat of arms and inscription, glass foot damaged, 12in (31cm).
$400-750

An Epping Forest Centenary flagon, London 1978, 41oz.
$500-900

Accompanied by certificate signed by the Lord Mayor of London.

A Victorian baluster wine ewer, E & J Barnard, London 1865, 12in (30cm), 22.8oz.
$900-1,700

A Victorian vase shape wine ewer, C. F. Hancock & Co. London 1892, 12in (30.5cm), 26oz.
$900-1,700

A wine bottle carrier/coaster of steel mesh with brass edges, stamped with maker's initials in an oval *B*, c1860, 12½in (31cm) long.
$800-1,500

A rare George III double barrel cup, the two halves with gilt interiors combining to form a coopered cask, probably Peter Bateman, London 1813.
$1,200-2,100

A late Victorian novelty port bottle carrier, maker H.T. London 1890, 13in (33cm) long, 27oz.
$1,700-3,000

An unusual tole peinte double wine bottle carrier, the red ground decorated with oval landscape panels and gilt vine decoration, 19thC, 17in (43cm).
$600-1,200

A Channel Islands wine cup, engraved with initials, maker's mark RB, a fleur-de-lys and coronet above, struck also with a coronet and with an A with coronet above, Guernsey, c1695, 6in (14cm), 7oz 3dwt.
$3,200-6,000

See Richard H. Mayne, Old Channel Islands Silver, Plate 7, for similar marks.

A Russian gilt wine service, comprising: a circular waiter, 7in (18cm), and 6 stem cups, 3in (8cm) high, Moscow marks 1887, contained in original silk lined case.
$400-750

Make the most of Miller's

Every care has been taken to ensure the accuracy of descriptions and estimated valuations. Where an attribution is made within inverted commas (e.g. 'Chippendale') or is followed by the word 'style' (e.g. early Georgian style) it is intended to convey that, in the opinion of the publishers, the piece concerned is a later – though probably still antique – reproduction of the style so designated. Unless otherwise stated, any description which refers to 'a set', or 'a pair' includes a valuation for the entire set or the pair, even though the illustration may show only a single item.

Miscellaneous

An Edwardian silver animal pincushion, in the shape of a hedgehog, Birmingham 1904.
$200-450

A pair of Italian polychrome and giltwood dishes, supported on dancing goblins, late 19th/early 20thC, 9in (23cm).
$600-1,200

A glass and silver hip flask, Asprey, 1906.
$400-750

A sterling silver pincushion, by Tiffany & Co., 4in (10cm).
$600-1,200

A silver hip flask, 1873.
$500-900

A George III hot water jug, by Benjamin West, London 1772.
$600-1,200

A pair of pounce pots, by John McKay, Edinburgh 1798, 3oz.
$500-900

A Victorian cigar lighter, the rim engraved with a presentation inscription, by J.S. Hunt, stamped Hunt & Roskell late Storr, Mortimer & Hunt, on circular ebonised plinth, 1851, 5in (13cm), 18oz 17dwt.
$2,600-5,300

A rare French ivory and silver snuff rasp, engraved with a portrait of Mary Queen of Scots, the legend Maria Scotorum Regina 1567, early 18thC, 7½in (19cm).
$4,000-7,500

By descent to the present owner from William Forrester Cochrane, Factor to the Earl of Mar d.1792.

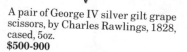

A pair of George IV silver gilt grape scissors, by Charles Rawlings, 1828, cased, 5oz.
$500-900

A Victorian novelty letter opener modelled as a sabre in its scabbard, detachable, by E.H. Stockwell, 1875, engraved with retailer's mark of Thornhill of 144 New Bond St, 5½in (13.5cm) long.
$300-600

A Victorian novelty cigar cutter, modelled as a monkey, unmarked, c1880, 5in (13cm) long.
$300-600

A Victorian novelty propelling pencil, by Sampson Mordan, modelled as an owl with coloured glass eyes, engraved with maker's name only 'S. Mordan & Co.,', c1880.
$200-450

A sugar urn, Philadelphia, with a pierced gallery and a tapering conical lid with an urn finial, on a flaring stem over a square base, the body engraved with foliage and script initials 'JCK', unmarked, minor solder repair to lid, 1785-1810, 9½in (24cm) high, 15oz..
$900-1,000

An ice bucket and serving spoon, by Gorham & Co., on conforming base and formed as an iceberg with applied icicles, surmounted with 2 polar bears, the spoon with pierced spade shaped bowl with cast polar bear handle in rope twist grip, 1871, 11in (27.5cm), 34.5oz.
$4,000-5,000

A strainer, American or English, the bowl pierced in a petal pattern, with 2 open scrolled handles, late 18thC, 7in (17.5cm) long, 2oz 10dwt.
$600-800

A rare marrow scoop, by Clark & Company, Augusta, Georgia, double ended, with a tapered flat handle, marked on reverse, 1830-42, 7in (17.5cm) long, 1oz.
$800,1,000

A pair of sugar nippers, American or English, with scrolled and spurred grips, the circular hinge engraved on one side with a patera and on the other with initials 'HI', marked on inside of tips, marked 'LS', mid/late 18thC, 5in (12.5cm) long, 1oz.
$800-1,000

r. A porringer, by William Simpkins, Boston, with a keyhole handle engraved with a crest, marked with name touch in centre of bowl, bruises, 1755-80, engraving possibly later, 5in (12.5cm) diam, 6oz.
$1,200-1,800

l. A porringer, by Jacob Hurd, Boston, with an everted brim and a keyhole handle engraved with a crest and contemporary initials 'AB', marked on back of handle with full name touch and marked on shoulder with surname touch, small repairs to bowl and handle joins, c1750-58, 5in (12.5cm) diam, 7oz.
$1,500-2,500

r. An American porringer, with keyhole handle engraved with script initials 'NW', unmarked, late 18th/early 19thC, 5½in (13cm) diam, 6oz 10dwt.
$700-1,000

An ice bucket, American, with two pierced handles, the flaring sides chased to simulate wood grain staves, encircled by applied straps, with a removable pierced strainer, the base stamped 'Sterling', late 19thC, 7in (17.5cm) wide, 21oz..
$600-700

l. A porringer, by William Hollingshead, Philadelphia, with an everted brim and a keyhole handle, the side engraved with script initials 'EEK', marked with initial touch on back of handle, 1760-85, 5½in (13cm) diam, 8oz.
$1,500-2,500

A punch strainer, by Benjamin Burt, Boston, with a moulded rim, 2 scrolled handles, the bowl with decorative piercing, mark struck on front of one handle, 1755-80, 11in (27.5cm) long, 4oz.
$4,000-4,500

A three bottle decanter holder, by Gorham & Co., retailed by Hyde & Goodrich, on foliate scroll supports, each circular caster engine turned and with foliate vacant cartouche, with beaded rim, the central ring handle capped with acanthus, c1860, 18in (45cm) high, 71oz.
$2,000-2,500

A Victorian silver centrepiece stand.
$600-1,200

A George III dish ring, the pierced collar frame finely chased and engraved with a frieze, Dublin, c1780, 8½in (21cm) diam., 18oz.
$1,600-2,800

An ivory box, the cover set with a compass in a gold frame, the interior containing a small ivory barometer and two small brushes, c1810, 7cm long.
$400-750

An Irish silver dish ring by E. Johnson, Dublin, in late 18thC style, dated 1896, 8in (20cm) diam.
$1,300-2,400

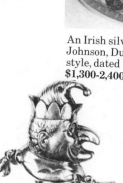

A rattle, formed as a jester, 2 bells, mother-of-pearl handle, stamped W.H.G., Chester.
$300-600

A small rattle shaped as a bear, 2 decorated bells, maker's mark C & N, Birmingham.
$200-450

A gilt rattle with a whistle, the mouth piece decorated with a castle, 4 gilt and one silver bell, coral mouth piece, maker's mark GU, England, 19thC.
$400-750

A George III pocket cheese scoop or apple corer, with plain handle and reversible screw-in blade, marks rubbed, 5in (12.5cm).
$200-450

A George IV silver mounted cut glass condiment jar on stand, by Paul Storr, London, 1825, together with another stand and mount, 1829, 5in (12.5cm) high, 2 stands 14oz.
$4,000-7,500

A German condiment with English import marks, modelled as a lady in 16thC costume, possibly Mary of Guise, import marks for 1913, 3½in (9.5cm) high.
$300-600

A George III mustard pot, by Crispin Fuller, London 1795, 3in (7.5cm), and spoon, London 1803 5oz
$400-750

A Victorian composite silver gilt dressing table set, by Charles Stuart Harris, William Comyns, Sampson Mordan, Rosenthal and Jacobs, etc., the rectangular box Dutch silver gilt coloured metal, 1885–1889.
$1,800-3,800

A four-piece silver and enamel dressing table set, 1909.
$600-1,200

l. A cut glass dressing table tidy with H.M. silver and enamel lid, monogram by artist.
$200-450

r. A cut glass dressing table tidy with H.M. silver and enamel panelled lid.
$150-300

An interesting Victorian novelty pepperette as Benjamin Disraeli, with sphinx shaped helmet, knee breeches and tail coat, standing beside a pyramid, maker H.W.D., London 1878, 155gm.
$3,200-6,000

A pair of Victorian cast novelty frog pepperettes, one bearing traces of gilding, each with realistically textured skin, A.C. London 1881, 2in (5cm).
$600-1,200

A fine Victorian silver stand with 3 glass bottles, and with rope border.
$600-1,200

A George III lyre shape toast rack, the oval base engraved initials, maker Nathaniel Smith & Co., Sheffield, 1798, 5oz.
$500-900

A George III oval boat shape 6-division toast rack, with crested initialled ring handle, by John Emes, London 1805, 7.5oz.
$400-750

A Louis Vuitton travelling case with silver gilt and tortoiseshell fittings, c1925.
$8,000-15,000

A pigskin beauty case by Mappin and Webb, with silver, gilt and crystal fittings, contained in a separate removable case, hallmarked 1943.
$1,600-2,800

l. A George III oval silver cruet stand.
$500-900

c. A heavy quality silver sugar box and scoop.
$800-1,500

r. A Victorian circular and footed silver dessert basket, 12in (30cm).
$400-750

A silver toast rack, spelling 'Toast', 1935.
400-750

A Regency rectangular egg cruet, by William Eley, with a set of 6 matching egg cups, bulls head crest, London 1820, together with a set of 6 George IV fiddle thread pattern eggspoons, makers Eley and Fearn, London 1824, 32oz.
$1,700-3,000

A Victorian rectangular basket design egg cruet, with 6 egg cups and a stand, presentation inscription and crested, by Robert Hennell III, London 1856, 9½in (24cm), 28oz.
$900-1,700

A George III Scottish butter pail, engraved with a crest below a motto between reeded bands, the interior gilt, maker's mark GMH in monogram, Edinburgh 1814, 5½in (14.5cm) across handles.
$1,200-2,100

A Continental cow creamer, probably Dutch, 19thC, 7in (18cm) long, 7oz.
$600-1,200

◁ An Edwardian table bell, formed as a lady with spreading skirts, 1905, 5½in (14cm), 15.5oz.
$800-1,500

◁ A snuff box whistle, in the form of a boar's head, London 1975, 1½in (4cm).
$200-450

A pair of Victorian presentation silver riding spurs, each inscribed 'Presented by Mr. H. Clayton to the Winner of the Salford Cup, 1887', hallmarked Birmingham 1846, maker's mark J.B., with fitted morocco leather covered case.
$600-1,200

An early George I cast candle snuffer and stand, maker Roger Kempton, London 1714, 7½in (19cm), 10oz 6dwt.
$4,000-7,500

A George IV silver strainer, maker's mark J.B., London 1828, 4in (10cm) diam., 4oz.
$400-750

An easel mirror with oval bevelled plate, London 1901, 24 by 18in (61 by 46cm).
$900-1,700

An Austrian cane handle modelled as a greyhound's head, by Georg Adam Scheid, also bearing German duty marks, mounted on wood cane, c1890.
$800-1,500

479

Candlesticks

A pair of Sheffield plate candlesticks, by M. Fenton & Co., c1779, 11½in (29cm).
$1,400-2,600

An early Sheffield plated taperstick, c1770, 7in (17.5cm).
$500-900

A pair of plated on copper table candlesticks, in the George II style, 9½in (23.5cm).
$300-600

A pair of Old Sheffield plate candlesticks, 10½in (26cm).
$180-300

A Victorian Sheffield plate table candelabrum, 28in (71cm).
$600-1,200

A pair of plated candelabra with sconces, 22in (56cm).
$500-900

Services

A pair of Sheffield plate candelabra, 21in (53cm) high.
$1,000-2,000

A Victorian electroplated four-piece tea and coffee service.
$500-900

A Victorian plated tea or coffee set.
$600-1,200

An electroplated four-piece tea and coffee service, Henry Wilkinson & Co., late 19thC.
$500-900

A James II ebonised striking bracket clock of phase III type, the finely engraved backplate signed 'Joseph Knibb Londini fecit', restorations, 12in (30cm).
$20,000-30,000

Above left A mid-Georgian walnut clock by Jno Melling Chester, 89in (225cm).
$20,000-45,000
Above right A seven day clock, dial signed Geo. Graham London, some restorations, 92in (232cm).
$60,000-120,000
Below A green-japanned clock, signed Newman Cartwright, early 18thC, 105in (265cm).
$10,000-18,000

A Royal presentation grande sonnerie spring clock by Thomas Tompion, c1700, 28in (71cm).
$500,000+
Presented, c1700 by William III of England to Cosimo III de Medici Grand Duke of Tuscany, and still not paid for at the time of the King's death, on the evidence of a petition in 1703 from the maker to Queen Anne.

An ebony veneered bracket clock, with glazed sides and solid back, signed 'Henricus Jones in the Temple, Fecit, late 17thC, 17in (43cm).
$36,000-66,000

A small George II ebonised grand sonnerie bracket clock, the moulded arched case with gilt brass mouldings, door fronting, the enamel dial signed Thos. Hughes London between strike/silent and calendar rings in the arch, the 7-pillar movement with triple fusee and chain, quarter strike on 6 bells, now with lever platform and signed engraved backplate, and a brass bound mahogany box, 10in (25cm) high.
$11,000-20,000

A George III scarlet and gold japanned bracket clock, made for the Turkish market, signed William Dunant London, 22½in (56cm) high.
$18,000-26,000

Left A French engraved brass carriage clock with porcelain dial, 8-day hour and half-hour striking and repeating movement, by Margaine, Paris, No.11506, late 19thC, 7in (17.5cm) high, in leather travelling case.
$6,000-12,000

An early George III ebonised striking bracket clock, the enamel mounted dial signed Robt. & Peter Higgs London, 17½in (43cm).
$14,000-24,000

A George III satinwood 'balloon' bracket clock, signed Richd. Webster Exchange Alley London, 24in (60cm).
$10,000-18,000

A lady's boudoir timepiece, 6½in (17cm).
$1,800-3,800

An 18ct gold open faced key wind watch.
$600-1,200

Left A French gilt brass and white marble perpetual calendar 4-glass mantel clock, the circular enamel dial with visible 'coup perdu' escapement and centre seconds, signed Breveté, Le Roy & Fils, Paris, the enamel calendar dial showing month, date, and in the centre day and phases of the moon, in a chased gilt mask, 19thC, 16½in (42cm) high.
$5,000-9,000

Below A rare month-going Vienna regulator with perpetual calendar, signed Meisterstück Des Ludwig Deffner in Wien, c1820, 61in (152cm).
$24,000-45,000

A George III ormolu, marble and biscuit porcelain mantel clock, the movement with a circlet of Roman numerals within an astrolabe on a plinth, inscribed Vulliamy, London 235, 12½in (32cm) high.
$14,000-24,000

Right An Austrian or Swiss Biedermeier ormolu mounted walnut and parquetry automaton table clock with organ, stamped HLR within a lozenge, restoration, 22in (55cm) high.
$34,000-54,000

l. A South German giltmetal tabernacle clock or Turmuhr, restorations, early 17thC, 19½in (48cm) high. **$24,000-42,000**

r. A South German silver-fronted Telleruhr, the circular movement signed Matthias Geill on backplate, 14in (35cm) high, excluding stand. **$14,000-24,000**

A Louis XIV tortoiseshell and gilt brass mounted 'Pendule de Voyage', the shaped case arched at the top, on 4 bun feet, signed along the base 'Duchesne A Paris', the gilt chapter ring mounted with enamel numerals and subsidiary regulating dial above, with pull quarter repeating on 2 bells, outside count-wheel strike, tulip pillars and signed shaped plates, 11in (28cm) high. **$10,000-18,000**

A gold cased repeating watch with Robin escapement, signed on the gold cuvette, Breguet No.2187, case No.2790/B 2187, with chain and key, 4.4cm diam, in a morocco fitted case by Dessoutter. **$50,000-90,000**

Above and right A fine and rare Swiss gold and enamel double-dial automaton watch, with quarter repeating on 'real bell', gold chain and two keys attached, c1800, 6cm. **$60,000-96,000**

485

A gold and diamond-set clock watch for the Turkish market, signed 'by Daniel de St Leu, Wtchmar to Her Majesty, London', in tortoiseshell veneered gilt metal protecting case, c1790, 2½in (6cm).
$50,000-90,000

A Swiss gold, hunter-cased, one-minute chronometer tourbillon watch, by F. William Dubois Locle, in leather case, c1840, 2in (5cm).
$60,000-95,000

A gold pocket chronometer, signed 'John Arnold & Son Inv. et fec. London No.357/658', maker's mark TH, London, 1788, 2in (5cm).
$14,000-24,000

A Swiss, gold and enamel, musical automaton verge watch, the unsigned bridge cock movement with diamond endstone, c1820, 2½in (6cm).
$20,000-45,000

Left A gentleman's size perpetual calendar gold chronograph watch by Patek Philippe, Geneve, plain 18ct case, no. 1518/674143, 3.5cm diam, on 18ct gold Rolex flexible bracelet.
$40,000-75,000

486

Above A gold and enamel, pair-cased watch with 3 outer cases, and gilt-metal chatelaine, the movement signed 'Geo. Musgrave, Taunton', the inner and outer cases hallmarked 1784, all in a later glazed display case, slight chip to bezel, 4.8cm diam.
$14,000-24,000

Left Top, a slim gold and enamel open faced key-wind watch.
$1,700-3,000

Below, an open faced keyless cylinder fob watch, the bar movement stamped Savoye Freres & Cie, and signed on the cuvette 'Faucard à Dinard', 3cm.
$300-600

Left A brass astrolabe comprising mater, rete, 3 latitude plates, pivoted alidade, pivoted rule for stellar co-ordinates and axis pin, signed 'GEORGIVS HARTMAN NORENBERGE FACIEBAT ANNO MD XXXII', 5in (13cm). $34,000-54,000

Right A gilt and silvered brass astrolabe comprising mater, rete, latitude plate pin with nut and alidade, probably German, late 16thC, 7in (17cm) diam. $18,000-26,000

Left An English brass nocturnal, calculated for latitude 50° 30′ N, unsigned, but bearing monogram *F*, index arm 5in (12.5cm). $20,000-30,000

A fruitwood, Gunter-type honary quadrant, unsigned, early 18thC, 5in (13cm) radius. $2,200-4,200

A gilt brass compendium, German, mid-16thC. $20,000-30,000

488

A rare brass trigonometer, the base rule with a linear scale 10-210 fitted with a slide secured by two screws, the reverse with miniature plumb bob and protractor, damaged, signed Philipus Danfrie, F, late 16thC, 15in (38cm) folded.
$74,000-120,000

Philipe Danfrie, described as an outstanding maker, fully described and illustrated his Trigonometre in Usage du graphomètre, published in Paris in 1597

A brass geared universal ring dial, probably from the workshop of Thomas Heath, London, the circular base with levelling screws, the geared meridian ring within annular support mounted on scroll brackets engraved with flowers, the base inset with compass and spirit levels (lacking needle and glass), engraved with degree scale graduated from 0° to 90° in each quadrant, and an outer scale graduated from 0° to 360°; the base engraved with table of the Equation of Time and reading to the nearest 5 minutes of arc by means of vernier on rim, English, mid-18thC, 14in (36cm).
$40,000-75,000

A gunner's caliper, one arm engraved with scale, the Weight of the cube Foot in, with symbols and owner's monogram, the other arm with gunner's scale, the reverse with pictorial representation of geometric solids, various scales, the tips of both arms with hardened steel points, signed I Rowley fecit, in original fishskin covered case, 7in (18cm) long.
$4,000-7,500

An unsigned armillary sphere demonstrating the apparent motion of the planets, the outer Zodiac calendar ring supporting 2 circles showing the position of fixed stars, the Pole Arctique and Pole Le l'Eclipque, possibly French, 16in (40cm) high.
$1,700-3,000

A cabinet of geological specimens in 2 trays, each specimen with printed paper label, the accompanying pamphlet entitled 'Catalog de la Nouvelle Collection des Roches du Mont-Blanc', Classe par M. le Professeur Jurine et M. Brard, early 19thC.
$2,000-4,500

A brass compound binocular microscope signed 'A Ross, London, No. 1772', with extensive range of accessories, in oak cabinet, mid-19thC. Cabinet 23in (59cm).
$4,000-7,500

A 2in (5cm) reflecting telescope, signed John Cuff, London, with 13½in (33cm) long body tube, in original oak case.
$4,500-9,000

A lacquered brass compound binocular microscope, by R&J Beck, London & Philadelphia, with oak case of accessories, late 19thC, 19in (48cm).
$4,000-7,500

A brass 'Grand Model' compound binocular microscope, with a collection of accessories and eyepieces, by W. Watson & Sons Ltd, in fitted mahogany case, 19in (47cm) high.
$4,000-7,500

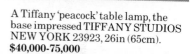

A Tiffany 'peacock' table lamp, the base impressed TIFFANY STUDIOS NEW YORK 23923, 26in (65cm).
$40,000-75,000

A magnolia leaded glass and bronze floor lamp, the shade impressed TIFFANY STUDIOS NEW YORK 1599, the base cast with a band of leaves and impressed TIFFANY STUDIOS NEW YORK 379, 80in (203cm) high to top of pig-tail finial.
$160,000-270,000

A Tiffany 'peony' leaded glass and bronze table lamp, the shade and base impressed with maker's marks and numbered 1505 and 550 respectively, 31in (79cm) high.
$50,000-90,000

A Tiffany 'apple blossom' leaded glass and bronze table lamp, shade and base impressed with maker's marks, the base numbered 7806, 26in (66cm) high.
$28,000-48,000

A Gallé double overlay cameo glass lamp, Gallé cameo signature to base and shade, c1900, 13in (32cm).
$18,000-26,000

A Gallé triple overlay cameo glass lamp, shade and base signed Gallé, 28in (71cm).
$20,000-45,000

Below Five Gallé cameo vases, all with signature.

Back row: 14in (35cm).
$1,200-2,100
12in (29cm).
$900-1,700

Front row: 7in (18cm).
$800-1,500
9in (23cm).
$1,800-3,800
7in (18cm).
$1,000-2,000

A Gallé 'blowout' lamp with bronze mount, base and shade signed Gallé, c1900, 18in (45cm).
$70,000-130,000

A Gallé marqueterie-de-verre vase, with incised chinoiserie signature, c1900, 14in (35cm).
$18,000-26,000

Five Tiffany Favrile vases, all inscribed, l.-r.:
$4,500-9,000 $12.000-21,000 $4,500-9,000
$4,500-9,000 $3,200-6,000

A plique à jour and metal lantern 13in (34cm).
$3,200-6,000

l. to r. Galle vase 19in (48cm). $8,000-15,000
Galle vase 22in (56cm). $8,000-13,500
Daum vase 20in (51cm). $4,500-9,000

A pâte-de-verre liquor service by G. Argy-Rousseau.
$4,500-9,000

A glass and brass vase attributed to
Loetz, in the manner of Hans
Christiansen, c1900, 15in (37cm).
$1,800-3,800

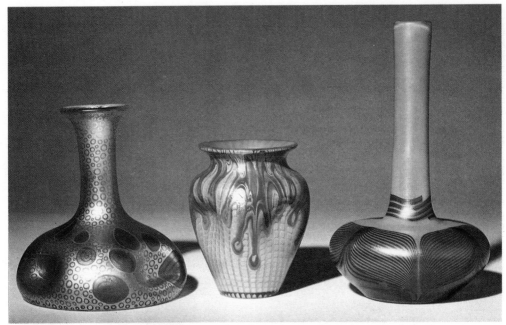

l. A vase designed by Kolomon Moser, 7in (17cm).
$2,600-5,300
c. A Loetz vase 8in (21cm).
$1,400-2,600
r. A Ferdinand Poschinger Glasshütten vase, engraved signature and 'Bayern No. 189', 10in (25cm).
$1,800-3,800

A Daum cameo glass vase 9in (22cm).
$1,700-3,000

A Gallé cameo glass vase 10in (25cm).
$3,200-6,000

A Gallé cameo glass vase 12in (30cm).
$1,800-3,800

A bronze lamp, 'L'Ombellifère' signed Leo Laporte-Blairsy, c1900, 20in (50cm).
$18,000-26,000

A leaded glass landscape panel by Tiffany Studios, 69 by 30in (179 by 78cm) excluding frame.
$50,000-90,000

Originally one of 10 panels commissioned as a window, and dispersed upon demolition of the house. The whereabouts of 4 of the panels unknown.

A collection of 11 Art Nouveau drinking glasses, few minor chips, 8in (21cm) and smaller.
$800-1,500

A pair of Orrefors mirrored doors by Simon Gate, inscribed Simon Gate Orrefors 1936, 84in (214cm) high.
$18,000-26,000

A mahogany display cabinet, designed by Carl Davis Richter, 65in (163cm).
$6,000-12,000

An Ernest Gimson bureau, with elaborately fitted interior, barber's-pole inlay, executed by Sidney Barnsley, 33in (83cm).
$24,000-54,000

A Sidney Barnsley walnut dresser with diamond pattern moulding, 75in (190cm) wide.
$10,000-18,000

Right An oak daybed by Charles Eastlake, with panelled sides, the headrest carved with daisies, and a gothic roundel, upholstered in green velvet on turned legs, 73in (185cm) long.
$8,000-13,500

A walnut extending dining table, with barber's pole inlay and plain octagonal moulded legs, and a set of 6 dining chairs with leather drop-in seats, by Ernest Gimson, executed by Sidney Barnsley, the table 114in (283.5cm) extended.
$20,000-45,000

A German teak desk, the rectangular top with rounded corners, covered in beige leather, the drawers oak-lined, with brass handles, stamped on one drawer Otto Fritzsche, Munchen, 45in (112cm) wide.
$1,800-3,800

A Martin Brothers stoneware tobacco jar and cover modelled as a grotesque cat, inscribed R. W. Martin & Brothers, London & Southall 5.1885.
$18,000-26,000

A Royal Doulton polychrome glazed stoneware, fountain figure, the 'Lily-Maid', inscribed Gilbert Bayes, 24in (61.5cm) high.
$18,000-26,000

A Rozenburg eggshell glazed vase, decorated by Sam Schellinck, crowned Rozenburg Den Haag and stork mark, painter's monogram and work order no. 459, c1902, 10½in (26.5cm).
$18,000-26,000

An unusual and elaborate plique-à-jour pendant necklace, unmarked but probably German, on baton chain, total length of pendant 6½in (15.5cm). $4,000-6,800

A Concord Watch Co. ladies' watch, yellow metal set with peridots, topaz, diamonds and pearls, and with diamond and pearl clasp. $4,000-7,500

A gold, diamond and plique-à-jour enamelled pendant. $6,000-12,000

Right A pair of gold, diamond and plique-a-jour enamelled ear pendants. $2,000-4,500

498

A baluster ewer, stamped 'Tiffany & Co makers', and 'Sterling Silver, 925-1000', pattern No. '14106', 1899-1900, 19in (48cm).
$2,200-4,200

A liqueur set comprising decanter and 6 cups, stamped with 935 German silver mark and PH, for Patriz Huber, c1900, decanter 7in (18cm).
$6,000-12,000

A bronze group of mermaid and fisherman, signed 'Ed.Lanteri' and dated '1898', 24in (60cm).
$3,200-6,000

A silver and enamelled picture frame stamped 'W.H.H.', for W. H. Haseler, Birmingham 1899, 11in (27cm).
$2,000-4,500

A white metal and enamel inkwell attributed to C. R. Ashbee, seven-sided on ball feet, 4in (11cm) high.
$4,500-9,000

An early William De Morgan tile panel consisting of 16 squares, painted on blanks from the 'Architectural Pottery, Poole, Dorset', 24in (61cm) square.
$1,300-2,400

A Tiffany Favrile oviform glass vase, signed 'LCT' and 'F183', 9in (24cm) high.
$2,000-4,500

A bronze and ivory figure, Bat Dancer, cold painted in green and yellow, inscribed signature on base F. Preiss, 9½in (24cm) high.
$7,000-12,000

An ivory figure, 'Nude', carved after a model by Ferdinand Preiss, 17½in (44cm) high.
$18,000-26,000

An Art Deco jade, lapis lazuli and mother-of-pearl table clock, signed by Cartier, 1216, base repaired.
$20,000-45,000

Three gilt bronze and ivory figures after models by A. Gori:

l. 'Exotic Dancer', inscribed in the bronze A. Gori, 15in (37.5cm).
$3,200-6,000

c. 'Flower Girl', inscribed A. Gory Salon Des Beaux Arts Paris, 14in (35cm).
$1,400-2,600

r. 'Flower Seller', inscribed A. Gori, 15in (38cm).
$6,000-12,000

A lacquered metal bowl on small raised circular foot, with rounded flaring body and everted rim, distressed gold body and coral red interior, signed in red lacquer Jean Dunand, c1925, 4in (10cm).
$1,800-3,800

A Carlton Ware oviform ginger jar and cover enriched with gilt decoration, printed marks Carlton Ware, Made in England 'Trade Mark', 12in (31.5cm).
$2,000-4,500

A Clarice Cliff vase, hand painted marks Inspiration by Clarice Cliff New Pottery Burslem England, hand painted signature Clarice Cliff, c1930, 16in (40cm).
$6,000-12,000

A pâte-de-verre vase with stylised moulded decoration of fish swimming through waves, moulded signature G. Argy-Rousseau, c1925, 6in (15cm).
$5,000-9,000

A Lalique butterscotch glass statuette, 'Thais', inscribed R. Lalique, 9in (22cm).
$7,000-12,000

Three Fauré vases, silver and thick enamel, with geometric abstract designs, signed C. Fauré Limoges, c1925.
$3,200-6,000

A white metal and enamel cigarette case, enamel signed F Zwichl, stamped marks 'made in Austria', c1920.
$1,700-3,000

A covered jug modelled as George Robey, 10in (25cm).
$8,000-13,500

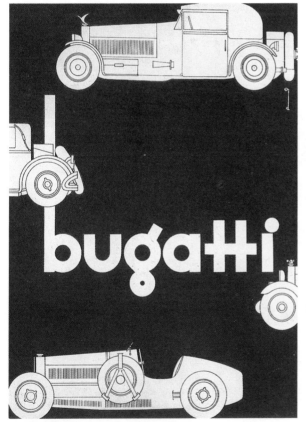

A poster design showing 4 different Bugatti models, signed with the artist's monogram, 21½ by 16in (53 by 39cm).
$8,000-15,000

Right An enamelled minaudiere caricaturing Enrico Caruso, enclosing compartments, a mirror, aides memoire and pencil, maker's marks 'Lacloche Freres Paris' and facsimile of Caruso's signature, 5in (12cm) long.
$5,000-9,000

It is thought that Caruso probably did his own caricature.

A silver and rosewood tea and coffee service by Charles Boynton, maker's and London marks for 1947, 77oz 17dwts.
$8,000-15,000

A bronze figure, 'Anagke', after a model by Gilbert Bayes, signed and dated 1918, 23in (59cm).
$20,000-45,000

A 78-piece silver table service by Charles Boynton, maker's and London marks for 1947, 154oz 11dwts.
$10,000-18,000

A complete Art Deco burr walnut bedroom suite, attributed to Jules Leleu, including telephone and cigarette case.
$20,000-45,000

Below A mahogany and satinwood baby grand piano by Eavestaff, inlaid metal inscription Healey, c1930, 56in (143cm) long.
$4,500-9,000

An illustration design dated 1926, 21in (42cm).
$1,300-2,400

504

Miscellaneous

An Elkington & Co., electrotype ink standish, 7½in (19cm) diam.
$300-600

An Elkington electrotype wedding scene from Much Ado About Nothing, engraved by Leonard Morel-Ladeuil, 1884, 16 by 22in (41 by 56cm).
$600-1,100

An Elkington plate shell shaped spoon warmer, 8in (20cm) diam.
$180-300

A Regency Sheffield plate meat dish and matching dish cover, 18in (46cm).
$600-1,200

A Victorian spoon warmer, in the form of a 16thC mortar, c1870, 6½in (16cm).
$400-750

A Victorian Sheffield plate centrepiece, c1860, 21in (53cm) high.
$800-1,500

A Sheffield plate Argyle, with beaded rim and water reservoir below, 19thC, 6½in (16cm) high.
$200-450

A large silver plated centrepiece and stand, by Elkington & Co., dated April 1851, and with original iron bound oak carrying case.
$4,500-9,000

Make the most of Miller's

Every care has been taken to ensure the accuracy of descriptions and estimated valuations. Price ranges in this book reflect what one should expect to pay for a similar example. When selling one can obviously expect a figure below. This will fluctuate according to a dealer's stock, saleability at a particular time, etc. It is always advisable to approach a reputable specialist dealer or an auction house which has specialist sales.

A table-centre candelabrum, 28½in (72cm) high.
$900-1,700

A Victorian plated table centrepiece.
$600-1,100

A George III Sheffield plate tea caddy, 5in (13cm).
$600-1,100

A wall mirror, plated, late 19thC, 25 by 16in (64 by 41cm).
$1,000-2,000

A travelling coffee set of cylindrical
form, with reeded girdles
comprising: coffee pot on stand,
cream jug and sugar bowl, by Hukin
and Heath, c1885.
$300-600

An E.P.B.M. tea urn, late 19thC,
18in (46cm) high.
$300-600

A silver plated tea urn, 19thC.
$500-900

A pair of large silver plated hearse
lamps, 43in (110cm) high.
$4,000-6,800

A late Victorian chamber pot.
$1,000-2,000

A Sheffield plate kettle, c1850–60.
$150-300

A plated cruet stand with 8 bottles.
$300-600

An old Sheffield plate wire-work
sugar basket.
$300-600

An old Sheffield plate box, depicting
Frederick the Great in profile
wearing armour, c1765.
$400-750

A Victorian novelty brandy
warmer, modelled as a witch's
cauldron, 13in (33.5cm) high.
$300-600

An old Sheffield plate fruit basket,
11in (28cm) wide.
$150-250

A Sheffield plate cake basket,
19thC, 15in (38cm) wide.
$150-300

A Sheffield plate tea tray,
early 19thC, 29in (74cm).
$500-900

A Victorian novelty condiment set,
moulded as a bird perched on a
branch, 5½in (14.5cm) high.
$300-600

A large tea tray, electroplated on
copper, 31in (78cm) wide.
$400-750

An old Sheffield plate wine
cooler, by Matthew Boulton
& Co., 9in (23cm) high.
$500-900

A pair of novelty biscuit boxes,
formed as melons, the three
segments each with their own
pierced cover, 13in (33cm) high.
$1,400-2,600

A Continental electroplated
cigarette case, c1900.
$400-750

A Victorian novelty condiment set,
modelled as a drayman standing
behind 3 condiments shaped as
barrels, 5½in (14cm) high.
$200-450

A Victorian electroplated meat
press, by Elkington & Co., 17½in
(44cm) screwed down, excluding
wood base.
$3,200-6,000

An Australian decoratively plated
mounted two-handled emu egg
trinket box, some damage, 19thC,
7in (18cm) high.
$1,800-3,800

A Continental electroplated
cigarette case, c1900.
$400-750

Tortoiseshell

A Jacobite tortoiseshell snuff box, the lid inset with a painted miniature portrait on glass of The Young Pretender, Charles Edward Stuart, gilt metal rims, 3½in (9cm).
$1,200-2,100

A gold mounted and gem set tortoiseshell parasol handle, late 19thC, 11½in (29cm) long, in fitted case.
$900-1,700

A French tortoiseshell and silver egg, 19thC.
$500-900

A late Victorian heart-shaped tortoiseshell/silver frame.
$600-1,200

Three tortoiseshell and silver frames. c1890.
Pair **$400-750**
Singles **$180-300**

Metal Brass

A pair of brass andirons, American, each with lemon shaped finial above a lemon shaped turning over a hexagonal standard, on spurred arched legs, with ball feet, the billet bars with conforming brass log stops, one billet marked with initials 'P.R.M.R.', 1800-10, 22½in (66cm) high.
$1,400-1,600

A pair of Regency gilt brass and bronze three-light candelabra, 20in (51cm) high.
$2,600-5,300

A fine pair of Federal brass andirons, Philadelphia or New York, each with double urn finial above a tapering columnar shaft over a plinth, on spur-arched cabriole legs with claw-and-ball feet and conforming log posts, 1790-1820, 30½in (76cm) high.
$2,500-3,000

A pair of Federal bell metal andirons, American, with vase shaped standard and tapering finial above a hexagonal plinth on spurred arched legs, and ball feet with conforming bell metal log stops, 1790-1810, 25in (62.5cm) high.
$3,500-4,000

A brass door porter, 16in (41cm) high.
$400-750

A Louis XV style brass, polished steel and cast iron fender, with 3 brass and steel implements.
$900-1,700

A brass tobacco box, Dutch, c1740, 5in (12.5cm).
$300-600

A brass tavern tobacco box, c1830.
$800-1,500

An unusual nickel plated brass solder testing balance, the support signed 'W. Butterworth, maker, Tutbury', with 9 cone solder samples in a glazed wall cabinet, 20in (51cm) wide, and an Austrian postal balance.
$300-600

A brass alms dish, German, c1550, 15in (38cm).
$800-1,500

A Regency brass music stand, with blue-painted and gilded rest, 60½in (153cm) high, fully extended.
$2,000-4,500

A pair of Anglo-Indian brass jardinières, 41in (102.5cm) high.
$4,000-7,500

A rare Volta brass pistol, with brass combustion cylinder conical reducer and brass electrode in a bone ivory collar, 19thC. ▷
$300-600

A pair of W & T Avery Ltd. snuff scales, to weigh 1lb. Class B. No. A189, with brass pans, together with a set of 5 weights.
$300-600

A pair of early Victorian lacquered brass postal scales, inscribed R. W. Winfield, Birmingham, 10½in (26.5cm).
$300-600

A pair of brass and steel sovereign weighing scales, 8 brass weights to weigh from 5–300 sovereigns, the latter and the scales stamped with the makers' name Vandome & Co., London, 27in (69.5cm) high, the oak box with makers' label.
$600-1,100

A Spanish gilt brass relief of the Young St. John The Baptist with his lamb in a wood, two nicks on edges and drilled at corners, the reverse bearing the inscription 'Divan. Unes.' 5½ by 4in (14 by 10cm).
$1,000-2,000

A pair of brass andirons, early 18thC, 29½in (77cm) high.
$6,000-12,000

A large brass mounted lodestone, 8in (20.5cm) high.
$5,000-9,000

A pair of German brass reliefs of the Judgement of Solomon, and David Anointed by Samuel, after the Master H.G., polished surfaces, 6½in (16.7cm), a copper electro-type relief of Darius's family before Alexander, after Charles Le Brun, late 16th/early 17thC, 3 by 4½in (8cm by 11.5cm).
$800-1,500

Bronze

An English bronze bust of a jester, in the style of John Cheere, ebonized wood pedestal and stand, early 18thC, 14in (36cm), with painted wood column, 19thC, 54½in (136cm) high.
$14,000-24,000

A parcel-silvered bronze figure of a trained seal, cast from a model by Marcel Bouraine, French, lower rear of base drilled, ball missing, early 20thC, 19in (48cm) high.
$1,400-2,600

A bronze figure of a Crusader, after E. Fremiet, inscribed 'Credo', signed, red marble plinth, 14½in (37cm) high.
$400-750

A large copper kettle, complete with spirit lamp, the carrying handles of white glass, 13in (33cm) high.
$200-450

A Louchet gilt bronze picture frame, stamped on the metal 'Louchet' and on the leather back 'Louchet, Ciseleur, 3 Rue Auber, Paris', 8½in (21cm) high.
$800-1,500

A French bronze statue of a lute player, known as 'Vendangeur Improvisant', cast from a model by Francisque Joseph Duret, patina slightly rubbed, 19thC, 36½in (92.5cm).
$3,200-6,000

An Arts and Crafts brass desk set by Margaret Gilmour, comprising: table blotter, 12 by 18in (30 by 45cm), pen tray, inkwell, stamp box and picture frame, stamped with 'GM' monogram.
$300-600

A Japanese bronze model of a prowling tiger, signed with a seal, 19thC, 10in (25.5cm) high.
$800-1,500

A Florentine bronze model of a frog, from the workshop of Giambologna and Pietro Tacca, hollow cast and probably having served as a fountain spout, shaped wooden base simulated porphyry, both sides of mouth worn, late 16th/early 17thC, 5in (14cm) high.
$10,000-18,000

A bronze figure, 'Cat Lapping', cast from a model by Rembrandt Bugatti, Italian, inscribed 'R. Bugatti (7)' and stamped with the Hébrard foundry cire perdue seal, rich dark brown patina, early 20thC, 6in (15cm) high.
$24,000-42,000

A pair of bronze dogs, modelled by A Dubucand, 19thC., 4½ by 5in (11.5 by 12.5cm).
$1,000-2,000

A painted Vienna bronze model of a young dog, 7in (18cm) long.
$600-1,200

Two bronze deer with antlers, 48in (122cm) high, including base.
$2,000-4,500

An animalier bronze of stallion and mare, P.J. Mene.
$3,200-6,000

A French bronze cockerel and farmyard scene, signed 'Arson', 19thC, 8½in (21cm) wide.
$600-1,100

A green-patinated bronze group, unsigned, 15½in (39cm).
$1,000-2,000

An English bronze group of 2 sleeping lovers, late 19thC, 4½ by 7½in (11 by 18.5cm).
$800-1,500

A bronzed head and shoulder bust of a young Roman, with impressed marks and signed B.S. Asche, 19thC, 27in (68.5cm).
$600-1,200

A bronze allegorical figure, after Emile Louis Picault, titled 'La Source Du Pactole', c1880, 24in (61cm).
$4,500-9,000

A French bronze statuette of the Neapolitan fisherboy, after Jean Baptiste Carpeaux, signed 'J.B. Carpeaux', and inscribed Susse Fres. Edt. Paris and stamped with the foundry seal flanked by P & B, late 19thC, 24in (61cm) high.
$7,000-12,000

A bronze figure of a man, signed 'Jobbagy' and stamped F. Dunn & Co., oars damaged, 19thC, 25in (63cm).
$1,000-2,000

A bronze figure of a labourer with sledge hammer, entitled 'Pax Et Labor', signed on base Picault, 19thC, 28in (71cm).
$1,200-2,100

A bronze figure of Mercury, on ebonised socle, early 19thC, 14in (35.5cm).
$18,000-26,000

A pair of bronze figures of Mercury and Fame, 19thC, 32½in (82.5cm) and 31½in (80.5cm).
$1,000-2,000

A bronze figure of the ballerina 'Nattova' by S. Yourievitch, early 20thC, 29in (73cm) high overall.
$2,200-4,200

◁

A Coalbrookdale bronze group, stamped 'Bell Fecit, Coalbrookdale' and bearing inscription 'A Gift from Mrs. Abraham Darby to Frederick Monks 1898', polished patination, 19thC, 32in (94cm).
$1,200-2,100

A pair of bronze figures, signed Felix Joubert, Sculpt, 1937, 112in (284cm) overall.
$11,000-20,000

A pair of bronze figures, by Kessler, 9in (23cm) high.
$400-750

An important cast bronze figure of Hercules and the Erymanthian boar, 19thC, 31in (78.5cm).
$1,300-2,400

An Italian bronze study, signed 'P. Chiapparelli, Fe Roma', on veined green marble plinth, 19thC, 24in (61cm) wide.
$1,600-2,800

A bronze statue 'Diana the Huntress', 19thC, 34in (86cm).
$1,700-3,000

A cold painted bronze figure of an Arab snake charmer, 3in (7.5cm). $600-1,200

A Japanese bronze figure on stand. $3,200-6,000

A pair of French ormolu and bronze candleholders, 19thC, 12½in (31.5cm) high. $1,000-2,000

A bronze group of a fox hunt, cast from a model by Isidore Jules Bonheur, French, inscribed 'I. Bonheur', stamped Fabr. Francais D'Art J. D'Estray, and */*, blackish brown patina, late 19thC, 19in (48cm) high. $8,000-15,000

An Austrian cold painted bronze figure of a bearded Arabian warrior sitting on a horse, 9in (23cm). $600-1,200

Two fragments from a Hispano-Visigothic bronze sword handle or terminal of a cross, set with malachite, almandines, other stones and gold, gemset and with a centre section of similar form, 6th or 7th Century A.D., 4½in (10.5cm) and 2½in (6.5cm). $1,600-2,800

A bronze figure of a rider upon a runaway horse, Santa Coloma, signed, 19thC, 15in (38cm) high. $2,600-5,300

An English bronze mortar, dated 1708, 6in (15cm) high. $800-1,500

A Paduan bronze triangular sandbox, in the style of Andrea Briosco, called Riccio, early 16thC, 3½in (8.5cm) high. $4,000-7,500

A bronze plaque depicting the flagellation, 4 armed soldiers scourging the haloed Christ, reeded edge with shell pendant, 16thC, 5½ by 4½in (14.5 by 11cm). $400-750

A collection of 12 Henth bronze weights, some bearing verification marks. $300-600

An English bronze cauldron on hoof feet, c1650. $600-1,200

513

A Regency bronze and ormolu inkstand, with blue glass liner, 3½in (9cm) wide.
$1,300-2,400

A pair of Chinese bronze vases, decorated with hens and foliage in low relief, 16in (40.5cm).
$600-1,100

A bronze cigarette box, cold painted bronze on brass base, 4in (10cm) high.
$800-1,500

A Shan bronze drum, cast with a ▷ star motif and numerous concentric bands, applied strap handles, 28in (71cm) diam.
$1,200-2,100

An English bronze posnet cooking pot, c1590, 6in (15cm) high.
$900-1,700

An Italian uniface bronze medal of Lorenzo the Magnificent De' Medici, after Niccolo Fiorentino, 3½in (8.5cm) diam, another of Lorenzo di Piero de Medici, Duke of Urbino, after Francesco da Sangallo, 3in (8cm) diam, and two after Selvi, of Lorenzo the Magnificent and Christina of Lorraine, 3in (8cm) diam.
$400-750

A green patinated bronze inkstand, with 2 square wells, matching letter rack and blotter, 19thC.
$600-1,200

Copper

A small English copper kettle, c1840, 6in (15cm).
$300-600

A copper kettle with swing handle, c1790.
$300-600

A copper kettle with fixed brass and copper handle, acorn finial, late 19thC, 13in (33cm).
$100-250

◁ A Georgian copper kettle, c1800, 11in (28cm).
$300-600

A copper kettle on original brass stand, c1800, 12in (30.5cm).
$600-1,100

A set of 4 Victorian copper baluster measures on flared feet, 1 pint to 1 gill.
$600-1,100

A Victorian copper tea kettle on stand with spirit burner, 7½in (19cm).
$200-450

A George IV copper samovar, warranted best London Manufacture No.29, 15in (38cm).
$300-600

An English copper spirit measure, ½ pint size, c1840, 4in (10cm) high.
$200-450

A late Georgian copper tea urn, with brass tap, c1830, 15in (38cm) high.
$200-450

A set of 10 graduated copper pans with steel handles and copper lids, some engraved initials NGC by Benham & Sons, Wigmore Street, London and Temple & Crook, Motcomb Street, S.W., 19thC, 14in (35.5cm) to 5in (12.5cm) diam.
$1,200-2,100

c. A copper and brass grape hod, 18thC, 30in (76cm) high.
$600-1,100

l. and r. A pair of cast brass and wrought iron firedogs, 26in (66cm) high.
$800-1,500

A set of 3 European gilded and copper dishes, early 19thC, two 20in (51cm) and one 25in (63.5cm).
$900-1,700

A moulded gilt copper cow weathervane, American, with cast zinc head, tubular mount, on later metal stand, 19thC, 27½in (68cm)..
$2,000-2,500

A copper coal scuttle.
$150-300

A copper urn with elephant handles, 24in (61cm).
$400-750

A Victorian copper and steel basket grate and fender en suite, bearing the registration number 75774, 34in (86cm) and 60½in (151cm) wide.
$1,200-2,100

A gilt copper electrotype frame housing a Limoges enamel plaque of the Virgin and Child Enthroned, after Bellini, the frame with an applied Holy Water stoup, top left hand corner of plaque damaged, traces of verdigris around stoup, 19thC, 25½ by 12in (64.5 by 30.5cm).
$2,000-4,500

A brass and copper jardinière, with a detachable liner, with a border of husk swags centred by cows' skulls, on 3 monopodiae supports headed with sphinxes, united by scrolling foliate cross stretchers and with honeysuckle and Babylonian mask ornament, 19thC, 36in (92cm) high.
$3,200-6,000

Based on the example excavated from Pompeii and now in Naples Museum.

A copper crucifix, the Corpus Christi applied separately, the foot with a peg for attachment, with traces of gilding, 12thC, 9½in (23.5cm) high, perspex stand.
$3,200-6,000

A copper electrotype model of the Vendôme Column, cast with a continuous spiralling relief of military manoeuvres inscribed 'Neapolio . Imp . Aug . Monumentum Belli Germanici Anno MDCCCV Trimestri Spatio Ductu Suo Proflugati Ex Aere Capto Gloriae Exercitus Maximi Dicavit', mid-19thC, 52in (132cm) high.
$3,200-6,000

Ormolu

A pair of Louis XVI ormolu figures of scantily-clad Bacchantes, 28in (71cm) high overall.
$5,000-9,000

A pair of ormolu ostrich candlesticks, 12in (31cm) high.
$1,300-2,400

A pair of Regency ormolu twelve-light candelabra, 24½in (62cm) high.
$7,000-12,000

A George III ormolu hall lantern, with arched glazed cylindrical body in waved frame, 30in (76cm) high, excluding chain suspension.
$11,000-18,000

A Russian ormolu and serpentine marble desk set, 18½in (47cm) wide.
$7,000-12,000

An Hungarian onyx and ormolu desk set.
$400-750

◁ An Empire ormolu cut-glass twelve-light chandelier, the nozzles fitted for electricity, 36in (92cm) high.
$2,000-4,500

set of 4 ormolu candlesticks with
shaped drip-pans, nozzles, shafts
nd swirling bases with rockwork
nd chased berried foliage, 11in
8cm) high.
3,200-6,000

A Regency ormolu inkstand, with a
pair of cut-glass bottles and 2
pentrays, 13in (33cm) wide.
$7,000-12,000

A pair of Regency ormolu urns,
10½in (27cm) high.
$9,000-15,000   ▷

Iron

set of 4 cast-iron garden urns,
0in (51cm) high.
,200-2,100

A pair of wrought iron lancet
shaped gates in the manner of
A.W.N. Pugin, c1840–45, 108in
(275cm) high.
$2,600-5,300

A pair of gilt painted wrought iron
and brass Communion rail gates,
attributed to Augustus Pugin,
19thC, 28in (71cm) high, with letter
of attribution.
$600-1,100

Continental tall iron strong box,
e lid and sides riveted with straps
nd twin handles, the front with a
rtouche, 17th/18thC, 14in (36cm)
ide.
900-1,700

A cast-iron statue of a blackamoor,
holding a snake on his left arm with
a base for a lamp, early 19thC.
$10,000-18,000

*Said to have been purchased from
the Duke of Cumberland's Lodge,
Windsor Great Park.*

A rare pair of iron candle snuffers
on stand, maker's mark Dowler,
18thC, 6in (15cm) high.
$1,800-3,800

pair of enamelled cast-iron door
tops in the form of a classical
unch with Toby and Judy with the
aby, 7½ by 12in (19 by 31cm).
300-600

A pair of Regency cast-iron
campana shaped garden urns, 20in
(51cm).
$800-1,500

A large wrought iron and painted
metal screen, possibly designed by
Skidmore, c1840–45, 90in (228cm)
high.
$800-1,500

A cast-iron garden seat, in the
Coalbrookdale style.
$1,200-2,100

A wrought iron weather vane,
18thC, 14in (36cm) high.
$600-1,100

A George III polished steel and cast-
iron basket grate, 35in (89cm) wide,
and a fender en suite, 46in (117cm)
wide.
$6,000-12,000

A pair of cast iron figural andirons,
New England, each in the form of a
woman with crossed arms, on
arched legs, late 18thC, 12in (29cm)
high.
$700-1,000

Pewter

A quart-size pewter tankard, c1790,
7½in (19cm) high.
$600-1,100

A Scottish pewter
chopin measure,
c1790, 8½in (22cm) hig
$1,000-2,000

An English quart-size barrel-
shaped tankard, c1820, 6½in
(16cm) high.
$400-900

An English half-pint
pewter double
volute lidded measure, c1780.
$300-600

A Normandy pewter measure,
c1800, 10in (25cm) high.
$500-900

A set of 5 West Country pewt◌
measures, 19thC, ½gall–½gi
$1,600-2,800

A set of 6 graduated haystack
measures, by Austen & Son, Cork,
with loop handles, 19thC,
½gall–½noggin.
$2,000-4,500

A pewter plate, inscribed 'Thomas's
Chop House Cornhill, c1800, 9in
(23cm) diam.
$1,600-2,800

A pewter charger, 17thC, 22in
(51cm) diam.
$1,000-2,000

wo beakers, the first by Ashbil riswold Meriden, Ct., 1807-35, the econd American, early 19thC, the rst with two bands of incised lines, ie second bell-shaped, with a coved ootrim, and two bands on incised nes, unmarked, 3in (7.5cm).
400-500

A tankard, New York or Philadelphia, with a narrow midband, and a domed lid with a scrolling thumbpiece, the S-shaped handle with a boot-heel terminal, unmarked, late 18th/early 19thC, 6in (15cm) high.
$3,000-4,000

A basin, by Robert Palethorp, Jr., Philadelphia, with a single reed brim, marked in centre with eagle and name touches, 1817-22, 10in (25cm) diam.
$1,000-1,200

dish, by Nathaniel Austin, harlestown, Massachusetts, with single reed brim, marked on back ith eagle touch and initial pseudo allmarks, some pitting, 1763-807, 15in (37.5cm) diam.
200-400

A tankard, by Henry Will, New York or Albany, the lid with a crenellated lip and a scroll thumbpiece, the S-scroll handle with a bud terminal, the rim and footrim moulded, marked on inside with Laughlin touch 491, marks worn, late 18thC, 7in (17.5cm) high.
$6,000-8,000

A teapot, by Morey and Ober, Boston, with a domed lid with finial a double scroll handle and a faceted scroll spout, 1852-55, 7½in (18cm) high.
$300-400

teapot, by Roswell Gleason, orchester, Massachusetts, apple iaped, with domed lid and lobed ooden finial, a partly fluted scroll out and a spurred wooden scroll andle with volute handle joins, on moulded circular foot rim, marked i bottom, 1821-71, 7½in (18cm) igh.
200-250

A teapot, by William Calder, Providence, R.I., pyriform, with domed conical lid and conical finial, a scroll handle and a faceted scroll spout, marked on base, 1817-56, 7in (17.5cm) high.
$2,800-3,000

A deep dish, with 'LOVE' touch, probably Philadelphia area, with a single reed brim, marked on back, 1750-1800, 13in (32.5cm) diam.
$800-900

chalice, by Timothy Brigden, lbany, New York, with tapering ylindrical cup over a baluster :em, on a domed and moulded foot, arked inside cup and on base, 816-19, 9in (22.5cm) high.
7,000-7,500

A plate, with 'LOVE' touch, probably Philadelphia area, with a single reed brim, marked on back, 1750-1800, 8in (20cm) diam.
$350-400

A beaker, by Thomas Boardman & Co., Hartford, with double incised midband, on a moulded foot, marked on base, 1822-25, 5in (12.5cm) high.
$800-900

Two basins, with unidentified eagle mark, the first with a narrow reed brim, marked in the centre of the bowl, the second with partial mark in the centre of bowl, repairs to rim, late 18th/early 19thC, 7½ and 8in (17.5 and 20cm) diam..
$500-600

A lighthouse coffee pot, by Israel Trask, Massachusetts, with domed lid and turned wood finial, a double scroll handle, a scroll spout, and with reeded and bright cut engraved banding, marked on base, c1813-56, 10½in (26cm) high.
$650-750

A flagon, by Oliver Trask, Beverly, Massachusetts, with a domed lid and knob finial, a curved spout, an S-scroll handle, marked on base, 1832-39, 11½in (28cm).
$600-800

A large plate, by Richard Austin, Boston, with a single reed brim, marked on back, 1793-1807, 12in (30cm) diam.
$500-550

A baptismal bowl, by Lorenzo Williams, Philadelphia, with an everted rim, on a stem over a stepped and domed circular foot, marked on base, 1838-42, 6½in (16cm) diam.
$800-900

A coffee pot, by Ashbil Griswold, Meriden, Connecticut, with reeded banding, with a domed lid, an S-shaped spout, and a double scroll handle, marked on bottom, 1807-35, 11½in (28cm) high.
$400-500

A flagon, by Thomas D Boardman, Hartford, with a stepped domed lid with an urn shaped finial, a double scroll handle with a scroll thumbpiece and a bud terminal, and a curved spout, the body with a raised mid-rib and a flaring foot, marked with eagle touch, name touch, and Hartford touch on base, 1804-60 and later, 13in (32.5cm).
$2,000-2,500

A flagon, by Israel Trask, Beverly, Massachusetts, with domed lid and disc finial, a curved spout, and an S-shaped handle with reeded banding at shoulder and foot, marked on base, repair to lid at hinge, c1813-56, 12in (30cm).
$700-1,000

A beaker, probably Ashbil Griswold, Meriden, Ct., with 2 bands of incised lines, partial mark on base, 1807-35, 3in (7.5cm) high.
$150-200

A coffee pot, by Boardman & Co., New York, with domed lid with wooden disc finial, a squared handle and an S-shaped spout, on a moulded circular foot, marked on base, 1825-27, 12in (30cm) high.
$500-600

Make the most of Miller's

When a large specialist well-publicised collection comes on the market, it tends to increase prices. Immediately after this, prices can fall slightly due to the main buyers having large stocks and the market being 'flooded'. This is usually temporary and does not affect very high quality items.

Four salts, early 19thC.
l. probably Philadelphia, with a pyriform bowl, the rim and footrim with beaded border, 2½in (5cm). lc. and rc. with circular bowls, on circular feet, unmarked, 3in (8cm). r. with an everted brim and engine turning, 2in (5cm).
$1,000-1,200

A rare spoon, probably by Francis Bassett II, New York, with straight rat-tail handle, marked with indistinct touch, probably Jacobs touch 33 on inside of bowl, 1749-1800, 6½in (16.5cm).
$1,000-1,100

A pair of fluid lamps, by Rufus Dunham, Westbrook, Maine, each with a double wick holder above a cylindrical font, on a tapering stem with a stepped circular foot, marked on base, 1837-60, 6in (16cm) high.
$750-1,000

Two pairs of fluid lamps, American, the centre pair with a single wick above a cylindrical font over narrow baluster stem, on a circular foot, the other pair each with a double wick holder above a cylindrical font with a scroll handle, unmarked, early 19thC, 5½in and 3in (13 and 7.5cm).
$550-750

A pair of fluid lamps, American, each with a brass double wick holder with pewter snuffers above a cylindrical font, on a baluster stem with a strap handle, over a dished circular base, unmarked, 1825-50, 8in (20cm).
$550-750

A pair of fluid lamps, by James H Putnam, Malden, Massachusetts, each with a flaring cylindrical font over a tapering stem, on a domed circular foot, marked on base, 1830-55, 8in (20cm).
$700-900

A pair of fluid lamps, by Roswell Gleason, Dorchester, Massachusetts, each with a double wick holder above an acorn font, on a baluster stem, over a circular foot, one wick holder without snuffers, 1821-71, ½in (24cm).
550-750

A bedpan, by Thomas D and Sherman Boardman, Hartford, with a baluster shaped handle, eagle touch struck twice on base, initial touch struck once on base, 1810-50, 17½in (44cm) long.
$400-500

A porringer, by Edward Danforth, Hartford, with a boss bottom and an old English handle, marked on handle with Laughlin touch 389, 1790-1820, 4in (11cm) diam.
$2,600-3,000

A porringer, by Joseph Belcher or Joseph Belcher, Jr., Newport, R.I., with a boss bottom and a crown handle, marked on handle with Laughlin touch 314, some wear and damage to handle, 1770-90, 5in (12.5cm) diam.
$1,500-2,000

A porringer, by David Melville, Newport, R.I., with a boss bottom and a flowered handle, marked on handle with Laughlin touch 322, mark worn, 1776-93, 5in (12cm) diam.
$1,200-1,500

A porringer, by Samuel or Samuel E. Hamlin, Providence, R.I., with boss bottom, and a flowered handle, marked on handle with Laughlin touch 336, 1780-1820, 4in (11cm) diam.
$800-900

A porringer, by Samuel or Samuel E. Hamlin, Providence, R.I., with boss bottom and a flowered handle, marked on handle with Laughlin touch 334, 1780-1820, 5in (12.5cm) diam.
$900-1,100

A porringer, by Thomas Danforth III, Stepney, Connecticut and Philadelphia, with a boss bottom and a flowered handle, marked on back of handle with Laughlin touch 368, pitted, small repair to bowl, 1780-1820, 5in (12cm) diam.
$800-1,200

A porringer, by William Billings, Providence, R.I., with a boss bottom and a flowered handle, marked on handle with Laughlin touch 346, repairs and bruises, 1791-1806, 4in (11cm) diam.
$900-1,200

A porringer, by Samuel or Samuel E. Hamlin, Providence, R.I., with boss bottom and an old English handle, marked on handle with Laughlin touch 337, 1780-1820, 4in (10cm).
$700-800

A porringer, by Gershom Jones, Providence, R.I., with a boss bottom and a flowered handle, marked on handle with Laughlin touch 341, repairs to bowl, 1774-1809, 5in (12cm) diam.
$1,600-2,000

A porringer, possibly by Richard Lee, Sr., or Richard Lee, Jr., Springfield, Vermont, with basin bottom and a tab handle with raised beaded decoration, unmarked, repair to handle, 1800-20, 6in (15cm) diam.
$1,800-2,000

A porringer, possibly by John, Joseph or Samuel Danforth, Connecticut, with a boss bottom and a dolphin handle, unmarked, 1780-1820, 5in (12.5cm) diam.
$100-300

A porringer, by David Melville, Newport, R.I., with a boss bottom and a flowered handle, marked on handle with Laughlin touch 322, 2 repairs to bowl, 1776-93, 5in (12.5cm) diam.
$1,500-2,800

A porringer, by Thomas Danforth III, Stepney, Connecticut and Philadelphia, with a boss bottom and an old English handle, marked on back of handle with Laughlin touch 368, 1780-1818, 4½in (11cm) diam.
$1,300-1,500

A porringer, by Thomas D and Sherman Boardman, Hartford, with a boss bottom and a flowered handle, marked on handle with Laughlin touch 428, 1810-50, 5in (12.5cm) diam.
$600-800

A porringer, by Joseph Danforth, Jr., Richmond, Virginia, with a boss bottom and a flowered handle, back of handle with incised 'JD' and star touch, similar to Laughlin touch 379, 1807-12, 5in (12.5cm) diam.
$1,800-2,000

A porringer, by Frederick Bassett, New York City or Hartford, with a boss bottom and an old English handle, marked on back of handle with Laughlin touch 468, 1770-90, 5in (12.5cm) diam.
$1,800-2,200

A pair of broad rimmed English chargers, stamped with 'hallmarks', touch of SB with fleur-de-lys (ad) verso, c1670, 20½in (51.5cm) diam., the rim 4in (10cm).
$2,600-5,300

l. An English latten trefid spoon, c1710, 6in (15cm).
$180-300

c. An English pewter slip-top spoon, c1650, 5½in (15cm).
$300-600

r. An English latten seal-top spoon, c1630, 5½in (15cm).
$300-600

A Dutch pewter chalice, c1620, 9in (23cm) high.
$1,000-2,000

A pair of pewter candlesticks, c1830, 8in (20cm) high.
$300-600

An English pewter salt and pepper set, with engraved crown over 'B' monogram, c1790, pepper 4½in (11.5cm) high.
$300-600

Locks and Keys

A group of Gothic keys, 3 to 6in (7.5 to 15cm),
top: iron, c1500   **$200-450**
l. bronze, c1300   **$500-900**
c. iron, c1400   **$200-450**
r. bronze, c1400   **$400-750**
bottom: iron, c1500   **$200-450**

A group of keys, all c1680:–
l. A French steel key, 3½in (9cm).
$300-600

lc. An English steel key.
$300-600

rc. An English steel key.
$200-450

r. A French steel key.
$200-450

Five steel keys, 19thC, 4in (10cm) approx.
l, lc, and r.   **$100-250**
c, and cr.   **$20-45**

Lead

An Italian lead metal of Niccolo Piccinino, possibly late 15thC after Pisanello, 3½in (8.8cm).
$200-450

A pair of English lead urns, one slightly sunken on its foot and bowl splitting at corners, late 17th/early 18thC, 43in (107cm).
$11,000-18,000

A pair of lead urns, the fluted baluster bodies applied with trailing foliage and hirsute mask heads, on tapering stands with circular naturalistic bases, slight damage, 18thC, 16in (40cm).
$300-600

A tôleware miniature tray, with hand painted scene, c1830, 9in (22.5cm) diam.
$200-450

A cold painted lead Arab group.
$200-450

A Victorian Pontypool coal scuttle, with picture of dog on glass panel to lid.
$1,200-2,100

Miscellaneous

A good Chinese export card case, chased in relief with people taking tea, the front applied with a cartouche inscribed 'Hilda, 1905', the reverse chased with birds amidst bamboo, by Luen Hing of Shanghai, c1905.
$300-600

A large pair of French spelter figures of children, by Miroy Freres, bearing metal labels numbered 4 and 5, late 19thC, 39in (99cm).
$1,300-2,400

An English tin horn lantern, c1800, 10in (25.5cm).
$300-600

A pair of Pontypool urns and covers, with gilt decoration and lion mask ring handles, 13in (33cm).
$3,200-6,000

An Indian chased white metal ink stand, with 2 glass bottles, ivory inlaid border to stand, 10½in (26.5cm) wide.
$300-600

A Victorian tôle coal box, the glazed lid decorated with a winter scene with tapering body and iron tripartite base, 19½in (49cm) wide.
$2,000-4,500

A cold painted spelter figure of a Middle Eastern girl dancer, after Louis Hottot, 31in (79cm).
$1,400-2,600

A gilt metal shaped oval casket and hinged cover, surmounted by a putto and with scroll handles and feet, printed with cherubs and flowers, 14in (35.5cm) wide.
$1,000-2,000

An unusual tôle peinte tea urn, the pierced quatrefoil base with a drawer for cinders, decorated overall with painted flowers and gilt sprays, 19thC.
$1,000-2,000

A National Fire Brigade's Union Chief Officer's plated helmet, with dragon and scroll cresting, crowned sunburst pattern badge, original lining and chin strap.
$1,000-2,000

A pair of lead-coloured metal figures of harvesters, 27in (68.5cm).
$600-1,200

A pair of Regency ormolu-mounted Pontypool chestnut urns, painted on a cream ground, 10½in (26.5cm) wide.
$1,200-2,100

An English tin candle mould, c1830, 9in (23cm).
$150-300

A patinated spelter bust of a young woman, entitled 'Time is Money', set with a clock with striking movement and enamelled chapter segments, slight damage to rear of base, 26in (66cm).
$800-1,500

A Trousse, comprising knife, and long and short fork, all with ivory handles bound with engraved brass, the leather sheath with tooled decoration, 17th/18thC.
$800-1,500

Two French or Italian uniface medals of Roman Empresses, one inscribed 'Albia Terentia Othonis Mater', the other 'Petronia AV: Vitellii Vxor', 17thC, 3½in (8.5cm) diam, and 7 French oval bronze plaquettes of Roman Emperors, 18thC, 2 by 1½in (5 by 4cm), and a bronze cast of a Renaissance cameo, 2½ by 1½in (6 by 4cm).
$400-750

An English tin wall sconce, c1800, 10in (25.5cm).
$200-450

A gilt brass chandelier, fitted for electricity, 19thC, 35in (90cm) high
$4,500-9,000

Ivory/Shell

l. A Malacca cane with ivory dog's head, silver collar.
$600-1,100

r. An ebony walking stick with ivory rabbit's head, gold collar.
$600-1,200

A pair of Shib decorated ivory tusks, 19thC, 14in (35.5cm).
$600-1,100

An ivory concentric ball novelty, 19thC, 18½in (47cm) high.
$1,300-2,400

A carved Dieppe ivory and silver gilt fork and spoon, 19thC.
$6,000-12,000

A French ivory diptych of the Nativity, Adoration of the Magi, Crucifixion and Coronation of the Virgin, arranged in 2 tiers beneath Gothic arches, Virgin's finger missing, overpainted and with new hinges, mid to late 14thC, 7 by 3½in (18 by 8.5cm) each panel.
$14,000-24,000

An ivory and ebony elephant thermometer, 1880.
$400-750

A fine Swiss 'Bears of Berne' chess set carved in ivory, one side natural, one brown stained, tiny defects to 2 weapons, 19thC, 3½in (9cm) height of kings, 2½in (6.5cm) height of pawns.
$18,000-26,000

A pair of Austrian fruitwood and ivory statuettes of 2 beggars, in the style of Simon Troger, minor defects, 18thC, 8in (20cm).
1,800-3,800

A Japanese carved ivory figure of a female deity playing a stringed instrument and seated upon a dragon, on oval base, 11in (28cm).
1,200-2,100

From l–r.
A German turned ivory ball of concentric spheres and spiked stars, minor damage, late 17th/early 18thC, 2½in (6cm) diam.
$1,000-2,000

An English turned ivory Auctioneer's gavel, 4½in (11.5cm).
$400-900

A mother-of-pearl vase and cover, minor losses, possibly 17thC German, 10½in (26.5cm) high.
$1,400-2,600

A German silver-mounted shell spoon, the handle formed from the spiral centre, 18th or early 19thC, 12½in (31cm).
$1,300-2,400

An English ivory gaming ball, in a turned wood box, the ball with numerous roundels (for painted numbers?), the box in 2 halves with a screw thread, minor chips to box, 18th/early 19thC, 4in (10cm) diam.
$2,000-4,500

A buffalo horn dinner gong, the two horn supports with plated mounts on wood plinth.
$400-750

A German ivory mirror case of Hercules and the Nemean Lion and Samson and the Lion, the central roundels within frames of vines which interlock, some cracks, probably early 16thC, 4½in (11.5cm), four parts.
$4,000-7,500

A Scottish horn table snuff mill, engraved 'May we never forget a Friend at a Pinch'.
$1,000-2,000

A good whales tooth scrimshaw, decorated in polychrome fashion with a three-masted sailing ship and a coconut tree, early 19thC, 5½in (14cm) long.
$400-750

A bone inlaid Moorish oval framed mirror on stand, 19thC, 58in (148cm) high.
$800-1,500

A Portuguese rhinoceros horn group of Orpheus charming the animals, carved and pierced with numerous animals, on an ivory mounted black-stained horn foliate plinth, 9in (23cm).
$1,200-2,100

A French ivory Dieppe figure of Napoleon, his chest opening to reveal a triptych depicting scenes from his campaigns, 12in (31cm).
$1,700-3,000

A group of 7 German bone panels of Salvator Mundi, the Virgin and Five Apostles, with stained wood frame, 17thC, 4½in (12cm).
$1,800-3,800

Marble

An Italian marble bust of the Fate Lachesis, sometimes ascribed to Michelangelo, late 16th/17thC, 29in (73cm).
$18,000-26,000

This amazing bust of one of three Fates was popular, judging from the existence of 3 other examples, 2 in marble and one in bronze.

A fine Roman white marble bust of the head of Laocöon, on a waisted grey marble pedestal inscribed 'Laocoon', late 17th/early 18thC, 27in (68.5cm).
$1,700-3,000

A French marble bust of a cherubic boy, clutching a doll of Punch inside his garment, marble socle; minor chips, late 18thC, 12in (30cm).
$3,200-6,000

A pair of carved marble figures of Mars and Minerva, each seated with shield and helmet, early 19thC, 22½ and 16in (57 and 41cm) high.
$2,600-5,300

A white marble portrait bust of a young lady, on veined yellow marble base, early 19thC, 16in (41cm).
$400-750

A French white marble statue of Antinous, left thumb cracked, 18thC, 25in (63cm).
$4,000-7,500

An English marble bust of Mercury, wearing the petasus and with curly hair, on marble socle, late 18th/early 19thC, 17in (43cm).
$1,300-2,400

A pair of white statuary marble busts of Grecian semi-clad young ladies, each standing on mottled brown and grey fluted plinths, Marshall Wood, signed and dated 1869, 27in (68.5cm) and 25½in (65cm) height of busts.
$6,000-12,000

A white marble sculpture of a standing naked Venus, her arms outstretched within a carved shell, 26in (66cm) high.
$900-1,700

A carved verte marble figure of a lion, late 18thC, 11in (28cm).
$500-900

A German ivory model of a recumbent dog, in the style of Loenhard Kern, on a wooden plinth veneered with tortoiseshell, end panels missing, possibly 17thC, 2 by 4½in (5 by 11cm).
$2,600-5,300

An English marble relief of Napoleon fleeing from the field of Waterloo, by Sir Richard Westmacott, R.A., carved in 3 sections with irregular joints, minor abrasions, early 19thC, 68 by 189in (173 by 480cm).
$100,000-200,000

Provenance: The Manor of Littleton, Shepperton, Middx.

A marble statuette of a maiden in classical dress, signed P. Barzanti Florence, 44in (110cm).
$4,000-7,500

A Roman marble fragment.
$800-1,500

A marble relief of a Roman Emperor, on a blue ground in giltwood frame, 8½ by 7in (21.5 by 18cm), and another similar, 7½ by 6in (19 by 15cm).
$4,000-7,500

A sculpture, Wise Owl, in figured grey marble, perching upon 3 books, 19thC, 13in (33cm).
$900-1,700

A pair of Watcombe terracotta jars and covers, each brightly painted between turquoise bands, slight damage, printed mark, c1880, 18in (46cm).
$600-1,100

Terracotta/Stone

A pair of French terracotta busts of a Satyr and a Bacchante, by Louis Delaville, signed on the reverses 'Delaville', on waisted square socles, marble plinths, late 18thC, 9in (23cm).
$7,000-12,000

Louis Delaville, 1763–1841, was a pupil of Boizot.

A pair of carved stone figures of Summer and Autumn, both damaged, late 17th/early 18thC, 37in (94cm).
$2,600-5,300

A William IV green porphyry pedestal, 15½in (40cm) wide.
$900-1,700

A Belgian terracotta bust of Socrates, by Charles Malaise, signed on the back, in the opening, 'Malaise', traces of paint, chipped around edges, late 18th/early 19thC, 12½in (31cm).
$2,600-5,300

Charles Malaise, 1775–1836, came from Brussels and was a pupil of Godecharle.

A French terracotta bust of an 18thC lady with dressed hair, 16in (40.5cm).
$4,000-6,800

A painted terracotta model of a pug with red and gold collar, 14½in (36.5cm) wide.
$4,500-9,000

A terracotta bust of a young lady, signed by the French sculptor 'Henri Alphonse Nelson', 19thC.
$600-1,100

A French terracotta bust of an 18thC boy with wig and cravat, on turned socle, 18in (46cm).
$5,000-9,000

A fine terracotta figure of an Indian musician, 19thC, 43in (107.5cm).
$1,600-2,800

A pair of terracotta Berber musicians, 18in (46cm).
$1,700-3,000

A German limewood high relief of the Virgin of the Immaculate Conception, several fingers damaged or missing, minor cracks and repairs, supported on a wooden post on a velvet-covered base, 15½in (40cm) high.
$8,000-15,000

An oak panel, 16thC.
$600-1,100

A larger than life-size terracotta pug dog.
$400-750

Woodcarvings

A pair of German polychrome wood reliefs of gambolling putti amidst foliage, paint flaking and minor defects, 17thC, 20 by 9in (51 by 23cm).
$1,800-3,800

An oak panel, 16thC.
$800-1,500

A fine carved limewood oval mirror, late 17thC.
$7,000-12,000

A New England carved wood and polychrome figure of a West Point Cadet, fitted with rifle, leather straps, small pieces missing, retaining most of its original polychrome finish, c1890, on later wooden base.
$900-1,000

A chip carved casket, English, c1680, 5in (13cm) high.
$600-1,200

A carved wooden figure of a long eared owl, 19thC, 22in (56cm).
$1,300-2,400

A large wooden model of a seated camel, naturalistically and finely carved, 19thC, 27½in (70cm) high.
$26,000-45,000

A pair of Italian parcel gilt and painted brackets, partly redecorated, 20in (51cm) wide.
$1,400-2,600

A carved bone handled umbrella, American, the curved handle grip reeded and carved with flowers, one side with a profile medallion of George Washington, the other with an American eagle and shield, with brass fittings and wooden spokes, now covered in a green moire, with tassel fringe, early 19thC, 38in (95cm) long.
$700-900

Miscellaneous

A Flemish oak statuette of the mourning Virgin, her hands clasped in prayer, chips on base, early 16thC, 33½in (85cm) high.
1,800-3,800

An Italian mosaic picture panel, with 4 pigeons drinking from a bronze bowl, 19thC, 5½ by 4in (14 by 10cm).
$600-1,200

An Italian alabaster bust of a little girl, wearing an embroidered bib and bonnet, minor chips, grimy, 17thC, 13½in (34cm) high.
$2,600-5,300

A Campanian neck amphora, from the Cassandra-Parrish Workshop, 350-340 B.C., 11½in (29cm).
$1,000-2,000

A Nottingham alabaster relief of the Resurrection, top edge missing, repaired crack, 14th or 15thC, 14½ by 11½in (36 by 29cm).
$9,000-15,000

A pair of Georgian straw-work pictures, of the Church and Parsonage at Chilton, Wiltshire, in giltwood frames, 7 by 9½in (18 by 24cm).
$1,800-3,800

A large Flemish alabaster relief of the Entombment, minor chips and repairs, 16thC, 39½ by 31½in (101 by 79.5cm).
$7,000-12,000

An Attic black figure neck amphora, by the Red Line painter, late 6th Century B.C., 10in (25cm).
$4,000-7,500

Pottery

An Attic black figure olpe, repaired and restored, late 6th Century B.C., 9in (22.5cm).
$600-1,200

A predynastic painted pottery jar, with reddish-brown concentric spirals and wavy bands, rim chipped, Naqada II, 6in (15cm) high.
$2,600-5,300

A Jemdat Nasr bichrome pottery jar, the upper half painted with red and brown panels, 5in (13cm).
$1,800-3,800

An Apulian hydria, associated with the Darius/Underworld Painter, c330 B.C., 12in (30.5cm) high.
$1,700-3,000

A glazed frit cosmetic jar and lid, the swivel lid attached with modern bronze pin, 9th-8th Century B.C., 2in (5cm) high.
$1,000-2,000

An Attic black figure Siana cup, by the C Painter, 2nd quarter of 6th Century B.C., 13½in (34cm) diam. across handles.
$10,000-18,000

A terracotta figure of Horus, 1st/2nd Century A.D., 7½in (18.5cm).
$300-600

A collection of turquoise glazed composition gaming pieces, mainly New Kingdom, Dynasty XVIII, ½in (1.5cm) high average.
$1,800-3,800

A baked clay cuneiform tablet, an administrative document, 3rd Millennium B.C., 3 by 2½in (7.5 by 7cm).
$8,000-13,500

A predynastic slate turtle palette, in the form of a stylised turtle, the head inlaid with shell eyes, one missing, Naqada II, 5in (12cm) diam.
$5,000-9,000

A terracotta figure of a female musician, 1st/2nd Century A.D., 7½in (19cm).
$200-450

An unusual Mochica figural group, with central prone figure, the arms held to the stomach, flanked by 2 heads of deities behind a pierced arched structure surmounted by 3 heads, with flat base, overall with traces of brown decoration, AD 100-500, 3½in (7.5cm) high.
$200-250

A Shipibo pottery effigy vessel, with rounded base, angular body and shoulder with 4 vertical ribs, moulded facial features, and painted in shades of brown, blue and red on cream with angular geometric designs, 13in (33cm) high.
$300-600

A Colima vessel in the form of a wide mouth jar encircled by 4 realistically rendered lobsters, with incised tails and spines, the front claws raised in relief, burnished red, 100 BC/AD 250, 11in (27.5cm) diam.
$1,500-2,000

A Paracas bottle, moulded in the form of a face, the arms extended down, the hands raised upwards, a brown ground with ochre, red and green, 300-100 BC, 5in (12.5cm) high.
$800-900

A Chimu blackware ring vessel, in the form of an animal holding its tail in its mouth, with moulded details, and cylindrical neck with flaring rim, AD 900-1100, 10in (25.5cm) high.
$600-700

A rare and unusual Muisca pendant/collar ornament, the curved collar with a row of 6 stylised birds contained within 6 rectangles, below a series of linear devices, AD 1500-1550, 5in (12.5cm) long.
$2,500-3,000

An unusual Paracas feline vessel, probably Ocucaje, moulded and incised in the form of a snake, the double heads have a feline quality, the details indicated with incised markings and ornamented overall in orange, brown and ochre, 700-400 BC.
$1,700-1,900

A middle Mochica figural vessel, in the form of a seated figure, the legs crossed, holds a weapon in the left hand, wears an elaborate cape and mask in the form of a puma, 2 serpents indicated on the headdress, the spout at the back, painted in buff, the details indicated in reddish brown pigment, AD 200-500, 9½in (24cm) high.
$1,200-1,500

A middle Mochica figural vessel, in the form of a seated figure, perhaps a prisoner, the figure crouching forward, the left hand to the stomach, the right hand covers the mouth, the spout at the head, painted in cream, orange and reddish brown, AD 200-500, 10in (25.5cm) high.
$1,100-1,300

A fine middle Mochica portrait head of a warrior, with pursed mouth, alert eyes, wearing an elaborate conical headdress, 2 eagles issue from each corner, a fall with feathers painted on the back, the spout at the top, painted in cream, brown and deep red, AD 200-500, 12½in (31.5cm) high.
$7,500-8,000

A Colima seated male figure, with hands resting on knees, massive lappet necklace, pierced ears, incised chin strap, headband and body cloth, burnished details, 100 BC/AD 250, 14in (35cm) high.
$1,500-1,800

Four stone mace heads, Costa Rican, 3 encrusted, one cleaned greyish-stone, one with human head, one with jaguar head, one with bird head, and one of stylised form, AD 800-1500, the largest 4in (10cm)
$800-1,200

A Colima standing female figure, with arms at the sides, incised loin sash and back drop, rectangular ears, crossed headband and incised coiffure, 100 BC/AD 250, 12in (30cm) high.
$800-1,200

A Nayarit seated figure, with small crossed legs, holding a corn (?) to the front, wearing necklace, nose and ear ornaments, and wide headband, with white painted details, 100 BC/AD 250, 8in (20cm) high.
$500-600

A middle Mochica painted stirrup vessel, the globular body moulded at the centre with an encircling rope pattern, the top moulded with various peanuts in relief, a cream base, the decoation indicated in reddish brown, AD 200-500, 11in (28cm) high.
$700-900

A middle Mochica stirrup vessel, the body with 4 registers containing stepped designs, the spout and handle ornamented with linear and eccentric lozenges, AD 200-800, 10in (25.5cm) high.
$600-900

An unusually early Mochica figural vessel, probably from Piura, in the form of 2 puma cubs at play, one grasps the other, each with long curvilinear tails, the eyes incised, burnished red, AD 100-500, 7in (17.5cm) high.
$900-1,000

A middle Mochica figural vessel, moulded in the form of a large peanut, with an eagle head, long beak, and incised eyes, a wide spout at the back of the head, with areas of white pigment on an orange ground, AD 200-500, 12in (30cm) high.
$1,000-1,500

A Mimbres black-on-white bowl, the interior painted overall with angular linear designs, parallel bands, stepped motifs and dots, kill-hole, AD 950-1150, 11in (27cm) diam.
$700-1,100

A Mimbres black-on-white bowl, the interior painted with a wide frieze of hooked wave motifs, stepped design and parallel lines, kill hole, AD 950-1150, 12in (30cm) diam.
$1,500-2,000

A classic Mimbres brown-on-white picture bowl, the interior painted with 2 fish-headed animals, the bodies with chequer design, parallel linear designs and rim bands, kill hole. AD 950-1150, 11in (27cm) diam.
$1,700-2,000

A classic Mimbres black-on-white picture bowl, the interior painted with a deer and long tailed fox, 2 angular geometric motifs infilled with parallel linear design, and rim bands, kill hole, AD 950-1150, 11½in (30cm) diam.
$1,500-2,000

A Casas Grandes polychrome jar, with rounded body, neck with a moulded human head, and painted in shades of brown on cream with various geometric designs, AD 1160-1260, 8in (20cm) diam.
$600-700

A Mayan polychrome pottery vase, with ring foot, basal shoulder, slightly flaring cylindrical body and painted in shades of brown on cream with 2 panels of dignitary heads wearing elaborate headdresses and a band of geometric motifs, AD 550-950, 6in (15cm) diam.
$600-700

A Nazca pottery bridge-spout vessel, painted in shades of tan, brown, grey and cream with 6 humming birds sucking nectar from flowerheads which form the bases of the spouts, 100 BC/AD 100, 4½in (11cm) high.
$400-700

A Paracas bridge-spout vessel, with incised and polychrome decoration, the body encircled by a double-headed serpent, the tongues extended, interspersed with circular motifs, at the centre a band of interlaced geometric designs, painted in red, green and ochre, 300-100 BC, 6in (15cm) diam.
$2,800-3,000

A Chavin greyware vessel, with stirrup spout, moulded in relief with 6 incised bosses and overlapping scale-like design, the spout delicately adorned, 700-400BC, 9in (22.5cm) high.
$3,100-3,300

A Mochica mask, in the form of a warrior's head, the eyes indicated with white pigment, the ears pierced, and 4 holes at the sides, AD 200-500, 7in (17cm) high.
$450-600

An early Lucanian red figure squat lekythos, early 4th Century B.C., 5in (13cm).
$1,000-2,000

A cream glazed composition shabti for the King's Son of Kush, Hori, in dark brown glaze, Dynasty XX, Seth-nakht-Rameses III, from Tell Basta, 4in (11cm).
$600-1,200

A Cypriot terracotta stylised figure of a female idol, Middle Bronze Age, 7in (18cm).
$400-900

A terracotta figure of Harpocrates riding a goose, Graeco-Roman, from Alexandria, 6in (15cm).
$600-1,200

A painted terracotta figure of Venus Pudica, repaired, Hellenistic, 3rd–1st Century B.C., 8in (20cm).
$800-1,500

A turquoise composition statuette of Bastet, an inscription down the back in brown glaze reading 'Recitation by Bastet, Mistress of Bubastis: Eye of Re', Lord of all the gods', Graeco-Roman, 6in (15cm) high.
$6,000-12,000

Metalware

A turquoise glazed composition shabti for Lieutenant, In-t3y, repaired, Dynasty XIX/XX, 5½in (14cm).
$1,800-3,800

A Coptic steatite oil lamp, in the form of a bird, 6th-7th Century A.D., 3½in (9.5cm) long.
$1,600-2,800

A Syrian pottery model wheeled wagon, 2nd–1st Millennium B.C., 10in (25.5cm).
$2,600-5,300

A Veraguas gold cormorant pendant, with flattened splayed tail and wings with incised linear designs, each wing ornamented with 6 spiral designs, the bird head with pointed beak, bead eyes, suspension loop at the back, A.D. 800-1500, the bar pin at a later date, 3in (7.5cm) high.
$9,500-11,000

A Chiriqui/Chibachi gold figural pendant, in the form of a standing human figure holding a wand, the eyes, nose and ear ornaments applied, the suspension loop damaged, AD 800-1550, 5in (12.5cm) high.
$3,000-4,000

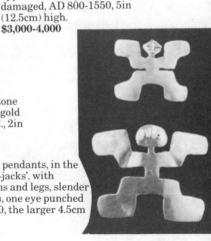

An Egyptian predynastic stone vase, encased in additional gold sheet, Naqada II, c3100 B.C., 2in (6cm) high.
$6,000-12,000

Two Tolima gold pendants, in the form of 'jumping-jacks', with fanciful long arms and legs, slender necks and waists, one eye punched out, AD 500-1500, the larger 4.5cm high.
$2,200-2,500

A bronze terminal in the form of a panther's head, early 1st Millennium B.C., 1½in (3cm) high.
$800-1,500

A rare Romano-British solid bronze figure of a standing stag, the eyes recessed for inlay, now missing, three legs damaged, 6½in (16.5cm) high, and a bronze stamped patera handle fragment, 1st Century A.D., from Southern England, 3½in (8.5cm) long.
$40,000-66,000

A bronze seated figure of the ram-headed God Khnum, 3in (7.5cm), another of a seated cat 2½in (6cm), a standing figure of Hathor, 3½in (9cm), a crouching figure of Harpocrates, 3½in (9cm), and a figure of a writhing crocodile, 4in (10cm) long, 4th–1st Century B.C.
$2,000-4,500

An Egyptian bronze head of a cat, broken away from a statue, 6th–4th Century B.C., 1½in (4cm).
$1,200-2,100

A bronze figure of a seated ibis, Ptolemaic Period, 3½in (9cm).
$1,000-2,000

A Canaanite bronze female votary, mid 2nd Millennium B.C., 3½in (9cm).
$2,600-5,300

A Greek cast bronze applique, late 5th/early 4th Century B.C., 1½in (3.5cm).
$6,000-12,000

A bronze figure of Osiris, Late Period, 13in (32cm).
$4,000-7,500

A gold and garnet ring, convex garnet intaglio, a crab, the sign of Cancer, 1st Century B.C./A.D.
$1,200-2,100

A bronze rein-guide in the form of an eagle's head above a naked youth wearing Phrygian cap, 5in (13cm) high, and another with square-shaped handles and spherical top, 5½in (14cm) high, East Roman, 2nd–3rd Century A.D.
$1,200-2,100

Two pairs of gold earrings, each hoop in the form of Eros wearing a girdle, head surmounted by a rosette, 2nd Century B.C.
$1,800-3,800

A Hellenistic gold ring, with mottled pink stone intaglio bearing robed youth holding staff, 1st Century B.C.
$800-1,500

A bronze lamp stand base, Roman, 11in (27cm) wide.
$1,200-2,100

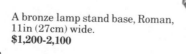

A bronze steelyard, mounted on perspex, 2nd–3rd Century A.D., 20in (51cm) high, 540gm.
$1,200-2,100

A fine Coptic bronze oil lamp, 5th Century A.D., 8in (20cm) long.
$4,000-7,500

A bronze lion-headed mask appliqué, probably from a chest, perspex mounted, 2nd–3rd Century A.D., 4½in (11.5cm) diam.
$400-750

A bronze mirror with 'Hathor' handle, Dynasty XVIII, 10in (25cm) high.
$10,000-18,000

A Villanovan bronze boat-shaped fibula, 7th Century B.C., 2in (5cm) long, an Anglo-Saxon bronze and enamel triangular brooch, 5th–6th Century A.D., 2in (6cm) long, and an Anglo-Saxon bronze key, 5th–6th Century A.D., 3½in (8.5cm).
$800-1,500

Marble

A large marble head of Venus, right eyebrow, nose and chin restored, 1st–2nd Century A.D., 17½in (44.5cm).
$18,000-26,000

A marble portrait head, possibly the Emperor Commodus, eyes with articulated pupils, mounted, late 2nd Century A.D., 9in (23cm).
$8,000-15,000

An East Roman marble architectural relief of a female mask, mounted, 2nd Century A.D., 10½in (26.5cm).
$8,000-15,000

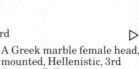

◁ A marble head and torso of a sleeping Eros, mounted, 2nd–3rd Century A.D., 12in (31cm).
$6,000-12,000

A Greek marble female head, mounted, Hellenistic, 3rd Century B.C.
$2,200-4,200

▷

A marble statue of Diana, restored, Roman, 2nd Century A.D. in the main, 37½in (95cm).
$14,000-24,000

▷

◁ A marble statue of Aphrodite and Cupid, repaired at neck and right arm, late 3rd Century A.D., 11½in (29cm).
$4,500-9,000

Miscellaneous

A translucent bluish-green glass beaker, 4in (10cm), and an almost colourless glass bowl, 3in (7.5cm), both 1st Century A.D.
$800-1,500

A Roman marble fragment from a relief in Greek style, 5in (13cm) high.
$800-1,500

A twin-handled green glass ungentarium, Romano-Syrian, 3rd-4th Century A.D., 5½in (13cm).
$400-900

A limestone head of a female votary, late 6th Century B.C., 6in (15cm).
$800-1,500

A translucent green glass bowl, 4in (10cm), a similar beaker, 3in (7.5cm), both 1st–2nd Century A.D., and a flask, with white swirling pattern, 3rd–4th Century A.D., 5½in (14cm).
$400-900

A fragmentary painted limestone erotic figurine, traces of red, brown and black pigment, 5th Century B.C., 3in (8cm) long.
$5,000-9,000

A limestone torso fragment of a female votary, late 6th Century B.C., 10in (25cm) high.
$800-1,500

A South Arabian limestone figure of a seated woman, mounted on perspex, 3rd–1st Century B.C., 8in (20cm).
$600-1,200

A gesso-painted linen mummy cloth, and another inscribed strip of mummy cloth, mounted behind glass and framed, Ptolemaic, 4th–1st Century B.C., 17 by 12in (43 by 31cm).
$1,000-2,000

A limestone relief fragment, from Sakkara, Old Kingdom, 8 by 5½in (20 by 14cm).
$400-900

A gesso-painted wooden foot end from an anthropoid coffin, Late New Kingdom, c1000–700 B.C., 11 by 10½in (28 by 26.5cm).
$1,300-2,400

Rugs & Carpets

A Romano-Egyptian encaustic on wood mummy portrait, repaired with some restoration, mounted and framed, 2nd Century A.D., 14 by 7in (35 by 19cm).
$2,000-4,500

An Agra mat, c1870, 36 by 36in (91 by 91cm).
$1,000-2,000

An Amritzar carpet, c1850, 144 by 106in (365 by 269cm).
$8,000-13,500

A triangular mosaic fragment, grotesque mask ornament, red, black, greenish grey and cream tesserae, set in concrete, Roman, 3rd–4th Century A.D., 16 by 15½in (41 by 39cm).
$800-1,500

An Aubusson rug, c1850, 84 by 48in (212.5 by 120cm).
$4,000-7,500

A Charles X Aubusson carpet, woven in pastel shades, the olive coloured ground with a pattern, the borders in pale blue on an ochre coloured ground, areas of restoration, 128 by 113in (325 by 287cm).
$4,500-9,000

A Belouch rug, the camel field woven with 4 brown and red rectangular medallions, enriched with silk, the kelim ends woven with 3 rows of scroll work, pile slightly low, 64 by 37in (160 by 92.5cm).
$800-1,500

A Bergama rug, c1850, 54 by 42in (135 by 105cm).
$3,200-6,000

A Baktiari nomadic rug, with 15 square panels of flowers and 3 borders, 71 by 55in (177.5 by 137.5cm).
$1,000-2,000

A Bessarabian kelim, c1900, 108 by 72in (272.5 by 182.5cm).
$6,000-12,000

A Bessarabian kelim, the mottled ivory field with sprays in a pale raspberry red border, one tiny hole, 78 by 60in (197.5 by 150cm).
$800-1,500

A Chinese rug, the royal blue field with clouds and Buddhist emblems around an Imperial five-clawed dragon, 109 by 67in (275 by 168cm).
$6,000-12,000

A Caucasian rug, the centre with blue field, with a yellow shaped border, red and ivory multiple borders with stylised animal figures, 71 by 47in (177.5 by 117.5cm).
$1,000-2,000

A Caucasian Khila Shirvan-Baku rug, with red and floral hexagonal medallion on midnight blue field, 56 by 37in (140 by 92.5cm).
$300-600

A Kirman carpet, the burgundy field with a stellar floral medallion with pendant mosque lamps, in a royal blue medallion and flowering vine border, areas of very slight wear, 202 by 139in (513 by 352cm).
$2,000-4,500

An Isfahan prayer rug, 88 by 56in (222.5 by 140cm).
$2,600-5,300

A Caucasian Kelim, c1850, 76 by 54in (193 by 135cm).
$5,000-9,000

An Isfahan rug, with ivory field, 89 by 60in (225 by 149cm).
$5,000-9,000

◁ A Gorevan carpet, the ivory floral field with a large madder and indigo centred medallion, 130 by 94in (330 by 241cm).
$1,600-2,800

A Kirman carpet, the shaded ice blue field with large cusped indigo floral radiating medallion, in a multiple ivory, burgundy and blue palmette and flowering vine border, 185 by 122in (469 by 309cm).
◁ $4,000-7,500

A silk Kashan rug, with golden yellow field, in a shaded apricot similar border between silvery floral stripes, 86 by 53in (218 by 135cm).
$10,000-18,000

A Caucasian rug, c1870, 96 by 54in (242.5 by 135cm).
$9,000-15,000 ▷

A Muslagham rug, Hamadan area, 78 by 54in (197.5 by 135cm).
$2,000-4,500

Karabagh rug, the terracotta
eld with Chelaberd medallions, 95
y 58in (241 by 145cm).
,000-7,500

GLOSSARY

Abrash	Variations of density in a colour seen in a carpet by irregular horizontal washes, can greatly add to the value.
Aniline	Chemical dye, a derivative of coal-tar, first produced in the 1860's, most common in the red-blue-purple range, colours tend to fade (orange-pink, for instance can fade to walnut-brown).
Boteh	Widespread pattern of Persian origin (original meaning 'cluster of leaves'), used in Europe in the Paisley pattern.
Ch'ang	Chinese endless knot, the inextricable knot of destiny.
Chrome dye	A fast synthetic dye now used in all the major rug weaving areas, colours do not fade.
Gol Henai Pattern	Floral pattern associated with Persian rugs, mainly found on Hamadan rugs.
Hejira (or Hijra)	The beginning of the Muhammedan calendar, 16 July, A.D. 622.
Herati Pattern	Also called the mahi or fish pattern. This common pattern originated in East Persia.
Jufti	'False' knot, either Turkish or Persian, whereby the knots are tied to four, not two, warp threads.
Kelim	Also spelled kilim, gilim, gelim. Principally from Anatolia.
Madder	Deep red-brown dye.
Palas	Caucasian name for kelim.
Palmette	A flowerhead of heart-shape with many radiating lobes or petals.
Sileh	A corruption of a now lost Caucasian place name. A form of Soumak, sileh pieces tend to be woven with rows of large S-motifs.
Soumak	Sumak, Summak, Sumacq, Sumakh, thought to be a corruption of Shemaka, town in south east Caucasus.
Spandrels	Architectural term for the space between the curve of an arch and the enclosing mouldings.
Swastika	A hooked cross. Chinese symbol for 10,000 (wan) and happiness.
Tiraz	Official weaving factory usually set up under Royal patronage.

A Kazak rug.
$600-1,200

A Kashan silk embossed and metal thread rug of vase design, 79 by 54in (200 by 134cm).
$12,000-21,000

A large Senneh corridor Kelim, the royal blue field with diagonal rows of multi-coloured stepped lozenge medallions in a triple blue, yellow and indigo flowering vine border, one area of slight repair, 222 by 61in (562 by 155cm).
$1,200-2,100

A Kurdish carpet, c1830, 144 by 72in (365 by 182.5cm).
$7,000-12,000

A Kashan rug, the red groun corners on a blue field with one main red ground border 80 by 54in (202.5 by 135cm)
$2,200-4,200

A Qashqai Kelim, the field divided into blood red, green and mustard yellow serrated panels in a light blue hooked lozenge border, 101 by 60in (255 by 152cm).
$1,700-3,000

A Kuba rug, c1870, 72 by 50in (180 by 125cm).
$5,000-9,000

A needlepoint rug, in crimson wool on a cream ground, lined, late 19thC, 70 by 49in (175 by 122cm).
$1,000-2,000

A needlepoint carpet, Continental, with khaki, black and multi-coloured variations, shows slight wear, repairs and backed, comprised of numerous panels sewn together, 19thC, 102 by 99in (259 by 250cm).
$4,000-7,500

A pair of fine Qum rugs, the ivory field around a scalloped blue floral medallion, surrounded by fluted columns, in an ivory palmette and vine border, a signature cartouche at one end, 86 by 54in (217.5 by 137cm).
$10,000-18,000

An antique Rescht panel, the indigo ground with 6 columns of burgundy scalloped floral medallions, a broad outer tomato red boteh stripe, backed, areas of splitting along seams, 138 by 85in (350 by 215cm).
$1,300-2,400

A silk Qum rug, the ivory field with 3 radiating open medallions surrounded by stylised vine, in an ivory serrated lozenge border between mock kufic stripes, 85 by 52in (215 by 132cm).
$6,000-12,000

A Turkoman Juval, woven in shades of rose and brown, with diagonal rows of small medallions, enriched with silk, deep fringe, in excellent condition, 12 by 43in (30 by 108cm).
$1,200-2,100

An antique Senneh rug, the ivory field with a central indigo herati pole medallion, the spandrels similar, in a yellow floral border between ivory similar stripes, 40 by 28in (102 by 72cm).
$4,000-6,800

A pair of antique Serapi runners, the field of each with a blood red lozenge with flowering plants around an indigo lozenge medallion, one dated AH 1300 (AD1883), 143 by 36in (360 by 90cm).
$3,200-6,000

A Shirvan rug, the indigo polychrome floral motif field enclosed by an ivory motif border, 58 by 44in (145 by 110cm).
$1,200-2,100

A Talish runner, the dark blue field woven with small red florets, the cream main border with bold florets, some wear, 93 by 39in (236 by 98cm).
$4,000-6,800

◁ A Tabriz rug, the madder field with a sky blue poled medallion and matching spandrels enclosed by a triple meander border, 68 by 48in (170 by 120cm).
$1,400-2,600

An antique Talish runner, the ▷ shaded light blue field, in an ivory border of cusped lozenges, areas of slight wear, one small repaired cut, 141 by 41in (356 by 103cm).
$3,200-6,000

A Shirvan rug with multiple floral decoration on an indigo field, ivory multi-coloured star border and twin guard stripes, 78 by 49in (197.5 by 122.5cm).
$1,300-2,400

An antique Yomut flatweave, the brick red field with columns of blue double hooked motifs divided by split lozenges, 120 by 74in (304 by 189cm).
$4,000-6,800

A Yugoslav Kelim, the raspberry red field with two stylised floral sprays in an ivory floral border, 109 by 69in (275 by 174cm).
$1,300-2,400

A Tabriz style carpet, the mustard yellow field with scrolling vine around large ivory cusped palmette medallions, in a broad peppermint green border, very slight staining, slightly dry, 159 by 142in (409 by 360cm).
$4,000-7,500

Textiles – Costume

A pair of North West American or Canadian Woodlands Indian moccasins, 19thC, 10in (25cm).
$1,000-2,000

An antique Tekke Turkoman carpet, the brick red field with 6 columns of linked Tekke guls divided by secondary linked cruciform guls, 155 by 104in (394 by 262cm).
$1,800-3,800

A pair of yellow silk shoes, embroidered in blue silk, lined, c1700.
$1,800-3,800

A fine and rare gentleman's banyan or dressing gown, of crimson silk damask, lined with emerald green silk, mid-18thC.
$12,000-21,000

A pair of green damask silk shoes, with ivory silk brocade, c1780.
$600-1,200

A Yomut carpet, the fox brown field with interlocking rows of guls, 139 by 91in (355 by 230cm).
$2,200-4,200

A pair of lady's shoes of mainly blue, orange and ivory silk brocade, c1700.
$1,800-3,800

A pair of braces of pale blue grosgrain, embroidered with trailing flowers, c1840.
$500-900

A rare pair of mules, of ochre coloured morocco bound in yellow silk, inscribed on the soles 'from The Princess Charlotte of Wales to Mrs . . .1814'.
$1,300-2,400

A fine calash of emerald green silk with 12 wired arches, late 18thC.
$1,200-2,100

l. A trilby hat of grey felt, trimmed with coral pink and black velvet, with traces of label, c1865.
$200-450

c. A bonnet of ivory satin and coral pink velvet, labelled Mrs. Seale, Milliner, 80 Oxford Street, c1865, and a bentwood hat box labelled William Whitley, Westbourne Grove.
$300-600

A Zejwa corridor carpet, the blue field woven with 4 large sunburst medallions, in shaded brown or cream, generally good condition but pile low, 125 by 53in (318 by 138cm).
$1,800-3,800

r. A young man's cap, of black wool with patent leather peak, lined with green and telescopic upper part, mid-19thC.
$200-450

A pair of lady's shoes of cornflower blue watered silk, c1850.
$300-600

A rare crinoline hoop of blue, pink, and grey striped cotton, with 4 whale bone hoops, c1760.
$10,000-18,000

A dress of pale pink silk, c1815.
$800-1,500

A corset of brown linen, stiffened with whale bones and bound with pale linen braid, c1770.
$2,000-4,500

An open robe of pale yellow silk ▷ lustre, woven with garlands of flowers, the neckline edged with 18thC Binche lace, the front of the bodice slightly altered.
$4,000-7,500

◁ An open robe and petticoat of green and white striped silk, trimmed with pinking, slightly altered, c1780.
$7,000-12,000

A suit of rust coloured wool, with deep cuffs and wide skirts and gilt buttons, comprising: coat, waistcoat with detached sleeves and breeches, c1760.
$11,000-18,000

A gentleman's waistcoat of cream silk, with 22 embroidered jacket buttons, late 18thC, and a garter.
$300-600

A Chinese Imperial robe, altered, 19thC.
$4,000-7,500

A red silk dress, with chiné print of flowers in black, and accompanying jacket, lined, bearing the maker's label Christian Dior, Paris, Automne-Hiver 1958.
$1,000-2,000

A mink chiffon dress, with front and back panels of lace, a silk imitation snakeskin belt and neckline trim, lined, bearing the maker's label Lucile Ltd., 11 rue de Penthièvre, Paris, c1910.
$1,200-2,100

An evening mantle or burnouse, by Liberty, made from an Indian embroidered shawl, fastened at the front with multi-coloured tassels and an Art Nouveau pewter clasp set with pink hardstone, lined with blue silk and labelled Liberty & Co., London and Paris, late 1880's.
$1,600-2,800

Believed to have belonged to the mother of Sir Edward Mortimer Archibald, a British Consul General in America, 1857–93.

An iridescent green silk taffeta dress bound in yellow silk, lined, bearing the maker's label Lucile Ltd., 11 rue de Penthièvre, Paris, c1910.
$1,600-2,800

Lucile (Lucy Wallace Duff Gordon) b1870, d1935 was the first London based designer to attain world celebrity and had ateliers in London, Paris and New York.

A cream gauze dress with black spot print, lined, bearing the maker's label Jeanne Lanuin Paris, Castillo, late 1950s, and accompanying petticoat.
$180-300

A cream gauze coat, probably silk and alpaca, with matching dress sprinkled with diamanté, each lined, bearing the maker's label Balenciaga, 10 Avenue George V, Paris, late 1950s.
$1,800-3,800

A picture of blue felt with silk and wool embroidered and applique, c1790, 12in (30cm) diam. framed and glazed.
$600-1,100

An embroidered picture, the linen ground worked in crimson wools and silks with mainly stem, buttonhole and running stitches, c1650, 19 by 22½in (48.5 by 57.5cm) framed and glazed.
$2,600-5,300

A petit point picture, worked in coloured wools and silks, c1770, 9in (23cm) square, framed and glazed.
$3,200-6,000

Embroidery

A rare silk-on-silk needlework picture, Philadelphia, worked in polychrome silk threads in a variety of embroidery stitches including satin, whip and French knots, on a silk ground, depicting a smiling sun and clouds above a tree with a squirrel and birds flanked by fruit trees, centering a leopard and a lion within a landscape with a butterfly, rabbits, a dog, flowers and strawberries, the eyes of the lion and leopard of glass beads, the silk ground fabric sewn to original borders of canvas and damask, 1750-60, 16½ by 17in (41 by 42.5cm).
$22,000-24,000

An old label affixed to the backing bears the inscription 'Loaned by Elizabeth A. Bringhurst, 1095 Park Place'

An applique quilt, French Tulip, worked in turkey red and medium green solid cottons against a well-quilted white ground with pierced zig-zag border, c1890.
$400-500

A silk work picture, worked in coloured silks on an ivory silk ground, late 18thC, framed and glazed, 18½in (47.5cm). ▷
$600-1,200

A pieced quilt, Broken Star, worked in rose shaded solid cottons against a pale pink ground, quilted with feather wreaths and diamonds, with pieced rose border, 1920s.
$500-700

Lace

A stumpwork picture, embroidered and applied in coloured silks and coiled metal thread with mainly tent, eye and satin stitches, c1660, 17 by 21in (43 by 53cm) framed and glazed.
$8,000-15,000

A length of reticella, early 17thC, 4½ by 46in (12 by 114cm).
$800-1,500

A petit point panel, 18thC, 20 by 25½in (51 by 64cm), now framed as a firescreen.
$3,200-6,000

A bertha of Brussels bobbin and needlepoint lace, a collar and a handkerchief with similar surround.
$200-450

A Brussels bobbin and needlepoint bertha collar, 19thC, and another.
$500-900

A silk needlework picture, 'The Moralist', 17in (43cm) square, in gilt frame, with a note on the back which records that the picture was worked by Mary Callaghan, and was finished in 1800.
$4,000-6,800

A Brussels point-de-gaze collar, late 19thC.
$400-750

A deep Youghal needlepoint flounce, 31½ by 160in (80 by 400cm).
$800-1,500

A woolwork ship's picture, of a British frigate in full sail, with embroidered label H.M.S. Emerald, 19thC, 16½ by 12½in (42 by 32cm), framed and glazed.
$800-1,500

A pair of joined Brussels bobbin lace lappets, c1750, mounted with seal inscribed Elise & Co., 170 Regent St, London, Antique & Modern Lace Warehouse, 41½in (104cm), and a similar edging, 2½ by 38½in (7 by 98cm).
$300-600

A pair of Brussels bobbin lace lappets, c1730, 21½in (54cm) long.
$500-900

A length of Mechlin edging, designed with sailing boats, cherubs, birds and flowers, c1740, 3 by 67in (8 by 168cm).
$600-1,100

A Carrickmacross bridal veil, with scalloped border, 19thC.
$400-750

Samplers

A needlework sampler, inscribed 'Margaret Neilsons sampler sewed in her tenth year taught by Mrs. Henderson, Miss Macredies School 1831. The rev. William Woodrow Minister of Dreghorn', early 19thC, 17 by 14in (43 by 37cm), mounted.
$2,200-4,200

A woolwork sampler by Elizabeth Shufflebottoms, 1832, 24in (61cm) square, in contemporary maple frame.
$800-1,500

A drawnthread and needlepoint lace linen sampler, late 17thC, 12½ by 7½in (31 by 19cm).
$500-900

A sampler worked by Rebekah Danford dated March 31st, 1788, 18 by 14in (46 by 37cm).
$500-900

A sampler by Peggy Kellbrick, dated 5th February 1836, 23 by 23in (58.5 by 58.5cm).
$2,600-5,300

A sampler worked in brightly coloured silks, in red, yellow, blue and green, with initials D.A. and D.G. and the date 1784, Dutch, 19 by 11in (48 by 28cm).
$900-1,700

A needlework sampler, decorated in coloured silks, holed, 18thC, 17 by 12½in (43 by 32cm).
$1,000-2,000

A sampler, c1842, 19 by 21in (47.5 by 52.5cm).
$900-1,700

A needlework sampler, by 'Mary Ann Hunter aged 14 years 1844', 26 by 16½in (66 by 42cm) in stained wood frame.
$600-1,200

A needlework sampler by Jane Brannan, age 9, 1829, the wool ground embroidered with coloured silks in mainly cross stitch, early 19thC, 16 by 12in (40.5 by 30cm), framed and glazed.
$600-1,200

A George IV needlework sampler, by E.H., slight holing, 1826, 17 by 12½in (43 by 32cm).
$800-1,500

A needlework sampler by 'Elizabeth Mawdsley, 1807', the wool ground embroidered mainly in cross stitch with coloured silks, early 19thC, 22½ by 16½in (56.5 by 42cm).
$1,400-2,600

A Brussels verdure tapestry, borders now lacking, 17thC, 164 by 72in (416 by 182cm).
$18,000-26,000

A Brussels tapestry, woven in silk and wool with the triumph of Mars, the sky partially rewoven, mid-18thC, 194 by 155 (492 by 393cm).
$12,000-21,000

A needlework sampler by Hannah Ransome, 1795, the wool ground embroidered in coloured silks, late 18thC, 14 by 11½in (35.5 by 28.5cm), framed and glazed.
$800-1,500

A panel of Brussels tapestry, woven mainly in blue, green and ivory wool, 17thC, 60 by 66in (150 by 166cm).
$1,000-2,000

Tapestries

A Flemish verdure tapestry, restorations, 17thC, 101 by 115in (255 by 290cm).
$5,000-9,000

A Flemish tapestry, depicting Athena, repairs, late 17th/early 18thC, 108 by 55in (272.5 by 137.5cm).
$2,200-4,200

A tapestry, worked with elegant children playing and picnicking, in fresh colours within a rococo frame enclosing pink flowers, with an outer border of dark green, French, 19thC, 68 by 88in (170 by 222.5cm).
$13,000-22,000

A pair of woven tapestry panels of pastoral scenes, in muted colours of blue, crimson, green and brown, 18thC, each 31 by 22in (79 by 56cm).
$1,200-2,100

An Aubusson tapestry, on a beige ground with shaped olive green borders, 90 by 56in (227.5 by 140cm).
$5,000-9,000

A tapestry of Diana, guild mark, D.T.W., 19thC, 76 by 81in (192.5 by 205cm).
$7,000-12,000

A tapestry woven in muted colours, with a Mannerist cartouche with a coat of arms, Spanish or Italian, 17thC, 94 by 99in (237.5 by 250cm).
$10,000-18,000

Curtains & Covers

A Persian cover, the cotton ground printed in indigo and madder, lined, early 19thC, 81 by 48in (204 by 120cm).
$200-450

A coverlet of filet squares, linked with lawn and having vandyked, fringed filet border, probably Italian, joined, c1900, 79 by 60in (200 by 150cm).
$180-300

A joined panel of green satin, embroidered in silver thread, with pairs of initials crowned and similar monograms at each corner, possibly a bed tester or coverlet, late 17th/early 18thC, 48 by 54in (120 by 135cm), framed.
$1,700-3,000

A cream cotton coverlet, printed in green, blue and red, with stylised tulips and anemones, padded and quilted, the reverse printed in red, late 19thC, 82 by 73in (208 by 186cm).
$400-750

A 'mosaic' patchwork cover composed of white, Turkey red and printed cottons, including dark ground and lilac, the cottons dating from 1800–45, 95 by 100in (240 by 252.5cm), unfinished with papers intact.
$300-600

A patchwork coverlet, designed with panels of worsted woven with mainly red, blue, grey and black in a striped design, the reverse of pale worsted, quilted, c1870, 113 by 91in (284 by 230cm).
$900-1,700

A Greek cover of undyed linen, embroidered in coloured silks, 17thC, 22½ by 46in (57 by 114cm), and another similar piece, probably Epirus, 20½in (52cm) square.
$800-1,500

A patchwork coverlet, quilted, early 19thC, 99 by 87in (250 by 220cm).
$400-750

An American patchwork coverlet, worked in squares of plain, printed and chiné silk and brocades, in a squared design bordered in pale yellow, inscribed with names including: Mary Blair, Blairville South Carolina, Mrs. C. E. Kennedy, William Blair Brigaley, Mary S. Bryan 1846, Lancaster Theodore Bagaley aged 3 year, lined in glazed blue cotton and quilted, made in Pennsylvania, mid-19thC, 107 by 111in (270 by 280cm).
$1,000-2,000

A linen coverlet, embroidered in chain stitch with mainly brown and pink wools, lined, the reverse embroidered with the initials, D.H. 1779, 100in (252cm) square.
$600-1,100

A patchwork quilt of log cabin design, worked with coloured, corded silks and brocades, lined, late 19thC, 99 by 83in (250 by 210cm).
$500-900

A patchwork coverlet, of red and white embroidered squares, embroidered with the date 1892, lined, 101 by 83in (256 by 210cm).
$500-900

A patchwork cover, worked with diamond-shaped pieces of plain and printed silks, brocades and velvets, mid-19thC, 93 by 79in (236 by 200cm).
$500-900

A Welsh coverlet, double woven in black, blue and cream wools, late 19thC, 84 by 71in (212 by 178cm).
$400-750

Woven in 1891 by the two sisters who lived at Maesgwyn House, Maesgwyn, Carmarthenshire, Wales, and who were mentioned in Under Milkwood by Dylan Thomas: 'Who milks the cows now at Maesgwyn'.

A patchwork coverlet, with hexagonal pieces of printed and plain cotton, c1860, 113 by 83in (286 by 210cm).
$500-900

A Durham quilt, worked in a waved feather pattern with alternating stripes of pink and white cotton, late 19thC, 90 by 80in (228 by 202cm).
$180-300

A large wool and silk challis shawl, printed all over in scarlet, aquamarine, shades of brown and cream with an elaborate floral and Paisley pattern, c1860, 128 by 63in (325 by 160cm).
$800-1,500

A crewel work bedspread, embroidered with scrolling foliage in dark and light blue wool on linen ground, holed.
$1,000-2,000

An Eastern quilted cream damask coverlet with tufted border, possibly Indian or Chinese in origin and made for the European market, late 17thC, 60 by 38in (150 by 95cm) and matching pillow cover with self covered wood buttons, 19 by 27in (47.5 by 67.5cm).
$4,500-9,000

A Mexican saltillo, worked mainly in red, blue and cream wools, 19thC, 48 by 79in (120 by 200cm).
$2,200-4,200

A Hanoi wall hanging of ivory silk embroidered in pastel silks, 48 by 53in (120 by 134cm).
$200-450

An altar cloth, finely embroidered with gold and silver thread, dated 1615 in English and Latin on each side, 26 by 26½in (66 by 67cm).
$1,000-2,000

A panel of linen and cotton, worked in coloured wools with crewel and tambour stitch, early 18thC, 70 by 87in (175 by 220cm) and the companion, and another 2, 89 by 32in (226 by 80cm).
$7,000-12,000

A set of three Aubusson portieres, with twisting blue ribbon on a sand coloured ground with pale eau-de-nil border, 19thC, 108in (274cm) drop.
$5,000-9,000

An altar frontal of crimson damask silk, the upper part and two falling panels of 17thC Italian cream silk applique, part fringed, lined, 41 by 66in (102 by 164cm).
$500-900

An Aubusson tapestry portiere pelmet, woven mainly in green, red and blue, 19thC, 44 by 114in (110 by 299cm) wide.
$1,400-2,600

A large hanging, formerly of cream velvet, worked in silver thread and sequins, Indian, late 19thC, 104 by 60in (264 by 150cm).
$500-900

A Victorian embroidered pelmet, worked in coloured wools, highlighted in silk, on a black ground, edged with twisted silk cord, 10½in (26.5cm) deep.
$13,000-22,000

A pair of linen curtains, embroidered in crewel work, with two pelmets en suite, Indian for the European market, 19thC, 104 by 59in (262.5 by 147.5cm).
$7,000-12,000

A Schleswig–Holstein wall hanging, of double woven blue wool and undyed linen, late 18thC, 65 by 37in (164 by 92cm).
$2,600-5,300

A rare wall hanging or valance, worked in coloured wools and silks, some repairs and re-working and overpainting, 16thC, 88in (222.5cm) wide.
$6,000-12,000

It is very unusual to find secular wall hangings of this period.

A long panel of Victorian beadwork densely worked in coloured beads with flowers, 9in (23cm) deep.
$400-750

A fine set of bed hangings, comprising one large panel, a pair of narrow curtains and a valance, of linen embroidered in brightly coloured red, blue, yellow and green wools, with flowering trees growing from rocky hillocks, English, 18thC, curtain 88 by 92in (222.5 by 232.5cm).
$11,000-18,000

Handkerchiefs

A satirical printed handkerchief, 'The Reformers attack on the Old Rotten Tree – of the Foul Nests of our Morants in Danger', printed in colour on silk, c1830, fragile.
$500-900

A silk handkerchief, commemorating the Peace of Rysbach, published by Charles Weston at the Nag's Head in Bishop's Gate Street, near Leaden Hall, 1713, fragile.
$600-1,100

Fans

A French fan with carved, pierced and gilded ivory sticks, c1770s, 11in (28cm) long, in a shaped framed and glazed case.
$500-900

A Chinese ivory brisé fan, c1790s, 10½in (27cm) long, and a box.
$1,200-2,100

A French fan with carved and pierced ivory sticks, c1760s, 10½in (26cm) long.
$1,300-2,400

A French fan with carved, pierced, silvered and gilt ivory sticks, the silk leaf painted with a central panel of Mars, Venus and Cupid, c1780s, 11in (28cm) long.
$600-1,200

A fan, the silk leaf painted with a military scene, probably the surrender of Fort St. Philip in Minorca by the English to the Spaniards, the ivory sticks pierced and silvered, French for the Spanish market, 1756, 10½in (26.5cm).
$1,000-2,000

Lord Blakeney (1672–1761) after seventy days' defence of an almost indefensible fortress, surrendered on the honourable terms, whereby his garrison was transported to Gibraltar and not made prisoners of war. He was 84 and had not gone to bed throughout the siege.

A fan with tortoiseshell sticks, c1880s, 12in (31cm) long, in a silk lined velvet box.
$300-600

A fan with black wood sticks and gauze leaf, applied with a velvet and lace mask, with cut-out eyes and nose, one guard inset with looking glass, the other with silvered metal container for scissors, buttonhook and pencil, the handle with attached powder puff, c1880s, 14in (36cm) long.
$600-1,100

A French fan with carved, pierced, silvered and gilt mother-of-pearl sticks, c1750s, 11½in (29cm) long.
$300-600

A fan with chinoiserie sticks of carved and pierced ivory, probably French, c1760s, 8½in (22cm) long.
$500-900

A French fan, with mother-of-pearl sticks, the leaf painted with an 18thC pastiche, signed 'B. Bisson de Récy', c1890s, 10½in (27cm) long.
$300-600

A fan with carved, pierced silvered and gilt mother-of-pearl sticks, the leaf of Brussels point-de-gaze, c1870s, 14½in (37cm) long, in original box.
$900-1,700

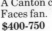

A Canton carved ivory Hundred Faces fan.
$400-750

A Japanese tortoiseshell fan, with gilt lacquered decoration.
$300-600

A Chinese mother-of-pearl brisé fan, c1840s, 7½in (18.5cm) long.
$600-1,100

An Italian fan with pierced ivory sticks, mainly in terracotta and yellow, c1770s, 11in (28cm) long.
$500-900

A painted fan, the leaf decorated with the Virgin and Child, the ivory and mother-of-pearl inlaid sticks with silver pique point, probably Italian, mid-18thC, 10½in (27cm).
$180-300

A fan, the chickenskin leaf painted with classical vignettes, with plain ivory sticks, Italian, c1780, 10½in (27cm), in contemporary pink paper-covered box, lacking lid.
$900-1,700

A Japanese fan, the stiffened cream cloth leaf printed and painted with figures.
$180-300

A fan, the leaf a hand-coloured etching with detailed Almanack for the year 1794, published 1st January, 1794, by John Cox and J. P. Crowder, Wood Street, with plain wooden sticks, damaged, 11in (28cm).
$400-750

A bone brisé fan, probably Dutch, c1730s, 8in (20cm) long.
$400-750

A pair of lacquered fans.
$500-900

A fan with wood sticks and carved guards, the printed hand-coloured leaf inscribed 'Vaughan's Quadrille Fan', c1790s, 11½in (29cm) long.
$900-1,700

An unusual Jamaican fan, the leaf composed of leaf-shaped panels of lace barke (Lagetta Lintearea), edged with cabbage barke (Orodoza Oleracea), and fringed with French cotton (Colotropie Procera), the sticks of tortoiseshell and trimmed with a tassel of penguin fibres, c1880, 15in (38cm).
$300-600

An autograph fan, the chickenskin leaf painted with a cat and signed by various members of European Royal Families, signed 'Karl' twice 'Thyra', 'Albert', etc with simulated blond tortoiseshell sticks, gilt and clouté with steel, 1903, 9in (23cm).
$1,200-2,100

A church printed fan, 1776, the leaf a hand-coloured etching with pious verses and quotations from the Scriptures, published by I. French, 47 Holborn Hill, June 1, 1776, inscribed 'Beauty like Flowers soon fades away, the charms of virtue ne'er decay', with bone sticks, 12in (31cm).
$800-1,500

A fan with carved, pierced and gilded mother-of-pearl sticks, the printed leaf after the painting of 'George III, Queen Charlotte and their six eldest children', by Johann Zoffany, c1860s, 10½in (27cm) long.
$200-450

A painted Spanish fan, the leaf decorated with mythological figures in a landscape, ivory red lacquer and cut steel guards, 18thC.
$200-450

Shawls

A shaped handscreen of catgut stained blue appliqué with featherwork birds holding sprays of flowers, with white metal handle, probably made in the Northern half of South America for the European market, 13in (33cm).
$6,000-12,000

This fan closely resembles the famous handscreen in the Messel/Rosse collection at the Fitzwilliam Museum. As to date, it is very difficult to pronounce – the fan in the Fitzwilliam has always been called 17thC – no portraits are known of ladies carrying such fans and until now no other such fan has been found. The colours of the feathers are as delicate as watercolour. They fade fast in the light. This fan is very fresh and is mounted on what appears to be catgut. Examples of English folding fans of catgut dating from the mid-18thC have been found. The provenance of this fan could point to an early 19thC date, the silver handle is probably not European and could date from as late as 1840.

A Kashmir shawl, the centre panel of blue pashmina, the border worked in coloured wools and silks, c1860, 76 by 67in (192 by 168cm).
$1,200-2,100

A Kashmir shawl, the ivory pashmina centre with boteh to either end woven in madder and indigo, c1800, 51 by 122in (128 by 310cm).
$800-1,500

A Kashmir shawl, the indigo pashmina ground woven with boteh to either end in mainly green, red and yellow, c1820, 53 by 103in (132 by 260cm).
$800-1,500

A shawl, with cream cashmere ground woven with cones and florets to the border and each corner in mainly red, blue, yellow and green, probably French, c1850, 66in (165cm) square.
$400-900

A Sumatra shawl, the ikat centre woven in red, black and ivory silks and gold thread in a striped design.
$800-1,500

Dolls – Wooden

A carved and turned painted wooden doll with carved ears, inset enamel eyes, pink cheeks, stitched brows and lashes with the remains of nailed-on wig, c1790–1810, 18½in (46cm) high.
$2,200-4,200

A fine and rare George II wooden doll, painted gesso-covered face, black enamelled eyes with red dots at each corner, painted eyelashes and line eyebrows with short brush strokes above and below, and stitched nailed wig, elongated 'fork' fingers, tip of nose and upper lip rubbed, slight damage to three fingers on one hand, re-dressed, 22in (56cm).
$20,000-30,000

A group of painted wooden headed dolls, 'There was an old woman who lived in a shoe', with silk clothing and shoe, early 19thC, 5in (13cm) long.
$300-600

A carved and painted wood figurehead in the form of a French Cantinière, 39½in (100cm) high.
$1,000-2,000

A turned and carved painted wooden doll, with inset blue enamel eyes, remains of wig base nailed to the head, with painted wooden legs and pink kid arms, wearing contemporary linen under-bodice, c1830, 12½in (31cm) high.
$1,300-2,400

Wax

A doll with wax head, arms and feet, natural brown hair, 19thC, 19in (47cm).
$300-600

A rare beeswax shoulder headed doll, the brown eyes wired between the legs, the stuffed body in original white dress, underclothes including pantalettes, with blue kid slippers, c1810, 17in (43cm) high.
$1,000-2,000

A wax over composition shoulder headed doll, the blue eyes wired from the waist, with original wig, the stuffed body with wax over composition limbs, in contemporary petticoat and straw bonnet and necklace.
$600-1,200

A wax composition doll, with closed mouth, sleeping blue eyes, fair wig, stuffed cloth body, voice box, with waxed composition lower limbs, in original white cotton and lace dress and coat and underclothes, 14in (35cm).
$600-1,100

A Victorian display case containing a wax head doll, standing among stuffed songbirds, butterflies and artificial flowers, larger birds below, mid-19thC, 31 by 34in (79 by 86cm).
$6,000-12,000

A wax headed pedlar doll modelled as an old crone, carrying a basket of wares including gloves, a brush, bellows, toasting fork, skeins of wool, fans, nutmeg grater, book and a purse, 19thC, 9½in (24cm) high, under dome.
$1,200-2,100

A wax over composition headed doll, with fixed pale blue eyes, the stuffed body with blue arms, wearing contemporary organdie dress, mid-19thC, 22in (56cm) high.
$400-750

A wax over composition shoulder headed doll, the stuffed body with yellow kid arms and separated fingers, in contemporary sprigged muslin dress, 1810–1815, 14in (36cm) high.
$600-1,100

A brown wax over composition headed doll, the stuffed body with brown wax over composition limbs, in original clothes, late 19thC, 10½in (27cm) high.
$500-900

Bru

An unusual black Bru bisque head doll, with mohair wig, cork pate, fixed paperweight eyes, pierced ears and open/closed mouth, marked Bru Jne, 13in (33cm).
$600-1,200

Gebruder Heubach

A bisque headed character doll, with blue intaglio eyes and blonde wig, the jointed composition body wearing blue tucked frock and petticoat, marked 14676 24 and stamped in green 43, by Heubach, 16in (41cm) high.
$2,000-4,500

An all bisque child doll, the open/closed mouth showing two upper teeth, the moulded blonde hair with three glazed blue bows, jointed at the shoulder and hip, marked 10490 3 and stamped 23, probably by Heubach, 9in (23cm) high.
$1,000-2,000

◁

A bisque headed character doll, with closed water melon mouth, blue googlie eyes and with tubby rigid limb composition body wearing a yellow striped tunic, marked 9578 2/0 and the Heubach square mark, 8½in (21.5cm).
$1,000-2,000

A bisque head doll on a bent limbed body, made in Germany by Ernst Heubach, 1865–1925, moulded 300–2. ▷
$500-900

Jumeau

A French bisque head closed mouth doll, on a jointed body, in original dress, by Jumeau, Paris, 1850–1899, marked 'Tete Jumeau', 26in (66cm) high.
$8000-13,500

A Dep Tete Jumeau bisque headed doll, impressed Dep 8, and marked 'Tete Jumeau' in red, with open mouth and moulded upper teeth, fingers, feet and body chipped, 19in (49cm).
$800-1,500

A bisque headed bébé, with closed mouth, fixed bulbous brown eyes, pierced applied ears and with jointed fixed wrist composition and wood body, marked EHJ and stamped on the body 'Jumeau Medaille D'or Paris', containing non-functioning voice box, 18½in (46cm) high.
$5,000-9,000

A French bisque head doll by Jumeau, with wig, with Mama/Papa voice box, inoperative, 24in (61cm).
$1,700-3,000

J. D. Kestner

A bisque headed character baby doll, with open closed mouth, brown sleeping eyes, short blonde wig and composition baby's body, with upturned big toes, contemporary clothes, marked 211 JDK, 15½in (39cm) high.
$1,200-2,100

Armand Marseille

l. A bisque headed character baby doll, with open closed mouth, brown sleeping eyes, short brown wig and composition baby's body, marked 211 JDK, 17in (43cm) high.
$800-1,500

r. A bisque headed character child doll, with closed mouth, blue sleeping eyes, later blonde hair wig and composition jointed toddler body, original socks and shoes, marked K*R SH115/A 42, 16½in (42cm) high.
$5,000-9,000

l. A bisque headed doll with moving glass eyes, open mouth, jointed composition body, marked 'Armand Marseille, Germany, A9M', 24in (61cm) high.
$400-750

r. A bisque headed doll with moving glass eyes, trembling tongue and composition body, marked 'Porzellan Fabrik Burggrub Daslachende Baby, 1930/3/ Made in Germany DRGM', 18in (45cm) high.
$900-1,700

An Armand Marseille musical/dancing bisque headed puppet doll, impressed 70.20,5, lower limbs stuffed, forearms wood.
$1,000-2,000

A bisque headed bent-limbed character bébé, by Armand Marseille, Kollesdorf, 1880–1925, moulded 996, 20in (51cm) high.
$400-900

An Armand Marseille bisque headed doll, with open and shut eyes, composition body and limbs, marked 980, 22in (56cm) high.
$400-750

An Armand Marseille bisque head googlie eyed doll, the straight limbed composition body dressed in printed cotton with matching hat, marked 323 A 11/0, 6½in (17cm).
$900-1,700

S.F.B.J.

l. A bisque headed doll with glass eyes, kid covered body and bisque hands, impressed mark on shoulder 501, 12in (31cm) high.
$600-1,200

r. A bisque headed doll with moving glass eyes, open mouth and composition body, marked S.F.B.J.60 Paris, 18in (45cm) high.
$300-600

A bisque headed child doll, with blue lashed sleeping eyes, pierced ears, blonde wig and jointed composition body wearing contemporary clothes, marked 'SFBJ Paris 14', also 'Bébé Français', 32in (81cm) high, in original box.
$1,700-3,000

A S.F.B.J. boy doll, with articulated limbs, some damage to hands, model 237, 18in (45cm).
$500-900

A bisque headed bent-limbed character bébé, by S.F.B.J. in Paris, 1899–1925, moulded 301, 8in (20cm) high.
$200-450

Simon & Halbig/ Kammer & Reinhardt

A bisque headed character doll, with closed mouth, brown lashed sleeping eyes, blonde wig and composition jointed body, marked 'K*R Simon and Halbig 117/A 39', the head 4¼in (11cm) high.
$3,200-6,000

A bisque headed character baby doll, the open mouth showing two glazed teeth and cardboard tongue, composition baby's body, marked 'K*R Simon and Halbig 122 42', 17in (43cm) high.
$900-1,700

A clockwork toy of a bisque headed doll, in original Scottish outfit, pulling a two-wheeled cart, marked '1079 Halbig S & H 7½', by Roullet Decamps.
$1,200-2,100

A small bisque headed doll, on a 1920s five-piece body, by Simon & Halbig, Grofenhain, 1870–1925, moulded 1079, 9in (23cm) high.
$500-900

A Simon & Halbig bisque headed doll with long brown mohair wig, fixed blue eyes, pierced ears, open mouth with upper teeth and jointed composition body dressed in original undergarments, marked SH 1079 2½, 11in (28cm).
$600-1,200

A bisque character doll's head, with closed mouth, blue sleeping eyes and with remains of body, marked '1488 Simon & Halbig 6', the head 4in (10cm) high.
$3,200-6,000

Miscellaneous

A bisque headed doll on a French style jointed body, in original clothes, by Simon & Halbig, Ohrdruf, 1870–1925, moulded 719 dep., 23in (58cm) high.
$1,600-2,800

A bisque headed jointed doll, made by Theo Recknagel in Alexandrinentan, 1886–1925, marked RA, 11in (29cm) high.
$300-600

CHARACTER DOLLS

★ in 1909 Kammer & Reinhardt introduced a large number of character dolls

★ these were modelled from life, showing all the nuances of childish temperament

★ a model was made and then a mould taken, which was used about fifty times

★ Simon and Halbig cast and painted the heads for many other manufacturers, including Kammer & Reinhardt, such heads are marked K & R, Simon & Halbig, or K & R, S & H and the model number

★ early K & R character dolls

are of exceptional quality

★ the French had remained supreme in the manufacture of dolls, in the 19thC, with Jumeau one of the main exponents

★ however, from the 1890's the Germans had perfected equal skills

★ after K & R introduced their characters many other makers followed: Heubach, Armand Marseille, Bruno Schmidt, Kestner, and S.F.B.J. (the Societe Francaise de Fabrication de Bebes et Jouets)

★ obviously these dolls were expensive and so they were hardly produced in large quantities

★ K & R Model 117 is usually considered to be one of the most desirable, in fact any 'pouty' doll is highly collectable

★ the most common is model 126

★ there are more Heubach characters than any other

★ as one gets nearer to the First World War quality tends to decrease and character dolls produced after the war are in many cases, poor quality.

A bisque headed closed mouth doll on a kid leather body, with its original Scottish outfit, made in Germany, c1885–1900, 7in (18cm) high.
$300-600

A printed cloth rag doll, modelled as a wounded First World War soldier, printed on the foot 'specially made for Boots, by Deans Rag Book Co Ltd, Hygienic stuffing, guaranteed British manufactured', 10½in (27cm) high.
$600-1,200

A cloth doll painted in oils, with attached cloth ears with cloth jointing at shoulder, elbow, thigh and knee, marked under the right arm 'Chase Stockingnet doll Trademark, made in the U.S.A.', 23in (58cm) high.
$400-900

A painted cloth doll, with brown painted hair, the stuffed body jointed at hip and shoulder, wearing cotton frock and cardigan, by Kathe Kruse, 17in (43cm) high.
$900-1,700

Make the most of Miller's

Miller's is completely different each year. Each edition contains completely NEW photographs. This is not an updated publication. We never repeat the same photograph.

A doll in original clothes, made in Germany by Kathe Kruse, at Bad Kosen, 1910–1925, 18in (45cm) high.
$600-1,200

A bisque headed bent-limbed character bébé, in original clothes, made in Germany by Otto Reinecke in Moschendorf, 1878–1925, marked P.M.914, 14in (36cm) high.
$500-900

A bisque shoulder headed poupard, with turned white wood handle, and original skirt and streamers, marked 3200 AM 10/OX DEP, 13in (33cm) high.
$600-1,200

A Steiff Infantryman, marked with Steiff button in the left ear, 9in (23cm).
$600-1,200

A bisque headed bébé, with pierced ears, animal skin wig and fixed wrists, jointed composition body, wearing contemporary home-made dark blue sailor suit, marked '0 by Jules Nicholas Steiner', 13in (33cm) high.
$4,000-6,800

A rare china headed doll, the neck swivelling inside the carton body portion, with squeaker in the centre of the body and with carton lower body portion and china limbs, thumb and feet damaged, c1860, 12½in (31cm) high.
$2,200-4,200

A bisque headed character boy doll, frowning brows, large ears, short blonde wig and jointed toddler body wearing white sailor suit, marked 'K*RS & H 115/A 42', 16in (41cm) high.
$4,000-7,500

A French fashion doll, the bisque head with swivel neck, cork pate, fair mohair wig, the gusseted kid body with stitched fingers, dressed in original undergarments, 18in (46cm).
$3,200-6,000

l. A bisque headed doll with moving glass eyes, open mouth, jointed composition body, marked on head 'A.M.4DEP, Made in Germany', 19in (47cm) high.
$400-900

r. A bisque headed doll with tinted complexion, moving glass eyes, open mouth, kid covered body and bisque hands, marked 370 AM DEP, 21in (53cm) high.
$600-1,100

A bisque headed doll, the unusual composition body with stuffed central body portion and upper legs, with jointed arms and fixed wrists, marked DEP, 13in (33cm) high.
$800-1,500

A boxed effigy of a queen, possibly Queen Elizabeth I, her composition hands and face finely modelled and painted, English, probably late 17thC, 12in (30.5cm) diam.
$1,000-2,000

This figure may perhaps be a form of May Day 'Lady Doll', a floral decorated doll, with early pagan origins, which was traditionally carried in procession on May Day in some country districts – see Pollock's Dictionary of English Dolls, *Robert Hale, 1982.*

A crudely carved wood doll, with blue enamel and nail eyes and jointed limbs, early 19thC, 15½in (39cm).
$300-600

A shoulder china doll of an Irish gentleman, gusseted kid body and china lower limbs, 13in (33cm), with blue and white spotted kerchief tied to a stick, containing 2 lace handkerchiefs, a yellow flower, a bag of Irish gold, a watch, a locket, 2 miniature books, one of Occasional Pieces by Lord Byron, and a miniature envelope containing a letter to 'Dearest Emy' dated Sept.1904.
$300-600

A composition headed ventriloquist dummy, contained in a collapsing painted wooden box, with articulated levers to the eyes, arms, upper and lower limbs, upper and lower lips, and the head, 10in (25cm) high.
$600-1,100

A bisque headed character doll, modelled as a laughing boy, with fixed wrist jointed composition body, wearing grey suit with red socks and black shoes, marked H128, 14in (36cm) high.
$600-1,200

Automata

An automaton mandolin player, the composition headed figure with movement to the neck, forearm and leg, with musical movement in base, stamped 'G. Vichy, Paris', 25½in (65cm) high.
$3,200-6,000

A bisque headed jester, hand-operated mechanical figure, the wire covered body with wooden hands and feet, in original alternate coloured blue and white costume, as the handle is turned, the music plays and he hits a ball, bearing shop label, 11in (29cm) high.
$1,400-2,600

An automaton picture of a negro boy.
$1,700-3,000

An automaton doll mandolin player, with bisque Jumeau head, bisque forearms and original clothes, automaton movements, with 2 rods controlling movement of the head and one arm respectively, damage to bisque shoulder section, 17in (43cm) high.
$3,200-6,000

A fine musical automaton, of a clown turning a somersault on the back of a chair, with two cam movement and musical movement concealed in the chair, 25in (64cm) high.
$9,000-15,000

A composition headed automaton, in original white silk trousers under a long red brocade coat, as he puffs his pipe moving it towards his mouth, his lower jaw moves and his eyes open and close as he moves his head, French, 1880, 30in (76cm) high.
$13,000-22,000

A musical automaton banjo player, the composition headed negro figure seated on a chair, with musical and automaton movements, in dilapidated condition, 22in (56cm) high.
$600-1,200

An automaton negro flute-player, with composition body and bisque head, the body containing musical and automaton movements, lacks flute, 24in (61cm) high.
$5,500-9,000

A French bisque head doll with swivel neck from The Waltzers Automation, one bisque arm damaged, 16½in (42cm).
$800-1,500

An automaton doll negro flute-player, with bisque head and painted forearms, in original clothes, with musical and automaton movements, with two cams controlling vertical and horizontal head movements, head cracked behind ear, 17½in (44cm) high.
$3,200-6,000

Dolls Houses

A printed paper-on-wood dolls' house, opening at the front to reveal four rooms, with contemporary papers, German, late 19thC, 28in (71cm) wide.
$800-1,500

A painted wood dolls' house, by G. & J. Lines, the front opening to reveal a six-roomed interior with central stair-well, fitted with electricity, 33in (84cm) wide.
$1,000-2,000

A folding dolls' house, by J.C. Russley of Hull, the front opening to reveal a two-roomed interior and stair-well, 23½in (60cm) wide, with a quantity of Art Deco furniture.
$1,700-3,000

A French painted wood dolls' house, the front opening to reveal a four-roomed interior with original wallpapers, one room with fireplace and piano, 19½in (49cm) wide.
$800-1,500

A Georgian style baby house, the back opening in three sections to reveal one upper and two lower rooms, May 1830, 28in (71cm) wide
$14,000-24,000

A papered brick and painted wood dolls' house, the back opening to reveal a four-roomed interior with stair-well, 31½in (80cm) wide.
$600-1,100

A German toy milliner's shop, with four free-standing paper dolls and a similar table centrepiece, displaying four hats, in original box with pictorial label, in good condition.
$2,600-5,300

A late Victorian pine dolls' house, the back with removable panels, 23in (58cm) wide, complete with a small quantity of dolls' furniture.
$14,000-24,000

A selection of dolls' bedroom furniture.
$100-250

A group of dolls' house tinplate items including a stove, saucepan, oval kettle, food warmer, etc.
$100-250

A quantity of dolls' house pewter and tinplate utensils.
$300-600

A large quantity of dolls' house furniture.
$600-1,200

An English colonial dolls' house, opening at the back to reveal three floors, 16in (40cm) wide, with some furniture.
$600-1,100

Two Victorian carved wooden dolls, 1½ and 6½in (4 and 17cm), and six miniature dolls with porcelain heads.
$500-900

A set of pale wood dolls' house furniture.
$300-600

Teddy Bears

A Steiff pale plush teddy bear, the straw stuffed body with elongated arms, back hump and felt pads, marked with Steiff button in the left ear, 17in (43cm).
$1,600-2,800

A Steiff blond plush teddy bear, marked with Steiff button in the left ear, 20in (51cm).
$2,000-4,500

A Steiff yellow plush teddy bear, marked with Steiff button in the left ear, 24in (60cm).
$2,600-5,300

A gold plush teddy bear, probably by Steiff, pads worn, 16in (40cm).
$600-1,200

A golden plush covered teddy bear, with button eyes and hump, long felt pads, the front unhooking to reveal a metal hot water bottle, contained in the body of the bear, by Steiff, 17in (43cm) high.
$2,600-5,300

Known as Admiral Beattie, this bear was illustrated in Therle Hughes Edwardiana for Collectors.

l. A plush covered teddy bear, with leather muzzle and collar, by Steiff, 13in (33cm) high.
$900-1,700

c. A golden curly plush covered bear, 'Nigel', with pronounced hump, 27in (69cm) high.
$500-900

r. A plush covered bear, with long cut snout, bearing Chad Valley button in right eye, marked Chad Valley Hygienic Toys, British.
$200-450

A good Steiff blond plush teddy bear, with growler, straw stuffed body with swivel joints, elongated arms and large feet, moth holes in felt pads, plush worn in patches, 17in (43cm).
$2,000-4,500

This teddy bear is called Sebastian.

A pale gold plush covered bear, square manufacturer's mark, possibly Deans, 19in (47cm) high.
$200-450

l. A dark plush teddy bear, probably by Steiff, 16in (40cm).
$900-1,700

c. A dark plush teddy bear with wide apart rounded ears, probably by Steiff, forepads worn, 13½in (34cm).
$800-1,500

r. A fine Steiff pale plush teddy bear, with a leather muzzle and lead, marked with Steiff button in the left ear, 13in (33cm).
$1,000-2,000

A short golden plush covered teddy bear, with brown eyes, felt pads, growler defective, c1910.
$500-900

Lead soldiers

Heyde large scale model of King George V, damaged, 1911, 10cm.
$300-600

Elastolin 30/16 Goering in party uniform, arm loose, 1938, 7cm.
$60-120

Three early Britains model Lifeguards and the Officer, damaged.
$40-90

Britains rare set 2124, Welsh Fusiliers at attention with mascot, some damage, 1957.
$600-1,200

Britains set No. 2076, 12th Royal Lancers, Prince of Wales' Officer on grey with sword, in original box.
$200-450

Heyde, 23 Prussian guards, damage, c1740.
$300-600

Britains Set No. 212, Royal Scots with piper.
$100-250

Britains Set No. 315, five 10th
Royal Hussars, Prince of Wales'
Own, in original box.
$300-600

A set of 9 Britains camels, with 8
Indian soldiers with drawn swords,
camels with some fatigue, the
Indian chiefs with broken swords.
$300-600

Britains Mountain Artillery, with 4
mules, disassembled gun, 7 gunners
and a mounted officer.
$150-250

Britains Set No. 1613, British
Infantry in gas masks, with officer,
in original box, 1937.
$150-250

Britains Set No. 35, Royal Marines
at the slope, 1947.
$150-300

Britains Set No. 82, Colours
and Pioneers of the Scots
Guards, 1953.
$100-250

Britains farmers gig
No. F28, with horse and
Britains Fordson tractor,
both unboxed.
$60-120

Britains, 4 Imperial Yeomanry,
with Boer Cavalry officer, 2 CIV's
with paper labels, and a Devon,
some damage.
$150-250

DIE-CAST MODELS

★ 1870-1900 flat and semi-
flat soldiers made by
Germans
★ Britains invented the
hollow cast technique
★ this led to wide range of
military figures
★ earliest had oval bases
and paper labels – now
rare
★ farm items gaining
popularity, but soldiers
still most desirable, zoo
animals still not so
desirable
★ original box adds
substantially to value

Britains from a set of Infantry of the
Line Band, and a set of Drums and
Bugler, damaged, 1933.
$100-250

Britains Set No. 1254, Royal
Engineers pontoon section, 1937.
$800-1,500

Britains Set No. 28, Mountain
Artillery with mule team and quick
firing gun, early version, in original
Whisstock box.
$400-750

Britains assorted footballers with
goalie, 2 linesmen, one arm
missing, referee, arm missing,
1938.
$200-450

Britains Salvation Army, 1938.
$900-1,700

Britains model hunt, 18 pieces,
unboxed.
$100-250

Britains Salvation Army, 1938.
$600-1,200

Britains Set No. 50,
types of the British
Army, including the
First Life Guard,
in original box.
$300-600

Britains Set No. 144, Royal Field
Artillery, early version, in original
box.
$800-1,500

Britains Set 9401, Her Majesty's
State Coach, in original box.
$300-600

Britains Eastern People, repainted
in the Britains style, 1953.
$150-250

Britains, a specially moulded and
painted Band of the Royal Fusiliers,
originally commissioned from
Britains by Mr. Poitier-Smith,
c1937, in excellent condition.
$3,200-6,000

Make the most of Miller's

*Unless otherwise stated,
any description which
refers to 'a set' or 'a pair'
includes a valuation for
the entire set or the pair,
even though the
illustration may show only
a single item.*

Tinplate

A printed and painted tinplate toy, 'Dancing Sailor', EPL 535, fitted with clockwork mechanism causing the sailor to sway from side to side, by Lehmann, c1920, 7½in (19.5cm).
$300-600

l. A printed and painted tinplate toy of a single engine wing monoplane, 'Heinkel-Kampffflugzeug He 70', No. 819B, by Lehmann, c1936, in original box.
$300-600

r. A printed and painted toy of a single engine low wing monoplane, 'Fchenellverkehrffflugzeug, Heinkel-Blitz, He 70', by Lehmann, c1936, in original box.
$300-600

A Lehmann tinplate clockwork auto bus, complete with bus driver, No. 590, one wheel missing, 8in (20cm) long.
$900-1,700

A printed and painted tinplate toy, 'Bulky Mule, The Stubborn Donkey', EPL 425, of a donkey and cart with clown driver, fitted with clockwork mechanism, causing the cart to advance and reverse erratically, by Lehmann, c1910, 7½in (20cm), in original box.
$300-600

A Lehmann tinplate clockwork delivery van, No. 550 and inscribed 'A.H.A.', damaged, 5½in (13cm) long.
$300-600

A printed and painted tinplate toy of Gustav the Miller, 'Mill and Miller', EPL No. 230, by Lehmann, weight in bag missing, c1920, 16½in (42cm).
$300-600

A painted tinplate model of a gentleman, 'Heavy Swell', EPL 525, with clockwork mechanism causing the gentleman to advance, by Lehmann, c1912, 9in (23cm).
$1,400-2,600

A Bavarian clockwork tinplate game of Baker St. Station, with 5 trains travelling between 2 terminii, BUU Series, boxed.
$500-900

A painted and felt covered tinplate dancing pig with a clown rider, 'Paddy and the Pig' EPL No. 500, with clockwork mechanism, by Lehmann, some damage, c1910, 5½in (14cm) long.
$600-1,200

A Bing tinplate clockwork Mercedes automobile, complete with key, 8½in (21cm) long.
$2,600-5,300

A printed and painted tinplate cable car, 'Rigi', EPL No. 795, 2 printed tinplate gentlemen passengers, by Lehmann, c1930, 4in (10.5cm) long.
$300-600

A Triang tinplate and bakelite clockwork toy cyclist, c1930, 8in (20cm) long.
$150-250

A printed and painted tinplate toy of a butterfly, with clockwork mechanism causing the insect to advance and flap its wings, by Fischer & Co, c1910, 7in (18cm) wingspan.
$200-450

A printed and tinplate model of a limousine, with driver, by Bing, fitted with clockwork motor, c1925, 10½in (27cm).
$900-1,700

A printed and painted tinplate woman, 'Busy Lizzy' fitted with clockwork mechanism causing the woman to rapidly polish a floor, possibly by Fischer & Co, mop missing, c1920, 7½in (19cm).
$300-600

A fine Bing hand enamelled tinplate 4-door saloon car, with a clockwork mechanism with operating hand brake, in claret with red lining, black cab with gold lining and red lined windows, red seats, German, lacks chauffeur, c1912.
$8000-13,500

A printed and painted tinplate 4-door limousine, with clockwork mechanism, by Tipp, c1928, 8in (20cm) long.
$600-1,200

A painted tinplate bear, by F. Martin, with clockwork mechanism, causing the bear to shuffle forward, French, the bear's central rod in its back broken, c1905, 8½in (22cm).
$300-600

l. A Crawford's printed tinplate motor car biscuit box, with original box, 11½in (29cm) long.
$800-1,500

c. A German tinplate char-a-banc, clockwork drive, stamped 'P.W.', windscreen broken off and one headlamp missing, c1920, 10½in (26.5cm) long.
$900-1,700

r. A Hudson Scott & Sons Carlisle tinplate motor car biscuit box, in red, 6½in (16.5cm) long.
$600-1,200

A printed tinplate model of a lorry, with clockwork motor, by Mettoy, c1950, 6½in (17cm) long, in original box.
$80-180

TOYS

- ★ musical automata were produced from the 18thC
- ★ some of the first were the singing birds
- ★ 18thC birds were enamelled with no feathers
- ★ there has been a glut of reproductions in the last year
- ★ 19thC clockwork nursery pictures are now highly desirable – always more so if in working order
- ★ many made in the 1880's and 1890's in tin
- ★ wooden arks have been made from the middle of the 18thC
- ★ mass produced arks arrived in 1800
- ★ the best period for the collector of arks is 1860's and 1870's
- ★ German arks always the best
- ★ many wooden, iron and papier-mache pull-along toys made especially in the 19thC
- ★ in the 19thC many cheap wind-up toys were produced – the most collectable by Fernand Martin
- ★ mechanical toy banks appeared in the 1870's mainly from America
- ★ the most desirable being in cast iron with moving parts, worked by the coin
- ★ many have a patent number

A Bing painted tinplate beer wagon.
$300-600

A fine printed and painted tinplate early fire engine, with clockwork mechanism, with 2 firemen, 3 missing, by Tipp, lacks bell, c1925, 11in (28cm) long.
$200-450

A printed tinplate model of Captain Campbell's Bluebird, by Gunther-man, c1930, 20in (51cm), in original box.
$1,000-2,000

A fine printed and painted tinplate model of a 4-door limousine, with clockwork mechanism and operating handbrake, by Tipp & Co, c1928, 12in (30cm) long.
$2,600-5,300

A German lithograph tinplate clockwork racing car, the tyres printed Dunlop Cord, number plate TC 959, printed monogram T.C.O.
$500-900

A German pre-First World War tinplate Sedan clockwork motor car, with driver and passenger, rusting, lacking steering column and one mud guard, 6½in (16.5cm).
$600-1,200

A Crawford's tinplate biscuit box, lid with grocer's scale, 8in (20cm) high.
$80-180

A fine painted tinplate bear standing on an early 3-wheel carriage, with fly wheel mechanism, German, c1905, 6in (15cm).
$900-1,700

A printed tinplate push along model of a two-door Coupe, German, c1930, 17in (43cm) long.
$400-900

A tinplate friction drive Cadillac 300 Saloon, Gama, mid-1950s, 12in (30cm).
$500-900

A rare 22d 'Meccano' delivery van, finished in yellow paintwork.
$1,000-2,000

A KKK, battery operated tinplate Million Bus, boxed.
$300-600

A remote control printed tinplate Sonicon Patrol Car, boxed.
$100-250

A printed and painted tinplate toy of 'Popeye the Sailor', No. 268, with clockwork mechanism, some very slight rusting, some paint peeled inside boat, some slight chipped paintwork, by the Hoge Mfg. Co. Inc., U.S.A., c1935, 14in (36cm).
$2,600-5,300

A German painted tinplate floor toy paddle boat, Starlight, finished in blue, red and yellow, 11½in (29cm).
$3,200-6,000

A German tinplate clockwork open limousine, the bodywork in yellow, brown and black, early 20thC, 10½in (27cm) long.
$1,200-2,100

An early painted tinplate toy of a roller skater, with clockwork mechanism, possibly French, some chipping of paintwork, c1903.
$800-1,500

An early German painted tinplate floor toy paddle boat, marked 'Douglas' with the national symbol for the Isle of Man below, finished in green, yellow, red and orange, 14½in (36cm).
$4,000-7,500

A French tinplate clockwork toy, in the form of an acrobat, 14in (35cm).
$900-1,700

A Kiddyphone tinplate toy gramophone by Bing, with circular case and conical horn.
$100-250

An Arnold printed and painted tinplate motor bike with rider, with clockwork mechanism, in red and silver, inscribed 'M.A.C.700', W. German, c1950, 7½in (18cm) long.
$1,000-2,000

A rare painted tinplate Bleriot monoplane, with painted tin pilot, German, c1903, 5½in (14cm) wingspan.
$1,000-2,000

A German tinplate diver, with rubber tube, 5in (12.5cm).
$100-250

A Kico printed and painted tinplate toy of a gentleman pool player, with clockwork mechanism housed underneath pool table, German, ball missing, c1912, 6in (15cm) long, in part original box.
$900-1,700

A German tin toy, for connection to steam engine water or sand wheel, 10in (25.5cm) high.
$150-300

A painted single funnel tinplate model of a liner, 'Cruise Liner', No. 856, finished in brown, red, white, grey and green, by Fleischmann, c1955, 21in (53cm).
$14,000-24,000

A tinplate clockwork car, British made, mid-1930s, 12in (30cm) long.
$150-300

An English tinplate airliner, late 1930s.
$100-250

A German tinplate clockwork toy, in the form of a man seated on a barrel-shaped cart drawn by a pig, 8in (20cm) long.
$400-750

A Spot-On, London Transport Route Master bus, boxed.
$800-1,500

A 4-door limousine, with clockwork mechanism and operating handbrake, finished in light green and green, yellow and black linino, by Karl Bub, lacks glazed windscreen, c1928, 15½in (39cm).
$2,600-5,300

A pre-war tin toy station in mint condition, 10in (25.5cm).
$300-600

Miscellaneous

A Chevrolet Station Wagon, friction motor, boxed.
$80-150

A Crescent, Scammell Scarab mechanical horse and Shell B.P. tanker, slight fatigue to cab, boxed.
$300-600

A Huntley & Palmer's 'Double Decker Biscuit Tin Bus', with clockwork mechanism, British, c1928, 9½in (24cm) long.
$2,600-5,300

A Marusan, clockwork tinplate NYC Police Car, boxed.
$200-450

A Carette lithograph limousine, with clockwork mechanism, in red and white, finished in cream, turquoise and gold lining, German, some rust and 2 front headlamps missing, c1911, 8½in (21cm) long.
$14,000-24,000

A Levy, clockwork motorcycle rider with lady passenger, 6in (15cm).
$3,200-6,000

Above. A clockwork saloon with driver, and automatic brake mechanism operated by the small 5th wheel, finished in blue and black with red detail, S. Gunthermann, roof missing, some damage, 9½in (24cm).
$2,600-5,300
Below. A Lehmann, Mars tricycle, No. 471.
$1,000-2,000

A Tasoy, friction Ford Fairlane 500, boxed.
$80-150

A Friction drive Ford Ambulance with siren, and Ford Highway Patrol car and a San, battery operated Fire Chief's car.
$100-250

An Opel, made in Japan, by
Yonezawa, c1960.
$600-1,200

Three boxed Dinky toys.
$150-300

A circus lorry, 23in (58.5cm) long.
$60-120

A Lesney
Yesteryear
model No. 9,
Fowler
showman's
engine, unboxed.
$60-120

A double decker bus by 'Minerva',
English, c1925.
$600-1,200

A Dinky pre-war No. 22b yellow
and green sports Coupé, with
painted gold metal wheels.
$800-1,500

A rare Dinky No. 22A red over
cream sports car, with blue metal
wheels.
$800-1,500

A rare Dinky 28n 'Marsh's
Sausages' delivery van, with metal
mounts, tinplate radiator, finished
in green paintwork.
$900-1,700

l. A selection of Lesney, Matchbox,
first series, including No. 5
'matchbox' London bus, No. 9 fire
engine, No. 10 mechanical horse,
No. 11 'Esso' tanker, No. 17 Bedford
removal van, No. 21 Bedford coach,
No. 27 Bedford articulated low
loader and 20 other Lesney toys, all
in original boxes, and 4 loose toys.
$400-900

r. Lesney, 'Models of Yesteryear',
including Y-1 Allchine traction
engine, Y-2 1911 'B', Y-3 1907 'E'
class tramcar and 2 others, all in
original boxes.
$300-600

A collection of Dinky commercial
vehicles, including 957 turntable
fire engine escape, 955 fire engine
with extending ladder, 60 Royal
Mail van, 442 tanker 'Esso', 421
electric articulated lorry, 290 cream
and green double decker bus, 414
rear tipping wagon, all in original
boxes; Corgi 119 HDL Hovercraft
SR-N1 in original box, and a
Daimler ambulance box.
$300-600

A Dinky model Guy van with
upright radiator grille, unboxed.
$100-250

A Dinky 265 Plymouth USA taxi,
and a 448 Chevrolet pick-up and
trailer, boxed.
$150-300

A selection of Dinky toys, most with slight fatigue.
$600-1,200

Dinky – 148 Ford Fairlane, 174 Hudson Hornet, 179 Studebaker President Sedan, boxed.
$80-150

A Victorian painted Noah's Ark, with 107 stained wood and carved animals and people, including Mr and Mrs Noah, German, slight damage, c1870, 18in (46cm) long.
$800-1,500

A painted wood Noah's Ark, with flat bottom and roof opening to reveal a hollow interior, with approx. 140 painted animals and figures, mid-19thC, 12in (30cm).
$1,200-2,100

A brightly painted wood Noah's Ark, with hollow interior, and approx. 700 painted animals and figures, early 19thC, 17½in (45cm) high.
$6,000-12,000

A Victorian skewbald toy pony, covered in horse hide with grey hair mane and tail, with leather bridle and breast plate, on a green painted wooden base and metal wheels, one missing, 19½in (49cm) high; and a ginger straw filled polar bear with glass eyes, stitched nose and mouth, on 4 metal wheels, 9½in (24cm) high.
$800-1,500

An early Lines Bros. pedal car, the wooden body painted suede grey with sprung chassis, some underparts cast G & JL, 39in (99cm) centrewheel to centrewheel.
$1,200-2,100

A pedal car, c1930.
$150-300

A selection of boxed Dinky toys.
$300-600

A selection of boxed Dinky toys.
$300-600

A wooden rocking horse, c1930, 34in (86cm) high.
$400-900

A velocipede, with front wheel mounted pedals and wood handles, the horse of painted wood, 35in (89cm).
$800-1,500

A child's wooden dog on wheels, German.
$150-300

A painted wooden rocking horse, American, the standing yellow and black painted figure with horse hair tail and mane and with tufted velvet saddle, mounted to rock forward and backward on the wooden platform, c1875, 53in (132.5cm) high.
$2,600-3,000

Pixyland, Felix the Cat, part of tail missing, 1926.
$80-150

A painted wood dapple grey 'pony size' rocking horse, with horse hair mane and tail, British, 56in (142cm) long.
$800-1,500

A rocking 'Muffin the Mule', 43in (107.5cm).
$150-300

A metal framed wood painted green doll's pram, with leathercloth interior, folding hood, wood handle and rubber tyred wheels, c1900, 28½in (73cm).
$300-600

An early Victorian wood and plaster rocking horse on wooden stand, 42in (105cm) high.
$900-1,700

A large dappled rocking horse, with red draylon padded saddle, repainted and some replacement parts, ear chipped, 51½in (131cm), height of head to ground.
$300-600

A toy wooden pony cart, the base pale green with green and black shaft, 35in (89cm) long.
$200-450

Churchers model fairground: hand built and constructed in wood, brass and cloth, resembling a real fairground in 1/12in scale, finished by hand in coloured enamels, complete with mains, driving motors and lights by a 12 volt transformer.
$7,000-12,000

A German Heinkel, made by Lehmann, in mint condition and boxed, late 1930s.
$600-1,100

A painted carved wood set of a fair, probably Erzebirge, Germany, late 19thC, in original wood box.
$2,000-4,500

A rare Heyde circus, some damage.
$600-1,100

A Victorian doll's pram, with wickerwork frame lined with canvas, and fitted collapsible hood, with South African makers tab, i.e. 'Handy House, Grand Hotel, Cape Town', two small tears to canvas.
$400-900

A French singing bird and cage, c1860, 12in (30cm).
$2,000-4,500

A painted wooden 3-wheeled perambulator, upholstered in black American cloth with wire frame for a hood, 3rd quarter 19thC, 52in (130cm).
$400-900

An American aeroplane by Kingsbury, c1920.
$400-900

A penny toy train, Japanese, c1920.
$300-600

A mechanical music moire screen, 'Ombro-Cinema', French, c1920.
$400-900

A painted metal early 2-funnel gunboat, with clockwork mechanism, finished in grey, red and green, by G. Carette, hull chipped and dented, lacking flag on rear of boat, c1904, 8in (20cm).
$300-600

A Taylor & Barratt Zoo Series, 'Chimpanzees' Tea Party', 1938, in original box.
$300-600

An early painted metal 4-wheel carriage, with lady rider on a grey horse, German, c1890, some chipping to paintwork, 8in (20cm) long.
$1,000-2,000

A rare Charbens set 519, Camp, comprising metal tent, 4 hikers, 2 cups and 2 saucers, 1938, in original box.
$600-1,200

A Japanese battery operated robot, mid-1960s.
$800-1,500

A rare metal headed bicycling toy modelled as a boy with blonde moulded hair, French, lacks clockwork central pivot mechanism, c1880, 8in (20cm) long.
$1,300-2,400

Two Sharps toffee men, and 3 cocoa cubs, kangaroo, duck and pig.
$400-750

A rare character figure, 'Felix the Cat'.
$600-1,100

A fine hand carved and stained wood clockwork toy of two animated dancers, The 'Juba' Dancers, the mechanism concealed in wood base causing the dancers to shuffle, U.S.A., c1874, 10in (25.5cm), in original wood box.
$1,200-2,100

A German street scene, The Leipsic Fair, with lithographed free-standing props of buildings and figures, in original box in excellent condition, complete with story booklet, mid-19thC.
$3,200-6,000

Nineteen various model road signs, 9 Dinky petrol pumps, 3 street lamps, 7 various figures, etc. 40, unboxed.
$100-250

A very rare French double magic lantern, called a Lampadorama, c1882.
$1,000-2,000

A carved and painted wooden carousel figure, modelled in the form of a pig with small tusks, painted with polychrome harness and saddle, restorations to paint, late 19th/early 20thC, 47in (117.5cm) long.
$1,100-1,300

A French polychrome boule lampascope, by Lapierre, c1880.
$200-450

▷

◁

A small German magic box with chromolitho label on the lid, c1880.
$150-300

A French magic box, c1880.
$300-600

A carved and painted whirligig, in the form of a jockey on horse jumping a fence, mounted on a rectangular wooden base, early 20thC, 19in (47.5cm) long, together with a carved and painted whirligig in the form of a man sawing wood, on later white metal base, 24in (60cm) high.
$300-400

A fine large half-section shipbuilders model of the Tramp Steamer 'Great City' completed by Roper & Sons Ltd. the shipbuilders, and Blair & Co Ltd the engineers, at Stockton-upon-Tees in 1914 for the Great Steam Ship Co Ltd, Cardiff, in glazed mahogany case with mirrored back, boat 110in (278cm) long, case 124in (310cm) long.
$4,000-7,500

A half-model of a steam trawler 'Good Luck', built by Cook, Welton & Gemmel Ltd, Beverley, 1912, in mahogany mirror back case, 41 by 17in (103 by 43cm).
$2,600-5,300

A Victorian sailing model of a 'J' class yacht 'Valiant', built by P. McQuade, restored, with original masts, spars and sails, 1895, 109in (276cm) high by 103in (258cm) long overall, on mahogany stand.
$900-1,700

A painted wood model of 'The Victory', with rigging, lifeboats, deck detail and cannon, 37in (93cm), in glazed case.
$500-900

A long model of SS Queen Mary, complete with Stewart & Turner steam engine and illustrated magazine, 60in (150cm).
$100-250

A model of a pond yacht.
$1,400-2,600

A shipbuilders model of a freighter 'St. Catherine', with full detail to rigging, winching, lifeboats, all of wooden construction, finished predominantly in pink and grey, mounted, on wooden plinth 50in (126cm) long overall.
$4,000-6,800

A prisoner-of-war bone ship model, with a carved figurehead, and flying an ensign at the stern, rigged at the stern with pull cords to 'secure' and 'run-out' the guns, 11½in (29cm) long overall, on stand, in ebonised glazed case.
$2,600-5,300

A fine Gebrüder Bing electric tram-car, with a staircase at either end, finished in red, yellow and black, 9in (23cm).
$1,800-3,800

A Bassett-Lowke 2-6-4 tank engine No. 2524 LMS.
$12,000-21,000

A spirit-fired 4-4-0 tank locomotive No. 88, by Bing, in wooden box.
$1,700-3,000

A modern cased model of the training ship 'Danmark'.
$800-1,500

A Bing engine for Bassett-Lowke, gauge 1, London and North Western Railway, c1920.
$14,000-24,000

A gauge 0 clockwork model of the London Midland and Scottish Railway 4-4-0 No. 2 tank locomotive No. 2107, in original claret livery, by Hornby, in original box.
$400-900

A very rare gauge 1 clockwork model of the London and North Western Railway 4-6-2 'Bowen-Cooke' tank locomotive No. 2663, in black livery, with three front lanterns, by Marklin for Bassett-Lowke, c1913.
$1,800-3,800

A gauge 1 clockwork model of the London and North Western Railway 4-4-2 'Precursor Tank' locomotive No. 44, in black livery, by Bing for Bassett-Lowke.
$800-1,500

A 3½in (9cm) gauge live steam coal-fired 0-4-0 tank locomotive, 'Juliet', together with a trailer with wooden seat, 20in (50cm) overall length of locomotive.
$600-1,100

A 3RE 0-4-0 German Railways pattern locomotive and tender No. 2990, by Bing, finished in black with red lining.
$400-750

A gauge 3 live steam spirit-fired model of the London and South Western Railway 4-4-0 locomotive and tender, finished in original green livery, with yellow and claret lining, by Bing for Bassett-Lowke, boiler scorched, paint worn, some flaking and chipping, LSWR repainted on locomotive sides, c1904.
$5,500-9,000

Bing for Bassett-Lowke: A fine c/w 4-4-0 GWR locomotive and six-wheeler 'Sydney', re-named Cape Town and re-numbered to 3397, tender marked Lowko, c1904.
$1,000-2,000

A scarce Bing gauge 1 live steam spirit-fired model of an early 2-2-0 'single' locomotive and tender, in original green and black livery with red lining, boiler badly scorched, paintwork worn and chipped, some parts missing, c1902.
$800-1,500

A 3½in (9cm) gauge 'Caledonian Tank' live model steam engine, 0-6-0, in blue livery with brass dome and tender.
$900-1,700

A model of an American 'Virginia' type steam locomotive and tender, 'The Rio Grande', maroon colour, with brass fittings throughout, '1865' painted on side of locomotive, 'Denver & Rio Grande Western 3517' painted on side of tender, 51in (128cm) long overall.
$800-1,500

Marklin: A 3RE 20 volts 4-4-0 LMS locomotive and 4-wheeler tender, with first/third class carriages and brake van, Bing controller.
$1,000-2,000

Bing: a spirit-fired 0-4-0 LNWR locomotive and tender No. 1942 with separated lamps, and a Bing gauge 1 signal.
$600-1,200

A 7¼in (18cm) gauge live steam powered 4-4-0 locomotive and tender, in LNER livery, locomotive 55in (138cm) long, tender 38in (95cm) long.
$2,600-5,300

A gauge 0 3-rail electric model of the SNCF Autorail, finished in cream over red and blue, in original box, by Hornby.
◁ **$600-1,100**

A Marklin working model tinplate horizontal steam engine, in original box.
$400-750

Three gauge 1 Midland Railway twin-bogie passenger cars, including two first class coaches, both lacking corridor connectors, in original red livery, with grey roofs, and a third class brake car, No. 2783, in original livery, all by Bing for Bassett-Lowke, c1927.
$800-1,500

▷

A model six column rotative beam engine, painted in green, with oak block base and panel, under glass case, c1850, 16 by 12in (40 by 30cm).
$400-750

A gauge 1 London and North Western Railway twin-bogie third class brake car, in original cream and brown livery, with white roof, side opening doors, by Bing for Bassett-Lowke, lacking corridor connectors, some slight chipping to paintwork, c1922.
$300-600

l. A gauge 0 Pots wagon No. 1914, with brake man's cabin, one lid missing, by Marklin, c1930.
$600-1,100

c. A rare gauge 0 bogie flat car, with early single propeller monoplane, with pilot, collapsible wings, by Marklin, c1930.
$600-1,100

r. A gauge 0 model of a Bordeaux No. 416 'Wagons Foudres' vat container wagon No. 1940, by Marklin, c1930.
$500-900

Two gauge 1 Great Northern Railway twin-bogie, teak, first/third class passenger cars, Nos. 2875, in original paintwork, with grey roofs, by Marklin, c1925.
$600-1,100

An English wooden model of an open-top bus, c1912, 24in (61cm) long.
$600-1,100

A Tipp & Co limousine, possibly a Rolls Royce, German, c1930.
$1,400-2,600

A Hornby '0' gauge clockwork model railway set and track, 17 pieces in all.
$1,700-3,000

A well-detailed upright model mountaineers steam engine, with brass, copper and wood fittings, with chain drive to the 5in (13cm) gauge undercarriage.
$800-1,500

A painted metal model of an Austin A40 roadster pedal car, with operating headlamps and horn, finished in light blue with chrome trim, British, one glass missing in lamp, no battery, c1950, 64in (160cm) long.
$1,800-3,800

A 1960s radio model of a 1934
Dussenberg.
$300-600

Chess Sets

A Meissen chess set, each modelled
as sea animals, enriched in iron red
and brownish-grey, all on circular
bases with gilt line, blue crossed
swords and impressed marks, from
¾in to 3½in (2 to 8.5cm) high.
$3,200-6,000

A 1/11th scale scratch built model of
a Centaur multi-role military
vehicle, half-track Land Rover,
fitted with a 3.5cc glow-plug engine
with full radio-control, complete
with radio controller, 20in (51cm)
long overall.
$1,700-3,000

An Anglo-Indian ivory
chess set, in the
mediaeval style, 19thC.
$20,000-30,000

A carved ivory chess set with one
set stained red, carved as officials
and warriors, the white bishops
probably replacements, one castle

and some of the small figures
restored, late Qing Dynasty,
highest figure 5in (12cm) high,
rectangular glass cover.
$600-1,200

A scale model of a milk float,
'Express Dairy – College Farm
Finchley', well finished with brass
lamps, churn and accessories,
ceramic driver, and Norwich
Pottery cart horse, 21½in (54cm)
long overall, with wood stand.
$1,000-2,000

A carved ivory chess set, one set
stained brown, all in a silk-lined
box opening to form the chess board,
incised with seal marks on the base,
box 24in (61cm) wide.
$1,400-2,600

A scale model of a Ferguson
TE20 tractor and plough,
tyres stamped 'Goodyear',
with the Ferguson plough
safety attachment, 16in
(40cm) long overall.
$600-1,200

An Indian miniature ivory chess set
with table stand, the octagonal
stand mounted with ivory, late
19thC, the stand 10in (26cm) wide,
the chessmen 1¼in (3cm) high.
$1,400-2,600

Games

An Anglo-Indian Vizagapatam
ivory and ebony games box, the
exterior inlaid with chess squares,
the sandalwood interior inlaid with
a backgammon board, with 30 ivory
and ebony draughts counters in a
ribbed ebony box, early 19thC,
18in (46cm) wide.
$2,600-5,300

Britains Set 1400, Bluebird Land
Speed Record car, in original box
(G, box G), 1938.
$400-750

Musical-Instruments

A silver mounted violoncello bow, by W.E. Hill & Sons, branded W.E. Hill & Sons, 72gm.
$1,700-3,000

A Strocello acoustic 'cello with 4 strings sounding through a diaphragm and horn, the diaphragm 7in (18cm) diam, 48in (120cm) high overall.
$2,000-4,500

An 8-keyed boxwood clarinet, stamped 'Astor & Co, 79 Cornhill, London' and marked with a unicorn's head, with ivory mounts and brass keys with square covers, ebony mouthpiece, 23½in (59.5cm) long.
$400-900

A rare ivory recorder, by Thomas Stanesby Junior, branded 'Stanesby/Junior/6'; the body piqué in gilt, the gold mounts chased with miniature hunting scenes, 12½in (31cm) long.
$60,000-100,000

A Black Forest organ clock, the 22-key 8-air barrel movement with 2 ranks of wood pipes controlled by manual stops, with 2-train clock movement striking on a bell, 93in (235cm).
$4,000-6,800

A gold-mounted violin bow, by Albert Nurnberger, branded Albert Nurnberger, an ivory face mounted with a gold and ebony frog with pearl eye and gold and ebony adjuster, 59gm.
$2,600-5,300

A Bechstein baby grand piano, No. 240150, the mahogany case on tapering square legs with brass casters, 56in (140cm).
$4,000-7,500

An Edwardian concertina, leather covered with gilt tooling, and metal pierced fret ends with keys, inscribed 'C. Jeffries, Maker, 12 Aldershot Road, Kilburn N.W.6', in a leather case.
$400-750

A portable street reed barrel organ, by Chiappa, playing 7 tunes, on 31 notes, with part rosewood veneered case, inlaid front panel, later fret and oak lid, 22in (56cm) wide.
$6,000-12,000

A Spanish 32-note miniature barrel piano with castanet and triangle, playing 6 tunes, in grained case with label of Enrique Salva Mane, Barcelona, 24in (61cm) wide, on wood handcart.
$1,000-2,000

A gold-mounted violin bow...

A good overstrung baby grand piano, by Archibald Ramsden, Leeds, with steel frame and mahogany case, 48in (120cm).
$3,200-6,000

A Victorian grand piano in burr walnut case, by John Broadwood & Sons, 83in (210cm) long.
$1,700-3,000

An 'Autoplayer' pianola, the upright mahogany case with hinged top, the iron frame stamped 35160, 63in (157cm) wide, with a quantity of pianola rolls and a beech two-handled piano stool.
$900-1,700

A Weber boudoir grand piano, the mahogany case on 3 pairs of fluted tapering square legs with brass casters, 66in (165cm).
$1,200-2,100

A pochette (kit violin), bearing a manuscript label, London 1766, 14½in (37cm) long overall, in wood box.
$1,600-2,800

A fine English walnut case spinet, by John Langshaw, Wigan, early 18thC.
$18,000-26,000

With a Victorian receipt for the instrument dated 1888.

A French violin, the one-piece back of almost horizontal flame, with grained table, ebony finger board and scroll finial with rosewood turners, complete with bow, c1900, length of back 14in (36cm), contained in a fitted case.
$300-600

A French violin by Joseph Hel, labelled 'Fait par Hel . . . Lille 1878' and branded 'J. Hel' on the inside back, length of back 14½in (36.5cm), in case.
$7,000-12,000

A French viola, labelled 'Bennettini . . . Milano 1881', the varnish of a gold-red colour, length of back 16in (40cm), in case.
$3,200-6,000

An English spinet, by Thomas Hitchcock, inscribed 'Thomas Hitchcock, Londini fecit No. 1102' in Virginia walnut case, with ebony and ivory keys, c1725, 74in (187.5cm) wide, on later oak stand.
$12,000-21,000

Compass: 5 octaves, GG-g³.

The upper and lower keys are inscribed H, and the reverse of the nameboard is inscribed H/1102/ 1725.

A violin by Honoré Derazey, bearing the maker's script brand on the inner back and labelled 'Joseph Guarnerius', c1870, length of back 14in (35cm).
$7,000-12,000

Varnish of a clear red-brown colour on a yellow ground.

A good viola by Frank H. Howard, bearing the maker's label in London, signed and dated 1928, L.O.B. 17in (43cm), in a fitted rectangular case, lined green velvet, with waterproof cover.
$3,200-6,000

A fine violin by Arthur Richardson, bearing the maker's label in Crediton, Devon, dated 1932, dated and numbered 208 on the centre inner back, L.O.B. 14in (35cm), with a bow in shaped blackwood case.
$4,000-6,800

The oil varnish of a clear rich red-brown colour on a yellow ground.

A fine French violin by Jean Baptiste Vuillaume, labelled 'Jean-Baptiste Vuillaume à Paris/Rue Croix des Petits Champs'; the length of back 14½in (36cm), in case.
$20,000-30,000

A violoncello, unlabelled, with two-piece back, early 20thC, L.O.B. 30in (76cm), with 2 nickel mounted violoncello bows, in a cloth carrying case.
$800-1,500

A good English violin by William E. Hill & Sons, with one-piece back, label inscribed 'William E. Hill & Sons, makers, 38 New Bond Street, London 1895, No. 92', 14in (35cm), with oak case.
$7,000-12,000

A fine English violin, by John Lott, unlabelled, the varnish of a red colour over a golden ground, length of back 14in (35.5cm), in case.
$32,000-54,000

An interesting violin, possibly Neapolitan school, faintly labelled, the varnish of a golden-brown colour, length of back 14½in (36.5cm), in case.
$4,500-9,000

A violoncello by John Betts, London, unlabelled, c1790, L.O.B. 30in (76cm), in a wood case by W. E. Hill & Sons.
$10,000-18,000

Boxes

A 12in (30cm) symphonion disc musical box with 'Sublime Harmony' combs, in walnut case with monochrome print in lid and disc storage drawer in base, with 35 discs.
$1,800-3,800

A 19in (48cm) upright symphonion disc musical box with 'Sublime Harmony' combs, coin-slot mechanism and walnut case of conventional design, lacks pediment, and 6 discs.
$4,000-6,800

A 16in (40cm) table polyphon disc musical box, with double combs and panelled walnut case with monochrome print in lid, with 20 discs.
$4,000-6,800

◁ A walnut cased musical box, the cylinder and comb movement marked B.H.A., with butterfly hammers striking on 3 bells, 19thC, 19in (48cm) wide.
$900-1,700

A rare changeable cylinder overture box, by Nicole Freres, with 5 cylinders, 3 overtures, one operatic airs and one dance, each playing 4 tunes, in crossbanded burr walnut case, 38in (96cm) wide, the cylinders 13 by 3in (33 by 7.5cm).
$10,000-18,000

◁ A 24½in (62cm) upright polyphon disc musical box with coin mechanism, side-wind motor and walnut case of typical form, with flat cornice, on disc-bin stand, 74½in (187cm) high, with 24 discs.
$8000-13,500

l. A 7½in (19cm) symphonion disc musical box, with single comb, in walnut case with monochrome print in lid, with 8 discs.
$500-900

c. A Pearl & Pearl crystal set, in mahogany box, with headphones, and two other items.
$100-250

r. A 7½in (19cm) symphonion table disc musical box, with single comb, in mahogany case with monochrome print inside lid and transfer decoration to top, with 24 discs.
$500-900

A French singing bird box, the feathered songbird with ivory beak, in enamelled case, No. 3771, with original key, late 19thC, 4½in (12cm).
$2,000-4,500

An early keywound Swiss cylinder music box, the movement with segmented comb, playing 4 airs, stamped 3568, cylinder 8½in (21cm), in mahogany case, 12in (30cm) wide.
$1,000-2,000

A bells-in-sight musical box, with 13in (33cm) cylinder playing 10 airs, with 9 bells with insect and bird strikers, in walnut case, 23in (58cm) long.
$1,700-3,000

A small automaton disc musical box, the single comb playing 5½in (14cm) discs and activating an automaton see-saw with cats in a glazed compartment, slight woodworm, 7½in (19cm), together with 12 discs.
$600-1,200

A 30in (75cm) cylinder music box, rosewood inlaid, with 10 airs, 6 bells and drum-in-sight, WO, mid-19thC, 19½in (49.5cm) cylinder.
$2,200-4,200

A square section bird cage of wire and turned wood construction containing automata bird in flight and one other pecking at a nut, box case containing musical box, 19thC, 17in (43cm) high.
$400-900

A small fairground organ with 58-note paper roll reed-organ action, in covered trolley on casters, 100in (250cm) wide, with 63 Angelus/Symphony rolls.
$4,000-7,500

A French key wound singing bird automaton, the tortoiseshell case with oval silver and parcel gilt engraved cover, late 19thC, 4in (10cm) wide, in original leather travelling case.
$900-1,700

A good symphonion table musical box, the case carved in rococo style, late 19thC, 19in (48cm) wide, with a quantity of discs.
$3,200-6,000

An automaton monkey violinist on a snuff box, the musical movement playing 2 airs, 20in (50cm) high overall.
$5,000-9,000

Phonographs

A Continental singing bird automaton, in repousse sterling silver gilt casket, decorated all over with floral swags, acanthus and cherubs, on 4 bun feet, late 19thC, 4½in (10cm) wide.
$1,300-2,400

A gilt metal singing bird musical box, 4in (10.5cm).
$1,300-2,400

An Edison Gem phonograph, with large horn, c1903.
$400-750

Transport

A 1924 Rolls-Royce Silver Ghost 40/50 HP 4-seat convertible limousine, coachwork by Barker, Reg. No. XR 3080, chassis No. 69EM, engine; 6-cylinder side valve, 7428 cc, 40/50 hp, 4-speed right-hand change sliding mesh gearbox, mechanical servo 4-wheel brakes, suspension semi-elliptic front and cantilever rear, wire wheels with dual sidemounted spares.
$74,000-120,000

A 1946 SS Jaguar 2½ litre sports saloon, Reg. No. HXK 465, chassis No. 510370, engine No. P385.
$5,000-9,000

A 1930 Riley Nine Monaco 4-door saloon, Reg. No. EO.4810, chassis No. 60/5426, engine No. 60/5426.
$7,000-12,000

A Morris Cowley Six saloon, first registered January 19th, 1934, in midnight blue and black.
$3,200-6,000

A 1934 Alvis Speed Twenty 4-seat tourer, coachwork by Vanden Plas, chassis No. 15797, engine No. 12474, engine; 6-cylinder, overhead valve, dual ignition, triple SU carburettors, 2511 cc, 87 bhp.
$32,000-57,000

A 1935 Standard 'Nine' saloon, engine No. A.52971, chassis No. 312792, capacity 1056 cc, date of original registration November 23rd, 1935.
$2,600-5,300

A 1930 Austin Seven 'Chummy', painted in primrose yellow and black, Reg. No. KR4012.
$7,000-12,000

A 1937 Leyland open fire appliance, Reg. No. XS.4860, engine No. 3609, engine; 6 cylinder, overhead valve, 4.9 litre, 30 hp, manual sliding mesh gearbox, 4-wheel brakes, semi-elliptic suspension.
$11,000-18,000

A 1938 Railton Straight Eight Fairmile drophead coupé, Reg. No. MG.5981, chassis No. 745447, engine No. 31747, engine; Hudson 8-cylinder in line, side valve, 4.2 litres, 100 bhp, three forward speed gearbox, 4-wheel hydraulic brakes, semi-elliptic suspension.
$11,000-18,000

The interesting registration number is one of a batch issued to University Motors and more often seen on the MGs that they sold.

A 1951 Singer Nine roadster, chassis No. 4AB 7159.
$4,000-7,500

A 1953 Bristol Type-403 2-door sports saloon, chassis No. 403/1444, engine No. 1542.
$3,200-6,000

A 1954 Bentley R-type Continental sports saloon, coachwork by H.J. Mulliner, chassis No. BC11C, engine No. BCD7, engine; 6-cylinder, inlet over exhaust valve, 4875 cc, power output undisclosed, independent coil spring front and semi-elliptic rear suspension with adjustable dampers.
$66,000-100,000

A 1955 Sunbeam Talbot MK.III drophead coupé, chassis No. A.3502211/9/HCO, engine No. A.350261/ODH50.
$2,200-4,200

A 1964 Sunbeam Alpine Mk.IV sports saloon convertible, chassis and engine No. B.9402783 H.R.O.
$1,000-2,000

A 1958 Bedford H.C.B. Angus Short Tender, ex Dumfries & Gallow Fire Service, Reg. No. LCS 149.
$2,200-4,200

A 1960 MGA 1600 sports 2-seater, chassis No. GHN/82765, engine No. 14057, engine; 4-cylinder, overhead valve, 1588 cc, gearbox, four-speed synchromesh, brakes, disc front drum rear, suspension, independent coil spring front, semi-elliptic rear.
$7,000-12,000

A 1962 Alvis TD21 foursome drophead coupé, chassis and engine No. 26733.
$5,500-9,000

This is one of 1,067 chassis of the TD21 series built between 1959 and 1962.

A 1907 Triumph 3½ HP solo motorcycle, engine No. 1203, frame No. 108056, Reg. No. XN 9022.
$4,000-7,500

A 1968 Aston Martin DB.6. Superleggera grand touring 4-seater, Reg. No. WGU 957G, chassis No. DB6.3485, engine No. 4003773.
$6,000-12,000

A 1909 Triumph 3½ HP solo motorcycle, engine No. 5658, frame No. 139731, Reg. No. AH 2226.
$3,200-6,000

A 1968 Jensen Interceptor Mk.I 2-door fixed head coupé, Reg. No. EDL 725F, chassis No. 115/2759, engine No. 752/15.B.
$3,200-6,000

A 1924 Excelsior 2½ HP standard solo motorcycle, engine No. J2169, frame No. J2197, Reg. No. KL 964.
$2,600-5,300

A Douglas model B 2¾ HP solo motorcycle, engine No. 038, frame No. 562730, Reg. No. P5524, c1910.
$4,000-6,800

A 1937 Brough superior 11-50 special 1150 cc motorcycle combination, engine No. LT2. F55863.5N, frame No. M81805, Reg. No. DKA 255.
$8,000-13,500

A 1926 Norton 16-H 490 cc solo motorcycle, engine No. 45357, frame No. 38987, Reg. No. PP 7097.
$3,200-6,000

A bicycle, with 54½in 136cm) diam. wheel with radial spokes, adjustable pedals mounted on the axle, and with iron backbone with mounting step, c1880.
$1,800-3,800

A nickel-plated brass mascot modelled as Charles Lindberg's Spirit of St. Louis, 6in (15cm) wingspan, on turned wood stand.
$1,200-2,100

l. A child's antique Penny Farthing bicycle with Dunlop saddle.
$600-1,100

r. A similar child's Penny Farthing bicycle.
$600-1,100

A nickel-plated brass mascot modelled as Charles Lindberg's Spirit of St. Louis, 6in (15cm) wingspan, on turned wood stand.

A West Country jingle.
$800-1,500

A plated Rolls Royce 'Kneeling Lady' mascot, fitted to correct radiator cap, for the 'Silver Wraith/Silver Dawn' range of cars, display base mounted.
$300-600

A twenty-two man manual horse-drawn fire appliance, by Shand Mason & Co, London, c1871, 126in (320cm) long overall.
$10,000-18,000

A small sized 'Old Bill' mascot with original nickel plating, the helmet signed 'Bruce Bairnsfather', 2½in (6cm) high, display base mounted.
$80-180

A Jaguar SS100 'Leaping Cat' mascot, the rocky base stamped 'Desmo' and 'Copyright', original chrome plating on brass, on correct radiator cap, the cat 7½in (19cm) long.
$200-450

A rare Lincoln-Imp silver plated brass motor car mascot, with blue beads for eyes, mounted to a radiator cap, 5½in (13.5cm) high.
$200-450

A Lalique clear glass mascot, moulded 'R. Lalique' and 'France' markings, damaged, 8in (20cm) high, 2½in (6cm) diam. base.
$400-750

A nickel plated 'Safety First' vintage accessory mascot, 5in (13cm) high, display base mounted.
$80-180

.A G.W.R. 4-6-0 4000 Star Class 'Knight of the Grand Cross' cast brass number plate 4018.
$900-1,700

Use the Index!

Because certain items might fit easily into any of a number of categories, the quickest and surest method of locating any entry is by reference to the index at the back of the book.

This has been fully cross-referenced for absolute simplicity.

Fishing

An unnamed angler's knife, with four tools.
$20-45

A 'Helical' line drier, by the Helical Co of Redditch, with four wooden arms, fixable into centre wooden holder and clamp.
$30-60

A Hardy 'Uniqua' trout fly reel, with ivorine handle, 1910 style check, 3in (8cm).
$60-120

A rare casting reel, the 'Kitchen's Patent', dated 1920, 4¾ by 3in (12 by 7.5cm).
$400-900

The only known example of a belt-driven multiplier.

A Brown Robertson lock-joint tool of aluminium, with 9 recesses for gripping jammed rod joints, 5 by 1in (12.5 by 2.5cm).
$20-45

An Arthur Allan spinet fixed spool reel, with half bail arm and open cogs, c1920, 2in (5cm) diam.
$30-60

◁
A Malloch 'Sun and Planet' reel, designed for harling on the Tay, sizes 2½ to 5in (6 to 12cm).
$150-300

Sport

A rare Hardy salmon size Spintac tackle box, of fine oak with five internal compartments and lift-out trace carrier, c1940-50, 8½ by 4½in (21 by 11cm).
$60-120

A Victorian archery target.
$150-300

A set of lignum vitae bowls.
$150-300

A pike trimmer from Lake Windermere, the red and white cork bearing owner's name, J. Wrigley, c1880, 4in (10cm).
$40-90

A good quality table croquet set.
$300-600

A late Victorian silver vesta case, moulded as a footballers leg and ball, 2in (5cm).
$900-1,700

Golfing

A pair of rare F.H. Ayres table tennis rackets, c1890, 17in (43cm) long.
$300-600

Two scarred head golf clubs, c1895.
$200-450 each

1. A Forgan putter, c1875.
$800-1,500

2. A McEwan spoon, c1870.
$3,200-6,000

3. A scarred head L.T. putter, c1890-1900.
$200-450

A Forgan putter, c1875.
$800-1,500

A feathery golf ball, c1840.
$2,200-4,200

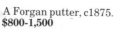

A 'hole in one' adjustable golf club, c1925.
$200-450

A brown glazed oviform single-handled jug, modelled with golfers in blue, green and brown, printed Royal Doulton marks, 9in (23cm).
$600-1,200

A golfing mug.
$150-300

A Royal Doulton 'Kingsware' oviform golfing mug, in green and amber, pink and yellow against a green and dark brown ground, c.m.l. & c., 5½in (14cm).
$600-1,200

A golfing mug, 'From Kirkstone Pass Inn, 1,500ft altitude'.
$150-300

A Royal Doulton teapot, sugar bowl and milk jug with silver rim, dated 1910.
$300-600

A golf trophy of Pam Barton, spelterware, 6in (15cm).
$200-450

A Copeland Spode teapot in royal blue.
$300-600

A spelter figure of a golfer, signed, 14in (35.5cm) high.
$800-1,500

A silverplate vesta case, enamelled in colours with a footballer before a goal, 1½in (4cm).
$200-450

A silverplate and enamel vesta case, inscribed 'Colman's Mustard', 2in (5cm).
$150-300

A silvered metal striker/lighter modelled as football boot and ball, 2¼in (5.5cm).
$80-180

A pair of copper-coloured spelter figures of a footballer and a goalkeeper, damage to goalkeeper's arm, 20in (50cm).
$300-600

A gold-coloured spelter group depicting four footballers, inscribed 'Un Match Interessant', some restoration, 13½in (34cm).
$600-1,200

A silver table lighter in the form of a football, upon circular foot, 2½in (6cm).
$150-250

A Football League Champions Southern Section Division 3 gold medal.
$300-600

A Scottish League Championship winners gold medal for 1922-23, won by Glasgow Rangers Football Club, and inscribed 'W. Robb'.
$500-900

▷ A canvas pigeon decoy.
$40-90

A Liverpool Cup winners gold medal for 1885, the reverse inscribed 'Everton F.C.– J. McG.'.
$200-450

Jack McGill was the first professional that Everton F.C. ever signed.

A Victorian 'Bussey' table tennis set.
$200-450

A Victorian sledge, 32in (80cm) long.
$150-300

A mahogany tennis racket press, c1900.
$200-450

A colourful metal golfer.
40-120

A Strauss mechanical toy, USA, 1930s, in original box.
150-300

Crafts

l. A silver 'hole in one' trophy.
$80-180

c. A silver toast rack.
$200-450

r. A silver golfing figure, 2in (5cm) high.
$80-180

A silver match striker case, 2in (5cm).
$150-300

A selection of spoons.
$60-120

A Royal Doulton ceramic trophy, 11½in (29cm).
$600-1,100

rare earthenware bowl, by Sir Frank Brangwyn, in rich russet with patches of iron-black on a yellow underglaze, 10in (25cm) diam.
200-450

set of four two-handled bowls, by Michael Cardew, covered in a rich dark brown glaze, impressed MC and Wenford Bridge seals, small rim chips, c1970, 5½in (13.5cm) average diam.
400-900

An earthenware mustard-coloured slip decorated rhyme tankard, by Michael Cardew, with strap handle, inscribed between incised borders, 'Brandy & Gin Swell out the Skin & Make A Man Feel Very Queer & Whenever I Puts Them Into My Guts I Always Wish They were Beer', impressed MC and Winchcombe Pottery seals, c1926, 5½in (13.5cm) high.
$600-1,200

A black stoneware bulbous vase, by John Leach, the saggar-fired matt black body with sandy and smooth textures, impressed JL seal and Muchelney, 8½in (22cm) high.
$400-750

A porcelain cut-sided bottle, by Shigeyoshi Ichino, covered in a pale celadon glaze, impressed Shige and St. Ives seal, c1968, 11in (28cm) high.
$300-600

A large stoneware lidded jar, by Michael Cardew, covered in a rich dark brown glaze, impressed MC and Wenford Bridge seals, c1970, 13in (33cm) high.
$800-1,500

tall stoneware vase, by Joanna Constantinidis, with burnished texture revealing manganese beneath a buff slip, impressed C seal, 1971, 26½in (66.5cm).
800-1,500

A stoneware cut-decorated bottle, by Janet Leach, with dark brown body with blackish-green glaze trails and splashes, impressed JL and St. Ives seals, c1958, 10in (25cm) high.
$600-1,100

An earthenware bowl, by Gertrude and Otto Natzler, on small foot and with horizontal ribs in a grey speckled celadon glaze streaked in brown, painted 'NATZLER', 6in (15cm) diam.
$1,500-2,000

An earthenware compote, by Gertrude and Otto Natzler, in a textured olive brown glaze with aquamarine crystalline highlights, on a conical base in a dark olive glaze, painted 'Natzler', 8in (29cm) diam.
$2,000-2,200

A 'Denaura' earthenware vase, by the Denver China and Pottery Company, modelled with overlapping flowers and long stems in a matte dark green glaze, stamped twice with firm's mark, painted 'DENAURA' and impressed 'DENVER 172 LF 172', 5in (12.5cm) high.
$1,000-1,200

An earthenware vase, by Arequipa, moulded with a frieze of sinuous leaves in a streaked mauve, light blue, pale green and tan glaze with white patches forming stylised iris blossoms, impressed with firm's mark and 'AREQUIPA CALIFORNIA 206 5', 7in (17.5cm) high.
$1,900-2,100

An earthenware vase, by Grand Feu, Los Angeles, in a 'Mission' glaze of various shades of brown, impressed 'GRAND FEU POTTERY L.A., CAL.' and inscribed '713', 5½in (13cm) diam.
$1,500-2,000

A large stoneware footed bowl, by Margaret Rey, covered in a specked buff glaze with bold iron-brown decoration, impressed seal, c1930, 13in (33cm).
$900-1,700

A porcelain sgraffito bottle, by Lucie Rie, covered in a bronze manganese glaze, with matt cobalt blue on the inner rim and shoulders, impressed LR seal, c1980, 10in (25cm) high.
$1,700-3,000

An earthenware handbuilt coiled amphora, by Fiona Salazar, decorated in burnished black, brick-red and amber slips, painted 'Fiona Salazar', c1984, 11in (28cm).
$500-900

A porcelain sgraffito bowl, by Lucie Rie, with a matt manganese glaze, impressed LR seal, c1978, 8½in (21cm) diam.
$6,000-12,000

A stoneware beaker-shaped vase, by William Staite Murray, covered in a creamy-buff glaze with charcoal grey decoration, impressed M seal, c1930, 5½in (14cm).
$400-900

A raku deep circular bowl, by Martin Smith, decorated in grey and pink, minor chips to rim, c1977, 9½in (24cm) diam.
$900-1,700

Tribal Art

An Eastern European native silver belt, applied with coral, silver floral bosses and blue and green champlevé enamels.
$300-600

A Benin wood box, ornately carved, a good patina overall, 19 by 4in (48.5 by 10.5cm).
$600-1,100

A fur ivory bracelet, with stained circular motifs between 2 engraved linear bands, 3in (7.5cm) diam, and 2 other ivory items.
$80-150

A Rajasthan cloth, in purple and browns on a red ground, attached khaki border, 58½in (146cm) square.
$800-1,500

A Tlingit wool fringed blanket, Chilkat, dyed in yellow, turquoise and white on a black field, 66 by 33½in (166 by 85cm).
$8,000-13,500

A Bambara wood horseman, the rider carved with the arms free of the body, crusty to glossy dark brown patina, 17in (43cm) high.
$800-1,500

A Poto knife, metal bound hilt with large wood double knob finial, 27in (68cm) long.
$300-600

A guro wood mask, with pierced slit eyes, incised raised brows, surmounted by two horns, serrated border, glossy dark brown patina, 12½in (32cm) high.
$600-1,100

A Plains feather war bonnet, comprising 28 eagle feathers with green stroud binding, and polychrome beaded headband, with red, white and blue ribbons attached.
$600-1,200

A classic Achiri Challapta pancho, Achiri Region, Province of Pacajes, Department of La Paz, Aymara Group, natural dyed alpaca, the central black field with 6 horizontal linear bands woven in blue, white, pink, yellow and green, the edge with multi-coloured fringe, late 19thC, 56 by 66in (140 by 165cm).
$1,300-1,500

A fine Sioux hide and cloth baby carrier, the upper hide section decorated with red dyed quillwork and beaded edge, the interior lined with printed cotton, in excellent condition, mounted, 29in (72.5cm) high.
$2,200-2,500

A Jalisco pottery kneeling female figure, the body modelled with skirt, tunic and headgear, 13in (33cm) high.
$600-1,200

An African carved wood fertility god, a kneeling female figure with tall head-dress, an infant on her back, with covered cooking pot supported by 2 small kneeling figures on circular base, 26in (65cm) high.
$9,000-15,000

A fine Haida mountain goat spoon, the handle intricately carved with a raven surmounted by 3 well-carved faces peering over the top of its head, in turn surmounted by a seated figure of a bear supporting a small hawk on top of its head, the wings of the raven incised with totemic symbols and its tail portraying a face carved in relief, the handle fastened to the ladle with 3 copper rivets, and mounted on a metal base, 11½in (28cm) high.
$3,500-4,000

Four Hupa twined baskets, including 3 of hemispherical form and one of cylindrical form, woven in shades of brown and cream with angular geometric designs, and one with a rim of red glass beads, the larger 6½in (17cm) diam.
$150-300

A matrimonial Urku/wedding overskirt, Bolivar Region, Provence of Arque, Department of Cochabamba, Aymara Group, the central red and green field flanked by 2 wide bands, the design band in the left panel is executed in double cloth typical of the Bolivar region and the right panel with a central design band in pebble weave typical of the Challa region, late 19thC, 48 by 53in (120 by 132.5cm).
$1,500-1,700

An aymara, Ahuayo, Department of Oruro, the mahogany field with a central band containing avain motifs, woven in white, purple, yellow, pink and blue, the 2 edges with bands containing avian motifs in green and gold, early 19thC, 44½ by 50in (112 by 127cm).
$1,300-1,500

A Llacota/Mans mantle, Aymara Group, Department of Potosi, natural dyed alpaca, a central brown field, the sides with linear bands in yellowish-gold and various shades of purple, mid-19thC, 43 by 44in (107 by 110cm).
$1,300-1,500

An Eskimo walrus tusk cribbage board, engraved with a village scene, hunters with animal, sleds and fish, 22in (56cm) long.
$600-800

A pair of Sioux beaded hide boy's breeches, with overall white, green, red, blue and yellow beadwork in geometric designs and crosses, 18in (45cm) long.
$600-900

A Tlingit twined spruce root basket, woven in red, yellow, blue and purple, with 3 parallel bands of crosses and angular geometric designs, 7½in (18cm) diam.
$400-600

Lesser Sumba Island, Indonesia, tortoiseshell comb, with elaborate animal and avian motifs, 7in (17.5cm) high.
$3,200-6,000

A large Nez Perce cornhusk bag, embroidered in dyed grass, one side woven with 6 stepped triangles, in the centre a series of 3 stepped devices resembling trees, on the reverse, stylised butterflies, woven in shades of red, purple, green, yellow, turquoise and black, 22½in (56cm).
$500-700

An Attu twined basket, embroidered in red, purple and blue with small triangles, and fitted lid with knob, 7½in (18cm) high.
$300-400

A Sioux beaded hide vest, decorated overall with green, red and blue geometric motifs, and 2 American flags, on a white beaded ground, 18in (45cm) high.
$900-1,100

A pair of Yoruba female Ibeji figures, with a string of blue beads around the necks, well patinated elongated faces with ridged tripartite coiffures, 11½in (29cm) high.
$600-1,100

A fine and rare Yoruba bronze group, for the Ogboni cult, of a seated male figure, probably a priest, the male attendant holding a pair of edan Ogboni, the female her breasts, probably from Ilorin, c1900, 8½in (22cm).
$1,300-2,400

A Bambara wood marionette figure, comprising a highly stylised 4-legged female, surmounted by tiers of elongated heads decreasing in size, decorated overall with pierced and punched panels of brass, copper and white metal, 67in (168cm).
$1,000-2,000

A Yaka wood female figure, with abdominal fetish cavity, traces of yellow about the eyes and white to the ears, glossy brown patina, 18½in (47cm) high.
$400-750

A large Watam canoe prow, carved in the form of a crocodile with incised curvilinear decoration, 48½in (121cm) long.
$200-450

A Loango ivory tusk, spirally carved in relief with native figures, some wearing European clothing, 11½in (29cm) long.
$150-300

A Cameroon circular wood stool, the support pierced and carved with 3 tiers of bat heads, scorched ornament, Tikar/Babanki-Kijem, 16½in (41.5cm).
$900-1,700

A Southern Plains hide quiver, decorated at each end with beadwork in blue, yellow and red on a green ground, a wood bow and two arrows, 34in (86cm).
$600-1,200

A Loango hippopotamus tooth, finely carved in low relief on one side, and in the Chinese manner on the other, creamy yellow patina, 13½in (34cm) long.
$600-1,200

A Loango ivory tusk, spirally carved with figures, most of whom are fighting, seated female figure finial, cracks, 9½in (24cm) long.
$600-1,200

Ephemera – Pop

The Beatles – 'One & One is Two', a Dick James Music single-sided demo disc, 1964, in (?) original sleeve.
$600-1,200

A coloured aquatint of Buddy Holly and others, No. 7 of 10 artist's proofs, numbered, titled, signed and dated by the artist, David Oxtoby, 1977, plate area 27 by 21in (68 by 53cm), framed and glazed.
$300-600

A colour transparency collection, comprising approx. 5,000 labelled transparencies, 2¼in (5.5cm) square, protected by transparent bags and protecting card mounts, in twelve card index drawers.
$14,000-24,000

603

Cigarette Cards

Jung Nickel, No. 328, No. 329 and No. 331, women in hats and costume, G to F.
$300-600

One of only 8 Beatles' dresses worn by usherettes for the Royal Premiere of 'Help' in July 1965, sleeveless with pink and white polka dots, with ink signatures of all 4 members, Ringo Starr signing twice, and those of Cynthia Lennon and Brian Epstein.
$3,200-6,000

Mela Koehler, No. 310, No. 312 and No. 315, women in costume, G to F.
$200-450

Mela Koehler, No. 375 and No. 589, women in hats and costume, G to F.
$200-450

Maria Likarz, No. 722, No. 777 and No. 781, women in hats and costume, G to F.
$200-450

Mela Koehler, Nos 519-523, women in costume with dogs before patterned backgrounds, G to F.
$600-1,100

Wills, Cricketers 1896, a complete set of 50.
$1,800-3,800

Baker, Beauties of All Nations 1899, a set of 25.
$150-300

BLACK CAT CIGARETTES

Wills, Cricketers Series 1901, a complete set of 50.
$200-450

Gallaher, Royalty Series, a complete set.
$200-450

Carreras, Women on War Work, a set of 50.
$150-300

Arnold Nechanski, No. 891 and No. theatrical designs, G to F.
$150-300

Cope, Dickens Gallery, a complete set of 50.
$200-450

Postcards & Posters

Raphael Tuck, Celebrated Posters No. 1501, Ogden's Guinea Gold Cigarettes and A Country Girl at Daly's Theatre.
$80-180

Raphael Tuck, Celebrated Posters No. 1501, Rowntree's Elect Cocoa, No. 1501, Dewar's and No. 1506, Mazawattee Cocoa.
$150-300

Marilyn Monroe, 'The Seven Year Itch', a polychrome film poster, 1955, small clean tear at folds, 30 by 40in (76 by 100cm).
$200-450

A postcard showing flooding in Southsea High St, and others (about 1,000) in one album.
$400-750

Louis Wain, The Meeting Between a Puppy and a Kitten, signed, watercolour heightened with white, 7½ by 11½in (19 by 29cm).
$400-1,500

A signed photograph of Vivien Leigh.
$300-600

George Ernest Studdy, I'm Much Slicker When There Aint A Moon!, signed and inscribed, pencil, pen, black ink and watercolour heightened with white, unframed, 10½ by 15in (26.5 by 38cm).
$600-1,500

George Ernest Studdy, Can't We Think of Anything Nice To Do?, signed, inscribed, pencil, pen, black ink and watercolour, heightened with white, unframed, 10½ by 15in (26.5 by 38cm).
$200-450

Louis Wain, Ginger Tomcat, signed, pencil and coloured chalks, pastel, unframed, 9 by 7in (23 by 18cm).
$1,400-2,600

William Henry ▷ Walker, A Fairy Bower, signed, pen, black ink and watercolour, unframed, 10 by 5in (25 by 12.5cm).
$1,600-2,800

Cecil Aldin, In Disgrace; A Welcome Surprise; The Favoured One; and Dutch Boys Fishing, signed, with inscriptions on reverse, pencil and watercolour heightened with white, unframed, 11½ by 9in (29 by 23cm).
$1,600-2,800

◁ Ethel Larcombe, Gathering Roses, signed with monogram, pencil and watercolour heightened with white, unframed, 20 by 15in (50 by 38cm).
$800-1,500

English School: There was an Old Woman who lived in a Shoe, pen and black ink, 9 by 13in (23 by 33cm).
$150-300

Ethel Larcombe, The Mistress with her Page, signed with monogram, watercolour, unframed, 20 by 15in (50 by 38cm).
$600-1,100

Ernest Howard Shepard, Adversaries in The Bad Old Days, signed with initials and inscribed, pen and black ink, unframed, 14 by 10in (35 by 25cm).
$800-1,500

Ronald Searle, Alls Well that ends Well, signed and inscribed, pen, brown and red ink, brown washes, published Punch, September 30th, 1953, 11 by 14in (28 by 35cm).
$400-1,200

Ethel Larcombe, The Blue of Heaven is !arger than the Cloud, signed with monogram and inscribed, pencil and watercolour, unframed, 9½ by 6in (24 by 15cm), and another unframed watercolour by the same artist.
$400-750

William Henry Walker, Pan, signed, pen, black ink and watercolour, unframed, 10 by 7in (25 by 18cm).
$1,300-2,400

Edward Jeffrey Irving Ardizzone, The Fight on its Bridge, inscribed, further inscribed 'Milldale, Chapt. XIV', No. 2, pencil and pen and black ink, 7 by 10½in (18 by 26cm).
$400-900

Ronald Searle, Twelfth Night, signed, inscribed and dated 1954, further inscribed 'Punch Theatre', brush, pen, brown ink and brown washes, published Punch, January 13th, 1954, 11 by 14in (28 by 35cm).
$400-900

Osbert Lancaster, 'Personally I don't believe a word of this thin man stuff – I know damn well just what the old Gauguin of Fleet St is up to', signed twice, inscribed, further inscribed 'Specially Commissioned . . .', brush, pen, brown ink and blue crayon, on three sheets, 9½ by 22in (24 by 55cm).
$400-900

A German magic poster of one of the most famous magicians, c1930.
$200-450

A 'Player's Weights' poster, signed 'Winks', 19½ by 29½in (49 by 74cm).
$40-90

Disneyalia

Snow White and the Seven Dwarfs, eight polychrome moulded plaster figures, bases stamped or printed 'G. Leonardi by Permission of Walt Disney Mickey Mouse Ltd', some chipped, one repaired, c1937, 12 and 7-8in (31 and 18-20cm) high.
$300-600

Snow White and the Seven Dwarfs, with an EPNS souvenir spoon, Snow White possibly repainted, 1939.
$200-450

Vulture from Robin Hood, gouache on full celluloid, 12 by 15½in (31 by 39cm).
$300-600

Scripophily

Hen, from Robin Hood, gouache on full celluloid, 12 by 15½in (31 by 39cm).
$200-450

National Bank: £1 specimen 1870, GVF.
$200-450

Penny, from The Rescuers, gouache on full celluloid, 12 by 15in (31 by 38cm).
$200-450

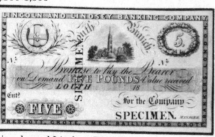

Barclays Bank: 1924 (c) original artwork in brown and blue on light card for £1 note, view of Douglas harbour on reverse, VF.
$800-1,500

£10 proof on paper for Belfast 1830 (c), VF.
$200-450 ▷

Lincoln and Lindsey Banking Company: £5 proof on card (G.S369A) plus a letter from the Bank dated 1839 and instructing Perkins, Bacon and Petch to print and deliver 4,000 £5 notes, GVF.
$150-250

£1 and £3 1881, plus £1 1882, all proofs on paper with the signature area cut out, VF-EF.
$200-450

1819 – 10 roubles State Assignat (P.A18), V.G.
$180-300

USA: Bank of the United States of America 1832 share certificate signed by 'Biddle', slight stains on fold, small tears, and repaired badly with sellotape, scarce, F.
$200-450 ▷

◁

Newmarket Bank: £5 1899 (G.2061c) overstamped 'Cancelled' twice, VF.
$80-180

1862 $2 (p.129), F.
$150-300

Argentina: 1880 Banco Otero & Ca.
20 pesos proof (P.–), engraved by
Bradbury Wilkinson, EF.
$200-450

Channel Tubular Railway
Preliminary Co Ltd, 1892 five
bearer shares, VF-EF.
$200-450

Azores: 1905 5 milreis prata
VG.
$180-300

Trinidad: 1 March 1939 Barclays
Bank $5 (P.S102), pinholes top left
corner, otherwise crisp, GVF.
$180-300

Oriental – Bamboo

A carved bamboo incense stick
holder, densely carved and pierced
with entwined 'chilong' dragons,
the hardwood ends with cylindrical
stoppers, mid Qing Dynasty, 9in
(23cm) long.
$2,200-4,200

A carved bamboo group of Shoulao,
surrounded by seven young
attendants, 17th/18thC, 13in
(32.5cm) high.
$1,000-2,000

A Cantonese enamel scalloped
bowl, decorated in imitation lapis
lazuli and filled with ivory balls,
11½in (29cm) diam.
$5,500-9,000

Cloisonné & Enamel

A fine small oviform cloisonné
enamel vase, decorated in colours
and aventurine on a dark blue
ground, with silver rims, slightly
bruised, signed on the base 'Murase
seizo', Meiji period, 5in (12cm) high.
$1,600-2,800

A pair of Japanese cloisonné
vases, decorated on a yellow
ground, thumbnail chip to
one vase, 19thC,
46in (115cm).
$11,000-18,000

A pair of Chinese cloisonné vases
with sky blue ground, on a highly
decorated ground of red and pale
pink, late 19thC, 12in (31cm) high.
$600-1,100

A pair of cloisonné enamel vases
and covers, on a pale blue ground,
6in (15cm).
$600-1,200

Make the most of Miller's

*Price ranges in this book
reflect what one should
expect to pay for a similar
example. When selling one
can obviously expect a
figure below. This will
fluctuate according to a
dealer's stock, saleability
at a particular time, etc. It
is always advisable to
approach a reputable
specialist dealer or an
auction house which has
specialist sales.*

A pair of cloisonné enamel censers
and detachable covers, with
turquoise bodies, red crests and
multi-coloured wings, standing on
fixed gilt bronze stands, minor
damage, 18th/19thC, 11½in
(28.5cm) high overall.
$3,200-6,000

Furniture

A pair of cloisonné enamel figures of hawks standing on turquoise rockwork, with black, white and mottled grey feather markings and lime-green eyes, minor pitting, 18in (45cm) wide.
$4,500-9,000

A Japanese black lacquer table cabinet, the interior with an arrangement of drawers, c1870, 19½in (48cm) wide.
$1,000-2,000

A Japanese cherrywood display cabinet, 19thC, 50in (125cm).
$2,200-4,200

A pair of Japanese lacquer cabinets on stands, 19in (47cm).
$1,200-2,100

A composite suite of Chinese carved pierced hardwood furniture, each piece profusely pierced and carved, the arms in the form of dragons, raised on carved legs with animals masks and feet, 7 pieces.
$4,000-6,800

A carved padoukwood three-piece suite.
$1,200-2,100

A Japanese bronze miniature four-fold screen, the panels decorated with inset enamel, gold and silver, together with a wooden stand, 19thC, 9in (23cm) wide, fully extended.
$1,000-2,000

A Huali altar table, the top inset with three burr-wood panels, Qing Dynasty, 33in (83cm).
$2,200-4,200

A Chinese hardwood whatnot, with six cleated shelves on curvilinear supports, 26in (65cm) wide.
$1,200-2,100

A Japanese lacquer four-tier whatnot, with 2 pairs of doors, brass mounts and gilt foliate decoration, 38in (95cm).
$2,200-4,200

Glass

A hair crystal bottle with irregularly scattered black rutile needles, stopper.
$600-1,200

A Beijing red overlay glass flattened bottle, carved with 3 'qilong' forming a continuous pattern of irregular circles, the clear body with snowstorm inclusions, with stopper.
$600-1,100

An inside-painted glass bottle, painted on both sides, inscribed and signed 'Ye Zhongsan', with stopper.
$800-1,500

A pair of Beijing overlay violet-blue milk-ground glass baluster vases, late Qing Dynasty, 10½in (26cm) high.
$1,700-3,000

A Chinese reverse painted glass panel, colourfully decorated, 19thC, 20 by 14in (50 by 35cm), wooden frame.
$600-1,100

A smoked crystal figure of a hawk, perched on a rocky outcrop, 9in (23cm) high.
$500-900

Ivory

A fine Tokyo school ivory carving of a lady dressed in a kimono, a little boy climbing on her back, age cracks, signed 'Koraku', 19thC, 10in (25.5cm) high.
$1,800-3,800

Horn

A horn bottle, carved in low relief, minor repair, stopper.
$800-1,500

Inros

A Japanese five-case inro, decorated with various coloured lacquer, with attached ojime Netsuke, late 19thC, 3¼in (8cm).
$500-900

A three-case gold sprinkled roironuri inro, decorated in hiramakie and kinji, with a tasselled Chinese style fan, signed in gold hiramakie on a gyobu ground, Kyoto Kokaku ke (family), okuru (gift to) Kimura Shozaburo, slightly scratched, tiny chips, early 19thC, with attached pink coral bead ojime.
$1,600-2,800

A wood and ivory carving of a drum seller, with roped sandals on his feet, stained hair and eye detail, signed on a rectangular red tablet Kazuyuki, late 19thC, 10½in (26cm).
$2,200-4,200

A sectional ivory okimono of a basket weaver and his wife, signed on an oval red tablet, Eitoku, late 19thC, 4in (10cm) high.
$1,200-2,100

A fine ivory carving of Kannon, engraved and stained detail, base of figure slightly cracked, signed Shunyosai Nobuyuki to, late 19thC, 5½in (14cm).
$1,200-2,100

A Japanese carved ivory rectangular plaque, in pierced hardwood frame and stand, red lacquer seal, c1900, 16in (40.5cm) wide.
$1,200-2,100

A stained ivory censer and fluted cover, the details inlaid in shell and other materials, signed on the reverse of the cover Tamayuki, Meiji period, wood stand, 11½in (29cm) high.
$2,000-4,500

A carved ivory figure of a fisherman on natural base, 15½in (39cm) high.
$2,200-4,200

An ivory medical figure of a maiden lying naked except for a pair of shoes, signed, hardwood stand, 7in (19cm) long.
$1,200-2,100

An ivory tusk carving of a barge, with a shi-shi mask and a phoenix, signed on a red lacquer tablet, carved wood stand, 16in (40.5cm) long.
$1,000-2,000

A set of 5 ivory groups, each group of musicians playing various instruments, on carved hardwood stands, 6in (15cm) high.
$1,200-2,100

A pair of ivory tusk vases, with Shibayama decoration, metal mounts and carved wood bases, 12in (30.5cm) high.
$2,600-5,300

Jade

A white jade bottle, carved in low relief on both sides with grazing horses, rose quartz domed stopper, 3in (7.5cm).
$600-1,100

An unusual jade boulder, carved as a Daoist cave, with Daoist Immortals and 'lehan' grouped around Budai seated on a plinth behind a smoking censer, late Qing Dynasty, 13½in (34cm) wide.
$6,000-12,000

A carnelian oval box and cover, carved in the form of a cicada, 2½in (6.5cm) long, and a carnelian pendant, pierced for suspension, 2½in (6cm), 19thC.
$800-1,500

Lacquer

A rare pair of Chinese Cinnabar lacquer boxes, each surmounted with a Dog of Fo, in red lacquer on a black lacquer diaper ground, each containing 3 stacking boxes, late 18thC, 10½in (26.5cm).
$6,000-12,000

A massive dark green 'new jade' carving of Shoulao, wearing a simple cap and long flowing robes, 32½in (83cm) high.
$1,800-3,800

A rectangular Roironuri cabinet, decorated in gold, silver, red, brown and black hiramakie, takamakie, nashiji and heidatsu, some old wear and damage, one carrying handle missing, 19thC, 17½ by 11in (45 by 28cm).
$3,200-6,000

A Momoyama period rectangular black lacquered wood casket with hinged cover, decorated in gold lacquer and shell inlay, original Kanagu with possible hasp replacement, normal old damage due to wear, c1600.
$3,200-6,000

A rectangular tabako-bon decorated in gold and silver hiramakie, hirame and heidatsu on a yasuriko ground, with nashiji interiors, the top incorporating two silvered metal liners with silver covers decorated en suite to the box, silvered metal carrying handle, slightly chipped and cracked, late 19thC, 8in (20cm) wide.
$1,400-2,600

Metal

A fine bronze figure of Ebisu, his kimono decorated in gilt nikubori, unsigned but probably by Miyao, late 19thC, wood stand, 23in (58.5cm) high.
$3,200-6,000

A Japanese bronze figure of a Samurai in armour, the dress highlighted in gold, standing on a shaped wooden plinth, late 19thC, 13in (33cm).
$1,700-3,000

A bronze of a temple dog, 7in (18cm).
$400-750

A bronze group of toads, naturalistically cast and chased, 3½in (9cm) long.
$800-1,500

l. A good Japanese inlaid and onlaid bronze baluster vase, signed on a panel, 18in (46cm).
$900-1,700

c. A large Japanese bronze baluster vase, table lamp conversion available, 21½in (54.5cm) high.
$400-750

r. A Chinese porcelain vase, decorated in coloured enamels within green key patterned borders, basal hairline crack, 17in (43cm) high.
$400-750

A bronze conservatory fountain, the body cast in the form of a knarled old tree trunk with entwined fiery dragon surmounting, 19thC, 35 by 26in (89 by 66cm), standing on an oak table with heavily carved cabriole supports and pad feet.
$10,000-18,000

A Japanese bronze of a trumpeting elephant with ivory tusks, on stand, 9in (23cm) overall.
$400-750

An important large Chinese silver water carrier in the form of a winged dragon, the whole with alternate plain and punched scales, standing upon scaled bird's clawed feet with 3 front and one rear toe, 19in (48cm) high, 152oz approx.
$28,000-48,000

A pair of massive North European bronze lions, on oblong bases, greenish patina, original pitting, late 17th/early 18thC, 54in (136cm).
$90,000-160,000

Ajax Committing Suicide, late 17th C.
$50,000-90,000

A French statuette of a dancing putto, some damage, late 16thC, 10in (24.5cm).
$70,000-130,000

An unsigned bronze group of an 18thC scientist seated on a rococo style chair, beside plate electrical machine, marble base, 19thC, 12in (30cm) wide.
$2,000-4,500

An Italian gilt-bronze hunting group, in the style of the Master of the Bull Hunt, late 17th/early 18thC, 19in (48cm).
$5,000-9,000

A French gilt-bronze group of the Three Graces, on rosso antico plinth, early 19thC, 17in (43cm) high.
$14,000-24,000

An Italian bronze door-knocker in the form of a pouncing lion, late 16th/early 17thC, 13in (34cm) long.
$10,000-18,000

A gold snuff box with miniature of Napoleon, 1810.
$40,000-75,000

Above: A French copper-gilt crozier, with velvet covered wooden stand, gilding rubbed, some losses, 15thC, 65in (163cm) overall.
$6,000-12,000

Right: A George II silver-gilt two-handled cup and cover engraved with coat-of-arms and crest, by Benjamin Godfrey, 1738, 12¼in (31cm), 81oz.
$14,000-24,000

An English bronze bust of Gracie Doncaster, known as the 'Age of Innocence', cast from a model by Alfred Drury, integrally cast flared base on shaped marble plinth, greenish patina to bronze, fine casting crack running round base, dated 1897, 26in (66cm) high excluding plinth.
$18,000-26,000

A pair of large Louis XV candlesticks, the bases with accolé coats-of-arms, Nicholas Besnier, Paris, sockets possibly English 18thC replacements, 10¼in (26cm), 72oz. **$30,000-60,000**

The arms are those of Bateman accolé with Spencer

A William and Mary double quart lidded tankard engraved with a contemporary coat-of-arms within a cartouche, the moulded cover with cast wing thumbpiece, cast cut card front, scroll handle, maker's mark F.S. with pellet above and below, London 1689, 8½in (21cm) high, 48oz.
$30,000-54,000

A fine tureen and cover designed by Georg Jensen, stamped Georg Jensen 337B, 52in (132cm) wide, 63oz 16dwt. **$40,000-75,000**

Apprentices were required to make a similar version of this tureen, known as the Rosenbonbonnière, before they could become master silversmiths at Georg Jensen

A Victorian pilgrim bottle, the shoulders applied with female masks with scrolls and acanthus and hung with a chain, the front engraved with the Royal arms of Edward, Prince of Wales, maker's mark TWD, London, 1894, 21½in (53cm), 152oz.
$20,000-30,000

A pair of Victorian six-light candelabra by Barnard Brothers in the style of Paul Storr, the shaped circular bases cast and chased in high relief with lions' masks, flowers and foliate scrolls on matted ground, bases stamped 'Thomas, 153 New Bond St' fully marked, London 1872, 28in (70cm) high, 430oz.
$40,000-75,000

A pair of George IV wine coolers by Paul Storr, plain removable collars and plated liners, marked on bases and collars, London, 1826, 11in (29cm) high, 150oz.
$20,000-45,000
The arms are those of Robyns of Staffordshire and Worcestershire. The crest of two dolphins, forms the design for the handles.

A Regency four-piece tea and coffee service by Paul Storr, later engraved crest, fully marked London 1809-11, 121oz.
$24,000-45,000

A large tazza designed by Georg Jensen, stamped marks Georg Jensen G1925, 264, 10½in (28cm) high, 35oz 12dwt.
$8,000-15,000

A George IV soup tureen, cover and stand, top of stand engraved with Royal coat-of-arms, Ed. Farrell, London 1823, 17in (43cm), 203oz.
$60,000-120,000

A George III silver-gilt tea tray by John Crouch and Thomas Hannam, later armorials in the style of Walter Jackson, London, 1784, 29½in (74cm) long, 173oz.
$30,000-50,000

A set of 24 silver-gilt dinner plates by Martin-Guillaume Biennais, Paris, 1809-19, 9½in (24cm), 442oz.
$32,000-57,000

A pair of Roman busts, after the antique, with fiorito alabaster shoulders, 17thC, 36in (91cm).
$70,000-130,000

An Italian marble bust of a Roman Emperor, the shoulders of variegated marble on a cement core, minor damage, 17thC, 36in (92cm).
$36,000-57,000

A Florentine marble bust of the Infant Christ, unfinished, by Mino da Fiesole, late 15thC, 8½in (21cm).
$14,000-24,000

An Italian marble head of a bearded Roman, possibly Geta, 17thC, some damage, 13in (33.5cm).
$3,200-6,000

Left: An Italian marble statue of Paolina Borghese Bonaparte as Venus Victrix, reclining on a painted wooden chaise longue, attributed to Adamo Tadolini, minor repairs, early 19thC, 36in (90cm) long.
$20,000-45,000

617

A pair of Roman black marble
and pietra dura pedestals,
late 16th/early 17thC, 48½in
(121cm) high.
$6,000-12,000

A Hereford sandstone statue of a seated knight wearing
chain mail, with a seated dog at his side, the back flat and
unworked, slightly weathered and with consequent losses,
13thC, 55in (137cm), and another, left, his hand on his
heart, a medallion around his neck, the back flat and
unworked, slightly weathered.
$56,000-90,000 each

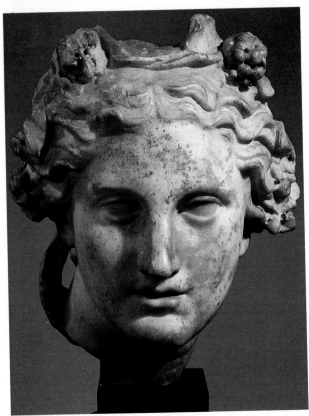

A marble head of a Maenad, her wavy hair entwined with ivy
tendrils and berries, a lock escaping below the nape of the neck,
the eyes with unarticulated pupils, a Roman copy after a Greek
original of 4th Century B.C., 10in (26cm) high.
$40,000-75,000

A George III ormolu-mounted blue john
pot pourri vase, with foliate handles,
the pierced domed cover cast with
foliage and with berried finial, on
spreading socle with laurel leaf collar,
on a square plinth outlined with black
and white marble, 19½in (48cm) high.
$18,000-26,000

An Attic black-figure amphora, near
the Antimenes group, domed lid
repaired, late 6th Century B.C., 13¾in
(34cm) high.
$18,000-26,000

l. A bronze figure of Anubis, the jackal-headed god, on marble
stand, 6th/4th Century B.C.
$4,500-9,000

r. A bronze figure of Harpocrates, on marble base, 4th/2nd
Century B.C., 5¾in (15cm) high.
$6,000-12,000

An inscribed bronze measuring jar, inscribed 'the good god,
Menkheperre, beloved of Amen-re, given life', 1490-
1436B.C., 6in (15cm) high.
$20,000-30,000

An Etruscan bronze figure of a striding warrior, with incised
decoration, right arm raised in striking position, spear missing,
5th Century B.C., 10in (25cm) high.
$190,000-300,000

A serpentine royal shabti of King Senkamenisken, bearing 6 lines from Ch.6 of the Book of the Dead, 643-623B.C., 7½in (18cm) high.
$12,000-21,000

Senkamenisken was the grandson of King Taharqa and was buried at Nuri

A Hellenistic hollow gold bracelet with central Herakles knot motif, 3rd Century B.C., 2¾in (7cm) diam. 55gm.
$20,000-30,000

An Egyptian bronze figure of a seated cat, modern gold hooped earrings, on marble base, 5th/4th Century B.C., 7¼in (18cm) high.
$90,000-150,000

Right An Egyptian bronze figure of Horus the falcon, with finely chased wings and one eye encircled with gold, on hollow rectangular base, 6th-4th Century B.C., 5¾in (15cm) high.
$6,000-12,000

An Egyptian turquoise-glazed model of hippopotamus and baby, 5½in (14cm) long, Dynasty XII, 1991-1778 B.C.
$24,000-45,000

A silk and cotton Heriz carpet, very slight overall wear, 203in (515cm).
$60,000-96,000

A silk Heriz rug, the ivory field with a waisted and cusped brick-red palmette medallion, a shaded steel-blue vine border, excellent condition, 72 by 53in (180 by 133cm).
$28,000-48,000

A Hamadan carpet, the field with columns of flowerheads, dated AH 1304 (AD1886), 124 by 80in (314 by 204cm).
$8,000-15,000

An Isfahan carpet, the ivory field with palmettes and floral sprays around a blood-red and beige cusped floral medallion with pendants, the blue spandrels with arabesques and palmettes, in a blood-red palmette and vine border between ivory and blue floral stripes, slightly stained, 172 by 126in (436 by 320cm).
$28,000-48,000

Right A silk Khotan saph, the field with 8 alternating blood-red and light blue prayer arches with plants with floral mihrabs, 161 by 32in (408 by 110cm).
$10,000-18,000

An Aubusson rug, 119 by 77in (300 by 195cm).
$6,000-12,000

A Bidjar rug, 80 by 53in (202 by 134cm).
$6,000-12,000

Left A Talish runner, 142 by 35in (360 by 88cm).
$5,000-9,000

Right A Chinese embossed carpet, 151 by 141in (383 by 358cm).
$8,000-15,000

Left A Kashan silk embossed prayer rug of Tree of Life design, the sandy mihrab with blossoming shrubs with birds, within floral spandrels and ogee prayer arch, enclosed by a main cartouche and arabesque floral meander border, 76 by 52in (192 by 130cm).
$12,000-21,000

Right A Ziegler carpet, the ivory field with an open floral medallion in a blue-grey similar border, 200 by 149in (508 by 379cm).
$26,000-45,000

Left A Bessarabian kilim carpet, in the Empire style, the sky blue ground covered by an ivory spoke-like centre medallion and graduated ivory spheres, with surrounding grape wreath and flaming torchere and caduceus spandrels, with a brown primary border, backed, 163 by 156in (414 by 396cm).
$50,000-90,000

Below A part silk Isfahan carpet, tomato red field with indigo and ivory concentric roundels, 128 by 82in (314 by 208cm).
$50,000-90,000

Above A Ziegler carpet, the blood-red field with palmettes and floral sprays around floral medallions, in a blue flowering vine border between floral stripes, 173 by 150in (440 by 320cm).
$10,000-18,000

A Donegal carpet, the ivory field with a broad white border of floral sprays and scrolls, 158 by 114in (401 by 289cm).
$11,000-20,000

A silk and metal thread Kum Kapu prayer rug, signed Zare Agha, excellent condition, 72 by 48in (180 by 120cm).
$100,000-200,000

Below A Meshed part silk carpet, the burgundy field with large flowering trees with a variety of birds in an indigo palmette and vine border between yellow flowering vine stripes, 116 by 93in (294 by 241cm).
$20,000-30,000

An Ushak carpet, 177 by 146in (450 by 370cm).
$1,700-3,000

A Greek Kilim woven in 2 parts, the royal blue field with columns of large floral roundels in a large open floral spray border, 169 by 150in (429 by 382cm).
$5,000-9,000

A Kirman pictorial rug, the beige field and crimson border with rows of 101 portrait oval medallions of Kings of Persia with inscriptions, 84 by 55in (213 by 138cm).
$6,000-12,000

A silk Souf Kashan prayer rug, with royal blue mihrab, vertical crease line of wear, 79 by 51in (200 by 128cm).
$10,000-18,000

Left A Qum silk carpet, with ivory field, blood-red panel and blue medallion, and boteh border, 155 by 115in (394 by 290cm).
$30,000-50,000

Right A silk Tabriz carpet, the blood-red field with a centre column of blue scalloped palmettes, with ivory medallions, in an indigo border, 72 by 50in (180 by 125cm).
$26,000-45,000

Left An Axminster carpet with flower heads, floral swags and ribbons around a yellow central roundel, in an outer mottled purple floral frame, with a broad brown floral border, areas of slight wear and repair, 324 by 197in (822 by 500cm). **$12,000-21,000**

Below A silk Tabriz prayer rug, the brick-red field with 2 flower vases, in an ivory palmette frame, an indigo floral arcade above, in an indigo boteh border between stripes, repaired, 96 by 65in (242 by 162cm). **$18,000-26,000**

A Ziegler carpet, 230 by 165in (584 by 419cm). **$6,000-12,000**

Right A fine Sileh, the blood-red field with 2 columns of indigo and ivory stylised dragon motifs surrounded by stylised floral motifs, in a reciprocal skittle pattern border, 92 by 80in (232 by 202cm). **$10,000-18,000**

Left A verdure tapestry, 18thC, 154in (390cm).
$14,000-24,000

Right A Brussels tapestry woven in silk and wool in well preserved tones with the family of Darius prostrate before Alexander the Great,169 by 271in (404 by 628cm).
$12,000-21,000

There is a similar but smaller panel of this subject at Hampton Court woven by Judocus de Vos after Le Brun.

Left A Flemish verdure tapestry woven with various scenes in a forest, the fruiting borders with masks and various animals and birds on a sunlit pool, seated figures beneath drapery, possible Oudenarde, reduced, a little re-weaving, late 16thC, 101 by 263in (255 by 668cm).
$36,000-57,000

Right A pair of tapestries, woven in silk and wool showing statues in trellis-work pagodas, beside rivers, possibly Berlin, late 18thC, lacking borders 126 by 92in (320 by 232cm).
$6,000-12,000

627

A Dutch tapestry woven in silks and wool with Christ and the woman caught in adultery, mid-16thC, 94in (236cm) high.
$24,000-45,000

A pair of Aubusson entre fenêtres, cord-bound edges, backed, 151 by 49in (384 by 124cm).
$3,200-6,000

Right: A French composite needlework panel, 96 by 59in (244 by 150cm).
$4,500-9,000

Below: A sampler by Catherine Fitz-simone, dated 1807, 18in (45cm).
$800-1,500

Right: A sampler by Peggy Kelbrick, in excellent condition, dated 1836, maple frame, 28in (70cm) square.
$2,600-5,300

An undated sampler by Ann Davies aged 11, with French knots, cross stitch and satin stitch worked in coloured wools, c1810, 14 by 10in (35 by 25cm).
$400-900

A silk map sampler of England by I Toghill, dated 1787 in original gilt frame, 12in (30cm).
$200-450

A Scottish sampler by Marion Weir, dated 1842 in rosewood frame, 20 by 24in (50 by 60cm).
$1,300-2,400

An earthenware footed bowl by Michael Cardew, impressed marks, c1935, 10in (26cm) diam.
$1,800-3,800

A buff stoneware spade form by Hans Coper, the interior revealing amber beneath manganese glaze, HC seal, 1973, 11in (28cm) high.
$8,000-15,000

Two stoneware vases and a bottle by Hans Coper:-
l. A vase, impressed HC seal, c1965, 13in (33cm) high.
$12,000-21,000

c. A vase, impressed HC seal, c1952, 10in (26cm) high.
$20,000-30,000

r. A bottle, impressed HC seal, c1965, 11in (29.5cm).
$14,000-24,000

A glass sculpture in 2 sections, 'Split Triangle', each section engraved Colin Read 1985 R 140 A&B, 36in (90cm) long.
$8,000-15,000

Above: Two bowls by Lucie Rie:

l. A stoneware bowl, impressed LR seal, c1980, 13in (32cm).
$9,000-15,000

r. A porcelain sgraffito footed bowl, impressed LR seal, c1966, 13in (33cm).
$6,000-12,000

Right: A rectangular stoneware slab bottle by Bernard Leach, impressed BL and St Ives seals, c 1955, 8in (19cm) high.
$800-1,500

Above: A massive 'famille rose' Canton enamel dish, the reverse with flowers, foliage, rockwork and an inscription with the date 'jiwei' year (1739), 31in (77cm) diam.
$12,000-21,000

A large cloisonné oviform vase on wooden stand, late 19thC, 37in (92cm).
$4,000-6,800

Right: A pair of cloisonné enamel vases of double gourd shape, early 19thC, 13in (33cm) high.
$8,000-15,000

An Ando cloisonné and plique-à-jour bowl, late Meiji/Taisho period, 7½in (18.5cm) square, with wood stand and fitted wooden box.
$4,500-9,000

l. An Ando cloisonné vase, signed in seal form, factory mark, 12in (33cm). **$24,000-45,000**
r. An Ando cloisonné vase, late Meiji period, 15in (37cm). **$4,000-7,500**

A German sporting crossbow with steel bow, worn and damaged, the crossbow early 17thC, the cranequin late 16thC.
$10,000-18,000

A carved nephrite figure by Fabergé, in fitted case stamped Wartski, London, 11.5cm.
$90,000-160,000

A hardstone figure of John Bull, signed Fabergé, workmaster Henrik Wigström, St. Petersburg, 1896-1908, repair to right boot, 12cm, in original fitted case with Imperial Warrant mark.
$90,000-150,000

A George III satinwood and tulipwood tea caddy, crossbanded lid with foliate ormolu handle and cavetto border, the interior with 3 chinoiserie painted tôle canisters, the front, sides and back crossbanded in tulipwood, c1790, 6in (15cm) high.
$7,000-12,000

Left A George III Pontypool or Usk scarlet hot water kettle and brazier, c1800, 18in (46cm). **$1,800-3,800**
And a similar coal scuttle, 14in (36cm). **$2,600-5,300**

Right above A rare ivory recorder, by Thomas Stanesby Junior, branded Stanesby/Junior/6, 12in (31cm) long.
$50,000-90,000

A Greek icon of Saint Paraskeva, depicted half-length, holding a cross in her right hand and wearing a dark brown maphorion on a gilt ground, the lower border depicting 3 scenes from her martyrdom, early 16thC, 24 by 16½in (60 by 41cm).
$10,000-18,000

A pair of Royal doors, depicting the Annunciation and Four Doctors of the Church, Northern Greek or Balkan, 17thC, 49½ by 15in (125 by 38cm).
$12,000-21,000

Above A Bwa wood cock mask, 30in (76cm).
$8,000-15,000

Right A rare kaka wood paternity figure, with child on father's back, thick crusty patina, 28in (70cm).
$14,000-24,000

A Tibetan gilt copper repoussé figure of Padmasambhava on separate lotus base, Khatvanga missing, late 18thC, 28in (71cm).
$9,000-15,000

633

Left A large Ming cloisonné enamel deep dish, decorated with red and yellow 5-clawed dragons, minor pitting, integral cloisonné enamel mark at the base centre, 20in (50cm) diam.
$34,000-54,000

Below A large late Ming gilt-lacquered bronze figure of Guandi, seated wearing flowing robes over his armour, holding his belt in his right hand, supported on a base with a tortoise and snake, areas of gilding remaining, old damage, 16th/early 17thC, 28in (70cm) high.
$4,000-7,500

A pine base, with 4 glazed doors at the front with 4 shelves (not shown), the back open, also with 4 shelves, probably English, superb carving with intricate woodwork and joints, c1850.
$1,600-2,800

A large Korean inlaid silver-flecked brown lacquer box and cover, the top and sides inset in mother-of-pearl and wire, minor damage, 18thC, 13½ by 26½in (33 by 65.5cm).
$6,000-12,000

A large contemporary wood netsuke, boldly carved as a foreigner carrying a stag across his shoulders, with stained ivory and lacquer inlay, signed 'Seihosai Meikei'.
$20,000-45,000

A silver-inlaid bronze shroud weight, Han Dynasty, 3in (7cm) wide.
$90,000-150,000

A steel-mounted saddle etched in the manner of Jörg Sorg of Augsburg, wood and leather frame, Augsburg, c1550. **$8,000-15,000**

Netsuke

A fine Chinese gold splashed bronze vase, 17thC.
$6,000-12,000

A finely patinated ivory netsuke, of a professional sneezer seated tickling himself with a stick, age cracks, signed Ryuko, and kao, early/mid-19thC.
$900-1,700

An ivory netsuke of an ape, his arms holding a section of bamboo across his back, his fur engraved with stained detail, tiny chip, unsigned, Kyoto School, early 19thC.
$600-1,200

An ivory netsuke of Hotei, holding an uchiwa with a karako climbing on his back, inscribed Okakoto, early 19thC.
$400-750

An okimono-style ivory netsuke, of the Annamese tribute elephant richly caparisoned in Shibayama-style inlay, signed on a gilt tablet Shibayama, 19thC.
$1,800-3,800

An ivory netsuke of a coiled snake, eyes inset in dark horn, inscribed Toshitsugu, late 19thC.
$1,000-2,000

An ivory netsuke of Daikoku, his kimono and hat inlaid in Shibayama style, stained hair and eye details, signed on a rectangular red tablet Masatamo, late 19thC.
$600-1,100

An ivory netsuke of a catfish, its eyes inlaid in coloured horn and metal foil, inscribed on a raised oval panel Masanao, probably Meiji-Taisho period.
$1,600-2,800

A well carved ivory netsuke of a large rat, eyes inset in dark horn, a smaller rat on his back, small chips, inscribed Okatomo, 19thC.
$1,700-3,000

A well carved boxwood netsuke of a snail, crawling over a well-bucket bound with rope, the material bearing a three-tone effect, signed Shigemasa, early 19thC.
$3,200-6,000

A finely detailed wood netsuke of a cicada on half a walnut, unsigned, 19thC.
$800-1,500

Yoshichika; a carved boxwood netsuke of a bell-shaped flowerhead, the underside enclosing 7 ebonised free carved seed pods, signed in panel, 4cm, and a carved boxwood netsuke in the form of numerous interwoven fruits, unsigned, some stalks cracked, 4cm wide.
$400-900

Tsuba

Wood

A Japanese hardwood circular plaque, finely decorated and inlaid with carved ivory, mother-of-pearl and gilt-decorated lacquer.
$800-1,500

A large presentation tsuba, signed Nemoto, the word on the flag held by the child says 'Hanamiren', the edge with cloisonné inlay, the faces with mother-of-pearl Shibayama decoration, gilt grounds, signatures, 4½ by 4in (11 by 10cm).
$2,600-5,300

A painted wood 'No' mask of Kumasaka, his eyes applied with gilt metal, slightly damaged, signed on the reverse Deme Eiman, 19thC, 8in (20.5cm).
$1,200-2,100

A boxwood case of Napiers bones, containing 9 four-sided rods engraved on all sides, and an end triple rod engraved on 2 sides only, the whole sliding into a case decorated with geometrical lines, 3½in (9cm).
$600-1,200

Miscellaneous

A set of 3 oriental silk screen panels, floral and bird decoration, late 19thC, 30 by 17in (76 by 43cm).
$1,400-2,600

A Cantonese densely carved tortoiseshell circular box and cover, 19thC, 5½in (14.5cm).
$1,400-2,600

Russian – Works of Art

A Russian porcelain octafoil dish for the Order of St. Andrew, mock Meissen mark, mid-19thC, 11in (29cm) diam.
$600-1,200

A Russian Imperial dish, with later Soviet motifs, brightly painted, with motto 'In the hands, hammer, scythe, book' painted after a dish 'The Literacy' by A. Shchkotina-Pototskaya, with underglaze Imperial Factory mark, Period of Nicholas II and later Soviet marks, 1921.
$1,400-2,600

A pair of Imperial porcelain dinner plates from the Kremlin Service, by the Imperial Porcelain Factory, Period of Nicholas I, 1825-1855, each with the blue underglaze cypher of Nicholas I, gilt worn, 9in (24cm) diam.
$1,600-2,800

A Russian Imperial dish, with later Soviet motifs, painted with a commissar standing before the Petrograd Palace Square, the borders painted with red and black Cyrillic inscription 'Petrograd, Uritsky Square', painted after a dish 'the Commissar' by A. Shchkotina-Pototskaya, with over-glaze Imperial Factory mark, Period of Nicholas II and later Soviet marks, with minor chip, 1922.
$1,700-3,000

A silver niello crucifix, centred by the Saviour on the Cross flanked by oval panels nielloed with the half-length figures of the Virgin and Saint John, God the Father above, and Jerusalem below, maker's mark A.B., Moscow, 1791, 16½in (42cm) high, 27oz 10dwt.
$1,800-3,800

A biscuit figure of a peasant, wearing a white blouse over a printed blue tunic, by the Gardner Factory, Moscow, with impressed and stamped red factory mark, repair to bench and base repainted, late 19thC, 5½in (14cm) high.
$800-1,500

A biscuit figure of a Garmochka player, seated on a wooden bench, dressed in a white embroidered tunic, blue britches and beige overcoat, on a green rectangular base, by the Gardner Factory, with red factory mark, Moscow, his right boot repaired, c1880-1890, 7in (16cm) high.
$900-1,700

A parcel-gilt niello kovsh, the exterior of the bowl overall nielloed with Italianate landscape, with gilt interior, Vologda 1816, assay-master Semen Klishin, with unrecorded maker's mark Cyrillic (?) G, split to rim, 7½in (18.5cm) long, 8oz 8dwt.
$4,000-6,800

A parcel-gilt covered beaker on 3 ball feet, with bulbous panels repoussé and chased with rocaille on matte ground, signed with the initials of Andrei Kostrinsky, Moscow, feet repaired, c1750, 6¼in (16cm) high, 7oz 10dwt.
$2,000-4,500

A pair of tapering cylindrical silver beakers, the body engraved with a wide band of arabesques below a reeded rim signed with initials of Timofei Silianov and Andrei Kostrinsky, Moscow, 1751, 4oz 17dwt.
$1,800-3,800

A silver-gilt sugar sack, chased to simulate a hessian sack, the top folded down, signed with the Imperial Warrant Mark of Sazikov, Moscow, 1860, 2½in (5.5cm) high, 8oz 2dwt.
$2,000-4,500

A circular silver niello sugar bowl, depicting views of the Kremlin, on stippled ground, with swing handle, by M. Sokolov, Moscow, c1890, 4in (10cm) diam., 8oz.
$600-1,200

A silver tea glass holder, chased with a troika scene on spreading base and with C-scroll handle, with gilt interior, by Fabergé, Moscow, 1899-1908, 4½in (11.5cm) high, 4oz 15dwt.
$800-1,500

A small jewelled Continental or Russian metal-gilt mounted coconut cup, on spreading foot, the coconut body carved and set with 6 coloured stones at intervals, within a beaded border further decorated with green enamel rosettes, coral and coloured stones, 17thC, 3in (6.5cm) diam.
$1,200-2,100

A shaped triangular silver-gilt picture frame, signed 'Fabergé Moscow 1894', with wooden back and easel strut, 7½in (19cm) high.
$8000-13,500

An unusual Russian lacquered purse, the side painted with a peasant couple conversing by a wicket fence, 3in (7.5cm).
$400-750

A Russian cloisonné enamel egg cup, decorated in red, green, white, mauve and three shades of blue, stamped twice apparently with the mark of August Hollming, the foot with the mark of Pavel Ovchinnikov, c1910, 3½in (9cm) high.
$800-1,500

A pair of Russian cloisonné spoons enamelled in pastel shades of pink, blue, mauve and green on a frosted background with white enamel bead borders, maker's mark VA, Cyrillic, c1900, 8in (20cm) long.
$1,000-2,000

A Russian spice box of customary form.
$600-1,100

The Apostle Peter, from an iconastas, wearing a brown himation over a dark green chiton, with gilt halo, on ivory ground, Northern, 17thC, 31½ by 12½in (80 by 32cm).
$3,200-6,000

The Smolensk Mother of God, painted with dark brown, green, ochre and gilt highlights on a tan ground within red borders, 18thC, 12 by 10in (31 by 26cm).
$1,800-3,800

A diptych of the Virgin of the Sign and Saint Nicholas, naturalistically painted within a metal case enamelled with blue, green, yellow and white within white pellet borders, with suspension ring and clasp, 18thC, 3½in (8.5cm) wide extended.
$1,800-3,800

A Greek triptych, painted in cinnabar and dark green on gilt grounds, Greek Islands, 18thC, 15¼in (38cm) wide extended.
$2,000-4,500

The Virgin Smolenskaya, finely painted and covered with a repoussé and chased riza, with ornately designed haloes, the lower border applied with two inscribed nielloed plaques, signed with initials of Vasili Iakovlev, Moscow, 1803, 14½ by 12in (36 by 31cm).
$2,000-4,500

The Vladimir Mother of God, painted in brown with gilt highlights, on an ivory ground, the borders depicting a guardian angel and a Chosen Saint, covered with a repoussé and chased parcel-gilt riza, 19thC, the riza probably Riga, 1857, 12 by 10½in (31 by 26cm).
$3,200-6,000

A miniature parcel-gilt triptych, maker's mark Cyrillic G S, Moscow, c1880, 3½in (8.5cm) wide extended.
$1,400-2,600

The Vernicle, naturalistically painted, covered with a parcel-gilt riza chased to simulate cloth, 19thC, maker's mark Cyrillic E L, the riza c1880, 12 by 10in (31 by 25cm).
$800-1,500

The Tikhvin Mother of God, naturalistically painted and covered with a finely chased and repoussé parcel-gilt riza, maker's mark Cyrillic S G, in wooden kiot, Moscow, c1880, 11 by 9in (28 by 23cm).
$2,200-4,200

The Virgin Bogolubskaya, brightly painted before a monastery, with applied vari-colour cloisonné enamel halo and champlevé enamel plaque, 19thC, the riza signed with the initials of Ivan Alekseev, Moscow, c1890, 10½ by 9in (26 by 23cm).
$2,000-4,500

One half-litre Tokaj Eszencia – Vintage 1848 – Tokaj Hegyaljai Bortermeld, the intact label states 'Very Sweet King of Kings of Old Tokaj Wine' and '30° proof'.
$600-1,200

Wine

Two bottles: Château Lafite – Vintage 1874 – Pauillac, 1er cru classé, recorked by Whitwham & Co. 18 July 1980, reference numbers 432 and 434, original labels intact, bin-soiled and tattered but legible, wax capsules, the bottles have the vintage embossed in a glass button attached to the shoulder, original corks attached to the necks, both bottles appear to have excellent colour, one bottle with neck level, one with top-shoulder level.
$4,000-7,500

One magnum: Château Mouton Rothschild – Vintage 1878, Pauillac, 1er cru classé, recorked by Whitwham & Co. 18th July 1980, reference number 448, original label bin-soiled but intact and legible, wax capsule, appears to have excellent deep colour, neck level, very rare.
$4,500-9,000

Clos de Gamont – Vintage 1914 – Cahors, Jouffreau et Fils, Prayssac, excellent general appearance with good colour and neck level.
$400-900
◁

Two bottles: Simi Sonoma County Cabernet Sauvignon – Vintage 1935 – perfect neck levels.
$900-1,700

One bottle: Château Pétrus – Vintage 1948 – Pomerol, excellent general appearance with high-shoulder level, normal for age.
$900-1,700

One bottle: Château d'Yquem – Vintage 1929 – Sauternes, 1er grand cru classé, excellent general appearance, with high-shoulder level, normal for age, typical dark-tea colour.
$600-1,200

One bottle: Beaulieu Vineyard Cabernet Sauvignon – Vintage 1956 – private reserve, Georges de Latour, excellent general appearance with neck level and good mature colour.
$600-1,200

Five bottles: Heitz Cellar Martha's Vineyard Cabernet Sauvignon – Vintage 1968, excellent general appearance with perfect neck levels.
$1,600-2,800

A plated two-branch student's oil lamp, with green tinted shades.
$400-750

A bronze candelabrum, with two tôle shades and domed base stamped 'VR' below a crown, fitted for electricity, 24in (61cm) high.
$2,200-4,200

A Regency bronze candlestick, fitted for electricity, with pleated green silk shade, 30½in (78cm) high including shade.
$2,200-4,200

A late Georgian silver-plated Corinthian column lamp with stepped base and card shade, 30½in (78cm) high including shade.
$2,200-4,200

A Restauration bronze and ormolu candlestick, fitted for electricity, with pleated and fringed green silk shade, 21in (54cm) high including shade.
$1,200-2,100

A Tiffany bronze table lamp, with mottled palm tree style telescopic stem and three-light shade, both impressed Tiffany Studios, New York, 1651, 35in (88cm) high, fully extended, shade 19in (48cm) diam.
$4,000-7,500

A tôle urn decorated in lacquer, fitted for electricity, with coffee-coloured silk shade, 27½in (69cm) high including shade.
£1,300-1,500

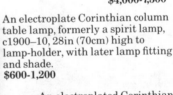

An electroplate Corinthian column table lamp, formerly a spirit lamp, c1900–10, 28in (70cm) high to lamp-holder, with later lamp fitting and shade.
$600-1,200

An electroplated Corinthian column table lamp, formerly a spirit lamp, late 19thC, 25in (63cm) high to lamp-holder, with later lamp fitting and shade.
$800-1,500

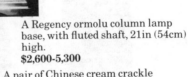

A Regency ormolu column lamp base, with fluted shaft, 21in (54cm) high.
$2,600-5,300

A pair of Chinese cream crackle glazed lamps, applied with biscuit lion's mask handles, the chinoiserie giltmetal mounts signed 'F. Barbedienne', the oil lamps now converted to electricity, 17in (43cm) high.
$1,200-2,100

A silver-plated Corinthian column table lamp, with opaque glass shade.
$300-600

A Regency carved wood and painted torchere, now fitted for electricity.
$1,300-2,400

A heavy cast Victorian standard lamp, with original oil, telescopic, with painted shade, 1891, 21in (53cm) across base.
$900-1,700

A good quality Victorian brass telescopic standard lamp.
$400-750

A silvered brass Corinthian column lamp, with stepped base, 19thC, fitted for electricity, 31½in (79cm) high.
$1,800-3,800

A particularly fine Palissy-ware model of an elephant forming the base of an oil lamp, the elephant fully draped with howdah and mahoot, with original shade, 16½in (41cm) high excluding lamp and shade.
$4,000-7,500

So called Majolica wares which are decorated in transparent coloured glazes should perhaps be more correctly termed Palissy-ware. True majolica employs an overglaze painting in opaque colours.

A pair of Louis XVI ormolu mounted candelabra, on dove grey marble bases.
$5,000-9,000

A pair of French giltmetal candelabra, with blue porcelain bodies, late 19thC, 32in (80cm) high.
$4,500-9,000

A pair of English candelabra, on red marble bases, with bronze putti, c1830.
$1,200-2,100

A pair of Swedish candlesticks, 18thC, 7½in (19cm) high.
$500-900

A German ceramic oil lamp, in the form of an owl with acorns, late 19thC.
$1,200-2,100

A heavy cast French ormolu three-branch floor standing candelabrum, with basket-work shelf and ornate tripod base.
$900-1,700

Papier Mâché

A pair of papier mâché wine coasters, the red grounds decorated in red on black between black and gilt bands, 5in (13cm) diam.
$1,600-2,800

A single wine coaster, decorated in green and gilt on a black ground, rim chip, 5½in (13cm) diam.
$400-750

A pair of black papier mâché wine coasters, 5in (13cm) diam.
$800-1,500

A pair of papier mâché wine coasters, the red grounds embellished in gilt and black with a band of oak leaves, the sides moulded in relief with a slender rib, 5in (12.5cm) diam.
$800-1,500

A Victorian large papier mâché tray, decorated in gilt, enriched with mother-of-pearl on a black ground and on a folding stand with splayed supports, 31½in (80cm) wide.
$1,000-2,000

A papier mâché tray, the reverse bearing the label T. Simpson & Co., early 19thC, 30½in (76cm) wide.
$1,700-3,000

A set of three graduated papier mâché trays, decorated on a black ground, 19thC, 30in (75cm) largest.
$1,800-3,800

A good black lacquered papier mâché tray, painted in enamel colours, slight damage, mid-19thC, 31½in (80cm).
$1,300-2,400

A set of three graduated Victorian papier mâché trays, the turned borders of each decorated with gilt foliate scrolls and mother-of-pearl inlay, the largest 30in (75cm) wide.
$1,000-2,000

A papier mâché tray, with raised rim, the whole decorated on a black ground, 19thC, 30½in (76cm) wide.
$3,200-6,000

A papier mâché tray, painted with a rustic scene, after George Morland, early 19thC, on later supports, 31½in (79cm).
$1,300-2,400

◁ A papier mâché tray, of extended octagonal form, stamped Clay, King ST. Covt Garden, 19thC.
$2,000-4,500

A Victorian papier mâché bread tray, 16½in (41cm) wide, and a rectangular Victorian papier mâché inkstand, fitted with two glass bottles and a pen tray, standing on four bun feet, stamped Jennens & Bettridge, London, 12½in (32cm) wide.
$400-750

A Victorian papier mâché tray, 31in (77cm) wide.
$800-1,500

A Victorian papier mâché tray, the centre decorated with a painted and mother-of-pearl inlay, the reverse stamped Jennens & Bettridge, 2nd Quality, 31in (77cm) wide.
$800-1,500

Two Victorian papier mâché tea trays.
$1,600-2,800

A papier mâché tray, early 19thC, 30in (75cm) wide.
$1,200-2,100

A good Continental painted papier mâché box, decorated on a gold ground, 19thC, 8½in (22cm) wide.
$1,200-2,100

A fine papier mâché games box, the lid inlaid with mother-of-pearl and set above an interior fitted with four similarly decorated small boxes and a larger central one, the base of the exterior stamped Jennens & Bettridge Patent Pearl, mid-19thC, 11 by 10in (27.5 by 25cm).
$2,000-4,500

A Victorian papier mâché tea caddy, decorated with painted and gilt flowers and foliage, above a compartmented interior, 7in (18cm) wide.
$300-600

A pair of oval papier mâché dishes, signed 'D. Cox', the scalloped borders of each heightened with gilt foliate scrolls, 10½in (26cm) wide.
$1,000-2,000

A pair of black papier mâché decanter stands, with oval gilt painted panel decoration, late 18thC.
$1,400-2,600

A pair of Victorian papier mâché hand screens, on giltwood and ebonised handles, 9½in (24cm) wide.
$200-450

A pair of Victorian papier mâché hand screens, each painted with an Oriental landscape and heightened in gilt, on turned giltwood handles, 9in (22cm) wide.
$1,000-2,000

A pair of papier mâché Wolverhampton face screens, with ivory handles, c1840, 14in (35cm) long.
$600-1,200

A pair of Victorian papier mâché hand screens, on turned giltwood handles, 9in (22.5cm) wide.
$300-600

Sewing

A Palais Royal lemon-wood sewing casket, complete, c1820, 6½in (16cm) wide.
$1,200-2,100

A Patent Friction Taylor hand lockstitch sewing machine, with separate bobbin-winder.
$400-750

A Grover & Baker hand sewing machine, on mahogany base board with brass Patent plaque, with patents to 1863.
$2,000-4,500

'La Populaire, système Avrial' sewing machine, in carrying case, with wooden treadle and associated clamps, together with set of instructions.
$2,000-4,500

'The Challenge' sewing machine manufactured by Joseph Harris of Oriel House, Bull Street, Birmingham, with gilt decoration, registration mark 12th Feb. 1871, on wood base, with wooden carrying case.
$300-600

A carved and stained turned bone bobbin inscribed 'A gift from my brother George Mark', another 'John Bunyan', two named 'Thomas' and 'Ann' and three others, mounted.
$180-300

Nine carved and stained turned bone bobbins, inscribed, three named 'Sarah', 'John' and 'Richard', each with spangles.
$600-1,200

An Edwardian pin cushion, Birmingham, 1908.
$400-750

An Edwardian button hook, Birmingham, 1908.
$100-250

A carved and stained turned bone bobbin inscribed 'Kiss me quick and don't look shy'; one 'Diana Freeman'; one 'King Richard'; one 'George Gren'; and four others, each with spangles.
$300-600

Miniatures

An oval miniature, indian ink on vellum, by James Ferguson of a young lady, c1750, 2½in (6cm), in a turned wooden frame.
$500-900

'Lovers strolling in a country park', English School, c1790, 2 by 1½in (5 by 3.5cm), in a gold pendant frame with hairwork reverse.
$400-900

A miniature of Margaret Campbell, wife of Robert Dun Eglington, c1840, 6in (15cm) high.
$600-1,200

An oval miniature, by Richard Cosway of a gentleman, with blue eyes and brown hair, wearing a blue cloak with lace jabot, c1765, 3cm, in a gold slide frame.
$400-900

A portrait of a gentleman, in a gold enamel frame, set with hair on reverse, c1800.
$600-1,200

A rectangular miniature by Charles Foot Taylor of a seated lady, holding an open miniature case in one hand, c1845, 4½ by 3in (11 by 8cm), cased.
$400-900

An oval miniature, by Richard Crosse of a gentleman, c1770, 3.5cm, in a gold slide frame.
$1,000-2,000

Empress Marie Louise, by Peter Mayr, signed and dated 1810, giltmetal mounts, 7cm high, in rectangular gilt wood frame.
$4,000-7,500

An oval portrait miniature of a young man, the reverse set with a seed pearl and gilt thread mounted hair locket panel, in gold mount, 19thC, 7 by 6cm.
$600-1,200

A miniature portrait of Soloman Dayrolles, French, c1780, 3in (7.5cm), in a tooled red morocco case.
$600-1,200

A circular miniature by Kolfmann of Mlle Tassin, wearing a lace inset red décolleté frock, signed and dated 1820, 5.5cm, in wooden frame.
$500-900

An oval miniature by N.H. of a young girl, wearing a white frock with floral and 'gothic' background, signed with the initials and dated 1900, 4½in (11cm), in gilt metal surround.
$300-600

A pair of silhouette paintings 'On the Road to the Races 1830' and 'Returning from the Races', black painted on glass, 15 by 11in (38 by 28cm).
$1,700-3,000

An oval enamel miniature after Lampi, of the Empress Catherine II, wearing a pink jacket over a white frock and ermine cloak with the sash of St. Andrews and the Imperial Crown, 3in (7.5cm), in chased silver frame with paste surround, the surmount in the form of the Imperial Crown.
$1,000-2,000

A miniature portrait, said to be of Hersey, Marchioness of Linlithgow as a child, in a gold and blue enamel frame, in leather folding case.
$400-900

A wax profile portrait relief of George III, wearing ceremonial garments, within gilt surround, glazed and within turned wood frame, 8½in (21.5cm) diam.
$400-900

A gentleman by Heinrich Schoedl, signed, gilt metal frame, 3in (7.5cm) high.
$600-1,200

A gentleman, said to be John Miller, facing left, wearing a black coat and spotted waistcoat, 2½ by 2in (6 by 5cm).
$400-900

Coins

Norwich, Dunham & Yallop, Goldsmiths, 1793 (last figure of date over-cut on a 2), obv. arms of Norwich, rev. shop front, (D & H 29).
$1,000-2,000

Lady Byron by F. Read, wearing a black dress with lace collar, a red stole and holding a posy of flowers, 3½ by 2in (9 by 5.5cm), in a fitted tooled leather case.
$600-1,200

An oval miniature by George Engleheart of Mrs Herries, wearing a lace-trimmed lilac décolleté frock, 4cm, in a gilt metal surround.
$1,700-3,000

A pair of glazed wax octagonal reliefs, one of Robert Adam after Tassie, 6 by 4½in (15 by 11.5cm).
$1,800-3,800

A pair of Victorian wax reliefs of Queen Victoria and Prince Albert, in mahogany frame, 6 by 8½in (15 by 21.5cm).
$400-900

Suffolk, Ipswich, Penny, 1796, but of Cardinal Wolsey left, rev. Conder's Drapery Warehouse, etc. (D & H 11; Schw.ll(i)).
$600-1,200

Suffolk, Ipswich, Penny, 1797, view
of Wolsey Gate, rev. cypher IMC (D
& H 14).
$500-900

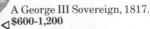

A George IV Sovereign, 1822. ▷
$600-1,200

A George III Sovereign, 1817.
◁**$600-1,200**

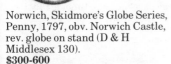

Norwich, Skidmore's Globe Series,
Penny, 1797, obv. Norwich Castle,
rev. globe on stand (D & H
Middlesex 130).
$300-600

Cornwall, West Wheal Mine,
Penny, view of St. Michael's Mount,
rev. West Wheal Fortune – One
Penny Token, Prince of Wales'
feathers issuing from coronet,
(D.15).
$900-1,700

Austrian, Salzburg, Wolf Dietrich ▷
von Raitenau, Klippe Double-
thaler, 1593, St. Rudbert seated,
shield of arms before, rev. four
winds blowing at tower.
$500-900

Brazil, John V, 10,000-Reis, 1725,
Minas Gerais (V. 39; F.34).
$1,200-2,100
◁

Norwich, Dinmore & Son, obv.
bottle, rev. Hope standing, plain
edge, gilt-proof, (D & H 24c).
$400-900

Germany, Saxony, Johann Georg I,
Double-thaler, 1617, half-figure
right, rev. helmeted arms (Dav.
7590a).
$600-1,200

◁

Germany, Hesse-Darmstadt,
Ludwig X, Thaler, 1793, civilian
bust right, rev. crowned and
supported arms, (Dav. 2337).
$1,800-3,800

Germany, Hamburg, Admiralty
Portugalöser, on the launch of a
new convoy ship, 1736, gold, by D.
Haesling, (Gaedechens 1815; Forrer
Vol II, p.375).
$4,000-7,500

Italy, Subalpine Republic, 20-
Francs, L'AN 10 (=1801), on the
victory of Marengo (F.1172).
$1,000-2,000

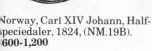

Norway, Carl XIV Johann, Half-
speciedaler, 1824, (NM.19B).
600-1,200

Puerto Rico, Alfonso XIII (of Spain),
Peso, 1895, (C & C 16036).
$1,200-2,100

▷

Malta, Emmanuel Pinto, 20-Scudi, 1764, crowned arms of the Order and Grand Master, rev. St. John holding banner, Paschal lamb at his feet (R & S 22; F35).
$900-1,700

Spain, Charles III, 8-Escudos, 1773 PJ, Madrid (C & C. 11550; F.137).
$2,600-5,300

Sarawak, Charles J. Brooke, Proof 20-Cents, 1906 H (Pr.5; Y.11).
$400-750

Roman Republic, Janus/Prow series, c250-225 B.C., as (T & V pl.35,51).
$800-1,500

U.S.A., Half-Dollar, 1807, Heraldic Eagle reverse.
$800-1,500

Sweden, Oscar I, Riksdaler, 1853 (SM.33; Dav.354).
$400-900

Malta, Emmanuel de Rohan, 20-Scudi, 1778, cuirassed bust right, rev. arms of the Order and of the de Rohan family on oval shields, edge decorated with leaves (R & S.3; F.43).
$900-1,700

U.S.A., 3-Dollars, 1854.
$1,200-2,100

Switzerland, Lucerne, 4-Franken, 1814 (Dav 364).
$400-900

Pine Furniture – Beds

A bedstead with high ships sides, 19thC, 72in (180cm) long.
$300-600

A two-door Irish bed cupboard, with panelled sides, c1840, 48 by 78in (120 by 197.5cm).
$1,000-2,000

A German bed, c1890, 75½in (191cm) long.
$300-600

An Irish settle bed, which opens out to a bed, c1840, 72in (182.5cm) long.
$400-900

Bookcases

A stripped pine bookcase on cupboard, 84in (212.5cm) high.
$1,200-2,100

A European blind top bureau bookcase, with plain interior indicating provincial construction, c1800, 42in (105cm).
$1,400-2,600

A Victorian glazed secretaire bookcase, etched glass doors, fitted interior, c1820.
$1,800-3,800

Chairs

A rocking chair, c1860, 34in (85cm) high.
$200-450

An 'American' action beech rocking chair, all woodwork and metalwork original, re-upholstered, c1850.
$600-1,100

An American pine and bleached mahogany rocking chair, on original casters, c1900, 42in (105cm) high.
$300-600

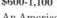

A pine high chair which converts to a play pen, c1920.
$200-450

An elm, ash and oak Yorkshire spindle-back rocking chair, 42in (105cm) high.
$500-900

A pine chair with new cane seat, 31½in (78cm) high.
$150-300

A set of 4 pine chairs, 32in (80cm).
$300-600

Chests

A Victorian chest of drawers with shaped gallery back, 33in (82.5cm).
$150-300

A selection of traditional Orkney chairs with original straw backs,

ladies chair with drawer.
$400-750

gentleman's chair with hood, very rare.
$800-1,500

child's chair.
$300-600

A Georgian chest of drawers, c1790, 48 by 42in (120 by 105cm).
$300-600

A pine coffer dated 1715, carved 'In this chest are the books and maps belonging to the Commission of Severs for the Eastern park of the County of Kent, 1715', with original escutcheons, feet replaced, 19 by 78in (47.5 by 197.5cm).
$800-1,500

An original bow-fronted chest, with graduated drawers, 18thC, 36in (90cm).
$1,200-2,100

An Irish astragal glazed two-part planner chest, c1850, 72 by 48in (180 by 120cm).
$1,600-2,800

A Georgian chest of drawers, with high bracket feet and original brass handles, 39in (97.5cm) high.
$600-1,200

A 3 piece bedroom suite, comprising chest of drawers, 45 by 46in (112.5 by 115cm), wardrobe, 89 by 49 (225 by 122.5cm) and a dressing table, 64 by 50in (160 by 125cm).
$2,000-4,500

A two-drawer mule chest, c1860.
$300-600

A Welsh mule chest, c1820, 22 by 35in (55 by 87.5cm).
$300-600

A chemist's shop flight of drawers, with original knobs, 19thC.
$400-750

Cupboards

A rustic Irish food cupboard, with oak frame and pine, early 18thC, 51in (127.5cm).
$1,000-2,000

A German chest of drawers with turned columns, original handles and fittings, c1850, 34 by 43in (85 by 108cm).
$800-1,500

Europes largest Antique and Country Pine Showroom!

WE NOW HAVE - 3 SUPER SHOWROOMS - IN SOUTHERN ENGLAND!
★ Europe's Largest - STOCKWELL, LONDON ★ Europe's Second Largest - CAMBERWELL, LONDON
★ Over the Border - BECKENHAM, KENT

★ THE ANTIQUE
HUNDREDS OF ITEMS FROM ALL OVER THE UK AND EUROPE, STRIPPED AND RESTORED TO A VERY HIGH STANDARD.

★ THE REPRODUCTION
TABLES, DRESSERS, ROBES, CHEST OF DRAWERS, etc. VERY POPULAR IN THE USA. BELIEVED TO BE THE LARGEST
SELECTION OF HIGH QUALITY REPRODUCTION PINE UNDER ONE ROOF.

★ THE ARCHITECTURAL
FIRE SURROUNDS - DOORS - ROOM DIVIDERS - SHUTTERS - TELEPHONE BOXES - VICTORIAN STREET LAMPS - PEWS -
COMPLETE CHURCH INTERIORS - PANELLING - PORCHES CHIMNEY POTS.

★ THE MISCELLANEOUS
BARROWS - DOG CARTS - WHEELS etc.

★ THE STRIPPING
RETAIL AND TRADE: ALL PINE DOORS AND FURNITURE - CAST FIRES - RADIATORS - GATES - RAILINGS etc.
And many other items including ROCKING HORSES - SHEEP and FLYING PIGS.

★ THE SHIPPING
2 ft, 20 ft and 40 ft CONTAINERS PACKED AND SHIPPED.

To receive a copy of our bi-monthly 'ANTIQUE BULLETIN', write to:-

BUILT ON REPUTATION ANTIQUE and COUNTRY PINE ESTABLISHED 1971

187-191 CLAPHAM ROAD, STOCKWELL, LONDON SW9 0QE, ENGLAND
Telephone: 01-274 0300 (10 lines) - *Open 7 days a week*
CAMBERWELL: THE OLD CHURCH, WREN RD, LONDON SE5 8QS   BECKENHAM: 22 HIGH ST, BECKENHAM, KENT

653

An Irish 4-door cupboard with arched and decorated interior, c1780, 94 by 50in (237.5 by 125cm). **$3,200-6,000**

A Northern Irish panelled food cupboard, c1800, 78 by 58in (197.5 by 145cm). **$1,300-2,400**

An Irish 4-door astragal glazed cupboard, with carved interior, c1830, 78 by 48in (197.5 by 120cm). **$1,600-2,800**

A large Victorian housekeeper's cupboard, on unusual 9-drawer base, c1840, 78in (197.5cm). **$1,400-2,600**

A pot cupboard, 29 by 16½in (72.5 by 40cm). **$200-450**

A bedside cabinet with gallery top, c1900, 31 by 14in (77.5 by 35cm). **$200-450**

A linen press with panelled doors and beading, 46in (115cm), and base with original dark stained handles, c1820. **$1,000-2,000**

A drum pot cupboard with marble top, c1840, 15½in (38cm) diam. **$400-750**

A Dutch linen press, with pin hinged doors, mahogany carved pelmet and original fittings, c1790, 87 by 57in (220 by 142.5cm). **$5,000-9,000**

A Dutch bowfront corner cabinet, the broken pediment above a pair of cupboard doors, the lower section with 5 frieze drawers and 2 cupboard doors below, on bracket feet, 18thC, 40in (101cm). **$600-1,200**

A corner cupboard, made up from old wood, 63 by 30in (157.5 by 75cm). **$400-750**

A large Irish 4-door cupboard, with panelled sides and rope-twist frame c1840–50, 78 by 54in (197.5 by 135cm). **$1,800-3,800**

Desks

A Georgian pine bureau, the top drawer acts as a support for the writing leaf, oak interior, c1800.
$1,300-2,400

A late Georgian slope-top estate desk, with bank of drawers, c1800-30.
$400-900

A pitch pine desk, c1860, 42 by 42in (105 by 105cm).
$800-1,500

Dressers

A pine bureau. 24in (60cm).
$400-900

A North Wales pot-board dresser, c1780, 78 by 68in (197.5 by 170cm).
$2,200-4,200

An Irish dresser, with rope-twist shelves, c1840, 75 by 66in (190 by 165cm).
$1,200-2,100

A Welsh breakfront dresser, Anglesey, c1830, 80 by 63in (202.5 by 157.5cm).
$2,200-4,200

A small chiffonier, c1820, 45 by 38in (112.5 by 95cm).
$600-1,100

An Irish fiddle front dresser with 3 drawers, c1840, 78 by 66in (198 by 165cm).
$1,300-2,400

A Yorkshire serpentine front dresser, c1850, 50 by 54in (125 by 135cm).
$1,000-2,000

A narrow cottage spice dresser, c1860, 34in (85cm).
$600-1,200

> ### Use the Index!
> *Because certain items might fit easily into any of a number of categories, the quickest and surest method of locating any entry is by reference to the index at the back of the book.*
> *This has been fully cross-referenced for absolute simplicity.*

An Irish hanging dresser rack with bevelled drawers, c1850, 66 by 60in (165 by 150cm).
$600-1,200

A North Country enclosed dresser, 19thC.
$1,000-2,000

A one-piece Irish dresser with plate rack, c1860, 54in (135cm).
$1,000-2,000

A Lancashire pine dresser, with 3 bowfront drawers, c1860, 59 by 57½in (147.5 by 143cm).
$900-1,700

A William IV chiffonier, with two drawers and side pillars.
$600-1,100

An Irish dog kennel dresser, c1850, 78 by 60in (198 by 150cm).
$1,200-2,100

A large Irish arched base dresser, c1840, 78 by 60in (198 by 150cm).
$1,200-2,100

A Welsh chiffonier, c1830, 68 by 55in (170 by 137.5cm).
$1,700-3,000

Dressing Tables

A dressing chest, with original handles and fittings, c1840, 44 by 41in (110 by 102.5cm).
$600-1,100

A Victorian dressing chest, c1880, 62 by 42in (155 by 105cm).
$600-1,100

A hand stripped 'satinwood' dressing chest, c1890, 63 by 36in (157.5 by 90cm).
$400-900

Mirrors

A pine and elm dressing table mirror, c1860, 24 by 22in (60 by 55cm).
$200-450

A carved mirror, 27 by 23in (67.5 by 57.5cm).
$200-450

A carved mirror, 34½ by 30in (86 by 75cm).
$300-600

A Dutch settle, c1880, 44½ by 40in (111 by 100cm).
$400-750

Settles

A church pew, c1850, 33 by 64in (82.5 by 160cm).
$400-750

A Georgian bowfronted settle, 69in (172.5cm) wide.
$800-1,500

Sideboards

A North Country sideboard, c1880, 36 by 58in (90 by 145cm).
$800-1,500

Stools

A pine stool, 19½ by 18in (48 by 45cm).
$80-150

A pine stool, 27in (67.5cm) high.
$150-250

Tables

A Georgian sycamore topped carving table with 2 drawers and 6 legs, c1810.
$1,300-2,400

A Georgian cricket table, c1820, 29in (72.5cm) diam.
$300-600

A sloping desk stool, 29½ by 16in (73 by 40cm).
$150-250

An English pine table, c1860, 30 by 96in (75 by 242.5cm).
$1,200-2,100

A bed table, c1860, 28½in (71cm).
$100-250

An octagonal table, 47½in (118cm) diam.
$800-1,500

A Regency side table with original handles, 29½ by 32in (74 by 80cm).
$200-450

Wardrobes

A hand stripped 'satinwood' wardrobe, c1890, 79 by 48in (200 by 120cm).
$600-1,100

An arched door wardrobe, with shelves on one side, 54in (135cm).
$800-1,500

A carved Austrian double wardrobe with one full width drawer, c1860, 42in (105cm).
$900-1,700

A wine cupboard, with 2 raised and fielded panelled doors, on bracket feet, 18thC, 48in (120cm) wide.
$900-1,700

A marble topped washstand, with green tiles, c1860, 46½ by 36½in (116 by 90cm).
$300-600

Washstands

A washstand, c1860, 30 by 36in (75 by 90cm).
$200-450

A double washstand, c1860, 39 by 45in (97.5 by 112.5cm).
$200-450

A marble topped washstand with cupboard, c1850, 49 by 42in (122.5 by 105cm).
$500-900

Miscellaneous

A blanket box fitted with candle box and 2 drawers, c1860, 21½ by 43in (53 by 107.5cm).
$200-450

A Georgian lady's work box fitted with a sliding shelf, 30½ by 20½in (76 by 51cm).
$300-600

An Irish panelled grain bin with 3 secret compartments, c1800, 60 by 48cm (160 by 120cm).
$800-1,500

An Irish cheese press, with 4 doors and 2 drawers, c1850, 78 by 66in (197.5 by 165cm).
$1,200-2,100

A pine box, 11 by 20in (27.5 by 50cm).
$80-150

A large dough bin, with scrubbed top used for a work surface, c1820, 34 by 50½in (85 by 126cm).
$600-1,100

Pine shelves, c1860. 48 by 33in (120 by 82.5cm).
$200-450

Pine steps, 49in (122.5cm) high.
$80-150

A pine Liberty shelf, 31 by 20in (77.5 by 50cm).
$150-250

A pine mystery object, 31 by 24in (77.5 by 60cm).
$100-250

A towel rail, 35 by 22in (87.5 by 55cm).
$80-150

A George III pine fireplace with gesso applications.
$1,300-2,400

An adjustable easel, on a trestle base, with casters, 92 by 29in (232.5 by 72.5cm).
$1,700-3,000

A rare pine longcase clock, Scandinavian, Swiss origin, c1810, 79½in (201cm) high.
$1,800-3,800

A Flemish painted pine cabinet, the sides with linen-fold panels and the front decorated in high relief with a central fall-front flanked by cupboards, 19thC, 47 by 55½in (118 by 138cm).
$1,600-2,800

Kitchenalia

A sycamore flour scoop, 18thC, 10in (25cm) long.
$60-120

A small sycamore spoon, 18thC, 7in (17.5cm).
$40-90

An English seal top spoon with maker's mark, c1600, 6in (15cm) long.
$300-600

A sycamore measure or water dipper, 18thC, 5in (12.5cm) diam.
$80-150

An ice cream wafer maker as used before the War.
$30-60

A sycamore ladle, 18thC, 14½in (35cm) long.
$60-120

A wooden scoop for flour, etc.
$40-75

A German ladle, the bowl made from a shell, c1800, 15in (37.5cm) long.
$150-300

A metal whisk with collar for altering span of whisk.
$10-20

A handmade wire utensil suitable for many purposes; whisk, fish slice, server, made from wire netting and wire.
$10-20

A Danish wooden flour scoop.
$40-90

Two eel forks, with wooden handles.
$100-250

Two Yorkshire pottery jelly moulds.
$30-60

A toasting fork, blacksmith made.
$20-45

A wooden pestle and mortar.
$40-90

A walnut pestle and mortar, c1800,
6½in (16cm) high.
$900-1,700

An unusual Danish mortar, with
heavy steel ball for crushing herbs,
etc. 14in (35cm) diam.
$180-300

An oatmeal roller, 19thC, 26in
(65cm) long.
$60-120

A tôle-ware coffee pot, early 19thC,
10in (25cm) high.
$400-750

A good walnut platter, late 18thC,
11in (29cm) diam.
$400-750

A Virol jar, 'a preparation of bone
marrow, an ideal fat food for
children and invalids'.
$10-20

A treen round pierced bowl, with a
central brass inlaid panel, early
19thC, 10in (25cm).
$600-1,100

A sycamore skimmer, 6in (15cm)
diam.
$60-120

A treen wooden bowl, 10in (25cm)
diam.
$150-250

A 'Lazy Susan' oak cheese board,
carved with acorns, 22in (55cm)
diam.
$400-750

Make the most of Miller's

*Every care has been taken
to ensure the accuracy of
descriptions and
estimated valuations.
Where an attribution is
made within inverted
commas (e.g.
'Chippendale') or is
followed by the word
'style' (e.g. early Georgian
style) it is intended to
convey that, in the opinion
of the publishers, the piece
concerned is a later –
though probably still
antique – reproduction of
the style so designated.
Unless otherwise stated,
any description which
refers to 'a set', or 'a pair'
includes a valuation for
the entire set or the pair,
even though the
illustration may show only
a single item.*

A set of Art Nouveau style scales, by Salter.
$40-75

A treen string box.
$100-250

A German cherry-pipper, 10in (25cm) high.
$40-75

A wooden darning mushroom.
$11-20

A wooden clamp.
$20-45

A Danish wooden meat press, 14in (35cm) long.
$60-120

An African wooden mixing bowl on legs, 13in (33cm) high, 15in (38cm) diam.
$150-250

An Irish wrought iron rushlight candleholder, c1780.
$300-600

A wooden money box shaped like a pail, an early souvenir marked 'Present from Blackpool', made in the Lake District, Bobbin Mills.
$40-75

A late Victorian Maypole Tea tin, 6 by 5 by 7in (15 by 12.5 by 17.5cm).
$80-150

A French wrought iron candleholder, c1760, 8in (20cm) high.
$300-600

Three English wooden based rushlight holders, c1760, approx. 9in (22.5cm) high.
$200-450 each

A pair of flat irons.
$10-18 each

A wrought iron oat-cake spit stand.
$200-450

An English iron and wood rushlight holder, c1760, 7in (17.5cm) high.
$300-600

A Yorkshire brass and metal fire-front trivet.
$150-250

Tools

A rosewood box plane, with cast brass sole plate and steel blade by Hearnshaw Bros., 7½in (19cm) long.
$180-300

1. A beechwood compass plane with concentric top, adjustable steel sole and Mathieson iron.
$100-250

2. A Dutch beechwood brace with eleven bits in pads.
$300-600

3. A Dutch plough with iron bow-nuts and carved date 1785 in a panel.
$600-1,200

4. A Dutch plough with wing nuts, the toe stamped 'I†R, Ryke' and 'KP', dated 1790 in shaped panel.
$800-1,500

Two hogscraper iron candlesticks, c1820, 7 and 8in (17.5 and 20cm) high.
$80-180

An A1 dovetailed steel panel plane, by Norris, with Patent Adjustment, 15½in (39cm) long.
$600-1,200

An unusual cast iron jack plane with beechwood wedge and handle, with adjustable front sole, 14¼in (35.5cm) long.
$80-180

A panel-raising plane, by Gabriel (zb), with adjustable fence and depth-stop and iron by Green.
$200-450

Make the most of Miller's

Price ranges in this book reflect what one should expect to pay for a similar example. When selling one can obviously expect a figure below. This will fluctuate according to a dealer's stock, saleability at a particular time, etc. It is always advisable to approach a reputable specialist dealer or an auction house which has specialist sales.

A rare ogee plane, by Richard Mealing, (Zb), early 18thC, 10½in (26cm) long.
$800-1,500

A fielding plane, by Wm. Toone, (-1740-), the stock rebated on both sides.
$800-1,500

A brass block plane with ebony infill and wedge, the sole 7in (17cm) long.
$200-450

A bronze chariot plane with mahogany foregrip and wedge, the sole 5in (13cm) long.
$200-450

A beechwood double-bound octagon lever pad brace, by Robert Marples, with brass baluster and ebony head with inlaid ivory ring.
$400-900

A handled bridle plough by Mathieson, Edinburgh, with steel bridle and original varnish finish, and an off-the-bench wedge-stem sash fillister by the same maker, in similar condition, c1930.
$900-1,700

A brass framed ebony ultimatum brace, by Robert Marples, Sheffield, 13in (33cm) long.
$200-450

A Norris 50G coffin-sided gunmetal smoother with steel sole, Patent adjustment and walnut closed handle.
$900-1,700

A small draw-knife, by Maw & Staley, with mahogany handles, the blade 5in (13cm) long.
$80-180

A gentleman's tool kit by Holtzapffel of London, c1850.
$2,600-5,300

Sundry Trades

A tin hanging shoe-cleaning box, 7in (17.5cm) wide.
$10-20

A five-inch centre lathe, by Holtzapffel & Deyerlein, No.1048, complete with accessories and reconstructed treadle, the bed 44½in (111cm) long overall.
$1,000-2,000

A shoemaker's pattern.
$40-75

A shoemaker's pattern.
$40-75

Two Victorian hat-maker's blocks.
$100-250

Agriculture

Thomas Clark's Patented crimping machine, composed of a green painted cast iron frame, supporting two brass rollers, 9½in (24cm) high.
$150-300

A hop measure, 35in (88cm) high.
$80-150

A Scandinavian painted flax-cutter.
$40-90

A hop scuppett, 23in (58cm) wide.
$150-250

A teasing panel of nails for combing wool, 24in (60cm) long.
$40-90

A German wool-winder, 27in (68cm) high.
$80-180

A flax-basher, 24in (60cm) long.
$30-60

An elm milking stool, 18thC, 8 by 15in (20 by 38cm).
$100-250

An oak bushel measure, complete with Orkney Customs & Excise stamp on every stave, 19thC.
$150-250

Drinking Vessels

A Scandinavian fruitwood skala, the rim painted with the initials 'W J W' and dated '1871', 11½in (29cm).
$600-1,200

A coconut treen cup, 6in (15cm) high.
$80-180

A horn beaker.
$30-60

The Dining Room

A rosewood salt, c1820, 3½in (9cm) high.
$200-450

A good Georgian mahogany wine coaster, 6½in (15cm) diam.
$300-600

A pair of fruitwood wine coasters, c1780, 3in (7.5cm) high.
$300-600

Miscellaneous

A mahogany smoker's compendium, with snuff pot in the top, pipe rack in the middle and tobacco jar in the base, c1860, 15½in (39cm) high.
$1,700-3,000

A treen watch stand on circular base, with ivory mounts on turned pillars and stretchers, mid-19thC.
$80-180

A pepper box, 5½in (14cm) high.
$60-120

A pair of carved bellows, probably Scandinavian, 18th/19thC, 25½in (64cm).
$200-450

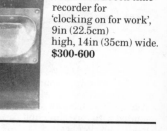

A Gledhill Brook time recorder for 'clocking on for work', 9in (22.5cm) high, 14in (35cm) wide.
$300-600

Arms & Armour – Armour

A rare left-hand tilting gauntlet, late 16thC, 13in (33cm).
$3,200-6,000

An Italian half-chanfron of bright steel, shaped to the upper part of the horse's head and boxed above and below the flanged eye-openings, slight surface cracking in places, late 16thC, 15in (37cm) high.
$1,300-2,400

An Italian comb morion of one piece, the skull with a row of lining rivets with brass rosette washers, the whole surface etched with trophies of arms against a granular ground and within gilt borders, probably Milanese, the skull with old internal patch, c1570, 12in (30cm) high.
$3,200-6,000

A Commonwealth steel lobster tail helmet, with adjustable nose guard and pointed peak, one ear flap missing, 17thC, 10½in (26cm), with wood stand.
$900-1,700

A copy of a suit of German Gothic style armour, 19thC, helmet of later date, 69in (173cm) high.
$4,500-9,000

A pair of crane-neck rowel spurs of iron, with figure-eight terminals, large rowel of sixteen points, original buckles and hooks, incomplete on one spur, and with considerable remains of gilding throughout, probably German, early 17thC, 6in (15cm).
$1,300-2,400

▷

A very rare French model armour, manufactured by Granger of Paris, c1870, 12in (30cm) overall.
$1,700-3,000

A close helmet of blued steel, plume-holder missing, pivoted chin-piece with turned and roped upper border, retaining nuts replaced, neck-guard of two plates front and rear, both the lower plates replaced, retaining much original blued finish, probably French, late 16thC, 12½in (32cm) high.
$9,000-15,000

A composite cuirassier half-armour of bright steel, comprising close helmet, gorget, breast-plate struck with London Armourers' Company mark at the neck, full arm defences including fingered gauntlets, back-plate and tassets extending to below the knee, many rivets replaced by nuts and bolts throughout, some plates loose, basically mid-17thC.
$5,500-9,000

A mace, the head with seven flanges, the points of two slightly damaged, probably German, 16thC, 24½in (61cm).
$3,200-6,000

A Persian chiselled and damascened steel kulah khud and dhai, the former fitted with two plume-holders, central spike, the latter with four steel bosses, 19thC, 11in (29cm) high and 18in (45cm) diam.
$6,000-12,000

Cannon

A pair of iron ship's cannon, the tapered ringed barrels with the initials B.P. with crown above, each mounted with rope rings and stays, barrels 43in (107.5cm).
$3,200-6,000

The initials B.P. are probably for Bailey-Pegg, makers to the Crown.

A rare brace of Spanish brass ship's cannon barrels, the vent plane of one bearing the Royal Cypher of Charles IV, 1788-1808, the trunnion ends of one marked no.399, the other CORBRE DE RIO TINTO & P.129, the barrel weighing approx. 130 lbs, dark age patina, a near pair, late 18thC, bores 3in (7.5cm) diam., 31in (78cm) overall.
$4,000-7,500

An English cannon, 18thC, 80in (200cm) wide.
$2,000-4,500

A German left-hand dagger, with original indented grip bound with steel wire and with two Turks' heads, probably late 16thC, 16in (40cm).
$1,800-3,800

Crossbows

Bayonets, Daggers & Knives

A huntsman's plug bayonet, probably Spanish, the grip with brass pommel, in its original brass mounted green leather sheath, minor blade rust, tip of point broken, 19thC, blade 7in (18cm).
$80-150

A large Flemish crossbow with steel bow struck with a mark, a unicorn's head, string replaced, the handles both inset with a Spanish (?) coin, the claws struck with a mark, rubbed, 17thC, 45in (113cm).
$5,500-9,000

A Spanish left-hand dagger, the broad ricasso struck with three marks and pierced with two holes for sword breaking, the grip bound with copper wire, probably by Francisco Perez of Toledo, late 17thC, 22½in (56cm).
$4,000-6,800

An unusual dagger, with tapering blade inlaid with silver and set with turquoises on both sides, decorated gilt on a black ground, the inner side engraved on a black ground, with wooden handle, probably replaced, Japanese made for export, the blade probably Bhutanese, 17th/18thC, 17½in (44cm).
$900-1,700

A Georgian Naval dirk, c1820.
$500-900

A selection of fighting knives, Dutch, M.E.C., Italian, Commandos.
1 **$80-150**
2 **$150-300**
3 **$400-750**
4 **$500-900**
5 **$500-900**
6 **$600-1,200**

A Scottish Officer's dirk set of the Argyll and Sutherland Highlanders.
$1,400-2,600

Swords – European

A Nazi R.A.D. Mans Dagger, by 'AXT und Hauerfabrik Solingen', also marked 'R.A.J.D.', plated mounts, staghorn grip, stamped on lower grip mount 'R.166', in its steel sheath with plated mounts, stamped on throat mount 'BG 1230', GC, minor sheath painted finish wear.
$400-750

A Nazi S.A. dagger, by 'E.P.&S', blade retaining virtually all original polish, GS mounts, in its metal sheath with single hanging strap and belt clip, some minor wear to painted sheath finish, tip of chape dented.
$300-600

◁ A Viking sword, in excavated condition, retaining fragments of its wooden scabbard, pommel missing, late 9th/10thC, blade 28in (70cm).
$2,000-4,500

A mediaeval sword in excavated ▷ condition, with bold wheel pommel of latten, later leather-covered grip, late 13th/early 14thC, blade 34in (85cm).
$6,000-12,000

A Nazi Kriegsmarine Officer's dirk, by Eickhorn Original, Solingen, with brass plated hilt, in its brassed scabbard, some damage to portepee, blade 10in (25cm).
$300-600

A swept hilt rapier, the blade of flattened diamond section with twin central fullers and struck each side with a mark, the faceted hilt chiselled with scallop shells on the outer face, wire bound grip with Turks' heads, probably French, one hilt bar cracked and one Turk's head lacking, late 16thC, blade 45in (112.5cm).
$1,700-3,000

A mediaeval sword with flat tapering double-edged shortened blade, with a series of marks inlaid in brass, brass incomplete, one side with running wolf mark, also inscription in Naskhi script, 14thC, with later wooden grips, blade 30in (75cm).
$20,000-30,000

A Charles II hunting hanger, c1680.
$1,200-2,100

An English silver smallsword with etched 31½in (80cm) colichemarde blade, lion passant mark.
$1,400-2,600

Swords – Eastern inc. Japanese

t A Mameluke sabre, blade 33in (84cm) long, housed in brass mounted hide-covered scabbard with inscription.
$1,700-3,000

c A George III court sword.
$150-300

b A Victorian General Officer's Mameluke sabre, by Hawkes & Co. Ltd., 30½in (77cm) blade inscribed: 'To F.D.B. from H.C.S. on appointment to the 18th Hussars, 6th Nov. 1883'.
$1,700-3,000

A Persian jambiya, with carved ivory hilt, inscribed 'Osno', with Persian inscriptions above and below, in original cloth-covered wooden scabbard, cloth worn, with chased silver mounts, early 19thC, 14in (35.5cm).
$1,800-3,800

An Arab shamshir with curved watered Persian blade, silver hilt with applied gold decoration, silver pommel replaced, in leather covered scabbard with gold and silver mounts, the blade probably 18thC, blade 31in (79cm).
$2,000-4,500

A Turkish kindjal, with foliate brass inlay, in a purple cloth-covered wooden sheath with 2 large pierced silver chapes, 21½in (55cm) long overall.
$800-1,500

A court tachi, with suguba hamon signed 'Inouye Izumi no Kami Kunisada' and dated 1668, blade 25½in (64.5cm).
$2,000-4,500

An Arab jambiya, the hilt entirely sheathed in gold decorated and applied with 2 small stones, contained in gold covered scabbard decorated en suite, slight damage to hilt, blade 6in (15cm).
$1,200-2,100

A Japanese short sword, the hilt with applied parcel gilt bronze mounts, the lacquered scabbard with parcel gilt bronze mounts and brass hilted knife, 14in (35.5cm) long overall.
$400-750

A Daisho, the katana with copper tsuba inlaid with engraved gold panels, with brown mottled lacquered scabbard, late 19thC, blade 28½in (72.5cm).
$1,800-3,800

Firearms – Blunderbusses

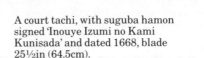

A flintlock blunderbuss by Bunney, 14in (35.5cm) brass barrel.
$1,300-2,400

An Indian fullstocked flintlock blunderbuss breast pistol, top jaw and screw missing, stock cracked by front of lock, a 'sleeper' with dark age patina, c1850, barrel 11in (28cm), muzzle 1¼in (3cm) diam.
$200-450

An Irish over-and-under double barrelled percussion blunderbuss, by 'Kavanagh Dublin', c1850, barrel 13½in (34cm), muzzle 2⅛in (6cm) diam.
$2,000-4,500

Muskets & Sporting Guns

A matchlock musket, signed, barrel with moulded muzzle inlaid in silver, replacement steel ramrod, 38½in (98cm).
$1,300-2,400

A German wheel-lock sporting gun, with slender octagonal sighted barrel struck on the breech with 3 acorn marks and with a further mark, 'HE' conjoined (New Støckel 2821), unsigned, late 17thC, 35½in (90cm).
$6,000-12,000

An English 16 bore fullstocked flintlock fowling piece, some pitting, c1780, 39in (99cm) barrel.
$800-1,500

A South American (Mexican) fullstocked matchlock carbine, the octagonal steel barrel with a brass trumpet muzzle to give the impression of being a blunderbuss, the serpentine and pan cover replaced, some rust and pitting, stock bruised, c1800, 25½in (64.5cm) barrel.
$600-1,200

A dog lock musket, with 2 stage 42½in (106cm) barrel, octagonal at the breech, the plain lock with dog catch, later wood ramrod, some defects, 59in (147cm) long overall.
$1,300-2,400

A French D.B. flintlock sporting gun with gold damascened barrels engraved 'Canon Tordu' along the gilt rib, with maker's marks on the breech and retaining much original blue, by Brunon l'âiné à Caen, c1790, 30in (76cm) barrel.
$4,000-7,500

A 12 bore fullstocked flintlock sporting carbine, by Newton, Grantham, with silver foresight, the breech flat struck with maker's mark WN and crowned P mark of a private Birmingham Proof House, requires restoration, c1780, 25in (63.5cm) barrel.
$800-1,500

A Birmingham proved 7 bore halfstocked percussion wildfowling gun, by Robert Gill, c1830, the patent breech with platinum safety plug and inlaid platinum band, barrel 31½in (80cm).
$800-1,500

A 12 bore 2¾in (7cm), boxlock ejector gun by Charles Hellis & Sons, No. 2978, in leather case with accessories and a wooden bird carrier.
$1,600-2,800

A Herzegovenian Miquelet.
$900-1,700

A Persian blunderbuss.
$600-1,100

Rifles

A composite wheel-lock sporting rifle, the breech struck with a mark, New Støckel 1044, and retaining traces of engraving and maker's signature, by Johann Stifter of Prague, some repairs, late 17thC, 32½in (82.5cm) barrel.
$4,000-6,800

A Turkish flintlock rifle, decorated with gold, the butt inlaid with green and white horn and brass pellets and rosettes, the fore-end with green horn cap, ramrod missing, c1800, 36½in (92.5cm) barrel.
$1,700-3,000

A rare London proved 16 bore fullstocked Manton Patent percussion tube lock sporting rifle, converted from flintlock, marked Jam.s Wilkinson London, the lockplate engraved John Manton & Son, some damage, c1820, 21in (53cm) barrel.
$1,000-2,000

A 12 bore D.B. percussion 'cape' rifle, engraved steel mounts including rectangular patchbox cover engraved with a lion, and original brass-mounted ramrod, signed Deans, London, Birmingham proof marks, c1860, 30in (76cm) barrel.
$1,700-3,000

A good double barrelled 40 bore percussion express rifle, damascus barrels signed on the rib J. Purdey, 314 Oxford Street, London, complete with brass tipped wooden ramrod, Serial No. 5194 for 1856, retaining some original colour overall, 30½in (77.5cm) barrel.
$3,200-6,000

An Irish 40 bore over-and-under percussion sporting rifle, with original horn-tipped ramrods, by Wm. & Jn. Rigby, Dublin, No.8715, some rust pitting, c1841, 30in (76cm) barrel.
$1,700-3,000

Pistols

A military wheel lock pistol, with some restoration, 23½in (59cm) overall length.
$3,200-6,000

A pair of Swedish flintlock holster pistols, with long barrels signed 'Felix Meier in Wienn' on the sighting flats, with pierced silver escutcheons with coronet above, horn fore-end caps, and original horn-tipped ramrods, one fore-end an old replacement, some wear throughout, early 18thC, 21in (53.5cm).
$5,000-9,000

A brace of Continental military holster pistols, barrels with large brass blade fore sights, plain locks, full stocked with plain brass mounts and complete with their steel ramrods, probably Danish or Norwegian, both butts drilled through and one fore-end with contemporary repair, c1750, 13in (33cm) barrel.
$1,800-3,800

A pair of silver mounted flintlock holster pistols, by John Brazier, London, London silver hallmarks for 1751, maker's mark of James Brooker, one cock associated, the other repaired, ramrods replaced, 13½in (34cm).
$4,000-7,500

A Scottish all steel flintlock belt pistol, with signed lock by Thomas Murdoch, London proof marks, steel and trigger associated, ramrod later, late 18thC, 12½in (32cm).
$1,300-2,400

A Black Watch regulation all-metal flintlock belt pistol, by John Waters, Birmingham proof marks, ramrod-pipe and ramrod replaced, c1790, 12in (30.5cm).
$1,000-2,000

A pair of flintlock holster pistols, sighted octagonal barrels signed Towler, Dublin, contained in baize-lined mahogany case with brass swing handle complete with copper flask and cleaning rod, one fore-end damaged, one cock repaired and cock retaining screw missing, 9½in (23.5cm) barrel.
$1,300-2,400

A brace of Cavalry Officers double barrelled flintlock holster pistols, by D. Egg.
$6,000-12,000

An unusual pair of Irish small flintlock pistols, with engraved case-hardened patent breeches with gold lines and platinum vent, signed engraved bolted locks with rollers, and 'French' cocks, one missing, by William Dempsey, Dublin, much original finish, c1820, 6in (14.5cm).
$6,000-12,000

A pair of flintlock 'Manstopper' pistols, by H. Nock.
$1,800-3,800

A Danish Lobnitz percussion pistol.
$1,800-3,800

A pair of Scottish percussion belt pistols, signed Campbell, steel parts re-blued and one ramrod replaced, 6½in (17cm) barrel.
$3,200-6,000

A pair of percussion cap saw handled target pistols by H.W. Mortimer & Co., converted from flintlock, the browned 10in (25.5cm) barrels signed H.W. Mortimer & Co. London, Gun Makers to His Majesty, 15½in (39.5cm) overall length without extension, with some accessories in a later fitted case.
$3,200-6,000

A pair of Officer's double barrelled percussion belt pistols by Staudenmayer.
$2,200-2,400

A fine pair of percussion pistols, by John Dickson & Son, proof marks, Nos. 4070/1, late 19thC, 16in (40.5cm).
$3,200-6,000

A pair of Belgian percussion rifle target pistols, in original lined and fitted mahogany case with accessories, corner lid missing, Liège proof, c1850, 15in (38cm).
$4,000-7,500

A Colt five-shot percussion pocket revolver, Serial No. 8154 on all parts, contained in red lined mahogany case complete with all accessories, 5in (12.5cm) barrel.
$3,200-6,000

The pistol retains nearly all its blueing and colour hardening.

A pair of cased percussion pistols with dagger, by Fenton.
$1,200-2,100

Medals

An important group of four 'reduced size' stars':

1. The Most Ancient and Most Noble Order of the Thistle (K.T.), pierced silver cross with gold centre and gold brooch fittings, elliptical, 6.2 by 5.5cm.

2. The Most Illustrious Order of St. Patrick (K.P.) pierced silver star with gold centre, slight green enamel damage to trefoil, 6cm.

3. The Most Exalted Order of the Star of India, Knight Grand Commander (G.C.S.I.) the star worked entirely in gold, 6cm.

4. The Most Distinguished Order of St. Michael and St. George, Knight Grand Cross (G.C.M.G.) silver, silver gilt, gold centre and enamels, with gold brooch fittings, 6cm.
$18,000-26,000

Pair: Sepy Sundar Singh, 36th Bengal Infantry, Indian Order of Merit, 3rd Class, Military Division, lacking its silver riband buckle, reverse inscribed '352 Lce. Naick Sundar Singh Indian Contingent British Central Africa' and officially engraved '3rd. Class Order of Merit', Central Africa, one clasp, light contact marks, 1894-98.
$2,600-5,300

Six: M.B.E. 2nd type mil., 1939-45 star, Atlantic star, Burma star with Pacific bar, War, N.G.S. 1915 1 bar S.E. Asia 1945-46 (Sen. Gd. Gnr. J. M. Bell M.B.E. R.N.) GVF, mounted as worn, together with set of miniatures Palestine, 1945-48 bar replaces S.E. Asia.
$300-600

An Indian Mutiny medal, Defence of Lucknow 32nd Lt. Infantry.
$14,000-24,000

A Waterloo medal, 79th Regt.
$18,000-26,000

A Crimea medal 4th Dragoons Light Brigade Charge Survivor.
$3,200-6,000

Pair: Guardsman I. Glendenning, Coldstream Guards, Military Medal, E.II.R., 2nd type, General Service Medal, 1962, one clasp, Northern Ireland, an edge bruise to each medal.
$1,600-2,800

Drums

A 16th/5th Queens Lancers side drum.
$6,000-12,000

Helmets

Saxony, Heavy Cavalry Troopers helmet.
$2,600-5,300

A Victorian Officers helmet, Royal Horse Artillery.
$2,600-5,300

6th Dragoon Guards, The Carabiniers, Officer's gilt helmet, with chin chain.
$1,300-2,400

A Yeomanry Cavalry Officers metal helmet to the Fife Light Horse.
$1,400-2,600

17th Duke of Cambridge's Own Lancers Officers chapka, lance cap, with white swan's feather plume, gold bullion boss bears embroidered George V cypher, corded gilt plume socket modified, and chin chain lined with white leather.
$2,200-4,200

A Prussian Infantry Reservist Officer's Pickelhaube, gilt brass HP, brass leather backed chinscales, both cockades, original silk and leather lining, GC, some stitching of neck and peak mounts damaged, some wear to patent leather finish.
$400-750

A Prussian Infantryman's NCO's Pickelhaube, gilt brass HP, brass leather backed chinscales, brass spike and mounts, leather lining, state cockade GC, some wear to patent leather finish, neck and peak guard leather age congealed.
$200-450

French Dragoons of the Line, Trumpeter's brass helmet of 1830 pattern with correct red chenille, but some non-regulation features, including the white poupette.
$800-1,500

French Cuirassiers Trooper's helmet of heavy polished steel, with brass mounts, red hair tuft and a red hackle-plume, helmet impressed beneath mane, A. Godillot and 83 and 57.
$800-1,500

Militaria – Badges/Plates

A gilt shako badge and a belt plate, the 10th North Lincoln Regiment, 19thC.
$600-1,100

A Victorian Officers helmet plate, the Border Regt.
$600-1,200

A Victorian Officers Home Service helmet to the Royal Irish, 1878 Pattern.
$600-1,200

A good officer's silvered 1869 pattern shako plate, universal Militia Pattern, near VGC.
$80-180

On the whole, during the past twelve months, jewellery prices have remained steady, with occasional ripples of excitement in the trade, when a rare, authenticated piece came onto the market, and an astronomical price was paid. This often bears no relation to the actual intrinsic value of the item, but rather to the fact that there are many people who have a strong desire to own a rare item, and can afford to go on bidding far beyond its actual market value. Nevertheless, there are still many pieces of good secondhand as well as Antique and Victorian jewellery which are excellent value. Quality of workmanship, together with excellent condition are the main criteria on which to judge an item's value; shoddy workmanship, obvious damage, and poor quality repair work can drastically reduce the value of all items of jewellery.

A turquoise and white enamel and split seed pearl brooch/pendant set in gold.
$800-1,500

Any damage would reduce a similar item to a fraction of this price.

An Art Deco period pendant, with pavé set diamonds, and a fine 'fancy' yellow diamond in the centre of the flower motif.
$8,000-13,500

Good examples of this period are especially sought after, but still extremely good value, due to the quality of the stones which were used.

A Victorian period 15ct gold black enamel Mourning brooch, set with diamonds in perfect condition.
$900-1,700

Mourning jewellery had been worn for very many years before the death of Queen Victoria's beloved Prince Albert, but after his death, the fashion for wearing black jewellery to commemorate the death of a loved one almost overwhelmed the jewellery craftsmen of the day. Rings, necklaces, brooches and earrings were made in their thousands, from Whitby Jet, French Jet (black glass), black enamel and black onyx. Often the details of the deceased were engraved on the back of the item, together with a lock of hair placed within a specially made recess covered by a tiny piece of closely fitting glass. A large quantity of this type of jewellery has survived until the present day, and can still be bought very reasonably, primarily because it does not enjoy a wide appeal, due to what some feel to be its 'morbid' associations.

Oriental baroque pearls set in decorated gold 'wirework' on gold neck chain, c1920.
$200-450

A 15ct. gold brooch set with freshwater seed pearl, requires restoration.
$180-300

The above in perfect condition.
$400-750

A turquoise, gold and seed pearl bracelet, c1880.
$900-1,700

Many examples of this style of bracelet are to be found and, according to age, condition and the stone set within them, prices range from £100 for gold and about £30 for silver. Victorian gilded base metal examples even cheaper.

A Victorian gold necklace set with various coloured agates, interlinked by short lengths of gold chain.
$400-750

A Victorian agate brooch set in gilded metal.
$80-150

An exceptionally fine Florentine mosaic brooch, in gold Castellani style mount.
$800-1,500   *'H*

A heavy quality Victorian silver locket and collarette, Registered Design Mark.
$300-600

A Victorian diamond-set gold hinged half-hoop bangle.
$1,600-2,800

A 15ct gold, diamond and seed pearl mounted hinged bangle, with applied foliate decoration and safety chain.
$600-1,200

A snake bracelet, 18ct with diamonds, and ruby eyes, 1860, in original box.
$9,000-15,000

An Edwardian diamond, onyx and pearl bracelet, by Dussaussoy, Paris.
$13,000-22,000

A diamond mounted bracelet of tapering rectangular links, millegrain and pavé-set with brilliant cut stones.
$5,000-9,000

A gold ram's head hinged bangle, decorated all over with granulation and wirework, maker's mark C.B., c1865.
$1,600-2,800

A gold, ruby and diamond bracelet, set with circular and rose cut diamonds and calibré cut rubies on a gold bracelet.
$13,000-22,000

A Victorian gold hinged bangle, set with diagonal rows of coral and half pearls, interspersed with rose diamonds.
$1,200-2,100

A diamond line bracelet, set with 40 slightly graduating circular cut diamonds.
$2,200-4,200

A Georgian gold Halley's comet brooch, set with a central emerald, bordered by rose cut diamonds.
$600-1,200

A gold, opal and diamond brooch, pavé set with brilliant and rose cut diamonds, oval and circular opals.
$1,200-2,100

A gold brooch, by Castellani, set with a grey agate scarab, signed, small chips, 19thC.
$1,000-2,000

A Victorian gold and shell cameo bracelet.
$1,600-2,800

A 15ct gold brooch, with onyx stone cameo of Diana in 3 colours, c1860.
$1,700-3,000

A Victorian diamond feather brooch.
$3,200-6,000

A gold brooch with rose diamonds, 19thC.
$800-1,500

A carved shell cameo, 19thC, 2¼in (6cm).
$300-600

A Victorian diamond frog brooch, set with cushion and rose diamonds.
$900-1,700

A Victorian gold, white and dark blue enamelled knot brooch with 17 diamonds, and a pair of similar earrings.
$1,000-2,000

A Victorian diamond and sapphire bee brooch.
$5,000-9,000

A Victorian mosaic demi parure, consisting of a brooch/pendant, earrings and two buttons, in original fitted case, Italian, c1870.
$3,200-6,000

PEARLS

★ pearls have been a favourite form of adornment since the earliest recorded times. Whether they are the beautiful natural oriental pearls taken from the oyster beds of the Far East, or the exquisite little fresh water seed pearls found in profusion in our British rivers since early Roman times, or the cultured pearl, which has been imported and sold in this country since the 1920's, all are highly desirable and all are found inside a shell fish or mollusc

★ the only difference between a natural pearl and a cultured pearl is that in a cultured pearl, the nucleus has been introduced by hand to the oyster, and with a natural pearl it has been formed by accident

★ all pearls from shell fish will feel slightly 'gritty' when rubbed gently along your natural teeth, whilst any artificial variety will feel smooth

★ the only method of identifying natural pearls from the cultured variety is by x-ray or with an endiscope in a gem testing laboratory

A Victorian rose diamond, sapphire, ruby and half pearl butterfly brooch, mounted in silver and gold.
$1,000-2,000

A late Victorian gold, silver, and diamond flower brooch, pavé set with brilliant and rose cut stones.
$3,200-6,000

A 15ct Victorian snake bracelet, with emerald eyes, cabochon garnet, boxed.
$1,600-2,800

A Victorian diamond set bee brooch, with ruby eyes.
$1,000-2,000

A diamond and blue enamel lapel brooch, with rose diamond and blue enamel oval brooch with central initial and coronet.
$600-1,200

An enamelled and diamond mounted regimental brooch, of the Royal Poona Horse Regiment, decorated with red enamel and pavé set with rose diamonds.
$400-900

A Victorian diamond and pearl brooch.
$1,800-3,800

A diamond brooch, set with 10 varying sized collet set circular cut diamonds within pavé set diamond scrollwork.
$6,000-12,000

A pearl and diamond target brooch/pendant.
$1,800-3,800

A modern 9ct gold diamond and ruby bar brooch, in the form of a diamond set fox mask with ruby eyes set on a riding crop.
$400-750

A diamond and ruby brooch, with central ruby flanked by two rows of full cut brilliant diamonds.
$4,000-7,500

A piece of silver cocktail jewellery.
$400-750

A fine quality aquamarine and diamond brooch, with 5 central graduated emerald-cut aquamarines flanked by full brilliant diamonds, terminating at either end with lozenge shaped aquamarines, by Cartier, London.
$5,000-9,000

A platinum and diamond bow.
$4,000-7,500

A pair of Victorian gold carbuncle and diamond fly pendant earrings, inscribed and dated 1871, in original fitted case.
$1,000-2,000

A pair of Victorian gold earrings.
$600-1,100

A pair of diamond flower pendant earrings.
$3,200-6,000

A pair of sapphire earclips, each approx. 5 carats with 10 stone diamond surrounds.
$8000-13,500

A pair of 18ct amethyst and diamond earrings.
$1,300-2,400

And a 15ct amethyst brooch.
$1,000-2,000

A Turkoman Afghanistan necklace, 19thC.
$800-1,500

A topaz necklace and cruciform pendant with earrings en suite, possibly Italian.
$1,700-3,000

A pair of diamond pendant earrings, each with a line of square set brilliants, suspending a single pear shaped diamond in millegrain setting.
$11,000-18,000

An 18ct gold and diamond snake necklace, c1940's.
$10,000-18,000

An 18ct ruby and diamond necklace, c1940's.
$4,500-9,000

A late Victorian diamond necklace.
$6,000-12,000

A late Victorian gold and diamond rivière with 62 graduated 'old mine' brilliants in silver collet settings.
$6,000-12,000

A French 18ct gold enamel and red pearl frame stone cameo, c1850.
$5,000-9,000

An unusual German 'angel' pendant necklace, by Paul Wunderlich, with a central formalised and headless female form with hinged outspread wings on wirework collar, with original receipt for 1979, and fitted case.
$400-900

A gold enamel and pearl pendant cross by Carlo Giulliano, c1860.
$5,000-9,000

A Victorian 29 stone diamond circular target pendant suspended on a diamond set knife edge bar, with detachable brooch pin.
$3,200-6,000

A gold and enamel pendant, set with diamonds and pearls, by Arthur Phillips, c1860.
$2,000-4,500

A gold enamel and pearl pendant cross by Carlo Giulliano, c1860.
$4,000-7,500

An early Victorian French silver brooch, set with miniature portrait and coloured pastes.
$200-450

A Victorian 15ct gold locket, decorated with coloured enamel star design, inset with split seed pearls.
$800-1,500

A 15ct belcher link neck chain.
$400-900

A golden brown amber necklace, restrung in the 'flapper style' of the 1920/30s.
$200-450

A matching pair of earrings with 9ct screw fittings.
$100-250

Amber is the fossilized resin of prehistoric pine trees originating in the Baltic regions. Much of the amber used in Victorian jewellery came from Sicily, whilst quite large amounts have been picked up on the beaches of Norfolk, washed down over a period of time. Always cut 'en cabochon' and often containing the remains of prehistoric insects, vegetation and even fish scales.

Many substances have been produced to simulate precious stones, but in Victorian and Edwardian times great use was made of 'paste' stones, often originating in France. They are made from a very soft lead glass, which when new will pass very well for the 'real thing' in artificial light, but because of its softness will very soon become scratched and lose its original lustre. Often the presence of distinctive 'glass bubbles' will confirm that these stones are artificial.

This must be the most popular design of Victorian locket ever made, and many have stood the test of time by surviving in mint condition, comparing very favourably in price to their modern counterpart. Price will be drastically reduced by any damage or missing stones, etc.

A Boucheron diamond bow.
$4,000-7,500

A very fine 15ct gold citrine intaglio carved seal ring, depicting a slave in prayer with motto in French carved around the edge, 19thC.
$800-1,500

Seal rings have been a popular form of jewellery since ancient times and have been made in a variety of metals both precious and base, and set with all manner of real and imitation stones including glass.

A 15ct gold Victorian brooch/pendant, set with split seed pearls and peridot, in perfect condition.
$800-1,500

This type of brooch was considered highly suitable for a young lady of the Victorian period. It was considered very unladylike for an unmarried woman to wear diamonds, and even if married, it was considered vulgar and ostentatious to wear diamonds in the day time!

DIAMONDS

The 'brilliant cut' for diamonds was invented in the 17th century by a Venetian lapidary named Vincenzo Peruzzi and remained basically much the same for the next 200 years. Most of the diamonds found in Georgian and Victorian jewellery are cut in this way, or if not, the 'rose cut' was used. This is a semi-spherical dome shape of triangular facets (usually 24 or 12 in all) culminating in a point. (Even tiny off-cuts of diamonds were made use of, and were commonly known as 'chips'.) Size was considered of much more importance than colour or quality, and most of the diamonds used in antique jewellery originated in East India or South America. (The stones mined in Brazil sometimes had a definite yellowy tinge, and were commonly known as 'Whisky' diamonds for obvious reasons.) With the discovery of diamonds in South Africa in the mid-19th century there was a shift in the whole world market, and to this day the majority of diamonds come from there.

An Italian gold and Roman mosaic pendant cross, with central circular panel with dove motif.
$600-1,200

An Edwardian style silver and gold mounted diamond open work pendant, with centre heart shaped opal and opal drop, on silver neckchain.
$800-1,500

A gold, silver and diamond circular locket pendant, pavé set with 'old mine' brilliant cut stones, the reverse with glazed cover, late 19thC.
$1,800-3,800

An Edwardian gold, peridot and diamond pendant, of openwork scroll design, pavé and millegrain set with brilliant and rose cut diamonds, key-stone, octagonal and marquise-cut peridots.
$1,400-2,600

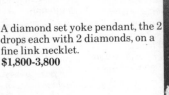

A diamond set yoke pendant, the 2 drops each with 2 diamonds, on a fine link necklet.
$1,800-3,800

A single stone diamond ring, the circular cut diamond in yellow and white 18ct gold mount.
$5,000-9,000

A gold pendant with enamel portrait of a gypsy, set with rose diamonds, with black enamel and rose diamond surround, the whole mounted on a diamond set pendant with non-contemporary decoration and chain loop.
$1,600-2,800

A gold and half stone shell-shaped pendant, with pierced textured gold mount, applied with diamond set scrollwork.
$600-1,200

A Victorian diamond and enamel pendant, centred by a 6 pointed rose diamond star within a blue enamel surround, all on a shaped raised panel with white enamel beading, and similar pendant ring.
$1,200-2,100

An emerald and diamond pendant, pavé set with brilliant cut diamonds, calibré and cushion shaped emeralds, on a fine chain.
$3,200-6,000

A diamond footballer charm, set with baguette diamonds, emeralds, sapphires and rubies.
$1,000-2,000

A Faberge set of 4 gold, platinum and sapphire buttons, each with a single oval cabochon sapphire, millegrain set on a cagework frame with bolt rings to convert to a pair of cuff-links, workmaster August Holming, in fitted case.
$8,000-15,000

A single stone diamond ring, the circular cut diamond with pierced diamond shoulders, plain hoop.
$4,000-7,500

DIRECTORY OF INTERNATIONAL AUCTIONEERS

This directory is by no means complete. Any auctioneer who holds frequent sales should contact us for inclusion in the 1988 edition. Entries must be received by April 1987. There is, of course, no charge for this listing.

AMERICA

Associated Appraisers Inc.
915 Industrial Bank
Building
Providence, RI 02906
Tel: (401) 331-9391

Barridoff Galleries
242 Middle Street
Portland, ME 04 101
Tel: (207) 772-5011

Butterfield & Butterfield
1244 Sutter Street
San Francisco, CA 94109
Tel: (415) 673-1362

California Book Auction
Galleries
358 Golden Gate Avenue
San Francisco, CA 94102
Tel: (415) 775-0424

C. B. Charles Galleries, Inc.
825 Woodward Avenue
Pontiac, MI 48053
Tel: (313) 338-9023

Christie's East
219 East 67th Street
New York, NY 10021
Tel: (212) 570-4141

Representative Offices:
California:
9350 Wilshire Boulevard
Beverly Hills, CA 902 12
Tel: (213) 275-5534

Florida:
225 Fern Street
West Palm Beach, FL 33401
Tel: (305) 833-6592

Mid-Atlantic:
638 Morris Avenue
Bryn Mawr, PA 19010
Tel: (215) 525-5493

Washington:
1422 27th Street N.W.
Washington, DC 20007
Tel: (202)965-2066

Midwest:
46 East Elm Street
Chicago, IL 60611
Tel: (312) 787-2765

DuMochelle Art Galleries
409 East Jefferson
Detroit, MI 48226
Tel: (313) 963-6255

John C. Edelmann
Galleries, Inc.
123 East 77th Street

New York, NY 10021
Tel: (212) 628-1700/1735

Robert C. Eldred Co. Inc.
Box 796
East Dennis, MA 02641
Tel: (617) 385-3116/3377

1808-10 Chestnut Street
Philadelphia, PA 19103
Tel: (215) 563-9275

Garth's Auctions, Inc.
2690 Stratford Road
Delaware, OH 43015
Tel: (614) 362-4771/
369-5085

Kelley's Auction Service
P.O. Box 125
Woburn, MA 01801
Tel: (617) 272-9167

Northgate Gallery
5520 Highway 153

Chattanooga, TN 37443
Tel: (615) 842-4177

O'Gallerie, Inc.
537 S.E. Ash Street
Portland, OR 97214
Tel: (503) 238-0202

Stalker and Boos, Inc.
280 North Woodward
Avenue
Birmingham, MI 48011
Tel: (313) 646-4560

Swann Galleries, Inc.
104 East 26th Street
New York, NY 10021
Tel: (212) 254-4710

Trosby Auction Galleries
81 Peachtree Park Drive
Atlanta, GA 30326
Tel: (404) 351-4400

C. T. Bevensee Auction
Service
P.O. Box 492
Botsford, CT 06404
Tel: (203) 426-6698

Bridges Antiques and
Auctions
Highway 46
P.O. Box 52A
Sanford, FL 32771
Tel: (305) 323-2801/322-
0095

Brookline Auction Gallery
Proctor Hill Road, Route
130
Brookline, NH 03033
Tel: (603) 673-4474/4153

Phillips
867 Madison Avenue
New York, NY 10021
Tel: (212) 570-4830

525 East 72nd Street
New York, NY 10021
Tel: (212) 570-4852

Representative Office:
6 Faneuil Hall
Marketplace
Boston, MA 02109
Tel: (617) 227-6145

Robert W. Skinner, Inc.
Main Street
Bolton, MA 01740
Tel: (617) 779-5528

585 Boylston Street
Boston, MA 02116
Tel: (617) 236-1700

C. G. Sloan & Co.
715 13th Street N.W.
Washington, DC 20005
Tel: (202) 628-1468

Branch Office:
403 North Charles Street
Baltimore, MD 21201
Tel: (301)547-1177

Sotheby Parke Bernet, Inc.
980 Madison Avenue
New York, NY 10021
Tel: (212) 472-3400

1334 York Avenue
New York, NY 10021

171 East 84th Street
New York, NY 10028

Mid-Atlantic:
1630 Locust Street
Philadelphia, PA 19103
Tel: (215) 735-7886

Washington:
2903 M Street N.W.
Washington, DC 20007
Tel: (202) 298-8400

Southeast:
155 Worth Avenue
Palm Beach, FL 33480
Tel: (305) 658-3555

Midwest:
700 North Michigan
Avenue
Chicago, IL 60611
Tel: (312) 280-0185

Southwest:
Galleria Post Oak
5015 Westheimer Road
Houston, TX 77056
Tel: (713) 623-0010

Northwest:
210 Post Street
San Francisco, CA 94108
Tel: (415) 986-4982

Pacific Area:
Suite 117
850 West Hind Drive
Honolulu, Hawaii 96821
Tel: (808) 373-9166

R. W. Bronstein Corp.
3666 Main Street
Buffalo, NY 14226
Tel: (716) 835-7666/7408

Brzostek's Auction Service
2052 Lamson Road
Phoenix, NY 13135
Tel: (315) 678-2542

Buckingham Galleries, Ltd.
4350 Dawson Street
San Diego, CA 92115
Tel: (714) 283-7286

Bushell's Auction
2006 2nd Avenue
Seattle, WA 98121
Tel: (206) 622-5833

Canton Barn Auctions
79 Old Canton Road
Canton, CT 06019
Tel: (203) 693-4901/379-
0500

Fred Clark Auctioneer, Inc.
P.O. Box 124, Route 14
Scotland, CT 06264
Tel: (203) 423-3939/0594

Cockrum Auctions
2701 North Highway 94
St. Charles, MO 63301
Tel: (314) 723-9511

George Cole, Auctioneers
and Appraisers
14 Green Street
Kingston, NY 12401
Tel: (914) 338-2367

Conestoga Auction
Company, Inc.
P.O. Box 1
Manheim, PA 17545
Tel: (717) 898-7284

Cook's Auction Gallery
Route 58
Halifax, MA 02338
Tel: (617) 293-3445/
866-3243

Douglas Galleries
Route 5
South Deerfield, MA 01373
Tel: (413) 665-2877

The Fine Arts Company of

Philadelphia, Inc.
2317 Chestnut Street
Philadelphia, PA, 19103
Tel: (215) 564-3644

George S. Foster III
Route 28
Epsom, NH 03234
Tel: (603) 736-9240

Fred's Auction House
92 Pleasant Street
Leominster, MA 01453
Tel: (617) 534-9004

Col. K. R. French and Co.
Inc.
166 Bedford Road
Armonk, NY 10504
Tel: (914) 273-3674

Gilbert Auctions
River Road
Garrison, NY 10524
Tel: (914) 424-3657

Grandma's House
4712 Dudley
Wheatridge, CO 80033
Tel: (303) 423-3640
534-2847

The William Haber Art
Collection, Inc.
139-11 Queens Boulevard
Jamaica, NY 11435
Tel: (212) 739-1000

Charlton Hall Galleries,
Inc.
930 Gervais Street
Columbia, SC 29201
Tel: (803) 252-7927/779-
5678

Harbor Auction Gallery
238 Bank Street
New London, CT 06355
Tel: (203) 443-0868

Harmer's of San Francisco,
Inc.
49 Geary Street
San Francisco, CA 94102
Tel: (415) 391-8244

Harris Auction Galleries
873-875 North Howard
Street
Baltimore, MD 21201
Tel: (301) 728-7040

William F. Hill Auction
Sales
Route 16
East Hardwick, VT 05834
Tel: (802) 472-6308

The House Clinic
P.O. Box 13013A
Orlando, Fl 32859
Tel: (305) 859-1770/
851-2979

Iroquois Auctions
Box 66, Broad Street
Port Henry, NY 12974
Tel: (518) 942-3355

Julia's Auction Service
Route 201, Skowhegan Road
Fairfield, ME 04937
Tel: (207) 453-9725

Kennedy Antique Auction
Galleries, Inc.
1088 Huff Road
Atlanta, GA 30318
Tel: (404) 351-4464

Kinzie Galleries Auction
Service
1002 3rd Avenue

683

Duncansville, PA 16835
Tel: (814) 695-3479

R. L. Loveless Associates,
Inc.
4223 Clover Street
Honeoye Falls, NY 14472
Tel: (716) 624-1648/1556

Lubin Galleries
30 West 26th Street
New York, NY 10010
Tel: (212) 924-3777

Maison Auction Co., Inc.
128 East Street
Wallingford, CT 06492
Tel: (203) 269-8007

Joel L. Malter and Co., Inc.
Suite 518, 16661 Ventura
Boulevard

Encino, CA 91316
Tel: (213) 784-7772/2181

David W. Mapes, Inc.
82 Front Street
Binghamton, NY 13905
Tel: (607) 724-6741/
862-9365

Mechanical Music Center,
Inc.
25 Kings Highway North
Darien, CT 06820
Tel: (203) 655-9510

Milwaukee Auction
Galleries
4747 West Bradley Road
Milwaukee, WI 53223
Tel: (414) 355-5054

Wayne Mock, Inc.
Box 37
Tamworth, NH 03886
Tel: (603) 323-8057

William F. Moon and
Company
12 Lewis Road, RFD 1
North Attleboro, MA 02760
Tel: (617) 761-8003

New England Rare Coin
Auctions
89 Devonshire Street
Boston, MA 02109
Tel: (617) 227-8800

Park City Auction Service
925 Wood Street
Bridgeport, CT 06604
Tel: (203) 333-5251

Pennypacker Auction
Centre
1540 New Holland Road
Kenhorst, Reading, PA
19607
Tel: (215) 777-5890/6121

Quickie Auction House
Route 3
Osseo, MN 55369
Tel: (612) 428-4378

R & S Estate Liquidations
Box 205
Newton Center, MA 02159
Tel: (617) 244-6616

Bill Rinaldi Auctions
Bedell Road
Poughkeepsie, NY 12601
Tel: (914) 454-9613

Roan, Inc.
Box 118, RD 3
Logan Station, PA 17728
Tel: (717) 494-0170

Rockland Auction Services,
Inc.
72 Pomona Road
Suffern, NY 10901
Tel: (914) 354-3914/2723

Rose Galleries, Inc.
1123 West County Road B
Roseville, MN 55113
Tel: (612) 484-1415

Rosvall Auction Company
1238 & 1248 South

Broadway
Denver, CO 80210
Tel: (303) 777-2032/
722-4028

Sigmund Rothschild
27 West 67th Street
New York, NY 10023
Tel: (212) 873-5522

Vince Runowich Auctions
2312 4th Street North
St. Petersburg, FL 33704
Tel: (813) 895-3548

Sage Auction Gallery
Route 9A
Chester, CT 06412
Tel: (203) 526-3036

San Antonio Auction
Gallery
5096 Bianco
San Antonio, TX 78216
Tel: (512) 342-3800

San Francisco Auction
Gallery
1217 Sutter Street
San Francisco, CA 94109
Tel: (415) 441-3800

Emory Sanders
New London, NH 03257
Tel: (603) 526-6326

Sandwich Auction House
15 Tupper Road
Sandwich, MA 02563
Tel: (617) 888-1926/5675

Schafer Auction Gallery
82 Bradley Road
Madison, CT 06443
Tel: (203) 245-4173

Schmidt's Antiques
5138 West Michigan
Avenue
Ypsilanti, MI 48 197
Tel: (313) 434-2660

Shore Galleries, Inc.
3318 West Devon
Lincolnwood, IL 60659
Tel: (312) 676-2900

Shute's Auction Gallery
70 Accord Park Drive
Norwell, MA 02061
Tel: (617) 871-3414/
238-0586

Robert A. Siegel Auction
Galleries, Inc.
120 East 56th Street
New York, NY 10022
Tel: (212) 753-6421/2/3

Stack's Rare Coin Auctions
123 West 57th Street
New York, NY 10019
Tel: (212) 583-2580

Sterling Auction Gallery
62 North Second Avenue
Raritan, NJ 08869
Tel: (201) 685-9565/
464-4047

Stremmel Auctions, Inc.
2152 Prater Way
Sparks, NV 89431
Tel: (702) 331-1035

Philip Swedler & Son
850 Grand Avenue
New Haven, CT 06511
Tel: (203) 624-2202/562-
5065

Tepper Galleries
110 East 25th Street
New York, NY 10010
Tel: (212) 677-5300/1/2

Trend Galleries, Inc.
2784 Merrick Road
Bellmore, NY 11710
Tel: (516) 221-5588

Valle-McLeod Gallery
3303 Kirby Drive
Houston, TX 77098
Tel: (713) 523-8309/8310

The Watnot Auction
Box 78
Mellenville, NY 12544
Tel: (518) 672-7576

Adam A. Wechsler & Son
905-9 E Street NW
Washington, DC 20004
Tel: (202) 628-1281

White Plains Auction
Rooms
572 North Broadway
White Plains, NY 10603
Tel: (914) 428-2255

The Wilson Galleries
P.O. Box 102
Fort Defiance, VA 24437
Tel: (703) 885-4292

Helen Winter Associates
355 Farmington Avenue
Plainville, CT 06062
Tel: (203) 747-0714/
677-0848

Richard Withington, Inc.
Hillsboro, NH 03244
Tel: (603) 464-3232

Richard Wolffers, Inc.
127 Kearny Street
San Francisco, CA 94 108
Tel: (415) 781-5127

Samuel Yudkin and
Associates
1125 King Street
Alexandria, VA 22314
Tel: (703) 549-9330

AUSTRALIA

A.S.A. Stamps Co. Pty. Ltd.
138-140 Rundle Mall
National Bank Building
Adelaide,
South Australia 5001
Tel: 223-2951

Associated Auctioneers Pty.
Ltd.
800-810 Parramatta Road
Lewisham, New South
Wales 2049
Tel: 560-5899

G. J. Brain Auctioneers Pty.
Ltd.
122 Harrington Street
Sydney,
New South Wales 2000
Tel: 271701

Bright Slater Pty. Ltd.
Box 205 G.P.O.
Lower Ground Floor
Brisbane Club Building,
Isles Lane
Brisbane, Queensland 4000
Tel: 312415

Christie, Manson & Woods
(Australia) Ltd.
298 New South Head Road,
Double Bay
Sydney,
New South Wales 2028
Tel: 326-1422

William S. Ellenden Pty.
Ltd.
67-73 Wentworth Avenue
Sydney,
New South Wales 2000
Tel: 211-4035/211-4477

Bruce Granger Auctions
10 Hopetoun Street
Huristone Park,
New South Wales 2193
Tel: 559-4767

Johnson Bros. Auctioneers
& Real Estate Agents
328 Main Road
Glenorchy, Tasmania 7011
Tel: 725166 492909

James A. Johnson & Co.
92 Boronia Road
Vermont, Victoria 3133
Tel: 877-2754/874-3632

Jolly Barry Pty. Ltd.
212 Glenmore Road
Paddington,
New South Wales 2021
Tel: 357-4494

James R. Lawson Pty. Ltd.
236 Castlereagh Street
Sydney, New South Wales
Tel: 266408

Mason Greene & Associates
91-101 Leveson Street
North Melbourne,
Victoria 3051
Tel: 329-9911

Mercantile Art Auctions
317 Pacific Highway
North Sydney,
New South Wales 2060
Tel: 922-3610/922-3608

James R. Newall Auctions
Pty. Ltd.
164 Military Road
Neutral Bay,
New South Wales 2089
Tel: 903023/902587
(Sydney ex.)

P. L. Pickles & Co. Pty. Ltd.
655 Pacific Highway
Killara,
New South Wales 2071
Tel: 498-8069/498-2775

Sotheby Parke Bernet
Group Ltd.
115 Collins Street
Melbourne, Victoria 3000
Tel: (03) 63 39 00

H. E. Wells & Sons
326 Rokeby Road
Subiaco, West Australia
Tel: 3819448/3819040

Young Family Estates Pty.
Ltd.
229 Camberwell Road
East Hawthorn,
Melbourne 2123
Tel: 821433

NEW ZEALAND

Devereaux & Culley Ltd.
200 Dominion Road
Mt. Eden, Auckland
Tel: 687429/687112

Alex Harris Ltd.
P.O. Box 510
377 Princes Street, Dunedin
Tel: 773955/740703

Roger Moat Ltd.
College Hill and Beaumont
Street
Auckland
Tel: 37 1588/37 1686/
37 1595

New Zealand Stamp
Auctions
P.O. Box 3496
Queen and Wyndham
Streets
Auckland
Tel: 375490/375498

Alistair Robb Coin Auctions
La Aitken Street, Box 3705
Wellington
Tel: 727-141

Dunbar Sloane Ltd.
32 Waring Taylor Street,
Wellington
Tel: 721-367

Thornton Auctions Ltd.
89 Albert Street,
Auckland 1
Tel: 30888 (3 lines)

Daniel J. Visser
109 and 90 Worchester
Street
Christchurch
Tel: 68853/67297

AUSTRIA

Christie's
Ziehrerplatz 4/22
A-1030 Vienna
Tel: (0222) 73 26 44

BELGIUM

Christie, Manson & Woods
(Belgium) Ltd.
33 Boulevard de Waterloo
B-1000 Brussels
Tel: (02) 512-8765/512-8830

Sotheby Parke Bernet
Belgium
Rue de l'Abbaye 32
1050 Brussels
Tel: 343 50 07

CANADA

A-1 Auctioneer Evaluation
Services Ltd.
P.O. Box 926
Saint John, N.B. E2L 4C3
Tel: (508) 762-0559

Appleton Auctioneers Ltd.
1238 Seymour Street
Vancouver, B.C. V6B 3N9
Tel: (604) 685-1715

Ashton Auction Service
P.O. Box 500
Ashton, Ontario, KOA 180
Tel: (613) 257-1575

Canada Book Auctions
35 Front Street East
Toronto, Ontario M5E 1B3
Tel: (416) 368-4326

Christie's International Ltd.
Suite 2002, 1055 West
Georgia Street
Vancouver, B.C. V6E 3P3
Tel: (604) 685-2126

Miller & Johnson
Auctioneers Ltd.
2882 Gottingen Street
Halifax,
Nova Scotia B3K 3E2
Tel: (902) 425-3366/
425-3606

Phillips Ward-Price Ltd.
76 Davenport Road
Toronto, Ontario M5R 1H3
Tel: (416) 923-9876

Sotheby Parke Bernet
(Canada), Inc.
156 Front Street
Toronto, Ontario M5J 2L6
Tel: (416) 596-0300

Representative:
David Brown
2321 Granville Street
Vancouver, B.C. V6H 3G4
Tel: (604) 736-6363

DENMARK

Kunsthallens
Kunstauktioner A/S
Købmagergade 11
DK 1150 Copenhagen
Tel: (01) 13 85 69

Nellemann & Thomsen
Neilgade 45
DK-8000 Aarhus
Tel: (06) 12 06 66/12 00 02

FRANCE

Ader, Picard, Tajan
12, rue Favart
75002 Paris
Tel: 261.80.07

Artus
15, rue de la Grange-
Batelière
75009 Paris
Tel: 523.12.03

Audap
32, rue Drouot
75009 Paris
Tel: 742.78.01

Bondu
17, rue Drouot
75009 Paris
Tel: 770.36.16

Boscher, Gossart
3, rue d'Amboise
75009 Paris
Tel: 260.87.87

Briest
15, rue Drouot
75009 Paris
Tel: 770.66.29

de Cagny
4, rue Drouot
75009 Paris
Tel: 246.00.07

Charbonneaux
134, rue du Faubourg Saint-
Honoré
75008 Paris
Tel: 359.66.57

Chayette
10, rue Rossini
75009 Paris
Tel: 770.38.89

Delaporte, Rieunier
159, rue Montmartre
75002 Paris
Tel: 508.41.83

Delorme
3, rue Penthièvre
75008 Paris
Tel: 265.57.63

Godeau
32, rue Drouot
75009 Paris
Tel: 770.67.68

Gros
22, rue Drouot
75009 Paris
Tel: 770.83.04

Langlade
12, rue Descombes
75017 Paris
Tel: 227.00.91

Loudmer, Poulain
73, rue de Faubourg Saint-
Honoré
75008 Paris
Tel: 266.90.01

Maignan
6, rue de la Michodière
75002 Paris
Tel: 742.71.52

Maringe
16, rue de Provence
75009 Paris
Tel: 770.61.15

Marlio
7, rue Ernest-Renan
75015 Paris
Tel: 734.81.13

Paul Martin & Jacques
Martin
3, impasse des Chevau-
Legers
78000 Versailles
Tel: 950.58.08

Bonhams
Baron Foran,
Duc de Saint-Bar
2, rue Bellanger
92200 Neuilly sur Seine
Tel: (1) 637-1329

Christie's
Princess Jeanne-Marie de
Broglie
17, rue de Lille
75007 Paris
Tel: (331) 261-1247

Sotheby's
Rear Admiral J. A.
Templeton-Cotill, C.B.
3, rue de Miromesnil
75008 Paris
Tel: (1) 266-4060

MONACO

Sotheby Parke-Bernet
Group
P.O. Box 45 Sporting
d'Hiver
Place du Casino,
Monte Carlo
Tel: (93) 30 88 80

HONG KONG

Sotheby Parke Bernet
(Hong Kong) Ltd.
P.O. Box 83
705 Lane Crawford House
64-70 Queen's Road Central
Hong Kong
Tel: 22-5454

ITALY

Christie's (International)
S.A.
Palazzo Massimo
Lancellotti
Piazza Navona 114
00186 Rome
Tel: 6541217

Christie's (Italy) S.R.1.
9 Via Borgogna
20144 Milan
Tel: 794712

Finarte S.P.A.
Piazzetta Bossi 4
20121 Milan
Tel: 877041

Finarte S.P.A.
Via delle Quattro
Fontane 20
Rome
Tel: 463564

Palazzo Internationale delle
Aste ed Esposizioni, S.P.A.
Palazzo Corsini
Il Prato 56
Florence
Tel: 293000

Sotheby Parke Bernet Italia
26 Via Gino Capponi
50121 Florence
Tel: 571410

Sotheby Parke Bernet Italia
Via Montenapoleone 3
20121 Milan
Tel: 783907

Sotheby Parke Bernet Italia
Palazzo Taverna
Via di Monte Giordano 36
00186 Rome
Tel: 656 1670/6547400

THE NETHERLANDS

Christie, Manson & Woods
Ltd.
Rokin 91
1012 KL Amsterdam
Tel: (020) 23 15 05

Sotheby Mak Van Waay
B.V.
102 Rokin
1012 KZ Amsterdam
Tel: 24 62 15

Van Dieten Stamp Auctions
B.V.
2 Tournooiveld
2511 CX The Hague
Tel: 70-464312/70-648658

SINGAPORE and MALAYSIA

Victor & Morris Pte. Ltd.
39 Talok Ayer Street
Republic of Singapore
Tel: 94844

SOUTH AFRICA

Ashbey's Galleries
43-47 Church Street
Cape Town 8001
Tel: 22-7527

Claremart Auction Centre
47 Main Road
Claremont, Cape Town 7700
Tel: 66-8826/66-8804

Ford & Van Niekerk Pty.
Ltd.
156 Main Road
P.O. Box 8
Plumstead, Cape Town
Tel: 71-3384

Sotheby Park Bernet South
Africa Pty. Ltd.
Total House, Smit and
Rissik Streets
P.O. Box 310010
Braamfontein 2017
Tel: 39-3726

SPAIN

Juan R. Cayon
41 Fuencarral
Madrid 14
Tel: 221 08 32/221 43 72/222
95 98

Christie's International Ltd.
Casado del Alisal 5
Madrid
Tel: (01) 228-9300

Sotheby Parke Bernet & Co.
Scursal de Espana
Calle del Prado 18
Madrid 14
Tel: 232-6488/232-6572

SWITZERLAND

Daniel Beney
Avenue des Mousquines 2
CH- 1005 Lausanne
Tel: (021) 22 28 64

Blanc
Arcade Hotel Beau-Rivage,
Box 84
CH- 1001 Lausanne
Tel: (021) 27 32 55/26 86 20

Christie's (International)
S.A.
8 Place de la Taconnerie
CH-1204 Geneva
Tel: (022) 28 25 44

Steinwiesplatz
CH-8032 Zurich
Tel: (01) 69 05 05

Auktionshaus
Doblaschofsky AG.
Monbijoustrasse 28/30
CH-3001 Berne
Tel: (031) 25 23 72/73/74

Galerie Fischer
Haldenstrasse 19
CH-6006 Lucerne
Tel: (041) 22 57 72/73

Germann Auktionshaus
Zeitweg 67
CH-8032 Zurich
Tel: (01) 32 83 58/32 01 12

Haus der Bücher AG
Baumleingasse 18
CH-4051 Basel
Tel: (061) 23 30 88

Adolph Hess AG
Haldenstrasse 5
CH-6006 Lucerne
Tel: (041) 22 43 92/22 45 35

Auktionshaus Peter
Ineichen
C.F. Meyerstrasse 14
CH-8002 Zurich
Tel: (01) 201-3017

Galerie Koller AG
Ramistrasse 8
CH-8001 Zurich
Tel: (01) 47 50 40

Koller St. Gallen
St. Gallen
Tel: (071) 23 42 40

Galerie Koller,
New York Office, Inc.
575 Madison Avenue,
Suite 1006
New York, NY 10022
Tel: (212) 486-1484

Kornfeld & Co.
Laupenstrasse 49
CH-3008 Berne
Tel: (031) 25 46 73

Phillips Son & Neale SA
6 Rue de la Cité
CH-1204 Geneva
Tel: (022) 28 68 28

Christian Rosset
Salle des Ventes,
29 Rue du Rhone
CH-1204 Geneva
Tel: (022) 28 96 33/34

Schweizerische Gesellschaft
der Freunde von
Kunstauktionen
11 Werdmühlestrasse
Ch-8001 Zurich
Tel: (01) 211-4789

Sotheby Parke Bernet AG
20 Bleicherweg
CH-8022 Zurich
Tel: (01) 202-0011

24 Rue de la Cité
CH-1024 Geneva
Tel: (022) 21 33 77

Dr. Erich Steinfels,
Auktionen
Rämistrasse 6
CH-8001 Zurich
Tel: (01) 252-1233 (wine)
       (01) 34 1233 (fine art)

Frank Sternberg
Bahnhofstrasse 84
CH-8001 Zurich
Tel: (01) 211-7980

Jürg Stucker Gallery Ltd.
Alter Aargauerstalden 30
CH-3006 Berne
Tel: (031) 44 00 44

Uto Auktions AG
Lavaterstrasse 11
CH-8027 Zurich
Tel: (01) 202-9444

WEST GERMANY

Galerie Gerda Bassenge
Erdener Strasses 5a
D-1000 West Berlin 33
Tel: (030) 892 19 32/
891 29 09

Kunstauktionen Waltraud
Boltz
Bahnhof Strasse 25-27
D-8580 Bayreuth
Tel: (0921) 206 16

Brandes
Wolfenbütteler Strasse 12
D-3300 Braunschweig 1
Tel: (0531) 737 32

Gernot Dorau
Johann-Georg Strasse 2
D-1000 Berlin 31
Tel: (030) 892 61 98

F. Dörling
Neuer Wall 40-41
D-2000 Hamburg 36
Tel: (040) 36 46 70/36 52 82

Roland A. Exner
Kunsthandel-Auktionen
Am Ihmeufer
D-3000 Hannover 91
Tel: (0511) 44 44 84

Hartung & Karl
Karolinenplatz 5a
D-8000 Munich 2
Tel: (089) 28 40 34

Hauswedell & Nolte
Pöseldorfer Weg 1
D-2000 Hamburg 13
Tel: (040) 44 83 66

Karl & Faber
Amiraplatz 3
(Luitpoldblock)
D-8000 Munich 2
Tel: (089) 22 18 65/66

Graf Klenau Ohg Nachf
Maximilian Strasse 32
D-8000 Munich 1
Tel: (089) 22 22 81/82

Numismatik Lanz
München
Promenadeplatz 9
D-8000 Munich 2
Tel: (089) 29 90 70

Kunsthaus Lempertz
Neumarkt 3
D-5000 Cologne 1
Tel: (0221) 21 02 51/52

Stuttgarter
Kunstauktionshaus
Dr. Fritz Nagel
Mörikestrasse 17-19
D-7000 Stuttgart 1
Tel: (0711) 61 33 87/77

Neumeister Münchener
Kunstauktionshaus KG
Barer Strasse 37
D-8000 Munich 40
Tel: (089) 28 30 11

Petzold KG- Photographica
Maximilian Strasse 36
D-8900 Augsburg 11
Tel: (0821) 3 37 25

Reiss & Auvermann
Zum Talblick 2
D-6246 Glashütten im
Taunus 1
Tel: (06174) 69 47/48

Gus Schiele Auktions-
Galerie
Ottostrasse 7 (Neuer
Kunstblock)
D-8000 Munich 2
Tel: (089) 59 41 92

Gus Schiele Auktions-
Galerie
Paulinen Strasse 47
D-7000 Stuttgart 1
Tel: (0711) 61 63 77

J. A. Stargardt
Universitäts Strasse 27
D-3550 Marburg
Tel: (06421) 234 52

AuktionshausTietjen & Co.
Spitaler Strasse 30
D-2000 Hamburg 1
Tel: (040) 33 03 68/69

Aachener Auktionshaus
Crott & Schmelzer
Pont Strasse 21
Aachen
Tel: (0241) 369 00

Kunstauktionen Rainer
Baumann
Obere Woerthstrasse 7-11
Nuremberg
Tel: (0911) 20 48 47

August Bödiger oHG
Oxford Strasse 4
Bonn
Tel: (0228) 63 69 40

Bolland & Marotz
Feldören 19
Bremen
Tel: (0421) 32 18 11

Bongartz Gelgen Auktionen
Münsterplatz 27
Aachen
Tel: (0241) 206 19

Christie's International Ltd.
Düsseldorf:
Alt Pempelfort 11a
D-4000 Düsseldorf
Tel: (0211) 35 05 77

Hamburg:
Wenzelstrasse 21
D-2000 Hamburg 60
Tel: (4940) 279-0866

Munich:
Maximilianstrasse 20
D-8000 Munich 22
Tel: (089) 22 95 39

Württenberg:
Schloss Langenburg
D-7183 Langenburg

Sotheby Parke Bernet
G.m.b.H.
Munich:
Odeonsplatz 16
D-8000 Munich 22
Tel: (089) 22 23 75/6

Kunstauktion Jürgen
Fischer
Alexander Strasse 11
Heilbronn
Tel: (07 131) 785 23

Galerie Göbig
Ritterhaus Strasse 5
(am Thermalbad)
ad Nauheim
Tel: (Frankfurt)
(611) 77 40 80

Knut Günther
Auf der Kömerwiese 19-21
Frankfurt
Tel: (0611) 55 32 92/
55 70 22

Antiquitaeten Lothar
Heubel
Odenthaler Strasse 371
Cologne
Tel: (0221) 60 18 25

Hildener Auktionshaus und
Kunstgalerie
Klusenhof 12
Hilden
Tel: (02103) 602 00

INDEX

Aalto, Alvar 392
Abraham (Liverpool) 383
Act of Parliament clocks 371
Adam, Rosyth 448
Adams, Rosyth 448
Adams (London) 379
Adams, Dudley 377
Adams, George 449
Adnet, A.J.J. 433
Agra 539
agriculture 666
alabaster 532
albarelli 65
Alcock & Co. 13
Aldin, Cecil 605
Aldridge, Edward 435
ale glasses 186–7
Alekseev, Ivan 640
Allam, Robert 371
Allan, Arthur 596
Allen, Thomas 352
Allshorn (London) 380
alms boxes 586
alms dishes 509
altar tables 609
American China
  Manufactury,
  Philadelphia,
  Pennsylvania
  133
amphoras 423, 532, 600, 619
Amritzar 539
Anderson, David 431
Anderson (New York) 281
andirons 484, 510, 518
Angell, George 449
Angell, John 455, 461
Angell, Joseph 446, 455, 461,
  466
anglers' knives 596
Anthony, Joseph Jr. 437
antiquities 532–9, 617–20
  marble 538, 617–18
  metalware 536–8, 618–19
  miscellaneous 538–9
  pottery 532–6
apothecaries' bottles 188
appliqué 537
Archambo, Peter 435, 445
archery targets 596
architects' tables 331
Ardizzone, Edward Jeffrey
  Irving 606
Arequipa 600
Argyle 505
Argy-Rousseau, G. 493, 502
armchairs 193–4, 197,
  225–8, 272–80, 297, 300,
  394–6, 430
  open 268–278
  upholstered 278–80
armillary spheres 489
armoires 205, 313–17
arms and armour 509, 513,
  667–75
  armour 667–8
  badges 675
  cannon 668
  crossbows 668
  daggers 668–9
  firearms 670–4
  helmets 675
  medals 674
  pistols 509, 672
  rifles 672
  swords 513, 669–70
Arnhem clock sets 391
Arnold, John Roger, & Son
  486
Arras 99
art deco 420–33
  ceramics 420–5, 427–8
  clocks 431
  figures 425–9
  furniture 429–30
  glass 431
  jewellery 431
  metal 432
  miscellaneous 433
  vases 420–1, 423–5, 432
artists' boxes 590
art nouveau 387–410
  boxes 407–8
  carpets 387

ceramics 387–91
  chairs 392
  clocks 391–2
  dishes 398
  furniture 392–3
  glass 397–9
  jarinières 387, 389
  jewellery 400–1
  jugs 391, 397, 403, 406,
    410
  lamps 401–3
  Martinware 403–404
  metal 404–8
  Moorcroft 408–9
  posters 410
  silver 405
  spirit flasks 470
  vases 387–91, 397–9,
    403–4, 407–10
Arts and Crafts movement
  401, 405
Asche, B.S. 512
Ash, Claudius and Sons 382
Ash, Thomas 441, 466
Ashbee, C.R. 500
ashtrays 422
Ashworth Bros. 74
Astbury 76
astrolabes 488
Aubusson 540, 622, 628
Aulenti, Gae 434
Ault 388
Austin, Josiah 454
Austin, Nathaniel 519
Austin, Richard 520
automata 485, 561–2, 632
automaton clocks 370, 374
Axminster 626
Aynsworth (London) 375

Babb, Nicholson 433
bachelors' chests 300, 302
bacon seats 205
badges 675
Baker 604
Baktiari 540
Ball, Black & Co. 436–7
Ballard, A.K. 66
Ballard, O.K. 66
balloon clocks 483
balusters 408
bamboo 608
bangles 677
banqueting tables 337
baptismal bowls 520
Baradelle (Paris) 382
Bard, Conrad, & Son,
  Philadelphia 468
Bardin, Thomas 378
Barker, Robert 471
Barker, Susanna 471
Barlow, Hannah 509
Barnard, Edward 460
Barnard, Edward and Sons
  473
Barnard, E.J. and W. 440–1,
  447, 455, 460–1, 474, 615
Barnard, W.J. 406, 453, 459
Barnish, William 352
Barnsley, Sidney 393, 496–7
barographs 382
barometers 376
Barraud (London) 352
Bartlett, Samuel 454
Bartmann krugs 71
Bartram, James 222
Bary, Thomas-Michel 446
basket grates 516, 518
baskets 91, 435–6, 479,
  506–7
Bassett II, Francis 521
Bassett, Frederick 523
Bassett-Lowke 576
Bateman, Ann 473
Bateman, Hester 446, 466,
  471
Bateman, Peter 473–4
Bateman, William 467
Bates, Theodore Charles 586
Bayes, Gilbert 497, 504
Bayeux 112
Bayley, Edward 360
Bayley, Richard 456

Bayreuth 63
beakers
  glass 538
  horn 666
  pewter 519–20
  porcelain 44
  silver 436, 639
beauty cases 478
Becchi, Alessandro 434
Bechstein 581
Beck, R. and J. 490
Becker, Gustav 375, 383
bedroom suites 504, 652
beds 189–90, 244–5, 650
beds pointer 244
bedside cabinets 654
bedside cupboards 314, 430
bed tables 659
Belcher, Joseph 522
Bell, Edward 352
Bell, Joseph 457
Belleek 112, 132, 140
Bellman, William 352
bellows 667
bells 60, 479
Belouch 540
belts 601
bench tables 215
Benham and Froud 405
Bennett, Murrle, & Co.
  400–1
Bennettini 582
Benson, W.A.S. 401
Bentley, Eli 354
bergeres 226, 274, 277,
  279–80
Berlin 99, 131, 136, 145–6
Berliner 585
Berlin pointers 99
Berry, John 353
Berthelot, John 446
Besnier, Nicholas 615
Bessarabian 540, 623
Bettridge, John 438
Betts, John 583
Bible boxes 586
bicycles 586
Bidjar 622
Biennais, Martin-Guillaume
  616
Bigelow and Kennard 402
Billings, William 522
Bing 586–70, 577–9
Binns, Charles F. 421
binocular microscopes 490
birdcage stands 346
birds 40, 403
Birkle Bros. 371
biscuit boxes 407
biscuit jars 15
Blachford, Samuel 459
blackamoors 329
Blackwell, London 381
Blake, H. 353
Blake, John 352
blanket boxes 301, 660
blankets 601
Bloor 115
bluejohn 618
blunderbusses 670–1
Boardman, Sherman 521,
  523
Boardman, Thomas D. 521,
  523
Boardman, Thomas, & Co.,
  Hartford 519–20
bobbins 646
bonbonnières 591
bonheurs du jour 245
bonnets 544
bookcases 222, 246–55, 394,
  651
  dwarf 248–9
  open 248
  pedestal 251
  revolving 249
bookcases pointer 249
bookstands 248
Boscobel 590
Boteler, J.W., and Brothers
  126
Böttger 42, 102

bottles
  glass 399, 416, 610
  oriental 53, 161, 610–11
  porcelain 161, 599
  pottery 91
  silver 615
  stoneware 600, 630
bottle stands 473
Boucheron 400
Boulton, Matthew 443, 453,
  471, 507
Bouvier, Charles 298
Bow
  bowls 91
  candlesticks 94
  centrepieces 96
  dishes 124
  figures 43, 122–14
  ink pots 43
  mugs 135
  sauceboats 138–9
Bow pointers 107, 113
bowls
  art nouveau 388, 403,
    405–6, 409
  cloisonné 631
  glass 179, 418, 537
  metal 502
  oriental 52, 157–161, 608
  porcelain 44, 48, 91–2, 630
  pottery 9, 13, 37, 40, 388,
    631
  silver 438
  stoneware 403, 411, 600,
    630
  wood 662–3
boxes
  art nouveau 407–8
  glass 416–17
  ivory 477, 588
  jade 611
  lacquer 416–17
  papier mâché 645
  porcelain 44, 93, 423
  silver 407, 438–40
  silver plate 506–7
  tortoiseshell 638
  wood 589, 601
Boynton, Charles 504
bracelets 400, 431, 601, 620,
  676–8
braces 544
bracket clocks 360–4, 482–3
bracket clocks pointer 361
brackets 327, 531
Brander, G.F. 378
brandy warners 506
Brangwyn 424, 599
Brannan 423
brass 405, 432, 508
Brazier, John 672
breakfast sets 425
breakfront bookcases 190,
  232, 246, 248–9, 251
breakfront cabinets 392
breakfront sideboards 329
Breguet 485
Bretby 387
Breveté, Le Roy, & Fils 484
Brewer, John 45
Brigden, Timothy 519
Bristol 40, 60, 124
Broadwood, John, & Sons
  581
bronze
  art nouveau 404–5
  busts 614
  dishes 432
  figures 404, 425–9, 504,
    510–12, 537, 619–20,
    634, 612
  lamps 495
  vases 432, 514, 612, 637
brooches 400–1, 431, 498,
  676–81
Brown, Nathaniel 353
Brown, Robert 459
Brownfield 71, 80
Bru 557
Bruce, William 458
Brussa, Osvaldo 60
brush rests 54
Brussels 42

Bruton, Thomas 355
Bub, Karl 571
buffets 217, 313, 320, 350
bureau bookcases 190, 221,
    246–8, 651
bureau cabinets 192, 232,
    246, 259–61
bureaux 191–2, 221, 255–61,
    393, 496, 656
bureaux pointers 256–8
bureaux de dames 258
bureaux on stands 257
bureaux plats 237
Burnham and Root 408
Burrows, G. 461
Burt, Benjamin 476
Burwash, William 443, 469
Bustelli, F.A. 50
busts
    bronze 404, 510, 512, 614
    ivory 528
    marble 529, 617
    metal 526
    pottery 10–11, 14, 427
    stone 530
    terracotta 422, 532
Butler, Frank 411
butter churns 38
butter dishes 154
butter pails 479
butter tubs 46, 145–6
button hooks 646
buttons 410, 682

cabinet desks 320
cabinets
    art deco 429–30
    art nouveau 392–3
    dwarf 267, 269–70
    oak and country 192
    oriental 612
    pine 660
    side 220
cabinets on chests 230,
    259–60, 307, 430
cabinets on stands 220,
    262–6, 309, 609
caddies 76, 94
caddy spoons 451–2
Cafe, John 441, 446
Cafe, William 442
Calder, William 519
Caldwell, E.F. & Co.,
    New York 437
calipers 489
cameos 678, 680
cameras 384–6
campaign beakers 436
campaign chairs 294
campaign chests 305
Campbell 673
candelabra
    art nouveau 407
    bronze 508, 642
    glass 179–80
    ormolu 516
    porcelain 95–6, 643
    silver 440–1, 615
    silver plate 480, 505
candle holders 513, 663
candle moulds 526
candle snuffers 479, 517
candlestands 214, 346–7
candlesticks
    art nouveau 405, 408
    brass 405
    bronze 642
    glass 180–1
    iron 664
    ormolu 516–17, 642
    pewter 524
    pottery 38
    silver 441–4, 615
    silver plate 480
canes 479, 527
Canner, Christopher 465
cannon 668
canterburies 271–2
canterburies pointer 271
Canton & Shanghai 456
caps 544
carafes 59, 182
card cases 440, 525
Cardew, Michael 599, 630
card tables 232, 236, 238,
    333–4
card tables pointer 332
Carette, Georges 571, 575

Carlton ware 387, 420–1
car mascots 595
Carne, John 353
Carpeaux, Jean-Baptiste 404
carpets 387, 433, 540–4,
    621–6
carpets glossary 541
Carreras 604
carriage clocks 364–6, 483
Carrier, Albert 41
Carrington & Co. 374
Cartier 501
cartoons 410
Cartwright, Newmann 482
carvings 433
carving tables 653
Cary (London) 380
Casartelli, J. 378
caskets
    metal 526
    silver 440
    wood 262, 531, 590, 612
cassoni 311
Castellani 677
Castelli 64, 73
casters 444
casting reels 596
cathedral clocks 375
cats 388
Caucasian 540
Caughley 100, 124, 131–3,
    135, 138
Caughley pointer 124
cauldrons 513
Cayre, Joseph 355
ceiling domes 419
cellarets 350
cellos 581
censers 608–11
centre pieces 96–7, 444, 477,
    505
centre tables 233–4, 236,
    335–6
ceramics 387–91
Cetta, J. 376
Chaffers, Richard 44, 101
chairs
    arm 193–4, 197, 225–8,
    272–80, 297, 300, 430
    art nouveau 392
    campaign 294
    child's 294
    corner 194
    dining 194–5, 224–5, 277,
    281–93, 299
    hall 293–4
    lounge 434
    oak and country 193–7
    pine 651
    side 195–6, 224, 226,
    294–300
    wainscot 193
    Windsor 195–7
chairs pointer 291, 296
chaises longues 326, 434
chalices 519, 524
Chamberlain, Robert 47,
    106, 130, 140, 144
chamberpots 506
chandeliers 401, 515, 526
character dolls 559
chargers 389, 518, 524
Charpentier (Paris) 374
Chawner, Henry 455, 467
Chedel (Paris) 366
cheese boards 662
cheese presses 660
cheese scoops 477
Chelsea
    bowls 44, 100
    candlesticks 95
    jardinières 132
    plates 43, 124
    services 140
    tureens 145
Chelsea pointers 125
Chermayeff, S. 430
cherry pippers 663
Chesne, Claudius de 353
chess sets 527, 580
chestnut baskets 47
chests 198–200, 229, 300–6,
    311, 396, 651–2
    bombé 306
    dwarf 303, 306
chest of drawers 199–200,
    217, 304, 306, 309, 652
chests on chests 200, 222,
    306–8

chests pointer 304
chests on stands 199, 308–9
cheval mirrors 325
cheverets 340
Chiappa 581
Chiapparelli, P. 512
chiffoniers 267–70, 656–7
*Chinese dynasties and marks
    pointer* 178
Chinese porcelain pointers
    162, 174
Chiparus, Demetre 425–6,
    428–29
Chiparus, Gazan 432
Chollar, Thomas P. 66
chondrometers 383
christening sets 406
Christian, Philip 133
Christofle 434
chromolithographs 433
chronograph watches 486
chronometers 376, 486
Chun Yao 157
cigar cases 439
cigar cutters 410, 475
cigarette boxes 514
cigarette cards 604
cigarette cases 432, 439, 503,
    507, 591
cigar lighters 475
clamps 663
claret jugs 58, 474
clarinets 581
Clark, William 355
Clark & Company, Augusta,
    Georgia 476
Clarkson (London) 379
clerks' desks 320
Clews 86
Clichy 60
Cliff, Clarice 424–5, 502
clock cases 97, 387
clocks
    Act of Parliament 371
    art nouveau 391–2
    bracket 360–4, 482–3
    carriage 364–6, 483
    dial 375
    garnitures 373–4
    glass 419
    lantern 370
    longcase 352–60, 482, 660
    mantel 366–70, 391, 484
    miscellaneous 374–5,
    391–2
    regulators 360, 484
    skeleton 370–1
    table 374, 391, 484, 501
    wall 371–3
clocks pointers 352–3, 358,
    361
cloisonné enamel 608–9, 631
cloth 601
clothes presses 316
coal boxes 351, 525
Coalbrookdale 91, 114, 146
Coalport 100, 125, 133, 140,
    146
coal scuttles 515, 525
coasters 473
coats 546
cocktail shakers 432
coffee pots
    pewter 520
    porcelain 48
    pottery 42, 76
    silver 445, 447, 467
    tôle 475
coffee services 387, 461–4
coffee sets 420, 432, 556
coffers 198–200, 311, 652
coffers on stands 229
coins 648–50
Coker, Ebenezer 442–3, 458
Cole, Thomas 374
Coleman, C. 380
Colinet, C.J.R. 425
Collet, Edward-Louis 426
Collier, David 355
Colston, Richard 355
comb morion 667
commemorative 11–15, 411
commodes 229–30, 311–13
compacts 400
companion sets 587
compendiums 488
comports 387, 445
compotes 436–7, 600
Comyns, W. 436, 477

concertinas 581
Concord Watch Co. 498
condiment jars 477
condiment sets 407, 507
conservatory tables 336
console tables 235, 336
Constantinidis, Joanna 599
Cooke, Welton & Gemma Ltd
    577
Cookson, Isaac 446
Cooper, W. 376
Cope 604
Copeland 114, 140, 387, 597
Copeland, Elizabeth E. 407
Coper, Hans 630
copper 510, 514–16
cordial glasses 186
corkscrews 471
corner cabinets 654
corner chairs 194
corner cupboards 203–5,
    314–15, 393, 656
corner cupboards pointer 314
corsets 545
cosmetic boxes 586
costume 544–6
Cosway, Richard 647
cottages 15–16, 98
Cottell (Crewkerne) 355
Courtauld, Augustine 457
Courtauld, Samuel 441
court cupboards 201, 202–5
cow creamers 16–18, 39, 479
Cox & Coombs 379
cradles 245
crafts 599–600
Crane, Walter 389
Cranendonck, I. de 379
Creak, George 448
cream boats 155
cream jugs 58
cream pitchers 437, 454
creamware
    jugs 12
    plates 62
    tea caddies 76
    teapots 11, 77
    tureens 79
    vases 81
creamware pointer 12
credenzas 270–1
credenzas pointer 271
Crescent 571
Crespell, S 443
crested china 156
crested china pointers 156
Creswick, T., J. and N. 444
cricket tables 215, 658
crimping machines 666
crinoline hoops 545
croquet sets 596
cross bows 632, 668
Crosse, Richard 647
crosses 405
Crossley, Richard 448
Crouch, I. John 457–9, 468,
    616
croziers 614
crucifixes 516, 639
cruets 422, 479, 506
Crump, Francis 465
crystal sets 592
Cuff, John 490
cupboards 201–6, 313–17,
    392–3, 652–6
cups
    glass 432
    oriental 161–2, 639
    porcelain 49, 51, 99–106
    silver 407, 447–8, 614
    wood 666
Currier, Edmund 357
curtains 550–2
cutlery 448–51
cutlery boxes 587
Cuzner, Bernard 400
cylinder bookcases 248
cylinder bureaux 225, 248,
    257–9
Cyrillic 640

daggers 668–9
daisho 670
Dali, Salvador 434
Dancer, J.B. 380
Danforth, Edward 522
Danforth, Joseph 523
Danforth, Thomas 522–3

Danfrie, Philipus 489
Daniel, H. & R. 125
D'Argental 397
darning mushrooms 663
Daum 493–4
Daum, Nancy 397
Davenport 141
davenports 238, 317–18
davenports pointers 318
Davies, Ann 629
Davies, Margaret 412–14
Davis, Moss & Co. 440
Dax 428
Day, Robin 430
days beds 496
Deacon, Samuel 355
Deans (London) 672
Deans Rag Book Co. Ltd 560
Decamps 574
decanter boxes 587
decanters 58, 181–3, 431
decanter stands 473, 645
decoys 598
Deffener, Ludwig 484
de Lamerie, Paul 457
Delaville, Louis 530
Delft
    Bristol 40, 63, 78, 83–4
    Dublin 81
    Dutch 62–3, 73, 76
    English 9
    Lambeth 36, 65
    Liverpool 9, 38, 61, 78, 83
Della Robbia 387
De morgan, William 389,
    391, 500
Dempsey, William 673
dental instruments 382
dentists' cabinets 261
Denver China and Pottery
    Company 600
Denziloe, John 466
Derazey, Honoré 582
Derby
    candlesticks 95
    coffee cans 100–1
    dishes 126
    figures 107–9, 114–16
    jardinières 138
    plates 125–6
    services 44–5, 141
    stirrup cups 100
    tureens 145
    vases 146–7
Derby, Royal Crown 95
Derby pointers 108
Deruta 42
desks 222, 319–20, 393–4,
    434, 497, 656
desk sets 510, 516
dessert baskets 478
dessert services 44–5
dessert sets 399
detectors 592
deudarns 206
De Vez 397
dial clocks 375
dials 377
diamonds pointer 681
Dickson, John & Son 673
die-cast models pointer 565
dining chairs 194–5, 224–5,
    277, 281–93, 299
dining room suites 430
dining tables 212–13, 233,
    336–7, 497
dinner gongs 527
dinner services 47, 424
diptych 527
dirks 669
dishes
    art nouveau 398
    copper 515
    enamel 631, 634
    glass 398, 419
    oriental 53, 57, 638
    papier mâché 645
    pewter 519
    porcelain 47, 155
    pottery 12, 42, 62, 421
    silver 452–3, 475
    silver plate 505
    stoneware 600
dish rings 477
Disneyalia 607
display cabinets 192, 264–6,
    393, 489, 496, 609
Doccia 138
Dodd, P.G. & Son 360

Dollond (London) 379
dolls 556–61
dolls' houses 562–3
Donald, W. 355
Donegal 624
door knobs 407–8
door knockers 614
door porters 508
doors 495, 633
door stops 517
Doulton 74, 411–12
Doulton pointers 411
Doulton, Royal 412–15, 597,
    599
    figures 497
        HN1747, HN1945,
        HN2085, HN2086,
        HN2087, HN2088 412
        HN379, HN733,
        HN1267, HN1708,
        HN1740, HN1834,
        HN1927, HN1943,
        HN2191, HN2712 413
        HN88, HN100, HN301,
        HN423, HN610,
        HN1204, HN1222,
        HN1361, HN1365,
        HN2115, HN2122 414
    figures pointer 412
    jugs 13, 415
    plates 47
dower chests 325–6
dragon jars 56
dram glasses 187
drawing compendiums 382
draw knives 665
draw-leaf tables 215
Dresden 97, 109, 137
dress clips 431
Dresser, Christopher 388–9,
    405–6, 408
dressers 206–10, 217, 320,
    496, 656–7
dresses 545–6
dressing chests 303–4, 306,
    657
dressing gowns 544
dressing mirrors 324
dressing stools 331
dressing tables 657
dressing table sets 477–8,
    586
dressing table tidies 478
dressing table trays 407
drinking glasses 183–7, 495
drinking sets 405
drop-leaf tables 212–13, 338
drug jars 64–5
drum pot cupboards 654
drums 514, 674
drum tables 236, 338
Drury, Alfred 614
Dubacand, A. 511
Duchesne (Paris) 485
dumb waiters 320–1
dumb waiters pointers 321
Dunand, Jean 502
Dunant, William 483
Dunham, Rufus 42
Dunn, F. & Co. 512
Du Paquier, Claudius
    Innocentius 105
Durst, Alan Lydiat 433
Dussaussoy 677
Dutton (London) 371

earclips 679
ear pendants 498
earrings 537, 679–81
easels 660
East, John 445
Eastlake, Charles 496
Eaton, William 445, 457,
    460, 463
Eavestaff 504
Edison 584–5
Edmonds & Company,
    Charlestown,
    Massachusetts 66
Edouard, Guy 406
Edwards, Edward 439
effigies 561
Egg, D. 673
eggs 508
Eickhorn Original 669
elbow chairs 221
electrical 591–2
Eley, William 479

Eley and Fearn 449
Elkington & Co. 445, 505,
    507
Elliot, George 360
Elliott, William 453, 469
Elton 387
embroidery 546–7
Emery, Stephen 444
Emes, John 447, 453, 478
Emes & Barnard 472
enamels 408, 591, 608
encriers 416–17
Engleheart, George 648
Engler (Bordeaux) 369
epergnes 445
ephemera 603–8
Erfurt 80
Erikson, Ruth 402
escritoires 261
etagères 240, 350
Evans (London) 381
Evans & Wormall 381
Evans, W.F., and Sons 371
Ewen, John 471
Ewenny 71, 80, 84
ewers 55, 162, 387–8, 454,
    499

Fabergé 632, 639
face screens 646
faience 65, 74–5, 80
fairings 107
fairyland lustre 92
famille rose 55, 631
famille verte 54–5
fans 553–5
Farquhar, William 376
Farrell, Edward Cornelius
    616
Faubourg St Denis 142
fauteuils 277
Favrile 399, 493, 500
Feline, Edward 446, 452
Fenton 674
Fenton, Jonathon 66
Fenton, M. & Co. 480
Ferguson, James 647
fibulas 538
Fiesole, Mino da 617
figures
    animal 19–23, 43, 107–12
    art deco 425–9
    bronze 404, 425–9, 504,
        510–13, 537, 612,
        619–20, 634
    glass 610
    ivory 428–9, 501, 527–8,
        611
    limestone 539
    marble 529
    metal 526
    oriental 52–4, 162–4, 609
    ormolu 516
    people 23–35, 112–23
    plaster 433
    porcelain 48–9, 107–23,
        639
    pottery 19–35, 39, 52–4,
        89–90, 415, 423, 426–7,
        536
    silver 599
    spelter 525, 597–8
    Staffordshire 19–34, 39
    stone 530, 632
    stoneware 411, 497
    terracotta 530, 532–4, 536
    tribal 601–3
    Wedgwood 41
    wood 433, 531, 633
Finney (Liverpool) 356
firearms 670–4
fire dogs 515
fireplaces 321, 660
firescreens 325–6
fire tools 351
Fischer & Co. 568
Fish, Henry 361
fish bowls 55–6
fishing 596
Fisler, Ebenezer 356
Fitz-Simone, Catherine 628
Fladgate, John 361
flagons 474, 520
flasks 60, 389, 415, 475
flatware 14–15, 36, 61–4,
    124–31, 164–8
flatware services 450
Flavelle, Henry 472
flax-bashers 666

flax–cutters 666
Fleischmann 571
Flight, Barr and Barr 47,
    106, 150
flintlocks 671
floor lamps 491
flour scoops 661
fluid lamps 521
folding chairs 225
Foley 387–8, 420
folio stands 330
fonts 330
Forbes, William Garret 435
forks 661–2
Fornasetti, Piero 423, 434
Fothergill (Knaresborough)
    356
Fothergill, John 471
Fountain, William 458
fountains 612
Fox, Charles 436, 446, 457,
    461, 473
Fox, Charles T. 443, 446,
    453, 473
Fox, George 443, 453, 473
Fox, Mordecai 444
fragments 529, 538
frames 508, 516
Frankenthal 48, 94, 100,
    116, 126
Frankenthal pointer 116
Fraureuth 423
Fray, James 471
Frisbee, William 467
Fritzsche, Otto 497
Frodsham, Charles 361
fruit baskets 506
Fulda 48
Fuller, Crispin 471, 477
furniture
    art deco 429–30
    art nouveau 392–3
    beds 189–90, 244–5, 650
    bonheurs du jour 245
    bookcases 246–55, 651
    breakfront bookcases 190,
        232, 246, 248–9, 251
    bureaux 191–2, 217,
        221–2, 255–61, 393, 496,
        656
    cabinets on chests 259–60,
        307, 430
    cabinets on stands 217,
        262–3, 309, 609
    canterburies 271–2
    chairs 193–7, 224–8,
        272–300, 651
    chests 198–200, 217,
        300–6, 311, 651–2
    chests on chests 200, 222,
        306–8
    chests on stands 199,
        308–9
    commodes 229–30, 311–13
    cupboards 201–6, 313–17,
        392–3, 652–6
    desks 319–20, 393, 434,
        656
    davenports 317–18
    display cabinets 192,
        264–6, 393, 496, 609
    dressers 206–10, 217, 320,
        496, 656–7
    dumb waiters 320–1
    fireplaces 321
    globes 377–8
    lowboys 212–13, 322
    mirrors 231, 322–5, 479,
        505, 531, 538, 658
    miscellaneous 351
    oak and country 189–215
    oriental 609
    pine 650–61
    screens 325–6, 517, 609,
        638
    secretaire bookcases
        252–5, 651
    secretaire cabinets 220–1,
        259–62
    settees 226, 326–7
    shelves 327
    sideboards 327–9, 392,
        430, 658
    side cabinets 192, 217,
        267–71
    stands 215, 329–30, 393
    steps 330
    stools 210–11, 228, 330–1,
        603, 658

tables 211–15, 217, 232–8, 331–49, 497
teapoys 349
wardrobes 317, 659
wellington chests 311
washstands 349–50, 659
whatnots 350, 609
wine coolers 131, 350–1, 473, 507
Furstenburg 91, 137

Gallaher 604
Gallé, Emile 388, 392–8, 401, 492–4
Galloway, J. 355
games 580
games tables 238, 338
gaming balls 527
gaming pieces 533
Garbe, Richard 413
garden fountains 41
garden furniture 327
garden seats 57, 169, 518
garden stools 389
garden urns 517
Gardiner, Baldwin 454
Gardner Factory 639
garnitures 38, 51, 373–4, 398, 406
Garrard, Robert 460, 472
Gate, Simon 495
gateleg tables 211–13, 233, 236, 339
gates 517
Gaudron (Paris) 368
gauntlets 667
gavels 527
Geill, Matthias 485
generators 383
Gibbons, John 465
Gibson, W. 443
Gill, Robert 671
Gillow & Company334
Gilmour, Margaret 510
Gimson, Ernest 496–7
ginger jars 421, 423–4, 502
Guilliano, Carlo 680
glass
    art nouveau 397–9
    bottles 399, 416, 755
    bowls 179, 418, 539
    boxes 416, 17
    candelabra 280–1
    candlesticks 280–1
    decanters 181–3
    dishes 419
    drinking glasses 183–7
    figures 610
    flasks 60
    inkwells 416–17
    jugs 58
    mugs 59
    oriental 610
    paperweights 188
    scent bottles 188, 416–17
    sculptures 630
    vases 188, 397–9, 417–18, 500, 610
Glasshüten 494
Gleason, Roswell 519, 521
globes 238, 377–8
Glynne, R. 377
goblets 183, 399, 456
Godrey, Benjamin 614
Gogerty (London) 379
gold 614, 620
Goldscheider 423, 427–8
golfing 597, 599
Gorevan 541
Gorham & Co. 461–2, 476
Gorham Manufacturing Co., Providence 437, 458, 468, 470
Gori, A. 501
Goss china 156
Goss china pointers 156
Gould, Christopher 361
Gould, William 442
Graham, Geo. 482
Graham, John 435
grain bins 660
Grainger, George 134
Grainger, Lee & Co. 136
gramophones 585–6
Grand Feu, Los Angeles 600
Granger 668
Green, James 356
Green, John & Co. 443
Greene & Greene 396

Griffiths, E.J. 413
Grimalde & Johnson 366
Griswold, Ashbil 519–20
groups
    bamboo 608
    bronze 499, 511–13, 603, 612, 613–14
    horn 528
    lead 525
    porcelain 50, 414
    pottery 38–9, 391, 411
    spelter 598
Grover & Baker 646
Grueby 402
Guild of Handicrafts 405, 410
guns 671
Gunthermann 569, 571
Gurschner, Gustav 405, 426
gyroscopes 382

Hackwood, William 41
Hagen, Ernest 275
half-chanfrons 667
Halfhide, A.E. 365
Hall 592
Hall, Martin & Co. 464
hall benches 330
hall chairs 293–4
Hamadam 621
Hamilton, Robert 466
Hamilton & Co. 468
Hamley (London) 574
Hamlin, Samuel 522
Hampson (Bolton) 356
Hanau 71
Hancock, C.F., & Co. 474
handkerchiefs 553
Handel 402
Hands, D. & C. 447
handscreens 555, 645
hangers 669
hanging cupboards 201, 204–5, 314, 317
Hannam, Thomas 459
Hannoversch-Münden 75
Hans (Paris) 372
Hardy 596
Harradine, L. 412–14
Harris, C.S. 436, 477
Harris, Jeffery 361
Harris, Joseph 646
Harrison, Thomas 355
Hartman, Georgius 488
Haseler, W.H. 499
Haselwood, Elizabeth 447
hat and coat stands 330
hat-maker's blocks 665
hats 544
Hausmaler 147
Haviland, Theodore 422
Haviland & Co, Limoges 126
Hawkes & Co. 670
Heal, Ambrose 393, 430
Hearnshaw Bros. 664
Heath, Thomas 489
Heath & Middleton 406, 443
Heeley, Benjamin 356
Heer-Schofield Company, Baltimore 452
Hel, Joseph 582
Helical Co. 596
Hellis, Charles & Sons 671
helmets 675, 526, 667–8, 675
Hennell, Robert 467, 479
Henry, Guillaume 447
Henry, S. 383
Herberts, John William 383
Herculaneum 68
Heriz 621
Heubach, Gebrüder 557
Heyer, William B. 442
Heywood Brothers, Gardner, Massachusetts 254
Hicks, J. 382, 472
Hicks and Meigh 81
Higgins, Francis 449
Higgs, Robt and Peter 483
Hill, Edward 254
Hill, Thomas 254
Hill, W.E., & Sons 581–2
Hille 430
Hilliard & Thomason 439
hinges 432
hip flasks 470
Hispano-Moresque 42, 62
Hitchcock, Thomas 582
Höchst 116–17
Höchst pointer 117

hods 515
Hoge Mfg. Co. 569
Holaday, Sarah 465
Holland, Son and Slater 463
Hollingshead, John 354
Hollingshead, Joseph 354
Hollingshead, William 476
Holmes, Thomas 356
Holmes, William 447, 457
Holtzapffel 665
Holtzapffel & Deyerlein 665
Hooke, C.W. 356
hop measures 666
horn 610
Hornby 578–9
Höroldt, J.G. 48
horse spills 22
Houle, John 435
Hovander 439
Howard, Frank H. 582
Howard & Sons 335
Howden, Francis 471
Howell, James, & co. 367
Hubatsch 423
Huber, Patriz 499
Hughes, Thos. 483
Hukin & Heath 405–6, 506
humidores 406
Hunt, John Mortimer 466
Hunt, J.S. 440, 472, 475
Hunt & Roskell 374, 456, 466
Huntley & Palmer 571
Hurd, Jacob 476
Hutton, William & Sons 406–7
Hyde (Bristol) 378
Hyde and Goodrich, New Orleans 454, 476
hydria 532

Iakovlev, Vasili 640
ice pails 131, 476
Ichino, Shigeyoshi 599
icons 633
illustrations 433, 504
Imari 56–7
incense stick holders 608
ink pots 43
inkstands 453–4, 505, 514, 517, 525, 587
inkwells 131, 155, 500
inros 610
Intarsio ware 387–8, 420
irons 663
ironstone 70, 80–2
Isfahan 540–1, 621, 623
ivory 428–9, 501, 527–8, 587–8, 610–11

Jackfield 67
Jacobs 477
Jacot, Henri 365–6
jade 611
Jaeger le Coultre 391
jambiya 670
Japanese art periods pointer 168
Japy frères 373
Jardinières
    art nouveau 19, 393, 397
    brass 509, 516
    oriental 169
    porcelain 132
    pottery 19, 41
    wood 329, 393
jars
    oriental 170–1
    pottery 52, 64–5, 532, 662
    stoneware 599–600
    terracotta 530
Jarvie, Robert 406
Jarvis, James 376
Jasperware 86
Jeffries, C. 581
jelly moulds 661
Jennens, J.C., & Son 373
Jennens & Bettridge 644
Jensen, George 432, 464, 615–16
jewellery 400–1, 431, 498, 676–81
Jian Yao 157
jingles 595
Joel, Betty 430
Johnson, E. 477
Johnson, H. 383
Johnson, W. & A.K. 377

Jones, Ball & Co., Boston 454
Jones, George 9, 75, 80, 86
Jones, Gershom 522
Jones, Henricus 482
Jones, Henry 361
Jones, John II 438
Joubert, Felix 512
Joubert, Francois 447
jugs
    art deco 424
    art nouveau 391, 397, 403, 406, 410
    commemorative 11, 13–14, 411
    creamware 12
    glass 397, 406
    oriental 55
    porcelain 47, 51, 132–5, 153
    pottery 11–14, 37, 67–71, 403, 410, 415, 424, 503, 597
    silver 455, 475
    Toby 38, 39
jukeboxes 586
Jumeau, Emile 557
Juval 543

Kähler, Hermann 428
Kakiemon 44, 57, 91
Kalo 406
Kammer & Reinhardt 559, 585
Kander, Charles F. 452
Kandler, J.J. 49–50
Karabagh 541
Karland, Nikols 449
Kashan 541–2, 622, 625
Kauba, C. 410, 425
Kavanagh 671
Kazak 542
Kelbrik, Peggy 628
Kelim 541–3
Kempton, Roger 479
Kessler 512
Kestner, J.D. 557–8
kettles 405, 506, 510, 514–15, 632
keys 524
Khotan 621
Kico 570
Kilim 624
kindjal 670
King, Jessie M. 400, 410
Kingsbury 575
Kirk, Samuel 474
Kirman 540–1, 625
kitchenalia 661–7
Klinger, J.G. 377
Kloster-Veilsdorf 94, 109, 119
knife boxes 587
knives 601
Knox, Archibald 391–2
Knox, John 356
Koehler, Mela 604
Kolfmann 647
koros 57
Kostrinsky, Andrei 639
Kovsh 639
KPM 136, 423
Krider, Peter L. 468
Kruse, Kathe 560
Kuba 542
Kullberg, Victor 376
Kum Kapu 624
Kurdish 542
Kusmitshev, Antip 449
Kyoto-Satsuma 57

lace 547–8
lace boxes 590
Lacloche Frères 431, 503
lacquer 589, 611–12, 634
ladles 450, 661
Lake Windermere 596
Lakin & Poole 24
Lalique, René 401, 416–19, 502, 595
Lalique, René, pointer 416
Lallemant 422
Lambert 592
lamps
    art deco 425–6
    art nouveau 401–4
    bronze 418, 491–2
    pewter 521

postwar 434
  silverplate 506,642
lampshades 401,433
lamp stand bases 536
lamp tables 347
Lancaster, Osbert 606
Langlands, John 456
Langlands & Robertson 471
Langlois 112
Langman, J. 443
Langshaw, John 582
Lanteri, Ed. 499
lantern clocks 370
lanterns 423,493,516,525
Lanz, J.W. 48
Lapierre 576
Laporte-Blairsy, Leo 495
Larche, Raoul 404
Larcombe, Ethel 605–6
lathes 665
Laughlin, John Jnr. 459
Laurel 426
Lautier, Benjamin 362
Lawrence & Co. 438
Lawson, William 358
Leach, Bernard 630
Leach, Janet 599
Leach, John 599
lead 524–5
lead soldiers 564–6
Lebrun 457
Lederer, Hugo 426
Lee, Richard 523
Leeds 77
Le Faguays 426
Lefevre 388
Legras 398
Lehmann 567,571,574
lekythos 137
Leleu, G. 401
Le Nove 103,116
Lenci 422,427–8
Lesney Yesteryear 572
letter balances 383
letter boxes 590
letter openers 475
Le Verrier, M. 425
Levy 571
Lias, I.H. and G. 460
Liberty & Co. 392,400,
  406–7
library bookcases 249–50
library globes 238
library steps 330
library tables 233–4,339,
  347,394
lighters 598
lighting 643
Likarz, Maria 604
Limehouse pointer 101
limewood 531
Limbach (Hull) 117,376
Limoges 423,502
line driers 596
linen presses 316–17 393,
  654
Lines Bros. 573
Linthorpe 388–9
lions 42,613
liqueur sets 499
liquor services 493
Liverpool
  bowls 9,101
  candlesticks 38
  dishes 126
  jugs 68,133,138
  mugs 44
  sauceboats 138
Liverpool pointers 101
livery cupboards 202–4
Lloyd, Philip 362
lockets 676,681
Locle, F. William Dubois 486
lock-joint tools 596
locks 524
lodestones 510
Loetz 398–9,493
Logan, George 420
Lomax, James 358
longcase clocks 352–60,482,
  660
longcase clocks pointer 358
Longton Hall 44,91,101,
  109,146
loo tables 339–40
Loring, Joseph 465
Lott, John 583
lounge suites 327
loving cups 18,415

lowboys 212–13,322
Lowestoft 153–5
Lowestoft pointers 153–5
Ludwigsburg 109,116–17
Ludwigsburg pointer 109
Luneville 42
lustres 181

MacDonald, Barbara 425
Macintyre Moorcroft pointer
  409
McKay, John 475
Mackennal, Bertram 404
McQuade, P. 577
magazine stands 395
maiolica
  bowls 9
  dishes 62,87,89
  ewers 89
  figures 20,90
  jardinières 87
  jugs 90
  stands 88
  teapots 78
  tureens 80
  vases 90
  wall brackets 86
Malloch 596
Mane, Enrique Salva 581
mantel clocks 366–70,391,
  484
mantles 545
Manton, John & Son 672
Maple & Co. 358
Mappin and Webb 364,438,
  444,463,478
marble 528–30,538,617–18
Marcolini 110,127
Marconi 592
Margaine, François-Arsène
  365,483
Marklin 578–9
Marples, Robert 665
Marquand & Co., New York
  458
marrow scoops 476
Marseille, Armand 558
Marsh & Tatham 232
Marshall, John 448
Marshall & Sons 464
Marti and Cie 373
Martin, F. 431,568
Martin, R.W. & Brothers 497
Martin & Hall 463
Martin Brothers 403–4,497
Marusan 571
Masatamo 612
mascots 408,419,595
masks 423,433,538,601,
  633,638
Mason 70,82
Masonicalia 454
matchlock carbines 671
match strikers 599
Mathieson 665
Mathsson, Bruno 434
Maw & Co. 389
Maw & Staley 665
Mayr, Peter 647
Mealing, Richard 664
measures 515,518,661,666
measuring jars 619
meat presses 507,663
mechanical toys 559
medallions 401
medals 514,526,598,674
medical instruments 380–2
Meikei, Seihosai 636
Meir, John & Son 80
Meissen
  baskets 91
  bowls 48,51,101–3
  boxes 93
  butter tubs 146
  candlesticks 95–6
  clock cases 97
  cups 51,102–4
  dishes 126–7
  figures 49–50,109–111,
    117–19
  ice pails 131
  jugs 133–4
  plates 49,126–7
  sauce boats 139
  services 141
  snuff boxes 49–50
  tea caddies 51,94
  tea pots 145
  tureens 146

vases 147–8
Meissen pointer 102
Melling, Jno 482
Melville, David 522–3
Mene, Pierre Jules 511
Mennecy 122
menus 410
Merritt 592
Meshed 593
Messter, Edward 383
metalware
  art nouveau 404–8
  brass 405,432,508,
    509–10
  bronze 510–14
  copper 514–16
  iron 517–18
  lead 524–5
  miscellaneous 525–6
  ormolu 516–17
  pewter 518,524
Métayer, Louis 49
metronomes 586
Mettoy 568
Meunier (Paris) 370
Meyr's Neffe 399
microphones 592
microscopes 379–80,490
militaria 675
milking stools 666
Mills, Nathaniel 438,440
minaudières 431,503
Ming 53–5,634
miniatures 647–8
Minton
  bowls 89
  dishes 87
  ewers 89
  figures 90,120
  garden fountains 41
  garden seats 389
  jardinières 41,87–8,389
  jugs 90
  pottery 389
  services 45
  stick stands 88
  teapots 90
  vases 41,147
Minton maiolica pointer 86
mirrors
  art nouveau 393
  bronze 538
  silver 479
  silver plate 505
  wood 231,322–5,531,658
mirrors pointer 323
mirror cases 528
mirrors on stands 528
Miyao 612
moccasins 544
models
  bronze 511
  copper 516
  ivory 529
  oriental 56–7
  pottery 52,536,620
  silver 455–6
  terracotta 530
  wood 531
Molins 426
Mondehare, J. 362
Monell & Williams,
  New York 462
money boxes 38,84–5,663
money scales 383
Montini 429
Moorcroft, William 408–9
Moorcroft MacIntyre 409–10
Moorcroft pointer 408
Moore, John C. & Son 467
Moore & Son & Thompson
  380
Moore Company 455
Mordan, Sampson 60,439,
  460,475,477
Moreau, Louis Auguste 427
Morey and Ober, Boston 519
Morrison, Jas. 445
mortars 513
Mortimer, H.W. & Co. 673
Mortimer & Hunt 452
mosaic fragments 539
Moser 494
mother-of-pearl 586
motorcycles 594–5
Mourgue, Olivier 434
mugs
  commemorative 13

glass 59
  porcelain 135–6,155
  pottery 13,19,44,72,415,
    597
  silver 456
  Wemyss 82
mule chests 199–200,304,
  652
mules 544
Müller (Twickenham) 365
Muller Croismaire 399
Müller Frères 398–9
mummy cloths 539
Murdoch, Thomas 673
Murray, James 362
Murray, William Straite 600
Musgrave, Geo. 487
musical boxes 374,583–4
musical instruments 581–3
music stands 329,393,509
music stools 331
muskets 671
Muslagham 541
mustard pots 457,477

Nailsea 59
Nantgarw 128,144
Naples 93,137
Nash, Eliezer 438
Nash, Paul 420
Nast 51
Natzler, Gertrude 600
Natzler, Otto 600
Nechanski, Arnold 604
necklaces 400,431,498,676,
  680–1
needlework tables 340
nests of tables 340
netsuke 636–7
Neuss, Johann Georg 441
Neve, John 375
Nevers 10
Nevers faience pointer 10
Newbold, Thomas 438
New Hall 128,140
Newton 671
Newton & Co. 382
Nicholls, John 362
Nicole Frères 583
Nicolson, John 448
nightlights 419
Nock, H. 673
nocturnals 488
Noke, C.J. 413–15
Norris, Joseph 370
Northcote, Hannah 473
Northern (Hull) 378
Northern celadon 53
number plates 595
Nurnberger, Albert 581
nursing chairs 299
nutmeg graters 439
Nymphenburg 50,93–4,120,
  128
Nymphenburg pointer 94

oak 531
oak and country furniture
  beds 189–90
  bookcases 190
  bureaux 191–2
  cabinets 192
  chairs 193–7
  chests 198–200
  cupboards 201–6
  dressers 206–10,217
  miscellaneous 215
  stools 210–11
  tables 211–15
occasional tables 234,340
Ochies 428
octagonal seats 331
octagon lever pad braces 665
Öfner, J. 432
Ohr, George 421
oil lamps 536,642–3
Okakoto 637
olpe 532
ophthalmoscope 383
organ clocks 581
organs 581
Oriental
  bamboo 608
  cloisonné enamel 608
  furniture 609
  glass 610
  horn 610
  ivory 610–11
  jade 611

lacquer 611–12
metal 612
netsuke 637
tsuba 638
wood 638
Oriental pottery & porcelain
bottles 161
bowls 157–61
cups 161
ewers 162
figures 162–4
flatware 164–8
garden seats 169
jardinières 169
jars 170–1
miscellaneous 177
tea & coffee pots 172
tureens 173
vases 173
Oriental pottery and
porcelain
pointers 162
ormolu 516–17
Ouline 426
Ovchinnikov, Pavel 639
owls 403, 411

Pace, Thomas 362
Pages, Francis 457
Palethorpe, Robert Jr. 519
palettes 533
Palmer (London) 376
panels 410, 433, 495, 531,
610, 628
pans 515
paper cases 439
paperweights 188
papier mâché 240, 643–5
parasols 508
Parian ware pointer 121
Paris 131, 142
Parker and Wakelin 435
parquetry tables 341
partners' desks 393
pastille burners 15–16, 98
Pastorelli (London) 376
patch boxes 591
pâte-de-verre 502
Paterson, J.A. 358
Patrick, J. 376
Payne, John 465, 467
Payne (London) 367
Pearce, R. 461
pearls pointer 678
pearlware 9–10, 12, 18, 37,
62, 72–3, 83–4
pedestals 240, 530, 618
pedestal desks 319
pedestal sideboards 328–9
pedestal tables 341
Pemberton, Samuel 438–9,
440, 451
Pembroke tables 234, 341–2
Pembroke tables pointer 341
pendants 400–1, 498, 676,
680–2
pendules de voyage 485
pepperettes 478
pepperpots 667
Perigal, Francis 360
Perl, Karl 425
Perry and Co. 408
pestle and mortars 662
Peterson, Abraham 435
pews 658
pewter 405–6, 518, 524
Pfalz-Zweibrucken 121
Philippe, Patek 486
Philippe, R. 428
Phillips, Arthur 680
Phipps & Robinson 438–9,
471
phonographs 584–5
Phyfe, Duncan 332, 348
pianolas 581
pianos 240, 504, 581
Picault 512
picture clocks 375
picture frames 406, 499, 510,
639
picture panels 531
pictures 532, 546
pier glasses 323
pier tables 235, 342
pike trimmers 596
Pilkington Lancastrian 389
pillar clocks 375
Pilleau, Peze 466
pincushions 475, 646

pine furniture
bases 634
beds 650
bookcases 651
chairs 651
chests 651
cupboards 652–6
desks 656
dressers 656–7
dressing tables 657
mirrors 658
miscellaneous 660
sideboards 658
stools 658
tables 658–9
wardrobes 659
washstands 659
Pinxton 45, 92, 128
pistols 509, 672–4
pitchers 454
Pitts, William 435, 444, 460
planes 383, 664–5
planner chests 652
plaques
art deco 424
art nouveau 404
bronze 513
enamel 513
ivory 610
oriental 638
porcelain 136–8
pottery 37, 40, 72–3, 82,
424
stone 433
plates
oriental 55, 57, 638
pewter 518–20
porcelain 49
pottery 14–15, 36, 46,
61–3, 388, 423
silver 457, 616
platters 662
Plichta 82
plique à jour 493
ploughs 665
Plymouth 121
pochettes 582
pole screens 240, 325
Pollock, John 459
Ponti, Gio. 434
Pontifax, Daniel 458
Pontypool 525–6, 632
pop ephemera 603–4
porcelain
baskets 91
bottles 161, 599
bowls 91–2, 157–61
boxes 44, 93, 423
butter tubs 146
caddies 94
candelabra 95–6
centrepieces 96–7
clock cases 97
cottages 98
crested china 156
cups 99–106, 161
ewers 162
fairings 107
figures 107–32, 162–4
flatware 124–31, 164–8
garden seats 169
Goss china 156
ice pails 131
inkwells 131
jardinières 132, 169
jars 170–1
jugs 47, 51, 132–5, 153
Lowestoft 153–5
miscellaneous 177
mugs 135–6
oriental 157–77
plaques 136–8
pots 138
sauceboats 138–9
services 140–4
tea and coffee pots 145,
172
tureens 145–6, 173
vases 146–52, 173–6
porcelain pointers 162
porringers 476, 522–3
Poshinger, Ferdinand 494
postcards 605–6
posters 410, 503, 605–6
postwar 434
pots 73, 138
pottery
bowls 9–10, 37

busts 10–11
candlesticks 38
commemorative 11–15
cottages 15–16
cow creamers 16–18
cups 18
figures – animals 19–23,
162–3
figures – people 23–35,
163–4
flatware 36, 61–4
jardinières 387, 389
jars 52, 64–5, 532, 662
jugs 11–14, 37, 67–71, 403,
410, 415, 424, 503, 597
miscellaneous 83–90
mugs 72–3
oriental 157–77
plaques 37, 72–3
pots 73, 475
services 74–5
tankards 75
tea-caddies 76
tea/coffee pots 76–8
tiles 37, 78–9
Toby jugs 71
tureens 79–80
vases 41, 80–1, 387–91
Wemyss 82–3
pouring vessels 389
powder boxes 49
Prattware
bowls 9
busts 10
cow creamers 17
figures 21, 24, 39
jugs 68
tea caddies 76
watch holders 85
prayer rugs 622, 624, 626
Preiss, Frederick 428–9, 501
Presidential dinner service
plates 126
press cupboards 317
pressed glass 180
Priest, John 442
propelling pencils 475
prows 603
punch bowls 56–7, 92, 437
purses 639
Putnam, James H. 521
putters 597
puzzles 410

quadrants 488
quilts 546
quivers 603
Qum 542–3, 625

radios 591–2
radios pointer 592
Raingo Frères 369
Ramsden, Archibald 581
Ramsden, Omar 400
rapiers 669
Rapin, Henri 423
ratafia glasses 187
rattles 477
Rawlings, Charles 475
Rawlings & Sumner 472
Rayment, Richard 358
Read, Colin 630
Read, F. 648
reading chairs 225
reading tables 342
receivers 592
Recknagel, Theo. 559
recorders 581, 632
Redlich & Co, Canterbury
437, 461
reels, fishing 596
refectory tables 217
refrigerators 434
regulator clocks 360
Reid, William 459
Reily, Charles and Mary 439
Reily, John 471
Rein, F.C., & Son 382
Reinecke, Otto 560
Reinicke, P. 50
reliefs 509–10, 529–32, 538
rent tables 215
Rescht 542
Rhead, Frederick 388, 420
Rhenish 71
Richards, Samuel 468
Richardson, Arthur 582
Richardson, Joseph Jnr 454
Richardson, Richard 471

Richter, Carl Davis 496
riding spurs 479
Ridgway 142
Rie, Lucie 600, 630
rifles 672
Rigby, Wm., & Jn. 672
rings 537, 682
Rivière, M. Guiraud 425–7
Roberts (Otley) 358
Roberts, Samuel & Co. 458
Robertson, Ann 473
Robertson, Brown 596
Robertson, William 460
robes 545
Robins, John 467
Robins, Thomas 469
Robinson, John 458
Robinson and Leadbeater 11,
14
Rochard 427
rocking chairs 300, 651
Rockingham 46, 84, 121
Rogers 79
Rohlfs, Charles 394
rollers 662
rolling pins 60
roll top desks 320
Roper & Sons Ltd 577
Rosenthal 422–3, 428, 477
Roskell, Robert Allan 466
Ross, A. 490
Rothwell 77
Round, J. and Son 444
Rowbotham, John & Co. 443
Roycroft 402, 406
Royal Dux 121, 391, 427–8
Rozenburg 497
Rugg, Richard 458
rugs 540–3, 620–2, 625
rugs and carpets glossary
541
runners 622
rushlight candleholders
663–4
Ruskin 423
Russell, Thomas, & Son 376
Russian works of art 638–40
Ryuko 637

sabres 670
Saddler, E. 37
saddles 636
Safavid 42
St. Leu, David de 486
St. Louis 60
Salazar, Fiona 600
salon chairs 297–300
salt and pepper sets 524
Salt & Son 381
Salter, William 389
saltglaze
bowls 18, 37
figures 24
jugs 14, 67–8
mugs 72
tea caddies 76
salts 37, 59, 406, 456–7, 521,
666
salts bottles 188
salvers 454, 457–9
samovars 515
samplers 548–9, 628–9
Samson 112, 148
Samson, Edme et Cie pointer
112
Samuel, H. 372
Sancai 53
sand boxes 513
Sanders, Benjamin 455
Sandoz, Edouard Marcel
422–3
sauceboats 43, 138–9, 480
saucers 49, 51, 407, 421
Savory, Joseph and Albert
461
Savoye Frères & Cie 487
Sayre, John 447
Sazikov 639
scales 509, 663
Scavini 428
scent bottles 60, 188, 416–17,
460
scent phials 60
Scheidt, Georg Anton 479
Schellinck, Sam 497
Schindler, P.E. 49
Schliepstein, Gerhard 422,
428
Schmidt-Hofer 426

Schoedl, Heinrich 648
Schutz, Georg 434
scientific instruments
  cameras 384–6
  dental 382
  dials 377
  globes 377–8
  medical 380–2
  microscopes 379–80, 490
  miscellaneous 382–3
  surveying 378–9
  telescopes 379, 490
  viewers 386
scissors 475
screens 325–6, 394, 517, 609, 638, 660
scrimshaw 528
scripophily 607
sculptures 422, 529–30
scuppetts 666
Searle, Ronald 606
Secessionist ware 389
secrétaires 349
secrétaires à abattant 261
secrétaire bookcases 252–5, 651
secrétaire cabinets 220–1, 259–62
secrétaire chests 229, 303, 305
sectors 382
Seger, Ernst 429
Senneh 543
Serapi 543
services 74–5, 140–4, 461–4, 480
serving tables 215, 343
settees 226, 326–7
Settle, James and Thomas 473
settles 198, 392, 394, 658
Sèvres
  bottles 91
  centrepieces 97
  clock cases 97
  cups 51, 103–5
  figures 122
  garnitures 148
  inkstands 131
  jardinières 132
  jugs 134, 391
  lanterns 423
  plates 128
  services 142–3
  teapots 145
  vases 148–9
Sèvres pointer 104
sewing 646
sewing boxes 587–8
sewing caskets 646
sewing machines 646
sewing tables 237, 348
Seymour, John 256, 298
Seymour, Thomas 256, 298
S.F.B.J. 558
shabti 536, 620
shamshirs 670
Shaw, John 438
Shaw, Thomas 358
Shaw, W.C. 360
shawls 555
Shchkotina-Pototskaya, A. 638
Sheffield, J. & T. 444
shell 527–8
Shelley 420–1
shelves 327, 660
Shenfelder, D.P. 66
Shepard, Ernest Howard 606
Sherratt, Obadiah 19, 22, 28–9, 38–40, 72
Shibayama 637
Shigemasa 637
Shirvan 543
shoe-cleaning boxes 665
shoemakers' patterns 665
shoes 544–5
Shoulds, Samuel 357
Sibley, Richard 453, 457, 469
sideboards 327–9, 392, 430, 658
side cabinets 192, 220, 267–71
side chairs 195–6, 224, 226, 294–300, 395–6
side tables 213–14, 234–5, 333, 343–4, 659
signal box timepieces 375

Sileh 626
silver
  art nouveau 405
  baskets 435–6
  beakers 436, 639
  belts 601
  bowls 436–8
  boxes 407, 438–40
  caddy spoons 451–2
  candelabra 440–1, 615
  candlesticks 441–4, 615
  casters 444
  centrepieces 444
  coffee pots 445
  cups 447–8
  cutlery 448–51
  dishes 452–3
  inkstands 453–5
  jugs 455
  miscellaneous 475–9
  models 455–6
  mugs 456
  salts 456–7
  salvers 456–7
  sauceboats 459–60
  scent bottles 460
  services 461–4, 616
  tankards 465–6, 615
  tea caddies 466–7
  tea kettles 467
  teapots 467–8
  tea sets 407
  trays 468–9, 616
  tureens 469, 615–6
  vases 407
silver plate 480, 505–7
silver tables 344
Simmance, Eliza 412
Simon & Halbig 559
Simpkins, William 476
sirens 383
skalas 666
skeleton clocks 370–1
skimmers 662
Skinner, John 362
slant front desks 255, 257
Slater, Walter 387
sledges 598
slipware 18, 22
Smiley, Thomas 457
Smith, Beck & Beck 379
Smith, Joseph 465
Smith, Martin 600
Smith, Nathaniel & Co. 478
Smith, Stephen 448
Smith & Nicholson 455
smoker's compendium 667
snooker tables 351
snuff boxes
  enamel 591
  gold 614
  porcelain 49–50, 93
  silver 438, 479
  tortoiseshell 508
  wood 589
snuff mills 528
snuff rasps 475
sofas 226, 326, 430, 434
sofa tables 235, 344–5
sofa tables pointer 344
Sokolov, M. 639
Sorley, R. & W. 374
Sorney, André 430
Soumaine, Simeon 444
spelter 525–6, 597–8
spice boxes 640
spill vases 15, 22, 81
Spilsbury, Francis 456
spirit bottles 58
spirit decanters 58
Spode 72, 80, 96, 105, 131–2, 140, 149, 597
sponge-ware 80
spoons 405, 450, 521, 524, 527, 599, 640, 661
spoon-warmers 403, 505
sport 596–9
spurs 667
Staffordshire
  bowls 9
  busts 10–11
  cow creamers 16–18
  figures 19–34
    animals 19–23, 112
    people 23–35, 39
    garnitures 38
    jars 65
    jugs 67–70
    mugs 72

services 74–5
stirrup cups 18
tea caddies 76
tiles 37
tureens 79–80
vases 15
Victorian figures
  ballet 33–4
  circus 33–4
  crime 34
  exploration 32–3
  military 32–3
  naval 32–3
  opera 33–5
  politicians 31–2
  religious 33
  royalty 30–1
  sport 35
  statesmen 31–2
  theatre 33–5
Staffordshire pointers 14, 30
stained glass 399
standard lamps 643
Standring (Bolton) 359
stands 215, 329–30, 393, 396
Stanesby, Thomas 581, 632
Starr, Theodore B. 470
stationery boxes 589
statues 510, 517, 529, 538, 617–18
statuettes 418, 502, 512, 527, 531, 536, 613
Staudenmayer 673
Steiff 563
Steiner, Jules 560
Steinway & Sons 240
steps 330, 660
Steward, John 471
Stewart, John 66
Stickley, Gustav 392, 394–6
stick stands 329
Stifter, Johann 672
stirrup cups 18
stirrup vessels 534
Stockwell, E.H. 475
stoneware
  bowls 411
  dishes 24
  figures 411, 530
  jugs 11, 14, 71
  mugs 72
  vases 15, 403–4, 412, 597–9
stools 210–11, 228, 330–1, 395, 603, 658
stools pointer 331
storage chests 305
Storr, Paul 456, 460, 469, 477, 616
strainers 476, 479
Strasbourg 123
Stretch, Peter 354
Strocello 581
strong boxes 517, 589, 663
Stroud, William 468
Studdy, George Ernest 605
Stumbels, William 359
sucriers 58
sugar baskets 506
sugar bowls 51, 437, 461, 639
sugar boxes 48, 478
sugar nippers 476
sugar urns 476
suits 545
suites 609
Sullivan, Louis H. 407–8
Summers, William 435, 440
Sumner, William 448
Sunderland 70
surveying instruments 378–9
Sutherland tables 345
Sutton, Henry 383
Swansea 70, 129, 133, 149
Swansea pointer 129
sweetmeat glasses 187
Sweetser Co., New York 470
Swift, J. 380
Swift, John 446
swords 513, 669–70

tabako-bon 612
Taber, Stephen 354
tabernacle clocks 485
table à deux plateaux 393
table bureaux 255
table cabinets 609
table clocks 391, 501
table lamps 402, 491, 642

table legs pointer 189
table lighters 432
tables
  architects 331
  card 232, 236, 238, 333–4
  centre 233–4, 236, 335–6
  circular 233
  console 235, 336
  cricket 215, 658
  dining 212–3, 233, 336–9, 497
  draw-leaf 215
  drop-leaf 212–13, 338
  drum 338
  games 238, 338
  gateleg 211–13, 233, 236, 339
  lamp 347
  library 233–4, 339, 347
  loo 339–40
  needlework 340
  nests of 340
  oak & country 211–15
  occasional 234, 340
  pedestal 341
  Pembroke 234, 341–2
  pier 234, 342
  pine 658–9
  reading 342
  refectory 213–14, 217
  serving 215, 343
  side 213–14, 234–5, 333, 343–4, 659
  silver 344
  sofa 235, 344–5
  Sutherland 345
  tea 215, 345–6
  tripod 237, 346–7
  wake 347
  wine 347
  work 347–8
  writing 237, 349
table tennis sets 598
tablets 536
tables à écrire 349
table services 432, 504
tabourets 394, 396
Tabriz 543, 625–6
tachi 670
tackle boxes 596
Talish 543, 622
talking clocks 375
tallboy chests 229
tallboys 200, 204, 306–9
tall-case clocks 354, 357
tambour desks 256
tankards
  pewter 518–19
  pottery 75, 599
  silver 465–6, 615
tantalus 587
tapestries 549–50, 627–8
Tasoy 571
Taylor, Charles Foot 647
Taylor, E.A. 393
Taylor, Jasper 362
Taylor, Joseph 440, 451
Taylor and Perry 438
tazzas 432, 616
teabowls 18, 51, 54, 100–3, 106
tea and coffee pots 172
tea and coffee services 51, 461–2, 504, 616
tea caddies
  papier mâché 645
  porcelain 51, 155
  pottery 76
  silver 466–7
  silver plate 505
  tortoiseshell 588–9
  tea-glass holders 639
  wood 588, 632
tea kettles 467
teapots
  art deco 420, 432
  pewter 519
  porcelain 48–9, 154, 434
  pottery 11, 37, 76–8, 415, 597
  silver 432, 461–4, 467–8
teapoys 349
tea services
  art deco 420, 424
  silver 461–2
teasets 407, 421, 434
teaspoons 405
tea tables 215, 345–6
tea tins 663

tea urns 506, 515, 526
teddy bears 563–4
teeth 603
telephones 433
telephone tables 394
telescopes 379, 496
telescopes pointer 379
televisors 592
Telleruhr 485
tennis racket presses 598
tennis rackets 597
terracotta 388, 422, 530–1
Terrey, I.E. 472
Terrey, John Edward 463
tester bedsteads 245
testing balances 509
tête-à-têtes 45
textiles
  costume 544–6
  covers 550–2
  curtains 550–2
  embroidery 546–7
  fans 553–4
  handkerchiefs 553
  lace 547–8
  samplers 548–9
  shawls 555
  tapestries 549–50
thermometers 527
Thompson & Capper 381
Thomson, William 462
Thropp & Taylor 438
Thuringia 122
Thwaites, James 359
Thwaites, John 375
Thwaites & Reed 360
Tiffany, L.C. 403
Tiffany & Co. New York
  clocks 366
  glass 399
  metal 407
  silver 447, 450, 462, 467, 469–70, 475, 499
Tiffany studios 401, 405, 491, 495
tile panels 42
tiles 78–9, 391, 403, 500
Timbrell, Robert 447, 457
timepieces 484
time recorders 667
tin 525–6
Tingley, Samuel 454
tinplate toys 567–9
Tinworth, George 412
Tipp & Co. 568–9, 579
Tittensor, H. 414
toast racks 478–9, 599
tobacco boxes 84, 439, 509, 589
tobacco jars 65, 388, 409, 497
Toby jugs 38, 89
toilet cases 586
toilet cupboards 314
toilet mirrors 324–5
tôle 525, 642, 662
tôle peinte 240, 526
Tompion, Thomas 482
tool kits 665
tools 664–5
Toone, Wm. 664
Tooth, Henry 388
torchères 238, 330, 642
tortoiseshell 508, 587–90, 638
Toshitsugu 637
tourbillon watches 486
Tournai 129
towel rails 660
Towler (Dublin) 673
toys 564–76
toys pointer 568
Traies, William 452
Transitional Wares pointer 165
transport 593–5
Trask, Israel 520
Trask, Oliver 520
travelling cases 478
travelling chests 311
trays
  lead 525
  papier mâché 240, 644–5
  pewter 406
  silver 453, 468–9, 616
  silver plate 507
Tressemanes and Vogt, Limoges 126
trestle tables 215
Treusch, Ernst 432

tribal art 601–3
trigonometers 489
tripod tables 237, 346–7
trivets 664
trophies 597–9
trousses 526
tsuba 638
tub bergeres 226
Tuck, Raphael 605
Tucker & Hemphill China 134
Tucker, William 133
Tunbridgeware 587
tureens
  art nouveau 405
  oriental 173
  porcelain 42–3, 145–6
  pottery 79–80
  silver 469, 615–16
Turin 64
Turkoman 544
turret clocks 375
tusks 527, 603
tusk vases 611
typewriters 592

umbrellas 531
ungentarium 539
Unger Brothers 400
Urbino 64
urns
  copper 515
  lead 525
  metalware 526, 642
  ormolu 517
  pottery 41
  wood 329
urn tables 351
Ushak 624

Valentines 590
Valery, J. 368
Van Briggle 391
Van Erp, Dirk 402
vanity cases 586
vases
  art deco 420–1, 423–5, 432
  art nouveau 387–91, 397–9, 403–4, 407, 409–10
  bluejohn 618
  bronze 432, 514, 612, 637
  cloisonné 631
  glass 188, 397–9, 417–18, 492–4, 500, 610
  oriental 53–7, 173–7, 608
  pewter 405
  porcelain 44–5, 146–52, 154, 422
  pottery 41, 80–2, 387–91, 423–4, 497, 502
  shell 527
  silver 407
  stone 536
  stoneware 15, 403–4, 412, 597–9, 630
ventriloquist dummy 561
verandah seats 327
Vernon, Barbara 415
vesta cases 439, 596, 598
Vienna 105, 129, 137–8, 143
Vienna pointer 105
Vienna regulator 484
vinaigrettes 438, 508, 591
Vincennes 51, 104
violas 582
violins 582–3, 586
violoncellos 582–3
vitae cases 596
vitrines 263, 265
Volkstedt 93
Volkstedt-Rudolstadt 122
voluters 383
Vuillaume, Jean Baptiste 582
Vuilliamy, Justin 363, 367, 484

Waals, Peter 430
Wadsworth, John 389
Wain, Louis 421, 605
wainscot chairs 193
Wainwright, John 359
waistcoats 545
Wakelin, Edward 460
wake tables 347
Walker, William Henry 605–6
Walker & Hall 440, 468–9

walking sticks 527
Wall, Dr. 135
wall appliqués 591
wall brackets 86
wall clocks 371–3
wall masks 422
wall sconces 526
Walton, John 21, 25–7, 85
war bonnets 601
Ward, Richard 363
wardrobes 317, 659
washstands 349–50, 659
waste paper baskets 351
watches 431, 485–7, 498
watch holders 85
watch stands 667
Waters, James 455
Waters, John 673
Watson, John 441, 443
Watson, Samuel 363
Watson, Thomas 465
Watson & Sons Ltd 490
wax dolls 556–7
weathervanes 515, 518
Weber 581
Webster, Richd. 483
Wedgwood
  bowls 9, 12
  busts 11
  comports 85
  figures 41
  inkstands 86
  jugs 67, 71
  medallions 73
  plaques 73
  plates 61–2
  services 75
  vases 81
Wedgwood & Bentley 72, 81, 85
Wedgwood pointer 75
weights 60, 513
Weir, Marion 629
wellington chests 311
Wells, J. 363
Wemyss 82–3
Wemyss pointer 82
Wendler, Kurt 423
West, Benjamin 475
West, James 359
Westerwald 71
what-nots 350, 609
Whieldon 16, 22, 40, 67–8, 71, 76–7
Whipham, Thomas 456
Whipple, J. & Co. 463
whisks 661
White, H.M. 426
white metal 525
Whyte, David 457
Wiener Werkstätte 399
Wigström, Henrik 632
Wilde, Abraham 466
Wilkinson, Henry & Co. 463, 480
Will, Henry 519
Willard, Aaron 354, 357, 369
Willard, Alex G. 357
Williams, Lorenzo 520
Williams, S. 363
Wills 604
Wiltberger, Christian 445, 468
Windmills, J. 359
window seats 228, 326, 330
Windsor chairs 195–7
wine 641
wine antiques 471–4
wine bottle carriers 474
wine coasters 643, 666–7
wine coolers 131, 237, 350–1, 473, 507, 616
wine coolers pointer 350
wine cupboards 659
wine cups 54
wine ewers 474
wine funnels 45, 473
wine glasses 58–60, 183–7
wine labels 471–2
wine services 474
wine tables 347
Winsor & Newton Ltd 590
Winters, Christian 357
Wisker (York) 376
WMF 478
Wollek, C. 427
Wood, David 367–8
Wood, Enoch 21, 25, 28, 29
Wood, Enoch, pointer 21

Wood, Ralph
  figures 10, 19, 20–1, 23–4, 29
  jugs 38, 68, 71
  plaques 72
  teapots 77
  vases 80
Wood, Ralph (younger) 19, 24
Wood, Samuel 444
Wood and Caldwell 22–3
Wood & Hughes, New York 454
wood carvings 531
Woolford, James 433
wool-winders 666
Worcester
  baskets 47
  bottles 91
  bowls 92
  candlesticks 96
  centrepieces 97
  cups 106
  dishes 46–7, 129–30
  jardinières 132
  jugs 46, 133–4
  mugs 136
  plates 47, 129–30
  sauceboats 139
  services 47, 143–4
  tea caddies 94
  vases 45–6, 149–52
Worcester, First Period 46, 136, 139, 144
Worcester pointers 92
Worcester, Royal
  candlesticks 96
  centrepieces 97
  cups 106
  dishes 130
  figures 123
  plaques 138
  plates 130
  vases 150–2, 421
work boxes 587, 660
work tables 347–8
Wren, John 456
Wright, Frank Lloyd 402
Wright, Thomas 377
Wright, William 359, 364
writing boxes 589
writing desks 320, 349
writing sets 589
writing tables 237, 349
Wrockwardine 59
Wucai 157
Wunderlich, Paul 680
Wylie and Lochhead 393

Yardley, W. 359
Yomut 543–4
Yonezawa 572
Yorke, Edward 445
Young, Samuel 359
Younge, S.C., & Co. 473

Zeiss, Carl 379
Zejwa 544
Ziegler 623, 626
Zwichl, F. 503